David Ebsworth is the pen name of writer Dave
and Regional Secretary for the Transport & Ge
has travelled a great deal within western Europe
States, in China, Nicaragua and Colombia. He
has lived for the past thirty years in Wrexham wi
four adult children and nine grandchildren. Sinc
the couple have spent about six months of each year in southern Spain. Dave
began to write seriously in 2009.

The
JACOBITES'
APPRENTICE

DAVID EBSWORTH

SilverWood

First published by SilverWood Books 2012
www.silverwoodbooks.co.uk

Copyright © David Ebsworth 2012

ISBN 978-1-78132-009-9

British Library Cataloguing in Publication Data
A CIP catalogue record for this book is available from the British Library

Set in Sabon and Baskerville Italic by SilverWood Books
Printed in England on paper from responsible sources

Cover artwork shows: castle by Patrick Guénett, paintbucket by Vladimir Yudin,
paintbrushes and dagger by Stanislav Stasyuk (all courtesy of DepositPhotos).

Dedicated to Ann Mary, my ideal reader

Prologue

Aran was just thirteen years old when he was taken on one of the estate carts to Chester. He had slept overnight in the vehicle so that, at five o' the clock next morning, he could catch the Fly Wagon to Manchester. And for such a journey, there *was* just the Fly Wagon – unless, of course, you were ample and proficient enough to go by horse or private carriage.

Aran had been embittered at that age, the only extant child of parents who had, in death, each abandoned him. His father had passed first, just three years previously, taken by a pulmonary infection that, according to his mother, had been the decisive legacy of a wound to his chest, received during service with the military. To the English mind, his country might have seemed like nothing more than an extension of their own shires, but Wales still supplied some of the worthiest soldiers in their blood-red army, and his father had been one of them.

By that time, a certain Josiah Redmond had assumed the squirearchy within the village, and Aran's mother had already been employed on the estate, soon finding work in the new hall itself. Then, in November of the year 1721, she gave birth to the boy, the only one of her children to survive infancy.

It had been an important year. Robert Walpole had recently become Prime Minister and, in an age when communications cantered faster each year, a new mail service had been established between every major northern town to London so that it was now possible to send a letter from, say, Chester to London, and receive a reply, within ten days at the most.

Aran had spent his early years running errands for the Squire, or working in his gardens, or gathering a limited education from Josiah Redmond's house-keeper. But then his mother, too, had died.

Josiah Redmond, he had discovered, was part of a family business based in Manchester. They were manufacturers of fustian cloth, amongst other things, owning several small warehouses and managing a network of weavers along the River Irk, making up finished cloth from imported Irish yarn. Since Squire Redmond himself was now too old, at this stage, to manage the business, it was operated by his much younger brother, Titus.

The Squire had some opaque affection for Aran but, with meagre pertinent resource locally, he had decided that the boy would be best placed with Titus Redmond's family. He had carefully given him four shillings and

1

a sixpence to pay for the journey. This was a gargantuan sum, but he was determined that Aran should make the long journey in at least some comfort.

He had thus soon been stowed inside the Fly Wagon along with bales of imported silk, a crate of porcelain table ware, twelve casks of salted pork, and two other passengers, an overweight merchant and a thin, bespectacled gentleman afflicted with some scabrous skin disease. The smell of pork fat had greased all within, and the constantly shifting bales whispered and groaned at anything with which they came in contact. They were sheltered from the weather by a tarpaulin, and from chimerical footpads by a double-shotted chaperon, but nothing could protect them from the nauseous motion of the wagon on the rutted highway. In consequence they had, by turns initially, disgorged over the side and moaned in their miseries. The carters stopped several times, once at Warrington, a comely village, to change horses and, on other occasions, to relieve themselves at the wayside.

The bespectacled traveller had said almost nothing throughout the entire journey, simply farting fulsomely and frequently. However, the merchant, like many of his class, was a gregarious fellow who had taken it upon himself to engage Aran in some sparkling conceit.

'Did you know,' he had asked the boy, 'that there is a land in which dwell only Rogues on the one hand and the Righteous on the other?'

'No, sir,' Aran had replied.

The merchant had delved in the pocket of his waistcoat and withdrawn an ostentatious silver snuffbox, its bone lid carved with the image of a horned ram. He had flicked open the lid and, sprinkling the powdered tobacco onto the back of his hand, snorted the weed first through his right nostril and then through his left. His upper lip and the sides of his nose were permanently discoloured from the substance. And such was his addiction that the inhalation ceased long ago to make him sneeze.

'In all truth,' said the merchant, 'it was your melancholic demeanour that caused me to recall the land of Rogues and the Righteous.'

'I apologise, sir,' Aran had replied, 'but I do not know this fabled land of which you speak.'

'Well, now let me see. In this land there are only Rogues and the Righteous. The Rogues always lie, of course, and the Righteous may only tell the truth. So, imagine yourself in this land.'

'How can the Rogues be told apart from the Righteous?' Aran asked.

'A pertinent question,' replied the merchant, 'for it is certainly important to know the difference, is it not?'

'They may not be distinguished by their dress?'

'They dress identically.'

'Then I should question them.'

'Fine idea, my young friend. Let us suppose that, initially, you meet a modest group – three, let us say.'

'I shall ask how many Righteous are amongst them.'

And so the riddle played itself out over the long miles until, finally, Aran arrived at the correct solution. A process of logical deduction. Only one Rogue present. Two of the Righteous.

The merchant had slapped his thigh. 'God's Hooks, boy. You are a whetted one, despite your years.'

They had made reasonable progress, despite the desperate condition of the route, arriving on Deansgate Street in Manchester at around ten o' the clock that evening. The merchant fumbled for his purse, produced some copper coins. He pressed them into the boy's palm.

'Thankyou, sir,' he said. 'But I cannot accept.'

'Nonsense, lad,' replied the merchant. 'It was worth every penny for the entertainment that you afforded me. But perhaps a word of advice before we part. For Manchester is a misbegotten midden. Like all growing towns it attracts more than its own share of scoundrels too. Why, you may even have to confront some of them. If so, you would do well to recall the riddle I set you. Remember always that you may learn much of value from life's rogues, as well as from the seemingly righteous. So long, of course, as you can distinguish between the two.'

Chapter One

Maria-Louise Redmond believes there are only two kinds of people in this world: those who make a difference, and those who do not. It is possible for individuals of superior status to leave no discernible footprint at all on the sands of our lives whilst, sometimes, those from the most apologetic origins can erect absolute breakwaters against a tidal wave of events crashing against the cowering nation. *And I am such a person*, thinks Maria-Louise Redmond, knowing that in the Great Rebellion developing through these early days of 1744 she has a status far beyond that of simply a Manchester merchant's wife.

Today, she leaves their patrician house in Market Street Lane through the rear entrance, and walks down steps into the walled garden. In company with her eldest daughter, Rosina, now aged nineteen, she takes the brick path past a wicker windbreak that protects the Bramleys and the Pearmains. They exit a polished gate and skirt the remains of coppice to come onto a confined lane that leads towards the new church. She bruises her pinched fingertips along the harsh edges of the outer wall, and the chiselled hide of a flanking hornbeam.

Mother and daughter are each swaddled in burdensome winter coats against the acrid cold, their boot soles protected by pattens against the stubborn snow. It is exacting to discern their features within the furs wrapped about their heads, but it is still possible to see that Maria-Louise, the shorter of the two women, has one set of quintessential Irish characteristics, while Rosina has another, still representative of her ancestry but as distinct from her mother's as it would be possible to find. The mother's features are fey, a description that she fears since, whilst it might denote the elfin qualities of the *Sidhe* from her emotional homeland, she associates it closely with the sense that it portrays for their Highland allies: fated to die. The daughter, on the other hand, has sea-green eyes framed by high and prominent cheekbones, while ringlets of burnished copper spill provocatively from her hood.

Maria-Louise has travelled widely in her thirty-eight years and visited more than one major metropolis, but she has never forgotten the impression made upon her by Manchester when she saw it first, unable to understand the favourable impression that it made upon Defoe, whom she never had the honour of meeting, but for whose works she has respect.

So, to describe Manchester as 'the greatest mere village in England' is, for her, akin to calling the Pacific Ocean a pond. She understands villages. Villages are peaceful and make loneliness an outlaw, whereas Manchester…

'We should find somewhere more tranquil again,' she says absently to her daughter. Her accent remains distinctly Irish, but her daughter's is closer to the Lancastrian dialects prevalent throughout the County.

'La, mother!' replies Rosina, 'You are so provincial. I would simply die for want of companionship.'

'We all know the sort of companionship you crave, my dear. Best to keep it between ourselves, do you not think?'

'Provincial *and* old-fashioned, mama. But not so very different else although, now I think of it, I *do* also have the better taste.'

'You mean the French affectations that pass for good form these days?' says Maria-Louise. 'I declare, Rosina, that they will not serve. We shall be brought low, like Ancient Rome itself, by French decadence.'

'Yet you do not reject the French porcelain and chintz that now adorn the house? Mister Addison says that *le goût* simply reflects the beauty of God's Creation. He maintains that bringing us closer to the polite arts will protect us from that sort of vulgar opulence that you fear. Why else would you devote such attention to my music lessons?'

'Do not mistake me, my dear. I have the greatest faith in good taste, yet I simply cannot find it in your generation's curious obsession with all things French.'

They have picked their way through the frigid mud and patches of remaining snow, littered with the random wastes of the town, so that she can leave a note for her husband at one of his warehouses. She notices that amongst the men at work here today is the Welsh boy, Aran Owen – a boy no longer, of course, for he is a tall and handsome twenty-two year old now. He has completed an apprenticeship with Scatterbuck the printer, secured for him by Titus once his letters were learned. Nonetheless, he is still helping with the business here in much of his free time, because he has an astute mind for these things and because he is obedient to the family. Her husband values this obedience. She recalls how Aran had first arrived, ten years earlier, another of her brother-in-law's strays. And she feels some guilt since, for a while, they had made this warehouse his dog-patch. The warehouse occupies the ground floor, whilst the upper storey consists of a tack room, a tool room, and a small, empty hayloft to which Aran had been directed for his living quarters. There had been barely space for a palliasse, left upon the floor, a piss and dung bucket, a camphor-scented chest to hold his lean belongings, and a porcelain washbowl. But, Lord bless him, he had still been absurdly grateful for, as he had said, it was palatial when compared with the hovel in which he had been raised. *He has grown agreeable though, all the same*, she thinks.

The building leans forward rakishly, pensive and care-worn, as though too much activity will spill it tumbling into the thoroughfare. It is held erect only by the pressure and support of its flanking companions, a private house on one side and a bawdy den, another of her husband's enterprises, on the other. The beams and rafters are grey and web-strewn, riddled with worm and mildew so that, when the outer doors are opened, its foetid breath adds to the already insalubrious air of the street beyond.

Maria-Louise thinks to mention Aran Owen to her daughter, but recalls that there is antipathy between them. In any case, they must almost retrace their steps to arrive at the house of Mrs Starkey, Rosina's harpsichord teacher. It would be easy enough to arrange for Mrs Starkey to conduct her lessons at the Redmonds' home, for they now have their own harpsichord installed, but it suits her purpose this way.

'I trust, ma'am, that you will return punctually this week to collect your daughter?' says Mrs Starkey.

'You must be enjoying a veritable surplus of harpsichord students if they are now queuing so, one after the other, Mrs Starkey. I give you joy of it!'

'I may not have another student but you pay for one hour of my services, ma'am...'

'And one hour shall I take,' Maria-Louise interrupted. 'Not one moment longer.'

'With respect, Mrs Redmond, you were last week just over an hour and one quarter, and the week before that...'

'You need not fear, Mrs Starkey,' says Rosina, 'for my mother's assignations take less time each week. She practises her own arts also, you see!' She smiles. Her mother smiles too, delighted that her daughter can display such wit. But there is a serious side to Rosina's implied criticism and there is an issue here for Maria-Louise herself. So her next stop takes her to Roman Entry, and the private room serving as the Catholic chapel where clandestine Mass is attended. Today, though, she makes simple Confession, or as much of it as she dares.

Yet this delays her still further so that she now hurries to the home of James Bradley, her husband's rival in many respects, close to the Byroms' house on Hanging Ditch. She should hate him, of course, for he is also prominent amongst the town's Whig faction, supporters of the Hanoverian usurper. Yet he has been her *inamorato* for longer than she cares to remember. So long that Bradley's servants treat her as a familiar visitor, hastening her to the salon that serves as their regular trysting place.

She does not have to wait long before James Bradley himself enters. This burly, solid, seasoned gentleman is sporting a turquoise silk waistcoat and matching breeches. His powdered hair is tied back with a broad, black ribbon, for he does not favour periwigs. She stretches up to touch it as he, in turn, reaches for her within the folds of her coat. They take each other with a rutting passion, against the wall and, afterwards, she wipes herself.

'I swear that your passions increase with every year that passes, my dear,' he says. 'But I have never really known, indeed I *still* do not know, whether I rank higher in your passions than the deluded views to which you cling.'

'Delusion? To support the True King of this realm, rather than the Hanoverian usurper?'

'Not a Stuart monarch these sixty years gone. Only those Jacobite *banditti* descendants of the line so roundly rejected by the people of this country. The *people*, my dear! And a *people* so tired of the Stuarts that they invited a Dutchman to rule. Invited a Dutchman! Does that mean nothing to you?'

Unconsciously, she reprises the history of it all. The last of the Stuart Kings, James the Second, *Jacobus* in Latin, and his supporters henceforth, in perpetuity, Jacobites. James deposed in favour of his son-in-law, Stadtholder William of Orange, and the bloodline finally passing to distant relatives, the Electors of Hanover. The Hanoverian line, on the other hand, had continued through George the Second, who has now been on the throne these seventeen years past, since '27. She sighs.

'The *people* will not continue to tolerate these Hanover turnips of yours. Indeed not!'

The Cause runs deep in her blood, for her father had fought alongside James the Second at the Boyne in 1690 and was later dispossessed, along with many others. James himself had died, in exile, in 1701, but Jacobite support had then transferred to his only son, James Francis Edward Stuart, also exiled, with his mother, in France.

'I think you are mistaken, *cara mia*. Part of this town is split entirely down the middle, but the *people*?' He sucks his teeth with a thin whistling sound as he does whenever a thought vexes him. 'The *people* mostly could not give a hurried fuck for *either* side in this issue. They *do* care, however, that there is a French invasion fleet sitting in the Channel, simply awaiting any sign of insurrection on the part of your Jacobite friends.'

'How very philosophical,' she says. 'And, of course, you have no political leanings of your own? No vested interest in keeping the Hanover Rats in place? Difficult for you to build so many fine new dwellings if you no longer have access to the land sales! And without this construction enterprise, what façade would there be for your own more questionable activities? Yet, if it gives you comfort, you should know that I do not give a fig for the French and would not thank them for their interference.'

'Hypocrisy does not become you, Maria-Louise. Your *banditti* friends know fine well that they can never win *without* French support. And you think that the Jacobite cause is much more than an excuse for your husband to run his bawdy palaces, his geneva-houses, and Heaven only knows what besides? Fustian manufacturer my arse! Which brings us, I suppose, to the other reason for your visit. It cannot be to celebrate my birthday since that was three days past. So in what sort of *espionage* are you engaged today?'

'La! I missed your birthing day? Then I shall make it up to you. But, for now, I need just the merest tidbit of information,' says Maria. 'I hear that the Excise collectors are due to visit again. It would be, well, helpful, to know when their visit might take place.'

'God blind me, my dear. You want me to help your husband conceal his contraband? You really are quite the thing.'

'There are certain things that I must do for the Cause,' she says.

'For the Cause?' he laughs. 'That hardly flatters *me*, my dear. Do you not enjoy our meetings at least a little?'

'You are perfectly capable of flattering yourself, James,' she says. 'But mixing business with pleasure is no bad thing.'

'There are those who would describe your activities as business, pure and simple. It is called *whoring*, I believe.'

She makes a gesture with her shoulders and smiles, wide and thin-lipped.

'It causes me no discomfort that any should think me so. My manservant, O'Farrell, returned bloodied to the house some days ago. He had been fighting, of course. He eventually owned that he had overheard somebody describe me as a whore.'

'Sweet of him to defend your honour.'

'I told him he was a fool. On that basis he would have to fight every day of his life!'

Bradley sucks at his teeth again. He wonders why she *really* wants this information but then it is hardly a secret and the whole town will know before long. And so he confirms that the Excise men will be in Manchester on Lady Day itself, at the end of next month. They part rapidly, allowing her to collect Rosina from Mrs Starkey's only a few minutes beyond her allotted time, and she returns home.

As usual, Titus Redmond is waiting impatiently for her return.

'So!' he says, when they are at last alone. 'Did you discover what we need to know?'

'Of course, my love.' She describes her news and each detail of the way in which she had discovered it.

'You really *are* a bitch on heat, are you not?' he says. 'And thank God for it, too!'

Chapter Two

Dudley Striker sits his bay mare at the spot where the River Mersey arrives from its origins at Mottram and converges with the Tame and the Goyt, just above the market town of Stockport. From here the river winds west under Stockport Bridge, flows down into a constricted sandstone gorge, then snakes south and west again to Didsbury and Stretford. In that area, he knows, there is a stretch with no fewer than forty fording places before the river reaches the morass of Chat Moss, seven or eight miles wide in each direction. On it goes to Warrington with its generous bridge, the last on the river. He smiles with the assured knowledge that, if threatened by a Jacobite army, the Hanoverians will destroy the bridges, at Warrington and elsewhere, whilst totally ignoring the crossing places that the Jacobites will certainly prefer to use.

To the east are the high moorlands where, it is said, there are silent villages in the Pennine Chain where Sinister Arts are still practised as part of the Old Religion. The snows are yet deep up there and Striker shivers involuntarily, blowing into his cupped hands before pulling his redingote more closely about himself.

He turns the horse south towards Higher Poynton, not far from Stockport, for he is informed that those of the True Faith sometimes frequent the White Swan there. The inn is ancient but there is stabling here. The place is grey with the scent of wood smoke from the blistering hearth. It is already busy.

'Might I take your coat, master?' asks the innkeeper, but Striker barely acknowledges him. Instead, he lifts the coat's tails and turns his backside to the fire for several minutes. Finally, he removes a psalter from its pocket and drapes the redingote over the nearest unoccupied bench.

The innkeeper gestures towards the psalter. 'Is it the Lord's business that brings you here, sir?'

'My business is my own. You have food?'

'Conies in a broth, master. Some cheeses. Local. And some kidneys with mushroom. If I could suggest...'

'Must I pay extra for the suggestions, innkeeper? No matter. Then it will be the broth. A flask of heated wine too.'

The innkeeper decides to make no further comment and Striker is left in peace, opening the prayer book to Psalm 91. He who dwells in the shelter

10

of the Most High will rest in the shadow of the Almighty. Reading is so good for the soul.

The broth arrives, along with the spiced wine and stale bread. Striker surreptitiously makes the sign, yet not so surreptitiously that it fails to catch the innkeeper's eye. As he services the needs of other customers, he considers Striker's black clothes, clerical and yet...

He decides to try again.

'Forgive me, master,' he says, 'but your business, your own of course, as you say...'

'My own, as I have said,' replies Striker. 'You understand the word privacy, innkeeper?'

'But several of us here share the Faith, sir, if you don't mind me saying. And if you could stand the company...?'

Striker closes the psalter. Very well. If he must!

He is joined by three others and Striker endures endless minutes of meaningless trivia while the innkeeper brings further flagons of wine and small beer, along with a bowl of water, placed in the middle of the table.

'A toast to the King, perhaps,' says one of the men, raising a tankard above the bowl.

Striker slams his hand on the table edge, suddenly beside himself with laughter.

'Give you joy, gentlemen!' he says, regaining control of himself. 'No need for this pretence amongst us, my friends. If we will toast the King's health, we should do so openly. No need for this, this...' and he gestures towards the bowl. 'No gentlemen, let us raise our draughts and toast the Good King James!'

'Good King James,' they say. Or 'The King Over The Water,' depending on their preference.

'Then we are right to think that your business concerns us, master? Utmost secrecy, of course...' says the innkeeper.

'We hear rumours,' says another. 'Great happenings and the promise of the True King's return perhaps. The French fleet waiting to bring him.'

Striker spreads his hands to caution them. 'What can I tell you? I have explained that my enterprise is a private one.'

'But this enterprise is also the King's enterprise?'

'Yes,' says Striker with reluctance. 'That much is certainly true.' Though Striker is a man thrifty with the truth. Truth is a rare and precious commodity, to be used sparingly.

'Then you should know that there are many of us hereabouts who would come out if the King does indeed return.'

A hundred or more, they reckon. Reliable men. Arms available besides.

'You should be less liberal with your intelligence, my friends. But leaderless men?' Striker frowns, dismissing the idea as preposterous. They are

11

like children, he thinks, committed to a confidence but desperate to share it.

The men look at each other, unsure how to proceed, even whether to proceed. But they are concerned that they might have lost the stranger's favour.

'Go on,' says one of them. They go on, for there seems to be no going about at this point.

'Not leaderless, master,' says another.

Striker returns his attention to them, smiling his interest with as much sincerity as he can muster.

'A leader too,' he says. 'Somebody of substance, I trust?'

A moment's reluctance and then, they volunteer, 'Sir Peter Leighton, of Lymewood Hall.'

Striker has heard of him already, of course, but knows little about the estate and so he spends some time gathering facts. All the facts he needs, seeking the weakness in their enthusiasm, and finding it. For whilst Sir Peter may be loyal to James Francis Edward Stuart, his son is an ardent Hanoverian. Moreover, apart from these followers, faithful as they might be, it seems that only Sir Peter holds them together. Important to speak with him as soon as possible then, and he finally allows the discussion to swing in this direction, suggesting a meeting.

'Today?' they ask.

'Is there something wrong with today?' asks Striker. 'Perhaps the King's business can wait until tomorrow? Or next week?'

No, of course not. They apologise, seek to reassure him. One of them will ride directly to Lymewood and ascertain whether Sir Peter would be amenable to meeting at the inn? At the Hall itself?

'I think not,' says Striker. 'I have news for Sir Peter's ears alone, and we need to meet in strict security. But I have a suggestion. On the way here I passed a ruined croft, just off the Stockport Road, perhaps a mile north.'

They know the place. 'Then sunset,' suggests Striker. He will wait for one hour. No more.

The men move quickly, anxious to be about their business, but Striker reaches out to the innkeeper.

'Just one more thing,' he says.

'Master?'

'That cheese you mentioned. A good Cheshire product, I surmise? Then cut me a decent piece to carry away with me, and another flagon of spiced wine while I wait'

By sunset, he has tethered the mare just beyond the tumbled stones of the croft, and he has spread a kerchief on the wall itself. He gazes down into the wooded gulley beyond. Upon the kerchief he has placed the cheese, and he amuses himself by carving thin slices with a paring knife. He waits for a while, but not over-long, until Sir Peter Leighton arrives, mounted, overweight, fine dressed. It takes some effort for him to dismount and he approaches Striker cautiously, sweating ire.

'I am not accustomed,' says the gentleman, when he has regained his composure, 'to being summoned from my own holding, sir. I have shown you the respect due to a royal messenger, if such you should be. But this is a strange choice of meeting place,'

Yet you came, thinks Striker. 'Strange circumstances under which we meet, Sir Peter, and I beseech that you may forgive the manner of your invitation since it was, as you suggest, royally intended.'

'You have the advantage, sir. The men who issued your invitation, if invitation it can be called, could not even give me your name.'

'My name is not important at this stage, Sir Peter. And those men have done great service today. For they tell me that, if Good King James is able to return, you will lead them out on his behalf?'

Sir Peter Leighton maintains his own counsel but Striker hardly needs his confirmation since he has spent the afternoon checking his facts most carefully. Everything that the innkeeper's companions have told him is correct. Sir Peter has arms a-plenty and is held in sufficient esteem to lead a sizeable body of men in the Cause. But he is largely isolated from the rest of his class. It is doubtful that anybody would replace him if he were lost. Striker decides on a different approach.

'Will you share some food, Sir Peter?' he says. 'For I swear this is the finest cheese that Cheshire has ever offered. Indeed, it is like your good self, a rarity in this County. No, I insist! I would be mortally offended should you refuse.'

Sir Peter reluctantly accepts, reaching for the piece of cheese that Striker proffers on the tip of his paring knife. But Striker raises his other hand to check him.

'Please, Sir Peter! No need to sully your hands,' he says, offering the cheese so that His Lordship may simply take the morsel between his teeth. Sir Peter leans forward to receive it and looks only mildly surprised when Striker rapidly flicks his wrist twice. With the first movement, to the right, he sends the cheese morsel sailing across the width of the croft, as Sir Peter's eyes follow its motion slowly through the air. With the second, to the left, Striker neatly slices through the vein of the other man's neck and his voice-box both.

He meets the startled gaze, watches as Sir Peter lifts both hands to his neck, then gently pushes him backwards over the ruined wall, careful to avoid the fountain of gore that follows his fall.

'First blood to His Majesty, King George, I think!' says Striker.

Chapter Three

If he had discovered Francis Bacon at a younger age, Aran Owen might not have been so troubled by the doubts that rained unremittingly upon his first months as a journeyman printer, his apprenticeship finally over but now confronted with the task of making his own reputation and way in the world. 'If a man will begin with certainties,' Bacon had written, 'he shall end in doubts; but if he will be content to begin with doubts, he shall end in certainties.' Content? He is certainly not content, but at least he has learned to adjust to this further development in his life, and to usefully combine his artistic talents with his trade skills.

Strangely, a breakthrough has come as a result of the competition between the town's many apothecaries. Mister Bue in Top Salford, across the river, had therefore commissioned a splendid trade card – a flyer, in truth, for which Aran crafted a traditional scene, with babe swaddled tightly to a board and suspended from a low beam whilst the proud mother continues with her house-keeping. The text advocates Bue's own unguent of salts for cleansing the slippery fluids from the skin of a new born, as well as the use of Pennington's oil of almond purge, an extremely efficacious way to cleanse the child of its long-hoarded excrement. The card's principal claim, though, is that Mister Bue now stocks the world-famous Anodyne Necklace, which helps so much in the reduction of infant mortality through the avoidance of stress in the cutting of babies' teeth. Aran has thus been able to also include a second smaller design, showing a representation of the necklace itself, just above a commendation from no less renowned a physician than Doctor Paul Chamberlen himself, the very author of the necklace.

Within weeks, this innovative teething aid, after being confined to sale within London for so many years, has been on sale at no less than twelve apothecaries within Manchester, and Aran Owen has been required to produce trade leaflets for each of them. It is hardly the artistic patronage of which he dreams, but a beginning none the less.

The printing has been undertaken at the establishment of Adam Scatterbuck, under whose guidance Aran has served his apprenticeship. And now, Scatterbuck and Aran Owen are united again in a different enterprise, this time in one of the warehouses owned by Titus Redmond. This warehouse is packed tight with bales of imported Irish linen yarn, due to be transported across town to Long Millgate, with its noxious open sewers, and the cottages where quantities of warp and raw cotton will be left for each family's weaving loom. Tied batches of any finished cloth, coarse fustian, will later be collected and the family paid for the carding, roving, spinning and weaving that they have undertaken – about eighteen shillings for each twelve pounds of woven yarn, plus ninepence for each pound of weft spun. From the cottages, the woven cloth is transferred further along the Irk's bank, to the pee-stained stench of the small fulling mill where the cloth is cleaned and finished before being dyed in simple colours.

Titus has summoned here a select group to meet him – Aran Owen and Adam Scatterbuck, along with two others, Francis Townley and Jacob Driscoll. Aran knows them to differing degrees. Townley, most recently returned to Manchester, is Redmond's principal link to the most militant of the Lancashire Jacobites. Scatterbuck, Titus Redmond's personal *confidant* though their relationship is a strange one. And Driscoll, the pit-dog. Yet Aran senses himself the junior partner here, flattered that he is chosen for this inner sanctum, delighted as always to dispatch even the smallest part of his debt to the family, but unsure of his role. They are all dressed against the weather for the damp warehouse, as well as the mood, is even colder than the street, and they are thankful that such meetings are always mercifully short. Titus Redmond is not known for his lengthy speeches.

It is his custom, though, to find himself a comfortable throne on which to sit atop the bales of linen yarn whilst his audience stands below. His face has more cracks and creases than the tumbled walls of Old Man Castle, and he teases the end of a military moustache even though he has never served a day in his life.

'If the bristle offends you,' says Scatterbuck, 'you should have it shaved.'

'It distinguishes me.'

'You are distinguished enough without,' says Aran, hoping to lighten the atmosphere, although he knows that Redmond would not have gathered this particular group without serious cause.

'I *am* distinguished,' says Titus, 'as are we all here, with the exception of Master Owen, by our Faith – and *he* is Welsh, Our Lady defend him. Enough distinction for *any* man.'

Aran accepts the taunt well enough though he is seldom pleased to be reminded of his roots for, while his accent still betrays traces of his origins, he has worked every day of the past nine years to become a true Lancastrian.

'No laughin' matter, bein' distinguished as Catholics,' growls Jacob Driscoll.

Aran is always reminded of his school books whenever he sees Jacob enraged in this way. Titus may be a Catholic but he had certainly been sufficiently connected with the Warden of Chetham Hospital College – a charitable school for the area's luckier orphans – to fulfil his older brother's wish and secure young Aran a place. The boy qualified as an orphan, but he had most definitely not been a citizen of the parishes that were beneficiaries of this establishment, and could normally, therefore, not have gained entry. But he had soon been installed in one of the school's ten dormitories, sharing that peculiar and dubious honour of being one of the deserving and, thus, privileged poor.

Along with his fellows, Aran had studied Virgil's *Aeneid*, or the works of Cicero and Ovid, always with the assistance of Lily's Latin *Grammar*. Molière or Cervantes in translation. Other times, students were required to study Bailey's *Dictionary*, and to test their spelling skills against its incalculable number of entries, or to have their arithmetic improved by a growing familiarisation with algebra or Pythagorean theorems. Meanwhile, Aran's writing had been improved by reproducing sections of Eachard's *Roman History*, or Abbé Bannier's *Mythology*, in English translation, of course.

But it had been their study of the natural philosophies that particularly attracted him. On the one hand, the school had acquired the recently published two-volume edition of Miller's *Gardener's and Botanist's Dictionary*. A special edition with illustrations from the work of Maria Sibylla Merian. These were reproductions of her original watercolours and Aran had been entranced by their intricacy, spending endless hours by candle-stub attempting their imitation. On the other hand, the Chetham's Library also held a valuable copy of Philippe de Thaon's *Bestiaire*, And there he had found the picture of a simian which now comes to mind whenever Aran encounters Jacob Driscoll. Driscoll is thirty-three years old, horse-faced and morose, ape-like arms over-long for his body.

'And when, Jacob,' says Titus, 'we are no *longer* distinguished, when the Whigs of this town see me as an equal, rather than as a Catholic, then I shall shave it.'

'Pox on it, Titus!' shouts Francis Townley. 'Are we summoned for no other purpose than to discuss your facial hair?' Townley is two years older than Jacob Driscoll, a person of some notoriety in the town for he had once been a child page to the Dowager Queen of Spain. It had made him precocious and he has never recovered. Inheriting his father's fortune much earlier than had been good for him, he had later found it necessary to seek service abroad, entering French military service in the Régiment de Limousin. It has left him with an affectation for elaborate dress.

'One day, Francis, your impatience will see you swing, I swear it will! No,' says Titus, 'I have news.'

'More news,' says Scatterbuck, 'and not a decent broadsheet in this hinterland within which to print it.' Scatterbuck is the oldest of the gathering, his clothes ill-fitting. His rolling, lumpen face is permanently shaded with printer's ink and a fine slick of sweat, smeared regularly by a stained kerchief. Titus weighs his comment for a moment.

'There are times when you manage to inspire me, Adam. But let me not digress. This news is urgent enough even for *you*, for Sir Peter Leighton is struck down.'

'Infirm?' asks Driscoll.

'Of the worst kind, for he is slain – murdered as bold as brass.'

'Not a robbery then?' says Aran.

'*Assassinato!*' says Townley, and Titus Redmond smiles sardonically in confirmation.

'No clues,' he says, 'bating the ramble of so-called witnesses claiming this as the handiwork of some transient priest. They could not even describe the fellow.'

'God's Hooks!' says Townley. 'Then it has begun at last!'

'Tha' thinks this good news?' says Jacob Driscoll. 'Tha' Frenchified fop...'

'Fop?' Townley shouts. 'By our Lady, sir...'

'Put up, Townley,' says Titus. 'And *you*, Jacob – moderate yourself or, by God, you'll answer for it.' None of them, even Townley, will dispute Titus Redmond's authority.

'But Leighton was t' only 'ope for 'oldin' together our friends in Cheshire,' says Driscoll, still glowering at Townley, resentful of his French sympathies, for Jacob Driscoll believes himself justified in despising all things French. During the previous Jacobite Rising, in the Year '15, Driscoll's father had been a gentleman of substance amongst the Lancashire supporters of the Stuarts. Promised support from the French that had never materialised, the Rising had been brutally put down and Driscoll's father executed, the deed witnessed by his son, just five years of age at the time. He chews this memory again now, while Adam Scatterbuck considers the implications of Titus Redmond's news.

'Rain and troubles alike can each bring clearer skies in their wake,' says Scatterbuck. 'Rain and troubles alike can also be great levellers, reducing us in our search for shelter and safety, uniting us in our miseries and discomforts. Unless I am mistaken, Titus, you will have spoken with our friends elsewhere.'

'For somebody who looks such a fool, Adam, you so often have the right of it! As it happens, I have met our Welsh Lord, just yesterday evening. Sir Watkin Williams Wynn,' he says, pronouncing each part of the name deliberately, stressing the first letter each time. 'Name like a wet quim, but he *has* asked us to consider two initiatives...'

He jumps down from his throne of yarn bales, dragging some of them aside to discover small wooden crates beyond. These crates are square-sided, measuring some thirty-six inches on each dimension, more cumbersome than heavy. Each crate is marked identically with a red, stencilled monkey and oriental design, or character, with a red, octagonal surround, the mark of the Swedish East India Company. Aran Owen knows these crates. He knows the contents. Tea. He admires the miracle of *camellia sinensis*, that over three thousand varieties can be produced from just one shrub. Just one shrub but, depending on where it is grown, on the nature of the soil in which it is planted, or the climate in which it is nurtured, hundreds of variations in the flavour and texture of the leaf can be produced. Depending on how they are withered, dried, allowed to ferment and exposed to the elements in the process will produce either Black or Green teas. And the white shades, Oolongs. Very rare, dried by steaming for the colour to be reduced and, because it is rare – almost without price.

'First thing,' says Titus. 'Sir Watkin suggests that we do some more damage to the income of the Hanover rats by stepping up this little commercial enterprise of ours. If the war goes on much longer, they'll be weakened for want of finances.'

'And we cannot now have long to wait for the next turn of events, with the French and English fleets glaring at each other across the Channel,' says Francis Townley. Titus stares coldly at Jacob Driscoll, silencing any further outburst against the French. 'Yet with no disrespect intended, sir, I fail to see, by the Mass, how some exercise in contraband…'

'Because finance is the very fabric of war, sir,' says Scatterbuck, 'as I am sure your service for King Louis must have taught you. With the French invasion fleet already assembled, it seems hard to credit that they will not land an army on English soil before too long, but this time we must be certain that, with or without the French, the Cause will benefit from a leaner Hanoverian purse!'

'Stuff, gentlemen!' says Titus, impatiently. 'I do not mean to rail against this company yet it is crucial that all should understand fully. It will not serve else! Aran, remind our good friends, if you please, about the finer points.'

Both Townley and Driscoll have objections rising in their throats, neither of them inclined to lessons from the younger man, but checked by Redmond's extended finger, menacing each in turn.

'Well,' says Aran, 'as we all know, one of the main sources of revenue for the Government, for the Hanoverian Government that is, stems from the Customs duty imposed on luxury imports, and the biggest single contribution comes from the duty on tea.'

'As you put it so eloquently, Master Owen,' says Townley, 'we all *know* this. The bigger problem for our Friends in Exile is how to gain value from the Treasury Silver that King James managed to transfer abroad, now that the Hanoverians have devalued it at a stroke with their bloody Gold Standard. Is that not the problem in the fabric of our finances, Scatterbuck?'

'But we are learning' says Aran, 'to bend this apparent set-back to our proper devices – using the silver to buy tea from the Far East, where silver maintains its value. We bring the tea into England, as contraband, denying a small fortune in revenue to the Government. And, finally, the sale of *our* tea, at prices that undercut the legal trade, produces profit in gold that can be used at home to further the Cause.'

'And all of this,' says Titus, 'conducted through a whole network of operations, like our own, around much of the coast, and managed by the

Swedes, in willing and successful competition with the fucking *British* East India Company, thereby denying further profits to the state. And the task of expanding our select circle of customers falls to you, Aran.'

A gesture of confidence from his master that causes Aran to colour slightly, yet he catches too the sneering responses from both Driscoll and Townley.

'What, Jacob?' says Titus. 'You think I should have given this task to *you*? This requires delicacy, and your own strengths tend more towards dealing with those Manxmen who pass for smugglers. And you, Townley...'

'Fie, you think I have some design on these mercantile duties?'

'No sir!' says Titus. 'You, sir, were intended to represent our interests in dealing with those politician cunny-suckers. All that poxing work to force Walpole's resignation. For what?'

'To replace him with that bubble Pelham!' Scatterbuck says.

'No better than Walpole was! But Sir Watkin Williams Wynn,' Titus exaggerates the words once more, 'has a surprise in store for our good friend Pelham.'

'We start taking the Excise off them as well as the Customs duty?' suggests Aran.

Titus pats him on the shoulder. 'Smart man!' he says. The Excise duty is another major contributor to the realm's revenue, with taxes raised on beer, malt, hops, soap, candles, leather and other commodities, gathered locally by an appointed worthy in each town or district, then collected by travelling officials. In Manchester, the Excise is gathered by a certain Mistress Cooper, proprietor of the Old Coffee House, frequented by the Whigs and herself a Whig supporter, but universally respected for her general impartiality 'But we will do nothing in the town itself,' Titus continues. 'We cannot risk an offence to Mistress Cooper.'

'Then we wait until the Excise is collected and, well, divert it?' Francis Townley suggests.

'And by a strange coincidence,' says Titus, 'we know almost exactly when that collection will take place. During the last week in March, on Lady Day itself. When the Quarter Day taxes are collected, including all the year-end outstanding debts, it will amount to a pretty penny. It seems they have no intention of leaving such a large sum in town for too long. A job for *you*, Jacob, I think! To scare the Excise men just a little.'

The gathering breaks up soon afterwards, with secrecies sworn between each of them, so that only Titus Redmond and Jacob Driscoll remain to secure the premises.

'You know, Jacob, I have a mind to call next door and collect my profits from the bawdy house. Maybe one of our bulk-mongers can help cure this itch in my pricker at the same time!'

Chapter Four

'Music has charms to soothe a savage breast,' according to Congreve. And John Byrom, being an admirer of this eminent playwright, has chosen to follow his example this Shrovetide for several reasons. First, he abhors the base and illicit practices, and particularly Throwing at Cocks, which normally mark a week of northern carnevale preceding the beginning of Lent. Second, he looks constantly for ways in which this divided town may set aside its differences from time to time and, traditionally, the performance of public entertainments has betimes served this purpose to good effect. And, third, he feels it his personal mission to bring cultural enlightenment to the benighted local citizenry.

Mister Byrom has influence, too, and has thus persuaded this year's Constables that they should pay the Bellman to cry the event about town for, he argues, it is civic news. Besides, they need some distraction, for the Bellman has been engaged all of the previous week with news of the war. The London papers full of it also. First, that violent storms in the Channel have scattered English and French fleets alike, so any chance of invasion set aside. But, second, that Admiral Mathews has been badly beaten at Toulon and forced to retire on Menorca, leaving the Spaniards in control of the Mediterranean.

So the Bellman has made his rounds amongst the major thoroughfares and commercial streets, many lined on both sides with all manner of shops and emporiums. *Tonight, at the Commerce Exchange, a Dramatick Entertainment...* Two or three storey buildings lean towards each other so that they almost form archways above the lanes. Periwig makers and milliners; toymen and tailors; haggars and hucksters; sugar bakers and shag makers; whitesmiths and woollen drapers; chandlers and chocolate-houses. And he has been forced to compete, this Bellman, voice and clapper alike, against the town's cacophony of sound. *Neat feet and lights*, calls the offal seller, her barrow spilling over with tripe and trotters. *Flints and steels*, from a one-legged trader, his tray of fire strikes slung about his neck. *Kit-cats. Lovely kit-cats*, cries the pieman, pushing another dish of mutton pasties into his mobile oven. *Your Honours! Messieurs!* shouts the nosegay seller, exposing more of her attributes than seems respectable. In *this* Manchester, the scent of gut fat licks against rosemary and wafts across meat juices, backed by the essence of hot pastry.

Many of these scents now also fill the Commerce Exchange itself, as the audience gathers for the evening's performance and bring with them the food and drink that they will either consume if they are happy with the entertainment, or use as constructive criticism if they are not! There is little chance of unhappiness tonight though for Mister Byrom has astutely sponsored and arranged for a singular piece of theatre to be presented. The first staging in Manchester of John Gay's *The Beggar's Opera*, complete with travelling recitalists and an exceptional tenor undertaking the part of MacHeath.

The crowd gathers, passing through the enormous columns of the recently constructed Exchange and mounting the wide staircase to the first floor space where the Court Leet gathers twice each year and which, between meetings, serves as the town's principal theatre and concert hall. Such is the crowd, in fact, that the Borough Reeve and his two Constables are concerned that the floor might not support their weight, but Byrom assures them, with all the certainty that his reputation commands, that they have nothing to fear.

After all, he *is* a Fellow of the Royal Society, is he not? A published author besides, and his book does *sell* very well! During the past eighteen years, Byrom has popularised the use of shorthand with this volume. A great development, which has quite properly resulted in both his election to the Society and also his receipt of a Parliamentary Licence, giving him sole rights to teach his system, *and* the sole rights to levy a fee on those to whom he allows a franchise.

Surely, therefore, nothing can stand in the way of a successful evening and yet it is possible that Mister Byrom has lacked imagination here, an accusation frequently cast in his direction. For this Ballad Opera is not without its opponents, equally likely to factionalise any audience rather than unite them. It is, after all, written as a parody of the part played by Sir Robert Walpole in the South Seas Company affair though, by now, most of the play's anti-Whig sentiment has lost its sting.

At the head of the stairs stand the gentlemen merchants, the very Whigs against whom the piece was initially conceived, gathered around James Bradley and his fellow Jurors, the town elders from the Court Leet. John Clowes, Robert Jobb and others. They have already exhausted debate about events abroad. The perfidious French. Still technically no declaration of war yet actively engaged against Britain this last year and more. Deserved the thrashing at Dettingen. Never believed that there *would* be an invasion! And they move to more immediate concerns.

'I had the misfortune to see one of the original performances,' says Jobb, 'at Lincoln's Inn Field, with that warbler Fenton playing Polly Peachum. Tits like pumpkins but dreadful voice!'

'With the Italian divas you usually get decent tits and a good soprano besides,' says Bradley. 'But we're not treated to Opera of *any* sort very often. Churlish to miss the opportunity...'

21

'And speaking of tits...' says John Clowes, directing their attentions to the small group just climbing the stairs.

Maria-Louise Redmond's dress is, indeed, low-cut but no more than is fashionable, and she lifts the hoops supporting her skirts of flowered silk, revealing her stockings of green, worked with clocks of gold thread. Her face is whitened and rouged tonight, her lips bee-stung with *Ceruse*, shoulders and breasts alike powdered to match her coiffure.

She is accompanied tonight by Adam Scatterbuck since Titus will not, of course, attend such events, preferring the lavish attentions of a doxy or two whenever the chance allows. In any case, he too is absorbed with thoughts of the French. As they reach the top of the staircase, Bradley steps forward to take and kiss her hand.

'It seems,' he whispers, indicating his companions with his eyes, 'that I am not alone in wishing to fuck you.'

'It is only fair,' she replies, 'given that Titus and myself are trying to perform the same act with each of their businesses.' And she honours them with her sweetest smile, unlike Rosina, just a few steps behind her mother and suddenly deep in conversation with Jacob Driscoll. Her lace-gloved hand rests on his right arm, while Aran Owen does his very best to keep station on her other side. He thinks that she looks distinctly less precocious than usual tonight, in a dress of green satin, also hooped after the fashion, and her hair combed high in ringlets. She spurns the leaded powder that her mother favours, but follows the vogue of wearing a black taffeta heart-shaped patch near the corner of her left eye – a public statement of her passion on the one hand, and her Tory politics on the other. And tonight the politics run high, for she does not share her mother's muted delight that the French have shown, yet again, an inability to aid their Cause.

'Keep me from those cankerous Whigs,' she says, and Jacob steers her away from Bradley's group. Poor Jacob! He looks uncomfortable at the best of times but tonight more so, his hair held back in a Tie Wig, the queue encased in a black satin bag and his clothes fitting even worse than Adam Scatterbuck's. Impossible for him, however, to miss the chance of such intimacy with Rosina. But now he seems confused, looking for some alternative route so he can comply with her wishes.

'Look!' says Aran, trying to help and, at the same time, steal a march on Jacob. 'Stubbs – we could go and introduce ourselves.'

George Stubbs is barely twenty but establishing a prodigious reputation as an artist and presently on a short visit to Manchester from his native Liverpool. Aran has already taken an opportunity to make himself known, been awed by the other's tranquil maturity, jealous that he can already make his way as a portraitist.

'I hope that he is better able to apply his skills than to work on silly trade bills,' Rosina says. 'Anodyne necklaces indeed! Empiric remedies. Did it never

22

occur to you, Master Owen, that families able to afford five shillings for such a frippery are unlikely to have much difficulty sustaining their children in the first place?'

Deflated, he trails meekly behind Rosina, having to endure a sarcastic grin from Driscoll, whom she guides away from George Stubbs as well, heading instead for Elizabeth Cooper. Mistress Cooper is evidently pleased to see her and Rosina, in turn, displays no obvious sign of animosity to this Whig collector of the Hanoverians' Excise.

'Mistress Cooper,' she says, attempting to mask her sarcasm, 'I understand that Turnip George intends to simplify the Excise digest – so that, in future, only we Tories need to pay?'

'I understand that he was *completely* shocked to find that we have Whiggish friends who are still paying,' Elizabeth replies, pleased to share the jest. Her heavy brocade dress in somewhat out of fashion but it is hooped in the oval style. She is tall and fair, sports a small patch too, in Spanish leather, but unlike Rosina she shows her politics by wearing it on the right side of her nose.

'Tha' knows,' says Jacob Driscoll, 'that it 'as been a difficult year. Seems we may need more time than usual to gather t' Excise duty from our own produce, Mistress.'

'La, Mister Driscoll!' Elizabeth Cooper replies, 'I think that Titus Redmond has several women in his employ who are *far* more qualified than myself to advise on how a gentleman's extension may be handled.' And she turns to a conversation with local church leaders leaving an amused Rosina and her embarrassed entourage to pass within the auditorium.

For the Bellman, still on duty, is now calling the performance's opening. Temporary boxes have been constructed above the sides of the hall but the majority stand in a solid circle, hardly breaking their conversations, while the Beggar and the Player, joint narrators, introduce the Opera. Witty. Then, 'Play away the overture!'

Act One, in which Peachum, both thief-catcher *and* fence complains that his thieves are unproductive. His wife protests that one of them, Bob Booty has been very productive indeed.

The Tories in the audience roar with laughter, for Bob Booty has also been Robert Walpole's nickname for some years and, despite no longer holding office, the satire still has resonance.

Meanwhile, the Peachums discover, the famous Highwayman MacHeath apparently intends to marry their daughter, Polly.

'By the Mass,' says James Bradley to his friends, 'does MacHeath not remind you of Titus Redmond? I'd not let him marry any daughter of mine.'

Back on the makeshift stage, the Peachums conclude that the match may make sense if they can discover MacHeath's treasure and kill him for it.

In the box shared by Elizabeth Cooper and the assorted clergy, there are gasps of indignation at this want of moral standards.

'It is little wonder,' says the Reverend Doctor John Clayton, 'that the Bishop of York has forbidden performances of this travesty!'

'You seem to be enjoying it well enough, Reverend,' says Elizabeth. She looks with disdain on Clayton, his face powdered to cover the premature corruption beneath. He has all the mannerisms of a dandy and carries an ornate ivory walking cane which, periodically, he uses to scratch at the vermin within his full-bodied wig. To Elizabeth, he carries the stench of both internal and political decay.

Clayton is a Chaplain at the Collegiate Church, Christ's Church, now strongly associated with the Tory cause, its congregation being Episcopalian – High Church Anglicans, largely out of favour with the Presbyterian majority within the Protestant Faith. Clayton's sympathies lie with the Non-Jurors, who will not renounce their allegiance to the Jacobite Cause and are not, therefore, recognised by the establishment, and particularly by the Government, to pursue their Ministry. Still, Clayton continues as the Anglicans' High Priest although, as an open advocate of Jacobitism, he remains largely ineligible to take part in either the legal processes of the town or the election of its officials. Elizabeth supposes that she should feel some sympathy for the man, so recently widowed and bereft of his second son – yet he simply disgusts her, along with his fellows at the Collegiate Church.

Like most other Presbyterians in town, Elizabeth worships at Manchester's new church, Saint Ann's although, even there, the Rector is also strongly inclined towards Non-Jurist principles – Joseph Hoole, an unlikely ally for Reverend Clayton.

'There is still much to enjoy in the performance,' he says, 'without being influenced by its morality. The Church is under attack on all sides, my dear, and we should understand our enemies so that we may defeat them.'

His Assistant Curates are Ben Nichols and Tom Lewthwaite, frequently at odds with their Rector and the Non-Jurors but united on this point at least.

'The Rector is absolutely right, Mistress Cooper,' says Lewthwaite. 'You were present, I think, when Mister Wesley delivered his sermon?'

John Wesley has recently completed his second visit to the town. He had preached at St Ann's Church and, whilst heckled by some of the congregation, his evangelical Methodist attacks on corrupt clergymen, and the failure of the established churches to call sinners into repentance, were aimed mainly at the Catholic Faith – and therefore well received by the majority, despite the lack of any meaningful distinction between Catholicism and the High Church Anglicans.

'Personally,' says Clayton, 'I account Wesley a good friend. We were at Oxford together, did you know? Hardly a manifestation of the anti-Christ. He *does* have a tendency to act as though he were still undertaking missionary work amongst the savages. La, I have bespoke him many times on the matter

24

yet he will insist on acting as though we are some lawless gang of rogues operating beyond the Pale...'

There is a short break before the opening of Act Two while the modest scenery is changed, and Elizabeth Cooper takes the opportunity to excuse herself. She steps down from the box, pays her respects to John Byrom and his family in the adjoining box, and almost collides with Rosina Redmond who has also managed temporarily to escape the attentions of both Driscoll *and* Master Aran Owen.

'It is unusual indeed,' says Elizabeth, 'to find you without a veritable coterie of gentlemen escorts.'

'Clearly not a problem that we share,' replies Rosina, but instantly regrets the sharpness of her tongue. 'I apologise. I only meant...'

'I take no offence, Rosina,' says Elizabeth, and she laughs at the situation. 'Shall I tell you a secret? I enjoy the company of men admirably enough, but often only in measured doses. And, d'you know, I do not believe that I have ever counted one amongst my friends.'

'You have rejected all men as friends then, Mistress Cooper?'

'La! Not at all. Though I think that, in society, there can often be a fear that some of us, once we understand the benefits of female friendship, may choose not to marry or follow normal traditions.'

'There are too many differences between us, I think,' says Rosina, 'for you and I to ever be friends.'

'Fie upon it! What stuff! We *shall* be friends, Rosina, I am perfectly sure of it.'

She touches Rosina's arm and smiles warmly just as Act Two commences.

MacHeath is now in a tavern where he is surrounded by women of dubious virtue, discovering too late, that two of them, Jenny Diver and Suky Tawdry, have contracted with Peachum to capture him, and he becomes a prisoner in Newgate prison.

'By all that is Holy!' exclaims Reverend Clayton. 'Diver and Tawdry indeed! Breech-clad bawds I'll be bound. Practitioners of the Silent Sin.'

'Sapphists, you think?' says Hoole.

'What else?' says Clayton. 'Tawdry. As Flawed as Saint Audrey's Lace. Is that not the meaning? Tribady, sir. Nothing less than tribady.'

'Oh my goodness!'

The prison is run by Peachum's associate, the corrupt Jailer Lockit, whose daughter, Lucy, helps MacHeath to escape by stealing her father's keys. Lockit and Peachum discover MacHeath's hiding place and decide to split his fortune.

Intermission, and the local traders have excelled themselves for, outside the building, braziers have been lit and refreshments prepared.

Elizabeth looks for Rosina again, hoping to continue their discussion, but finds that James Bradley has gently taken her arm.

'I need to speak with you, my dear,' he says. 'Come, let us sample the food while we talk. That scent of rosemary denotes savouried eels unless I am mistaken.'

'A dish to which I have never fully taken,' says Elizabeth. 'They flourish so in the Irk but I cannot stop myself from thinking of the questionable wastes that I have so frequently seen spilling into the river from the fulling mills and dye-house there.'

'Yes,' says Bradley. 'Strange that so many items of note here in Manchester should be nurtured by the town's effluent. Which reminds me…' He pauses at a second stall, rich with the mixed and complementary aromas of trout with bacon, a traditional local recipe, and one more suited to Elizabeth's tastes. 'I have some news about the Redmonds,' he continues, when she has sampled the trout and pronounced that it is admirable.

'Concerning the Excise collection, I assume,' she says.

Yes, he is afraid so. Too many questions asked. He has a suspicion, no more than that, but since the Excise men are due very soon, he will arrange for the Constables to be on hand for her protection.

Not far away, a crowd is gathering around different stalls, where keepsakes and mementos of the evening are on sale. Images of Polly Peachum adorn fans and small firescreens while a series of broadsides feature all the major characters, along with extracts of the more popular scores, an enterprise of collaboration once again, between Adam Scatterbuck and Aran Owen.

'Beyond my wildest expectations,' says Scatterbuck. 'Handsomely done, Master Owen.'

'I never believed that we could finish them in time,' says Aran.

'They are fine images indeed, Aran. Very fine,' says Maria-Louise, and she touches his cheek with rare and genuine affection that moves him considerably. He has never been sure of his relationship with Mrs Redmond. For some time when he first arrived in Manchester she was simply aloof, polite enough but no more. Although, in truth, he had never *expected* more.

'This leaves me with a problem though, ma'am,' says Scatterbuck, 'for I cannot leave these rogues with all the proceeds of our work. Perhaps if either Master Owen or myself…'

'Think nothing of it, Mister Scatterbuck. I am sure that Master Owen will ensure my safe return home. Is that not so, Aran?'

Aran agrees, of course, and the Bellman calls everybody back for the Third and Final Act, in which Polly visits Lucy to try to reach an agreement about their rivalry for MacHeath's affections, but Lucy has decided to poison her. Polly narrowly avoids the poisoned draught, and the two girls find out that MacHeath has been recaptured.

In the final scenes, Lucy and Polly each plead with their respective fathers for MacHeath's life. However, MacHeath now finds that four more pregnant women each claim him as their husband. He declares that he is ready to be

26

hanged although, to satisfy the audience, the villain is reprieved, and all are invited to a dance of celebration, to celebrate his wedding to Polly.

And so it ends. The audience dances, with only a few exceptions and Aran Owen is, at first, one of them.

'It would be chivalrous, Master Owen,' says Maria-Louise Redmond, 'if my companion should invite me to dance.' Thus they dance and, as they dance, a strange thing passes between the younger man and the older woman. Something that neither of them might have expected and, before long, not really able to recall how the initiative was taken, they are below, in the deserted market area of the ground floor. Behind a column, he grapples with the hoops of her skirts, lifting them up so that they almost hide her ecstatic features, straining over them to smear the *Ceruse* from her bee-stung lips with his frantic kisses, groping within the endless layers of petticoat until, finally, he is able to feel the soft down of her bare cunny.

But as quickly as it began, it also ends. He finds that he cannot continue. Passions aroused physically but, within, he thinks only of...

'Rosina?' she asks him, ecstasy now replaced with some annoyance.

'It does not seem...'

'Proper, I think is the word you might have been seeking. But I tell you, Master Owen, that Rosina will not have you, whereas I most certainly *shall!*'

He stammers some foolish apologies while, outside, Rosina Redmond has just left the building in company with Jacob Driscoll and Mistress Elizabeth Cooper. Driscoll is keen to be alone with the younger woman. He is a man hardened by many experiences in life but, with her, he becomes docile, adoring, almost canine in his affections.

'Have you seen the sequel, perchance?' asks Elizabeth and, of course, Rosina has not.

'You would enjoy it, I am sure. More wonderful tunes. It is set in the West Indies and simply called *Polly*. MacHeath has been sentenced to Transportation but escaped and become a pirate, while poor Polly has been kidnapped and threatened with being sold into slavery. She too escapes, dressed as a boy and eventually discovers that perhaps a boy is exactly what God intended her to be.'

'An improbable story, I think,' says Rosina while Driscoll bids Mistress Cooper farewell, until their next meeting.

'Ah yes,' says Elizabeth. 'I am sure that we will meet again shortly, Mister Driscoll, and hopefully under equally pleasant circumstances. And Polly's story is less improbable than you might imagine.'

And, at that moment, something strange also passes between Elizabeth Cooper and Rosina Redmond.

'You must visit me, Rosina,' says Elizabeth.

'Oh, I *shall* do so!' says the young Miss Redmond.

Chapter Five

'I have seen the spectre in that exact place,' says Francis Townley, pointing petulantly to the far end of this extraordinary room, where the afternoon sunlight bursts against the dark panelling.

He is standing in the oak-lined Long Gallery of his birthplace, near Burnley's Calder. Even Titus must admit, despite his rancour at having to travel such a distance for the meeting, that the Hall is impressive, a large three-storey mansion built around an open court.

'Francis always had a vivid imagination as a youngster,' says Townley's brother, John, senior to his sibling by a good ten years. Titus has taken an instant liking to this elder Townley, a man with a more open and intelligent face than Francis, with his crook-tooth'd tendency to spittle. *Now, this man is a fighter*, he thinks. And, indeed, he is. A serving officer in the Black Musketeer company of the French Guard Cavalry, formerly a Captain in Rothe's Regiment of the Irish Brigade in French service.

Sir Watkin Williams Wynn comes to stand alongside Francis, puts a hand on his shoulder. 'And your spectre must be one of these gentlemen, I collect?' He gestures to the portraits of Townley ancestors, set within each of the wall panels around them.

'Here,' says John. 'My namesake. Sir John Townley. He apparently enclosed some of the Common Land and has been punished, in death, by walking these rooms every seven years to inflict grief on the family.'

'I understand that you, too, are prone to appear periodically, Captain, just like the Townley boggart.' The speaker is another of the Welsh party, the lawyer David Morgan. From his background, Titus knows that he too must be in his late-forties yet he seems considerably younger. And he is evidently surprised that *each* of the Townley brothers has been on the verge of responding to him.

'You must needs remember, Mister Morgan,' says John, 'that my brother is also still *Captain* Townley. He may not presently be active in his regiment but he remains entitled to his rank. And, yes, my duties to King Louis enable me only infrequent visits to England. Yet hopefully as the harbinger of better news, when I *am* able to appear.'

'While the boggart to which you refer so lightly is a harbinger of an entirely different kind,' says Francis. 'My family feels its hand gripping our hearts too frequently to merely set it aside as an invention of our imaginations.' And he casts a glance of almost open contempt towards his brother.

'It was not my intention to treat lightly the recent woes of your family, gentlemen,' says David Morgan. 'Sir Watkin has, of course, told us a little on our journey north. I offer you sincere condolences.'

Titus had been reluctant to meet here for this very reason. *Pox'd place is accursed for certain*, he thinks. *You can feel it from the moment you enter.* The Hall has, until recently, been in the hands of the Townleys' nephew, William. But William had died just two years previously, at the age of twenty-seven, and exactly seven years from the death of his father, their eldest brother, Richard.

'I knew your brother well,' says Sir Watkin. 'And Mister Morgan tells me that he took a keen interest in his trial.'

'I believe,' says Morgan, 'that it inspired me to study the law. Though I was a poor student. I may have been bred to the law, but I confess that I have never pretended to much knowledge that way. And then came the Rising in '15. I would have come out, was on my way once I heard that Forster was moving south with a Jacobite army. But all over before it was begun. The surrender at Preston, the fighting there. And then news of the trials for treason. Treason, mind! Yet news of Richard Townley defending himself against all those petty-foggers trickled through even to Pen-y-Graig. And such a defence. Astonishing.'

'A certain amount of mythology always attends these matters, do you not find, Mister Morgan?' says John Townley. 'For, while it is true that Richard defended himself in the court proper, he had needs employed a whole army of lawyers, or so it seemed to us, to help him in the preparation. There were days when the Hall seemed full to bursting with them. Do you recall, Francis?'

'I was still small,' says his brother, 'not yet eight years old. And they seemed like so many black-winged crows, flapping about the house. Too young to understand, but they frightened me more than the spectre has *ever* done. But Brother Richard was a great hero to me then. Why, he had fought for the True King! Yet I recall him weeping like a woman when the oaks in the parkland had to be felled so he might pay the butcher's bill from those lawyers, Mister Morgan.'

But there was enough left in the coffers for Brother Richard to virtually reconstruct two entire wings just a few years later, thinks Titus. *And your family might have lost a few oaks, while mine lost almost everything.* Such company he keeps. The Townley brothers may not have been senior enough to inherit the Hall and estates, as Richard had done, but their father had left them an inheritance sufficient to keep each in relative comfort. Both had chosen to supplement their inheritance through foreign service but the clothes of Francis Townley, at least, speak of extravagance. His brother more sombrely dressed, although still with a style that suits his position, and then, of course, there is Sir Watkin. A florid man, a life-long Tory and Member of Parliament for Denbighshire for more years than Titus cares to remember. Twenty-five or thirty, he supposes. Apart from the spell when he was unseated through corruption and vote-rigging by the Whigs in '41. He was back soon enough though. And Titus supposes that, as one of the four wealthiest men in the Realm, Sir Watkin Williams Wynn may not have been too troubled by his temporary absence from the House.

So what brings you here, Sir Watkin? thinks Titus. *The rest of us I understand.* The Townleys are Catholic Royalists bred in the bone. Morgan is a High Church romantic who lays all the ills of the poor and the dispossessed at the door of the State. It happens to be a Hanoverian State just now. And Titus? Yes, Catholic too, but from as different a background to these Townleys as may be possible. For people like him, his Faith is an anchor that binds him to the river bed, but an anchor set to hold him fast not by his own hand yet, rather, by the cunny-lickers who hold power, who still fear Papism as though it were the plague. *But you, Sir Watkin?* Titus Redmond is no fool and understands that, at times, folk may become attached to a particular cause simply by chance, rather than circumstance. He has seen such adherents before, fears them in many ways for, whilst some of these may sway with the wind and change sides as frequently as their clothing, others who come to a cause by accident are frequently able to construct for themselves a set of roots which then come to bind them far more securely than the natural disaffections felt by, say, Morgan, the Townleys or even himself. He wonders whether Sir Watkin might be such a one, for he can see no obvious connection between the Baronet and the Jacobite Cause that he has espoused with relentless fervour for twenty years and more. This is not simply his Tory affiliation since, as Titus knows well, there are *far* more High Church Tories who oppose the Stuarts than those who would seek their restoration. And such has been the case since Bishop Atterbury's failed lunatic plot in '22 to kidnap the Royal Family and have them replaced.

John Townley is, by now, leading them towards the Great Dining Room where supper is promised, and explaining some of the Hall's history.

'Yet, Sir Watkin,' he says, 'you, yourself, have one of those fine London houses built by Charles Downing, I fancy?'

'In the very street that bears his name. Yes, at Number Fourteen. An excellent location. So near to the centre of things. It serves my purpose very well. Mister Morgan and myself are able to meet at regular intervals. He has rooms in Shoreditch and helps me greatly with the Independent Electors' Club. The numbers grow each week and I think we can promise a good showing from our London Jacobites, Captain, when the time comes.'

'But I think, sir,' says Morgan, 'that it might give a false impression if we were to place over-much emphasis on the London situation. If it is not indiscreet to say so, there is a general belief among our people that, when the time *does* arrive, any attempt will come once again from the north. That the matter will be settled long before we need to consider London. And that, therefore, it is our fellows in Wales who may be more pertinent to the outcome.'

'I think we may safely assume, gentlemen, with some degree of certainty,' says John Townley, 'that, once there is no longer any obstacle to separate a Jacobite force from the Capital, it will be hard to find an inhabitant of that dissolute city who will not profess himself a life-long supporter of the True King. But Their Majesties are in one mind on this matter, both convinced that it will once again be the Highland Clans on whom the whole thing turns, along with the Lowland Scots. They will not all come out, of course, but the portents are positive and, assuming that events run broadly to plan, the next crucial issue becomes the border crossing. Much will depend on the reaction of the English, naturally, and the thing may rest with a purely tactical decision. All the same, it is more than likely that a march south will bring us through Lancashire rather than Yorkshire, Mister Redmond. I have heard my brother's views many times, as you can imagine, but you sir, how do you see the level of support on which we might rely?'

The company has descended now to the entrance-hall, itself a monument to Richard Townley who had ordered the removal of all the upper floors in this part of the middle, south-western wing, to create an impressive open space stretching up through the full three storeys of the building, handsome stone staircases with ornate iron balustrades climbing to each of the higher landings beyond.

Titus strokes his moustache for a moment, absorbing the opulence of his surroundings. 'And I assume, Captain,' he says, 'that you would expect me to speak plainly. I am a man of few words, as your brother will have told you, and most of those few were never designed for gentle ears. But I am a merchant, straight and simple, at least to my allies. I deal with profit and loss, so I see this whole affair in much the same way.'

'The military and the financial mind are never so far apart, I find,' says Sir Watkin, though he seems dubious about this proposed intervention from Titus.

'In that case,' Titus says, 'let me begin with the situation in Scotland, so far as I understand it. The Stuarts are a Scottish dynasty. They chime strongly with those who resent English rule, and particularly Hanoverian English rule. Scots Catholics, as well as your Episcopalian High Churchmen, have a peculiarly bad time of things since Presbyterianism has become, by law, the state church in Scotland. Catholics are strong amongst the Highland Clans while the Episcopalians are strong along the eastern coastlands of Aberdeen, Banff, Murray, East Lothian. But the old days when the Borders would rise at the drop of a hat to support the Stuarts have long gone. Glasgow, Renfrew, Lanark and Dumfries are more Hanoverian than Westminster. They have embraced Presbyterianism in such a way that they would *never* fight for a

Catholic monarch. And then, so many of the Clan Chiefs are reliant on England for their trade that they will not dare come out against the Hanoverians, whilst others will calculate that it is best to stay at home so that they might better plunder the homes of any absent neighbours. All told, I think you would be fortunate to raise ten thousand between the Highlands and Lowlands alike.'

'Better than twice that number were raised in '15,' says Francis Townley, 'with less preparation, and without the recent excesses of the Hanoverians to help us recruit.'

'Thirty years ago, Francis,' said his brother. 'Things have changed. And Mister Redmond's accountancy is important. Our Scottish friends have long memories. The thing that they remember most is that they were betrayed by the failure of enough Jacobites south of the border to come out in their support. No, Sir Watkin, I mean no offence to any here. It matters not whether they are right but their collective memory recalls it so.'

'And I, too, intend no offence, Captain Townley,' says Williams Wynn, 'when I say that the memory *south* of the Scottish border collects, rather, the number of times when we have been promised assistance by the French that has never materialised.'

'I am no official emissary, sir,' Townley replies, 'yet I think I can promise you a different outcome on this occasion.'

'I had a firm commitment to that effect from King Louis himself,' says Sir Watkin. 'But I had to be honest with him in return. Sir John Glynne and his Flintshire men are strong for the True King. Hundreds of them. I tell you that their blood is up although, as loyal as they might be, they will rise only if His Highness returns accompanied by a French army. I told them this at Versailles.'

Titus imagines the response which this dependency upon the French would evoke in his own household, from Maria-Louise especially, whilst Jacob Driscoll and his Ormschurch men would be enraged by any French involvement.

'French help may be welcome, Sir Watkin,' he says, 'but such dependency is another matter. Our balance sheet must show precisely the amount of support on which we can rely without foreign assistance, and it should be healthy enough to show that we can overcome the Hanoverians independently.' He marks off the reasons on his fingers. 'There are many here who will not come out if the French are involved, simply because they fear subservience to yet another foreign power. If we cannot deliver a Stuart restoration ourselves, how in fuck's name would they ever be able to rule the country afterwards? And if the French are unable to invade, whatever the reason, must we then resign ourselves to Hanoverian supremacy forever?'

'There is no question of French interference in the affairs of Britain, Mister Redmond,' says John Townley. 'King James is in possession of a sworn declaration from His Highness, King Louis, that his country has no imperial designs in this regard, that any French forces would be withdrawn as soon as the Stuarts are restored to the throne, and that French support is simply a recognition of the old alliance between Scotland, the Stuarts in particular, and France. Although perhaps interference is the wrong word, since conditions *do* exist of which, I assume, you gentlemen are aware?'

Titus finds that he is apparently the only one of the company who does not readily confirm knowledge of these *conditions*.

'I trust that there is nothing that has been kept from us?' he says.

'On the contrary, sir,' says Sir Watkin. 'The very purpose of my visit here, before meeting His Grace, the Duke of Perth, at Carlisle, was to bring welcome news, I think, to our comrades in Lancashire. Since the recent arrests, it seemed indiscreet to convey such news in any other way except in person.'

Titus recalls that fifteen thousand French troops had stood ready at Dunkirk, ready for a landing in Essex. In the middle of February, King George had informed Parliament about the planned invasion and a loyal address had been passed, though it was far from unanimous, supporting the Hanoverians in their commitment to thwart the French. The weather had intervened, however, as it so often does in English history, and the French fleet under Admiral de Roquefort had been scattered. Within days, arrests of suspected Jacobites had taken place, although surprisingly few of any note, and the Whigs were openly planning an Act to outlaw correspondence with the Stuarts. Discretion on the part of Williams Wynn therefore seems perfectly understandable to Titus Redmond, but he wonders how it transpires that Francis Townley has travelled here from Manchester with him, is clearly aware of the conditions of which his brother has spoken, but has said nothing to Titus himself in this regard. *Cunny-sucker*, thinks Titus. *Driscoll is right not to trust the prick!*

'These are dangerous times, Sir Watkin,' he says. 'Hardly the point at which important news can be entrusted to an express.'

'And this news in peculiar. I give you joy of it, for we are now assured that a landing will take place within the coming year and that, when the Stuart forces arrive, they will be led by the Young Prince, Charles Edward. King James has signed a Declaration. In truth, there were many Tory hands who helped with the drafting and I am proud to have played no insignificant part in the process. Yet we all agreed that the restoration would be, well smoother let us say, if there were fewer associations with the past. King James will therefore abdicate in favour of the Prince as soon as he reaches London. I have myself seen the signed Declaration. It was in Charles Edward's hands when he joined the invasion fleet last month. Such a wasted opportunity, yet I had counselled against the timing over and over again. February in the Channel. La! No sane man would have planned it so.'

'He carries the Declaration from King Louis also,' says Francis Townley. 'Confirming that the French have no territorial designs on England. This should be proof enough, Titus, even for Jacob Driscoll, that our French allies act only from good intent and, also, that this time they will surely come.'

'It is not Jacob Driscoll alone, Francis, who has cause to doubt the French,' says Titus, and he can almost hear Maria-Louise whispering in his ear. 'They did not come in '15. They did not come, as promised, four years later. And now, after all this time, they have not come this year either. But Jacob's strength, and the strength of many hundreds more in Lancashire, is that they will come out regardless of whether or not the French invade. But only so long as the balance sheet is in our favour, Sir Watkin. There can be no equivocation any more. The Scots must know that they can count on Lancashire. Lancashire must know that it can count on Wales. And we must all know that we can count on the Young Prince and London, both!'

'There is work to be done in Northumberland, Yorkshire and Ireland too,' says Sir Watkin. 'The very reason that I now repair to Carlisle. I should have been there earlier had I not been forced to deal with those damn'd ranters. Methodist Association of Wales, indeed! But those coves will not raise their heads again now awhile, I think.'

'At least, not until their heads are a little less bloodied,' says the lawyer, David Morgan, with a smile of satisfaction. I think, however, that I should point out for the sake of precision, Mister Redmond, that the failure in the Year '19, at least, cannot be laid at the door of the French.'

'I think we all understand Mister Redmond's point very well,' says John Townley. 'It is merely splitting hairs that the venture in '19 was led by the Spanish. The weather again, gentlemen, of course. That they succeeded in landing only two ships from a fleet of twenty-seven should give us pause for thought. But the entire thing collapsed due to lack of organised support amongst the Jacobites themselves, here in Britain. And if they had been organised, you would argue, sir, they should not have needed Spanish or French assistance to begin with. Am I correct? But there are two other factors to take into account now. The first is that, though the news may not have broken yet, King George will be receiving formal notification from His Majesty, King Louis, of course, that a state of war now exists between France and England.'

'Astonishing,' says Morgan, 'that hostilities can have proceeded these several years past without our countries deeming themselves to actually be at war. Why, Captain Townley, you were at Dettingen last June, I collect. A full-scale battle, with German George leading the Hanoverian army in person. Against a foe with whom we were not even at war. Astonishing, I protest.'

'We had a bad time of it at Dettingen. Noailles is a good commander. It would have been a fine trap. But Gramont lacks patience. He ordered the attack by the King's Horse too early, before the English were fully surrounded. Still, we drove them back, one regiment after another. It was the Austrians who saved them. Such a counter-attack. We lost many in the river though my own company found some decent ground on which to rally and reform.

But the lesson for us is that the English army is weak. If they can be brought to battle on more favourable ground, with less formidable allies, they can be beat. And once they are beat, the way lies open for a rising here. The mood will be right for it amongst the people.'

'But the other side of this coin, gentlemen,' says Titus, 'is undoubtedly that, with war declared, any act on the part of our friends here will now be treated as treason without any shadow of doubt. And we should take heed from Sir Peter Leighton's murder. Newcastle and Pelham have unleashed a new breed against us.'

John Townley looks grave, nods his head repeatedly. 'Newcastle has recruited an entire network of spies and skulkers,' he says. 'We have never seen its like before. And such fellows they are, too. Sir Peter's murder is a good example. The authorities have declared it a robbery, yet he was plainly lured to a place of assassination. And there is not even a hue and cry. I tell you that Newcastle has given these coves some form of *carte blanche*. He has even managed to insinuate them within our own people. I may not say too much on the matter. Indeed, I do not *know* too much, in truth. But it was certainly a clerk in the French Foreign Office, acting as part of this network, who passed the information to Newcastle about the invasion fleet. As you are aware, Sir Watkin, he implicated yourself, as well as the Duke of Beaufort and Lord Barrymore, in the process.'

'I have been expecting arrest or worse ever since,' says Sir Watkin. He is about to say more, until Cecilia Townley, William's widow, brings word that supper is served in the dining room above, on the first floor of the north wing. Two years after her husband's death, she still wears mourning clothes, and her thin mood darkens the room. The Townley brothers speak with her in gentle tones, play with the children while she, in turn, expresses concern for John's safety in particular. In a while, she clears the plates and Sir Watkin asks Titus to brief him on progress with their plans for raising funds.

'I fancy that Captain Townley understands the process well enough,' says Titus, 'since Francis is part of the planning team in Manchester. Put simply, though, we are using devalued Stuart silver to buy tea, then bringing it into the country but avoiding paying any duty at the point of entry. We sell the tea at a calculated price across the country, wherever we can do so safely. There are simply insufficient Excise Officer whoresons to threaten the trade. The Stuart silver thus becomes Hanoverian gold, and revenue for the Cause here in England.'

'There are others engaged in the same enterprise all across England,' says Sir Watkin, 'yet none on the scale of the Manchester initiative. Mister Redmond must be praised for his zeal. I had suggested to him also that, with the French fleet in the Channel, we might assume a more direct intervention, is that not so, sir? Yet I must allow that, with the attempt now deferred, it may be prudent to postpone this activity too.'

'Our plans are in place, gentlemen,' says Titus, ' and Lady Day is almost upon us. No, we shall proceed. The year-end Excise collection in Manchester is too large a prize to ignore at this juncture. The Prince's attempt may be postponed but it must still be imminent. And, once again, the more revenue we can raise for the Cause, the less reliance we shall have on others for its success.'

The Widow Townley returns with wine for the company.

'Ah!' says Francis. 'Let us take a bumper, toast the True King and our enterprise too.' Cups of claret are raised. 'And my Commission, John,' Titus hears him whisper to his brother. 'What does the King say about my Commission?' John Townley gives him some reassurance, tells him that he should have no concern in that regard. There is an understanding, but he must have patience.

'Well, to Lady Day!' says Sir Watkin. 'But you will have a care, sir, I trust. You have heard news from the south? Some excess shown by your counterparts there, I collect. Two over-diligent Excise men thrown in a well and stoned to death, they say. Meanwhile, myself, Beaufort, Barrymore and Orrery shall continue in our efforts amongst our Party to garner support for the Restoration.'

'But this is still not the official Tory line?' says Titus. 'Cunny-licking politicians!'

'Well, let us say that we are the significant minority!' says David Morgan. 'And all Remitters, each providing further subscription to the Cause.'

'Barrymore will not be much help, I fear, apart from financially,' says Williams Wynn. 'He was well placed at Marbury and Rock Savage to assume leadership of the Cheshire men. But he cannot even trust his own son, neither, a damn'd Whig of all things. Yet Flintshire will come with us and I think we have Shrewsbury too. It was the Saxe-Gotha woman who finally made the difference in Wales, I think. Do you not agree, Mister Morgan?'

Morgan does indeed. It was injury enough to his countrymen when a Hanoverian was invested as Prince of Wales, but when Frederick had married Augusta of Saxe-Gotha and she became his Princess at the age of twenty-five, without a single word of English, let alone Welsh, significant insult was added. That and the Courts of Justice Act, too, the attempts by the Chief Justice to make sure that all legal proceedings should be conducted only in English. Better that than in French or Latin perhaps. But such a slight against all those for whom Welsh is their only language. The thin end of a very long wedge, he assures them.

The woes of Morgan's countrymen continue while they return to the entrance-hall and the Green Room beyond, where he and the Townley brothers each take a pipe of tobacco, and Sir Watkin several pinches of snuff. These, at least, are habits that Titus Redmond has never formed and he cares not one jot about minor affronts to Welsh sensibilities. Instead, he has returned his attention to Sir Watkin Williams Wynn and the more significant matter of motivation. *You, Sir Watkin. The Duke of Beaufort. The Earl of Barrymore. And Lord Orrery, the Earl of Cork. The leaders of the Tory Remitters. Probably the four richest people in Britain,* he thinks. *And not one of you has more influence with the Crown than I myself. You plan to buy the Throne, Sir Watkin. Well, that is a game that more of us might yet play!*

Chapter Six

The Manchester coffee houses can compete with those of London neither in their number nor in their refinement but they share the fundamental features of such establishments throughout the country, attracting individuals of like minds and common interests to particular locations. So, on any given day, one may find the Tories, Episcopalians and Jacobites at the White Rose in Deansgate Street, and the Whigs, Presbyterians and Hanoverians at Elizabeth Cooper's Old Coffee House near the Exchange. Unsurprisingly, Mistress Cooper's establishment is the only one that will admit women, albeit only in the evenings, once they have begun to serve tea.

So thinks Aran, and tea is a commodity about which he now understands a great deal. He had long ago learned to use his wits to improve the dispatch digest for Titus Redmond's regular customers – twenty pounds of *Singo* and fifteen pounds of *Flowery Assam Congou* for the White Rose in Manchester itself; thirty pounds of *Darjeeling Bobea* and twenty-five pounds of *Hyson* for Thackeray's in Bristol, with similar amounts for Partridge in Norwich; one hundred and fifty pounds each of *Twankay* and *Tippy Pekoe* for the markets in York, Leeds or Harrogate; forty pounds of *Souchong* or *Golden Gunpowder* for the McClelland coffee houses in distant Edinburgh. He had soon come to realise the extent to which this expensive commodity has developed into a valuable market, with just a pound of the leaves costing the equivalent of several months pay for any normal working family and therefore well beyond the reach of all but the most wealthy.

But Elizabeth Cooper is not amongst the list of Redmond's recipients, particularly since her establishment also serves as the Customs and Excise House for the port of Manchester. Still, Aran welcomes the opportunity to visit her premises, has always admired the ambience although, normally, he would be expected to patronise the White Rose.

Today, though, as he opens the freshly varnished outer door of the Old Coffee House, a biting gust of urgent, early morning wind tumbles the blue tobacco haze that clings constantly to the oak timbers of its low ceiling. He pays the penny entrance fee to the crippled ancient on his high stool near the door, declining the proffered free clay pipe available from the racks behind. The entrance fee entitles him to go straight to the yawning brick hearth and carefully lift the steaming lids on both the coffee and chocolate pots, savouring the essence that emanates from each before deciding on the chocolate and, wrapping a cloth around the long, elaborate handle, he pours himself as generous a bowl as he can manage, knowing that he shall have to pay extra for further servings. Blowing gently on the contents, he seeks to reach that perfect balance between avoiding scald damage to his palate whilst maintaining the chocolate's warming temperature for as long as possible, and he takes up his station, leaning against the fireside's brickwork wall to survey the assortment of the day's customers.

It is a particularly wide assortment, as well, since the Bellman has been crying about the town for two days past.

This is to give notice to all the burgesses of this town that they are desired to present themselves this Lady Day to the Excise House, at Mistress Cooper's, in Market Street Lane, for the proper payment of any Duty collected in the pursuance of their enterprise, and also for the perusal of their annual accompts.

So here are the counting tables, manned by the counting officers and supervised by the Borough Reeve, Jeremiah Bower, assisted by the town's Constables, Miles Bower and Robert Hibbert. Here are some of the Invalids, those retired soldiers living in quarters at Shudehill, and still sporting odd items of uniform for, on occasions, and probably today, they serve as the town's militia. Here is Mistress Elizabeth Cooper, business-like in darkened calico to denote her official position as the local Excise Collector, accompanied by James Bradley.

'I resent my establishment assuming the air of an armed camp, Mister Bradley,' she says.

'Redmond has some scheme in mind,' replies Bradley, sucking at his teeth. 'But he will bite off more that he can chew this time.'

'Titus Redmond may be many things but he is no fool. He *must* know that he would risk all by drawing scrutiny to himself on the very day when the Excise Officers are in town!'

'Then you might explain to me,' says Bradley, 'the reason that we are honoured with the presence of young Master Owen?'

Aran can see them, of course, and can discern that they are talking about him, yet he is more concerned with some customers here who are strangers, keeping their own counsel in one of the darkened corners. But concern quickly becomes *ennui* and, in reverie, his mind turns to thoughts of Maria-Louise Redmond. How could he be so foolish? he wonders. How so nearly tainted his loyalty to Titus? And she...?

He puts this painful woolgathering aside, returns his primary concern to the worthies of the town, account books at the ready. All those 'first buyers' who must queue now to pay Excise on goods received from manufacturers, suppliers or markets and then pass the cost to their customers. The innkeepers for gin, spirits and cider; the victuallers for coffee, chocolate, tea and salt: the chandlers for soap and candles; and the butchers for any animal, down to the smallest pigeon or coney that may be intended for slaughter.

Finally, Aran notes the entrance of young Daniel Sourwood, Scatterbuck's new first-year apprentice, and he remembers very well the devoirs of his own apprenticeship in its first year. The printing trade might not have been his first choice and how fortunate, he thinks, to have been like Stubbs, apprenticed to a painter and engraver. But printing has its own artificial attractions. Besides, he thinks, how churlish an ingrate would a fellow be to quibble so when his patron, having first secured him an education, later went on to arrange his indenture. There is no denying that Aran has worked hard to repay at least a small part of his debt to Titus Redmond, has helped in his enterprise every spare moment since his first day in Manchester. A debt, he thinks, so nearly made meaningless in his fumble with Maria-Louise. Yet working hard is a natural talent for him. So, at Scatterbuck's, he had first learned to clean and brush. It is what apprentices do in their first year. Cleaning and brushing. Collecting the water, too. And then there is the type to keep clean, the new Caslon, straight from the foundry. Perfect! Fits the beds as prettily as any could wish. And the printer itself. A Blaeu machine, imported specially. Later in the year, there are the bell-like daubers, their insides packed tight with cotton. They hold the ink for spreading on the type, after it has been put to bed, of course. So, between runs, the junior apprentice is responsible for changing the wads. Washing and drying the dirty stuff too.

All these duties Daniel Sourwood can perform admirably but he is here today because he is also a prodigious runner, a regular winner in the Annual Fair Pedestrianism Contests. He pays his penny and joins Aran at the fireside, electing the coffee over the chocolate.

'Are you going to tell me what this is all about?' he asks.

'God's Hooks, Daniel,' says Aran, 'but you are a scrawny fellow, How much do you weigh? No. No matter. Enjoy your coffee and listen.'

Sourwood pulls at his cheap linsey-woolsey jacket and looks timidly about the room.

'Shortly, some more fellows will enter to collect sacks from those counting officers,' says Aran.

'How much?'

'What do you mean? The sacks?'

'No,' says Sourwood. 'I mean, how much shall I be paid? This being, well...'

'I chose you for this work because, in discussion with Mister Scatterbuck about your progress, he told me that you are a person of some integrity and...'

'Scatterbuck involved in this?'

'No, he is not! I simply asked him...'

'How *much*?'

'I am happy that you should be paid one golden guinea once the task is done but there is nothing illicit in this activity, Daniel, I must assure you!'

'In a pig's arse!' says Sourwood just as the Excise Officers arrive, to be greeted by Mistress Cooper, by Bradley and by the Reeve. The queue is still long, so they are shown to a table where refreshments will be served, and Aran has time to describe the role that Daniel must play.

These fellows, explains Aran, will leave during the afternoon and take one of the roads out of town, probably to Salford and beyond but there is no telling how their itinerary has been planned. In any case, once their route is certain, Sourwood will retrace his steps and return here. But he will not enter. Instead, he will turn into the alley behind the coffee house and there he will find a gentleman. He will check that this is the correct gentleman by asking his name, to which he will receive the answer, 'Dubliner.' Sourwood will give this gentleman details of the road taken by the Officers and he shall receive his guinea. Simple!

Aran Owen has been entrusted with some significant intelligence concerning Titus Redmond's plan, but he does not know the gentleman in question. He *does* know that Redmond's contacts in Dublin have had enough time to identify the young man as a possible accomplice, a perfect choice apparently since he has recently frittered away an entire inheritance on fine clothes, gambling and good-natured whores. He has been disowned by his family and must now flee to London. But he has been persuaded that a detour through Manchester might be profitable to him.

So, finally, the pieces are in place and, at last, the collections are complete. The Excise Officers are able to leave with over eight thousand guineas collected in gold and silver coin, with just a few promissory notes, loaded into saddle-bags on their pack-horses, and led off, escorted by the Constables.

Aran sends Daniel Sourwood in pursuit with a reminder about his instructions and is content that he has carried out his own part admirably. He may trouble himself briefly about Sourwood's assumption of criminality in the venture but he recalls Titus Redmond's imperfect translation of Horace, 'It is only grievous to be caught.' And the fringes of criminality seem to drape themselves frequently about his patron in the same way that Titus is wont to drape his arm about Aran's shoulder. *Fie lad!* he will say. *There is nothing criminal in giving the world that which it desires. Whoring and strong liquor are physicks as venerable as time itself.* The town may fear Titus Redmond a little but there is no harm in him. And, if this current caper might stretch the normal boundaries, it will only be for the furtherance of the Cause. His teachers at Chetham's may have approached the subject with caution but there is little doubt about their loyalties, and it is a powerful source of legitimacy for political views when they are shared by such eminent academics. At the same time, being Welsh, Aran has no particular affection for the English establishment but, in some troubled and whispering way, it is his status as an orphan that has driven him to so readily accept the tenets of Jacobitism. The Hanoverian army destroyed his father, regardless of any contrary views that his father himself may have felt, and the death of his father caused his mother, also, to abandon him. He is bereaved, therefore, by the Hanoverians as surely as though they had visited Josiah Redmond's estates and executed his parents before his very eyes. And being bereft, he joins the ranks of all the other dispossessed who find a unifying medium for revenge through the Jacobite Cause. So he will perform this simple task for the Cause, and perform it well.

Yet he has forgotten about the customers who had been strangers to him and fails to notice as one of them, a particularly well-dressed man but with nondescript features, rises from the darkened corner and follows young Sourwood from the coffee house. And Dudley Striker pauses only long enough so that he may permanently commit Aran Owen's features to his prodigious memory.

Chapter Seven

Titus Redmond leaves his house in Market Street Lane and smiles to himself as he watches the town's traders hurrying towards the Old Coffee House to pay their Excise duties.

Lick-spittles! he thinks. If only they knew. Lady Day, the start of the year, fiscal and otherwise. And *this* year, by Our Lady...

He contemplates whistling for a Chair but finally elects to walk. The wind is strong and he ties a scarf around his tricorne, knotting it beneath his chin. Clouds chase each other across the Spring sky and he picks his way around a midden that somebody has deposited in the Lane.

Filthy whoresons! If the Court Leet Jurors were doing their job properly, they would find this scum and...

A pig crosses his path and snuffles its way into the midden. Thank God for the pigs at least. Without them he dreads to think what the condition of the town might be.

He makes another visit to his bordello, the one that helps to keep his warehouse erect. The building also serves as a geneva house, and above its door hangs an enormous wooden flagon, covered with leather and bound about with bronze. At each of the upstairs windows an animal-gut condum flutters, tied to the frame by its pink retaining ribbons. Outside the front door there is a stretch of paving with scurvy-grass growing between the cracks and around the base of an ancient trough, empty of water but filled with every manner of detritus.

At this time of day most of his bunters and bulk-mongers are taking a well-deserved rest but Mother Blossom, as usual, does not miss the chance to proposition him. She might be ancient but he has sometimes waxed his wick within her experience although, on this occasion, he is anxious to speak with Adam Scatterbuck as soon as possible. Or perhaps he is simply anxious about other matters. In either case, he rapidly collects the Quarter Day rents and payments due to him and moves on.

Titus has never shared his wife's passion for romantic drama but he *has* learned to admire her particular heroine, Aphra Behn – a Catholic too, of course, a fanatical supporter of the Stuarts. And then along had come that so-called 'Glorious Revolution', in which the highest and finest of English Society, Whigs and Tories alike, had invited a Dutch prince to invade their own country to depose the existing Stuart King, James the Second. *Before my time, of course,* thinks Titus, *but only just.* William the Dutchman had led the invasion in the name of his wife, Mary – who was the King's own daughter, a Protestant daughter. Titus hawks and spits. And it had literally killed poor Aphra Behn when William's invading army had moved on London early in the Year '89. James had fled to France while William and Mary were crowned King and Queen. And so the first successful invasion of England since that other William, known as the Conqueror, had been completed.

But he principally admires Behn's writing attacking the Whigs and their impact on the world of business. 'Come away – poverty is catching', she had written, and he is determined that it should never catch *him.* He is not complacent about his modest success but he has overcome hurdles in life, turned them to his advantage, and helped by Maria-Louise.

Let the cunny-suckers sneer at them, he thinks. There is nobody in Manchester, or anywhere else, whose opinion he would either seek or respect. Except Maria-Louise, of course, but he quickly puts the thought back into a box. He recalls, instead, the way in which he had helped to restore the family's fortunes after his father had been arrested and put on trial in Manchester for their supposed support for the Jacobite Cause in the Year '15, only to be acquitted for lack of evidence. It may not have been such a drama for the public as the Townley trial but, by God, the Redmonds had suffered more deeply as a result. They had been in the fustian trade even then and the Redmonds had been recognised as one of the finer families of Lancashire – at least until the trial. Afterwards, all those 'loyal friends' of his father had simply deserted him and this precious damn'd town had thrown such a celebration at his father's downfall...

Cunny-suckers, he thinks again. Turned his father into a drooling fool. Good that it took him so little time to die.

His brother, Josiah, had just about managed to salvage the fustian business but, at the age of fifteen, Titus had chosen a different path.

Meanwhile, the English Crown had passed, in turn, from William and Mary, to Mary's sister, Anne, and finally, in the Year '14, to George, the Elector of Hanover – German George, George the First of England.

That lick-spittle could not even speak a word of the language but the new hope of the Jacobites, James Francis Edward, had planned an invasion, assisted by a mighty French army, gifted to him by Louis XIV, who recognised the twenty-six year old Stuart as *le prétendant*, the rightful claimant to the English throne. On this basis, the Scots had raised an army and some had marched south into Lancashire to await the arrival of James and the French forces.

In Manchester, street violence and mob rule had become the order of the day, with gang warfare breaking out frequently on the part of disaffected Tories and Jacobites on one side, and loyalist Whigs on the other. And into this chaos stepped a young Titus Redmond. Let his brother strive within the stinking piss of the fustian trade! Here was a better way to restore fortunes. If the town needed weapons, Titus would secure them. If they needed false courage to stoke the fires of their hatred, Titus would manage the geneva-houses to provide the fuel. And if the morality of the town slipped away, the baser needs of its male citizens would also grow – so the bawdy houses would need to grow also.

There had been open riots in the Year '15 across Manchester and at least twenty other English towns, and many Jacobite supporters, Jacob Driscoll's father amongst them, had paid the ultimate price.

But Titus Redmond had simply profiteered around the fringes, amused to find that his respect amongst the local burgesses had increased in direct proportion to the declining level of morals. At least, he is respected up to a point, the point at which the honest burgesses recall that he is a Papist.

The French army had not materialised. The Scots army had been roundly defeated at Sheriffmuir and the English Jacobites defeated at Preston but, in the following seven years, Titus had continued to build his own empire.

He continues now past the Commerce Exchange, sees the developing queue at Mistress Cooper's and, thinking of his Catholicism, he stops at the barber-chirurgeon to have his moustache trimmed. Whitlock weighs his coins when the trim is completed, while Titus also weighs the prospects for his own plan – wonders how Aran Owen and Jacob Driscoll will play their parts.

And then there is the Dubliner, of course.

Strange that he should have been able to use Maria-Louise's Irish contacts to find a suitable player. Her family might have been dispossessed but they remain well-connected with Catholic friends in Ireland. They had been one of the principal families there, of course, moving first to Liverpool in an effort to find a new life. But that most Loyalist of towns, a Whigs' Paradise, is no place for a decent Catholic and, after a brief visit to London, they had finally settled in Manchester.

Titus and Maria-Louise had met in 1722 and been married the following year, just before her father, old James FitzWilliam, had discovered the true nature of the Redmonds' business interests. The veteran soldier had gone to meet Our Lord with a final curse against Titus Redmond upon his lips and Maria-Louise herself had eventually grasped that Titus was not only a pimp for the town's bawds but also one of their fondest clients. But children had still followed, Rosina in the Year '24, then three more daughters besides.

Still, there are less discerning members of the FitzWilliam clan in Dublin, happy to help him or anybody else that will further the Jacobites' Cause.

He passes the new wharf almost without noticing, ignoring greetings from the master of the *Swift*, the trim Manx ketch presently unloading the Redmonds' latest cargo.

Past more gin-shops, the potters, and Gilbady the boat-builder, until he reaches Scatterbuck's place. A second-year apprentice works simultaneously on binding a large volume with two green paper-covered boards, whilst also serving a customer seeking a particular popular ballad. Titus Redmond is ushered through the passage, into the print room for his meeting with Adam Scatterbuck who greets him with a wave of his kerchief before using it to wipe his perspiring brow.

'Titus!' he says. 'A great honour, upon my word!'

'By the Mass, Scatterbuck, this no royal visit. But my thanks, incidentally, for allowing me the use of young Sourwood.'

'No need for thanks. No need,' he lowers his voice. 'Have you news?'

'Too early yet. And best left alone.' Titus feigns concern about security but, in truth, he is more bitten by a rare weakness, for he is a victim of superstition. His wife has infected him with her Irish belief that *bad sess* might befall when issues requiring a measure of fortune are discussed openly – and how much more likely when the issue is, itself, one relating to taxation. Such an irony. 'No,' he says. 'It is a different piece of business that brings me here.'

'You need not tell me – you are interested in my idea?'

'You were right, we have no newspaper for the town – apart from the *Magazine* I suppose?'

'Newspaper – the *Magazine*? I think not, Titus. It sells at three ha'pence for a monthly edition. Over-priced, clearly over-priced. And then the name! *Magazine*, eh? What irony! A repository for explosive articles is precisely *not* what the *Magazine* represents.'

'You have a better idea?'

'Of course,' says Scatterbuck. 'A broadsheet for Manchester. Local news. Maybe some County news, too. One or two London pieces, when we can get them. Some advertisements...'

'But what about the taxes? Broadsheets are going out of business every day because of the pox'd taxes,' says Titus Redmond.

'Blasted Stamp Duty! Just another way for those bloody Hanover turnips to censor us.'

'Don't be a fool, Scatterbuck. The Whigs must pay taxes on their broadsides too.'

'Of course. They tax everybody just the same. But you know where they have erred, Titus? Four pages, a penny tax, eh? But six pages, now. How much tax on *six* pages?'

'A penny ha'penny? Tuppence?' says Titus, and Scatterbuck laughs into his kerchief.

'They did not bloody think that anybody would produce a *six* page newspaper, now, did they? So no Stamp Duty on six pages! Is that not rich? And these clowns are supposed to be running the country. They might be fine for governing Dutchmen and Germans, eh, Titus?'

'And we can fill six pages?'

'Oh, yes, I think so, for here is the secret. We'll print six pages all right, but each edition will be spread over three weeks. Two pages each week, you see? There is nothing in their bloody Stamp Act that says the paper must be bought all in one piece. We produce two pages each week, and we charge a penny for the first two pages. Next week, pages three and four. Another penny. Third week, pages five and six. A penny. The customers get the satisfaction of knowing that half their money does not go in tax, and we do not have to charge them extra to cover the Stamp Duty. In exchange, we give them a good old-fashioned *Coranto*.'

'Then go to it!' says Titus. 'We will provide the capital, of course – within reason!'

'Reason, you say! Reason! A strange word in this age. But at least we may be able to use this new organ as a means to strike back at their God Damn'd Penal Laws.'

'Why should I care about that?' says Titus. 'The Penal Laws are an annoyance – but for men of enterprise, Scatterbuck... men like you and me, we can work around them.'

'But we still have friends elsewhere, Titus. What about them?' Redmond merely shrugs his shoulders, picking at his teeth with a small sliver of wood. 'You recall the Disleys?' asks Scatterbuck. 'In Somerset? We heard a while ago that old Barnaby died, leaving his property to be shared equally amongst his sons.'

'Barnaby Disley?' says Titus Redmond. 'He was a fool. Two decent older boys though. But the youngest son – Edward, I think – became a Protestant, did he not?'

'It split the family, Titus. But now Edward's been able to contest the Will, using the same Penal Laws, and claiming that, as a Protestant, he was entitled to inherit it all. The Courts have upheld his claim. It's left Barnaby's widow and the other boys without a florin. In *this* day and age.'

'Life is a whore!'

'But as a Catholic yourself, Titus...'

'I've told you before, I'm a Catholic only through obstinacy, not devotion,' says Redmond.

'You might take a different view once the Hanover rats start to impose the code more fully – and they *will*, you know!'

But at this moment, Titus Redmond is more concerned with events elsewhere, hoping that the simple act of considering a matter cannot, in itself, attract *bad sess*.

Chapter Eight

'Beware the fury of a patient man,' John Dryden had said, and patience had been just the first of many lessons to be assimilated by Dudley Striker in the frontier territory of the Thirteen Colonies. He had seen only four summers when his father, reduced by debt, had spent the last of their funds on a passage from Ireland, initially taking up a land grant in New Jersey and, soon afterwards, accepting an offer of one hundred acres within the Valley of Virginia. But his infant memory had retained recollections of his homeland and he had been positive that he could touch the scents and sounds of Tipperary amongst the white pine, red cedar and bitternut hickory of the valley's woodlands. They described themselves as 'settlers' but had settled uneasily amongst the earlier Puritan pioneers, and the presence of these newcomers had, in turn, unsettled the local savages who claimed this land as their own.

The savages, of course, had no more right to it than the Irish or Germans, for they had themselves simply taken it from the weaker tribes that had been there before. These local Tuscaroras, however, now lived modestly by farming, sharing their produce freely when times were difficult for the colonists who, in turn, largely allowed the native Americans to walk hungry past their doors whenever the roles were reversed. For the most part, the savages were treated with antipathy and, at best, arrogance. Yet they bore it well, not through deference or passivity, Striker had realised, but through patience since, once he had learned enough *Skarure* to communicate within their own values – and this Iroquoian tongue had come easily to him – he was able to see the presence and the moral deficiencies of his fellows through their eyes, as a temporary aberration in the natural rhythms of the world, one that would pass soon enough. As a result, direct conflict between the colonists and the Tuscarora was a rarity and so, in 1728, whilst also trading as a brewer, already largely self-educated, at the age of seventeen Dudley Striker had readily agreed to join the newly-formed militia.

He applies the lesson of patience now, upon the streets of Manchester, as he follows young Daniel Sourwood, though not yet knowing his name, from the Old Coffee House. He watches the boy go off in pursuit of the Excise men and their escort, those worthy but hapless Constables, Bower and Hibbert, and he reasons that the boy will return in due course to advise his accomplice – the cove whose features he has so carefully remarked at Mistress Cooper's.

Striker has no need to follow either the Constables *or* the boy, for he already knows their route. They are bound for Warrington since this road will take the Excise duty most quickly to its nearest safe destination. Dudley Striker simply wants to know the strength of any particular threat to its security if, indeed, such threat exists.

Despite the slating rain driven into town on the biting wind, he can see the small cavalcade, the boy some distance behind, as it nears the lower reach of Market Street Lane and turns north along Deansgate, at which point Sourwood runs back towards the Exchange. Instead of entering the coffee house again though, he ducks into the narrow alley alongside. Striker is momentarily concerned since he does not know whether there is another exit, so he embraces the shadows, skulking as he has been taught so effectively, until he is able to see the boy again, shaking the rainfall from his garments and now gesturing westwards to a heavily muffled rider mounted on a roan cob. From his build and general demeanour, this rider seems little older than the boy himself but he clatters out of the alley, takes his bearings, and then also follows the initial route of the Excise men. He disappears momentarily amongst the warehouses below the Lane and emerges soon afterwards with a second rider, also muffled against the weather, although this will not be sufficient to disguise him should Striker ever need to find the man. *What monstrous arms that fellow has,* he thinks. *I should know him anywhere with no single other detail to discern him.* But they set about their business with a decent enough will, he supposes, walking their horses as easily as may be, and attracting no particular attention.

Stealth, he is reminded. His second lesson from the colony's savages although, this time not from the Tuscarora. It was a matter of ancient tradition that the Valley of Virginia formed roughly the mid-point on the long war-path between the implacably opposed tribes of the Catawba from the South and the Lenape Delaware in the North. At different times, small groups of one or the other would magically materialise outside the settler cabins. And these were a breed apart, all sinew and dark-eyed, paint and shaven heads. Not for them the passive waiting for trade to be offered, at the whim of the whites. These fellows demanded trade, silently, simply, through their presence alone. They received the respect that they deserved, and a boyish Dudley Striker had recognised within them some sense of fellow-feeling, particularly with the Lenape, though this may have been that he could make himself more easily understood in *Skarure* by the Algonquian-speaking Delaware than he could in the Siouan dialect of the Catawba. So he entered into a trade with them – strong-brewed ale on one side, stealth and forest-craft on the other.

He is surprised to note now, an ocean away, that the two men following the pack train are not without a certain stealth of their own, for the Excise men have reached the sandstone and buttressed bridge over the Irwell to Salford, pausing so that the Constables may take cautious stock of the situation around them, assessing whether any danger might be pursuing them. Miraculously, their pursuers have quite disappeared, Striker observes, only to emerge again minutes later once their chase is away on the road to Pendleton Green and Eccles. He knows this road intimately, of course. He has scouted along it several times. Yet he is still surprised at the ease with which the ape-like fellow and his young companion can, themselves, use its contours to avoid the frequent backward glances of those they pursue. So, lesson three. Think yourself as one with the enemy. This thoroughfare carries a quantity of traffic despite its rude condition. No turnpike this, and sometimes little better than a rutted lane in its remoter sections, yet there is a regular stream of horses, carts, mules and those a-foot, certainly in this stretch to the bridge at Barton. But beyond, he wonders? *Yes, my dears*, he thinks. There is the ground below Fox Hill, a perfect killing ground as the Lenape might have considered it.

Some young men learn the value, or otherwise, of life through their first hunting forays, killing game birds or rabbits perhaps, and thus developing a life-long abhorrence of violence in all its forms, whilst the same practice amongst others may serve only to nurture an unconscious tolerance of things violent, justifying them as survival instincts. For Dudley Striker, however, the quarry in his early hunting forays had usually been other human beings. For he had eventually prevailed upon his new friends to let him accompany them in their forays against the Catawba. He hums a half-remembered fiddle tune to help idle away the long journey as he traverses Barton Bridge, recalling the Delawares' all-consuming sheer ecstasy in their feats of weaponry, in their frequently re-told martial exploits, in their skirmishes, in their rapine, in their mutilation of the foe – an ecstasy from which he drank as readily as mother's milk.

Shall he sense the ecstasy today then? Lesson four. Ecstasy in death. He has observed the two riders easing off the road some time back, dropping down to some poachers' path on the bank of the narrow Mersey that they might use to gain ground and overtake the Excise men unseen, waiting for them somewhere below him, amongst the willow, birch and alder that cover the base of Fox Hill, linking both river and road to the wastes of Chat Moss to the north. This is no fork of the Shenandoah, not the same place where the vengeful Catawba had caught the returning Lenape unawares, sent most of them to blood-soaked oblivion, but something here brings the massacre to mind.

He does not see the robbery itself, as it holds no importance for him. The Excise duty is one thing, but it is the path on which it will later set him that matters more. In any event, his imagination of the scene will be easily accurate. The Excise men and the Constables reaching the wooded area, still cautious yet more relaxed in their saddles since they are now more than half the distance to Warrington. Only a couple of hours more against they can turn over the responsibility to others. Cautious, yet glad of the respite provided by the trees from the driven sleet that has attacked them persistently on the road thus far. Surprised and frightened when the two muffled riders appear from the gathering gloom with pistol and blunderbuss. The Constables fumbling for their own weapons and cursing because, as officers elected for one year only, the town's Court Leet has decided that it is not worth the expenditure to train them in how the weapons might be used. The Excise men, more brutish bravos by far, ready to offer violence in return for any received yet still caught at a disadvantage and driven away from the road, deeper into the woodland at gun-point. Dismounted, down, face amongst the leaves and undergrowth. Hands behind their backs and feet together. The apparently younger of the two men binding them while the other threatens and pacifies them with his weapon, tethers their horses securely. Then the escape, leading the pack animals behind them, the younger laughing as his inner tensions and taut nerves escape him. Never a sign of emotion from the older footpad.

Emotion, thinks Striker. *Shall I ever experience such emotion again as I discovered in Virginia?* By the mid-'30s, a British peer, Lord Fairfax, had successfully claimed five million acres covering Virginia's Northern Neck including land worked by the Strikers. With his father dead, his Lenape brethren slaughtered and his older siblings lacking the will to resist Fairfax, Dudley Striker returned to England with a commendation from his militia commander. He had led an erratic life, resumed his studies whenever he was able, but entirely ignored by the military that he had sought to join, for he harbours a dream of becoming an officer, a gentleman. Then, in the Year '43, the new administration had been seeking to recruit agents against the developing Jacobite threat, and Striker was greedily accepted to this role. No commission, of course, but perhaps, in time…

He sees them, from his vantage point on Fox Hill, breaking from the trees at a point where they meld into the slough of Chat Moss, taking a narrow causeway that gradually disappears amongst the hummocks of the marshland morass.

The Excise men and their useless Constable escort shall free themselves in due course, he figures, so Striker spurs his bay mare down the slope, through the trees and onto the causeway. They will not travel too far, surely, in this direction since they must intend to return with their prize to Manchester. And these pathways, almost invisible, may be known to the older fellow – but in the fast-approaching darkness? He dismounts, peering closely at the prints wherever he can find them. They have dismounted too, he sees. But where? He strains his senses; hears whispered voices; tethers to a bush of furze or broom; mounts a small bank to his left, avoiding a pool that would otherwise surely betray his presence; and finds himself atop a natural amphitheatre, with the pack horses below him and the two thieves beyond.

Striker watches as the long-limbed fellow – for it is surely he – removes a bag of coin from one of the stolen saddle-bags and whispers some further urgency in the younger man's ear but then stops, suddenly alert.

Dudley Striker has made no noise, given away nothing, he is certain. Yet this cove senses that he is observed. Striker dissolves into his surroundings and, for a moment, is convinced that he remains undetected, but the man thrusts the purse into his companion's hands and pulling back the hammer on the blunderbuss, begins to stalk forward towards the rising edge of the hollow.

Striker rises like a wraith, smoothly easing a brace of pistols from within his riding cloak and, before, his potential attacker has the least chance of levelling his own barrel, he has sent a ball from each of them hammering towards his target. Pandemonium amongst the horses.

Flames in the fading light.

The man lets fall the blunderbuss, clutches at his own redingote once, then a second time, yet is still able, much to Striker's consternation, to turn and run towards his horse, leaping for the saddle and spurring the beast to action, up the far side and away.

'Fucking whoreson!' cries Dudley Striker, leaping down to capture the blunderbuss just rapidly enough to prevent the second footpad from drawing a pistol of his own. The noise of his fellow's escape fades to the distance, the horses subside and silence returns to the Moss.

Striker gazes coldly into the eyes of this young man and meets insolence there, some arrogance, but no fear. *I protest*, he thinks, *that I could learn to like him!*

'Your name?' says Striker. 'And you will tell me true or, by God...'

'I could give you *any* name, and you would be none the wiser.'

Interdum stultus opportune loquitur. Sometimes a fool speaks to the point.

'I fear that you are not attending me,' says Striker. 'You will tell me your name and I will see in your eyes either truth or falsehood. Survival, my young friend, depends on your response.'

The Dubliner weighs options, and Striker becomes impatient. He switches the blunderbuss to his left hand, draws sword with his right. He dislikes the sword, has never really learned its use except as a form of theatrical accessory for it carries a certain authority here in Europe, he finds. So he wields it with all the outward appearance of the most practised sword-sharp. Striker's real work, however, is with powder, flint and shot in as many pistols as a man may reasonably carry, or else it is up-close and personal, work with knife or hatchet.

'Let me help in your deliberation, though the Lord alone knows why I should trouble myself. If you fail to give me your name you will surely perish where you stand. And if I simply wished to commit an arrest, I could find more entertaining ways to discover your identity.

'My name is MacLaine,' says the young man. 'Jamie MacLaine.'

Dublin? asks Striker, and MacLaine affirms. He himself is a Tipperary man, admits Striker, though you would not know it from his accent. Too many years in the Colonies have removed the least trace of a lilt. At his most charming, it takes Striker little time to ascertain that MacLaine can provide no information that he does not already possess. Anonymous instruction issued in Dublin. A considerable amount of waiting on consecutive days at a location in Manchester. A message delivered by an unknown boy and a poor description – but, thankfully, Striker already knows the boy in question as well as the features of the young man who sent him on his errand. And the other cully, the boy's simian companion? He has been careful to keep his identity to himself, has hardly shared even a word to pass the time. Striker makes a decision that Jamie MacLaine shall live. It makes him feel beneficent.

'But the purse,' says Striker, gesturing with his sword tip, 'stays with me. You understand? And if I ever hear that you have breathed a word of our encounter…'

MacLaine provides an assurance, and he reluctantly provides the bag of coin. It is hardly a fortune, thinks Striker, but it may help offset the strange reluctance of my masters to meet my disbursements.

'Forgive my impertinence,' says MacLaine, 'but you are also a Gentleman of the Road?'

'Yes, strange is it not?' says Striker. 'I can barely recall the last incidence of highway robbery in these parts, and now come three of us on the same day. How typical of life, would you not agree? But one more thing. You have neither the finesse nor the predilection to succeed as a footpad, James MacLaine. You should ideally seek an alternative career. Do you mind me?'

The Dubliner mumbles some appropriate response, begins to mount, but is forestalled by Striker who drives the butt of the blunderbuss into the back of MacLaine's head, leaving him senseless on the ground. Bad enough to have just one of these fellows potentially lurking out there in the darkness, he thinks, at which point Striker finally feels able to put up his blade. He considers the pack horses and the fortune that they carry, playing out the possibilities, seeing himself return to the Valley of Virginia, wealthy enough to challenge even Lord Fairfax for ownership of those sweet lands. But there really *is* only one scenario that will serve. A pity, he thinks, but at least there is the purse…

A shame, too, about Jamie MacLaine, for Striker has seen the young man's future writ clear in his eyes. He could not be precise, of course, but if some finer prescience had shown him that MacLaine will swing at Tyburn, a dismally failed Road Agent, just six years later, he would not be surprised.

53

Chapter Nine

Elizabeth Cooper has been preoccupied since the Excise men and the Constables left the coffee house during the early part of the afternoon. The responsibility for collection of the Excise in Manchester rests, when all is said and done, with her. A responsibility that she fulfils at the close of each Quarter. Yet this Lady Day, this Year-end, she feels the weight of outside events pulling on that responsibility in a manner that she does not fully understand. Some half-spoken danger intimated by James Bradley and implications that the source of this danger might lie at Titus Redmond's door, yet nothing specific, and Bradley himself has not returned either. She does so hope that he has erred in his opinions. There can be no doubt that Redmond is a dishonest rogue, masquerading as a *politico*. Good Heavens, as a Jacobite, forsooth. To justify his illicit trading. But he is hardly alone in that and Manchester has a certain reputation for independence of spirit. It may be galling that Titus and many others manage to avoid paying the Excise but she has long shared the view that this hidden economy, a complex web, is ultimately good for the common wealth of the town.

To suppose that the Redmonds have somehow crossed a line today, into a form of open rebellion against the Crown, is unthinkable. How *would* such a thing impact on her relationship with Rosina, she wonders. Dear, sweet Rosina. She finds that she has come to dote on her, quite insanely.

Yet nor can she ignore James Bradley's astute comment about the presence of Master Owen in the coffee house earlier. That younger boy too, quite obviously conspiring with him in some way despite their juvenile attempts to pretend ignorance of each other. Adam Scatterbuck's apprentice indeed!

She calls on Crableck, the door-keeper, to light the lanthorns, for it is full dark now and the candles, already burning for some hours past, are no longer sufficient to dispel the gloom. Business is brisk, too, and she takes great delight in contemplating how profitable the establishment has become since the days when her mean-spirited father had practised linen drapery here. She had never expected to inherit from him, neither in respect of the premises nor, indeed, his devoirs as Excise collector. Yet there had been no compunction on the part of the Court Leet to deny her in either regard, nor to prevent her converting the shop to a coffee house. She has always been popular and respected, outspoken perhaps for a woman but, once more, this is hardly unusual in Manchester.

She pauses to deal with a complaint from the Assistant Curates at the new church, Mister Nichols and Mister Lewthwaite, that 'the chocolate may be somewhat cold.' Quietly notes that they have almost finished their respective saucers. Too penny-pinching to pay the price of a second, she thinks, yet smiles and moves the pots closer to the fire, fetching them another portion in any case. *Should they not have more important matters with which to concern themselves on this special day?* she wonders.

She has returned to thinking about Rosina when Lewthwaite disturbs her reverie.

'Ah,' he says, 'a customer that we might not expect to see in *your* establishment, Mistress Cooper.'

Elizabeth turns to see the unmistakable red ringlets of Rosina Redmond near the door, moves quickly to prevent her paying the penny entrance fee to old Crableck, almost beside herself with pleasure. Uncontained joy illuminates her features as she takes each of the younger woman's hands.

'La, Rosina!' she says. 'It is so *very* handsome to see you. Handsome indeed.'

'I felt the need for some convalescence, and remembered your invitation that I might visit,' says Rosina. 'The house has been intolerably tense today, and nobody shall tell me the reason. It has made me feel so terribly blue.'

'Then we will send for the good doctor and have him prepare a prophylactic bottle for you. I take them from him frequently and they would serve admirably to banish your dyspepsias.'

Rosina realises that Mistress Cooper is still holding her hands, both arms outstretched and she registers that other customers are observing them. She eases her fingers as politely as she is able from Elizabeth's grip.

'That is kind, Mistress,' she says, 'although in truth I should prefer a *saucière* of tea?'

'Oh fie, my dear. Then tea you shall have. Upon my word, what better place to come for tea than… Oh, but my goodness,' she laughs lightly. 'I should not be discussing tea with the daughter of Titus Redmond! What *would* my customers think?'

'A pox on your customers,' says Rosina, but quietly, enjoying the amusing intimacy. 'Whigs to the last dregs of their chocolate, every one of them. Let them go hang!'

'Then you would see poor Mistress Cooper destitute and crawling to the Parish? How cruel. But there! Another thing. You greet me as *Mistress* when, at the Exchange, we had got on so famously. You *must* call me Elizabeth. Not *Mistress*, please!' And she leans forward, so that she can whisper privately, seductively, 'At the least, not just *yet.*'

Rosina searches for a response, but Elizabeth is already drawing her across the room, between groups of customers, many of whom regard her with almost open hostility.

'You are likely to lose customers in any case, simply by providing 'hospitality to a Redmond,' says Rosina.

'Oh my dear! If you sense a certain *frisson*, far more likely that it emanates from your being a woman. I have tried so, but these gentlemen persist in viewing establishments of this kind as entirely their own domain. Yet I recall you mentioned a particular atmosphere in your house today?'

'You may not approve of Papa or his enterprises but they serve a cause that is precious to me. I know that he cares for me, for my sisters also, but there are days when his business absorbs him, disquiets him so, yet I should not wish to engage in the appearance of disloyalty against him.'

'It is neither for me to approve nor disapprove. But I should truly like to understand this cause to which you adhere so closely. You are a beautiful and fashionable young woman, Rosina, though it seems that you are beguiled by some dated controversy that is no longer germane.'

'Beguiled, you say?' replies Rosina, accepting the tea that has been proffered. 'You make me seem a simpleton without views of my own. But I tell you, Elizabeth, that I care not one fig for history. It simply enrages me. I cannot properly find the words. That those who share my Faith can still be used in such a vile way, restricted in how we should live.'

'Yet the Penal Laws are hardly applied. They are themselves *passé*. When was the last time that we heard of any Catholic prevented from travelling beyond five miles from their home? There is a new age coming, Rosina, that will finally sweep away these antiquated decrees.'

'If that were true, my father and those like him should no longer be denied their place amongst the burgesses of the town...'

'I cannot believe that he suffers so ill from lacking a place within the Court Leet. La! If I were a man I should count such a denial a positive blessing.'

'Still,' says Rosina, 'such bigotry cannot be borne. And if supporting the Stuarts is the only way in which to be rid of it then, like all the Catholics of this County, I shall respond in kind.'

'Well, I fear for all our futures, Rosina, and fear also that an end to bigotry might not be as imminent as you believe. As women, we must deal with bigotry every day of our lives. And even from the Church. Your own especially. I am so very vexed that we are still often perceived as mere chattel.'

'And I fear that the decorum of *some* women has done little to dispel that assumption!'

'Fie, I cannot imagine to whom you refer,' says Elizabeth, demure and smiling, knowing the reputation of Maria-Louise Redmond as well as any in the town. 'But tell me, do you not have admirers of your own? You seem rarely abroad without the attentions of a veritable procession.'

'Hardly a procession,' says Rosina. 'For so long I believed that it was the portion of all women to be pursued. My mother, you know...' and she looks imploringly to Elizabeth, is gratified that, from Mistress Cooper's demeanour, she need not explain further. 'Now my admirers seem restricted either to those who assume I have trod the same path as my mother, or by Jacob Driscoll and that prating fool, Aran Owen.'

'Ah, Driscoll,' says Elizabeth. 'He is a deep cove, I think, but seems to have some genuine affection for you.'

'I like Jacob well enough, but he is so *old*.'

'Yes, a year or so older than myself, I mind.'

'Oh, I apologise! I simply meant...'

Elizabeth Cooper laughs once more.

'No,' she says. 'You have the right of it! I *feel* old. Yet... Well, my dear, not quite *so* old in your company.' She touches Rosina's wrist as she speaks, admiring the girl's emerald eyes, the fine shape of her face. 'Yet you speak ill of Master Owen? He is more nearly your own age, well-established for his years, and a certain rugged charm I think.'

'La! He is *Welsh*. And my father uses him like a Prodigal, though when he first arrived he could not tolerate the boy. Cursed my Uncle Josiah for sending him. My mother would not entertain him in the house. Insisted upon him living at the warehouse until Papa arranged a place for him at Chetham's. Chetham's mind! How I should have loved to study there. Can you imagine? Wasting such an education on a Welsh boy? But now Papa, who values so little, seems to think that Master Owen is some gift of providence, and my mother... Well, I can hardly bring myself to describe the way she seems to feel for him now. While Master Owen himself boasts about his art, speaks of capturing my beauty on canvas. I declare! A vulgar Welshman.'

'But cannot be that vulgar if he admires your beauty so!' says Elizabeth. 'What is it that Congreve advises? *There is in true beauty something which vulgar souls cannot admire.* I own myself perfectly jealous by his attentions to you.'

'You should not speak so plainly,' says Rosina.

'In my own establishment I shall speak as I feel and, besides, these *men* are too absorbed in themselves to pay any attention to respectable Mistress Cooper. Those that would have shagged me have long abandoned the attempt and choose to see me simply as some desiccated spinster. How shocked they would be if they knew what passions pulse in my veins. What ambition. La! How shocked.'

'And you truly think that I am beautiful?'

'My dear, what can I tell you?' says Elizabeth. 'Is it not true that women are unique in being able to admire beauty in other women? It is a gift that men do not share. For only a certain *type* of man is able to admire beauty in other men.'

'Sodomites,' whispers Rosina.

'There are kinder words for such men, my sweet. Yet women are universally able to appreciate another woman's beauty. They might despise them for it, but they appreciate it none the less. And sometimes we are able to discern something beyond mere beauty, something beyond the beauty that a *man* might see in a woman he lusts after. It is the beauty that an artist may observe in the natural world, captured in the wing of a butterfly perhaps. If Master Owen is *truly* an artist, then he will see within you the same beauty that I myself perceive whenever I look at you, Miss Rosina Redmond.'

Rosina is both flattered by Elizabeth's blandishment and also surprised to find herself prompted to consider Aran Owen anew, through Mistress Cooper's eyes. She is diverted, however, by the entrance of James Bradley, shaking the rain from his outer garments and his wig, whilst accepting a pipe from Crableck before gazing about the room and, his gaze having finally settled upon the two women, sauntering to their table.

'A lecher if ever I saw one,' whispers Rosina, as Elizabeth stands to greet him.

'Mister Bradley,' she says. 'I trust that the day has passed more peacefully than you had feared?'

'Mistress Cooper,' says Bradley, bending the knee and pressing his lips to her hand. 'And Miss Redmond too, with charms to match those of your mother, I durst say!'

'Less freely surrendered than my mother's, sir, I assure you.'

'Surrender is certainly something about which your dear mother is an expert, my sweet. Such gay abandon,' he says. 'But I had not expected to see you here, of all people. Such a welcome surprise. And you, Elizabeth, what friends you have. Fie upon it! You amuse me so.'

'I live to amuse my customers, sir. It is an honest enough profession. But you have news of the day?' asks Elizabeth.

'No, none, yet...'

There is turmoil out on the street. Commotion that penetrates even the clamorous din of the Old Coffee House. Sounds of a horse ridden fast to the threshold. Raised voices as Constable Bower stumbles through the door. The Excise men attacked on the King's Highway, he says. A brave defence forlorn against professional footpads. Himself and Hibbert so rudely handled. The Excise itself stolen yet miraculously returned by a stranger. A modest hero who would accept neither reward nor notoriety. A hero who has agreed to accompany the Excise men safely to Warrington while he, Bower, dispatched home to bring word of this infamy. The villains dispatched too, according to their rescuer, the one sent to meet his Maker, the other peppered with ball and wont to perish somewhere in the mire of Chat Moss.

'Just as you had feared,' says Elizabeth Cooper. 'Yet you cannot still believe...'

She turns towards Rosina Redmond, clinging to her arm from the moment that Bower had first entered.

'What I believe, Mistress Cooper,' says Bradley, his tongue protruding further than usual as he sucks his teeth, and regards Rosina coldly, 'is that, this being Lent and Titus Redmond a Papist, he should have been more abstemious.'

Chapter Ten

Lancaster, with its castle, has always had a fearsome reputation and is frequently referred to as 'Hanging Town' for, it is said, the Lancaster Sessions have sent more souls to the gallows than anywhere else outside London.

Arriving as a prisoner at the arched entrance to the Castle's great twin-towered gatehouse requires no reminder that those who go further should abandon all hope. The towers rise above you to a height of over seventy feet from their massive sloping plinths, and the gatehouse is so large that no light ever penetrates to the middle of the bone-chilling entrance tunnel. From there, the fortunate will be taken to the comparative comfort of the dungeons beneath the court rooms in the Lungess Tower Keep, whilst the rest will find themselves, as did Aran Owen and Daniel Sourwood, in the Well Tower. There, the long and narrow cells are communal, stacked one upon the other, with gratings in the floor, so that those above are choked by the smoke from fires lit by those below, whilst those below must constantly beware the bodily wastes of fellow-prisoners in the upper levels.

Sourwood has suffered especially, for he is constantly taunted by their gaoler, the Assizes only meeting twice each year and, whilst Aran and Daniel have not suffered the terrible winter conditions of those often forced to await the March Sessions, they are still six months away from the next and Aran is not sure whether the younger man will survive that long.

Several days have passed since Aran and Sourwood had exchanged their covert messages in the Old Coffee House. A real jape, entrusted with the simple but important task by Titus Redmond, in advancement of the worthy cause, to help relieve the Hanoverians of their accursed Excise. But then the rumours of robbery on the open highway. Rumours of fighting, of shots exchanged. Rumours of killing, that Jacob Driscoll is one of the fatalities. Yet surely Driscoll is with friends in Ormschurch runs the counter-tattle.

In the dark before dawn, Aran Owen had been sleeping, a troubled sleep, at his lodgings in Fennel Street, Mistress Evesworth's establishment where each lodger must empty their own chamber pot, every day, she insists. Liquids in the barrel at the front of the house, since the fullers will pay her a penny a bucket for the contents, solid night soil to be burned in the brazier. But sleep rudely ruptured, hammering at the door, raised voices below, then his own room invaded. The Borough Reeve again, Jeremiah Bower, and the

Constables, Bower's brother Miles and Robert Hibbert. The darkness broken by the bright yellow uniform coat of the Beadle, tipping him roughly with his staff, in the name of the law. Barely a word spoken, he had been dragged to the street, roughly bound, and tumbled into the back of a borrowed dung-cart on top of another occupant, a whimpering Daniel Sourwood. Within a short while, Aran's limbs had become insensate, a thin soaking rain, and a situation made worse when eventually a halt called so that the two prisoners could be allowed to sit, only to find the blood racing back to their extremities as the cause of greater agony. Meanwhile, the ropes had continued to chafe wrists and ankles into open sores, while Daniel had alternated between whimperings, curses upon Aran for involving him in such foolery, and sullen silences.

They had travelled north, their mounted escort hurrying the cart along, hour after painful hour until, finally, stopping overnight at Preston's House of Correction where Aran and Daniel had spent an equally uncomfortable night, more whining, more imprecations, before a second day's journey to Lancaster and its fearsome castle. There, they had been manacled by the gaoler and neck irons applied before the ropes had been cut, the wounds now aggravated still further by their fetters. By your lordships' leave, explains the gaoler, he could always find his way clear to ease the manacles, remove them altogether if your lordships have the garnish – but, of course, no such means exist.

Their cell door is two inches thick, solid oak reinforced with iron, ancient, scratched and scored by those previously incarcerated within, and the current occupants, apart from Aran and Sourwood, are a mixed group. No debtors here since debtors are housed elsewhere but, rather, those accused of more serious and potentially capital crimes to be considered by the Assize: two children, one aged seven, the other perhaps four years older, taken for stealing; a man from Penrith, taken during the winter for illegally cutting down a tree when his fuel supply was exhausted; and a woman, now barely recognisable as such, taken for stealing a sheep. None of them have had the means to purchase comforts from the gaoler, no kindling for a meagre fire, no meat to supplement the thin gruel but at least the children are not manacled. They show a keen interest in the newcomers, of course, hoping that they will have a coin to spare, anything that they can trade, but they soon lose interest, return to the corner that they have shared these days past, avoiding the shit-rimmed grating.

Aran Owen tries time and again to raise Sourwood's morale, taking a leadership role as, he thinks, Titus would expect of him. The Redmonds will not leave them here to rot, he says. These cunny-lickers have no cause to hold them. They simply need remain steadfast and all will be well. But these failed attempts serve only to leave himself feeling lost and lonely. And, as the loneliness drives him deep within himself, he recalls his parents. *Why is it,* he wonders, *that I seem to miss them and value them more now than when they died?* The truth, he thinks, is that we never truly appreciate those we love until they are lost, despite this fact being so clearly self-evident. *The loss is exaggerated*, he decides, *since it is surely a loss at differing levels. I lose a father, then a mother and, at the same time, I lose something of myself, being no longer even a son.*

Yet Aran Owen knows that he had been fortunate, finding reprieve in his eventual acceptance by the Redmonds. It had taken time, but he had finally come to earn the trust of Titus himself, a man for whom trust was in limited supply. His recent carnal encounter with Maria-Louise may have challenged his reciprocation of this trust but it continues to vex him in another way since it has exercised his imagination every day since the night of the performance at the Exchange. *What about my loyalty to this woman? I have a debt to repay in that direction also.* A sense of guilt washes this thought too since it is no longer dreams of Rosina that comfort him.

Aran cannot recall sleeping in the Lancaster prison cell yet he must have slept at some stage for he is awoken by a prodding at his legs with the toe of a boot. A slender man, silken waistcoat, cropped hair but Aran does not recognise him. Silent, the man gestures for the gaoler to remove him from the cell, leads the way out to the small room beyond, sits Aran at a table.

'Master Aran Owen, I believe, upon my soul!' says the man.

'Why am I here?' says Aran, barely able to speak, his mouth and throat parched.

'Gaoler, some water, I beg you, for our young friend. Ah, why are you here, you ask? Because, Master Owen, you are a thief – or, at the least, a thief's accomplice. Whilst I... I am a thief-catcher, I presume you would say. Polly Peachum's papa brought to life! An irony, is it not?'

Aran wonders whether he has met this man at *The Beggar's Opera* yet he cannot recall, is sure that he would remember the contradiction between the falsely amiable features and those lifeless eyes.

'I am no thief, and you, I suspect, are no thief-taker. Who are you?'

'You know, Master Owen, I have great faith that we are assured a long and mutually beneficial relationship. And quite proper that we should therefore effect befitting introductions at its beginning. You, of course, need none such for I fear that I already know more about you than you know yourself. For my part, I am Striker. Dudley Striker. Give you joy of my name, sir, for few are privileged to share it!'

'I doubt that our relationship will endure too long Mister Striker. We may be some months from the Session but you have no evidence, no evidence I say, to link me with any theft. You might know my name by some rogue's trickery but...'

'Fie, Master Owen,' says Striker with an insipid smile, 'I need no trickery. A short *résumé*, perhaps. First, I am an agent of the Crown, the legitimate Crown, mind, and therefore unimpeachable as a witness. Second, I personally observed your young friend, Sourwood, passing a private message to one of the footpads who so foolishly attempted highway robbery of the King's Excise. A message that I had previously seen conveyed to Sourwood by you, Aran Owen. By *you*, sir! This places you as an accomplice and there is not an Assize in this land, by the Tits of the Virgin, most certainly not that which sits in Lancaster, that could fail to agree with me. And your name, by the way? Trickery, upon my word, how amusing! The old cripple in the coffee house gave me both your names in less time that it takes to spit.'

'It took you long enough, then, to have us dragged from our beds,' said Aran, his mind weighing Striker's words, trying to maintain some lucidity of thought when, in fact, he was stricken with the inward panic of irrationality. 'And this...' his gaze takes in the whole room. 'If you are so certain of your facts, why interrogate me more?'

'I had hoped to learn more of the ape-like fellow – Driscoll, I think, by name. Hoped that he would crawl home to die so that I could verify your master's involvement more easily. But, alas, I fear that the Moss will have swallowed his corpse by now. So, in his continued and, I hope, permanent absence, yourself and Sourwood are the only remaining links to friend Redmond. Valuable commodities, therefore. And then I thought to myself, *Striker, one of these young fellows could be a source of long-term education to you.* Upon my soul, it came to me like a vision. A perfect miniature vision.'

Aran steadies himself, reaches within for a point on which he can rally his courage. 'I have studied the art of miniaturisation myself,' he says, with more bravura than he feels. 'I discovered Nicholas Hilliard's treatise on the subject and practiced for some time, following his rules and procedures, using watercolour on vellum. I favour crisp lines in rich tones. And I paste the results on to a playing card, to stiffen the end-product, against cutting it to size. Simple but effective.'

'How wonderful to have an education, even one to which you were not entitled, as I understand. I envy you for I have had to provide my own. But education will mutually benefit us here, Master Owen. I mind that it may cost you, yet I assure you that, if you are unable or unwilling to provide me with the intelligence that I require... Well, for you the cost of education may be high, but the price of ignorance, assumed or otherwise, will be incalculable.'

Striker gestures for the gaoler to return Aran to the cell, instructs him to bring out Sourwood in his place. And after Daniel has been dragged away, cursing and protesting his innocence, he is left only with his thoughts. He uses them once more to shield himself. Thinks of his apprenticeship again. Time passes slowly as he plays and re-plays his experiences until, finally, the cell door opens once more. Daniel Sourwood thrust back inside, inconsolable. Striker wipes his fingers with a fine lace kerchief.

'Disgusting little boot-rag has soiled himself,' he says. 'Confirms for me, though, that it was *you*, Master Owen, who hired him to follow those noble Excise officers and then pass information to your Dubliner friend. Bring him!'

Aran is lifted to his feet by the gaoler but, on this occasion, he is escorted from the Well Tower altogether, across to the hall that serves to accommodate the Sessions.

'This,' says Striker, 'is where you shall answer for your crime, Master Owen. Imagine the scene. The judge, a hanging judge I do not doubt, there upon the bench. Accompanied by his doxies as likely as not. And you, here, alone...'

Aran Owen can feel his courage ebbing fast. His legs have assumed the consistency of marrow fat. He tries to conjure masterpieces conveying heroism but none will come to mind.

'Do you know, Master Owen, from how many capital crimes we are able to select one that befits your own actions? Why, upon my soul, there are upwards of two hundred available to us!'

'Including one that will see those two children in my cell swing, as well?' says Aran.

'Such hypocrisy from one so young,' says Striker. 'Why, it is only a year since a similar pair were brought to the dance in York, and the event caused so little remark that the newspapers printed no mention. They will *swing*, as you put it so delicately, or they may be lucky and escape with a branding. Show him, Gaoler.'

The gaoler unlocked an adjoining room where Aran could see a small open hearth and, hanging alongside, a range of instruments, branding irons, from which he selected one and returned to Striker.

'You see?' he said. 'Justice is swift here in Lancaster. It answers admirably, I find. The hangman always here on duty for the Assize so that any found guilty of lesser infringements can be marked accordingly.' Striker takes the iron from the gaoler, takes Aran's right hand and presses the brand hard into the ball of his thumb. The action is so rapid that Aran's instincts are left all askew, and he almost imagines for a moment that the branding iron has been applied red hot, can almost feel the pain searing his flesh. But when the brand is removed, there is simply a white indentation, a letter 'M'.

'Malefactor,' says Striker. 'A Fair Mark, do you think, Gaoler? Even without the heat, I say! But no such luxury for you, Master Owen – though I suppose you would not see it so, for such branding would almost certainly cost you the use of your right hand. No more portraiture for you, methinks.'

'You enjoy this, Mister Striker? A true agent of the Hanoverians, I see. Cells full of starving folk, simply trying to survive. And you, with your two hundred capital offences. Proud of them too, I durst say! No wonder this country is ready to rise up on behalf of the Stuarts.'

'A further attempt at irony, I must assume, although for my own part I am driven neither by religion nor by political faction. Yet I tell you, Master Owen, that you are deluded to think a Stuart Ascendancy would bring some liberation to the poor of this land, for it was never thus when they held sway previously. I count myself a poor student, but I am devoted to Rapin's *History of England*. A first-hand account of the depredations inflicted upon the people by the *good* King James the Second. So much so that it was Whigs and Tories alike that invited Dutch William here to depose him, the people so pleased to see him that the entire nation stood by and let William walk in with an army of fifteen thousand invaders and not so much as a kiss my arse! The will of the people, Aran Owen, and now here *you* are, involved in a crime *against* the people.'

'I have told you already, that I committed no crime – and it is no crime to love my country but despise its rulers.'

'A point of merest sophistry, and not one likely to amuse His Honour. And you know what awaits you thereafter, Master Owen. No Malefactor brand for you, my friend. Nor even the rope-end jig. For your theft was a crime against the Crown – a treasonable offence. And you must surely see the humour in this? Who says, Gaoler, that our system of jurisprudence wants humour, eh? For nothing could be more fitting than that somebody so devoted to drawing, our young friend here, should meet his end by himself being *drawn*.'

'They could not...' says Aran, but the colour has now drained from him.

'What else can you expect?' says Striker. 'And a punishment favoured so highly by this 'Size. Why, I have seen it performed in so many variations. Those with influence, position, may escape its worst aspects of course, either left to die by the rope or dispatched by the executioner's mallet before the process is begun. But for common traitors like yourself, Master Owen, the hangman will delight in cutting you down against you lose consciousness, then applying his blade to your guts and dragging forth your living entrails to burn them while you watch.'

Exhaustion, blood loss from his chafing wounds, lack of sustenance, uncontrollable terror. Aran Owen feels these factors swim about him, icy sweat on his brow, Striker's voice becoming distant. Then falling, senseless, swooning at his interrogator's feet. Water on his cheeks, Striker's voice regaining its focus, lifted to his feet then settled in a chair within the adjoining room. He knows at this moment that Striker speaks the truth, that he cannot endure the thought of a fate so cruel. Every sinew within him turns now to securing his release for, if he can once win his freedom, he is certain that Titus Redmond can arrange to preserve him from falling back into the hands of this monster.

'Such a delicate disposition,' says Striker. 'The artist in you, I assume. Such feminine feelings you must possess! Yet ready, I hope, to co-operate a little? Surely a price worth paying to avoid the blades.'

'You spoke of providing education,' says Aran. 'You want more information? But I seem to know only that of which you are already sensible.'

'You misunderstand me, my friend – and I promised at the outset that we *should* be friends, did I not? No, I had entirely determined that yourself, along with the shite-stained youth back in your cell, Jacob Driscoll too, why even Titus Redmond himself... that all of you are simply small fish in a reasonably large pond. That it is catching the larger fish which would earn me the most reward. Thus, I shall throw you back, Master Owen, in a manner of speaking. But I shall return to your pond periodically, to consider how you are growing. And you, in turn, will help me to better understand those larger fish of which I've spoken.'

'You will not ask me to betray the Redmonds themselves?' asks Aran. He determines that such a question will help him allay any suspicions that Striker may harbour, implying that he would want to remain loyal to the family whilst perhaps, just perhaps, being willing to save himself by betraying others.

'I doubt there is *anything*, my dear, that you could usefully tell me about Titus Redmond though I must confess some amazement that a parcel of mere merchants could be so involved in such treasonable activities. Manchester is a strange town, I fear. No, it is the upper echelon of this conspiracy that I must seek to purge, and the only salvation for *you*, Master Owen, is to work on my behalf in this enterprise. Are we agreed? Excellent, then all that remains is to find some token that we might exchange, binding us together, so to speak.'

Aran senses something in Striker's demeanour, the same contradiction between the outward amiability and the hidden menace, masked behind those reptilian eyes, made more disquieting still by the eyes themselves now being alive with fire.

'A token?' says Aran. 'I am happy to pledge my word upon it, sir.'

'Word upon it? Fie, Master Owen. We barely know each other yet here we are, embarking upon an arrangement that, for my part at least, I take as seriously as a betrothal. But no rings to bind us. What a pity. Ah, but wait! Those manacles of yours...'

Striker's gaze is fixed upon the Gaoler's tools, those used for fastening fetters, the hammers, the tongs, the pincers.

'Gaoler,' he says, 'I expect that those instruments are the very same that you might use to free Master Owen from these vile accoutrements. Yes? Then lay on, my good man. Release him – and *that* shall be my token to you, Friend Aran.'

I have misjudged then, thinks Aran Owen. *And yet I sense that this arrangement may not be so easily sealed.*

'What about Daniel Sourwood?' he says, as the Gaoler continues his work. 'It would look suspicious if I were released and he not'

'Upon my word, Aran, I have been pondering that same problem. But I do not think that it poses too great a difficulty. You are released on the basis that you convinced the authorities of your ignorance in the matter. Sourwood too, of course. Yet I have a separate problem there for, whilst you and I are

65

now associates, I would prefer to else remain as invisible as possible. You follow my drift, I see. Thus your young friend may need to spend a few days in the House of Correction back in Manchester, awaiting further interrogation or some similar pretence. And then, when my affairs have taken me from the place, he can be released. Yes, released.'

Aran seeks hard for the words *within* Striker's words, for he realises that this man inhabits different depths than himself. But the manacles and the neck-iron finally come free and he sees that Striker's pledge is good after all. He mumbles some thanks.

'It is nothing, my friend,' says Striker. 'The merest token on my part as I have said. But what token might *you* be willing to give, I wonder? No ring to give poor Striker, that much is certain!' He picks up the manacles and throws them into the corner. 'I wonder! You do realise, Master Owen that should you run, try to break our bargain in any way, that I will find you. And let me promise you this...'

He picks a pair of blackened pincers from the workbench, motions to the Gaoler who seizes Aran from behind in a mechanical grip, and takes Aran's right hand. He applies the pincer jaws to the young man's little finger.

'I promise you. That if I ever need to hunt you down, Aran Owen, I shall take every one of your womanly fingers, these artful fingers, and then I shall take your eyes. A pretty picture then you'll make. You understand me? Good. And if, for some reason I cannot find you, I will settle upon Titus Redmond's bitches in your stead. His whore first, and then each of the daughters.'

Aran protests that he has no such intention, sees vivid images of himself mutilated. Maria-Louise vilely handled. Rosina. Finds himself trapped.

'I am inclined to believe you, Master Owen, and it would be a great shame to spoil the hand of an artist as a mere token.' He releases Aran's hand, stares into his eyes a moment, deep cold penetrating wide and acrid fear. 'Yet some token I still desire. A point to be made, I think, so that you shall understand Dudley Striker more fully.' The Gaoler's grip becomes even stronger, and Striker takes Aran's left hand instead, stretches it as far away as he is able, looking at it with some disdain. '*Castigo te non quod odio habeum, sed quod amem.*' I chastise thee not out of hatred, but out of love.

He applies the pincers to the left index finger, and Aran Owen's animal scream of pain reverberates, on and on, through the otherwise impenetrable stones of Lancaster's fine castle.

Chapter Eleven

Daniel Sourwood's short life had been terminated by the act of suspension. Bradley, peering through flickering link-light, recognises the classic symptoms from previous events that he has witnessed, gibbet jigs and the like. The victim's face engorged, turned blue through lack of air. The blood mark blossoms on cheeks and in the eyes from burst capillaries. The protruding tongue. The stench of piss and shit evacuated as the sphincter muscles relax. The Angel Lust erection, not always present but certainly evident here. Poor little bastard, thinks Bradley, that this was probably his first and last proximity to a shag.

But the overriding symptom is naturally the crushed trachea, purple beneath the noose whose bitter end, the twisted cuff and sleeve of a linen shirt, remains tied to the window bars within the Manchester House of Correction's only cell.

The turnkey has discovered the boy's body in the pre-dawn morning, cut him down and sent immediately for the Constables who, in turn, have gathered together as many of the Court Leet Jurors as they could rouse. By rights, there should be a physician present too in cases of suspected suicide but, with none available, an apothecary is pressed into service, pours pepper into Sourwood's mouth to check for signs of vitality, an absurd exercise in the circumstance.

'God's teeth, what a prick!' says Robert Jobb and Bradley is genuinely unsure whether he refers to the apothecary or to Sourwood's *post mortem* erection.

'Ingenious to use his own shift for a noose,' says John Clowes, loosening the garment's rolled body and other sleeve from around Daniel's neck.

'He must have *been* a bloody genius,' says Bradley, 'to have fashioned the noose, climbed the wall to attach it and then given himself the drop!'

'Fie upon it, Bradley! Perfectly feasible, I should say,' opines Clowes.

'I take your meaning though,' says Jobb. 'Nothing here to stand upon. It would have been the devil's own job. Yet I have seen suicides undertake desperate measures before to end their miserable existence.'

'The entire case stinks to High Heaven,' says Bradley.

'Well I agree, but the boy *has* shat himself,' laughs Clowes.

Bradley ignores him. 'What was Sourwood doing here in the first place?' he says. 'The Reeve instructed, in the name of the Lord Lieutenant, to hold him here pending further investigation? Master Aran Owen returned unseen to the town and immediately sequestered by the Redmonds? Redmond himself still at liberty? I tell you, gentlemen, that we must have serious doubts about too readily declaring this a self-murder!'

'The boy was alone in his cell, Bradley!' says Clowes. 'Alone, I say. How possibly *not* self-murther? And he was within his senses, so far as we can judge…'

'I agree,' says Robert Jobb. 'Let us be done with the business. Unpleasant enough to deal with such a thing at the best of times. Primitive. Positively primitive.'

Bradley reluctantly agrees, sends the Constables to hire a sledge and make the necessary arrangements at Ancoats whilst he and the other Jurors return briefly to the turnkey's cramped quarters and offices so that their verdict and report can be formally recorded and the necessary process properly set in train. It is no minor matter to dispose of a suicide but Bradley is more consumed by Titus Redmond's apparent success in escaping justice. Consumed too with the thought that the Lord Lieutenant of Lancashire has sent an express confirming that he will visit the town this very day, and Bradley only hopes that His Fucking Lordship will not arrive until after the appointed hour for his weekly tryst with Maria-Louise. He might stand at least *some* chance, he thinks, of discovering more about this complicated business from Maria-Louise than any other source. And, meanwhile, he has his *own* business to attend, a few problems to resolve.

He arranges to meet the Jurors again at mid-day, and leaves the turnkey with some simple tasks, preparing the corpse, gathering tools and a couple of lads to help with the ceremonials. Then he makes his way to the new street, still without name until the Court Leet approve his suggestions, where his fine terrace is slowly rising from the ground.

Manchester has followed the same path as many much larger towns and cities, dealing with its urban growth by packing a large number of dwellings into a limited amount of space, and the brick-built terrace has provided the perfect solution. There is demand, too, from each *stratum* of their society. Narrow modest terraces for those with narrow modest incomes. Broad four-storey luxury for those with wealth to match. Bradley's terrace is the latter variety, and will be adorned with sloping slate roofs hidden behind stone parapets.

At least, he thinks, they *may* be so adorned if only he can get the fucking carpenters to grasp the concept of sash windows constructed to a vaguely uniform size to match each floor, short on the ground level for stability of the structure, tall and elegantly expansive on the first floor to match the importance of the rooms within, and square for the upper storeys. So he rants and rails upon the site, boxing ears wherever he finds it necessary, dares these so-called craftsmen to try him, uses his considerable size to intimidate, and all the while wonders why he has not had the fortune to be Adams in London, or John Wood with his fine crescents in Bath, or George Dance in Dublin. Each of them part of a dynasty. Sons to partner them, to inherit. But Bradley has no such children. He simply has Maria-Louise. His misfortune that he has only ever formed one strong attachment, and that to a woman already married to bloody Redmond.

I want to know, she had said all those years ago, what it is that attracts Titus to his whores. So Bradley had taught her some of the jilts' tricks he had learned. But you will use them to pleasure *him*, Bradley had later complained. Oh no, she intended only to punish Titus, though he might not know it, by denying him these pleasures for she remained utterly devoted to him, the father of her children. Yet she had eventually confessed her *ménage* with Bradley to her husband and, astonished, found that it had not offended him in the least. Quite the contrary, he had encouraged her, seemed totally oblivious to any lack of fidelity.

Ironically, it was Bradley's success as a builder that had brought them together, for he had won the contract to complete the Commerce and Commodities Exchange and the whole town had gathered at the rout organised in '29 to celebrate its opening. Well, at least in his own eyes he had won the contract. Acquired might be a better description, for the contract had initially been awarded by Sir Oswald Mosley to a certain Joseph Childers. But Childers had suffered a terrible accident and plunged to his death from the scaffolding poles whilst working alone on some finer points of the design. Such a tragedy. But it had brought Bradley to the attention of the town's burgesses and he had been elected to the Court Leet for the first time at the following Michaelmas. There had been the unfortunate business of the Workhouse scheme soon afterwards, of course. It had almost brought him to ruin through those damn'd High Churchmen. But he had recovered in time. He had served as a Juror almost continuously ever since and the function had helped him consolidate his position. He is now the town's foremost builder, but *only* that. While Dance and Woods can style themselves as architects, or planners, or whatever they wish, Bradley is still defined simply by his indentures, his dual occupation a bricklayer-cum-builder. His father was a builder, started as a bricklayer too, then a bricklayers' gaffer. Like George Dance, he had been born the son of a freeman, so had not even truly needed to serve an apprenticeship but he had gone through the system in any case, then later purchased a further Freedom, in Manchester, when he had moved here from Droylsden. He had also learned to fight on the building sites – he is good at it.

So he cuffs the carpenters to meek submission, sets them back to the task at hand and, once satisfied that his instruction is finally followed, he returns to his own modest palace on Hanging Ditch to find Maria-Louise already there before him.

'Fie, James! The town is awash with gossip about Daniel Sourwood. It must be true, I assume, if it has kept you so long. A suicide, they say?'

'A suicide indeed!' he replies. 'But, in truth, I have been detained elsewhere.'

'La!' she says, her elfin features now ablaze with impatience. 'Mistress Starkey is waspish at the best of times but she will be intolerable, intolerable I say, if I am yet again late returning for Rosina.'

'The harpsichord lessons?' he says. The tip of his tongue protrudes as he reaches for her. 'Perhaps your daughter would be better engaged learning to master a different instrument.' He presses his rising manhood against her.

'You begin to tire of me perhaps?'

'Well, my dear, a little variety never harmed an honest soul.' He finds himself thinking of Rosina and, surprisingly perhaps, it stimulates his arousal. Thoughts of Elizabeth Cooper have the same effect upon him, he finds, though he understands this even less. He is almost certain that she, at least, is a tribade and has many times considered that he might convert her from the Silent Sin if only…

Their passion is quickly slaked, almost a mechanical routine and both are preoccupied with other matters. He pours wine once they are both composed.

'So no errands to run for your husband today, my dear? No *espionage* to undertake?'

'We are all set upon the *same* errand today, I think. Tell me about Sourwood.'

'How so? Does Titus believe that the boy could have divulged something in death that might, after all, incriminate him? Intriguing. But today I think we play a different game. I will tell *you* something of Sourwood's demise though, first, you must tell *me* whatever you are able on the subject of Master Owen's mysterious disappearance from our society. I miss his presence so terribly.'

Her features cloud. 'You need not feign ignorance on *that* subject, sir. I imagine that if anybody knows what befell Aran Owen in Lancaster, it will be yourself!' she says.

'More intriguing yet!' says Bradley. 'I see that, in fact, each of us is blind in this. But you must know his location?'

She studies him a moment before replying, has never properly known when he is being disingenuous, but accepts his ignorance here at face value. 'He is in my house and under our care, though he is incapable of much intercourse. He is fevered. We fear infection to his injury…' Bradley's interest is clearly pricked. 'You did not know?' she continues. 'He has lost a finger in some gruesome treatment, that much is clear, though he insists when lucid that it was a bizarre accident.'

'So much for his blossoming career as a painter then!'

'It is no laughing matter! Fortunately it is his left hand that is maimed but he will certainly be incapacitated for some time. And I had so hoped to prevail upon you. A small commission for him perhaps. The murals that you propose for the Commodities Exchange perhaps?'

There is only Bradley that she knows who can force so much sarcasm into a fit of laughter and he is still trying to bring himself under control when a servant brings the news that Sir Edward Stanley has arrived, earlier than expected. Maria-Louise is ushered almost immediately through one set of doors, complaining that she still has no intelligence on Sourwood while Bradley, equally lacking intelligence about Jacob Driscoll's fate, adjusts himself to composure, throws open another entrance to his panelled drawing room in time to admit the shuffling bulk of the Eleventh Earl of Derby, now in his mid-fifties and, some say, already approaching his dotage.

'Give you good afternoon, My Lord!' says Bradley, containing his dislike for the Earl. The man is a Tory at heart, after all is said and done. Yet he reminds himself that Sir Edward is not tainted with the Manchester disease, where all Tories seem necessarily Jacobites too.

'Entertaining the Redmond woman I gather?' says Sir Edward, without even the slightest nod towards a formality of greeting. 'Entertaining, Mister Bradley? Do I have the thing correct?'

'It is a liaison that assists me, My Lord, to gather intelligence and the like. I appreciate that there is a certain lack...'

'Naive, sir. Naive. 'Tis the only way that I can think to describe it. Entire town knows about it, I understand. Perhaps even the entire County. Even Redmond himself?'

'I allow that it is not a matter which can be readily understood but it is personal to me and, as I have said, it grants a certain purpose to my office here.'

'Purpose you say? Hardly enough purpose, it seems, to prevent this self-murder, I understand. Certain that the boy killed himself?'

'The act seems impractical to me,' says Bradley, 'yet the turnkey swears that the boy was locked securely in his cell – though I am still unsure exactly *why* he was in the House of Correction in the first place.'

'Satisfied that he were sane, however?'

'I did not see the boy when he was returned from Lancaster, but the turnkey claims that, apart from being understandably distraught, he was perfectly sensible of his situation.'

'If he were sane then the act were criminal and you have to proceed according to the requirements of the law.'

And now the boy's mother, thinks Bradley, already a widow and supported only by Sourwood's meagre wage, will come to the bloody Parish, another drain on the public purse. 'Yes, My Lord, the arrangements are made for noon.'

'No disciple of Wesley, yet I aver that he were correct in styling suicide as the English fury. Support his solution also, though it may seem extreme.'

Wesley had written, 'Only let a law be made and rigorously executed, that the body of every self-murderer, Lord or peasant, shall be hanged in chains, and the English fury will cease at once.'

'Self-murder is a diabolical practice, and the scriptures confirm it!'

Bradley considers that the Earl of Derby's view might be somewhat eccentric since hanging a dead body in chains seems, to him, a relatively mild alternative to the procedure that Bradley himself will be later required to supervise. Personally, he favours the more tolerant opinion of Alexander Pope and others towards the matter of suicide. But there is nothing to be gained from a philosophical debate and he needs to use this interview for other purposes.

'Of course. And the Court Leet will carry out the duties required in regard to young Sourwood,' he says. 'Yet I wonder whether Your Lordship might grace me with some understanding about how he came to be released. The other Jurors are concerned that the Assize has not met to consider the implication of Sourwood and one other in the attempted theft of the King's Excise yet here they both are, returned to the town under most unusual circumstances.'

'You are concerned about these two or, rather, about Redmond? The fellow, I gather, could tumble into a midden and find that which would turn him a golden guinea. What makes him dangerous, it seems, is that within a week half the town would be following his example.'

'He is certainly a natural leader to certain types within the town, My Lord,' says Bradley.

'Leader you say? A leader of rabble, sir, is no leader at all!' Sir Edward Stanley is hardly an unassuming man for one who was allegedly surprised to find himself succeeding his distant relative, James Stanley, to the House of Lords in '36. He had been elected to the House of Commons for Lancashire nine years earlier, a staunch Tory, and claims to have given up this seat reluctantly. Another accident of birth, thinks Bradley. Who are they, after all, these Stanleys of Bickerstaffe? 'It is to defend the County from such rabble,' continues Sir Edward, 'that His Highness has seen fit to make me Lord Lieutenant.'

Bradley masks his contempt. An honorary appointment. No role in the actual government of the County, yet responsible whenever war might threaten for the local defence of Lancashire. The post has been vacant for the past eight years.

'You mean to raise the militia, My Lord?' says Bradley, knowing that this at least is within the jurisdiction of the Lord Lieutenant. This and ensuring the efficiency of the yeomanry.

'Premature, sir. Premature. Situation is under control for the moment, I am assured, yet was it to worsen, if the damn'd French had not been scattered...' Sir Edward rails a while against the evils of civil war. Another English disease it seems. Centuries of it. Lancaster against York. Tudor turmoil. The Great Rebellion, Parliament pitted against the Crown. The Glorious Revolution.

And the Jacobite Rising in the Year '15. 'People are tired of it, Mister Bradley. Sick to the stomach, I say. But if it takes yet another to be finally rid of this evil then so be it!'

'But should such occasion arise, Titus Redmond and his associates would be in the thick of it. I had assumed that we would rid ourselves of this hydra whilst we can still do so with ease.'

'His Grace, the Duke of Newcastle, sees the matter differently. Believes that ridding ourselves of Redmond would indeed simply be akin to removing a head, only to find it replaced by more. He advises to strike for the heart, the principle schemers, and has set his agents against this very task.'

'It was such an agent, we assume, who averted the theft of the Excise duty, My Lord? Yet to set Redmond's accomplices free, to leave Redmond himself at liberty when we all know of his complicity in the matter.'

'Then we should put the Excise men about his business perhaps. His Grace would not object, I think, was Redmond to be restricted in his activities. The flow of gold to the Jacobites slowed a trifle.'

'A difficult route to follow, perhaps. I was simply suggesting a more direct course,' says Bradley, knowing at the same time that he has spoken too hastily, registered too late the sly undertone in Sir Edward's comment.

'Damn your eyes, sir! You think me a simpleton? If you was to set the Excise men loose on Redmond's affairs, there's no telling that they might not stumble upon your own. Is that not the case? This whole town is riddled with corruption. Why, they tell me that sometimes you have timbers imported here on the very same vessels that land Redmond's tea, so that you might avoid the duty together.'

'The Court Leet will attempt to follow whichever course you think most prudent, My Lord, and we could easily point an investigation in the proper direction, but I was thinking more that Sir Oswald might place certain obstacles...' Sir Oswald Mosley is Lord of the Manor in Manchester, officially responsible for the operation of the Court Leet as the organ of local government for the town.

'Mosley's loyalties are certainly a matter for some delicacy,' says Sir Edward. He does not say, *Else I should not be speaking with the likes of James Bradley,* but his implication is clear.

'More reason perhaps that we should be taken into confidence. If we had some direct contact with this Agent of the Crown, for example, we might effect some mutual initiative?' Bradley thinks, *This so-called hero who may have returned the Excise duty but has failed to produce any perpetrator.*

'His Grace maintains personal contact with his Agents. He insists that it should remain so. I am not willing to undermine his wishes in the matter, nor take the issue any further. No, Mister Bradley, we must find another route to tackle Redmond.'

Unwilling or unable, thinks Bradley. It is well-known that the First Duke of Newcastle, Thomas Pelham, takes very personal control of his duties as Secretary of State, despite a certain reputation for indecisiveness in earlier years. Worse, appeals against his decisions are almost impossible since it is his brother, Henry Pelham, who now holds the more senior post of First Minister in place of Walpole.

'A pity,' says Bradley. 'But if we are not able to work directly with the Crown Agent then myself and those others of the Court Leet that I can trust will find some other way.'

'Quite so! And was you, for instance, to attempt some financial inducement to Mister Redmond or others like him, I am certain that I could prevail upon his Grace to provide the necessary recompense.'

Bribery. Hardly a way to crack such as Titus Redmond, much less a fanatic like Francis Townley. It is almost droll, the idea that they might be further rewarded for their calumnies. But the inspiration to take some local initiative intrigues James Bradley.

The drawing room clock chimes the hour and Bradley excuses himself. The suicide to attend, His Lordship will recall, and the Earl of Derby makes it clear that he will not be joining Bradley in the proceedings. Not quite the thing. He must stay in contact, however, and report directly to Sir Edward as matters progress.

At the House of Correction, Daniel Sourwood's blue cheese body has been brought forth and laid upon a sledge. Bradley averts his gaze. 'Cover him,' he says, knowing that the corpse should technically remain exposed to public view.

'But, sir...' says the turnkey.

'For mercy's sake, just do it!' Glances are exchanged between his fellow-Jurors, the Constables, the Beadle, the workmen. And the grim procession begins, soon joined along the route by many Congregationalists from the new church, St Ann's, including the Assistant Curates, Benjamin Nichols and Thomas Lewthwaite. But there is no attendance from their Rector, Joseph Hoole. No presence either from the Collegiate Church. Elizabeth Cooper pays her respects though, and the whole of the Byrom family it seems. John Byrom himself, so tall that he could almost be a grotesque. His younger daughters on whom he dotes. The eldest daughter, Beppy. How could God have been so parsimonious when he considered the degree of attractiveness to be afforded that woman? Bradley wonders. Then notices that Lewthwaite and Nichols have taken up station behind the sledge.

'You shall not grant him any prayers, gentlemen. It is forbidden, as you well know!' says Bradley.

'That which passes privately in my mind cannot offend the Law, Mister Bradley,' says Nichols.

'In any case,' says Lewthwaite, 'we have each studied our scripture. There are seven suicides contained therein, from Samson to Judas, and neither

Old Testament nor New forbids it, I find.'

'The duties of the Court Leet do not include room for theological banter, gentlemen, though I gather that St Augustine had a different interpretation. Whether we like it or not, Church and State are one on this. Suicide, as Gilpin puts it, is one of Satan's Temptations, and those that succumb must be treated accordingly.'

But I wish that it might be different, he thinks, as knots of silent spectators gather along the route. Long Millgate, following the line of the Irk, then south and east. Small holdings and enclosed fields beyond the houses. A fine spring day. Tiny yellow flowers of Ladies' Bedstraw on which the Virgin Mary gave birth to the Lord Jesus – and Jesus knows that Sourwood needs Her blessing this day. Meadow Daisies too, Sorrel, and the damp scent of Bear's Garlic mingling with its neighbouring lilac-pink Butterbur. Two miles or less to Ancoats, its own hamlet yet still within the township and parish, and the junction of lanes marked by Barlow Cross.

The pit is already dug, he notices, in the open and unhallowed ground alongside. Sourwood is not the first suicide to be buried here and he will surely not be the last. Efficient, thinks Bradley, for they would have struggled to complete the work with this crowd pressing in upon them. He is past astonishment at the propensities of the people for mawkish entertainment, their ability to gather unbidden in such numbers, hardly notices as the Constables attempt to keep them at a respectable distance while workmen roll Sourwood's body from the sledge. He *does* remark the hysterical screaming though. Widow Sourwood attempts to press past the Constables, is restrained by the Beadle. The mother cannot even be afforded a decent parting from her son, he thinks. There is no reason in this. No rhyme. Yet he recalls Alexander Pope again, likening suicides to the victims of war. 'Nor polish'd marble emulate thy face.'

Fitting, thinks Bradley. For whether Sourwood's own hand committed the final act or not, he has no doubt that he, too, is a victim of a war, though one still in the making. And in that moment the merest outline of a plan to deal with Titus Redmond begins to unravel within him. One final indignity, however. He knows that the workmen are poised for this duty, can still hear the boy's mother howling to the spring sky, can sense the silent apprehension within the crowd. None of these other Jurors will give the word, he knows, so he turns to the workmen, nods once and averts his eyes as they drive the wooden stake through Daniel Sourwood's lifeless heart, that he might be prevented from haunting those that still beat strong.

Chapter Twelve

The Redmonds' eldest daughters are quite too mature for childish antics, of course, but both the youngest have hurtled about the house since mid-morning, annoying any who will listen with questions about the rout that will take place at the house that evening to celebrate their father's birthing day. During the latter part of the day, they have been joined by the Byrom's youngest child, Dorothy, almost seventeen but closer in behaviour to Katherine Redmond, one year her junior.

'The Byrom girl vexes me so!' says Rosina to her father. She angrily closes a book of harpsichord notation lent to her by Mistress Starkey and stands from the instrument. 'She shrieks like a banshee or else prates endlessly about her father's importance and his past encounters with the Queen – as though this would somehow endear him to me.'

'He spends too much of his life in London, I think,' says Titus. And over-much inherited privilege in that family too, he thinks.

'You do not trust Mister Byrom, Papa?'

'By the Host! From a daughter of mine, indeed! Trust. Love. Truth. Words for poets and dreamers that have no substance. They are fluids, limited by the obstacles around which they flow.'

'You would take Mister Byrom's word for his actions, then, to the point only where somebody else might change them?'

Redmond thinks, *How could anybody place even conditional trust in a man who prays at the old church in the morning and the new church in the afternoon?* Astonishing though that he should attract such rumours. The very idea that he might have fucked Queen Caroline! Outrageous. 'Mister Byrom's word,' he says, 'or any other's, Rosina. Even your own, my dear.'

'Even Mama's?'

'*Especially* your Mama's!'

'You do not love her?'

'What, in the name of the Holy Virgin, is *love*? Your mother is the closest that I have ever come to finding friendship. I value her judgement above that of all others. She has mothered my four children. It may not qualify as *love*, Rosina, but it will serve. In any case, how is your charge today? Shall you persuade him to step a jig at the rout?'

'No charge of mine, Papa! And Mother guards him so jealously that a body could not get near enough to fathom his condition. As for dancing, he will always be a Welsh clod, Perhaps you should ask Maeve however for she, at least, seems able to penetrate Master Owen's sanctuary.'

Maeve is the babe of the household, still treated as such despite her thirteen years. There will be no more, thinks Titus. No sons now, and he therefore hopes that Aran might somehow... Yet Rosina seems to despise the lad so, and he shows no interest in either Anna-Marie or Katherine. Damn his eyes! Has he no bollocks? Enough, it seems, to withstand whatever torture was meted out to him at Lancaster for Aran has confided in Maria-Louise that the damage to his finger was no accident. How could it possibly have been so in any case? But he has sworn her to secrecy. Feels unmanned by his ill-treatment though seems to have given his inquisitors nothing. And, to be sure, he is released without even coming to the Session. Says that Daniel Sourwood likewise remained silent. Then why should Aran suffer torture and Sourwood not? And now the suicide. There is much still to ponder here. *Yet how can a man ponder anything with all this fucking noise?*

'Mistress Mudge!' he cries, as the sound of breaking crockery splinters about the house, and for the third time today by his reckoning. 'Shall we be forced to eat from the bare boards tonight? By God's Hooks, we shall certainly have no tableware left.' He leaves Rosina in the small parlour and climbs the rear staircase to find the housekeeper, Mag Mudge, on the first floor, his *piano nobile*, fumbling upon the carpet with a shattered serving dish, fortunately empty.

'Too bastard big,' she mumbles through the drooling ruin of her mouth.

Maria-Louise calls from the stair, two floors above. 'What treasure have I lost this time?' she shouts.

'The monstrosity with the crack-glazed apples,' he says. He cannot quite discern her response and a door slams above as she returns to her nursing duties.

'Mag, this will not serve!' he says.

'Not anymore,' she says. 'Broke. Too bastard big.'

'By the Mass, you know my meaning! You are broke too, yet in body only. Nothing wrong with your faculties, I think. And only a few hours left before the rout begins. How goes the work?'

'Bitch in the kitchen,' she drools, and pierces him with a glance from her blazing left eye, while its companion maintains a permanent focus on the tip of her nose. He explains to her yet again that Mistress Hepple has been contracted to help with cooking for the event simply to provide assistance to the family's own servants but Mudge has chosen to take it as a personal slight. *Yet God knows*, thinks Titus, *that we should never have been able to manage without extra help.*

'But the kitchen aside,' he says, 'shall we see the Entertaining Room?'

'All done,' she beams, but he takes her arm in any case, past the Grecian balusters at the top of the main stair, and into the long double room that serves for occasional dining and reception.

'As I thought,' he says, throwing open the double doors. 'Some of the curtains remain papered. Only half the couches have had their covers removed. The mantle-piece remains bare and there, on the floor, the china pieces that should adorn it still within their wrappings. Less than half-done!'

'Less than half a housekeeper,' she cackles, pulls her arm free, while Titus takes the opportunity of stopping Katherine and Maeve from yet another boisterous canter, sets them instead to helping Mistress Mudge and then seeks refuge in his private closet. His private domain, also on the first floor, but at the back of the house, next to the dressing room, and overlooking the garden.

Peace, he thinks, as he quietly locks the door, sits at a writing table and draws the cork from one of his own geneva jars. He has to own that he has become somewhat addicted to a glass or two, but sticks carefully to the original juniper-flavoured Dutch variety for which geneva is named rather than the rot-gut *gin* that he peddles so successfully amongst those who cannot afford a decent beverage. He throws back a shot, laughs at the memory of Maria-Louise's father and his incredulity when he first learned of his son-in-law's involvement in the trade. Stupid old cunny-licker almost had an apoplexy himself. Still, he shivers involuntarily. Maybe the geneva not so pure as he thinks. Maybe old FitzWilliam dancing on his grave. Maybe FitzWilliam's curse tugging at his destiny.

So the afternoon passes to early evening, with Titus alternating between his account books – his private management accounts sequestered here in his closet for nobody's eyes but his own – and supervising arrangements for the evening's rout, though supervision is perhaps too formal a description for a process which, in truth, centres mainly around checking that Mudge has left no more filled and forgotten chamber pots about the house.

Guests begin to arrive and the Redmonds' manservant, Phelim O'Farrell is on hand to usher them towards the ground floor dining room, tonight converted for cloaks, where they are collected by one of Mistress Hepple's nephew pages and grandly escorted up the elaborate winding stair that connects the reception hall to the *piano nobile* and the Entertaining Room where a second nephew offers a selection of wines and cordials. Maria-Louise is here too, extending welcomes while her daughters, even Rosina, swarm about her like butterflies.

Meanwhile, Titus begins to play the room. An uncanny ability. He can roister loudly with one group, seemingly absorbed entirely, yet registering the substance of even whispered discussion amongst others several yards away. Little escapes Titus Redmond on such occasions and these birthday *soirées* have become an annual event now for his Tory associates and chosen guests within the town.

He greets George Fletcher, a linen draper, with his wife, Susanna, already in conversation with Robert Gartside, another fustian manufacturer, attending tonight with his wife, Alice. Titus receives felicitations. They gossip about trade, the value of introducing even more Dutch looms to the town while Fletcher argues for more concentrated industry. Twenty years ago, he says, it would have been unthinkable for a draper to not only sell finished product but also, as he has done, to buy the raw materials and place the production with independent spinners and weavers. The only way to avoid the decline. The only way to counter the iniquitous taxes demanded by the Government on fustian to advantage the woollen trades. Fie upon it! Our own tax. The Manchester Act, indeed! Thruppence per yard. Peter Moss, also a linen draper, joins the conversation, accompanied by his wife, Mary. Factory milling, he says. The only way to proceed. Follow Wyatt's example in Birmingham.

But all the time he is registering the nearby discussion between Rosina and Elizabeth Cooper. Mistress Cooper hardly qualifies as part of the Tory faction but Rosina has insisted on an invitation for her, and Titus is curious about the reason. They chat about Sourwood's suicide, of course, Mistress Cooper appalled at the attitude of the Church, and particularly Wesley's astonishing views.

'But have you read Lydia Granger, my dear? *Modern Amours?*' says Elizabeth.

'It sounds hardly the reading for a young woman of good breeding,' says Rosina.

'It speaks rather of the effects that love can bring, often disastrous of course. Love unrequited can *be* such a disaster, do you not agree? And when it leads to broken-hearted suicide, how does the Church respond? With pity? No, I do believe that they fear the power of such *amour* just as the Catholic Church fears the influence of women in general!'

'You know that it disturbs me when you speak thus, Mistress. The Church of Rome respects and reveres women,' says Rosina. 'Why, it should be plain from the prominence of Our Lady.'

'What stuff! The Catholic Church is so fearful of women that, in Italy, it has created a market for castrated boys rather than allow a female singing voice to breech its male domain. The hypocrites condemn the practise of castration yet hire *castrati* for their Church choirs, more than two hundred in Rome's chapels alone.'

'But Saint Paul says, *Mulier taceat in ecclesia*. Women are to be silent in church. Corinthians tells us the same. The Holy Fathers say that such boys can imitate the Music of the Angels and are therefore blessed.'

'The Church of Rome attracts only two sorts of men to the Priesthood – the perfect and the pederast, and there are few who are perfect,' says Elizabeth. 'But see how disagreeable a discourse we have invented? And you have begun to call me Mistress again. It will not serve, Rosina. And you must promise never to leave *me* broken-hearted. Unrequited love indeed!'

Mistress Cooper leads his daughter away into the gathering and Titus ponders the exchange. He could almost swear that the woman was trying to *seduce* Rosina. A cunny-sucking tribade? He turns to seek out Maria-Louise but is intercepted by a tanned, broad man with blonde hair, tied and ribboned at the nape of his neck. Captain Axel Erikkson, lavishly dressed in coat and breeches of plum-coloured silk, stands near the head of an enormous Jacobean table, scented by gleaming beeswax and pushed against the long back wall of the room to accommodate the food. Give you Good Evening, he says, introducing the junior officers from his Swedish East Indiaman, presently at anchor in the Liver Pool. He enquires about the *décor* of the house. Palladian, of course. His voice carries little trace of accent and they talk easily about Erikkson's responsibility for their 'joint enterprise', his 'franchise', here in the North of England. The Captain is able to give reassurances that his Company will provide reliable service. A steady supply of tea, purchased at the best possible price in the Orient and, on the return voyage to Göteborg, their vessels putting in to a safe port, different ports on each journey, then transfer of the cargo to smaller vessels for the final stage. The Captain had expected to meet *Herr* Driscoll, however. He understands that Driscoll should be his main contact, as the person who...

But all the time he is focused on the game of *Ombre Renegado* taking place at one of the card tables. There are four players so that Daniel Holker has just dealt the cards, nine to each of the other three players in batches of three and, having tossed his five shillings into the pot, will now sit out the remainder of this hand.

'I have the dubious honour of being the eldest, gentlemen, so must lay down first, I think,' says Townley, the bidding done and slapping down the Queen of Coins and forcing Sydall to play his *Spadille*, the Ace of Swords and the only card high enough to prevent Townley from winning the hand. He has sacrificed, loses the next trick too as Sydall leads with his *Basto*, the Ace of Clubs.

'Not a good start, Francis,' says Chaddock. 'I might have expected a more astute opening after all those years playing with the French.'

'You should never under-estimate an opening gambit in *Ombre*, my friend, nor the French neither,' replies Townley, trumping Sydall's Ace of Cups with his own *Manille*, the Seven of Coins, for the third trick. 'You must not make the same mistake as Redmond or his Whore. You cannot be a true supporter of the Cause yet remain opposed to support from the French in our endeavour. They will give King George and his Sardinian friends a bloody nose before long. Mark my words!'

He takes the fourth trick with his *Punto*, the Ace of Coins, to the consternation of Thomas Sydall, who sees the hand slipping away from him.

'Oh, by the Mass...' snarls Thomas Chaddock.

Townley has taken the fifth with the Knave of Coins. 'I tell you that,

80

without support by the French, we cannot win a contest with the Hanoverians – and I suspect that the Redmonds know that very well!' He takes the sixth and seventh in quick succession, happy to surrender the final two tricks. *Sacada*. Townley, as *Ombre*, wins the game, picking up the dealer's original five shillings from the pot plus fifteen shillings each from Sydall and Chaddock.

Townley's turn to deal for the next hand and Titus ponders this exchange also. Personally, he could not give a fuck for the French one way or the other but Maria-Louise's opposition to French involvement in the Cause is well-known. Yet to call his wife a Whore, in his own home. There will be a reckoning with Master Townley but, for the time-being, Titus knows that he needs the fop, the natural leader for all the young disaffected of the town. He would prefer this role to fall to the older Townley brother but John has apparently returned to France and his regiment.

And here are the Non-Juror clergymen, Bishop Deacon, Reverend Clayton, and Joseph Hoole, Rector of St Ann's. Thomas Deacon introduces his wife, Sarah, a sickly woman, and some of their older sons. The suicide is discussed again, at some length, though Doctor Clayton is more concerned with the food recently laid but not yet serving along the length of the Jacobean table. Meats magnificent, no doubt, my dear friend. Such hams. Such hocks. Such fowls and tongues. Such sweetmeats. Such wines. Such efforts on the part of Mistress Hepple. But what of those who choose to abstain from flesh? Not only himself, of course. His good friend Byrom as well, a goodly number within this wonderful rout. Intends no slight, naturally, but had put the point to Mistress Mudge. Some cheese perhaps? Yet she had made a strange response, upon his soul! Sounded for all the world as though she had said, *bitch in the kitchen*, but of course he must have mistaken her. Poor lady. An act of considerable charity to employ the broken creature...

But all the time he is listening to Adam Scatterbuck, his good friend Adam, who has accosted the Redmonds' manservant, Phelim O'Farrell, distracting him from serving drinks to the guests. Titus had inherited O'Farrell as part of Maria-Louise's dowry for he had long served as a retainer for the FitzWilliams, his first language some Irish *brogue* and still has difficulty with English. *God's Hooks!* thinks Titus. *Can I do no better for servants than these two? This creaking Irishman who despises me. And Mudge!* The thought no sooner passes than Scatterbuck also mentions her name.

'Now,' he says, 'you must tell me, Phelim. Is it true what they say about Mudge and Titus? I have never dared ask him.'

'True, lordship. Fucks whores. Fucks Mudge. Then...' O'Farrell made a sudden sideways gesture with his head, tongue lolling from the side of his mouth in almost perfect imitation of Mudge's twisted features and clouded eye.

Lick-spittles, thinks Titus, but he cannot avoid the memory. Magdalen Mudge had been the best of his jilts. The *very* best. He had never known

81

whether Magdalen was truly her own name but those who visited his bawdy-house had taken to it, right enough, and she was soon established as 'the Sinner' to her customers or simply 'Mag' to the other girls. Titus had wet his own whistle there, of course, until the day that he had mistaken her suddenly slack jaw and rolling gaze for ecstasy, her loosely trailing arm for the effects of cheap geneva, and her dribbling dregs of speech for an expression of passion. By the time he had recognised the apoplexy, called for Mother Blossom, there was little that could be done for her. She had recovered some mobility but remained in this partly apoplectic state ever since and it was a rare moment of guilt, not charity, that had eventually placed her as their housekeeper. He had never discussed the incident with Maria-Louise, naturally. She had known the circumstance without him needing to describe it, mainly through her own understanding of him but also because O'Farrell was himself too closely acquainted with the town's bulk-mongers not to have revelled in the tale. And now Scatterbuck revelled in it also. His good friend, Adam. Adam, who has not displayed even a sentence of remorse following Sourwood's suicide. Why, he could almost swear…

'Sir,' he hears Aran Owen's voice behind him, turns to find his *protégé*, closely protected by Maria-Louise herself, naturally. There is a general murmur of interest and recognition from all guests in the vicinity, but Titus openly relieves his wife of her charge and takes Aran aside.

'Ah, the hero of the household!' says Titus. a rare display of genuine pleasure softening the deeply etched features.

'No hero, sir. I was unmanned, I think, when…' and he raises his left hand by way of illustration though the swathe of dressing hides all but a general impression of the injury. 'And I have been less than honest about the manner in which the wound was sustained, I fear.'

'At least you confided the truth of this abomination to my wife, however. No, no. You must not look so, for it was also proper that she should have shared the knowledge with her husband. Why, we have no secrets between us, I declare.'

Aran looks doubtful at this latter comment but Titus hastens to reassure him. He has sent an express too, this very day, to his brother for he knows that the Squire will want to have intelligence of the matter, though he has naturally spared him the details. But the hand itself? Doctor Hall, no less, had been summoned, of course. Eminent physician. Eminent. The very best, despite his politics. And at his wife's insistence. The prognosis is good. Hurts like the devil, he supposes. And this, Aran, is what life has become under the Hanoverians. Torture, no less. No better than the villain, Old Henry.

'Yet tell me about your tormentor,' he says, and places a confidential arm about Aran's shoulder. 'Who *was* this that practised so upon you? The gaoler perhaps, or some other?'

'Not the gaoler, sir, though he was certainly complicit. Some other fellow, though I could not see him clearly and was not told his name. Perhaps poor Sourwood…'

A spectre had passed across Aran's eyes. Not Sourwoods, thinks Titus. It was fear, he is sure. Recollection of the instruments, perhaps. Or something else?

'Sourwood cannot help us now, poor wretch,' says Titus. 'And Jacob is still sequestered in Ormschurch with his relatives, though he has written to me. Declares that this *hero* who saved the Excise duty must be some Agent of the Crown. Could he be the same, d'you think?' The spectre again, he notes. Fear indeed. 'We still do not know what happened to our Dublin friend either, of course, but Jacob is convinced that he must be dead. I shall have to inform his family, I suppose, though they shall think him no great loss. Well, we might have failed in our efforts on Lady Day, Aran, but your own part on behalf of the Cause was without blemish. Well…' He gestures vaguely towards Aran's damaged hand. 'Well, almost!'

Aran enquires about Driscoll's health, for he has heard that Jacob too may have been injured. Although the enquiry sounds lacking in any true feeling for Jacob's welfare. No, replies Titus, he is well. Jacob Driscoll has the luck of the Devil. Took two shots from this cove at point-blank range but so swaddled against the weather that each passed through his redingote without the slightest damage, though Titus suspects he did not know that at the time. Imagined himself gut-shot, he supposes.

'I was thinking about Jacob earlier,' says Aran. 'Did you know, sir, that there is a land in which dwell only Rogues on the one hand, and the Righteous on the other?'

'Not Manchester then,' says Titus, 'for you would be sorely tried to find anybody righteous in *this* place! A conundrum, though. Just the thing for a rout. You must tell me later. Ah, Mister Byrom, we were just discussing you.'

Titus notes that Maria-Louise has contrived to interrupt his discussion by bringing the larger part of the Byrom clan to meet him. John Byrom is in his early-fifties, the tallest man that Titus has ever met yet tending now towards a stoop, and a full-bodied wig, grey as though to denote advancing years. But his wife, Elisabeth, is still handsome. They formally present their two youngest daughters, Mary and Dorothy, though Byrom insists on embarrassing them by using their familiar names, Molly and Dolly, and despite the girls already being regular visitors to the Redmonds' house. Poor little devils, thinks Titus, and exchanges a knowing glance with Maria-Louise. Mister Byrom had commented on the musicians, she says. Quite enchanted. He had reminded her of his witty comment about the quarrel between Handel and Bononcini, said there was little difference between their music, since one went *tweedledum* and the other *tweedledee*. How charming! Byrom brushes aside the flattery, enquires after Aran's health. So unfortunate. And then the suicide. But Master Owen. He should value his opinion since he considers establishing an Academy

83

of Arts in the town. He has spent much time between the Royal Society and the St Martin's Lane Academy over the past few years, and it has inspired him. Inspired him, no less. Ah, but the food. A man hath no better thing under the sun than to eat, and to drink, and to be merry, he says.

'Yet with a better government, Papa, and less taxation, perhaps men should not have to work so hard to feed their families.' It is his eldest daughter, Elizabeth, standing close with her cousins, James Dawson and John Beswicke.

And all the time it has been *this* Byrom, Elizabeth, that has held Titus Redmond's attention. Elizabeth Byrom. Beppy, as her father calls her.

'Well, what d'you think?' Dawson had said. 'How many of the so-called Jacobites in town will turn their coats at the first sign of a reversal?'

'My father for one,' Beppy had replied. 'He is no true supporter. The Redmonds neither.'

'It amazes me that you are able to hold so true to your beliefs,' Beswicke had said.

'Oh, I am not alone here. There is a very distinct group of women in town with similar views. And take example from those Scots women of fame who, not being encumbered by the same legislation, hold a much more prominent and respected position in their society than may be possible in ours.'

Hardly the most beautiful young woman, thinks Titus. Features pinched and shrew-like, brown hair lacking lustre, despite the sharpness of her eyes. The sharpness of her tongue too. No true supporters? Where *has* she developed such views? Not from her father, that much is certain. He must speak with Rosina about dear Beppy!

But now Beppy Byrom's attention is focused on the dancing. La! she says. Do her cousins recall Lady Anne Bland's Dancing Academy? Weekly at St Ann's. The ladies chaperoned, naturally. Lady Anne herself a raving Hanoverian. Would dance in the streets at the Annual Fair with orange blossoms in her hair. Could not hold a candle to Lady Drake, of course. A *real* Jacobite. How *outré*!

And when he judges the moment propitious, Titus calls a temporary halt, judges *his* timing perfectly too, chooses his targets with care, thanks them for attending yet another Rout at the Redmonds. Begs for their indulgence, however. Could not let the evening pass without mentioning the Cause that unites so many of them here in his humble home. Delighted, naturally, to have his good friend and assistant, Aran Owen, returned to his household. Recalls that they occasionally develop schemes, raising funds for the purpose of keeping the honoured Stuart name from penury, though their latest scheme might have fallen somewhat short of its purpose. And this latter comment greeted with knowing smiles from most of the company. He therefore proposes a Subscription to the Cause as they have done in the past and will doubtless do again in future. On this occasion, however, the Subscription will have added purpose for part of it, he proposes, will help fund some memorial to Daniel Sourwood, presently condemned to his unmarked resting place at Barlow's Cross. The whole might not quite amount to eight thousand guineas, of course.

In the nature of these things, his guests begin to donate openly. Fifty pounds from Townley; seventy-five pounds each from Robert Gartside and Thomas Marsden; a collection of ten pounds and a few shillings from Chaddock, Sydall and some of their friends; sixty pounds from John Byrom, though only because he is pressed to it by his daughters; even five pounds from Mistress Cooper, but on strict condition that this Subscription goes only to the memorial for that poor boy; forty pounds each from George Fletcher and Peter Moss.

Not eight thousand guineas, thinks Titus, as the Subscription continues, but he can perhaps raise half that amount. No pittance to present to Sir Watkin Williams Wynn when next they meet. It will at least soften the loss of the Excise duty. And when other Subscriptions are added from Preston or beyond, why, it will speak for Lancashire's loyalty to the Cause. More, it will speak for *his* loyalty to the Cause. Might silence that cunny-licker Townley. Might silence Beppy fucking Byrom. But what of these new problems, he wonders. Elizabeth Cooper and his daughter? He almost thinks the unthinkable. And Adam Scatterbuck? Pox-faced Adam Scatterbuck. If he thinks he has latitude to mock him in his own home, he will need careful attention. And Aran Owen? Good, faithful Aran. What *was* it that fluttered behind his nervous gaze? And what *was* all that nonsense about rogues and the righteous? *Well, we shall see*, he thinks. *And when this Subscription speaks for my own loyalty, it shall bring other rewards in its wake.*

Some other recollection stirs Titus Redmond's memory.

'The rout has been a great success this year,' says Maria-Louise. 'And the subscription a great inspiration.'

'Yes,' he replies. 'But what would be your perfect recipe for such a rout, my dear?'

'Why,' she says, 'to take as many ladies and gentlemen as possible, and place them in a room with a low fire. Stir them well with some fine musicians. Add some books, some packs of playing cards. Season with some wit...'

'Or substitute flattery,' he says. 'It serves just as well as wit, and frequently cheaper to acquire.'

She smiles. 'Then allow the mixture to simmer for several hours.'

'Yes,' he says. 'Allow it to simmer and watch the scum rise to the surface!'

Chapter Thirteen

Three weeks have passed since the birthday rout and the house on Market Street Lane has returned to a semblance of normality. Maria-Louise has finally restored the Entertaining Room to full dress, the curtain pleats papered and smoothed, the shutters sealed, the couches covered, the candelabras and china back in storage, the Jacobean table hidden beneath its tarpaulin once more. Until next time, she thinks. Perhaps a dinner for family and close associates to mark Restoration Day at the end of next month. Although, truth be told, she prefers the room as she sees it now. More intimate somehow. Her own domain.

There has been damage in the process, of course. More porcelain lost. Mudge, naturally, and when the housekeeper has been scolded, why, such vehemence. She has stumped across the room, attempting to fix Maria-Louise with that milky cross-eyed stare, and muttered the most astonishing oaths. It amazes her that Mudge, now almost incapable of stringing together a coherent normal sentence, can yet blaspheme with articulate clarity. It amazes her, too, that after all this time, Mudge is still able to make *her* feel as though it is Maria-Louise who is the guilty element in this strange *ménage*. Mudge the injured party!

But, satisfied at last with the room's condition, she closes the double doors and climbs the stair to the third-storey, its bedchambers shared variously by the girls, Maeve in the smallest, while at this near end of the corridor, overhanging the stair itself, is the servant's garret occupied by O'Farrell, alongside the closet that has been allocated to Aran during his convalescence. She knocks lightly at the door and, when Aran bids her enter, she finds him busily drafting sketches at a small table, the only furniture that the tiny space is able to contain apart from his cot. He barely acknowledges her entrance, however.

'Give you good morning, my dear,' she says, pretending to lightness but anxious that, as with many previous days, she is doomed to leave again with a sense of rejection. Today, at least, she is rewarded with the semblance of a smile. A beginning, although Aran returns at once to his sketching. 'Ah, horses. And beautifully done. La, better than Stubbs by *any* reckoning!'

He laughs. Genuine mirth and the first that she has heard from him since Lancaster. Its glow warms her deep within.

'Stubbs will be the master of horses,' he says. 'I would not even qualify as an apprentice to him so far as horses are concerned. Yet horses I must produce, since Scatterbuck has determined to print the initial edition of his *Coranto* soon and intends to include notice of the Kersal Moor races. Hence he needs horses. Racing horses, no less. And has arranged for a plate to be etched.'

'Fame at last! Yet I am pleased to find you in better spirits at least. There have been so many days over the past weeks when your low mood has almost led me to rage. Irish intemperance. I may have been harsh at times, I fear.'

'No more than I deserved. Yet I felt betrayed. I had no desire that anybody else should know the truth of Lancaster. I confided in you alone, and then only when I was fevered from the wound.'

'And I have apologised to you, though I did not think that apology was needed. I see you as a friend, Aran. A dear friend. Yet you could not suppose that anybody would accept for long that your finger was damaged in an *accident*? Fie, your index finger, my love! People should want to know where on earth you had put it, that it should suffer so.' She is pleased to see him laugh once more. 'Yet I was more concerned that you should want to conceal the truth from my husband. He sent you on the errand which caused this, after all. I doubt that Titus would understand the word *guilt* yet he lives by his own code. And there is poor Sourwood too!'

'I feel responsible,' says Aran. 'For Sourwood, I mean. In Lancaster, I simply came to despise him, for he whimpered and cowered so. He blamed me for his situation. But he was just a boy. I should have considered that properly at the time. And he lifted wonderfully when he knew that we were being released. The return journey was harsher than the setting out, and I was hardly sensible for the most part. Yet he was mostly come to himself again. The rascal even asked me whether I thought Mister Redmond might recompense him for the time he had spent there. Even apologised.'

'Apologised? For what should he apologise?'

'Oh,' said Aran, as though recalling that he had said too much. 'I do not know, really. As I say, just a boy.'

'And knew that he would not be long in the House of Correction, I gather,' she said. 'But I still fail to understand why he should have been sent there in the first place. If he was released from Lancaster, saved from the Assize, then it was the strangest thing. And my husband has been unable to make neither head nor tail of it!'

His head turns, meets her gaze, and she knows with absolute certainty that there is more that he has not yet shared. *You have changed*, she thinks. *You have learned to conceal as I, too, have learned.* And she finds herself as anxious as he to leave this place in their relationship. But she has met Doctor Hall. They talked about his hand, now healing decently. Needs lighter dressings only, he says. The good doctor insists too that Aran should not forsake some light exercise and fresh air.

'Yes,' says Aran. 'He told me the same, yet did not prescribe any specific form of exercise. I have taken the air on several occasions, however. Went to see Scatterbuck. And also returned to Mistress Evesworth's to enquire after my lodgings. She says that my room is already let to another gentleman though, but I think she feels herself disgraced by the raid on her establishment. She could not look me in the eye, poor woman.'

'La, the only disgrace is that she has denied you lodging. Yet we shall find you something appropriate. Something intimate, my dear. And then I shall allow you to sketch my portrait. Perhaps even *déshabillé*. Or am I too old, too much the hag?' Old enough to be your mother, she thinks. What *am* I doing? But she pictures the three men in her life. Titus Redmond, her first real *amour*, and the man whom she had chosen to father her children, a bond between them that she cannot fully explain. James Bradley, to whom she had turned as a retaliation for her husband's fondness towards his bunters. A harmless diversion, he tells her, in the same way that other gentlemen might play at billiards or cards. And in exchange, Titus seems to recognise that she, too, needs the same intoxication, one that she sates with Bradley. A small price to pay considering her husband garners the additional advantage of regular intelligence from the Tory faction this way. Pillow talk, he calls it, yet God knows that she and Bradley have never employed the luxury of a pillow once in all the years of their association. Then, finally, there is Aran Owen. A most handsome young man who talks to her, at times, of art, literature, history, exactly as her father had done when she was a child. In a complex way, Aran is able to transport her back to years that she had thought lost. Lost with the passing of infancy. Lost with the duties of early motherhood. And she loves him for it.

'Old?' he says. 'I have never considered you thus though I fancy that you are simply grubbing for a compliment. And posing naked, madam? You are quite shameless. Though I understand that, at St Martin's Academy, it is an everyday occurrence for ladies to present their bodies for the study of its artists.'

'Should you not be green if I were to pose so for a group of students? La, jade green!'

'Jealous? When I already compete for your affections with a husband on the one hand and your *inamorato* on the other. Is that not how you describe Mister Bradley? That odious creature.'

'Then you see yourself competing for my affections?' she says. 'Progress indeed. For did I not say that I should have you? What then of my daughter. You no longer compete for *her* attention? Ah, I perceive that I have brought some colour to your pasty cheeks, Master Owen. It is *myself*, I think, who is yet in competition. Yet in your fevered ravings, it was not Rosina for whom you called!'

'You say that you see me as a friend. It is not a word that I would use lightly, though many do so. I cannot think that I ever *had* a friend before, but I am happy to reciprocate. I have thought of you as a friend also this long time past, yet never know how to address you since all the obvious possibilities seem too formal. Then what did I call you in my ravings?'

'Why,' says Maria-Louise, her elfin features ablaze with good humour, 'you had better consider me a friend given how vigorously you handled my quim at *The Beggar's Opera*. And should you truly care to know how you called for me? Why, with passionate groans and a polite *Mistress Redmond, Mistress Redmond*.' And she collapses in uncontrolled hilarity.

She leaves the house soon afterwards for her usual assignation with James Bradley but, for once, the prospect raises no excitement in her. Rosina, however, seems almost perpetually excited these days and her mother remarks the flush in the young woman's cheeks as they thread their way across town. The daughter's response is brusque, as usual. Too little time to prepare herself for the lesson at Mrs Starkey's, she says. Yet she practices her exercises with considerable vigour just now, thinks Maria-Louise. She has heard her, singing too. Loudly when she thinks herself alone. Aran Owen's favourite tunes, she has noted. Sees him now the hero. Perhaps, after all, if Aran is able to distract her from that Cooper woman. Perhaps the thing she fears...

They stop near the Exchange as a group of workmen attempt to unload the Maypole from a cart and heave it towards the alley that will lead them to Acre's Field. Another holiday, she thinks. Less than a week away. This time the Trade and Crafts Parade, the Sweeps' Procession, the Moorish Dancing. But she notices that some bystanders have now begun to help the workmen with their labours and there, unmistakeable, is Jacob Driscoll.

'La, Rosina. See, is that not Jacob?' she says, and they hurry to greet him.

'Give you joy of your return, Jacob,' she says, and he bows, kissing her hand as some dishevelled hair escapes from the ribbon that binds it, tumbles down across his horse-face.

'My father will be so *very* pleased to see you,' says Rosina.

'I 'ad 'oped that my return might cause *thee* some little pleasure too, Miss Rosina.' She blushes.

'We are *all* pleased to see you,' says Maria-Louise. 'But how was Ormschurch? It is such an age since I visited the town.'

'We 'ave many friends there, Mistress. Many good friends. In Lathom too. An' my family is there. Gave me lodgin'.'

'There were so many rumours,' says Rosina. 'And when my father received your note, he spoke of shots fired. Spoke of a lucky escape.'

'I was un'armed, my dear,' says Jacob, openly delighted by the tone of concern in Rosina's voice. 'Our Lady protected me that night, I reckon. A miracle. I shall meet that cove again someday an' there will be a reckonin' between us, tha' can be sure! But the Welshman, I understand. Not so lucky. And t' boy, Sourwood. Self-murder! 'Tis 'ard to believe.'

'Aran cannot give it credit either,' says Maria-Louise. 'You must visit him, Jacob. You may have had some differences in the past but he will be pleased to see you.'

'I shall, madam, if tha' wish it so. An' maybe, Miss Rosina, tha' would do me the honour of a turn around t' Maypole at the week's end?'

To her mother's surprise, Rosina seems happy to accept, and they continue their route to Mrs Starkey. *That pox'd woman is happy to take my shillings every week*, thinks Maria-Louise, now alone on her way to Hanging Ditch. *It should at least entitle me to some civility. Only a damn'd music teacher when all is said and done.* Her mood is generally lighter, however, for she perceives Rosina to have been less curt than usual. Interested, too, in both Aran *and* Jacob, she imagines. *Perhaps my fears about Rosina have no foundation.*

Yet when she reaches Bradley's house, her spirits darken, for there is no intimacy between them today. The first time. He receives her working at his desk, politely enough, refreshments served. Speaks indirectly, fixed upon his papers. The record of last Wednesday's Court Leet meeting. Thomas Walley now on the list of Jurors, despite his speech impediment. Various other people admitted as Burgesses. No, my dear, not your husband. Bitterness in his laughter. *We must both have to tolerate his moustache a little longer, it seems.* Fines for selling tainted meat. Three at twenty shillings. One at ten shillings. Fines for traders who have failed to clean under their stalls in the Market and Shambles. Thirty at two shillings and sixpence. Orders to remove dunghills and middings in Cockpithill Passage, Pool Court and Deansgate. Ten shillings fine for each offence. Several vagabonds and idle persons evicted from the town by the Constables. Expenses to be met.

'It seems that I have vexed you,' she says, when it is finally impossible to show any further interest in these *minutiae*.

'Time for a little honesty between us, perhaps?' he says, finally looking from his documents and sucking at his teeth.

'Honesty is a commodity that I have never thought lacking between us. Quite the reverse. Our relationship is surely the most brutally honest that one could imagine.'

'Yet we have trysted together these two weeks past without ever a word of this fucking Subscription proposed by your husband. And to add insult to my injuries, I had to discover the truth from Mistress Cooper, along with a few other interesting facts, I might add. But more of that anon.'

'I see that I owe you a profound apology, James. I had not realised that you would be so anxious to Subscribe. A prominent convert to the Cause. La! My husband will be so pleased.'

'Neither myself nor your husband give a farthing's fuck for *the Cause* beyond anything that may turn us a full shilling. You cannot really imagine that either of us would be greatly distracted from our Profit by the complexion of Government. We might have our allegiances, Whig or Tory, but we always hold more in common than that which separates us.'

'Me, for example.'

'Easier to hold a Jack a'Lanthorn. No, I was thinking about our shared need for a stable business foundation. We each rely on the trade of this town continuing to grow. To grow it needs a certain forwards momentum but not to the point where chaos prevails.'

'You propose some common ground between you? But it is late in the day for such a change of heart. You sense some refinement in the weather, perhaps. Yet I cannot imagine the gauge that has influenced you in this reversal.'

'I had not thought to consider the Lord Lieutenant of Lancashire as a weather gauge, my dear, though it is a fair analogy, for he signals turbulence ahead. He has charged me that, if the town cannot control itself, outside forces must do so on our behalf. There are those within your ranks, my sweet, who are dangerous to us all. Zealots like Townley, for example.'

'Townley would see us *all* sold to the French but he shall not prevail. No, it will be decent Jacobites from these islands who will overthrow the Hanoverians. But perhaps this is your fear, that George and his Pragmatic Allies will suffer imminent misfortune at the hands of the French. A dangerous time to have your Monarch at the head of an English army!'

'You believe that he will be lost in battle so that your *Prétendant* can simply step to the mark?' said Bradley. 'No, *cara mia*. Good King George had a lucky escape at Dettingen last year but we and our allies mauled the French badly in the end, did we not? And the action has now moved to the Kingdom of Sardinia in any case. Towards the Alps and Lombardy, I gather. With the Royal Navy to support the Sardinians, they must be expecting victory at any moment.'

'Their war in Europe has been rolling this way and that for the past four years but I wonder that England should have chosen to involve itself so closely in a contest between Austrian and Bavarian for the control of the Holy Roman Empire.'

'Why, it is the French, my dear. Is it not *always* the French? If they have decided to support the Bavarian then we must naturally support the Austrian. The foe of my enemy and so on. One way or the other, we are already at war with the French. And your husband's Subscription could easily be interpreted as supporting our adversary. It must not materialise, my dear, so that I can demonstrate to His Lordship that Manchester is under control.'

'My husband will never agree. He has made his own commitments and will not care one fig for the opinion of Edward Stanley. You must not presume to threaten us with *outside forces*, James. My husband can command his own support, zealots though some of them may be!'

'Ah, but he *must* agree, I think. You see, I believe that you are correct and that Titus Redmond could survive almost any form of open confrontation on the streets of our town. But there are more subtle influences at work here. What, say, if Titus was spirited away? Not here to lend his impressive talents to the leadership of your *banditti* rabble?'

Maria-Louise senses that their exchange has shifted to a different level. She must have a care lest her Irish tongue should reveal more than she intends. For his part, Bradley awaits reaction, receives no such reward, continues undaunted. More animated perhaps but undaunted.

'Let us consider a theatrical *scenario*,' he says, 'that might help to convince you. First, it was the merest convenience to declare Sourwood's death a suicide yet any further examination of the evidence could turn this to a cold-blooded murder in a moment.'

'You have said yourself that Daniel was securely locked in his cell. The turnkey confirms it!'

'Oh, Tyler is a simple soul,' says Bradley. 'Seems convinced now that he witnessed Jacob Driscoll loitering near the House of Correction on the eve of Sourwood's demise. May even admit to leaving his keys unattended a while.'

'But Jacob was...'

'Ormschurch? Yes, of course, but that is a modest detail, my dear. Half the town knows that Titus planned to liberate the Excise duty. Who else would have such motive in silencing Sourwood? And before you make further meaningless protest, you must see that the evidence needs to be no more than circumstantial for both Driscoll *and* your husband to be hauled off to Lancaster also. And Heaven *only* knows what treatment they should receive there.'

'I have never known Titus Redmond to fear either physical harm nor damage to his reputation. And without my husband's presence here, the very thing that you fear would come to pass. That Townley and his faction would shape the politics of the town.'

'A risk that His Lordship feels able to manage. And there is a second reason that may cause Titus to agree. He certainly cares nothing for his own well-being nor reputation. Nor even his wife's reputation, eh? But the well-being of his daughters. Now that *is* a different matter.'

Fear and anger rise in her with equal measure, an icy paralysis.

'He would turn this town to bloody ruin if harm befell his girls,' she says. 'You would not dare! And I would kill you myself, James Bradley, I swear I would. All this time...'

All this time! She has seen Bradley in many moods these dozen years past. She knows that, like her husband, he is a hard man. But she has seen other sides to him also, though never this one. This Bradley is a stranger and he causes her skin to crawl as he feigns shock at her reaction.

'My dear,' he says, ' did I mention *harm*? God's Hooks, no. But their reputation, a different matter altogether. And none of *my* doing. I had simply put some other matters directly to Mistress Cooper, she being an associate of mine, and reputation being such an important matter for *all* of us. Had you *no* inkling of Elizabeth's fondness for those of her own sex? I have never fully understood the Silent Sin, of course. Not uncommon, I understand.'

'Elizabeth Cooper's *pecadillos* are no concern of mine. Why, she has been a guest in my house. I might not enjoy her affiliations but she has never done me any wrong.'

'Though she tells me that she has a *particular* fondness for Rosina. Ah, I see from those other-worldly eyes that you already know this. Well, you must be a more liberal guardian than I should have assumed to allow her such hazard. Punishment so much less severe than for men with similar tendencies, of course. Yet to see her dragged through the street in disgrace, for instance. How should Titus react to *that*, my dear?'

'I do not know Elizabeth Cooper very well yet I cannot believe that she would have shared such intimacies with you, regardless of any association between you. You are a speculative man, James Bradley. A speculator in lands and properties, and I see now that you are a speculator in other ways too. I challenge you to bring forth any evidence of these matters and I shall act as no messenger for your proposals.'

'Evidence is no more relevant here than in the matter of Sourwood's death. A rumour is simply a pebble cast in a lake, its ripples scientifically predictable. And should you choose not to act as my messenger I would simply find another. Perhaps one bearing an additional piece of news. For how if, in the midst of all these rumours it should transpire that dearest Maeve was not Titus Redmond's daughter at all, but the child of a certain James Bradley? Nasty things, rumours. After all, sweet girl that she is, she favours nobody else in the family. Titus knows when our relationship began. It would not take him long to do the calculations. Very feasible, my dearest.'

'And all this to retain the favour of Sir Edward Stanley? To maintain your status within the Court Leet and gain future office for yourself? This lake of which you speak, sir, is no more than a piss puddle and you seem prepared to sacrifice much so that you may remain dominant within it. Well, sir, I shall not be your messenger and you may throw pebbles to your heart's content. But you shall be alone when you do so, James. Cold and alone!'

'I think not, Mistress. And my plan may be larger than you can credit. But, at this moment, I simply need the Subscription to disappear. Yet you should know that, if I am refused, the price will be much higher at the next turn around. And there might, of course, have been unnecessary suffering between. But for now, my dear, shall we not enjoy one final jape for old time's sake?'

Chapter Fourteen

The essence of Maria-Louise's good-natured mirth gathers in Aran's room long after she has left, mingling with the pastel tones of rose, lavender and a hint of wood smoke that breeze through his open window. It is a small window but south-facing and providing sufficient light to this simple cell.

He reaches beneath the narrow cot, bringing forth both the satchel that holds his materials and also the large pair of binding boards, manufactured for him some years ago by Adam Scatterbuck to preserve only his most prized sketches and paintings. Since the space within the boards is limited, it has provided a necessary discipline for him so that, with each improvement in his technique, an inferior effort is destroyed. But this twelve-month past, there has been an enshrined section on the inside of the back-board, hidden from the casual observer. Just sufficiently concealed to allow the sequestration of work that he would prefer to remain discreet.

Should he wish to paint Maria-Louise *désabillé*? he thinks. Why, he has already done so. And he removes several sketches from their concealment, admittedly not his finest, in which he has captured her undressed likeness from his imagination though, God knows, he is familiar enough with her form to feel confident about their accuracy. Insufficiently confident, however, to reveal their existence to Maria-Louise herself.

He stares at them with no real attention to the detail, occupied instead with an attempt to make sense of his feelings towards her, an attempt blocked by his recollection of the awareness that passed between them when she had speculated about Sourwood's suicide. There had been a fleeting moment when Aran had been tempted to reveal his full knowledge of Striker's involvement. That it had been Striker who had ordered Daniel's extended detention to facilitate his own departure from the area. That Sourwood had betrayed Titus and obviously been unable to live with the fact once he was returned to Manchester. But Striker's invisible yet constant presence had rendered him incapable of sharing any of this with Maria-Louise, friend though she might be. Worse, when she had looked to him for enlightenment she had seen only obfuscation in his eyes and he, for his part, knows that she had caught him short of honesty.

He holds up his left hand, regards it. Thinks again of Sourwood and Lancaster Castle. Begins to slowly remove the dressing, wincing as the final section comes unhappily away to reveal the index finger stump, swollen and distorted, that Doctor Hall has attempted to repair, here in this very attic. A brandy-induced fug inadequate to mitigate the pain. Pulling, prodding and stitching, with O'Farrell restraining him. Striker's surgical skills had at least been speedy.

There had been consolations though. Rosina's sweet renditions at the harpsichord below. Her treatment of him as though he were a hero of the Jacobite Cause. It had pleased him, inflated his pride, he must allow. Confused him afresh, too, for he harbours feelings for the daughter almost as deep as those for the mother. And he can distinguish the feelings towards both from any sense of particular lust, for he has known women in measure enough. Impossible to spend much time in Titus Redmond's company without being drawn also into the company of his bawds.

So what should I call her, he thinks, *in our moments of informal familiarity? This wife of my patron. This mother of the girl whose affections I also crave. This woman who has salved the wounds left by my own mother's loss.*

But from the very antipodes of the house, from the farthest side of this Redmond dwelling, he feels rather than hears reverberation from the lion-headed knocker at the front door. Distant, barely audible voices, and then silence until, minutes later, without formality, his door throws open and O'Farrell stands framed in the entrance. He says nothing for a moment, though not for want of breath, as he is fit beyond his age. No, it is rather that he gathers his limbs, cracking the joints at knee, ankle and elbow back into their more customary positions.

'No fecking servant for *you*, Master Welshman!' he says. 'Three fecking floors!'

'Why, Phelim,' says Aran, 'I believe your greeting is the closest that you have come to displaying affection for me. If you have a message, you could have called me.'

'No message. Come to see you. Driscoll. Fecker!'

'Jacob Driscoll, come to see *me*? By the Mass, a strange day indeed. I will come down, of course. But first, would you assist me in replacing this dressing, Phelim?'

The linen is replaced with the help of an entirely distinct O'Farrell, a temporarily gentle alternative while he binds the hand before creaking back to the stair, returned to his more natural state and muttering foreign profanities. Aran, meanwhile, adjusts his clothes and takes up his outside coat for he will attend to some other business, a trip to Mister Byrom's perhaps, once he has satisfied his curiosity concerning Jacob's visit.

He descends the white-washed stone staircase, private backbone of the house, but rather than follow it to the ground, he chooses to leave it at the first floor and take the hallway to the Entertainment Room, from whence he can make his grand appearance down the flight of richly carpeted steps to the entrance lobby. Driscoll waits there uneasily, his long arms folded across his chest.

'I 'ad news o' your 'and,' he says, lifting his own, while Aran is still half-way down the treads.

'Well, give *you* good morning too, Jacob Driscoll. The hand? A misfortune only, and you have had your own share of those, I think.' He had intended a friendly intimacy, since he does not relish the enmity that has grown between them, unbidden, over the years. But its effect is only to cloud Jacob's stretched features. He changes tack. 'Your family in Ormschurch. All well, I hope!'

'My family is my own affair. But I thank thee for tha' enquiry. Yet th' hand. No mere misfortune I 'eard.'

God's Hooks! thinks Aran. *I might as easily have taken an announcement in Scatterbuck's newspaper.* 'Mister Redmond, I collect, must have informed you then?' he says. 'Though I am anxious that the matter should not be subject to common gossip. I would appreciate it greatly, Jacob, if...'

'I met Miss Rosina and 'er mother,' says Jacob, almost as though he has not heard him. 'They said that tha' might appreciate a visit. By Our Lady, she greeted me so sweet-like. She 'as blown to full glory while I 'ave been away, it seems. And I shall mention tha' *misfortune* to no other. Why should I do so? Though I must give credit where such is due, I suppose, for I 'ad not envisaged thee as a man who would withstand torture so well.'

'If you intend a compliment, Jacob, it is welcome, though undeserved. Why, I was only recently thinking that the deed was hastily done. But welcome, as I have said. And all the more so since you, yourself, are worthy of such praise for your own adventures.'

Driscoll snorts, an equine braying sound. 'Compliment, says thee? Aye, maybe. But I was thinkin' more on Daniel Sourwood. Poor bugger. Suffered no such torment but still ended up t' suicide!'

The suspicion is plain to see, painted clear upon his words, and Aran's own guilt engenders a response that he knows to be inappropriate even as the syllables spill from his teeth.

'Perhaps there are things about Daniel Sourwood that you do not know, Jacob. *Poor bugger*, indeed! Or maybe you simply *pretend* ignorance. It has already been made obvious to me today that others in town, beside myself, should think it strange that Daniel remained in detention on his return to Manchester. What if there was concern that he might yet inform? Nobody would have better cause than *you*, Jacob to fear such a thing. Perhaps you *do* know the answer to our little conundrum!'

Driscoll's face assumes an attitude of stupefied consternation, roiling into rage and, finally, melting into amused annoyance whilst O'Farrell, hearing a raised voice, has brought his rasping limbs from the rear of the house to investigate.

'For tha' information, sir,' says Driscoll when he has finally collected himself, 'there's a dozen witnesses and more who will put me thirty miles away on t' night that Sourwood died. Why, Mister Owen, that wound 'as addled tha' brains unless I'm much mistaken. And 'ere was I, making this social visit simply from courtesy to Mistress Redmond and Miss Rosina. I should 'ave known better. An' thee, sir, must think tha'self fortunate to be under the protection of this 'ouse.'

He inclines his head briefly towards O'Farrell and is gone through the front door before Owen has a chance to consider an appropriate response. *What a ridiculous accusation to make,* he thinks. *And the more so since I had not previously even imagined that Jacob might have been involved in Daniel's demise.* But unbidden thoughts of this kind have a habit of developing their own life. They transmute from base ranting to gilded inspiration. Perhaps not such a stupid comment after all, he wonders. It would explain a great deal. Jacob escaped from Striker's ambuscade. The fate of the Dubliner unknown yet reasonably presumed perished. Jacob fearful of pursuit and capture. Aran and Daniel the only witnesses to connect him with the robbery, but only Sourwood perceived as a risk. And not even a denial from Driscoll's part. The conclusion now seems blindingly obvious. Yet it has still been incautious, at the least, to have voiced the matter in this way.

He takes time putting on his coat to allow Driscoll plenty of distance, gives O'Farrell brief details of his planned visits first to the Byroms' household, then later to the Redmonds' warehouse, and leaves.

He invokes the exchange with Jacob over and over again, living each line afresh while he passes into the Market Place. The half-timbered Booths dominate the middle of this irregular square, brooding around their central courtyard, grumbling against their desertion by the town's elders. The Court Leet no longer meets here since the Commerce Exchange has been constructed and even the tolls are not collected here now, as the office of the Collectors has shifted across to the fine three-storey building owned until recently by the Byroms and now extended to include John Shaw's Punch House, another favourite gathering place for the Jacobite and Tory factions. As he enters the square from the south, though, Aran is first greeted by the sight of the Conduit, still a wonder to him. It, too, stands unattended at this midday hour, its pumps firmly locked against illicit usage. But in the early morning, or again in the evening, it becomes almost the beating heart of Manchester as townspeople gather to collect their rations of fresh drinking water, conveyed here through clay pipes from the Isabella Spring. Here, too, the Corn Market meets, when in session, while on the far northern side of the square, stands the Shambles, its flesh boards empty today though it never quite escapes the smells of butchered meat. 'Whatsoever is sold in the shambles, that eat, asking no question for conscience sake.' Sound advice from Corinthians, thinks Aran.

And nor does the square ever escape the sounds of trade, even on days like this when the Market itself is not operational. The piemen are out in numbers at this time, crying their cooked pastry wares, while muscled dairy maids try to sell the last of their milk, claiming it still fresh, and the fish wives call *Six for Sixpence Mackerel*, though the street-wise know that the green darlings were twice this price earlier when still fit to eat. The cutler's basket rings with spoons sold and pewter collected; the pudding peddler's barrow stove belches heat with every sale; the potters, a whole family of them in fact, make music as they chime cups, plates, wash bowls, to ring their quality; and the stick sellers shout *Gimy Tarters!* not caring whether their birch wands are used to beat children, wives *or* carpets.

Aran has visited the new Byrom house on Hanging Dutch just once previously and it still impresses him. Two large front gables, black-timbered, with all the grandeur of a Manor House, are tipped with decoratively carved spirals and crowned with three chimney stacks. Beneath the gable attic windows, the main body of the house is crowned with fourteen frames of richly-painted roseate design, sitting atop the leaded mullion windows of the first storey, whilst the ground floor is raised well above street level on a paved terrace, protected at front by a solid stone wall and accessed by steps at each end. The formal entrance stands proud in the centre of the terrace area while a separate door for servants, trades and casual visitors stands at the lower, eastern corner. There are rumoured to be no fewer than thirty rooms in this house, including its kitchens, buttery and pantry, private rooms, garderobe, library and hall.

It is more awesome by far than Squire Redmond's house back in his own village and, today, it is alive with all the bustle and chaos that anybody knowing the Byroms would expect. The sons will be attending Clayton's Grammar School across the bridge in Salford, but the three girls are receiving some private tuition, though it seems to require each of them in turn to find excuse for getting in the way of the builders and decorators whose trestles, buckets and ladders form a regular procession from the reception hall to somewhere within the interior. John Byrom himself has been engaged in a game of chess with Doctor Clayton, clearly not in attendance himself at Saint Cyprian's today, but they have apparently quit the enterprise when Aran has been announced and welcome him now with concerned enquiry about his injury and health in general, but thankful that he has come to discuss the proposed Academy. It is the purpose of the decorators, naturally, to prepare the very room that Byrom has set aside to this end.

'And shall you not dine with us, Mister Owen?' says Byrom.

'I have already eaten, sir, I thank you.'

'It was an invitation to dine, Aran. Eating satisfies the stomach whilst dining satisfies the soul.'

It is clear that they should imagine so, thinks Aran, *in a house where no flesh is served*. Yet the meal is perfectly acceptable. A potage, plates of dressed asparagus, cheeses and apple pie, water served from their own well rather than the Conduit. There is discussion about the benefits of a Pythagorean diet. It serves the entire population well enough at Lent and on Fast Days, after all. Yet Mister Owen has come to discuss the Academy, of course, and there *have* been discussions at the coffee house. Neither the White Rose nor Mistress Cooper's can quite equate to Slaughter's in London, and they have no Hogarth to lead them, Byrom must allow. Yet he has brought with him that sense that drawing classes might carry to Manchester a similar sense of invention, the dissemination of new artistic ideals. They will need a system of subscription quite distinct from that of St Martin's, of course. He has reflected the principle in their announcement. They are also unlikely to fill their modest equivalent with the likes of Gravelot nor Roubiliac, yet perhaps Aran might be a likely substitute for young Thomas Gainsborough. Not that *he* is likely to come to anything, mind. *Far* too fond of landskips, and they will never answer. Yes, he understands that Gainsborough is still only sixteen years old but even so! And the announcement? Why, he has arranged that it should appear in Scatterbuck's first edition, though he is far from happy with the newspaper's support for the racing at Kersal Moor. Far from happy. He has tried to prevent it these several years past but so far to no avail. Failed, even though the land on which they occur borders that owned by this very family.

'But the subscription fees that you mention, sir,' says Aran. 'Perfectly reasonable, yet I wonder whether you might explain them in more detail?'

'Fie upon it, Mister Owen! Unless you require some didactic explanation, I protest that we need no such discussion, sirrah. I had hoped that you might become a founder-member, using your skills to occasionally assist with teaching the life-drawing classes, along with some modest stipend perhaps.'

'Your charity is generous but a stipend is unnecessary, I assure you. Why, I should be delighted, privileged indeed simply by the recognition, to help with the classes, though I do not believe that I have any great aptitude as a teacher. To be accepted into membership of the Academy is ample reward, gentlemen.'

'Charity?' says Clayton. 'Ah, now *there* is a subject for which Manchester is famous! Why, sir, the poor of this town receive so much charity that I wonder we have any person left who still warrants the title. I am certain that my good friend meant no charity, Mister Owen, and rather a simple commerce, mutually beneficial to each party, is that not so, John?'

'We can certainly leave the poor to their own devices, Reverend, I think. God has ordained the social order, after all. If he had not intended the poor to be amongst us, he would have ordered matters differently, one assumes. But He has also ordained that you should possess certain aptitudes, Mister Owen. A great talent in the making, we hear. And this being so, it would be remiss if we failed to put those talents to proper use. You are therefore, and herewith, accepted into membership of the Academy and we shall discuss the possibility of a stipend at a later date.'

Aran is properly grateful, awed by Byrom's confidence in his skills though not sufficiently so to forget that there are no professional art masters within the town. He cannot avoid the feeling therefore that he has been somewhat lauded by faint praise and, at an appropriate juncture, he offers his apologies and promises to return within the coming weeks so that details of the opening event might be settled. He makes his way across town once more to seek Titus Redmond at one of the warehouses. Hopefully, he will still have time to meet him before his patron decides upon a visit to the bawdy-house for he must now not only speak with Titus about his plans to develop the tea trade but also confess his recent accusations against Driscoll, for the implications of his outburst are just beginning to clarify.

But he is forestalled, no more than half-way to the Quay, by Titus Redmond himself, bound for Scatterbuck's to see the first edition of the new *Manchester Journal* roll from the press.

'A fortuitous encounter, Aran,' he cries. 'Come, man, shall you not accompany me? You can explain your plans for the business on the way and, afterwards, we shall each wax our wicks with the finest jilts that Manchester can offer. What say you? May even help to cure that glum demeanour!'

Aran falls into step beside Titus, makes his best excuse for declining Redmond's kind offer to share his jilts, and explains the reason for his demeanour with an apologetic rendition of his dialogue with Jacob, heightening the colour of Driscoll's own comments, now lending towards incitement in this more dramatic portrait of the event, and softening the tones of his own response. There is no daubing over the substance of his allegation, however, the outline showing in stark relief through the glaze that he applies to hide it.

'So, let us leave aside a moment your belief that Driscoll is capable of such killing,' says Titus, striding onwards but cool and calm as though he were in a debating chamber, 'but you consider also that he would act so from his own initiative? With no thought for the consequence to myself and my enterprise?'

'I owe Jacob an apology, sir. I see that plain. And in the aftermath, in trying to justify my hasty words, why, I see that I had also invented cause for the effect. But, more than this, I see that I owe *you* an apology also, sir. For of course Jacob would not act without your authority and the very idea that he may have taken such a step under your sanction is clearly unthinkable.'

'You must mark me well, Aran, for I am not a man to suffer cunny-suckers gladly. And I would not think twice about taking whatever steps I thought necessary to protect our enterprise or my family. But there *was* no necessity in this case. I was assured, assured by *you*, my young friend, that there was no risk from either yourself *or* Daniel Sourwood. You collect our conversation, I imagine? So unless you have some further light to shed upon the matter? No? Then I suggest that you leave me to soothe the Jacob's feathers and I will tell you when the time is ripe for your own apology to him. For my own part, I am pleased that some sense appears to have possessed you once more, and you can now explain this wonderful plan to me.'

They have stopped, briefly, so that Titus can regard him closely and Aran feels the dark eyes set in those deeply-etched features, searching his very soul. He senses Dudley Striker, somewhere within him, stealthily flitting between the shadows of his subconscious, hiding from Redmond's marauding gaze, urging Aran to evasion also.

'The plan?' he says. 'Of course, sir. Three things.' And as they continue along their route, he details the various strands of his thinking. He has never considered himself to be especially talented in these matters but he has always believed that patient hard work is an excellent substitute for intellectual capacity. So he has used his period of convalescence wisely. An express here, a contact there. First, he has followed Addison's axiom. 'There is nothing more requisite in business than dispatch.' There is no problem with the supply side of the business, since Captain Erikkson and the Swedish Company maintain an efficient flow of tea through Driscoll's network of smugglers. They *could* provide much more since the market is buoyant. But the business is constrained by the rate at which it can meet the demands of customers since it is wholly reliant on the established networks of Fly Wagons for their deliveries. The solution seems simple. The business should be expanded to include their own wagoners and haulage teams. Yes, there are risks and obstacles, but Aran deals with each of these patiently and precisely until Titus is convinced that the plan is sound. Second, Aran outlines the new picking system that he proposes for the warehouse itself. Simple, yet resolving the haphazard arrangement currently in place for the storage of stock. And third, he believes that they should consider expanding beyond their existing illicit trade and aim to win supply for those coffee houses in the north prepared to also pay the Excise.

'We would have to collect the Excise from them!' says Titus. 'Collect revenue for the Hanoverians? You have lost your wits once more, I do protest.'

'We would collect a modest amount, true. But might this not provide a screen of respectability behind which our other activities might be more secure?'

'It would certainly allow us legitimate contact with the other coffee houses. Lick-spittles, of course, but once we had them neatly on your hook, why, even the most upstanding would be hard-pressed to avoid the temptation of a little contraband amongst their documented goods.'

They agree the principles, commit to finalising the details later, and arrive at Scatterbuck's. It is a modest establishment with relatively restricted space, in which cleanliness is essential to the efficient operation of the process and to the presentation of the finished product. On the ground floor there are two rooms, the first entered from the street and serving as both a bookshop and binding room combined, with a short passage leading to the print room itself, and a narrow staircase to the upper floor, used purely for storage. The stone walls of each room are painted white and are otherwise unremarkable, except for the level of frenetic activity that they embrace. A second apprentice has been engaged, as well as a full-time press man, releasing Scatterbuck to spend more time writing articles and seeking new contracts. And the work has continued to grow, with a significant order from the Collegiate Church for their special *tête-bêche* edition Psalter and New Testament, printed head to tail, with the texts being inverted with respect to one another. The anomaly, naturally, is Scatterbuck himself, oblivious to the activity around him, each blemish of his skin outlined in smeared ink, but proudly displaying the first copy of the *Journal*.

'Give you joy of our enterprise, Titus!' he says. 'What think you? Is it not the quintessence of éclat? Simply the apogee of my vocation, a gazette *par excellence*.'

It is produced in three columns, of course, with each news item beginning with a large, factotum initial, and the normal range of articles and announcements.

> W BONNEY, *Saracen's Head Tavern, Market Street lane, respectfully informs his friends that he has on sale fine lively TURTLE just imported. Turtle dressed in Mugs to carry to any part of England.*

Aran searches for mention of the Academy, finds it on the second page.

> *At the house of Mister John Byrom, Hanging Ditch, on Friday, the 29th day of May, the opening of an Academy for the purpose of studying painting, design, draughtsmanship and drawing, which will avoid the failure of previous Academies elsewhere by ensuring that leading members shall not assume a superiority that fellow-students might not brook. All gentlemen prepar'd to accept this stricture shall be welcome to participate.*

'There is an astonishing amount of announcements,' says Aran. 'Did you invent them?'

'Outrageous accusation! You dispute my literary integrity? Opprobrium for my efforts at such an early stage? Why, sir, I was fair inundated by demand, no sooner had word of our venture escaped to the streets.'

> CAUTION. *Whereas my Wife, Judith FRISSON, has been contracting debts and otherwise misbehaving herself, I hereby caution all persons against trusting her, as I will not be accomptable for any of her debts. As Witness my hand. Henry FRISSON.*

'Frisson!' says Titus. 'I warned him against marrying that scold. The cunny-sucker would pay me no heed. I am surprised, though, that you have avoided the temptation to spread tattle about *me*, you bag of puss! I heard you at the rout, Scatterbuck, asking O'Farrell about my privacies.'

'An innocent enquiry about the health of Mistress Mudge, Titus. I assure you. No more than that...'

Aran intervenes with a suggestion that, in future editions, perhaps there might be space available for a riddle or similar conundrum. Swift's perhaps? *'I with borrow'd silver shine. What you see is none of mine.'*

'Fucking riddles,' says Titus. 'You will be wanting to rave about those pox'd Rogues and Righteous again should we give you space. God's Hooks, man, do you think we need to fill our columns with nonsense when there are serious matters to attend? See, this is better. A *courant* on the Hanoverians' war.'

> PELHAM, puppet PRIME MINISTER to the Hanoverian King, has announced that he will continue to prosecute the WAR against Bavaria, France and Spain, regardless of the cost, in a further speech to the House of Commons. Whilst this journal naturally supports the patriotic duties of our country, our readers will be alarm'd at the rising levels of taxation needed to support the WAR. A meeting of townspeople in the Bull's Head Inn has condemn'd the Hanoverian actions as a means to seize the silver concessions in Porto Bello, properly under the ownership of our exiled Good King James. The EDITOR seriously hopes that the CASUS BELLI for our present engagement should be more vigorously scrutinised and that the said PELHAM shall soon be brought down.

'Yet this seems lacking your normal fluidity, Adam? You have a second scribbler already?'

'Ah! Well it is certainly true that various potential contributors have offered themselves...'

'Your sweat has that rancid liar's stink, Scatterbuck. Who wrote this piece?'

'He insisted, Titus. Francis. Townley, of course,' says Scatterbuck, and he shifts yet more ink stain to his brow as he attempts to wipe away the offending perspiration.

'So Townley has become an investor in our enterprise then, has he? To have acquired such editorial rights? A pity that nobody chanced to inform me, do you not think?'

Aran has an affection for Scatterbuck and considers that he owes him some debt for the care that the older man lavished on his apprenticeship, though he could be a difficult master. He has a tendency to be verbose, however, and considers himself a polymath to equal even John Byrom whilst, in truth, the ambition of his own disciplines is not matched by achievement. The printer and publisher seems never quite comfortable within his clothes, that do not fit him admirably at the best of times. But now he appears to alternately inflate and then wilt within them as, at one instant, he swells his chest to confront Redmond and, at the next, he retreats into cowering subservience.

'I merely esteemed the efficacious rendition of assistance proffered by that gentleman,' says Scatterbuck. 'And for this relief, much thanks, as the Prince of Denmark would say. There can be no harm in honest assistance, surely. And Townley is, when all is done, a member of your innermost circle, Titus. Is he not?'

Aran carefully scans the next announcement in the heartbeat pending Redmond's retort.

The EDITOR is pleas'd to note that the esteem'd journal, the Gentleman's Magazine, has recently publish'd an article extolling the virtues of our fine town and detailing the 'substantial development' that has taken place these twenty years past.

'For a man who prizes his faculties so highly, Adam, you are a lack-witted lick-spittle at times!' says Titus. 'God defend me from my friends! And the best way to defend myself from friends like Townley is to keep them close, I must allow. But not *this* close! I have not invested in this pox'd plaything of yours simply so that Townley and his ranters might use it to propagate their own zeal. In future, you will print nothing that touches on the Hanoverians or our Cause that has not first been approved by me. And if I am not available, why, this former apprentice of your establishment shall stand in my stead.'

Aran looks up from the broadsheet, unsure whether he has heard his patron correctly but Titus confirms that it is indeed himself to whom he has referred. Reliable, he says. At least, for the most part. When his Welsh tongue fails to get the better of him, that is. And Scatterbuck accepts the admonition, relieved that it has been so slight, expresses fawning delight at the idea of working with Aran whenever it might be necessary.

'Now,' says Titus, 'what more is there? Ah, the races.'

The annual MANCHESTER RACES shall take place, despite recent objections, during the second weekend of JUNE, at KERSAL MOOR, and subscriptions are invited to support this EVENT.

The races to which John Byrom is so opposed, thinks Aran.

'And this?' asks Titus. 'From whence did this piece derive?'

At the Commerce Exchange, Manchester, on Monday, the 7th instant, to be seen, a person who performs the several most surprising things following, viz. first, he takes a common walking-

cane from any of the spectators, and thereon plays the music of every instrument now in use, and likewise sings to surprising perfection. Secondly, he presents you with a common wine bottle, that any of the spectators may first examine; this bottle is placed on a table in the middle of the stage, and he (without any equivocation) goes into it in sight of all the spectators, and sings in it; during his stay in the bottle any person may handle it, and see plainly that it does not exceed a common tavern bottle. Those on the stage or in the boxes may come in mask'd habits (if agreeable to them); and the performer (if desired) will inform them who they are. The EDITOR takes no responsibility for the veracity of these claims.

'A stranger,' says Scatterbuck. 'Travelling performer, he says. First performance outside London apparently. Astonishing claims, are they not? A wondrous spectacle, I am told.'

'Wondrous indeed!' says Titus. 'Well, Aran, this lick-spittle seems capable of even more invention and contortion than yourself, sir. Now tell me, what is the answer?'

Aran neither fully hears nor fully understands the question, for something has gripped him. Something cold and familiar. Where previously he had imagined Striker hiding in the recesses of his imagination, now he sees him standing proud in the light, that sardonic smile playing at his mouth. *A stranger?* he thinks. *A Bottle-Conjuror? Why should this bring Striker so vividly to mind?*

'Sir?' he says.

'Why, man, your riddle. You did mention Swift, I collect. *I with borrow'd silver shine. What you see is none of mine.* What is the answer?'

Chapter Fifteen

The house at Pool Fold, past the Cross, is more modest by far than her own, yet Rosina admires the quiet elegance with which Mrs Starkey has endowed it, and especially the music room where she now waits for her harpsichord lesson to commence. Its light heart helps to banish Rosina's customary annoyance at her mother's weekly dalliance and though Mrs Starkey is, she is sure, lacking any great means, the room has been decorated and furnished with great taste. A gilt-framed mirror in the *barocco* style hangs above the mantel, and the mantel itself caps a white fireplace carved in asymmetrical design to match the ceiling stucco. A simple Chinese vase and mandarin adorn the mantel shelf, and the walls are a shade of pearl, each of their panels edged in leaf, with central lozenges enclosing painted *jardinières*.

Apart from the harpsichord, there is simply one *fauteuil* and an occasional table, while the *clavecin* itself has been purchased from Mister Collins in Hanging Ditch, rather than the shop in Tib Lane, though he had not built the instrument itself but, rather, ordered its construction from a Swiss gentleman in London. The same gentlemen, in fact, who had later supplied Rosina's own. They are based on the Flemish Ruckers design but styled in the new fashion, veneered inside and out, elegant and restrained, with detailed inlay and marquetry in the keywell.

'La! At last,' says Mrs Starkey, who has been turning the pages of a finely engraved music book for some time. '*Les Barricades Mystérieuses*. I thought that you should enjoy it since they say that its title derives from the *divertissement* arranged by the Duchesse du Maine at which all the guests wore masks to celebrate the attendance of their clandestine guest, Good King James, naturally.'

'It is Couperin,' says Rosina, looking over Mrs Starkey's shoulder at the manuscript, the ornaments, the *notes inégales*. '*Rondo*. In B-flat. I should enjoy it of all things, though it seems complex.'

Mrs Starkey explains the main theme, and then each of the variations.

Rosina attempts the opening bars, thinking that her own life is one of variations dominated by a main theme, a turbulent one in which her own nature struggles against those of her parents. She may share their Faith, she may share their belief in the Cause, but otherwise she feels distant from them, and the greater the distance, the closer she senses herself drawn to

Elizabeth Cooper. She dreams of Elizabeth almost nightly now. Wicked dreams for the most part, though sometimes strangely interwoven with images of Aran Owen that she finds more difficult to recall. Mrs Starkey interrupts.

'Couperin *le Grand*,' she says. 'Exquisite. Though we should try some of the pieces by Clérambault, Dandrieu or Marchand over the coming weeks. So much more acceptable than the Germans, of course. Well, what can you expect from Lutherans?'

'I enjoyed the Corelli too,' says Rosina. 'It was so much more acceptable to Mama that I was studying an Italian. I fancy that she would be quite low if she knew that I was now fingering a Frenchman!'

'La! Miss Redmond!' says Mrs Starkey, using her hand to mimic the use of a fan and feigning embarrassment. They laugh together. 'There seem to be so many differences between yourself and your mother, my dear. She is very traditional in her outlook, I think. Is it very difficult for you? Though you may protest that it is no business on mine to put such a question, of course.'

Rosina weighs the level of impertinence in Mrs Starkey's enquiry. She is simply her music teacher, after all, though a fondness has grown between them over the months. The Starkeys are also Catholic, of course, and older than her parents but they have embraced *le goût* with as much fervour as their modest income will allow.

'It has become somewhat *less* difficult,' she says, 'since Mister Owen has been recuperating *chez nous*. Mama cannot escape the possibility, slight though it might be, that he shall become a fashionable artist at some stage so she has been quite shameless in pretending towards *le beau monde* in his presence. After all, if Our Lord has seen fit to grace us with such invention then modern good taste must surely be an imperative of Faith and its products must be virtuous. Yet my mother says that this is simply taking His name in vain, a mere excuse to argue *au français*.'

Mrs Starkey asks about Aran's injury. It is progressing well, she hopes. And she has heard from a reliable informant that the poor man is unable to return to his lodging, though she is hardly surprised. Mistress Evesworth would have been scandalised merely by the mud from the Constables' shoes upon her tiles, let alone by an arrest taking part on her premises, and entirely regardless of whether that arrest was warranted. But, then, perhaps she can be the bearer of good tidings for her husband had mentioned, just two days previously, that there are rooms available, well-appointed too, adjacent to the Punch House.

'Oh, give you thanks for this news!' says Rosina. 'I shall tell Mister Owen as soon as I am able but, for now, I should like to practise the Couperin once more. Would it not be the very thing if I could perform this on Restoration Day.'

'With four weeks of practise, my dear, I am certain that you shall have mastered it to perfection.'

And I must make a note in my diary, thinks Rosina, *to purchase some sheets of Clérambault too.* Her diary is precious to her, written in the shorthand code that she has learned from Beppy Byrom, with whom she shares a private tutor and a vigour for the Stuarts' Cause. She sees this Jacobite vigour as quite distinct from that of her parents, and from her mother in particular who, like many Jacobites, yearns for a return to privilege lost to their families with the exile of James the Second. For so many, it has become the creed of the distressed, of the redundant tradesman, of the failed enterprise, of the criminalised margins. A creed that calls upon them simply to reverse the order of things, to set matters back more than half a century so that all might be well again. And this was no aim to be achieved by mewling about the past yet, rather, by aggressive expansion of the vision into the present. *But what*, she thinks, *if the dream should fail?*

'Why,' says Mrs Starkey, 'next time, I shall also teach you how to voice the instrument. It has become too easy for people to rely on professional tuners, do you not think? Yet just imagine what might happen were you in the middle of a performance. You would be thought quite incompetent were you not able to make the necessary quill adjustments!'

Oh yes, thinks Rosina. *Incompetent. Indeed.*

And thoughts of adjustment fill her head as Maria-Louise returns to accompany her home but this is an agitated Mama, she notes, positively polite to Mrs Starkey though not, she suspects from any sense of propriety. *She is vexed*, she thinks. *Not at all herself. Almost bereft. Some lover's tiff with that salacious libertine Whig, I collect!*

Her mother is starched and tight-lipped as they pass the hatters and shuttle makers, tinmen and sugar bakers, grocers and pipe breakers, malters and pig keepers, drapers and smoke-jack makers, plasterers and cheesemongers, the haggars and brass founders. Rosina has become enamoured of the place. She feels affinity with Ireland, of course, but does not mourn its loss like Maria-Louise. Manchester is a growing place, become a modern town, and she is young enough not to see the detritus, the sometime sewerage, the middens nor the pigs that devour them, the deformity of many citizens, so numerous that the monster-mongers see no profit in them.

Let Mama seek her rural tranquility, she thinks, and wonders how her mother can remain unmoved by the time she had spent in London, brief though it may have been, or her two years in Paris studying with the children of an uncle, an Irish Brigade officer of Bulkeley's Foot, within the army of King Louis. *Yet she is not truly unmoved. Quite the contrary. She has been moved to hate towns and despise the French. La! An' I were only able to change places with her. To travel the capitals of Europe with Elizabeth as my companion.*

'I have been thinking about your education, Rosina,' says Maria-Louise, suddenly. 'You will collect that I had the great good fortune to finish in Paris.'

First Mrs Starkey, thinks Rosina, *and now Mama. Am I truly so thoroughly transparent?*

'I collect that you have never spoke a good word of that city, Mama, nor its inhabitants neither.'

'I do not suggest that *you* should go there, my dear. But my cousin Katherine is now in Geneva. Did I not say so? No, well, there she is, all the same.'

'Mama, it is scarce an hour since you left me with Mrs Starkey and you have expressed no previous concern about this matter. I can only assume that you have spent the intervening time in company with Mister Bradley. Am I to assume that the idea is somehow inspired by *him*?'

'There are matters that I must discuss with your father but, before I do so, I must put to you a question. A blunt question, my dear. I know that we lack intimacy at times, Rosina, but I care for you greatly. You must know this. Yet I have to ask...'

Rosina can almost see the question forming in her mother's mind. *Elizabeth Cooper has occupied me so much that Mama can somehow perceive the image of her also.*

'I intend no disrespect, Mama, yet I should take it amiss were either yourself or Papa to deem my friendship with Mistress Cooper an embarrassment. That she is a Whig should hardly concern you considering your own relations with Mister Bradley!'

'A Whig? Stuff, Rosina! It is more that she is apparently a Myra that concerns me. Or shall you tell me that you are not sensible of her sapphic passions? I could not blame you, I fancy, since she is not manly in the way of the Duchess of Newborough, nor others of her sort.'

'Elizabeth Cooper is my friend. Sapphic passions, indeed! She has never shown me anything but kindness. Yet you would brand her a tribade, a *lesbiana*, a nymph, simply on the word of Mister Bradley?'

'I am assured that she admitted as much herself. But I do not condemn her for it. It is well known that tribady is caused when young girls are seduced by older women already infected by this aberration. I am certain that Mistress Cooper must have been afflicted in the same way and I pity her for it, though it must be my duty to protect you from the same fate. Oh, fie upon it! What am I saying? You have *not*, my dear, I take it? Already, I mean. No venereal act?'

'I find it hard to believe that we are even *having* this conversation,' says Rosina.

'And *that*, my dear, is no apt denial!'

Her mother begins to sob, the first time that Rosina can ever recall such an occurrence. But they are returned now to the house, Titus still removing his coat as they enter. He is in good spirit following his return from Scatterbuck's, triumphantly displaying his copy of the *Journal* up to the instant when he finally becomes aware of his wife's distress.

109

Maria-Louise insists on urgent discussion in the fore-parlour, exiles both Mudge and O'Farrell to their respective quarters, the younger children to their rooms and Rosina to a chair in the entrance hall. Voices are raised but she can discern little of the detail though it is clear that the discussion extends well beyond herself and Elizabeth Cooper. There is a pit somewhere in her stomach and, within the pit, volcanic gases churn, sulphurous and flame-hot. This is not the hollow vacancy that she feels whenever she is separated from Elizabeth. Nor is it the rising tension that she experiences at the prospect of their meeting again. Not even the nervous excitement when they are together, or the empty frustrations of their parting. Those, she is aware, are exhibitions of immature infatuation. Her current state is one of quaking apprehension.

She wonders whether Aran Owen might be in his room and how he might react if she sought sanctuary there. *There is no shame in my friendship with Elizabeth,* she thinks, *yet Mama and Papa will not see it thus. And what has Elizabeth said that has caused all this? I cannot believe that she would have spoke intimately with that filth that Mama has chosen as her paramour.* She stands and begins to quietly ascend the staircase to the first floor but her parents' voices are raised again, seem to be moving closer, so that she runs down the flight once more, composes herself back upon the chair.

But they do not come. She can hear them still but muted urgency has overtaken strident argument. *I wish that Elizabeth were here with me. They would see then. Yet how* dare *they! Mama behaves like a strumpet with Bradley, and does not care who knows it. And Papa! He might as well simply bring still more of his jades to live with us for all the discretion that he displays in his fondness for the bawdy house.* And the sensation grows in her that her parents might not know how to confront the matter, might choose to simply ignore it. *On the other hand,* she thinks, *I could slip through that door and be gone. To Elizabeth. She would know the correct thing to do, I collect. Unless, indeed, she really* has *made some statement of betrayal to Mister Bradley.*

She stands again, careful to make no sound, and edges towards the front door, reaches for it, hears her mother's voice approaching the far side of the parlour door. *If I am to run, I must do so now.* The intricate handle of this near side of the parlour door begins to turn. *Run, Rosina.* The handle is released. The door remains closed. The argument within continues. *No,* she thinks. *This will not answer at all!* And, unbidden, she recalls John Donne. A piece that Elizabeth has read to her. 'For love all love of other sights controls, And makes one little room an everywhere.'

And *this* little room, thinks Rosina Redmond, is where she shall become a woman grown. She turns from thoughts of escape, takes five short steps across the polished floor and throws open the door of the parlour.

Chapter Sixteen

Sir Edward Stanley shifts his considerable bulk uncomfortably in his seat. *This damn'd bile*, he thinks. There have been small quantities of blood in his phlegm this se'nnight past and each visit to the jakes has been an occasion for searing pain in his gut. *I should take the opportunity to speak with Hall while I am in Manchester though, in truth, I should rather be shot of the place sooner rather than later. Perhaps when we reach Birmingham. Murchison is an admirable physician also.*

He notices that he has somehow laddered his finest silk stockings while waiting for the performance to begin. Little wonder in these makeshift crates passing for boxes lining the Commodities Exchange upper hall.

'Well, are you pleased that we have come, now you see the condition of the place, my dear?' he says.

'It may not be Drury Lane,' whispers his wife, Elizabeth, 'but I have never seen *Harlequin's Vagaries* and it would have been too bad of you, Edward, had we not come. You might not *like* Manchester but you cannot shun the town altogether, especially when we are so near.' She turns to John Clayton, across the empty seat between them. 'An unusual night for Pantomime, Reverend. Yet such an attendance!'

'In Manchester, Ladyship, *any* night might be suitable for Pantomime. Something in the nature of the town, I think. There is a heathen element here that you may have noticed, and these lyrical celebrations of ancient myth strike a certain chord. In London, too, of course. I collect that I should not be so fond of them myself, given my vocation, yet they amuse me so. Have you seen *Vagaries* already? No? Then you shall have a treat, for we saw a performance at the turn of the year. Same night as *The Recruiting Officer*. Farquhar's play?'

'Most of them here for the Conjuror, though, I imagine,' says Sir Edward, unable to avoid focus on Clayton's flaking skin. He could almost swear that the fellow was syphilitic. 'Such claims! You have seen the fellow, Reverend? Some mirror trickery, you think? My dear, you should think of some great monstrous musical instrument and challenge him to transmute his famous walking-cane into *that*, eh?'

'We may safely assume, Sir Edward,' says Clayton, 'that our plain Manchester folk shall have the most imaginative suggestions to make in relation to this walking-cane. For myself, I await with interest the Conjuror's contortionist entry to a common tavern bottle. Should he be able to meet *that* boast then the evening will, indeed, be a suitable tribute to Pan and the heathen ancients. Ah, but here is the rest of our company!'

Enter Sir Oswald Mosley, Lord of the Manor of Manchester, accompanied by his wife, Anne, and the family of John Byrom. Greetings are exchanged. 'Allow me to name...' but there are so many to remember that Sir Edward makes no attempt to do so. He enquires about Byrom himself though, absent from the group.

'John is in Cambridge, Lordship,' replies Elisabeth Byrom. 'He is so frequently out of town these days, often in London or Oxford, there is such demand for his shorthand tuition. Yet he will be home, I am sure, for young Ted's birthday next month.'

'And on this occasion he is undertaking some additional work for myself and Deacon, for we are determined on a new translation of Romans. There are so many obvious errors.'

Well, at the least, I shall not have to tolerate Byrom's company, thinks Sir Edward. He does not really like the cove. A dozen years previously, a new Workhouse had been approved by the Court Leet and a packed Town Meeting. Four storeys, no less. Enormous great thing. James Bradley had inspired the idea, of course, arranged to become elected as one of the trustees, and begun its construction. But Byrom and the High Churchmen had bitterly criticised the project, claiming that there were already sufficient facilities for the town's poor. A petition had therefore been gathered against the Workhouse and Sir Edward had been required to support it. A Committee had been established to hear evidence and the House had finally established that the project should be abandoned. Byrom had been feted on his return to Manchester with bells rung at the Collegiate Church. Sir Oswald's family had been key supporters, had employed Bradley as the builder in the first place, but then Sir Oswald himself been persuaded by the town's Tories to campaign against it. Sir Edward had been an opposition Tory himself at the time so had no great axe to grind in relation to the Workhouse. *Pity, all the same*, he thinks. *For the Court Leet was correct and Byrom were wrong. All his fine promises that the town could care for the poor without a Workhouse. And just look at the place! More beggars than the Constables is possibly able to shift.* His personal politics might still be Tory but his succession to the Earldom has, he likes to think, given him a broader view of the world. It has certainly distanced him from the more radical members of his Party. *And these High Church fellows – I wish we had sat somewhere else. Jacobites every one of them. All aglow too, I imagine, with our forces beat at Villafranca. And all this prattle about Saint Paul. Will Clayton never finish?* His discomfort is partially physical, otherwise political and social.

'I am sorry that our humble establishment can offer no greater luxury,

Sir Edward,' says Mosley. 'I am determined on a true gallery and some integral boxes but, at the moment, we have either these contrivances or the shilling seats, I am afraid.'

'What? Ah, no. Perfectly adequate, sir, I thank thee,' the Earl replies, but thinks that this is another dam'd Jacobite. The very fellow he has been instructed to keep under surveillance. How old *is* Sir Oswald in any case? He must be seventy by now, surely.

Sir Edward's wife is describing their lodgings to the other wives. Yes, she says, staying with Reynolds at Strangeways Hall. Odd muddle of a place. Half Tudor hall and half Palladian palace. And the lane from Hunts Bank to the estate. Such a trial.

A fie upon you woman, he thinks. *Had you not insisted on seeing this nonsense, we should be on our way to Birmingham by now*. Still, it has been useful, he supposes. It has given him a chance to speak with Francis Reynolds. Persuade him that he should stand for Parliament. Unlike his father, he is a loyal supporter of the Pelhams. But old Thomas had died two years earlier and Francis, he is sure, will help to put this place more firmly on the map.

Clayton has now shifted to a lecture on the nature of Pantomime itself. A celebratory imitation of Nature, as represented by the idolatrous deity of the Ancients. Pan, the shepherd of Arcadia. He quotes Dryden. 'Pan taught to join with wax unequal reeds; Pan loves the shepherds and the flocks he feeds.' The ladies are amused.

A fanfare. Great rollicking noise and tumblers introduce the first Act but chatter amongst the audience does not abate. The shilling spectators are familiar enough with this standard fare, even in Manchester, yet it is a welcome enough background to their gathering. Prometheus has just finished manufacturing his Man of Clay, but sings out his dissatisfaction at its lack of motion or meaning. Ribald rhymes about his creation's fine proportions. Such waste. If only he had the means to exercise them. The ladies feign embarrassment while the Chariot of the Sun sails the scenery sky. Prometheus snatches fire from its wheels as Doctor Clayton changes places with Elizabeth Stanley, allowing her to sit amongst the Byrom and Mosley womenfolk and he to enquire after the scientific nature of Sir Edward's visit to Birmingham since such, he understands from Her Ladyship, is the purpose of their journey. He understands that Sir Edward shares his own keen interest in scientific developments. His Lordship has such a reputation in these matters.

'Do you say so, sir?' replies Sir Edward. 'A modest reputation only, I am sure, if reputation it can truly be named.' Yet he glows at the recognition. And Clayton is perhaps not such a bad fellow. Not so *deeply* Jacobite, he imagines. 'Well, Reverend, the fact is that I had the good fortune to meet a colonial fellow. In Scotland. A presentation by Doctor Archibald Spencer. You know his work, of course?'

'Courses in Natural Philosophy, I collect,' says Clayton.

'An unconvincing show with experiments imperfectly performed, as it happens. Nonsense, of course. Electrical courses, indeed! But an interesting evening. This colonial fellow had some illustrations of the Flying Chair built for King Louis. A system of weights and pulleys so that he might ascend unassisted from floor to floor of his palace.'

'And you seek to emulate...?'

'Oh, good gracious! No, sir. The Earl of Derby's Flying Chair? Oh, fie. Elizabeth, my dear, you hear this?' Sir Edward's girth quivers with mirth. But he patiently explains that he is most taken by the fellow's design for a circulating stove, a closed firebox. It will provide more heat and less smoke than an ordinary open fireplace since baffles in the rear improve airflow. The houses both at Bickerstaffe and Rufford would benefit from one. Draughty places, both of them.

'Ah, the circulating stove,' says Clayton. 'Yes, I am familiar with the device. Yet the metallurgy is lacking, is it not? The cast sometimes cracks when the stove is fired, I fear, for lack of proper experimentation at the design stage. Such fellows as this colonial frequently display superficial ingenuity yet disappoint through their failure to adhere to strict experimental results as required by Boerhaave and Newton. In the model that I inspected the opening to the flue was in the floor of the stove. Can you imagine such a thing, Lordship?'

This fellow likes to come it the natural philosopher then, thinks Sir Edward.

'Ah,' he says, 'this man Franklin has improved on that design but the metallurgy still troubles me. Hence my visit to Birmingham. A foundry there has promised to resolve the matter. And then, perhaps, you might choose a circulating stove for Ancoats Hall too, Sir Oswald? Eh?'

But Sir Oswald has not followed the conversation. He has been following the Pantomime, apparently, as Mercury decides to punish Prometheus for his theft of the sun's fire, orders him chained to a rock where an enormous vulture, a hideous creature, shall prey upon his living heart.

'It all seems so terribly familiar,' says Sir Edward during the brief intermission preceding Act Two.

'A standard opening for Pantomime,' says Clayton, as the curtain lifts again.

'Who is the woman playing Columbine?' asks Elizabeth Stanley.

'Mrs Rawson, I think,' says Anne Mosley. 'An excellent singer.' And Columbine is, indeed, excellent. A clever solo performance which raises excitement and expectation for Harlequin's entrance.

'A wonderful performance, Sir Edward, do you not think?' says Mosley. 'And pleasing that my Exchange should be able to accommodate such performances.'

'Not really to my taste, Sir Oswald. Elizabeth is clearly enjoying the spectacle, however. And so far as the Exchange is concerned, I always admired your tenacity in having the place built. Remarkable edifice, though why in the name of Our Lord you should have chosen to construct it in the midst of this labyrinth of shit-strewn alleys I shall never understand. More cattle wandering the environs than in the grounds of Strangeways. I declare, sir. But you will excuse me, gentlemen, ladies? I fear that I must exercise my limbs a little. This damn'd bile, you know. No Reverend, no need to disturb yourself, I thank you. I shall return forthwith. If I can once free myself from this contraption...'

He has at last managed to catch James Bradley's eye, signed for him to meet outside, struggled to free his bulk from the box and lumbered through the crowd, waving aside the footman whom Francis Reynolds has assigned to accompany His Lordship, waving aside also those who would seek to detain him with greeting, fawning or favour to request, finding Bradley waiting below.

'Give you good evening, Bradley,' says Sir Edward. 'A fine one too, I see!'

'My Lord,' Bradley replies, with the merest inclination of his head in mockery of the bow to which the Earl feels entitled. He thinks Bradley an insolent fellow, likes him in truth no more than the High Churchmen and Jacobites. *Was there only a strong Tory faction in the town,* he often muses, *independent of those damn'd Jacobites. Yet they are all one here for the most part. A sorry state of affairs.* So he has no choice but to deal with these Whiggish types.

'Enjoying this Pantomime?' he feels obliged to ask though, in truth, he does not normally engage in polite chatter.

'I am usually more entertained by the audience, My Lord. I find that it is a satisfactory way to gauge the weather in town. The absence of *this* faction. The attendance of *that* family. The company that certain *individuals* keep amongst the crowd...'

'You do not refer to my *own* company, I trust, Mister Bradley?' Sir Edward feels his ire rising, his neck and lower cheeks enflamed.

'A gentleman in your own delicate position, Sir Edward, must needs be able to move freely amongst friend and foe alike. No, My Lord, I had merely been observing the absence of the Papists tonight and, in their absence, that particular persons seem to gravitate to new *liaisons*, let us say.'

'You speak in riddles, blast your eyes! Has this something to do with the confounded mess that you concocted around the Redmonds?'

'It is no mess, My Lord, I assure you. Quite the opposite.'

'Fie upon it, Mister Bradley! I had suggested some inducement to Redmond so that this damn'd Subscription of the Jacobites might be curtailed. And now I receive intelligence – and not from you, sir, but from the Duke of Newcastle himself – that you have embarked on some contrivance of your own. We spoke of inducement and *you* chose blackmail. And to what purpose, sir?'

'To the purpose, My Lord, which we intended. Certain information had come my way about the unnatural relationship betwixt Mistress Cooper – you will recall, Mistress Cooper, I collect – betwixt Mistress Cooper and the older Redmond girl…'

'Relationship, sir?' says Sir Edward. 'I wish you would speak plain. You mean, as the Spaniard would say, *donna con donna?*'

'Indeed, My Lord. At the risk of a certain crudeness, they apparently enjoy playing the Game of Flats together.'

'Vulgar phrase! Never really understood it. But was you in possession of any evidence it would be the duty of the Court Leet to act against these sapphist women, would it not?'

'Evidence is such a difficult word,' says Bradley. 'I had the information from Mistress Cooper herself but I had no witness to the discussion. Yet it seemed to me that I might allow Redmond to know that I was aware of his daughter's perversity.'

'Too disgusting to contemplate. Yet I recall the case of that Dragoon, served with the Iniskillings for years, and only discovered as a woman after his death. *Her* death, I should say. The *Courant* said that she was a lesbian, sir. The very word. But buried her with full military honours, none the less. When was that? Four years ago? Five? No more, I think.'

'I am sure that the practice must be widespread, My Lord. Yet here in Manchester it is still very much an aberration – and one that Redmond would not wish to see bandied about. Nor certain other matters either. I had picked up rumour of some involvement on the part of a Redmond man, one Jacob Driscoll, in the death of young Sourwood. You recall the suicide, Sir Edward. It is nonsense, of course, yet I thought that allowing Redmond to know of the rumour's existence might somehow cause him to think afresh about his own reputation. He is a man who craves respectability, after all.'

'Blackmail all the same, Mister Bradley. And where has it brought us, eh? Mistress Cooper is an important official in the town too. We could be hoisted on our own petard, sir.'

'Mistress Cooper flew at me in some rage, My Lord. That much is true. Accused me of embroidering her conversation with me. Yet the result was satisfying, I think. Redmond dispatched his younger daughters from the town at once. To Chorley and then to Southport I believe, and they have not yet returned. Meanwhile his household is in turmoil and there has been barely any activity amongst the Jacobites these weeks gone. Not even with the news of Villafranca.'

'His younger daughters? I do not understand how the *younger* daughters are involved. More riddles, sir. Yet the High Churchmen are in fine spirit, it seems. It is the same everywhere. They take joy at their own country's defeat by the French and Spanish. Outrageous, sir. And I hear that Redmond has started to purchase his own Fly Wagons so that he can run his illicit tea

116

wherever he damn'd well pleases. It does not seem to me that his activities are curtailed, sir. And, meanwhile, His Grace tells me that there are Jacobites springing up all over Wales, Scotland and Ireland as well.'

'But it is the Lancastrian Jacobites that most concern Your Lordship, I think. There are more Papists in this County than any other part of the realm except Ireland itself. And it is the Catholic activity here in Manchester, I believe, that may be curtailed by constraining Redmond. He has barely been seen since I passed my message to him. Nor his henchman, Driscoll, neither. No sign of any of them here tonight for example.'

'I can only imagine the manner in which you passed this *message*, sir. Yet you are correct about the Jacobites, Mister Bradley. It is to be hoped that our armies will be once more on the move against the French soon, and not encumbered this time by those damn'd Sardinians. His Grace believes that a decent victory will help stem the threat from the Stuarts too. Perhaps even terminate it for good. If only we can strike them a blow or two here at home also. Should like to believe that your stratagem might be effective yet at the same time you tell me they are curtailed, they manage to produce this new broadsheet and in its very first edition attack the progress of the war. It will not answer, sir! We should return to my original plan. Inducement, sir. Inducement. A company of Barrell's Regiment is due to pass through the town in the next week. I need to know whether I should guard against unrest, Mister Bradley, and *that* depends...'

But unrest, realises Sir Edward, might perhaps be more immediate, for there is a growing clamour above, that seems to have little relationship with appreciation for the performance. Some younger members of the audience have burst forth from the hall, run past them in great excitement to the lower level, gathered together some discarded fruits and vegetables left for the pigs to devour and started back up the stairs. At the same time, there is the harsh tone of a bell, a hand bell perhaps, in the distance.

'Fie upon you, gentlemen!' shouts Sir Edward, but the young fellows have pushed past both him and Bradley, disappeared within from whence the sound of outraged swarming is now unmistakable.

His concern for Elizabeth's safety lends agility to his age and weight and he forces his way back through the crowd, now blocking the doorway and seeming somehow more numerous than before, though this is clearly impossible.

'What is it?' he shouts to the footman, who has come to find him.

'End of the Pantomime, My Lord. The Bottle-Conjuror was announced but has not appeared. The audience has become ugly, Sir Edward.'

'Ugly indeed. Yet I do not know what they expect to gain by pelting rubbish at the stage in that way. Bradley! Your Constables, sir. And you...' He gestures at the footman, while Bradley dutifully turns back down the stairs to send word for Bower and Hibbert. 'Help me to escort Lady Stanley to safety.'

117

And Devil take the rest of them, he thinks. *Damn'd Jacobites*. But Elizabeth must be protected and so, assisted by the footman, he forces his way through the braying citizens. He is vaguely aware that somebody has ventured to the stage, another member of the Court Leet he thinks, in a bold attempt to restore some order but is rewarded simply with a further volley of missiles from the crowd.

'Make way for His Lordship, the Earl of Derby,' cries the footman, though barely audible.

'Fuck the Earl of Derby,' comes the response, and His Lordship turns impotently to confront his abusers, for it is impossible in this turmoil to discern the guilty party. However, he is bolstered to some degree by the edifying sight of the *Journal* being torn apart by various members of the audience, and Adam Scatterbuck's name being profaned for carrying the Bottle-Conjuror advertisement, other copies trampled underfoot and yet others balled into projectiles. *Scatterbuck may disclaim what he pleases*, thinks Sir Edward, *but the mob will blame him regardless, it seems. Such irony!* He takes advantage of a momentary lull and passage opened through the crowd as the Pantomime cast are permitted to leave, even applauded in parts, though the costumes of Harlequin, Columbine, Pantaloon and the rest have been heavily hidden beneath cloaks and travelling clothes. *No offence to yourselves, lordships!* the performers are told. Backs are slapped. Congratulations offered. Then their own entertainment resumes. Insults. Refunds demanded. But the footman and Sir Edward have slipped past, meeting the Reverend Doctor Clayton forcing a passage in the opposite direction for Elizabeth Stanley, closely followed by Sir Oswald Mosley and the rest of their company.

'My dear!' says Sir Edward. 'I knew that we should not have come. And you, Sir Oswald. You are Lord of this Manor, though it hardly deserves such a title...'

'La, Edward,' says his wife. 'There is no need to distress yourself. You see that I am quite well and both Reverend Clayton *and* Sir Oswald have played their part admirably in rescuing us from this unfortunate display – though I can hardly blame folk for their displeasure. This could have happened anywhere and I collect that we have seen it ourselves in London before today.'

'Quite so, and the authorities was on hand to restore order. There is the rub. The difference, my dear. But let us get you out of this place.'

'I can only apologise, Sir Edward,' says Mosley. 'I can only assume that the Constables are engaged elsewhere.'

In Manchester that should hardly surprise me, thinks Sir Edward but is restrained from saying so by pressure on his arm and a glance of rebuke from his wife.

And engaged elsewhere the Constables are indeed for, as the group descends the staircase from the Commodities Exchange, all attention is turned towards a glow in the south-eastern sky. Distant flames lick and lighten a pall of smoke at the edge of the town, and Constable Hibbert rushes to them, face blackened by soot.

'Mister Bradley's fine new terrace,' he gasps. 'Destroyed. Too far away from the wells, Conduit or river for the fire pump hoses to deliver any water. Destroyed, sirs.'

Sir Edward knows that Mosley is rightly proud of the town's fire pump and its volunteer Pumpmen. He boasts often that the leather pipes, all brass fittings and connections in the Newsham design, can deliver one hundred and sixty gallons each minute to the heart of a conflagration – but only so long as there is a source from which the water may be drawn. And also only so long as the fire's victim has been able to display the lead or copper plaque upon his wall, denoting that he has paid the insurance premium that, in turn, has funded the fire appliance.

'Well, Sir Oswald,' he says, 'what price your fine pump now, eh?' He does not wait for an answer or even seek satisfaction from Mosley's stricken demeanour. 'Yet I should be obliged was you to arrange for my lady wife to be returned to Strangeways Hall. No, my dear. No point in protest. I must go and see the damage for myself but shall give the blaze a wide berth, you may be sure. You, sir...!' A gesture to the footman. 'Fetch the Reynolds' chariot around and convey me at once to Bradley's terrace, or whatever is left of it!'

The small carriage arrives and sways a drunken path from the Commodities Exchange with Sir Edward seated inside, his arms outstretched, one to each side, in an effort to maintain stability. They lurch to one halt after another, first to avoid a trio of pigs, then blocked by a group of revellers intent on seeing the blaze for themselves, and finally confronted by an errant milch-cow that refuses to give way for His Lordship. Sir Edward recognises the first few by-ways, Market Street Lane of course, and then the sweeping detour to avoid St Ann's, but the outer parts of town are unfamiliar to him and the delays make him wonder whether, perhaps, he might indulge himself in a pinch of *rappee*. Elizabeth does not approve of the habit, naturally, but if he is going to be some time on his errand then all evidence of insufflation should have vanished by the time he returns to Strangeways. *In any* case, he thinks, *I have already confined myself to the Portuguese stuff on the advice that it will improve my damn'd eyes. I cannot imagine why the woman should be so set against it!* But the box is barely out of his pocket and the lid removed than the chariot jolts away again, with half the precious powder lost and the unmistakable stain of tobacco indelibly etched into the fabric of his breeches. 'God dammit, sir! Can you not be more careful?' he cries, and he has only just managed to pocket the remaining snuff when they reach their destination at last.

'Close enough!' shouts Sir Edward, as the chariot turns at the edge of an enclosure that, mercifully, still provides a natural break between Bradley's terrace and the rest of town. Sadly, however, two small cottages have not escaped the conflagration, their thatches alight and their occupants huddled silhouettes against flame and darkening sky, against smoke and gathering spectators. 'There fellow,' he says, leaning from the chariot and prodding the footman's shoulder. 'At the edge of the crowd. With the Pumpmen. Mister Bradley – you see him? Then take me there, blast your eyes! But carefully now. You are not to fright the horse.'

They approach cautiously until Sir Edward is able to make himself heard above the noise of the fire and the belated din of the Fire Bell, now peeling urgently somewhere back in the town centre. It is evident that, even in its ruin, Bradley has built a fine terrace. But flames have now consumed floor and staircase alike, roof trees, windows and doors. Much of the brick and stone-work still stands but will not survive the night.

Bradley leans against the fire pump, its leather hoses connected but impotently snaking to nowhere, its volunteer operatives watching the fire disconsolately.

They would be better occupied in taking the damn'd thing apart and returning to their beds, thinks Sir Edward. *But they cannot bring themselves to desert the scene, I collect.* Bradley turns and recognizes the Earl, walks to the chariot with head bowed and arms folded across his chest. 'My condolences, Mister Bradley. A bitter stroke, upon my word.'

'You believe that this is some mere misfortune, My Lord. Look at it! I am ruined.'

'The County knows you for a man of substance, sir. I regret your loss but, though it must be a grievous one, hardly ruinous, I imagine. You have a fire mark, I suppose? Insurance paid?'

'There are debts that you could hardly imagine, Sir Edward. And no insurance payment will compensate for my losses. But I regret speaking in such haste now, when I collect my words about inactivity on the part of the Jacobites.'

'I always try to avoid making statements that rebound upon me. Something I learned early in my years at the House. Yet you have gone from complete confidence in your plan of action to now believing Redmond and his *banditti* responsible for this fire. Deliberate fire-raising, you say?'

In the middle of the terrace, the façade begins to collapse.

'An act of arson, My Lord. Indeed. What else could it be? A political act. A treasonous act, Sir Edward.'

'A fie upon it, Mister Bradley. What a fellow you are!' Sir Edward smiles benignly. 'You must think me a real cull to believe that I could not see a claim for compensation forming in your mind. But you must set the thought aside, sir. The Duke will have none of it.'

'There *is* the small matter of the eight thousand guineas that I helped the Crown to retain, My Lord. I had simply thought that His Grace might be persuaded to offset some of my loss from that source.'

'Why, bless you sir! Even his own agent – who, after all was the *true* savior of the Excise duty – even *he* has seen no share of that purse! No, Mister Bradley. There will be no compensation. But we can at least be certain of one thing. If this *is* a political act, we can safely assume that we have a definitive answer from Titus Redmond to the proposals that you sent him.'

Chapter Seventeen

The evening had been unsettling before it was scarce begun. Elizabeth Cooper has no love for Pantomime. It disturbs her and has always done so since she saw her first performance, in London, twenty years before. She should have appreciated the capers of John Rich as Harlequin, she supposes, for his name is now legendary. Yet she found it grotesque, frightening. And now she is apparently also one of the few in town capable of seeing that the claims by this Bottle-Conjuror, set out in Adam Scatterbuck's *Journal*, must surely be a fraud. She has had to listen most of the day to her customers, intelligent folk for the most part, speculating on how the tricks might be accomplished, how a grown man might be compressed to fit within an ordinary bottle. What stuff! So, whilst she knows that she should have kept the coffee house open for the benefit of those customers when the performance is over, she fears that there will be little merriment amongst an Exchange audience that must surely feel itself trepanned.

She had worked fastidiously with Crableck, the crippled door-keeper, to clean, tidy and close the establishment early. She has been working hard these several weeks past, serving in the coffee house by day and evening, poring over her accompts late into the night, settling arrangements for the next Quarter Day's Excise payments whenever she cannot sleep, and using the time to contemplate ways in which she might develop her business. For sleep has eluded her frequently since Bradley had admitted his deeds to her. She had not seen Rosina for some time and, though she had gathered rumours of a problem within the Redmond household, she had not particularly associated this with Rosina. But she had expected to see her at the May Day festivities. Elizabeth had even harboured some hope that they might steal a dance together. A dance or maybe more. It had made her low when neither Rosina, nor any of the Redmond family, had appeared. She had mentioned the fact to Bradley, almost as an aside, and been surprised by the self-satisfaction that had spread across his features. He had muttered something about 'a good day's work' and she had pressed him for an explanation. He had been evasive, of course, and had attempted to gild certain aspects of his plan, such as Driscoll's alleged complicity in Sourwood's death, while dampening others. But she had been perceptive enough to see the flaws in the various iterations, pressed him further until, at last, she was satisfied that she had the truth from him.

Elizabeth Cooper is accustomed to compliments on the sharpness and wit of her tongue. She uses it to good effect with her more forward customers, though they have never felt the razor edge of it in the way that James Bradley did on that rain-soaked May Day morning. Such presumption! She has never considered Bradley a friend, though she considers that they have enjoyed a relationship of sorts, certainly from the time when he finally abandoned attempts to proposition her. More than professional associates, less than close friends. And she would never have trusted him with an intimate confidence. So to pretend that she would have shared a glimpse of her forbidden affection for another woman. Preposterous fellow! Dangerous too, for she has lived these intervening weeks with the fear that rumour might spread. And what then? Her reputation shot? Her business collapsed? The risk of trial and punishment? So she has buried herself in work, used it as a defence to drive away her worst nightmares, used it to hide too from blistering visions of Rosina Redmond.

She has imagined the very worst. Rosina forbidden to speak with her again. Rosina punished in despicable ways by her Papist father, by her licentious mother. Rosina dragged to the coffee house door for the inevitable confrontation. Rosina dispatched to some distant exile. Rosina believing that it was she, Elizabeth, who had betrayed her. Rosina suffering when, in fact, the two women had exchanged no more than a few shared moments of innuendo. Rosina in torment when, in truth, Elizabeth had no real idea whether her passion for the young woman was even reciprocated.

And then, quite suddenly, to unsettle Elizabeth still further on this already troubled evening, while she and Crableck had been about to lock the doors, Rosina Redmond had slipped inside and asked whether they might speak. Why, of course, she had said. Would she not care to wait upstairs while the work was completed below? A quizzical glance from Crableck. *That crook-back sees too much for his own good,* she thinks, as she dismisses him for the night. She pushes home the bolts behind him, turns the key, then stands with her back against the door for a spell to calm her racing pulse. All these weeks. And now, here she is! A face like stone, but here all the same.

Elizabeth surveys the coffee house itself, deeply inhaling the rich atmosphere. The bitter aromas of the coffee blends. The silken scents of the chocolate. The tart recollection of tobacco. The herbal essence of teas, mingled with the resinous remains from the hearth embers. They restore her as she crosses the slate slabs of the ground floor, converted in its entirety to meet the needs of her business, and passes through the kitchen that serves not only the coffee house but also her private apartments above. A stone stair takes her to the first floor dining room that is now become her parlour, decorated as finely as ever she can afford. The walls are painted in a dominant shade of rose, with some alcove panelling in ivory-white and the fireplace wall covered with a handsome paper, brocaded on its surface with a mixture of the same colours. On the fire mantel sits a musical snuff box, an Austrian silver *carillon à musique,* the lid inlaid with Ibex horn. A large rug, warm grey, covers much of the floor, exposing the polished boards only towards the skirtings. The whole effect, she thinks, is inviting and companionable, lit seductively, she hopes, by the vase-shaped lamps, Chinese porcelain, already burning since earlier in the evening. A slender mahogany table and two chairs, each with coverings in cream, rose and pale-blue *petit-point,* stand in the bow window, from which Elizabeth might gaze through distortions in the leaded glass to the street below. And the only other seating is a large couch, in burgundy velour, heavy with satin cushions that frame the nervously rigid figure of Rosina Redmond, apparently ignoring her arrival and seemingly intent upon the snuff box.

'Why, I realise now,' says Elizabeth, sharply, 'that it simply will not serve.' Rosina turns at the tone of her voice. 'It must all go! Every cushion. Each thread of fabric. All trace of colour. The entire *décor*! Until I can find an alternative scheme that might do justice to the vibrant shades of your hair. It is *precisely* the thing to brighten my dismal home. But I give you joy of it in any case, my dear, dismal or otherwise.'

'First you besmirch my good name, betray whatever friendship we might have enjoyed. To that, that... I cannot find words to describe your Mister Bradley. And now you mock me, Elizabeth. Is there nothing, in life, that you hold dear and serious?'

At one level, there is nothing Elizabeth Cooper wants more than to take this beautiful young woman in her arms and demonstrate the depth of her passions. Yet, at another, she feels a barrier between them now, of her own making. The fear of further complication and possible risk to her standing, her safety even, from involvement with this Jacobite's daughter. For the first time, she sees her this way. The daughter of a political foe. Still exquisitely desirable, but a potential menace.

'Rosina,' she says, 'I know exactly what was said between your mother and Mister Bradley. But he lied to her. In a quiet moment of discourse he had asked about my friendship with you. About whether it might compromise my position in the town. But he was talking politically, my dear. I naturally defended our friendship and he apparently chose to draw some inference from that about the depth of our relationship. He has a habit of twisting matters to his own ends, as you will have gathered.'

Rosina returns to the couch. Her anguish is plain.

'You naturally defended our friendship,' she says, 'whilst for my own part I have merely accepted that you were guilty of betraying it. Is that your inference, Elizabeth? Or should I address you more formally, as Mistress Cooper again perhaps, now that I have put such distance between us? I had hoped that, in coming here, I might indeed confirm that Bradley had lied, yet it never occurred to me that, in doing so, I should merely expose my own cupidity and paucity of character. I have been duped, it seems, and in addition I am unsure about the morals that I should draw from your words. What are they? That blood is only thicker than water in the most literal sense? I agree. That, on the other hand, a relationship freely entered, with deliberate commitment, can set bonds stronger than any accident of birth? I agree. But these are values that I transparently do not possess. I am not worthy of the friendship that you so instinctively sought to defend.'

'Your original question, I collect,' says Elizabeth, 'was whether there is anything that I hold dear and serious.' How should she deal with this? she wonders. Rosina's presence excites her. She lusts for her yet, at the same time, feels genuine affection for her too. But there is the risk. Always the risk. Worse now, for if Rosina has already shown such a lack of loyalty to her, how might she react in some other future crisis? She must reduce the risk. But she must also enjoy Rosina while she may. 'After my father's death,' she says, 'I was surprised to find that he had bequeathed his business to me. My mother inherited the premises so I cared for her and we continued to run the drapery, though it was an enterprise in which I had no real interest. It was connected too closely, I think, with unpleasant memories of my father. To my greater surprise, I discovered that father had made a recommendation to the Court Leet that I should assume his former duties as Excise collector, in the event that he should be unable to perform them further. And the Court Leet readily accepted. It pleased me to note that there are many other women Excise collectors about the country. And all the time, I dreamed of building a business truly my own. It was one of the Court Leet Jurors, I think, who first put the idea of the coffee house into my head and, when mother died, the premises became my own. The coffee house has been my life, Rosina. I hold it dear and serious. The best outside London, I am told. There is little that I would not do to protect it.'

'You guard the coffee house as jealously, then, as our friendship?' says Rosina. 'When I escaped from the house tonight, on the pretext of attending the Pantomime with Beppy, I had not expected to find myself contending for affection with your coffee beans and chocolates, madam.'

'And neither had I expected to find myself contending tonight as an alternative entertainment to that pox'd Bottle-Conjuror. Or should I be flattered that you must, at least, have considered me the most credible of the two? But see, you have named my coffee beans and chocolates to shame me, I fancy, for I find myself lacking in my duties as your hostess. And I collect that I once promised you the chance to sample one of my prophylactic bottles. Will you not take a few drops with me now, my dear? I must allow that their effect will be beneficial.'

Rosina seems uncertain but Elizabeth bids her wait and, taking one of the lamps, she lights her way to the closet near the stair that functions as her private office and dressing room. Her bottle of Sydenham's is half-empty but enough, she thinks, for their purpose. The local physicians are always happy to prescribe more in any case, though the price is rising. Why, after her previous visit, she had almost been tempted to settle for the Mithridate.

She takes the bottle and is about to leave the small room when another thought comes to her. Elizabeth has brushed against the clothes that she had folded this morning on top of the large trunk, a calico summer dress, some undergarments, stockings and the like. She moves them to a chair, opens the trunk lid and, undressing as quickly as she is able, dropping her own clothes to the floor, she replaces them with some gentleman's hose, a pair of plum-coloured silk knee breeches, a pair of buckled shoes, and a chambray shirt that she wears loose, workman-fashion, like a smock.

Her return incites a slight gasp from Rosina, then a badly stifled laugh. 'Why, sirrah,' she says, feigning fright. 'Pray tell me what you have done with my friend!'

Elizabeth puts down the bottle and struggles for a moment to fasten her hair in approximation of a Tie-Wig, astonished to find herself now embarrassed, wondering whether she might simply look foolish.

'Now you mock *me*,' she says. 'Wicked girl! I fancy that you will think me strange. I am always so much more comfortable dressed so, yet tonight I must allow to be anything *other* than comfortable.'

'Well, you certainly make the most handsome *chevalier* of my acquaintance, and I should hate to think you incommoded by my presence,' says Rosina. 'Yet if I make you uncomfortable, I could perhaps leave you to your privacy?'

'Without sampling the Sydenham's tincture? Fie upon you, miss, for I protest that you would have the Bellman crying my want of hospitality from now until Midsummer's Day. Here, let me pour you a little.' She takes a glass from the mahogany table, passes the draught to Elizabeth who sips cautiously.

'It reminds me of the theriac treacle with which Mama used to dose us against distempers. It is not unpleasant. I durst say that it is similar to the tonic that she now uses to ward against the megrims.'

'I should have thought your mother too robust to suffer so. And I am still waiting to discover how this matter with Bradley came about.'

'It must have been, what, three weeks ago now,' says Rosina, and Elizabeth sees that the tincture of sherry wine and opiate, the Sydenham's laudanum, has begun to work its wonders, for the younger woman is visibly more relaxed, reclining on the couch. 'We were returning from Mrs Starkey's. My harpsichord teacher. Well, anyway, Mother suddenly announced, in the middle of the street, that she wanted to send me to Geneva to stay with her cousin, Katherine. Then she began to tell me about her conversation with that lecher, Bradley. I did not know what to think, Elizabeth. At first, I wanted only to run here, to you. But later...'

'Later you began to wonder whether I had, after all, implicated you in some indecency.' Elizabeth joins her on the couch, slipping off the buckled shoes and folding her legs beneath her.

'Mama called you a Myra, compared you to the Duchess of Newborough, but I did not understand the reference.'

'A smutty little work called *The Toast*. The Duchess was cruelly satirised as a lesbian hag and your mother would be familiar with it since the book achieved some notoriety in Ireland. Lady Frances was herself from those parts, of course. I do not mind that she should brand me a tribade in this way but to compare me with a hag! What stuff! Yet it gives me some comfort to be reminded that Lady Frances survived the scandal tolerably well. Though she *is* a Duchess, of course.'

'She also asked whether there had been any venereal act between us.'

'She used that very term?'

'Without blushing,' says Rosina. 'Though for my own part I could have wished the ground to swallow me. When we returned to the house, I was made to wait in the hall while Mama told the whole story to my father. They were in the fore-parlour but I could hear a great deal and, again, I wanted to run. Yet this time it was not concern about your own part in the affair that restrained me. Quite the reverse. For I decided that, whatever had been said, whatever had been done, I must not allow myself to be shamed. That I must not be made guilty for feelings which, surely, Our Lady must have sown within me.'

'It was bravely done, my dear,' and Elizabeth reaches out to move a flame-red ringlet that has fallen across Rosina's forehead.

'I was in such a *ram you, damn you* humour that I must have appeared quite the ranter. Yet I do not recall much that I spoke to them. I refused to go to Geneva of course, or anywhere else for that matter. For her own part, my mother raged about Bradley threatening Papa. I do not care for Mister Bradley, I replied, but perhaps it is *your* relationship with *him* that threatens Papa. La, I said. What an example to set your children. She was quite beside herself. Then Papa said that he had always had suspicions about you. He said that he had thought your behaviour towards me odd at the rout. Mother said you had infected me in some way but Papa said that I must have been born that way, rather than infected, if I was indeed prone to tribady as well. He thought that, on this basis, my natural constitution could not be easily repressed but he hoped that, perhaps, I might learn normality. He suggested that I might see Doctor Hall since, after all, he had done such a good job repairing Aran Owen's hand. My mother raged about all the young men I could have chosen. By the Mass, said my father, I have no word for it! And I said, I expect that cunny-licking is equally appropriate in this case, too, Papa. Though I confess that I have not yet attempted the act.'

Elizabeth Cooper felt her reservations slipping away, at least for the time being, and not only due to the Sydenham's. She could not recall a moment when she had been so entertained and her cheeks streamed with tears of pure mirth as she bade Rosina repeat the parts of her account that amused her most.

'They forbade me to see you,' said Rosina, suddenly serious again, 'and

I did not demur since I still believed that you had colluded in some way with Bradley. It all became confusing since it seemed that there were other elements to the message that he had so obviously sent my mother to deliver.'

Elizabeth listens incredulously as Rosina details all that she can recall of the possibility that Jacob Driscoll might have been implicated in Sourwood's death and also of Bradley's claim that he might be Maeve's father. No, Rosina assures her, all of this has been kept from the younger girls, now both in Southport. But such a fiction. Bradley must surely have lost his wits. Unless, of course, there is truth to the rumour. And the story about Driscoll. No real evidence, of course. But there had definitely been something amiss with the Daniel Sourwood suicide. Something that did not quite fit, they both agree. And did she know, says Rosina, that it was not just Bradley who made the accusation? She had discovered that Aran Owen, too, had argued with Jacob over the very same thing. In any case, Jacob has fled the town once again. But her father is so very low. He has almost handed over the conduct of the business to Aran. It all remains within the family though, it seems. Rosina had set it all down in her diary. It is safe, however. In the shorthand that Beppy Byrom has taught her.

A diary? thinks Elizabeth Cooper. *She has written it all in a damn'd diary!* The words push themselves upwards through the warm haze of her spreading intoxication. They push themselves through the street noise outside. *There is such clamour on nights when there is a performance at the Exchange!* She can barely think, but knows that she will speak again with Bradley. It seems that they each have a problem here, perhaps one that has a mutually satisfactory solution.

But Rosina reaches for her, lays a slender hand on her knee, feels the texture of the plum-coloured silk, strokes it gently.

'Tell me, Elizabeth, to whom does a Protestant confess her sins?'

'Why, to God, of course. Yet we believe that no intermediary except Our Lord, Jesus Christ, is necessary to the process. We seek absolution through private prayer before God. Though we sometimes encourage confession to another when a wrong has been done to an individual *and* to God, both. Confession to God and to the person wrong'd, my dear. It is a simple enough creed, I think.'

Elizabeth feels herself aroused, moistened, thinks of John Donne again. 'Licence my roving hands, and let them go, Behind...before...above... between...below...'

The level of noise on the street is peculiar tonight, but she moves closer to Rosina's touch, imagines the delights of her clitoris.

'Did you have some particular sin in mind, my dearest?' she says. 'For I can show you absolution of a special kind.'

Yet how, she wonders, might one find any sort of satisfaction, any form of climactic peak, amidst such vulgar uproar. And now, that distant bell. Surely not the town's fire bell?

Chapter Eighteen

Striker rides on to the Camp Field through the thin haze of an early June morning that promises heat later in the day. The company drummer, a young boy, remarks him with screwed eyes while his small fingers tighten the skin. He looks hardly big enough to hold the thing, Striker muses, but finds himself in error as the youthful left hand takes up its intense, repetitive beat while the right rattles Reveille. It is almost a personal salute, and Striker takes his tricorne hat, sweeping it sideways and nodding his head in acknowledgement of the drummer's skill.

Smoke is already rising acrid from the cook fires, and the tents, stark and white against the mist, are immediately alive with activity. Scarlet coats and blue facings. Picquets returning to the lines, tired and hungry. The whores, bunters and bulk-mongers turned out against their will. The cattle too, resentful that they have been deprived of this pasture between the Deansgate Street and the river, sloping down towards the river.

The call to daily duty has barely rolled away, replaced by the cry of crows amongst the trees at the Irwell's margent, when Striker dismounts at the small marquee occupied by the company commander, and quite distinct from those of the other ranks. The Captain, too, looks barely older than his drummer-boy yet Striker knows that appearances are, in this case, deceptive.

'My compliments, sir,' he says, doffing his hat for a second time. 'Might I present my credentials?' and he takes two envelopes from within his coat, passing the first to the young officer who pauses before opening the letter just long enough for his man to assist him in securing an obviously new gorget about his throat. 'and give you joy of your Commission, Captain Wolfe. You were previously with the Twelfth, I collect?'

Wolfe covers his surprise quickly.

'You have the advantage of me, Mister...'

'The dispatch will explain my position, Captain, I believe.'

The Captain reads the letter, then a second time, checks the signature.

'This is a *carte blanche*. Signed by His grace, the Duke of Newcastle. And I assume that I may not know your name, sir?'

'I apologise for such a want of courtesy, Captain Wolfe, but it is a rude necessity, I assure you. But they tell me that you have seen action with the Twelfth?'

'At Dettingen, sir. Ensign then, of course. And a hot day we had of it, too. Damn'd hot. Though you seem to be a gentleman familiar yourself with hot deeds. Or perhaps I am mistook.'

'Some modest action in the Colonies, Captain. Nothing more. And how I envy you such a command. A company of Barrell's Regiment, new-raised in Lancaster. You have to lick them into shape before returning to Flanders, I imagine.'

'They completed their initial training well enough. They are a mixed bunch as you will appreciate. But you have still not explained the reason for your presence here. If, sir, you will also allow a certain lack of courtesy on my own part.'

'We are each men with schedules to follow, Captain, I protest! And my own business is simple enough. I merely need the loan of a few men for some work this evening. Healthy men, if you follow my drift.'

'You merely want the *loan* of some men, sir? Should you not do better to find such men on the streets of Manchester, for there are enough of them without honest employment, I understand. My own men, sir, are engaged upon the King's business. A *carte blanche* from the Secretary of State has no great authority within this camp.'

'Then this, perhaps...' And Striker proffers the second letter. Wolfe breaks a seal, sees that it bears the signature of his commanding officer. William Barrell, for whom this Regiment is currently named, has retired a few years previously, rewarded with the Governorship of some castle, to be succeeded by Lieutenant-Colonel Robert Rich. The letter confirms authority on the bearer in the King's name. 'I appreciate, Captain, that the circumstances are unusual and you must be thinking that I could somehow have acquired such a dispatch by any number of dishonest means. But I urge you to consider that, in such a case, I could put those letters to much better use than simply requesting the loan of a few men. And I assure you, sir, that they would be very *much* engaged in the King's business.'

'Yet business that might dishonour my Regiment, sir, I cannot brook. The Lord Lieutenant himself advised me to avoid difficulties in Manchester and I chose to camp here, rather than billet the men in town, precisely because of the Jacobite element in the place. This is, after all, the day on which those rabble celebrate the birthday of the Pretender. It has given occasion to open riot in previous years, I collect, and I would not have my men involved.'

'Then it would suit both our purposes admirably, Captain, if you were to confine your men to their quarters this evening, with the exception of the few I need. Your Regiment will not be dishonoured if they are without their uniforms. Yet it might be helpful if one of them were able to bring his hanger!'

Striker requires a few more minutes in the company of Captain Wolfe to quell his protests, to specify the sort of men he might need, and to make arrangements for a *rendezvous* with them in the evening. Then he repairs to the Market Square, stables his mount, and breaks his fast at the Punch House, a table near the windows, and amuses himself by reading the latest two pages of Scatterbuck's *Journal*. More gloating detail of the French and Spanish engagement with the British and their Sardinian allies at the end of April. The Sardinians had entrenched themselves along the heights at Villafranca to thwart the advance of their enemies into Lombardy, and had been bolstered by a small force of British regulars, marines and artillery specialists. Voltaire would say, 'Even in the Alps, we could still find Englishmen to fight us!' The result had been a costly stalemate but, with the defenders evacuated under the protection of the British Navy, the French and Spanish have been able to claim it as a victory, with Scatterbuck's editorial concentrating on the incompetence of the allied commanders, particularly the Sardinian Marquis of Susa, who had allowed himself to be captured.

There are more announcements about the races due to take place over the next few days at Kersal Moor and there is great speculation about the possible contenders for the Kersal Moor Great Stakes One Hundred Guineas, run over four miles for geldings.

More exhortations to supporters of the True King that they should light their windows this night, in celebration of James the Third's birthing day. Yet strange, he thinks, that these Jacobites should so readily forget the anniversary of their ignominious defeat, yes another one, at Glen Shiel in the Year '19 on this date also.

But Striker remains indebted to Scatterbuck all the same. It had been good of him to carry the Bottle-Conjuror announcement at short notice. The cully. La! What mummery. And such a blaze.

At last, he sees Aran Owen passing his window. He discards the broadsheet and moves quickly to the street to intercept him.

'Mister Owen!' he calls, ignoring the magic lantern images that pass across the sheet of Aran's features. Shock. Terror. Loathing. Trepidation. 'You have new lodging, I see. Mistress Evesworth tired of your unruly behaviour, I expect. No, I jest. No more than a jest. You must forgive my sense of humour. Yet shall there be no welcome between old friends, my dear? Nothing more than this unseemly concern that you might be observed in my company. Forsooth, I had not thought you such a scrub.'

'I should have trusted my hand,' says Aran, recovering his composure well, as Striker too observes. 'It has developed the ability to predict difficult days, foul weather and the like. It pained me like the very devil this morning yet the sky seemed so clear. I must remember, in future, that it might also herald your presence in the area, Striker.'

'A scrub with sharp thorns as well, I see. Yet your hand still bears a dressing. Not healing well, friend Aran? I could recommend a salve.'

Striker keeps pace beside his companion, though to the casual observer it might appear that there is no connection between them. Many of Striker's comments are seemingly directed towards the buildings on their left. His sentences, questions, responses are timed to occur when he is not observed so that the conversation between them is fragmented. He is dressed plainly, blends perfectly with the setting. And he notes that, since Aran also wishes to avoid being seen in *his* company, he has adopted a similar approach, without any prompting, to his own side of the dialogue. It is a difficult dialogue, naturally, but Striker is able to gather, at least, some minor pieces of intelligence. The injured hand, for example, though treated well in the beginning, is still prone to weeping and the finger stump refuses to heal completely. Business is brisk, though, with some minor commissions won, still mainly for trade card designs, hand bill illustrations and the like. Aran is defensive about the Old Pretender's birthday and about whether he will attend any of this evening's revelries in town to celebrate it. Aran is confused by Striker's reference to his father, himself a loyal redcoat in the Hanoverian army. And might Aran not easily have become one too if Striker had simply left him in Lancaster Gaol to rot? For many of those now drilling on the Camp Field have been recruited from that very place as an alternative to facing the Assize in September. Perhaps he and Sourwood both. He notes Aran's guilt at Sourwood's name and he recalls that other early morning in Manchester.

It had been simple enough to deprive old Tyler of his keys. A deep sleeper with or without his evening quota of strong ale. And the boy had accepted his fate passively, even smiled weakly at him as Striker unlocked the cell. Feeble struggle. Weak cry. Then submission. *Hush, my dear. Hush.* Striker's knee on his chest. Finger and thumb pinching nostrils closed and palm over Sourwood's mouth. Nearly. Nearly. Enough to make him insensible. Then the shirt. That sturdy apprentice's shirt. He had fashioned the makeshift noose and hauled the boy upright as he returned momentarily to consciousness. A tear. A single torn sob. Then he had inexplicably set a heel against the rough stones of the wall, heaving upwards as though to help Striker in his efforts. The knot secured. Striker taking a step backwards to survey the scene, dusting straw from his coat. He had noted the precise moment when Sourwood's innate and suppressed sense of survival had, finally, taken charge. Both heels now taking his weight against the upper edge of a stone. Fingers struggling to assist. *Too late, sweet boy.* Striker had kicked at Sourwood's ankles. The toes dancing a neat quadrille, sometimes almost succeeding in reaching the floor as the fabric had stretched taut. But not for long. The door had been re-locked, the keys replaced, and Tyler still sleeping soundly. Striker's identity had remained a secret still. At least, from everybody except Aran Owen.

'And guilty you *should* be!' says Striker. 'Such a waste of a young life. Though I hear rumour, Aran. Perhaps more than rumour. About our mutual friend, Jacob Driscoll. Though I had believed him peppered with pistol ball and lost on Chat Moss.'

'Oh, Jacob is very much alive, but he had no hand in Daniel's death.

Sourwood killed himself, plain and simple after all, though I still do not understand his reasoning. And Driscoll survived your marksmanship admirably, it seems. Though swears that he will have a reckoning with *you*, Striker!'

'I tremble at the very thought and thank you for the warning. You see, now, what it means to be friends? How easy to tend my needs? Why, I protest that you may find me no more difficult to cultivate than the flowers and herbage of old Josiah's gardens. Where was it again? Never mind. The place is unimportant. But the Squire now, Redmond's brother. You never mentioned him. An interesting gentleman, though far into his dotage now. He may be useful, do you not think so?'

Striker assesses the impact of his words. *So, he still cares for the fellow. Quite proper too, considering how much he owes the Squire. Aran might think that he owes a debt to Titus Redmond but how much more to the older brother.* And, yes, the implied threat has been recognised.

'You promised that I would not be asked to betray the Redmonds,' says Aran. 'Though I fail to see, in any event, how the Squire is relevant here.'

'A promise, my dear? I recall no such thing, though I certainly confirmed that I was more concerned with the upper echelons of this Jacobite conspiracy. And so I am. *Most* concerned. The Welsh connection, I find, may be more significant than I had first feared. Though I think that you are already sensible of the fact. Titus must speak with you frequently about his friend Sir Watkin Williams Wynn?' Striker may not be aware of the fact, but he spits the name in almost exactly the same way as Titus himself might do. And there is not just the Baronet, of course, but his coterie of associates. He has a tame artist of his own, Striker now recalls. One Richard Wilson, by name. But the more venomous are Morgan the meddling lawyer. Or Sir John Glynne, the Member for Flintshire. Then that damn'd Rector of Hawarden. All pulled together in the Cycle of the White Rose, their Jacobite Club flourishing on the Marches and in Wrecsam. 'I had thought that the greater threat rested with Cheshire but my master's intelligence was lacking in that regard. No, it is these Welsh fellows who interest me. And your sweet Lancastrians, too, naturally. But for the moment...'

'Cheshire?' says Aran. 'Sir Peter Leighton's murder! I should have thought of it sooner, Striker. It was *you*.'

'I may claim some modest part in that gentleman's demise, I must allow. But sirrah, such a look of horror on your face, sweet Aran! Did you think that this fledgling rebellion would be resolved without some blood shed? There will be rivers of it before the thing is done. We will bathe in it, you and I, my friend. Not the Williams Wynns of the world, mind. Clean hands for those gentlemen. And before you think it, lest you believe that Dudley Striker is some maniacal individual, you should know that I am only one of hundreds, yes *hundreds* of agents employed by *both* sides in this conflict. Lives are cheap,

Aran Owen. Now, let me explain your part in this!'

His instructions are clear, precise. Striker has received intelligence of a high-level meeting to take place soon, somewhere in the Manchester area, amongst the Jacobite leadership. Aran will know when it is due to take place and must send details of the meeting place to Striker, along with any relevant information about Welsh involvement in the gathering itself. But there is more. First, he must disguise his writing. Second, he must employ a simple code. *This* code. And he presents Aran with a copy of John Byrom's *New Universal Shorthand*. Such things amuse Striker. He is not sure, yet, how this particular strand will unfold but it is enough, for the moment, to savour the shock that he has delivered to Aran Owen. Divisions, divisions. All is not as it seems, he whispers, enigmatically, and finishes with advice that the encrypted message should be sealed in one of these envelopes, though he naturally does not reveal that they were recently acquired from Byrom's own writing desk. Nothing must be written on the outside of the envelope excepting a single letter 'S' and it must then be delivered to this man, the name and direction is written on the inside cover of the book, an express courier who will know what must be done. It is the only moment of direct intercourse between them and, as poor fortune would have it, the very one that Rosina Redmond has chosen to set foot, herself, on Market Street Lane. She is accompanied, as so frequently these days, by Phelim O'Farrell and Striker realises that there is no way to avoid an encounter, for she has plainly seen Aran and approaches them. *What sort of fool is he?* thinks Striker. *So evidently flustered by her presence still, despite...*

'Why, Aran Owen!' she cries. 'La! It has been *such* a time. Where *have* you been? And your new lodging? But forgive my interruption, gentlemen. You seemed so deep in discussion that I hardly dared intervene.'

'Rosina,' says Aran, now entirely at a loss. 'This is Mister...'

'Bradstreet, my dear,' says Striker, moving without effort to a gentle Irish lilt.

'You are from Ireland, Mister Bradstreet! Phelim, did you hear? What joy. What perfect joy. My own family counts itself blessed to share that privilege with you. You are a friend of Aran's, sir?'

'A business acquaintance, merely. Yet we have met on several occasions. And on each occasion, as I collect, whenever time has permitted us the occasional pleasantry, he has found cause to mention a certain *Miss Redmond* to me. Might I therefore assume that I now have the pleasure of meeting the object of his fascination in person? Ah, I see that I have been too fro'ward. Indiscreet, perhaps. My apologies. I had not intended to cause such consternation to you both.'

'A little fro'ward indeed, Mister Bradstreet, yet I account Aran as one of my dearest friends. But what business can you have that brings you all the way from Ireland? Is it possible that this might somehow be connected with my father's business interests also?'

'I am not familiar with your father, Miss Redmond. Just a humble Dubliner, though now plying my trade in Birmingham. A purveyor of fine pastries, though you could be forgiven for assuming my profession as otherwise. I am hoping to commission some portraiture from your talented young friend, my dear. My wife and children. Mister Owen has something of a reputation, you know.' *Perfect,* he thinks. *He has noted my reference to the Dubliner and will now add Driscoll's accomplice to the list of my assassinations. Wrongly, of course. But it will do no harm to my standing with him. He must be in no doubt. None at all. And this young woman. Who would have thought it possible? Though I should hazard a chance to turn her from tribady should I have half the opportunity.*

Striker realises suddenly that he has failed to pay attention to the Irish manservant, this creaking ancient with bones like dried timber. For O'Farrell, almost seeming able to hear his thoughts, is sniffing him, nostrils flared like some venerable deer-hound sensing danger. He mutters something beneath his breath. Did he truly say *'Tipperary'?* And there is something else for, since the Redmond girl had first joined them, Striker has been employing another of his talents. He has learned the skill of using his speech patterns to speed difficult encounters while, at the same time, employing his hands in a way that distracts the interlocutors eyes from his face. She may recall some vague impressions, a smile perhaps, a gesture, but she will never be able to describe even his most general features. But O'Farrell, he now sees, has never once averted his gaze from Striker's eyes.

'La! Birmingham, Aran,' says Rosina. 'Your fame is spreading. But are you staying for tonight's celebrations, Mister Bradstreet? We are just about to collect our cockades. Should you like me to collect one extra?'

'I am the True King's most loyal servant, my dear. And I hope to play the most active part in celebrating his birthday appropriately, though I may be promised elsewhere. All the same, I hope to have the pleasure of meeting you again.'

Aran Owen tenses and, in that moment, Rosina sees the book that he is holding.

'The *Universal Shorthand,* Aran? I had no idea that you were also a student of Mister Byrom,' she says.

'It was a gift from me, Miss Redmond,' says Striker before Aran has a chance to even consider a response. 'A clumsy one, I now see. I had considered that it might be appropriate, given the Manchester connection. And now I discover that Aran is a frequent visitor to the household of the great man himself. All the same, it was well-intended since it is, of course, Aran's own birthday in two days. But you do not need *me* to tell you that, of course! Still, I must leave you. Duty calls. I bid you a good day and, Mister Owen, I look forward to hearing from you in due course. You will not forget to contact me, I trust!'

And he escapes. But what *will* he do about O'Farrell, he wonders.

He spends some of the morning at the White Rose Coffee House, tucked amongst shops just around the corner, on Deansgate Street. And Striker settles himself with a copy of Theobald's *Double Falsehood,* though he finds it hard to accept the author's claim that the play has a foundation in Shakespeare.

Unlike Mistress Cooper's establishment, the White Rose is principally frequented by the town's Tories and High Church Episcopalians. Women may not imbibe here and the only female presence is the coffee woman, employed to ensure that customers receive only that for which they have paid. A severe old crone too, this one, with her stiff head-dress and long white shawl, though stained by countless spillages and reeking of stale tobacco.

Striker blends easily with the loners, the readers, the whisperers who take up one section of the tables but close enough that he can observe the two other main categories of adherents. First, the merchants, who use the place as a venue to conduct more intimate aspects of their trade. And, second, the wits, the poets, the literary folk who include, by the middle of the forenoon, John Byrom himself. Striker knows Byrom easily by sight and he listens to this chattering society now a while as they debate progress of the war. They congratulate Byrom on the birthing day of his son, Ted, two days earlier. And they recall the festivities of Restoration Day, unanimously applauding Miss Redmond's performance of the Couperin. The whisperers, however, say entirely different things about young Rosina, Striker notes. Yet there is nothing to be learned here. The coffee house crowd might profess themselves Jacobites but they will all be hidden beneath their beds when the thing begins in earnest. They will escape retribution too, though so far as Striker is concerned they are in some ways more culpable than any others. For these are the couch revolutionists who provide the encouragement, the mass, the substance to unrest though without ever the intention of risking themselves in its pursuit. *Byrom is typical of them,* he thinks. *How many fruitless hours I have spent following him simply to find that he is no more than a braggart! A clever one, but a braggart all the same. And if his wife only knew...*

But now comes Adam Scatterbuck, bidding good morning to the company and settling his less than fastidious form into a favourite corner where he will compile most of the articles for his next edition. Striker melds deeper within the shadows. He doubts that Scatterbuck will recall him as the cove who placed the announcement about the Bottle-Conjuror but there is little reason to chance the matter. He had wondered whether Bradley might, himself, have acted by now. After all, Striker has made sure that plenty have whispered in his ear during the past few weeks, placing the blame for the blaze squarely with the Redmonds. All this rumour, innuendo and blackmail that he loves so much. Does he not know that this is a time for action? *What can be the matter with the fellow?* he wonders. *Well, I shall simply have to assume some mandate on his behalf.*

136

He repairs to the Bull's Head Inn, back in the Market Place. His own lodgings are at the Ship, in Salford, but the Bull's Head is the true centre of Tory activity in town. Half-timbered, its distinctive gable a black and white herring-bone dominating the other buildings along the row, it is always a useful source of information for him. He climbs the five stone steps and loses himself in the haze within. If the White Rose is the place to conduct private business, the Bull's Head is something quite distinct. Apart from all else, the town's post office is here, set in one of the smaller rooms. And whilst the Commodities Exchange may provide neutral ground for the various factions to trade in common, those who prefer a more partisan approach will practice their commerce here. The Bull's Head provides a central point from which trade routes can be planned, for goods either inwards or outwards, using the various Fly Wagons coming and going through more than twenty different inns and taverns across Manchester and neighbouring Salford. Thirty end-destinations. Literally hundreds of stopping-places between. *And clever Aran Owen,* thinks Striker, *has succeeded in opening up yet five more routes on his master's behalf.*

Then, of course, there are all those other transport negotiations to undertake. For there are agents here, too, from the Quay and from the Navigation Company, setting the tolls for those distinctive sailing barges, the Mersey Flats, that make the return journey so regularly, between this town and Liverpool. There are twenty-one Flats with Manchester owners alone now. The *Molly,* the *Liberty,* the *Neptune,* and others. So that the Bull's Head is the heart of frequently complex transport deals and arrangements for the Tory business community involving the owners of the Fly Wagons, the agents of the Navigation Company, the boat owners and the merchants themselves. And here they are, colleagues, friends and associates of the Redmonds. The linen drapers, Fletcher, Dickenson and Moss. The fustian manufacturers, Gartside, Howarth, Bower, Chadwick and Marsden. A dozen more besides. They barter and babble in the Lancastrian to which Striker has now attuned his ear. They take food and thin beer. Jugged hare or veal. Kidneys and mushroom. Stewed fowl and vegetables. They drink cinnamon-spiced wine. They shake the lice from their wigs. They come and they go, smoking tobacco in their long clay pipes, taking snuff from their individual boxes and comparing blends. They fart and they belch.

Striker passes the time by indulging his fantasy. He will be a writer one day, for he has the necessary imagination. But such a writer! And his response to Miss Redmond was truly inspired. A purveyor of fine pastries indeed. He shall write a book on the subject. A Book of Receipts for Pastry, Cakes and Sweetmeats. Biscuits too perhaps.

By six o' the clock the Tory business community has largely completed its work and a new group of customers has begun to gather. Younger men for the most part, but not exclusively, and all of them sporting white ribbon, either pinned to a shoulder or in rosette form attached by the loop and button that cocks the brim of each tricorne hat. From time to time, young women will call from the street, often the wives or sweethearts of those within, seeking to sell any additional cockades that they might have made and Striker, along with a few others who do not yet possess this white emblem of the Jacobite, makes sure that he buys one.

I could hoist this entire insurrection, thinks Striker, *upon just one decent petard if I but had the means,* as the gathering is joined by many familiar faces. Francis Townley, of course, with his friends Holker, Sydall, Chaddock, and the Deacon boys. Whitlock he knows too, the barber-cum-chirurgeon. But a score of others beside, including a few who have at least some manner of authority about them. He will need to discover more about these men. So his *alter ego*, his trusted second self, Mister Bradstreet from Birmingham, will draw them into companionable revelation. He lays down some silver shillings. He is unlikely to ever receive recompense from his mean-fisted masters, and it is more than he can afford, in truth. But he needs to purchase wine for those now in his company. So that he might not celebrate this auspicious anniversary alone, he says, in Bradstreet's Irish lilt.

Backs are slapped and new-found friends are named. William Brettargh, giving him joy on this fifty-sixth birthday of Good King James. James the Third of England and Eighth of Scotland, if only the dear fellow could be allowed to take his throne. Bumpers are raised, the King toasted. Talk of the Palazzo Muti in Rome, now the residence in exile of the Stuarts. And young Charles Edward, so recently named Prince Regent. A good thing, they all agree.

But Mister Bradstreet, says a man introduced as John Collow, what brings *him* to Manchester? Why, pastries, sirrah. And Striker's purveyor of pies may expound lyrically on the theme of muffins, crumpets and pikelets. Flat-cake scones baked on stone and spiced with cheese, potato or both. Shortcakes and sweetmeats of every variety. But why here? There are pastry cooks a-plenty in Manchester. And Collow is slipped an unguent to salve any symptom of suspicion that might be forming. Pastry cooks and artists too, it seems. For Birmingham is so bereft, so lacking in refinery. Yet here, in this fine town, at no great distance from his own, Bradstreet has been directed to a young man of considerable talent so that his need for trade bills and family portraits may be satisfied. And the affability of the company grows at Aran's name, as good as a recommendation from Titus Redmond himself.

Yet, in the nature of Englishmen in any tavern, discussion soon turns to other distractions. To prize fighting, for instance. Bare-knuckle fighting. And not only prize fighting but wrestling too. For Whitlock, swaggering and staggering Whitlock, professes himself chief amongst the town's wrestlers. Catch-As-Catch-Can, of course. No Cumberland Backhold nonsense for a good Lancastrian. And if there is one commodity that Joshua Whitlock owns to excess, they all agree, it is bottom! Enough bottom to give you a bloody pate, Master Townley, slurs the barber, attempting to swing his walking stick in Townley's general direction. And Striker is impressed with the speedy reflex that brings Townley's own cane to parry the blow, ineffective though it might have been. His Bradstreet says so too, expresses admiration. A military man, he collects. Why, yes, says Thomas Chaddock. Francis has served with the French. An expert in the art of *canne de combat*. A cudgeller and singlestick fighter *par excellence*. There are frequently bouts here in the town. Perhaps he might stay long enough to see one? Several are planned for the Races. Though Chaddock's own interests lie more with the fortunes of the Duke of Bolton and his stables.

So Striker sifts and gathers, kneads and leavens, building his dossier of intelligence on these Jacobite *banditti* who, with yet more wine consumed, invite him to join them for some further celebration. As appears to be their custom on such occasions, they will attack the Dissenters' Meeting House in Pool Fold and, afterwards, perchance they will break a few windows that have been left unlit from lack of respect for King James. More bumpers are raised. The King Over the Water! And they hardly notice whether or not this nondescript purveyor of Birmingham pastries has joined them, as they stumble and spill to the Market Place. *No better than London Mohocks*, thinks Striker.

He returns to the Livery at Saint Mary's Gate and there takes a change of clothing from one of his saddle-bags. Mister Bradstreet's fine breeches and hose are replaced by workmen's pantaloons, spatterdashes and woollen stockings, bunched at the ankle. The fashionable frock is carefully folded in favour of coarse shirt and a buff waistcoat vest. An over-sized Monmouth cap substitutes for the wig and three-cornered hat. A small amount of dirt, but not too much, about the face and under the nails, completes Striker's transformation so that, when the appointed hour arrives, he enters the Woolpack as arranged, to meet Captain Wolfe's chosen men. And he could not have chosen better if he had undertaken the task himself. He has no difficulty in identifying them for they are five in number, each of them rum-looking, two of them Irish, all dressed in labouring clothes, and answering readily to his password. As instructed, one of them has brought a hanger, sensibly concealed beneath his coat, though it is not easy to fully conceal the thirty inches of blade and scabbard that the Regiment favours as its infantry sword of choice.

Striker explains their task. It is simple and no soldier could resist for, gentlemen, we shall visit a bawdy house. The best in Manchester! There is a small purse to be spent though he doubts whether they shall have to pay the bunters' fees but, yes, they may fuck their fill and give them joy of their efforts. Geneva too, if they must, though they must remain sensible of the need to keep their identity. If talk they must, they are all labourers, builders and the like, recently employed here in town until some god-damn'd fire had robbed them of their livelihood. Just enough saved between them for this final night of pleasure, then bound for Ireland or whatever home they choose to invent. But one of them must remain in the street, hidden as best he can, with the hanger. A precaution, nothing more, and whilst those within shall each be rewarded with a silver sovereign, the hanger-man will receive a golden guinea for his frustration, of course. Initial tensions disappear. The soldiers had imagined their task somewhat other, less pleasurable. Humping whores is work with which they feel comfortable. And payment in the bargain!

They wind through the streets, raucous and laughing as the hanger-man becomes the butt of endless jests, so that they become indistinguishable from the many other groups of revellers in town tonight. And Striker is amused that this evening of mischief, when the Jacobites indulge themselves by celebrating the Old Pretender's birthday through inflicting grief on good loyalists, should itself provide the diversion from his own activities. Activities that he considers to be in the service of King George. God bless him, too, for giving Striker the chance to indulge in them. He has already put the torch to Bradley's terrace and, he thinks, succeeded in sowing the seed that this was Redmond's work, a response to Bradley's blackmail attempt. And, now, *this* must look like Bradley's retaliation for the fire.

So they carefully approach Mother Blossom's, see that Redmond's weary warehouse is, as Striker had expected, locked and secured this night. He considers again whether a direct attack on the warehouse might have made a more pertinent point although, on balance, he thinks that His Grace, the Secretary of State, might at some stage prefer to sequester the contents for the Crown's own purpose. In any case, the timbers seem so worm-worn that the place is likely to collapse of its own volition before too long. And the bawdy den is such an attractive alternative.

Dubbins, the much maligned sword-bearer, is posted picquet at the nearest corner, and Striker enters with his four remaining associates, passing beneath the large wood-carved flagon that marks the place also as a gin palace. The house is larger within than it appears from the street, narrow but deep, with a small vestibule where outside coats may be hung and, behind, an antechamber where Mother Blossom herself bends over a table, apparently at her accounts. Plump and powdered. Scent and silks. A pair of double doors in the farther wall stand open to reveal a long salon, glimpses of the doxies themselves, and the noise of early customers.

Striker doubts that the trade is so well organised as London, where there are now lists available of recommended whores, along with their addresses, a description of their appearance and their particular talents, in publications like *The Covent Garden Magazine,* or *The Man of Fashion's Companion.* But then in London there would also be the risk that Titus Redmond and Mother Blossom might likely have been convicted of keeping a disorderly house, harbouring loose persons and pickpockets. No such likelihood here where people go to church, to the inn, to the coffee house, to the market, to the brothel, all entirely unremarked.

'Bid you good evening, m'lords!' says the woman. 'And fine, strong lads too. Though none that I recognise. Not from these parts, I collect? Drovers, perchance. Not tars. No red necks, I see. Oh. La! But curb the tongue, Mother Blossom. Keep your breath to cool the porridge, as they say.'

'Oh, my fine boys,' says Striker, his nostrils flaring at the scented air. 'The sweet smell of fecking corruption, eh?'

'Irish!' says the woman, with some indignation. 'Tha' might have known. Diggers, then.' Mother Blossom, Striker knows, had been born in Blackburn around the turn of the century, became a teenage prostitute and married a man called William Baker. During the following fifteen years she moved from prostitute to bawd, running her own brothels. Then, in the Year '30, she married a second husband, George Blossom, and two years later was brought before Lancaster Assizes, charged with bigamy, but also with the murder of a certain Beth Pooley, one of her girls, while attempting to carry out an abortion with a fork. The bigamy charge was dismissed on the grounds that her first marriage had not been consummated but, on the second charge, she was convicted of manslaughter and sentenced to hang. She was fortunate enough, however, to be pregnant at the time and instead served three years in that dank Lancaster hole. On her release she had come to Manchester and found work as a Madam running Redmond's bawdy house. Rumour has it that she has become a very rich woman. 'And no corruption here, sirs. Checked every week at Mother Blossom's. Physician visits regular, like. And there's the Earl's Protectors too for them as favours 'em. Washed clean after every use and fresh lanolin! Tha' can feel every stroke, m'lords. Every stroke.' She produces a fine-gut condum, pink ribboned, from a box on the table. 'A twelver each one. Highly recommended.'

A shilling well spent, too, thinks Striker, *if it helps to avoid the pox*. More use than the physician's visit. By the time the scabs appear, half of Manchester could have been infected. And then what? Would Titus Redmond lay down golden guineas for the mercury? He doubts it. *A night in the arms of Venus leads to a lifetime on Mercury.* 'Not a jobbing labourer among us,' he says. 'Each of us a good fist at his own trade.' He points at each of the soldiers in turn. 'Hod, hawk, trowel, square and plumb-bob. Trades madam. All trades. Or so we were until that fecking fire! This is our last night in Manchester though, ma'am, so need to make the most, eh? How much for a nice bit of sweet company.'

'Why, let Mother Blossom introduce thee to her ladies,' she says, moving towards the salon while her Flash-Man positions himself on guard at the front door.

So that must be husband George, thinks Striker. *A bit old to be her cock-pimp.* But the covey of drabs in his charge hardly look as though they

141

would give him much trouble. There are eight women in the room and two existing customers, both elderly and unknown to Striker. Both men have doxies with them, each in a state of undress and delivering hand-jobs amid a general atmosphere of bedlam as the remaining girls make lewd jests or sing loudly in accompaniment to a blind fiddler, screeching his reels and jigs incessantly from the far corner.

'That one is Mary,' says Mother Blossom, pointing to a dark-haired harpy with flowing ringlets down her back, languishing grey eyes and a tolerable complexion. 'She's a half-guinea piece. Extra for the fiddle and geneva. This one, Susannah. She may be older than you'd like but she gives more pleasure than a dozen girls half her age. Only four shillings.'

The introductions go on, with prices varying between the two extremes, and Striker is struck by the girls' anonymity, that these women would be entirely indistinguishable from the hundreds of other bulk-mongers working the streets, taverns and bawdy-houses of Manchester or similar towns, and the supposedly fifty thousand whores in London itself. Each of them slack-eyed with laudanum, geneva, or both. Homeless petty criminals. Young widows without sufficient annuity to survive. Evicted maidservants trying to raise the by-blows of former employers. Girls orphaned before reaching puberty. And Mother Blossom on hand to save them all. *We men have such propensity for misery-making*, thinks Striker. *Yet what drives me to the bawdies except the base need to indulge my cock in hole instead of hand!* But he is no pecksniff, no hypocrite. *Scornful dogs will eat dirty pudding*, he thinks. And though he may be a frequent visitor to such establishments, he has never escaped the intimate certainty that, while the women may flatter, jape and moan, each of them is a superior player to himself, masking the profound contempt for men that he knows is rooted within their very souls. Contempt and fear. Fear of the pox that might, at last, turn their brains to mush. Fear of the violence that men so frequently bring with them to such places. And tonight they are right to fear.

'You shall have no dickering from us about prices,' says Striker, 'for we seem to be looking down the barrel of your piece, Mistress. And you are, when all is done, the Mother Superior of this nunnery.'

'Mother Blossom's piece, tha' will find,' she says, 'is broader than a farthingale. And the only illness to afflict thee here shall be desire, my boys. But if any cares to sample Mother Blossom herself, she can promise some more delights. And Mother Blossom does not offer herself to every Turk who comes along. Not every tag, rag and longtail. And she, sir, is happy to dicker with a fine gentleman like tha'self all night long. All things in proportion, says she – for the right man, that is!'

'Well boys,' says Striker, 'when the sun shineth, make hay!'

Pitchers of gin are served and his four companions slowly settle with one or more of the women. Some disappear to an upstairs room but others simply couple where they stand, pulling off their clothes, especially now in the heat of summer and passion alike. He watches as a girl draws her pins and, with no stays to encumber her, removes everything but her shift. A soldier takes her on the couch, thighs opened, leaves her that way when he has spent, his semen frothed around the lips of her joke. And Striker allows himself to be led to an adjoining room by the old bawd herself, to her private drawing room. And draw him she does!

They are scarce alone before she hauls up her own buntlings, urging him to caress the sow-white bubbies. She heaves down his pantaloons, stiffens him and licks his flute while Striker, aroused but barely distracted and vaguely absurd, still sporting the Monmouth cap, surveys the room carefully, seeking out the likely repository of Mother Blossom's wealth and Titus Redmond's revenue. Nothing obvious but, as she turns him to the couch, seats him for a straddle, his backside feels a box lid, solid beneath the seat cushion.

'You mentioned the Earl's Protector, Mother,' he says. 'No offence intended, ma'am, but…'

She smiles and pouts, makes comments that mark her as a real brimstone, lewd and lascivious. But she moves from him to a lacquered dresser, all the same, unlocks it and dangles a condum from her fingers.

'Only the best for my special boys,' she says but, as she turns to Striker once more, she sees that he has pulled up his pantaloons and taken her small strong-box from beneath the couch. 'A dab!' she cries. 'A fucking Gypsy dab. Irish bastard. George! George!'

Striker steps forward towards the door and the woman leaps upon his back, heavy, attempts to gouge his eyes but succeeds only in twining her fingers in the cap's woollen folds.

'George!' she screams now, and the door opens. Striker can see little, a glimpse to the salon beyond, a halt to all intimate activity and the beginnings of sundry struggles as the doxies consider intervention, only to find themselves restrained by Barrell's finest. But he sees George Blossom well enough, framed in the doorway, cudgel in hand.

'For the love of God,' says Striker, proffering the stolen box to the Flash-Man. 'By Our Lady, take the damn'd thing!'

So George Blossom reaches for the box, an entirely understandable instinct, though he never receives it. For, as his guard drops, Striker smashes the heavy box against the man's nose, pulps it to a mess of blood and broken bone. Then a second time. And again, until he falls. The box is dropped on the cock-pimp's head so that Striker can deal with Blossom's bigamous wife, now clawing at his ear and beating a fist against his skull. Striker's hand slips within his vest and he pulls his paring knife, stabbing it in the knee that grips his right hip. A thin, high shriek. 'Gypsy fucking dabber!' But she falls to the floor, hands gripping the spouting wound that her customer has inflicted.

'This milch-cow cut my purse!' shouts Striker. And the pandemonium

143

intensifies. The blind fiddler begins to shout for help, calling on the Constables who, Striker knows, will now be thoroughly engaged elsewhere. Soldiers grapple with their clothes, dressing as quickly as they are able while defending themselves from the whores and sending the fiddler sprawling in the process. The two older sports attempt to pay the women for their pleasures, blustering and desperate to leave the place while Striker plunders the condom store in the lacquered dresser, pins his blade through the remaining Protectors to reveal the strong-box key ensconced beneath them. He heaves the key upwards, tossing it in the air to catch it with his left hand, smiling, sees George Blossom attempting without success to lift himself, sees the old bawd dragging herself back towards the couch, still clutching her wounded thigh.

'Cut-purse whores!' cries one of the soldiers. 'Pay them in kind.' And he swipes at one of the women, a savage blow that sends her crashing backwards to the wall.

'Wait!' Striker shouts. 'Not those.' *But a good idea, all the same*, he thinks. He remembers his time with the Lenape, the way that the tribal elders had dealt with the unfaithful wife of a favoured warrior. No punishment, of course, for the man with whom she had committed her offence, and Striker has no doubt that they had learned this particular barbarity from their European neighbours. He drums a devil's tattoo on the dresser a moment, turns to consider Mother Blossom as she curses him to hell. His thoughts are confused. The Lenape punishment for infidelity. A line of Shakespeare, *Othello* perhaps. 'Led by the nose, as asses are.' And an entirely inexplicable image of young Rosina Redmond.

So, while the chaos builds without, he steps quickly to the couch, places his foot firmly to trap the woman's wounded leg, seizes her by the throat, fingers and thumb squeezing her cheek bones. Her eyes roll, the whites showing naked fear. Silence.

'You have a bone in your throat now, Mother?' he says. 'No more words for me? You faithless...'

Faithless, he wonders. *Such a strange thought!* But he reaches forward with the paring knife in any case. She *is* Titus Redmond's favourite, he knows. Redmond's personal procuress. *A lesson for you, sir.* He pushes the knife, blade reversed, all the way inside one nostril, pulls upwards to split the flesh like orange peel. He repeats the operation with the other nostril while the bawd screams enough to wake the dead.

Striker releases her, picks up the fallen strong-box. He suspects that he may need to pay the soldiers more than he had intended from the contents but he needs them now and, without need of instruction, they keep his way to the vestibule clear. More curses now from Mother Blossom, though incoherent as gore flows down into her blasphemous mouth and she hobbles behind him,

But his escape from the bordello is blocked since, at that moment, the outer door is thrown open by Titus Redmond. Striker sees him recoil, stare quickly around the scene that greets him. The doxies. The blade in Striker's hand. And, finally, the spectacle of Mother Blossom's ruin. Striker is prepared for Redmond's reaction, for the violence that he sees building in the Jacobite's eyes. But he cannot be prepared for the tears that, to his astonishment, begin to spill over the creases and folds of Redmond's face. Their eyes meet through that veil. There is a moment of mutual recognition perhaps, before Titus coils to attack. Yet no attack follows since, in the doorway beyond, Dubbins raises the hanger to shoulder height and swings his blade to the back of Titus Redmond's head.

Chapter Nineteen

James Bradley gazes around the Hall at the burgesses and freemen gathered here for the first Town Meeting to be assembled in more years than he can recall. Manchester has no borough status of its own. It is a market town, part of Sir Oswald Mosley's Manor within the County Constituency of Lancashire. So those entitled to take part in Town Meetings are only those embraced by the County Franchise. Men exclusively, of course. Those who own land worth forty shillings, freehold. Those who are tenants of land *worth* forty shillings. And those who are freemen, a title that can be gained through completion of apprenticeship and subsequent admittance to the appropriate Trade Guild.

So here are the town's barber-surgeons, wax-makers, ropers, stringers, barkers, tanners, butchers, fleshers, cordwainers, shoe-makers, curriers, tallow chandlers, drapers, tailors, dyers, listers, fullers, felt-makers, cloth-workers, carpenters, joiners, wheelwrights, sawyers, coopers, masons, wallers, slaters, paviours, plasterers, bricklayers, mercers, grocers, haberdashers, ironmongers, salters, goldsmiths, plumbers, pewterers, potters, glaziers, painters, saddlers, upholsterers, skinners, glovers, whitesmiths, lorimers, locksmiths, cutlers, blacksmiths, weavers, and websters.

Oh, thinks Bradley. *And the printers, of course.* Such a shame that the town's only remaining printer is a Papist. Scatterbuck is therefore ineligible to attend the Town Meeting, regardless of his standing as a Freeman of his Guild. But then he sees Aran Owen amongst the gathering, together with Byrom. For he has forgotten that the Welshman is, himself, admitted to the Worshipful Company of Stationers, Printers, Booksellers and Newspaper-Makers.

Some are here, of course, through their honorary freedom of the town. Those who have gained such through being the son or apprentice of a freeman, or by marriage into a freeman's family.

But Bradley is still surprised by the numbers in attendance. He has no idea, in truth, how long the land value qualification has stood at forty shillings but it is numbered in centuries. Two hundred years? Three? However long it may be, the gradual devaluation of money means that there are annually more men covered by the Franchise. He does not care greatly whether the newcomers are rich or poor. He simply knows that a wider Franchise means greater risk of instability. He has heard the arguments in favour of democratical government. In many ways, he understands them. For the English political system is a true shambles. A butcher's yard of forty county constituencies and over two hundred borough constituencies, these latter alone falling into eight different categories. But he is troubled by the republican chatter that he hears in the coffee house and the newly-established Freemasonic Lodge. For what *is* democracy? Government by the people, based on liberty, equality and fraternity, as his Freemason friends seem to espouse? Or rule by the mob? *Dêmos*, people. *Kratos*, power. The Greek Ancients, who have given us the word, believed that they were establishing the former, government by the people. Discovered too late that they had, rather, built only the latter, rule by the ill-informed majority.

'Will Sir John be joining us, Sir Oswald?' says Bradley, whispering his question across the broad oak table of the Court Leet to the Lord of the Manor, whose task is also to preside over such meetings. He is now sixty-nine years old, ailing and camphorous. He scratches at his full-bodied wig.

'Expecting him. Certainly,' replies Sir Oswald, but Bradley knows that Sir John Bland will, at this time of the evening, be too engaged at the gaming table to concern himself with matters affecting the town's common-folk. The Mosleys have held this Manor for a century and a half and Sir Oswald had succeeded as its Lord upon the death of Lady Ann Bland since he had been the eldest and closest relative of her father, Sir Edward Mosley. Lady Bland had lived at Hulme Hall which, with Hough End Hall, had passed to her son, Sir John. Along with Francis Reynolds at Strangeways, these are the town's major landowners. Reynolds, at least, has troubled himself to attend. 'But as well to begin, Mister Bradley, you agree?' Bradley does, indeed, and Sir Oswald rises unsteadily to speak.

'Give you good evening, gentlemen,' he says. 'Can all hear me?' There is at least one rake at the rear of *any* gathering who will shout 'No!' and tonight is no exception. But Sir Oswald continues without paying him any heed. 'I thank you for your presence. Scot and lot, gentlemen! Obligations and responsibilities to our community. But this is not about taxation nor Excise duty, neither. No, gentlemen. Rather, mayhem and murther. Two weeks ago, merely yards from this very spot. And a se'nnight past I receive this express from the Lord Lieutenant. The Earl of Derby tells me, in his wisdom, that the militia are standing by to assist me should order require restoration in the town. He cites the Riot Act, gentlemen. The Riot Act.'

And glad he will be to intervene, thinks Bradley, recalling Sir Edward Stanley's instruction that Mosley's loyalties to the Crown are, to say the least, suspect. Sir Oswald had been made a Baronet by George the First himself in the Year '20 but over the intervening two decades had shifted steadily towards the Jacobite faction amongst the Tories. Yet he seems nervous tonight. Perhaps the size of the meeting. A gathering of several hundred can be difficult to control, particularly given the many differences amongst them.

'And you needs look no farther, Sir Oswald, to discover the cause of 'this threat,' shouts George Fletcher, the linen draper, pointing at Bradley. 'The Constables, I collect, have statements a-plenty to show that it was James Bradley's men involved in the mayhem at Mistress Blossom's. Yet he sits here still at your side, bold as brass.'

'No men of mine, George Fletcher!' says Bradley. 'But even had they been previously in my employ, it would not be enough to implicate me in this so-called mayhem. Have we forgot so soon that this was a brawl in a bawdy-den?'

'Mistress Blossom's is a respectable lodging house,' protests Thomas Tipping, a yarn merchant from Hanging Ditch, but is met by boisterous laughter that drowns his attempt to remind them of Titus Redmond's fate in the affair.

'I should remind the Town Meeting,' says Whig Attorney Matthew Liptrott, 'that no Affidavits have been sworn against Mister Bradley and I cannot countenance any slur upon his character.'

'He has been heard often enough casting blame on the Redmonds for the fire that destroyed his terrace, however. Is that not true, Bradley?' shouts Tipping.

'Gentlemen!' Francis Reynolds stands from his place at the oak table. 'I beg you. Sir Oswald has convened this meeting because the threat of the Riot Act is a real one. We need one voice in the matter and it serves no purpose to bandy accusations in this way.'

'Fine words, Mister Reynolds,' says Robert Jobb, stay maker, and Bradley's main supporter in the Court Leet. 'But Bradley has seen no justice from the fire that so nearly ruined him. Almost two months have passed and what word from the Constables? None. Though there cannot be a man in the room who would not lay blame for the arson at Titus Redmond's door.'

Robert Gartside, another fustian manufacturer, launches a spirited defence of his close friend, Redmond, damning to hell the perpetrators of the crime against him. But Bradley is thinking about the fire itself. He has to admit that he did not expect such a violent reaction to the message that he had sent to Titus. Perhaps he might have gone a little far with the attempt to implicate Driscoll in Sourwood's death. And he could genuinely claim no paternity for little Maeve, though the timing of his dalliance with Maria-Louise makes it at least a possibility. But sweet Rosina now. If there had been doubts about her tribady beforehand, there can surely be none remaining at this point. She and Elizabeth Cooper have been barely separable. Sweet Rosina, though. How strange. How troubling. Troubling, too, that he feels the absence of Maria-Louise so keenly and he wonders whether, given what has happened to her husband...

But Aran Owen has now joined the debate.

'I had no intent to speak at the meeting,' he said, 'since I am in attendance so that we may report the proceedings in the *Journal*.' One of

148

the check manufacturers, John Upton, interrupts with a caustic comment, asking whether the Welshman would not prefer to contort himself into a glass receptacle, since the town was still lacking the performance of a certain Bottle-Conjuror. 'But I find myself required to say a word on behalf of the Redmond family,' Aran continues. 'Mister Redmond himself always denied any involvement in the fire at Bradley's terrace. Now, there may be men in this room who are opponents of his, may even describe themselves as enemies. But there is not a single man present who could call Titus Redmond a liar. And his family does not deserve such accusations at this time of distress for them.'

John Clowes, the breeches maker, shouts, 'The Welshman's right. Redmond's no liar! Why, only last month I heard him admit at the Bull's Head how glad he would be to sell us to the Papist Pretender and French Louis, both. The man is an honest-to-goodness traitor and deserves all he's got. Can you imagine, gentlemen? Raising a subscription in his own house to finance a French army ag'in' us?'

'The true problem,' says the Reverend Doctor John Clayton, 'rests with the number of beggars and itinerants on our streets. Presbyterian charity has bred criminality in the very heart of our town. Why, Constable Bower was informing me that there is every reason to suspect that Mister Bradley's fire may easily have been set by one of these same idle-folk, seeking to warm himself through temporary accommodation in the unfinished premises.'

'And if your Episcopalian High Churchmen had not prevented the construction of a Workhouse for the town, we should not have such a problem with the unemployed and the vagrant,' replies Benjamin Nichols, Assistant Curate at St Ann's. 'Besides, there are few here, Doctor Clayton, who would have the temerity to deny that this increase in civil disorder is not the fault of *supporters* from the opposing factions represented here, even if blame cannot be directly attributed to their respective leaders. A plague on both houses, I say, for we should not tolerate being practised upon thus.'

'If anything,' says his colleague, Thomas Lewthwaite, 'it is the town's lack of morality that we must consider. And are both factions not equally responsible for this reprehensible state? There is hardly a street in the entire town without at least one bawdy-den and a couple of gin-houses. Though this can be no reason to countenance such violence. And murder, too, on the same evening. It must not be tolerated.'

Bradley watches as Thomas Walley, a clock maker, a Whig supporter, and a stammerer, engages in difficult private argument with William Fowden, a tin man and staunch Tory, though it remains unclear whether their disagreement relates to the points presently being disputed. In any case, the argument provokes Sir Oswald to call for order and remind the Town Meeting, once again, that it is convened to consider how best they might respond to the Earl of Derby's concerns.

'I say this,' shouts James Tomlinson, a miller. 'It's about the bloody

French! We've been fightin' them buggers for years, 'undreds o' years. An' now this bugger Redmond's been raisin' money for 'em. Is that right? Then I say this, that we should take up th' Earl o' Derby's offer and get the militia in 'ere, right quick. Redmond might be out o' the way but there's plenty more like 'im. And I dare say the bugger's subscription's still going strong. Bring in the militia, says me. Sort out every one o' the buggers!'

'The miller's right,' says Nathan Woolmer, a cabinet maker. 'Without the French always promising to be at their backs, the Jacobites wouldn't be so cock-sure of themselves.'

'Oh, and who do we think put William the Orangeman on the throne in '88?' says John Clough, the yarn merchant from Hunt's Bank. 'English yeomen, good and true? No, it was the bloody Dutch. And who keeps George on the throne if not his Hessians and Hanoverians? I tell you, gentlemen, that help from the French would be a small price to pay for the restoration of a true British monarch!'

'I'm with you, Mister,' says Abraham Howarth, a joiner. 'It's worse now that when we had Sir Bob Bluestring as First Minister. Stamp tax! Tea tax! Alcohol tax! Speak to any craftsman, small trader, or merchant seaman in this town, and I defy you to find even *one* of them a supporter of this Government. All we need is just a single spark and the whole country will turn against them – Whigs and Germans alike!'

'Stuff, sir!' says Joseph Bancroft, a smallware manufacture. 'The whole country indeed! You are dreaming, sir. And the taxes of which you speak are necessary only because the French are, once more, seeking to extend their influence across Europe. And when you speak of '88, it may be true that William was assisted by the Dutch, but we all gained from the process and no blood spilled in the making.'

'No bloodshed?' says John Clayton, angered almost beyond belief. 'Have we forgotten that William of Orange deposed the rightful king – a *Stuart* king? Have we forgotten the bloodshed inflicted on Ireland alone by William and his mob? And, speaking of Ireland, we should not forget the plight of our Catholic brethren so easily. Where are they tonight? Proscribed from attendance, gentlemen, that is where! We have been promised since the days of King William that this would be a society tolerant of individual religious rights, but those promises have been betrayed. They might, at the moment, not be applying *each* of their anti-Catholic laws, but they remain on the statute books. You all know them as well as I do.'

John Byrom speaks at last, as the entire gathering has known he will, at the apposite moment. 'The good Reverend Doctor makes a good point, gentlemen. I have just had the fortune to purchase a new horse in Cambridge. Black Jack he is named and paid ten pounds for him. But worth every penny, he made the return journey so pleasant. It is my second mount. Yet think upon the possibility that I might be a Catholic by faith. In this case, I should only be allowed one horse in any case and, even then, only if it is below the value of five pounds. Sheer iniquity. Yet, even then, I may not ride the beast beyond ten miles from my house, regardless of its quality. I am astonished.'

'For pity's sake!' says Bradley. 'Might we not deal with the topic that Sir Oswald has brought before us? We are threatened with the Riot Act and the imposition of the militia upon our town.'

'Then I say this, Mister Bradley,' says Byrom, 'if I may be permitted to quote from Virgil's *Aeneid*?' Bradley waves a hand at him in concession. 'I say this. *Aut haec in nostros fabricata est machina muros…*' Somebody shouts for him to speak English. 'Very well. *Either this machine is contrived against our liberties, or else there is some other mischief concealed within it.* So said the true-hearted Trojan Laocoon when he saw his townsmen considering whether they should admit and suffer the famous wooden horse of the Greeks. We must all defend the good ship *Manchester* against its storms. But to accept any form of militia intervention in our town cannot be borne. There is therefore only one solution, gentlemen. We must persuade the Earl of Derby that peace is restored and matters once again in hand. Which means, in turn, that there must be no repeat of recent hostilities, regardless of whoever may be culpable for them.'

There is general agreement from amongst the gathering, but also a voice of dissent, appropriately from the Reverend Joseph Mottershead. For the reverend gentleman was the leader of the town's Dissenters, those who had split from the Church of England a century ago because they would not conform to the strict rules of service. Their movement had grown rapidly and the first Dissenters' Meeting House had been built at Back Pool Fold in the town. It has an unhappy history, however, since in the Year '15 a Jacobite mob had sacked the place.

'I feel that I must speak at this point,' says Mottershead, and the gathering becomes hushed, for they know the personal grief that the Reverend must be feeling. 'In truth, I did not wish to attend but Reverend Clayton and Mister Byrom both speak of tolerance, yet my own church is frequently the subject of violent attack and the perpetrators always seem to escape with utter impunity. You have spent much time tonight on the subject of this business at Mistress Blossom's renowned house of ill-repute yet, at the same time, my own Meeting House, a House of God, gentlemen, was subject to yet another violation. Yet another group of *banditti* using some pretext that it was James Stuart's birthday so that they might run amok on our streets.'

'I feel for your loss, sir,' says Clayton, standing to lean on his stick. 'I truly feel for it. Yet it seems harsh that you, too, seem eager to lay the blame against a particular group within our society. For is it not true, sir, that the adherence of your own followers to such strange belief has made your Meeting House a target. Such conceit, sir, to deny the Trinity against the teachings of the Christian Church from the very time of its foundation!'

'It is the Trinitarian Doctrine, Mister Clayton, that has been the disgrace of the Christian name and turned Christianity, contrary to its very nature, to a society of sophists. As a Unitarian, my belief is simple. That Our Lord Christ, though himself divine, was entirely separate from God the Father. But I did not come here to expound some theological debating point. I came, rather, hoping that the death of my fellow-pastor may not have been entirely in vain. He was my son-in-law also, as you know.'

For, when the Jacobite gangs roaming the streets on the Old Pretender's birthday had rampaged through Pool Fold, for their annual sport against the Dissenters' Meeting House, young John Semple had tried to dissuade them. And amongst the rocks and cobbles hurled at the windows and doors, one of them had struck Semple on the forehead, slaying him instantly. The Constables had, at last, arrived on the scene but, at that stage, the mob had dispersed.

It is difficult, now, for Sir Oswald Mosley to hold the meeting together much longer.

'Gentlemen of Manchester,' he says. 'I must needs thank you for your attendance. In general, I agree with Mister Byrom and other speakers. Unthinkable that this Manor should fall under martial law. It is therefore my intent to return an express to Sir Edward with an assurance that I shall, myself, mobilise the Invalids to supplement our good Constables in their efforts. But this relies on the premise that, regardless of faction, there shall be an end to all violence. And our condolences, naturally, Reverend Mottershead, to yourself and your family. I am certain that we all feel your loss keenly.'

He asks that all those who support his proposition should say 'Aye' and is greeted with general agreement, some huzzahs, and a few wigs or tricorne hats tossed in the air. He promises that the Court Leet shall give urgent consideration to providing assistance with the damage done to the Dissenters' Meeting House. *Generous of him*, thinks Bradley, left with the dilemma that Redmond's supporters may not feel themselves bound by the Town Meeting's decision when so many of the Jacobites' leading protagonists have been excluded from the proceedings. Meanwhile, he cannot escape the sensation that many of those present have taken for granted that he was, after all, in some way responsible for the attack on Mother Blossom's.

Things had been going so well for him, too. He had almost secured enough support within the Court Leet to have himself appointed as Clerk of the Town Works, though he may have had to purchase the office. Worth almost any price, however. But what now? He will have to restore his former relationship with Elizabeth Cooper, perhaps, since her influence is still great. This had been clear to him earlier in the day, when she had overseen the collection of Midsummer Quarter Day rents and duties. He had been surprised by the confidence with which she had handled the many japes harking back to the events of Lady Day. She had done well. But then there is also Maria-Louise. He longs to see her again, regrets the way in which he had used her. And he wonders how she must be dealing with this latest trial, particularly as many of those leaving the Commodities Exchange seem so genuinely concerned about the state of Titus Redmond's health.

God's Hooks, he thinks. You might almost have imagined that it was Titus Redmond *himself* that had been killed!

Chapter Twenty

The letter that will evoke so many troubled thoughts had been delivered at noon, and Aran has carried it throughout the remnant of the day until, finally, he is able to break the seal when he returns to his lodgings overlooking John Shaw's Punch House.

Llanffynon Hall, July 7th, 1744
My dear boy: I had yours on Monday last by way of the letter from my sister-in-law in which she appraised me of her husband's condition. More anon in that regard but my immediate concern is that mine finds you well and finally established in the palatial new lodgings of which you spoke.

Aran rises from the small table that stands beneath the room's modest window, and opens it wide to allow the early evening breeze, hoping that it might dispel some of the overpowering heat that has accumulated through several hours of uninterrupted July sunshine beating against the outside glass. He has a view down into the market square, across to the Conduit and, immediately below, to the thatched roof of the Punch House itself, a recent extension to the main building in which Aran lives. The premises have belonged to the Byrom family for generations, and John Byrom himself is fond of reminding him that this was his own birthplace. With the move to their more opulent dwelling in Hanging Ditch, however, the house had provided letting opportunities for lodging rooms on the upper storey and a draper's shop at street level.

It is comfortable enough, Aran supposes, larger than his room at Mistress Evesworth's and certainly an improvement over the tiny space that he had occupied during his recovery at the Redmonds. But he crosses it in little more than six paces when he goes to open the door, wedging it ajar so that the breeze, once through the window, can better circulate and cool the interior. Like all lodging houses, the night can be intimate, for the wattle-and-daub interior walls are thin. They provide little insulation from the noise of adjoining rooms, so sleep is frequently interrupted by the creaking of warped oak floor planks, the hawking cough of a consumptive neighbour, the incontinent flow of piss to chamber pot, the raucous snoring of somebody along the landing. *Like somebody driving pigs*, he thinks. But he has become accustomed to it over the weeks, even the rank smells that rise from the market place itself.

He sets down the letter, briefly, on his bed while he folds his coat to lay it carefully within the large chest holding his possessions. The wall has no panelling, simple white broken only by irregular blackened timbers rising to the ceiling beams, just inches above his head. At least he can easily afford the rent, paid at each quarter-end by bill of exchange from the account that he holds with Mister Dickenson. There has been talk of a bank, though none has yet materialised. Still, Dickenson with some of the other merchants, and Childer the goldsmith, have been providing the service long enough, and never a difficulty, never a scandal, never a default, so far as he knows. No simple keepers of coin, these, but men whose promissory notes are as good as legal currency, issuers of endorsed receipts that may be converted back to gold or silver at any hour of the day or night without question.

Aran picks up the letter from the bed and sits again at the table.

For my own part, I find my seventy years weighing heavily against me and myself growing bitter at the passing of my days. Only the garden seems able to relieve my humour. Yet I recall your own affection for the grounds of Llanffynon at this season. It would give you joy, I know, to see the way in which these weeks of equatorial weather have assisted the orchards, and I declare that we must now possess the finest collection of fruit trees in Flintshire.

Aran sees himself struggling beneath the weight of fruit baskets on the gravel paths of Llanffynon Hall, through the yew walk, to the kitchen. Plums, apricots, apples or pears. Prized Edelsborsdorfers. Sweet Bon Chrétien d'Hiver. And, once the work is finally done, his mother shows him how to bring a pear's image to life, simple charcoal and a scrap of kitchen parchment, light and shade. He feels her loss sharply.

But my pastoral idyll has been most rudely shattered with the news of my brother's wounding, though Maria-Louise tells me little about his progress. Your own informs me that he is yet ailing but mending slowly, which gives me cause for still more concern. She says that he was attacked on the street whilst attending 'his' business, thus I conclude that she refers to the bawdy-house rather than 'our' business in the fustian. I must confess that I have never fully understood his affinity for such low-life and always expected that it would end badly. I have told him so. And now I am proven correct. How can such a thing be borne? And my sister-in-law such a virtuous woman as you, yourself, will have discovered.

The letter gives Aran pause, brings a smile to his lips. Yet, strangely, he agrees that he would, indeed, describe Maria-Louise as virtuous also. For he has seen the care that she lavishes upon Titus since the attack. She seems entirely capable of ignoring the location and circumstances of the crime. Her husband still believes that the ruffians encountered at Mother Blossom's were thugs hired by Bradley, and that to be struck down from behind in such a way is an act of cowardice to which Bradley alone might stoop. The sword blow to his head had, thankfully, been delivered without too much force, it seems. Some of its effect had been blunted, too, by Titus Redmond's wig and the angle of the blade, more flat than edge. But serious enough, and Doctor Hall has once more earned his fees. But the lasting injury does not seem entirely physical, and the good Doctor has been far from successful in his ministrations to Mother Blossom's mutilated features. So Titus has taken to his bed, morose and apathetic. Aran's dreams, however, have been stalked once again by Striker, and he fears that it may be himself, rather than Titus Redmond, who could most easily identify the attackers – or, at least, one of them.

The girls are much like their good mother, too, I collect and little Rosina took the trouble to enclose a note within the package. Most welcome, though I am barely acquainted with my niece. But she has written at length on the death of John Semple. A shocking event and one that, in itself, reminds me of the very reason that I retired from Manchester life. I knew Semple quite well and, whilst I have always believed that the Dissenters are heretics, he seemed, individually, a gentle and mannerly soul. Rosina, too, appears to be greatly moved by Semple's demise and, if she shares her mother's sweet nature, you might do worse that considering a proposal of marriage in that direction. Do you not think so, my boy?

Just two months ago, less, even the slightest suggestion of some permanent relationship with Rosina Redmond would have seemed a goal for which Aran might have sacrificed anything. Complicated by lusty feelings for her mother, naturally, but an exquisite preoccupation, all the same. Yet now there are rumours of the strangest sort. An atmosphere at the Redmonds' home that he could not even begin to describe. And at the Bull's Head, or in the Punch House, Townley and his friends speak openly such words as tribady, talk of lewd activity between Rosina and Elizabeth Cooper. They mock Titus, say that he is become feeble, unable to control the sexual meanderings of neither wife nor daughter. And Aran remains mute in the family's defence. He harbours noble intentions, obviously – of calling Townley out; of elopement with Rosina; of saving her from whatever spell Mistress Cooper must have woven about her; of finding some heroic way of demonstrating his worth to Maria-Louise. But intention is tin and purpose is plate, as they say.

In closing, I would also proffer a second piece of advice, hoping that you will not find it amiss on my part. Yet I have received a visit from the Rector of Hawarden, Richard Williams. He seeks my support in a certain cause with which, I am certain, you will be familiar. I believe that he speaks for others in the County, and elsewhere within the Principality, but I have reminded him merely that my age precludes involvement in such matters, whilst I simply remained silent on any question of monetary subscription which, I collect, must have been his true desire, and I suspect that the Reverend gentleman shall visit me again. I trust that I may not be placing you in any difficulty by writing to you thus, but I have seen so much misery arising from this particular, and would simply spare you, as a modest surrogate for both father and mother, from any grief in this regard.

In simple exhortation, therefore, that you should exercise caution at all times, I remain your humble yet inadequate guardian.

Josiah Redmond, Esquire

He folds the letter, lifts the lid on the chest to place it within, and thinks that Josiah's words of warning may just be a little late. Aran's thoughts turn to Striker once more, that waking nightmare that creeps at his heels like a sinister shade. He finds himself frequently looking over his shoulder these days, in apprehension, and does so now several times simply as he locks his room, leaves the lodgings and turns across the face of the building to mount the Punch House entrance steps.

Peering through the gloom as his eyes adjust from the outside brightness, he calls for six pennyworth of punch and, while the proprietor busies himself with lemon strainer, nutmeg grater and whalebone-handled ladle, Aran is greeted by Adam Scatterbuck. He calls for a second when he sees that Scatterbuck's own cup is now empty, and they pass a few agreeable minutes discussing the merits of John Shaw's concoctions. They bless the Hindu for bestowing such a gift upon them, and they bless the seafarers who brought the recipes back with them from their oriental travels. They argue about their preferences, Scatterbuck for Portobello, with its strong fusion of Jamaican rum, and Aran for Captain Radcliffe's, a more mellow blend of brandy and wine. And they exchange small-talk, an enquiry about Aran's hand, or Scatterbuck's progress in finding a new first-year apprentice which leads, inevitably, to recollections of Daniel Sourwood. Aran notes that Scatterbuck has rarely spoken of the boy. Well, says the other, if he is to be truly honest, he never cared for the fellow. He would not wish him dead, of course. But the boy always had an eye for the easy shilling. And yes, says Aran, he had noted this also. Scatterbuck must allow that he has sometimes wondered whether Sourwood had said more than was good for him in Lancaster Gaol, whether it was some guilt on his part that led him to take his life. Perhaps he is right, but Aran Owen does not permit the conversation to dwell on the point.

Meanwhile, this now being past six o' the clock, a mixed crowd of

157

customers has begun to gather, including a number of the doxies whom one would normally describe as 'good-natured girls', those with loose morals who, though not professional whores, are in truth little different in practice. Scatterbuck's eye is drawn by one in particular and Aran struggles to remind him that they are both here to conclude some professional business for they have still not provided coverage in the *Journal* about the Town Meeting and its outcome. It has become almost an embarrassment but Titus Redmond's reaction to the news of Sir Oswald Mosley's conclusion has been one of the rare moments of animation on his part subsequent to the attack.

'In all conscience,' says Scatterbuck, 'I am at a total loss. Sir Oswald presses me almost daily. Stresses the importance of our being seen to represent the rule of law in town. Yet Titus will have none of it, I fear. Will listen to no reason on the matter. In truth, rarely listens to me on any issue since the night of his birthday rout. I fear that I may have been indelicate, indiscreet in a discussion with O'Farrell. It was the influence of that fine claret, in truth. And I may be entirely wrong, but Titus will neither forgive nor forget even the most unintentional affront.'

'Yet he has set me to take his part in matters editorial for the *Journal* whenever it may be necessary. I saw him yesterday to discuss the new Fly Wagon route to Carlisle but he was at such an ebb that it was not worth the visit. I think we can safely assume that this may be just such a time of necessity and my advice, sir, is that you should publish the Town Meeting article as soon as possible. I will take responsibility for the decision and, if I am able to pour some oil on the waters between you, I shall gladly do so.'

Scatterbuck mutters his appreciation, promises to re-write the piece, perhaps phrase it differently, but Aran does not hear him for he has experienced a sudden certainty that they are no longer alone. He turns, looks up from his bench, to find Francis Townley standing behind him.

'What's this?' he says. 'Fie upon it! A conspiracy unless I miss my mark. Your pay-master will not be pleased with you, Adam, if you should dare flaunt his wishes. Not that I would blame him on this occasion. Fucking Town Meeting, indeed! And you, Mister Owen. You must think your credit with Titus is particularly high at the moment. But, by the Mass, I suppose that he has so much else to distract him that he would not notice one more slight. They tell me that he is still ailing, though the wound was minor, surely?'

'A deep one, sir,' says Aran. 'No threat to his life, perhaps, but you will know from your military experience that such head-wounds can take an unconscionable time to heal.'

'La!' says Townley. 'So you have added the physician's skill to your already legendary list of abilities, sirrah. Artist, printer, gentleman of enterprise. Oh, and the *Journal*, of course! How is our worthy broadsheet doing, by the way, Adam? Are we over the contagion from that Bottle-Conjuror announcement?'

'A temporary reduction in sales, Francis. Nothing more,' says Scatterbuck.

'Yet I do not recall that you have ever shared any ownership of the enterprise. Still, it is considerate that you should show such concern. I thank you for it, indeed I do!'

'Why, I had thought that my previous contribution to the sheet might at least afford me some small share-holding? And you have nobody else who can provide such immediate news on the war. Even as we speak, the French are moving against Sardinia and the rest of Hanover's allies. I could script another piece – unless, of course, Mister Owen has now also become an expert on matters military? Or could it be that the Redmonds will continue to show their phlegm against France by ignoring her successes. Not Titus, of course, for I doubt that he knows even the month from all I hear. But *Mistress* Redmond! Such an appropriate title in this case, do you not think? And an opportunity for Maria-Louise to exert some influence on the content of the *Journal*, I imagine.'

Aran feels a rare anger rising within him, stands blindly to confront Townley without any thought for the consequence of his action. Scatterbuck stands too, clutching at his arm in an attempt at restraint.

'Wait!' he says.

'No,' says Aran. 'Townley has gone too far.'

But Townley merely pushes him back to the bench.

'Sit yourself, sir,' he says, 'for you have not the mettle.'

At that same moment, John Shaw calls 'Eight o'clock, gentlemen and ladies, eight o'clock!' Closing time at the Punch House, strictly observed by the proprietor and, in the tradition of the place, he cracks a horsewhip behind the serving bar to underline his point while the maid, Molly Owen, stands ready with a water-bucket so that she may expedite the movement of any loiterer. And Townley has gone. Not even a backwards glance.

Humiliation. Belated recollection of all the barbs he might have employed to return Townley's own. Scatterbuck's admonishment that he should not have risen to the bait. For Townley is a dangerous blade-smith, is he not? And the admonishment damns Aran Owen by gratuitous pardon. It devours him, again and again, as they cross the Market Place, not too far from Pool Fold where Townley the dashing blade-smith, or at least the gang that runs at his back, have so recently killed poor Semple. He barely heeds Scatterbuck's endless flow of dialogue, nor even his farewell, when they reach the corner of Market Street Lane. Aran avoids a foul-heap and the hog that forages within it, crosses to the impressive double-frontage of the Redmonds' house. It does not stand in grandiose isolation, of course, for this section of the street outwardly declares the wealth of the town's most successful merchants, and here they are as plentiful upon the ground as pig-shit.

He climbs the steps to the outer door, to be greeted by the sound of Rosina at her harpsichord practice but, when he beats the knocker and O'Farrell opens for him, he has no sooner stepped into the entrance hall than the young woman appears from the fore-parlour to greet him.

'Oh, la!' she cries.' Aran Owen, you have been neglecting me.' She takes his arm and steers him back into the room, more animated than usual. *She is embarrassed*, he thinks. *This act of breathless excitement is no more than a screen.* But he enjoys her attentions all the same, though he wonders how he should react to the rumours about her. 'But you do not seem yourself, sir,' says Rosina. 'Troubled, one might say. I do hope that I have not caused you any discomfort by apprehending you so!'

'Not at all, my dear. A disagreeable exchange with Francis Townley at the Punch House while I was trying to conduct business with Scatterbuck, and I apologise if I have carried my ill-humour into your home. I am sure that it is not catching, though, and it gives me joy to see you again. You were practising, too, I collect.'

'I think Mistress Starkey would describe it more like paddling than practising. It is some Clérambault. The very devil!' She stands at the instrument and strikes the first bars. 'Yet you should pay no heed to Townley. He is a foolish fellow. For once, Mama's views and my own coincide on the matter.'

'There is yet some difficulty between yourself and your mother then?' he asks, immediately feeling himself foolish for putting the matter so bluntly.

'You know fine well that there is difficulty, Aran. Dissembling does not become you, sir. You frequent the Bull's Head, the Punch House and such other places where rumours are imbibed at a faster rate than porter or punch. Why, it would not surprise me to learn that your disagreement with Townley had itself some bearing on the matter.' He has to allow that she is correct, yet he does not confess that it has been the reputation of mother, rather than daughter, that sparked the fuse.

'A fie upon the fellow,' Rosina continues, 'but you have been a good friend to me, better than I have generally deserved and frequently repaid with indifference, I fear. So I would take this opportunity to speak plainly, sir, and hope that you will be able to understand. Nay, not understand, for that would be asking too much. But at least to hear a simple confession and think no worse of me for the telling.'

She still stands at the harpsichord, her fingers lightly touching occasional keys, but with a tremor to them now that was absent earlier. And her head, still proud and erect, now has a certain rigidity so that her moist eyes are fixed on a point somewhere high on the pale green wall. 'You will have heard rumours of a certain relationship between myself and Mistress Cooper,' she says, 'and I have to tell you...'

'My dear Rosina!' says Aran. 'If I might be allowed to interrupt you for a moment, I have to tell you that, yes, rumours abound at the moment. Some of them certainly speak ill of yourself and Mistress Cooper, though perhaps *ill* is not the correct word. I must confess a great degree of ignorance and I suppose that, like most others, I find difficulty with a young woman of such beauty and refinement as yourself – no, I do not intend to intrude upon your modesty yet I would ask that you permit me to finish – that a woman such as yourself should find more solace with one of your own fair sex. I dare not even think how such a thing would be considered in Llanffynon, yet I have lived in this place for long enough to know that there are so many things beyond my rude comprehension, and this is simply another. For me, personally, it is difficult because, at times, I had hoped... Well, hoped that there might be some place for an ignorant Welshman in your affections.'

Rosina's hands are now clasped before her, anguishing with each other, and a tear rolls down her cheek. Her mouth works, but no words come forth, and the moment is broken when O'Farrell enters, surveys the scene and announces that his master is waiting for Mister Owen to attend him. Aran promises that they will talk again later and lifts a finger, carefully, to catch the tear as it reaches the smooth curve of her neck. Then he turns and follows the manservant as O'Farrell's joints rasp and rattle up the flights of stairs to Titus Redmond's bedchamber. It is a fine room, at the front of the house. Even at this twilight time, sunlight still illuminates the Prussian blue interior woodwork, reflects from the polished floor, burnishes the black base-boards, and brightens the wool damask bed hangings that frame Titus himself where he sits propped against pillows, his head still swathed in bandage.

Aran takes a chair from near the window, a regal affair, covered complete in damask too, with a fringe of silver and golden silk threads along the lower edge. O'Farrell lifts the bed-cover, glances at the chamber pot below and, making some incomprehensible comment, takes it from the room. Normally, he would not have been allowed to depart without some offensive reproach from Titus but now the master merely observes him as he leaves and turns without any welcome to his visitor.

'So,' he says, 'you have been taking good care of my interests?' But the question is flat, without feeling. All the same, Aran greets him warmly and quickly lists some key issues. First, of course, the letter from Josiah. Kind of him to write, regards sent. Then the success of the new Fly Wagon route to Carlisle. Some points of note from the Waste Book, the daily diary for all the chronological transactions of the business. A few items of correspondence from the Letter and Bill Book. Brisk trade amongst the fustian manufacturers. And some news that Captain Eriksson has brought with him from a skipper recently returned from the East, that the Japanese have developed a new way of processing tea, steam-drying the leaves to produce a range of varieties to challenge the Chinese roast blends.

'He brought me the cups,' replies Titus, pointing at a dresser against the far wall. Aran stands and crosses the room and picks up one of the dainties, white porcelain and the finest that Aran has ever seen, paper-thin with a hint of blue to the opaque glaze. The base is without any glaze, however, but moulded in the form of a fantastical beast, a dragon, on its surface.

'Be careful, cunny-licker!' says Titus. 'It's *Shufu*. Four hundred years old, he tells me. The caddy too.' Another man might have been offended to be addressed so, but Aran simply smiles. It is the first sign of Redmond's former self that he has seen, and he welcomes it. The caddy is exquisite. Does Titus know, he wonders, that the word derives from the Chinese for one pound in weight. Might the fact amuse him? He thinks not, that it would likely provoke a further insult, so he sets the box back on the dresser and returns to the chair.

'The good captain tells me that the Swedish Company are beginning to seek other locations where tea might be successfully grown. Simply to meet the increasing demand. He says that the Russian Empress has agreed the regulation of the trade, with a three-hundred strong camel caravan plying back and forth, continuously, between St Petersburg and Xian. A journey of eleven thousand miles, sir. And Government policy to support the merchants, rather than tax them to oblivion! Yet they take their tea so differently there, topped with a lemon and drunk through a lump of sugar held between the teeth.'

'A pox on Pelham and his mandarins,' says Titus. 'And a regulated trade would be the death of it. It might be well for sugar-sucking Russians but not here, methinks.'

'Perhaps one day things will change,' says Aran. 'Perhaps one day we shall even convert Mister Wesley to a tea-drinker.'

'It would help if we could simply dissuade him from preaching against it. You must speak to Byrom, see if he can exert any influence on the scoundrel. Otherwise we shall never become truly rich, Aran, not with just two Penny Universities in the town. Yet tell me, have you taken the opportunity to visit the bawdy-house. They will not bring me news of Blossom, God damn their eyes.'

Aran offers apologies, for he has neglected the bawdy-house. In truth, he does not altogether see it as part of his responsibility, any more than he would dare interfere with Jacob Driscoll's arrangements with the smugglers. But he takes the opportunity, at least, to describe his meeting with Scatterbuck, explains the printer's dilemma, the pressure that he is experiencing from Sir Oswald to publish a piece on the Town Meeting, his concerns that he may have been indelicate during the birthday rout and therefore earned Titus Redmond's displeasure.

'Fuck the Town Meeting,' says Titus, 'and fuck that old fool too!'

'As it happens, Francis Townley seems to agree with you, on both counts.'

'Townley? What has Townley to do with this?'

'Why, nothing, I suppose. But he joined us at the Punch House to offer some advice about the *Journal*.'

'Your orders, sir, were to keep Francis Townley away from the *Journal* at all costs. Did you not mind that instruction, Mister Owen?'

'I collect the instruction well, sir, and we ended on terms which were far from amicable as a result. Yet he seems to think… He seems to think that you are a spent force, sir!'

All trace of despondent apathy slips from Titus Redmond's face and he tears the bandage from his head, revealing the stubble of his hair beneath.

'Spent?' he cries. 'That Frenchified lick-spittle will discover whether or not I am spent. My wife's late father, damn his soul, may have cursed me to hell but I will be fucked before I see the likes of Townley mock me there. And if that cunny-sucker ever agrees with me on *anything*, it is likely time that I should consider my position anew. Help me to get below.' So they gather his gown about him and descend the stairs, past an astonished Mag Mudge. She drags her useless right leg down to a small landing so that they might pass more easily, she drooling something incomprehensible about bastards and bitches, and Titus complaining that ill fortune follows those who pass on a stair. And who needs more ill fortune, he says, when you already have Mistress Mudge as a housekeeper?

On the ground floor, Aran is joined by O'Farrell and, between them, they help Titus across the reception hall and into the sitting room, that occupies the other half of the house frontage from the fore-parlour. They ease him onto the settee, with its daintily shaped but deceptively strong walnut legs, its scooped wings, seat and back upholstered with needlework tapestry. The room is rarely used and Aran has only once previously spent any time here, but he admires the marble chimney-piece, the blue and white delft tiles that surround it, the enormous mirrors that seem to double the interior dimensions, the beeswax candles mounted in their sconces around the walls. The walls themselves have been recently stripped of their original dark panelling to the bare plaster, and the surface smoothed, polished and painted in a shade of green verditer, flat-finished in the very latest fashion.

Rosina joins them, and Aran notices that her appearance causes Titus to slump lower on the sofa, his chin to sink upon his chest. For her own part, she has composed herself well, no sign now of her earlier distress.

'Where is your Mama?' he asks, his voice as flat as the paint.

'I am not her keeper, Papa. I have been practising in the fore-parlour. For her part, she may be practising elsewhere. I know only that she left the house some little while ago though I am unable to confirm her destination. It is seemingly only my own morals that require constant supervision.'

'Bull's Head, lordship' says O'Farrell. 'Letters to post if the fecker's not closed.'

The Bull's Head keeps later hours than those permitted to the Punch House but there are no regular opening times for the small post-room that the proprietors have set aside to serve the town. It is always a matter of luck alone whether you may find it open and operational.

'Then get yourself over there too, Phelim. Tell her I need her here as quickly as possible. And see whether Jacob Driscoll may be there also. It is

163

quite possible, though let us hope he is not at Old Nob's instead. Oh, and tell Mudge to light us, preferably without igniting the entire room.' O'Farrell touches a knuckle to his forehead and shambles out of the room. 'And *you*, miss, have no leave to speak to me thus in front of the servants. Nor in Mister Owen's company neither.'

'I doubt there is anything in this household that escapes Phelim's attention, Papa. And at least Aran attempts to understand me,' she says. 'He may talk stuff, but at least he tries.'

'He attempts to understand acts that defy nature, you mean? Men are hung for less. And I tell you this, Rosina.' He almost manages to raise himself from the sofa. 'That whatever faults may be laid at the feet of your Mama and myself, they are at least natural in the eyes of Our Lady. We shall answer for them in confession and before God. Why, even Aran here is not beyond dipping his wick at the bawdy-house from time to time, eh, my boy? No sin in it, I tell you.'

Aran smiles weakly and turns to examine the fire-piece more closely, hoping to somehow distance himself from this increasingly difficult exchange. It seems the best policy, although he would dearly love to explore Rosina's comment that he talks stuff. He tries to recall any words that might have given her the impression. At the same time, he feels an exaggerated need to make defence against her father's use of him as some weak excuse for bawdiness. It may indeed be the most natural thing to visit a doxy from time to time, but he would not have Rosina think badly of him through such amusement. Perhaps he shall speak privately with her anon.

'Men are hung for sodomy, father,' says Rosina. 'There is not even a name for the sin that you accuse myself and Elizabeth of committing. Yet you should know that Aran defended my honour in a dispute with Francis Townley this evening.'

Titus seems surprised, looks at Aran with a quizzical expression.

'Well,' says Aran, 'it was more properly the honour of the family that, I trust, was defended, although inadequately, I fear. He had said that your father is now a spent force but then went on to make some observations about general morality within the household.'

She looks disappointed, as though he had somehow let her down, but she does not respond. They hear Maria-Louise in the reception hall, opening the sitting room door, holding it open so that Mudge can shuffle past carrying a lighted taper.

'Please draw the curtains, Mistress Mudge, as soon as the candles are lit. Otherwise the Lane shall think that we are celebrating again. And perhaps we might. La! My husband raised from his sick-bed after so many weeks, and Aran Owen to visit us, both on the same evening.' She crosses the room, carrying a package and taking a thin shawl from her shoulders, uses a corner to dab at her forehead. 'Why, it is still so warm! I am sure that it will storm during the night.' Maria-Louise offers her hand to Aran, who kisses it lightly, bowing towards her as he does so. 'Give you good evening, sir,' she says, but acknowledges Rosina only with a terse nod. 'And you, husband. Feeling well enough to join us, I see. Though your colour yet lacks spirit. Perhaps you might fetch the master his cordial, Mudge, when you are done.'

There is another muttered reply as Mudge finally manages to light the last of the candles, blowing out the taper from the corner of her crooked mouth, so that a spark floats dangerously close to the flowered drapes. She pulls them closed as Titus sees the package in his wife's hand.

'I should prefer a drop of diddle,' he says. 'Yet you should not have been alone on the street at this hour with neither lanthorn nor link. Did O'Farrell not return with you? And what is this? There was post waiting at the Bull's Head?'

'Gin will do you no good,' says Maria-Louise. 'Mudge, the cordial if you please. And fetch tea, perhaps, for Mister Owen. Aran, you should enjoy a cup of chatter-broth?' He thanks her. 'Then we shall have a pot of *Bohea*, Mudge. And please make sure that the water is freshly boiled. Rosina, what ails you?'

'Nothing ails me, Mama. But if I am to be ignored in my own home then I should prefer to return to my music.'

'Then go, girl,' says her mother. Rosina bobs a curtsy in Aran's direction but does not meet his eye, leaves the room without a further word to either of her parents.

'She has apparently been discussing her condition with Aran,' says Titus, shifting to make himself more comfortable.

'A fie upon her!' says Maria-Louise. 'I cannot imagine what Aran must think of her. Nor what you must think of *us*. To allow such an affliction!'

'It is not a matter on which I would permit myself an opinion, in truth,' says Aran, 'since it is beyond my comprehension. Yet it seems harsh to describe her tendencies as affliction. If you shall forgive me, I think she leans more towards some condition of birth, some natural humour, perhaps, that may change with the passage of time.'

'Not while she spends so much time with that Myra! We forbade her, of course, but she is strong-willed. My own daughter, a tribade.'

'You know that my own views coincide with Aran's,' says her husband. 'We need to treat her condition in the correct way. It will become clear in due course, I hope. But the package, my dear. And where is Driscoll? I sent that shambling Irishman to find him.'

'I met O'Farrell at the Bull's Head,' she says, 'but Jacob was not there. Phelim has gone to find him. And this?' She lifts the package. 'It was not at the post-office. A rider met me in the street. An express from Sir Oswald, according to the boy.' She hands the packet to her husband, who turns it, examines the Mosley seal on the reverse, then begs an opener from Aran since it sits in a writing-box near the fire. There is a note, written on a single sheet

165

of carefully folded vellum, as well as a second envelope.

'I do not recognise the seal on this other,' says Titus, then unfolds the single sheet. 'Damn this candle-light. And this scrawl of Mosley's too. Aran, are there spectacles in the writing-box also? I have no real need of them, of course. Yes, those. I thank you.' He wears them self-consciously, looking first to Aran, then to Maria-Louise, though each pretends to notice nothing unusual. Aran, of course, has spent too much time examining the Waste Book and Accompts with Titus to be surprised by his weakening eyesight, and he understands the other man's vanity simply as a matter of pride. 'He says that this other is a letter from John Townley,' Titus continues. 'A meeting to take place at Ancoats Hall in August. The twentieth instant. What day is that, my dear? A Monday, I collect. He begs that I should make every possible effort to attend or, if I am yet indisposed, to send a trustee in my stead. The Townleys again. Lucky that I am not a superstitious man or I should believe that there was devilment at work, eh?' Yet he makes some small sign with his fingers, a ward against ill-fortune. 'A pity that Francis could not be more like his brother,' he says. 'But let us see what Townley Senior has to say. 'Ah, much the same as Mosley. He will be at Ancoats Hall on the twentieth. His journey conducted in the utmost secrecy. Vital that he should speak directly with *our people* in Manchester. Brother has informed him that I am indisposed, suggested that he... Why, the nerve of that cunny-sucker! That fucking lick-spittle! What a bubble he must think me!'

'Husband,' says Maria-Louise, sitting beside him on the sofa and easing him back against the cushions. 'You shall suffer an apoplexy. Please, you must not exert yourself so.'

Titus does, indeed, look gravely ill. All vestige of colour has now drained from his face but his neck seems to have become swollen, assumed a shade of deep crimson. Mudge arrives outside in the reception hall, kicks the door of the sitting room to gain admittance, and Aran opens to find her balancing a silver tray on the palm of her good left hand, using her right wrist to give some extra support. He takes the tray from her, thanks her, receives some admonishment in reply, carries it back into the room to set it down on a small table, mahogany and matching the carving of the settee. Maria-Louise has taken the letter from her husband, who has now lapsed into renewed torpor, his breathing become erratic.

'The cordial, Aran my dear,' she says. 'Would you mind?' Aran takes the glass to Titus, helps him sip a few drops, while Maria-Louise finishes reading. Francis Townley has suggested that, due to her husband's indisposition, he is willing to represent the faction's interests at the meeting. The writer has thanked his brother for those kindly intentions – a further outburst from Titus – yet believes that it would be more apposite for Titus to attend in person if that may be possible.

'Well,' says Aran. 'There is still a full month before the meeting.' He pours a cup of *Bohea* for Maria-Louise and another for himself, hears O'Farrell climbing the outside steps to the house, evidently in company with Jacob Driscoll. Aran wonders if he should make some excuse to leave, but he has left the moment too late. He receives the merest acknowledgement from Driscoll as the man enters and Jacob is at once delighted to see Titus risen from his sick-bed while also concerned to see him in such low humour.

'You heard about the Town Meeting, Jacob?' says Titus, recovering himself anew.

'I did so! Sir Oswald scared witless by t' prospect of militia in town. Callin' for peace and brotherly love, so I understand. With so many scores still to settle. Tha've a plan, sir?'

'My plan is revenge, Jacob. Sweet, throbbing revenge. Some lick-spittle has attacked me. Me *and* mine. Sir Oswald Cunny-Sucker has been pressing Scatterbuck to print up the Meeting's decision in the Journal but I was against the idea. All the same, Aran tells me that Francis Townley agrees with me on this. He has his own game to play, of course. But fuck him. We shall go along with Mosley for the nonce. Tell Scatterbuck he may proceed, Aran. And meanwhile, Jacob, you shall investigate. I still think that Bradley is behind the raid on Blossom's. That poor woman! How shall I ever face her?'

Aran is astonished that Titus should even consider facing her again, given the descriptions that he has received of her mutilated features. At the same time, he notices that Maria-Louise has distanced herself from her husband on the sofa, yet makes no comment on the matter. And, above all, Aran is relieved to find that he no longer needs to admit that he has *already* instructed Scatterbuck to publish.

'There are several matters of honour to defend here,' Titus continues. 'First, we must press ahead with the subscription. I had promised delivery of the Year-End Excise and failed. No, Jacob, no slight upon yourself. There was outside interference for which I had made no allowance. But if we could not deliver the eight thousand guineas to the Cause, I shall not be thwarted in my promise to raise the subscription.' He takes another sip of the cordial. It fortifies him. 'Second, our enterprise, our people, my person, have been subjected to a most villainous attack. It shall not be borne with impunity. You will find the perpetrators, Jacob.'

Panic and fear arise in Aran Owen by equal measure. He wonders whether Jacob Driscoll may be even remotely capable of the task but, remote or otherwise, he feels himself greatly enmeshed and at risk. Besides, there is the planned meeting at Ancoats Hall. Striker's instructions were precise. He should be informed by way of a coded letter, though Aran fails to see how anything useful may come of the intelligence. Impossible for Striker to infiltrate the meeting, he assumes, and a raid on the Hall during the meeting itself unthinkable. Sir Oswald is still Lord of the Manor and none of the likely attendees, with the possible exception of Captain John Townley, could be arraigned for any wrong.

'Third,' says Titus, 'there is young Francis. He has insulted myself and my household. Not once but on multiple occasions. And considers that I am a spent force, so much so that he now believes himself elevated to leadership of the entire Jacobite faction in Manchester. Oh, he *shall* be elevated, in truth, though not as he imagines. Cunny-licker! And, finally, there is the meeting at Ancoats Hall.'

'Meetin', sir?' asks Jacob, and Titus explains the letter from Sir Oswald. Jacob thinks for a moment. 'Well,' he says, ' let's 'ope that tha's fit and well again within t' month. But, if not, I would be 'appy to represent tha'self and t' family interests.'

Titus also takes time to ponder the matter, while O'Farrell pours a second cup of *Bohea* for his mistress, though he offers none to Aran. But as he straightens, his spine groaning painfully to the upright again, he utters a single word into the silence. A word that causes Aran almost to swoon.

'Bradstreet,' he says.

'Your pardon, Phelim,' says Maria-Louise. 'Did you say Bradstreet? Who or what, pray, is Bradstreet?' But O'Farrell simply turns towards Aran, as though awaiting an explanation from that quarter rather than giving one himself.

'You mean Mister Bradstreet from Birmingham?' says Aran. 'Though I believe that he is from Dublin originally. He visited me recently. A possible commission for his business. Why should he concern you, Phelim?' Aran struggles to control himself.

'Fecker says he's from Dublin. But he's Tipperary,' says O'Farrell.

'I am sure that this is an interesting distinction,' says Titus. 'But does it have relevance to this discussion, Phelim? God's Hooks, I *must* seek better servants.'

'Irish stranger, sir. Says Dublin but Tipperary. Something to hide. Day of the attack on your whores. Soldier, too.'

'The day of the attack?' says Aran. 'Why, I suppose that it might have been, though I cannot altogether collect the date. I was in company with Mister Bradstreet and came upon Miss Rosina and O'Farrell in the Market Place. But he is no soldier, Phelim. A purveyor of pastries. Beyond reproach, sir. Such an idea! Such stuff!'

'You see, Phelim?' says Titus. 'A purveyor of pies, man! By Our Lady, how could you think him a soldier?' But O'Farrell simply gives a snort of laughter and shakes his head. 'The very idea. That I should send Jacob to investigate some glorified pie-man.'

'Yet if Miss Rosina was present, sir,' says Driscoll, 'it may be worth askin' 'er for a description. And Mister Owen is such an artist that we might ask 'im to provide us with a likeness perchance. All perfectly innocent, I'm sure. But worth a look if I'm to investigate properly. An' tha' saw one of these

168

coves tha'self, sir, at Mother Blossom's. Tha' just never know. Besides, there's still that 'ackum I encountered at Chat Moss to be accounted for.'

Titus reminds Jacob that it had been dark when they had been so unexpectedly relieved of their prize, that Driscoll had confessed himself temporarily blinded by the flash of the pistol shots, while Titus can recall nothing of the man at Blossom's apart from his over-large Monmouth cap. Weasel features though. Hard. Peculiar smile, too. Yes, he says to O'Farrell. Ask his daughter to join them a moment.

'But you can hardly believe that Mister Bradstreet has any connection to these matters, surely!' says Aran. And he hears the tremor even in his own voice. He feels Titus Redmond's gaze upon him but the eyes are listless again.

'Well,' says Titus. 'I allow that it is unlikely. But we should not forget the fire at Bradley's Terrace neither, Jacob. You are *certain* that we had no part to play?'

'No more than with t' killin' of Sir Peter Leighton, sir. That's where this all started, so far as I can see. It would be interestin' to see whether we could jolt a few memories in Stockport.' Aran recalls Striker's confession of Sir Peter's murder, feels his world collapsing as a web begins to bind. 'But no,' Jacob continues. 'No part by any of our boys in t' fire. Certain of it. Though once Bradley started rumour-mongering about the girls, sir – beggin' tha' pardon, ma'am – we were bloody sore-tempted. By t' Mass we were!'

O'Farrell returns with Rosina, and her father enquires whether she might recall a certain Mister Bradstreet, an acquaintance of Aran's. Yes, she replies, still curt. She remembers him well, thought him a charming fellow. But so far as description goes, he could be almost anybody. A purveyor of pastries – yet, well, one would hardly have assumed him thus from his build. A gentleman prone to a more active trade, she would have assumed. Aran suggests that he travels a great deal but the logic is thin. Her father suggests a military man, perhaps, and she considers the proposition. A possibility, she allows, but too gracious in his comportment.

'The fellow at Blossoms could easily have been a soldier,' says Titus, working hard to recall the cove's features. 'And the sword. Short-bladed unless I am mistook. Yet that Company of Barrell's were all confined to camp. Something does not fit.'

'You cannot imagine, Papa, that Mister Bradstreet could have anything to do with your attack. La! He even presented Aran with a copy of Mister Byrom's shorthand tutor. I am certain that he can be vouchsafed.'

'Indeed, husband,' says Maria-Louise. 'It is understandable that you should seek revenge and protect the family's honour. Yet you clutch the merest piece of straw to think that any associate of Aran's could be responsible.'

'I would assume no such thing,' says Titus. 'But we know that Newcastle has agents everywhere. We know that some, at least, of those who attacked Mistress Blossom were Irish. Diggers and labourers they seemed. So your friend, Bradley, appeared the obvious suspect. Bradley is coward enough for such a deed though not, perhaps, in his character to be quite so obvious. And even somebody as astute as Mister Owen can be duped by a competent trickster. Still, unlikely that one of Newcastle's agents would be distributing Byrom's bloody book! Did the commission ever materialise, Aran?'

'Sir,' Aran replies, 'in truth it did not. Mister Bradstreet left for Birmingham, so far as I am aware, and I have heard no word from him since. I suppose it *may* be possible that he was merely practising upon me, knowing my connection with your business interests, but I can hardly credit such a thing. His familiarity with the pastry trade...'

'Well, 'e should 'ardly sport a label proclaiming 'imself an agent,' says Jacob Driscoll. 'And one thing's certain. There's at least one cold killer out there, and I mean to find 'im.'

'Very well,' says Titus. 'Then here we stand. If Aran vouches for Mister Bradstreet, that is good enough. But a likeness of him may still be helpful.' Aran agrees to produce such a likeness, relieved that his explanations are accepted. 'And Jacob shall investigate as I have suggested,' Titus continues. 'It was a kind suggestion too, Jacob, that you might relieve me of the burden for attending the meeting at Ancoats but I think a preferable plan might be for Maria-Louise to represent me. I am quite sure that I would be recovered sufficiently to travel there in person but it may serve me better to run awhile with Townley's view that I am still spent.'

Maria-Louise makes some protest, claiming that she would make an entirely inadequate envoy but Titus assures her that, from all those around him that he could trust, she is eminently the most able to carry out such a task. And Aran groans inwardly. He can think of no way to avoid informing Striker about the meeting. Images of the consequence from failure to do so play upon him, each worse than the previous. He fears Striker in a way that he would have thought impossible. But it is perfectly feasible that he might now place Maria-Louise in direct danger as a result of executing Striker's requirement. Perhaps he should find some way to dissuade her from this folly. Yet Titus is fatigued, suggests that they might continue the discussion during the coming weeks, and the opportunity is, for the moment, lost.

Rosina returns to the fore-parlour, O'Farrell to his duties, and Jacob to Old Nob's, taking a fond leave of the Redmonds but ignoring Aran. He, too, attempts to take his leave, needing time to consider this latest dilemma, but Titus bids him stay, and Aran fears that he may, after all, have to suffer still further inquisition about Bradstreet. Yet Titus has shifted his considerations to other matters.

'I did not have the chance to thank you, Aran, for the care that you have taken of my commerce,' he says. 'It goes without saying, I trust, that you have my total confidence. Yet we need to impose still further on your abilities, I find. First, my wife cannot attend the meeting at Ancoats Hall in the way that I have proposed.' Aran readily agrees. Yes, he says. He had imagined that Titus had not truly intended such a thing. 'Oh, she *shall* attend,' Titus continues, 'but you will accompany her. No protest, I pray. This is no time for false modesty. An eminently sensible arrangement. You shall be my eyes and ears whilst you, my dear, shall be my voice. And, by the way, as a second matter, I have spoken with Rosina about her condition.' Surprise shows on his wife's face. 'As you heard, Aran's opinion is similar to my own. Though I find myself shocked to say so, she must doubtless have some constitutional disposition towards her current tendencies. In which case, we need to be astute in the way that we deal with the matter. I can think of no better way of repressing those tendencies than by setting her in an entirely distinct situation, one that will place a duty upon her to change her ways, by the Grace of Our Lord. It is time, my dear, that our eldest should be found a husband!'

Chapter Twenty-One

Sir Edward Stanley, Earl of Derby, is late for the appointment, mops rivulets of sweat from his scarlet features, waddles up steps to the stone balcony before the entrance to Newcastle House. He glances back across Lincoln's Inn Fields, receives a salute from the sentries who guard the main door and asks that his compliments should be presented to the Secretary of State. He paces the black and white tiles of the foyer, takes a furtive pinch of snuff, looks up the double staircase, hopes that he will not have to climb even one of the three storeys, and is rewarded by being ushered to a ground floor office. More accurately, it is the private library that serves as an office for Thomas Pelham-Holles, First Duke of Newcastle-under-Lyme.

At fifty-one years of age, Pelham is still distinguished, his features sharp, athletic. His wig is long, full-bodied, his clothes dark and extravagantly expensive.

'Remember' he says to another man, sitting across from his writing desk. 'Credible role. Only one chance at this. Infiltrate them, Striker. Infiltrate. God knows, we have plenty of deserters. Choose one. Choose an identity.'

'I suspect my life may depend upon it,' says the other. 'Thus, so may you. I shall need a Welshman I think.'

'Welshman, yes. Good choice,' says Pelham. 'Ah, Sir Edward. Better late than not at all.' His tone is amicable enough but the censure is clear. The Earl of Derby is hardly accustomed to receiving such treatment and particularly before a stranger. As is usual in such circumstances, the hierarchy of their English class system will not allow Sir Edward to feel resentment towards his superior, so he determines that this other man, this Striker, is somehow responsible for his injured pride and therefore merits his displeasure. 'Mister Striker,' continues Pelham, 'allow me to name His Lordship. Earl of Derby, High Sheriff of Lancashire. Sir Edward, this is Striker. Valued associate.'

Striker rises slowly, bows deeply before Sir Edward, offers his most gracious smile.

'Sir Edward,' he says. 'I am a great admirer, My Lord.'

'Your servant, sir,' replies Sir Edward, but thinks that Striker must be one of the most obsequious coves that it has ever been his misfortune to encounter, then bows in turn to the Secretary of State. 'Your Grace,' he says, and takes the empty seat alongside Striker. He has not always been a great supporter

172

of Pelham, a *protégé* of Sir Robert Walpole, and served under him for more than twenty years until two years previously. Coming of age, in the Year '14, Pelham had become one of the greatest landowners in the kingdom, enjoying enormous patronage in the County of Sussex. He is a Whig, militant in his views. Yet Sir Edward knows him, too, for a man of direct action. He had exercised considerable personal influence in persuading Londoners to accept King George the First's accession to the throne. His own gangs of organised thugs had kept the Jacobite *banditti* off the streets. From that moment, he has pursued them ruthlessly, at one stage arresting and interrogating more than eight hundred people in Middlesex alone, barely escaping with his life when the Jacobites later tried to take reprisals.

Promoted by Walpole, Newcastle had been joined in government by his younger brother Henry Pelham. There is nothing unusual about brothers in politics, of course. The Gracchi, de Witts, Medici, van Montfoorts and Guises are all examples. But the Pelhams, despite sometimes intractable arguments, have survived better than most and they remain firm allies. They are, indeed, survivors for, in the recent General Election, with Walpole's fall from grace, Newcastle has retained his positions, first under the short-lived Lord Wilmington and then again when his brother himself became Prime Minister in '43.

'Striker has unusual talents, Sir Edward,' says Newcastle, rubbing a finger down the long bridge of his nose. 'Careful with his name, too, I collect. We are indeed privileged. But tea, sir? And your journey. Pray tell!'

The journey has been well. Very well indeed, for Sir Edward has a new two-horse chaise built by John Tull of London. He can drive it himself if necessary for it is remarkably easy on the rein. But he normally employs a postillion for ease of long journeys. Insisted on interviewing all of Tull's craftsmen, of course. The wheel-wrights, smiths, painters, carvers, gilders, curriers, and lace-makers. The timbers of the body are dry ash, the panels soft-grained mahogany, the roof and linings of finest deal board. This being its first summer, the panels have been well proven. The seat designed to accommodate his frame and the rabbets on the pillars have been so designed that the glass will never shatter regardless of the road's condition. And the springs, gentlemen! He can hardly tell them! Though there is a disadvantage, naturally, for Elizabeth now insists on accompanying him almost everywhere. And London. Well, the plays, the fashions. He shall return home a pauper. He pictures the chaise, gleaming yellow again now that the dust has been washed from it. Gleaming yellow and sporting the Stanley coat-of-arms. A bend supported by Gryphon and Stag beneath the coronet denoting his rank and bearing the family emblem of an eagle and child. Family motto 'Sans Changer', too, of course.

Newcastle seems to regret the civility of his enquiry now but Striker, while tea is poured and sipped, presses question after question. And

Sir Edward, almost despite himself, finds his opinion of the fellow softening with each response. Yes, he will use his time in London to resolve a minor medical problem. A damn'd bile. Discomfort in the nether regions. He has seen Hall in Manchester. Murchison in Birmingham too. But they have offered little comfort. And now Murchison has suggested some Jew. German Jew. Schomberg. Fenchurch Street. Newcastle has heard of him. Recently converted, he thinks. Striker sympathises. The journey must have been a trial for him. Delays, he imagines. But the only delays incurred when approaching the city. A goose-drive. Must have been ten thousand of the beasts, their feet all tarred and leathered to make the journey. For the rest, it had been plain sailing. Two hundred and twenty miles. The Companion had helped, naturally, showing all of the cross-roads, the milestones and the steep markers. Useful to know when to put on, when to take off again. Just one additional horse for the hills. Changed them frequently. So the Earl and Striker are soon deep within one of those frequent traveller debates about preferred routes and tales of the road.

'Loathe to intervene, gentlemen,' says Newcastle. 'Fear, however, that we must return to the business in hand.' He waves aside the pantomime apologies from both Striker and Sir Edward. 'Lancashire, sir. Mister Striker keeps me abreast. Special duties there.' Sir Edward allows himself to show a hint of surprise, enough to suggest that, as High Sheriff, he might have been informed. Yet he knows better than to challenge openly. In truth, he is more surprised that he has not heard of this Striker through his own network of intelligence. It may not be so sophisticated as Newcastle's but he has a certain pride in its efficacy. Bradley, for example, has never mentioned anybody of this name. He might not like the fellow. Too much the Whig. Comes it too much. But knows a thing or two. 'Yet your own appraisal, Sir Edward. How do things sit?'

'They are generally peaceful, Your Grace. Everywhere but Manchester it seems. You will know that we had a most brutal incident to mark the Old Pretender's birthday. Most brutal. A woman attacked and disfigured. A man killed. A man of God, too, though a Dissenter. And we have nothing to show for all the Constables' investigations.'

'Forgive me, Sir Edward,' says Striker, 'forgive such presumption on my part but it is my understanding that almost the town entire puts the blame for the first of those incidents squarely upon the shoulders of Mister Bradley. Or am I ill-informed?'

'There were a rumour of the sort yet I know Bradley. I cannot admit to liking the fellow but he is prominent in the Court Leet when all is said and done. I must allow that he seems to have motive since he were previously himself the victim of an arson. An act of treason, he says, lays the responsibility with a rival, one of the town's many Jacobites. Thus feels that he is owed compensation, Your Grace. I have set him straight on the matter, naturally.'

174

'Straight,' says Newcastle. 'Yes, quite. Gall of the fellow! So, arson. Mayhem. Murder. Short order. Ineffective Constables. And the Reeve, Sir Edward?'

'There is no evidence against Bradley, Your Grace. And the Reeve is one Jeremiah Bower. The Constables are Robert Hibbert and Bower's brother, Miles. Decent enough fellows but no real skill. The Lord of the Manor gives them little support neither I fear and the town is, well, difficult. Close-wove, you might say. Yet the Constables acquitted themselves well enough on Lady Day.'

'They were taken like conies in a wire, so far as I recall,' says Striker, almost to himself. 'An impudent contradiction, Sir Edward, I am aware. Apologies once more. But I think I may have the advantage of circumstance on my side here. I can assure you that they were trussed, skinned and ready for the pot when I came upon them.'

The Earl of Derby looks upon Striker with fresh eyes. The contradiction has, indeed, stung him, yet this is the fellow who thwarted the raid on the Manchester Excise duty. Another crime still unsolved, of course. Another mark against the town and, therefore, against the whole County. The County for which Sir Edward has certain responsibilities. Striker has pressed himself back against the fine green leather of his chair, smiles at him again. And Sir Edward realises a strange thing, that he is observing the other man's features for the first time since he entered the room, almost as though Striker has lifted a veil from before his face. Oh, he may have observed the smile, at once servile *and* insolent. But he has not observed the eyes. They are small, unrealistically dark, alive with dancing light, but cold light. Sunlight through ice, he thinks.

'Yes, impudent fellow, this Striker,' says Newcastle. 'But useful. Working for me less than a year. Already saved the Crown eight thousand guineas. Colonies before that. Dispenses justice like a Colonial. Professional liar, of course.' Striker acknowledges the compliment. 'Lies for his country, good as any Diplomat. Lies in the name of God, good as any Priest. Lies to send our enemies to their deaths, good as any General. And lies to save his own skin, good as any Politician. Eh, Striker? Eh?'

'Yet no culprits for the crime, Your Grace,' says Sir Edward, pleased that he can contradict both Striker *and* the Duke in his turn. 'Two men allegedly killed at Chat Moss. Yet we found no bodies. Two more taken to Lancaster. Then released without charge. One of them a suicide.'

'But Striker, like Our Lord, moves in mysterious ways. Striker? True?'

'If Your Grace insists,' replies Striker. That smile again. 'But one of them, an ape-like fellow, Driscoll by name, merely awaits retribution.'

Sir Edward is speechless, that the culprit of such a heinous offence should be known yet still at large is beyond comprehension. But the Secretary of State bids him to have patience, urges him to expand upon the situation beyond Manchester. They exchange intelligence about the leading Jacobites in both Preston and Ormschurch, give brief mention of the Townleys. But they return inevitably to discussion of Titus Redmond, his enterprises, the bawdy-house and the death of John Semple. Reverend Mottershead has written to the Secretary of State as a personal matter about the murder of his son-in-law, demands justice.

'I have advised him, Sir Edward. Shall leave no stone unturned. Please convey my wishes to Sir Oswald. I hold him responsible. Lord of the Manor. Constables must find the culprit.'

'Yes, Your Grace. You know that Sir Oswald were persuaded to arrange a Town Meeting, I collect? We hope that matters may settle somewhat, else I have told them that I shall be forced to mobilise the militia.'

'Must confess, Sir Edward. No confidence in Mosley, Runs with the Jacobite crowd. Certain, eh Striker?' Striker is afraid that His Grace may be right. 'And the war, gentlemen. Far from satisfactory. Sardinians thrashed at Casteldelfino!' There is a map of Europe on the wall behind the desk, and Newcastle traces a path to Piedmont. 'Held the French there last October. Fine show. But the Frenchies came back. Prince of Conti. Advanced along the Varaita. Pushed the Savoyards back. Tried a few counter-strokes, of course. All failed. Then get themselves trapped here. Pierrelongue. Not really Casteldelfino at all, truth be told. Thrashed, all the same. Fifteen hundred casualties. Meanwhile, here come the rest of the French and Spanish. Along the Stura. Outflank them. Now sitting pretty as you like. The whole region at their feet!'

'But we will give the Frenchies a taste of their own cordial on the northern front, I dare say,' says the Earl of Derby, receiving another encouraging smile from Striker.

'Kicked them out of Germany last year. Fallen back on Flanders, of course. Poor bloody Flanders. Bone-yard of Europe. Convenient for the French though. Ourselves and the Dutch too. Close to our base in Ostend. And His Royal Highness has promised new troops. Extra five thousand. But that depletes garrisons here. And how to hold it all together, eh? British. Dutch. Germans. Austrians. Need a Marlborough just to keep our *allies* in check. And Wade is no Marlborough!'

'Met him, Your Grace. A great engineer. He spoke once at the Society. A follower of natural philosophy. We may come to owe General Wade a great debt for his military roads in the Highlands perhaps.'

'Will speak of the Highlands in due course, Sir Edward. But even Wade's roads may prove to have a double-edge. Our main concern is Saxe. Eighty thousand Frenchmen. Strung between the Scheldt and the Sambre. Wade has fifty thousand in total. Arrived late for the campaign season. Recruits late too. Then arguments about disposition. End of May before they mustered at Brussels. Sat there like dummies while Saxe took Ypres from under our noses. Now threatens our supply lines. Has all the best options open to him.

Dutch and Austrians cannot bear to forsake any of their darling strongholds. Feet of clay. Admire the Austrians, of course. Never believed that we can win without them. Needed His Majesty's involvement though. Made sure that Wade called a council of war. Determined to bring Saxe to battle. Some of the old fire back in Wade's belly. And we have turned westwards at last. Crossed the Scheldt. Remains to be seen though whether Saxe will allow action to be forced on him. Entrenched now on the Lys. Between Menin and Courtrai. Also asked Lord Stair to intervene. See whether we might turn Saxe's tactics upon himself. March south perhaps. Threaten Picardy. We shall see!'

'You say that our garrisons here are now depleted, Your Grace. A parlous state. I so abhor this unrest. Our country deserves better.' Sir Edward is genuinely distressed. He blames the Whigs, of course, the Pelhams particularly. Obsessed, he thinks, with setting merchant above land-owner, dissenter above the established church, Parliament above Monarch. And where does this lead? Chaos and unrest, sir. And His Majesty himself a captive of these Old Corps Whigs. At least so far as domestic policy is concerned. They keep him diverted, allow him to indulge his Hanoverian and German predilections abroad. Let a Protestant nation be threatened elsewhere – with the exception of Prussia, of course – and George the Second will mount his charger and rush to its defence. He even extends this courtesy to Catholic Habsburgs should they give him the chance. And the Whigs encourage him. Why would they not, if it gives them free hand to insinuate their weak-minded policies at home? And they do not understand even the fundamental, that you cannot endow power and influence on any new element in society without first removing it from another. Have they never studied Machiavelli? Sir Edward can recite it at length. 'Nothing more difficult to take in hand, more perilous to conduct, or more uncertain in its success, than to take the lead in the introduction of a new order of things. Because the innovator has for enemies all those who have done well under the old conditions, and lukewarm defenders in those who may do well under the new. This coolness arises partly from fear of the opponents, who have the laws on their side, and partly from the incredulity of men, who do not readily believe in new things until they have had a long experience of them.' So their opponents gather indeed. Some with justification and others, the Jacobites prime amongst them, without. And the upshot, sir, will be more upheaval. He can feel it. But he does not express these thoughts openly. Indeed, does not need to, for they are arguments well-rehearsed already between Whig and Tory, even 'new' Tories like himself who wish to see some lasting conciliation of the arrangement 'twixt Crown and Parliament.

'And our country, Sir Edward,' says Newcastle, 'shall receive better. Administration will ensure it. Administration must ensure, too, that garrisons are supplemented. Your task as High Sheriff, eh? Lancashire could be prime. Prime, I say. Striker, you agree?'

'I am no military strategist, Your Grace. A humble farmer, gathering my crops of information and garnering them against the coming winter. Careful sowing, of course, in the first place. Noxious weeds to be removed as necessary. But, overall, it has been a productive season.'

Sir Edward considers the extent of Striker's weeding process and several uncomfortable images spring to his mind. 'I believe myself well-acquainted with the situation in Lancashire, Mister Striker,' he says. 'But are you abreast of the situation elsewhere, sir? My associates in Scotland say that the Duke of Perth has been active again. Talks openly of another rising in Scotland, they tell me. Shall we see them marching through Lancashire again, sir? That is my concern.'

'With Your Grace's permission?' says Striker and, receiving acquiescence from his master, he begins to set out some of the latest intelligence or at least, supposes Sir Edward, as much they have agreed to share with him. 'The Duke of Perth,' Striker continues, ' has gone so far as to invite Lord George Murray to lead the Jacobite forces whenever a rising may occur. But Murray is a sensible fellow. Passed the intelligence directly to the Government and has been made Deputy-Sheriff of Perthshire as a reward. So the Duke of Perth has experienced mixed fortunes. Been promised support by the Catholic Clans, of course. And they have established an Association, a Concert, not unlike that which the Duke of Beaufort has organised for England and Wales. Perth himself, of course. His uncle Lord John Drummond of Fairntower. Lord Lovat. Donald Cameron of Lochiel. Lord Linton. And John Murray of Broughton acting as intermediary between the Highlands and the Lowlands, between the Concert itself and the Pretender. More properly with their self-styled Prince, Charles Edward. The French allowed him to stay after the invasion fleet was scattered and your point is well-made, Sir Edward, for he has been badgering King Louis all year, assuring him that England can now be taken without civil war since it is so stripped of soldiers. Truth be told, my colleagues on the French mainland have lost track of him. But he is a rash young man, it seems. Has said that, regardless of all other considerations, he will come next summer, even if he only has a single footman for company.'

'So you see, Sir Edward?' says Newcastle. 'Important intelligence. Precious little standing between our gates and the barbarians saving Striker and a few like him. Yourself too, of course. Confidentiality, sir. Utmost secrecy, else there should be a rout. Panic amongst our people, eh? Militia must be prepared though. Strengthen them, sir, with whatever means at your disposal. Drill them. Drill them again.'

'Of course, Your Grace,' says the Earl of Derby. 'Yet is there no way to prevent a rising? You can rely on my discretion, sir. Naturally. But I must tell you that little of Mister Striker's intelligence was entirely unknown to me. Why, the very streets of Preston and Lancaster scream it daily. Arrest them, sir. Every treasonous dog in the pack.'

'Wish it were so simple!' says Newcastle. 'May be traitors, but not altogether fools. You agree, Striker? Evidence, sir. Evidence. Barely a written communication between them. Informants, of course. Always eager to sell their tattle. But never an affidavit. Never enough to send them to the Tower. Not now. Would never have done for the Tudors, of course. Nor the Stuarts neither, for that matter. More enlightened age, Sir Edward. Law demands it. Evidence, sir. So Striker must sow, gather and garner a little longer. Weeding where necessary, too. Had planned to send him back to the Colonies. A tidy little plan to divert the Frenchies at Louisberg. Will have to wait. Weeding to be done here first, eh?'

But there is something else, and Sir Edward stands on the edge of it. He is close enough to Government to understand the state of the economy. War is crippling the country with debt while the Jacobites – or, rather, the exiled House of Stuart – sits on a mountain of wealth. Silver, of course, so now with little value in England. Yet it finances their Cause to great effect. Some of it to pay directly for foreign support. Some of it converted to finance illicit activities here. Activities such as those conducted by the Redmonds and others like them. Turning Jacobite silver to valuable gold. So, what may be done? Easy, he supposes for Newcastle's network to simply weed out the perpetrators, these small fish at the lower end of the feeding chain. Alternatively, he might allow them to continue a while, then intercept the goods from which their profit is made, the alchemy performed. A third choice. Let them undertake the alchemy itself and merely seize the gold end-product from the upper echelons of the conspiracy when the time is ripe. This would have been Machiavelli's advice, he supposes. 'And money alone, so far from being a means of defence, will only render a prince the more liable to being plundered.' Yet Newcastle himself is, if anything, even more astute than Machiavelli. Oh, he may have a certain reputation for personal profligacy. But in Government? Might he not think of a fourth possibility? That the Jacobite silver, released from the grip of the Stuarts, could be put to work instead for the Hanoverians? Working in the same way, but now releasing revenue for the King? Leave them all in place? The traitors, or at least those who understand the enterprise and can make it function. The thought both appals and attracts the Earl of Derby, though it is mere speculation on his part, of course.

And while he ponders, barely attending to Newcastle or his further praise for Striker's talents, a courier is admitted. A letter, bearing a single letter 'S' and instruction that it should be delivered to the Secretary of State, for the attention of Mister Striker, who duly receives it from the hands of the Duke.

'Important dispatch, Striker?' asks Newcastle. Striker admits the possibility, tears the envelope, then studies the content.

Sir Edward stands, moves uncomfortably to the window, applies the kerchief to his forehead again, catches a glance of the page that Striker is holding. *Damn'dest thing*, he thinks. *Looks like some oriental scribble.*

'A few moments alone, Striker?' says Newcastle, and Sir Edward wonders whether this is an invitation for him to leave.

'No, Your Grace,' says Striker. 'No need whatsoever. And a matter that concerns Sir Edward directly. For it seems that we may no longer have any doubts about Sir Oswald Mosley's loyalties. He is apparently to host a meeting at Ancoats Hall this Monday next. An extremely delicate meeting of the Jacobite *banditti*. It comes a little late. A deliberate act on the part of a hesitant sub-gardener of mine, I fear. Yet he shall account for it in due course. Meanwhile, if I ride like the devil, I may yet be back in time. Occasion for some more weeding, perhaps!'

Chapter Twenty-Two

Sir Oswald Mosley has sent his own chariot to collect Maria-Louise and Aran for the meeting at Ancoats Hall. But Aran is disagreeably late. She does not know what troubles him so in recent weeks but he has become quite another person. Quite another, indeed. And she has needed his counsel on more than one occasion, simply to find it lacking. Apart from all else, while she had always doubted the wisdom of attending in place of Titus, she had initially found the idea more acceptable simply because it would provide such an opportunity for her to share some privacy with Aran himself, for he still ignites considerable passions in her. But then, with each week, self-doubt had multiplied and she had suggested to her husband on more than one occasion that he should consider the matter afresh. Titus had not been for turning however and, worse, he had even berated her for depriving him of a superior source of intelligence since she no longer had any tryst with Bradley.

So far as Maria-Louise herself was concerned, the arrangement seemed perfectly fair. Her husband's condition had prevented him from spending time at the bawdy-house and she, in exchange, had deprived herself of sexual adventures with James. Perfectly reasonable, albeit she doubted that further dalliance would in any case have been possible after their last encounter. It had not allayed her lust for Aran, naturally. In fact, her thirst for him was worse. But on the occasions when she had attempted some privacy with him, some minor intimacy, he had been cool towards her. She had thought to inflame him, perhaps, by sharing her husband's view that she should find some way to resume her relationship with Bradley. And he had laughed at her. La! Laughed at her! The scrub. She had made all manner of allowance for him. Perhaps he, too, was anxious about the meeting though, in truth, there seemed to be little about the event that might be troublesome. Captain Townley returned from France, it seemed, requesting a meeting with Sir Oswald and the presence of Titus too. Her husband had conveyed apologies, promised that Maria-Louise would attend, accompanied by Mister Owen, so that all of the Redmonds' interests might be properly represented. And a curt reply! It had seemed at first that their presence might not be required after all and she had been stung to think that fellow-supporters of the Cause could be so misogynistic they would baulk at the idea of meeting wife, rather than husband. She had reminded herself that this was England and that, in Captain Townley, she was dealing with somebody schooled by French culture – and both England and France were a long way removed from the norms of her native Ireland, whose matriarchal structures were respected and deep-rooted. But, within a short while, a further message had been received, confirming that Sir Oswald would be pleased to receive both herself and Mister Owen, and would dispatch his chariot at the appointed hour.

Yet the appointed hour has now come and gone by almost fifteen minutes. And whilst the chariot stands outside her front door, Aran Owen is still absent. The younger girls are running around the vehicle, naturally comparing its quality with their own more modest but still very serviceable conveyance. They admire the hammercloth hanging from the coachman's seat; the interior twill-woven wool cloth; the Spanish leathers; the fine carving of the red-lacquered footman's standard at the rear; the quality of the whip springs; the deeply waxed ebony panels; and the intricate design of the Mosley family crest.

Maria-Louise calls to Katherine and Maeve, cautioning them that the Lane is still alive with traffic. They should be more careful! And she studies herself in the side-window glass of the chariot for perhaps the tenth time, checking that the black taffeta patch remains secure, high on her left cheek, and adjusting the angle of her cap once more. She is not even sure that she likes the damn'd thing. It is muslin, dressed with a central pleat of red silk in the style of Mademoiselle de Fontanges, but it seems a little *outré* now, and she cannot imagine why she would have chosen to emulate the style of that French strumpet in the first place. It matches the dress though, a favourite sack-back, embroidered red silk with her best lace-trimmed *fichu* tucked under the ribbon bow of the bodice. She has eased the corset as much as she dares and the cane hoops that support her skirts at least allow her a fair amount of freedom. Alluring enough, she thinks, even to disturb Mister Owen from his low humour – if only the fellow would arrive!

Yet here he comes, at last. There are apologies. Excuses. She admires the cut of his suit. Invites Maeve and Katherine to comment also, and their comments are mercifully positive. Plain cloth, of course. Blue. Ornate *appliqué* on edges and pockets though, and the pockets at hip level. Waistcoat plain cream and breeches fastened below the knee. Fine silk stockings. He wears a lace cravat and his powdered wig is tied back with a matching bow. Elegant, she thinks, as he hands her up the steps and into the chariot. Titus has come out of the house, summons his daughters and gives his wife a wave of encouragement as Sir Oswald's footman takes station on the rear platform and the coachman sets them on their journey to Ancoats.

'Your husband seems much recovered,' says Aran, a little stiffly but thankfully without some of the distance that has distinguished their more recent exchanges.

'And yourself too, Mister Owen, if you will forgive the observation.

But yes. He has spoken of you frequently over the past few days though it seems you have vexed him?' She sees his defences rise again and he does not reply. 'Though only a minor matter, I think. He tells me that you teased him with a riddle. Swift, I collect. *I with borrow'd silver shine. What you see is none of mine.* He had considered that it was some covert criticism so was much relieved to know the answer. The moon, of course, is it not?' And she is rewarded by that lustrous smile that has been too long denied her.

'Yes,' he replies. 'Although in truth I had not realised that he did not already know. I told him rather as a reflection of my own condition, rather than his! And reflection is very apt in this sense, for I had received some minor praise – faint praise if truth be told – earlier in the day from Mister Byrom. It must have been three months ago or more. Yet it had occurred to me that any talent that I have been modestly able to display has only been visible due to the beneficence shone upon me by your husband, his family and, mostly, by yourself, ma'am.'

'I agree, of course!' she says, as seriously as she is able, further rewarded by the shock that she seems to have inflicted upon him. 'Yet I am cruelly repaid, it seems. Hardly a kind word between us for longer than I can recall. And then I appraise you of the plight in which my husband has set me – this damn'd business with Bradley – and you have the effrontery, the arrogance, the impudence to laugh at me, sir!' She feels her features, already elfin, diminutive, become even tighter, more pursed, as she confronts him with her most daunting expression. And to her annoyance, he laughs again. Damn the fellow! A scrub indeed.

'Maria-Louise, you astound me, ma'am! When you told me that your husband wanted you to resume with Bradley you could barely contain yourself. Why, if I had troubled to test your cunny again, I fancy I would have found it already damp with anticipation. No, lower your skirts, woman. That was not a proposition and I would not expect much discretion from either Sir Edward's coachman nor his footman neither. I need not remind you that we are not alone. But before you ask me, I assure you again that your *ménage* between husband and lover troubles me not one bit. I may not *understand* it, but it no longer troubles me. For our part, we have a friendship that I value. And if my recent behaviour has seemed boorish then I must beg you to recall that I am, indeed, a foreign rustic with manners to match. But I assure you that it has not been occasioned by any action on your own sweet part, yet rather by my apprehension at this evening's venture.'

She had not realised before, yet his accent changes, the Welsh surfaces, when he becomes animated, and she likes it. Yet she shares his apprehension about the meeting. At least, she assumes so.

'You must tell me, my sweet,' she says. 'Is it apprehension about the possible subject of the meeting that troubles you? For I confess that neither Titus nor myself have yet fathomed any reason to it. And if Captain Townley is involved, shall we perforce be required to suffer the company of Francis also? Or is it that you do not wish to attend at all? Perhaps you should have preferred to accompany my husband rather than myself?'

Aran is turned towards her on the double seat, but his gaze is directed through the window rather than at Maria-Louise, and his eyes are hooded, the brow furrowed with apprehension. She takes his right hand, regards it a moment, then lifts the knuckles to her breast, strokes them against the fabric until she feels her nipple liven beneath. She has his attention once more. The smile returns, though somewhat begrudged, she feels. But he makes no attempt to pull away the hand. Indeed, he spreads his fingers, caresses her gently a moment with the tips.

'I suppose we can all assume that, if the good Captain or Sir Oswald wished to speak with Titus initially, it must relate somehow to his enterprise and its relationship to the Cause but, beyond that, we will discover the detail soon enough. And so far as preference of company is concerned, I must allow that, on this one occasion, I should have preferred that you were somewhere else. It is no good slapping my hand so! A fie upon you, madam. Nor may you ask me to explain. Let us say, simply, that I have a premonition. Some sense that all may not be amicable this evening. You must needs be careful, my dear. We must each be careful.'

'You have some secret, sir? Something of which I should be aware? Perhaps you think that I did not see you deep in conversation with my husband on Saturday, though you spared precious little attention for *me*. It may have been Rosina's birthing day, but to dance around her so! Perfectly foolish. You know quite well that her sapphic passions lead her in a different direction. Or do you think that your Welshman's charms will deter her from further tribady?'

Rosina's birthday had been two days previously. A dismal affair, with a mutual decision that any major celebration would not be appropriate. Simply a few visitors, Jacob Driscoll and Aran Owen included, naturally. Apparently undeterred from their courtship of her. If courtship, indeed, it could be called! A pox on them both. If either had tried a little harder, put some fervour to their suit, perhaps Rosina might not have been so easily infected by the Cooper woman. And the scene, of course. Rosina declaring that she must visit Elizabeth, her father in a rage. It had settled, finally. Only a birthing day, when all is said and done. As good Catholics, they prefer to celebrate Feast Days in any case. All except Titus, who views his Faith so differently. And Rosina's Feast Day falls at the end of the month. *Santa Rosa de Lima*.

Aran has gently, at last, withdrawn his hand. 'I was speaking to your husband on another matter,' he says. 'Though it was, indeed, about Rosina. You will recall the day that we had the discussion about Mister Bradstreet and Titus confided in me that he was considering a match for your daughter.'

'La! Tell me that you did not take him seriously. Oh, I see that you *did*!'

It is absurd, she knows, but she is livid with jealousy. 'I suppose that you consider yourself some knight-errant in this matter. Some *Hidalgo de la Mancha*. My husband dangles doxies before your eyes, then rants about marriage for our daughter, the Myra – and suddenly she is become a Dulcinea! Well, I have told you before, young man. Rosina shall not have you. And what, pray, did my noble husband, my Sancho Panza, make of this generous offer, this noble sacrifice? A fie upon *you*, sir! Nothing now to say?'

The pause before Aran's reply seems eternal.

'He told me that Jacob Driscoll had put the very same proposition to him. That he needed to consider the matter carefully. Forbade me to mention the matter to his daughter, of course. Propriety, I believe he said.'

'Propriety, my arsehole! Jacob Driscoll I might understand for he is a poor dumb Lancastrian beast with slack wits. But *you*, sir! You have intellect. Culture. An artist. You are too young, sirrah, for this *Quijote* Quest.'

'As an artist, madam, it seems that I can do no better than gain admittance to Mister Byrom's Academy as an act of charity, with no subscription to pay. And my only purpose, it seems, is to save him an embarrassment. To complete a picture begun by Devis six years ago. He had only completed the merest outline. Left the rest unfinished. Clayton and his pupils at St Cyprian's Grammar School. Byrom himself under a tree, and his darling Edward on the school steps playing with a top. The most appalling cartoon. Yet I realise that I must undertake the work if I am to establish myself.'

'And you think that Mister Byrom will not credit Devis with the work?' says Maria-Louise. 'You are no great judge of character, I find, Mister Owen.' Yet she sees that the same flaw that drives him to complete the picture for Byrom and likely receive no acknowledgement for its execution is precisely that which drives him to pursue his suit for Rosina, knowing well that the prize will bear no relation to the promise.

'I bow to your superior appreciation of the human state, madam. I must suppose that there is method which eludes me in your passion for that blackguard Bradley. Or in following your husband's instructions as your cock-pimp so that he might be better informed of Bradley's schemes. Or that you still lust after the devil even though he has defamed your family, cast such doubt on the paternity of poor Maeve. Your *daughter*, madam!'

'You presume a great deal, sir! Too much. *Far* too much for one who claims to be untroubled by my relationships. Boorish, indeed. Scrub, indeed. Though these hardly serve. So let me tell you this, Mister Owen. That for all his faults, Mister Bradley is no Bob-Tail. He fucks me like a man, sir. There may be little romance about it but, in the final account, where does romance lead us? To the bed of a man more concerned with his doxies than his wife. Or the bed of a woman more concerned with playing the Game of Flats with another of her own sex. Have a care, Mister Owen! Remember the fate of our ingenious *Hidalgo*, I implore you.'

185

Yet even through the red mist of a battle-rage that would not have disgraced the legendary Cú Chulainn, she sees that his words are more a symptom of his anxiety than any true intent to slight her. And the realisation causes her to consider afresh his *premonition*. Is it possible that he knows more about the meeting than he allows? Could there genuinely be danger here? A silence has fallen between them as the chariot turns north-west into Ancoats Lane. Ten long, frigid minutes until they reach the Hall that stands at the Lane's end. Two storeys, the upper overhanging the ground floor. Tall attics within the high roof-space. The front consists of three gables, a solid square tower, like a keep, in the centre. The grounds sloping down by terraces to the Medlock. A venerable house, the oldest part timber-built. It had passed to Sir Oswald ten years previously, with the death of Lady Bland.

'Please, my dear,' whispers Aran, as Maria-Louise is handed down by the footman. 'Remember to be careful.'

She does not think that he deserves a response, her forgiveness. But she is at once moved by the genuine concern in his voice, now returned to its customary courtesy, and at the same time chilled that he could have been driven to speak to her in that way by whatever fear he is hiding.

But Captain Townley awaits at the top of the stairs leading to the arched stone entrance porch. He may be ten years older than his brother but he has the superior looks, she thinks. Though there is little about Francis with which one would need to compete. Crook-tooth'd, her husband calls him with cruel accuracy. Yet *this* Townley, this Black Musketeer, could be forgiven even his service with the French.

'Give you good evening and welcome, Mistress,' he says, bowing low from the waist and sweeping his right arm almost to the ground. 'And Mister Owen. A pleasure, sir.'

'Give you joy of it, Captain. My husband has spoken of you many times,' says Maria-Louise. 'Yet you find need to sport your blade even in polite company, I see?'

'A soldier's habit, madam. And I find that I have needed it most on those occasions when I might have expected it least. But I can remove it, should it cause you offence.'

She allows that there is no need, so the Captain escorts them into the Great Hall itself and, beyond, to a small room set along a narrow passage. Both Maria-Louise and Aran have each noted considerable activity around a larger salon as they pass through the house and, thus, neither is truly surprised when Townley closes the door and prepares to initiate a discussion between these three alone, having first requested that refreshments be brought.

'Before we begin,' says Maria-Louise, 'you will forgive me if I ask whether we are, in fact, to be graced by the company of Sir Oswald? And I only ask this since, as you will recall, Captain, there was initially some reluctance to meet with myself, rather than my husband.'

'And it was remiss of *me* that I failed to enquire after Mister Redmond's health, madam. I trust that he is at least somewhat improved. A cowardly attack and I only wish that I could have done more to assist him. But there was no intention to slight you personally, I can assure you. Yet you will know that I do not act alone in these matters, and those for whom I speak were simply caught unawares by the discovery that your husband was so badly indisposed.'

'And for whom, precisely, *do* you speak, Captain Townley? So far as I am aware, you serve King Louis.'

'I have the honour, indeed, to serve within the French Household Cavalry, Mistress. Yet I do not act as an envoy here for the French Crown. To speak plain, I am given leave to act on behalf of the True Prince of Wales, His Royal Highness, Prince Charles Edward. I carry significant word on his behalf. A message for your family, since he counts you amongst his most loyal subjects, while the gentlemen who accompany me have a different message for Sir Oswald. There is no slight here, madam. Simply the most efficient manner in which to utilise the short time available to us.'

'It is still the intention of King James to abdicate in favour of the Prince once he has reached London then?'

'Indeed, Mistress. The Declaration still stands, as does the Declaration from King Louis also. If you will forgive me, I was given to understand that this might be a major concern for you. Yet the French Crown is adamant that it has no territorial designs on England. Even now, with the war so far advanced, King Louis has other matters to concern him. I shall not trouble you, ma'am, with matters military. But the position in France just now...'

'La, Captain. You think that I can have no understanding of the situation? A mere woman, of course. And one, you have been warned, who is ill-disposed towards your French masters. Yet we understand the military position well enough. Marshal Saxe and your Frenchmen-in-Arms on the Lys. General Wade scurrying after him across the Scheldt.'

'I apologise again, ma'am. But the situation is more delicate than you could imagine. Madame de Châteauroux has seemingly decided that King Louis should do more to emulate the Sun King himself. Assume direct command of his forces, that manner of thing. So the Duchesse has been campaigning with him, along with her sister, Madame de Lauragais, of course. Their... How shall I put it? Their *adventures* have outraged our troops, to be blunt, and when the King finally removed himself and his companions to Metz, he fell gravely ill, just weeks past. The Bishop of Soissons, a good and honest man, intervened. Refused to administer the Last Rites unless His Majesty should rid himself of his concubines. The King has agreed, the good Bishop has declared His Majesty's penitence and Louis is recovered. A miracle. Queen Marie has joined him at Metz. It is delicate, as I have said, but the simple fact is that King Louis has now lost all interest in the conduct of the war. He has issued broad instructions to Saxe, re-affirmed previous edicts, including the

Declaration, and left his Ministers and Generals to prosecute his will while he, himself, concentrates on his convalescence. I tell you this because, with the King's current state of mind, it is even more unlikely now that any French army will take the field in the Jacobite Cause. And, meanwhile, the Prince has committed himself to a return next summer. Alone if need be. He calls, Mistress, on all his loyal subjects to assist him in this most noble enterprise.'

Maria-Louise must allow that this announcement seems difficult for Captain Townley. He is clearly a man of loyalties, and he has served the French Crown faithfully. So his gentle mockery of King Louis, feigned though it may be, must be designed to win her confidence. And it has served its purpose, she thinks, for her pulse has quickened at the news that the Cause might, at last, be free from foreign manipulation. Free, finally, to fulfil its own destiny.

'If His Royal Highness has forsaken the idea of French participation in our Cause,' says Aran, sharing her appreciation of this excellent news, 'it will be greeted with relief amongst many of his supporters, in Manchester and elsewhere. Though your brother might not agree and neither, I understand, would our friends in Wales.' It is a point well-made but Maria-Louise sees that he remains ill at ease, evidently unhappy from the moment that the door was closed.

'It would be misleading to say that he has forsaken the possibility, Mister Owen, for he knows that without French arms he will be hard-pushed to raise sufficient forces of our own. He has one more chance of funding the army that he needs, and that is really the basis for our meeting. But here is the problem that he faces. He correctly assesses that the endless tide of Whiggish propaganda is finally washing against him. beginning to take effect. These are the things that trouble him. The Whigs have dubbed his father as the *Pretender* because they allege that he was not truly James the Second's son. His Royal Highness, Prince Charles is now styled by them as the *Young* Pretender for much the same reason. They slight his mother for being Polish, despite the nobility of her birth. They cite his paternal grandmother's being Italian, that his great-grandmother was French. Anything to discredit. Anything to pour scorn on his candidature for the throne of England and Scotland. They have the effrontery to criticise his accent when the Hanovers can barely speak English at all! But it is working. Slowly but surely, our sources here inform us that, with the honourable exception of towns like your own, support may be slipping from our grasp.'

Maria-Louise doubts this conclusion though she has long held the view that the Prince's parents might have given him a more equitable start in life had they chosen not to burden Charles Edward Louis John Casimir Silvester Severino Maria Stuart with so many names for the amusement and mirth of his detractors.

'I am sure,' says Aran, 'that our friend, Adam Scatterbuck, would claim credit for countering their propaganda through his *Journal* but I doubt that we achieve much except delivering sermons to the already converted, and Manchester yet remains a town divided. Even amongst our own. And nothing divides us more surely than this issue of French invasion, or assistance, or call it what you may! You say that Prince Charles Edward has not altogether forsaken the possibility of raising a French army but Mister Redmond is unlikely to take the news kindly if you are suggesting that his enterprise must be bent to *that* purpose. Apologies, madam,' he turns to Maria-Louise. 'You can, of course, speak more intimately on your husband's behalf.'

'I see myself as representative of the Redmond *family* interests, Mister Owen. Neither my husband's nor my own. And beyond that the interests of many honest Jacobites. So I tell you this, Captain Townley, that the French Declaration may be helpful. Yet only so far as it goes. We have welcomed that they would have no territorial claim on England or Scotland should they be so inclined as to assist our Cause. But what of political claim? What of financial and mercantile claim? Sovereignty is not a matter of land alone. And we shall put ourselves neither to trouble nor risk in an escape from domination by Hanover simply to find our necks beneath the heel of Bourbon. Yet we understand the dilemma. The Welsh and others will not come out without a professional army at their backs. So be it! Then find *another* army, Captain Townley. Get thee to Connaught, sir, or a hundred other places where regiments may be raised to fight Hanover for faith and freedom, not fortune. Manchester will certainly supply such a regiment. And tell the Welsh this, that for every man they raise within their entire Principality, we shall match them from Manchester town alone!'

She senses that Aran has moved closer to her, protective though still nervous and keeping a respectful distance, while Townley is viewing her with new eyes. The fire of her passion for the Cause, as well as her mistrust for the French, burns bright within her and, she knows, it displays itself plain upon her features. And she understands men well enough too. Sees that the Captain now admires her in an entirely different way.

'I feel that I have been properly scolded, Mistress Redmond, though I would suffer such remonstration daily and gladly from such as yourself,' says Townley. 'And deservedly for I feel that I am guilty of explaining myself poorly. His Royal Highness is absolutely aware that victory will be difficult without considerable professional military support, though as you suggest it need not come necessarily from the French. I will naturally convey your opinions to him. For his own part, he seeks to assure his friends that he will allocate every remaining resource from the House of Stuart to this task. He will chance all on the endeavour, madam. I mentioned this matter to your husband in February. I speak of the Stuart silver, Mistress. Still safely guarded, though arrangements are presently in hand for its return along with Prince Charles Edward himself.'

'We have been efficiently transmuting Stuart silver to gold for a long

189

time, Captain,' says Aran, 'so I yet fail to understand the purpose of the meeting.' *He is anxious to be gone from here*, thinks Maria-Louise. *A fie upon the fellow. Hardly himself at all!*

'It is precisely because of the silver that we needed to meet, Mister Owen,' says Townley. 'For you are correct, and the process of using silver abroad, where silver standards remain prime, to buy tea and sell it for gold in England has worked well. But only by small degrees. Yet His Royal Highness now proposes that all the remaining Stuart treasury should be applied to the task. *All* of it, Mister Owen. And I do not believe that you can have any true concept of the amounts involved. You will each recall the tales that, when Newton held his position at the Royal Mint, he arranged for the recall of all silver coinage then in circulation. He claimed, of course, that this was necessary due to so much of it having been clipped when the coins became worn. But it simply provided a reason to reduce the amount of silver coinage in the economy even more and then, in '17, he went still further and introduced the new monetary standard. It was supposed to recognise the value of silver and gold alike, but in truth it has favoured the latter strongly so that, in the most subtle manner possible, and under the clever guise of Sir Isaac's patriotic efforts, the silver revenue of our exiled Stuarts was de-valued overnight. But, even so, you may be surprised to know that, at current prices, the remaining Stuart silver has a value of almost one million English pounds.'

It is a rare occasion for Maria-Louise, a moment of genuine surprise. She has been raised, naturally, on tales of the coffers with which James the Second had been able to flee the country, and there is frequent speculation about their value. But one million pounds exceeds any calculation that she has ever heard. And if this is the current exchange value, she is readily able to reckon its worth once it has been employed through the commercial and clandestine enterprise that the Cause conducts. Each twelve-month voyage to Canton and back will see a straight return of almost two hundred per cent on each guinea invested in tea whenever this product represents at least two-thirds of the cargo. Careful choice for the remaining third will pay for the voyage itself. So damask, taffeta, Nankeen cloth, silks, sago, rhubarb, mother-of-pearl, lacquers, arrack and porcelain. And she knows that Aran, standing silent beside her, will have reached precisely the same conclusion – or, at least, she hopes that he will have done so if he has finally regained his composure. He should, of course, have arrived at the point by a different route, counting tams of tea against taels of silver, but the result will have been the same, and he may understand the practical difficulties perhaps more sharply than herself.

'If I have this right,' says Aran, 'the Prince has declared his hand, promised to come within the year. Yet his fortune remains hidden abroad and, by the time that it is shipped back here, it will not be possible to organise our normal voyages through the Swedish Company in sufficient time to maximise its value. But I suppose that this will not concern him since silver to a value of one million pounds can still be spent here in England.'

'No, Mister Owen,' says Townley, 'it cannot. Apart from any other consideration, the risks involved in bringing such a cargo safely to these shores and then unloading them without interference, in advance of a rising, are entirely unacceptable. The next consideration for His Royal Highness is then the problem of government beyond any successful accession to the throne. It is highly likely that King George would do everything in his power to strip the country of its assets if we could not prevent his escape to Hanover or some other rat-hole. It would be less than prudent if we failed to ensure a significant sum put aside for the period in which the House of Stuart will need to be established afresh. So here is the plan that we need to discuss with you. First, King Louis has at least agreed to put vessels at the disposal of His Royal Highness to transport the silver for him. It is not widely known but His Holiness the Pope had put his personal bankers at the disposal of King James, and they have cared for the finances most wisely, as you might expect. Second, Prince Charles Edward has agreed with his father that as much as one quarter of the treasury might be allocated to raising the arms and men needed for our venture. Third, a further quarter will be invested through the Swedish Company so that, rather than one voyage per year to the Orient, as at present, they will equip as many as five voyages, for each of the next several years, in a way that will provide revenue for the country and resolve some of the debts accrued by Hanover and the Pelhams in waging their wars against our European friends. Fourth, the remaining half-million will be available to ensure an immediate exchequer for the day-to-day running of the country should the Hanovers, as we all expect, strip the coffers bare before their departure. Until London is taken, this sum will remain within the banking house used by the Swedish Company and be conveyed there from Rome, at the appropriate time, by the French vessels. And such is the extent of this investment that the bank will be prepared to advance a considerable amount in gold for the immediate needs of the Cause. I need not tell you both that this matter is one of utmost secrecy.'

'The Bank of Sweden is a reputable institution,' says Aran, 'and we have dealt with them frequently in the past. Yet I doubt the capacity of the Swedish Company to deliver the number of voyages that you require. The *Götheburg* and the *Friedericus* are certainly suitable for the purpose but beyond that they do not have sufficient vessels.'

'I have to tell you, Mister Owen, that the Company is in the process of commissioning many more vessels, all of them complying with the requirements of the Swedish Government, each outfitted in Sweden and every one of them flying the Swedish flag. And, through the advance that I mentioned, two of the Swedish Indiamen have already set out for Canton. This is not a matter of capacity on the Company's part, though perhaps there *may* be such a problem in relation to the ability of our enterprises in England to deal with the expanded trade that our investments would require. There are two things that we need to know, sir. First, whether there is genuine possibility that the consumption of tea is likely to expand further or, at the least, remain steady. Second – and I mean no offence here, Mistress – whether the Redmond family can maintain its previous level of activity in the trade through Manchester.'

'In short,' says Maria-Louise, 'you want to know whether your brother's account of my husband as a spent force may be accurate?'

'I find myself chastened once again, madam. But Francis is not alone in expressing concerns about Mister Redmond's health and humours. We have many other friends who assist us with our commercial activities yet none on such a level as those in Manchester. So you will understand, Mistress, that His Royal Highness needs to know whether Manchester can continue to meet our needs and, if not, whether we should consider some other with which to contract. We know Mister Owen's abilities, naturally, but I think even he would agree that the enterprise could not be sustained without Titus himself at the helm. I had hoped that a meeting with your husband might allay these fears but now here *you* are in his stead. It is a pure delight to meet you in person, naturally, but you will understand that this does nothing to satisfy our concerns.'

'Your concerns are without foundation, Captain,' says Maria-Louise. 'My husband may not yet have entirely recovered from his attack but he is regaining strength daily, while his faculties are entirely unimpaired, I can assure you. Should you wish to meet him in person, it can be easily arranged.' She knows that Titus will rage when he discovers the importance of the meeting, knows that he will blame everybody but himself for having chosen to absent himself from it, knows that she can barely grasp the extent to which trade expanded on such a scale will impact on the family's situation.

'And so far as scope for expansion is concerned,' says Aran, 'you must know that we are still far short of being able to meet the full demands of our customers. We are now supplying to the legal trade in addition to our former more select group of customers, and demand is growing on all fronts. It is remarkable but true. There seems no limit to the amount of tea that England is able to consume. Let us make profit for the Cause while we may, Captain. And give His Royal Highness joy of it!'

'I am greatly reassured to hear it, sir,' says Townley. 'And there is no need for me to meet your husband, Mistress, though I would have enjoyed the chance to renew my acquaintance with him. I suspect that he had his own reasons for sending such an ambassador in his place. But your own word is better than a bond, and please convey my best wishes to him when you report the details of our discussion. Yet there is one more thing that I must ask you to relay for me. And this also involves my brother. His Royal Highness is anxious that the foul propaganda against his good name should be countered or at least stemmed. In short, as you might say, he is concerned that his name should not become a by-word for unrest and mayhem. He understands that a man like Mister Redmond should be required to suffer neither insult nor injury lightly. And your husband has been practised upon in the most detestable manner. Yet there is only a short time to wait, now, before our New Age begins. It will bring opportunity for all manner of reckoning. So our Prince seeks forbearance on your husband's part, asks that he should do all in his power to ensure that peace, tranquillity and the rule of law should return to the streets of Manchester.'

'You accuse my husband, sir, of inciting unrest and mayhem? It is fortunate for you, Captain, that you face his ambassador and not his person.' Maria-Louise cannot imagine how she will even begin to convey Townley's words to Titus. And what stuff! It was not her husband who had been responsible for the endless investigations, rumour and allegations in the wake of John Semple's death.

'There *is* no accusation, Mistress,' says the Captain. 'And I assure you that there has been no greater embarrassment than my own in having to explain my brother's part in recent events. Fortunately, His Royal Highness has accepted that Francis was not responsible in person, and he has a certain affection for my brother. Yet he has placed him under a strict parole. Declared him accountable, though, from this moment for the actions of the young men who follow him. So far as your husband is concerned, the Prince is simply aware of the influence that he can bring to bear on others. He is respected, madam, at the highest level. And his part shall be rewarded in due course. Amply rewarded. But for the moment, His Royal Highness asks that men like Titus should begin to lay the foundations for our future society. And not in Manchester alone, I assure you. There are bridges to be built, old enmities to be set aside.'

She is still considering the possibilities. An end to the prohibitions against those of their Faith, perhaps. Her husband able to take his place at last amongst the burgesses of the town. A position on the Court Leet. The chance for Manchester to rise and Titus to rise with it. But she starts with alarm when the door to the room is thrust open by a man in similar attire to Townley, while poor Aran seems even more affected, almost ready to swoon.

'*Hélas! Nous sommes défaits,*' shouts the man. '*Il faut s'enfuir.*' We are undone. We have to get away. The Captain's hand moves instinctively to the hilt of his sword and Maria-Louise can see that, beyond the doorway, the passage from the Great Hall is now filled with anxious figures. More French is spoken and one man – she must assume it is a man – is being urged forward, struggling to free himself from an enormous riding cloak with which the others seem determined, although with reverence, to shroud him from prying eyes. And behind them, in the Great Hall itself, Sir Oswald Mosley is on his knees, arms outstretched as though in the grip of divine retribution.

'Mister Owen!' says Captain Townley. 'Sir, you must gather your wits now. My men say that the house is surrounded. Militia throughout the grounds. You must protect this lady for, God help me, I must be gone.'

Aran recovers himself a little, nods weakly at Townley, takes Maria-Louise gently but firmly by the arm.

'Good,' says the Captain. 'And it seems that Sir Oswald too might need some support. You will be questioned, sir, but you must say only that you were here to visit Sir Oswald, a mercantile matter. And by the Mass, get him off his knees, I beg you. For your part, Mistress, it grieves me that our meeting should have ended so abruptly.' His gaze turns towards the passage where his companions are now past this room but can still be heard quite plainly. 'I must help them. A Priest Hole and a hidden passage to Sir Oswald's ice-house on the Medlock bank. You will realise that I have been less than honest with you but I hope you will forgive me. The other meeting, between Sir Oswald and those... those *gentlemen*. It was necessary, I assure you!'

'I understand fully, Captain Townley,' says Maria-Louise, and her thoughts spin quickly between Aran's warning to be careful, his obvious anxiety throughout the meeting, the burden involved in conveying so many tidings to her husband, Townley's courtesy, the image of Sir Oswald still kneeling in silent supplication just beyond the passage, and the unavoidable conclusion about the identity of the Captain's companion. 'You must have no concern for us, sir,' she says, 'and I pray that we may meet again in due course. But, for now, I believe that His Royal Highness requires your immediate service!'

Chapter Twenty-Three

'I will not! Not, not, not!' shouts Rosina Redmond, unable to contain herself despite being upon the street and so obviously attracting the attention of other shoppers.

'I merely suggest that marriage may not be such a bad thing after all,' says Elizabeth Cooper, 'though I now regret even mentioning the matter. It simply seems evident to me that your father would only arrange such a thing through one of his circle, somebody already in his confidence. Somebody who would yet know your nature and therefore expect that completion of the vows would be limited so far as conjugal fulfilment is concerned.'

Rosina has come to recognise those honeyed tones of reason well from Mistress Cooper. She can be so damn'd persuasive. 'And why, pray, do you presume such a thing?' she says.

'La, my dear! It must be obvious. Your father needs the marriage so that he can lend the lie to Bradley's rumours about your tribady. But the rumours are abroad. Thus any man prepared to be a party in permanently dispelling them must also be a party to the plot. One of your father's circle, as I have said. Otherwise, litigation would follow. And the Good Lord knows that there have been sufficient examples of late. Barely a quarter goes by without some fellow taking to the Courts and complaining that his marital contract has been breached. The wife discovered as a sapphist. Evidence is called, though calling it such belittles the entire practise of the Law. Compensation demanded and awarded. The Scold's Bridle, or worse, as punishment for the woman. The broadsheets sated with the scandal. The rumour, presently modest in proportion, would mature to fact, grow beyond the boundaries of this sweet town to national notoriety.'

'That you can speak with such *sang froid* about the proposition astounds me,' says Rosina. 'One might almost imagine that you welcomed the thing.' It wounds her to say so, a morsel difficult to digest, caught somewhere in her gullet. And though she has spoken to wound, praying that Elizabeth might take the chance to dispel the accusation, she sees in her lover's eyes that the morsel may be meat.

'It was an observation, my sweet. Nothing more. Now get us to the milliner and see whether Brimstone has the bonnets that she promised.'

There! That gaiety again which Elizabeth has displayed so many times since Rosina broke the news to her about Titus Redmond's announcement. How can she react so when Rosina's own world has collapsed about her? It must be Mama's fault, she knows. Returned from a meeting at Ancoats Hall with Aran Owen. Full of fantasies about the Royal Prince. But all the other details supported by Aran. Captain Townley's message about a rising within the year. The fine part to be played by their family in the affair. The exhortation for order within the town. And Mama must have twisted and turned this latter point with great skill for father to have drawn the conclusion that *order* must somehow require an end to rumour or a nod towards respectability. A list of declarations had followed, most of them now forgotten by Rosina, 'bating his stated decision, against which he would brook no opposition, that she should marry. Marry! The word had chilled her heart, yet here is Elizabeth still chatting about the latest fashion in hats.

They have several milliners from which to choose, clustered together in Toad Lane, sharing space with various felt-makers, a mercer, a haberdasher and, uncomfortably, a smithy. But Brimstone is Elizabeth's favourite, being the largest of the hatters, her window well-dressed and her shop sign twice the size of the others.

'Is it symbolic, do you think,' whispers Elizabeth as they enter the establishment, 'that Mistress Brimstone's sign should be so large and she so small?' For there is the owner, a dwarf, working her way around the platforms, at the back of each table and display cabinet, setting her on a more equitable level with the half-dozen customers already admiring her goods. Rosina might normally find the comment amusing but not today, and even less so when Brimstone greets Elizabeth with respect yet graces herself merely with a glance of dwarfish disdain. The other customers too. *Give you good morning, Mistress Cooper*, they chorus, but barely the hint of a smile to acknowledge Rosina.

'I cannot believe that your father simply announced his intention in such a way!' says Elizabeth quietly. 'You must tell me more about this meeting between your mother and Sir Oswald. Such a mystery.' She peers into the cabinet with Brimstone's stock of buttons, ribbons and threads, not so extensive as the haberdasher's but adequate enough. 'Ah, you see, Miss Redmond,' loud and theatrical. 'Here are the new satins!' And she approaches the shelving with its bolts of fabric, taking the edge of an especially fine turquoise between thumb and finger.

'Mister Owen,' says Rosina, in hushed tones, 'has subsequently confessed that he heard Papa speak his mind on the issue more than a month ago yet considered that it was merely a momentary outburst. An outburst! The simple cull. And perhaps you can also explain why these women treat me like an outcast, whilst they shower such civility on *you*?'

'I fear you shall tire of me, sweet, if I continue to state the obvious. We share the iniquity of having been subjected to rumour but no more than that.

Your own position in our small society allows folk to take the rumour at its face-value until such time as it may be proved false, that will disappoint them for a short while. My own responsibility for the collection of their quarter-end duties and rents has disposed them to ignore the rumour, at least in public, until such time as it may be proved correct, that will provide them with a means to destroy me, a pleasure that they anticipate silently even as we speak.'

More customers have entered the store and politely enquire who might be last. Rosina waits while Elizabeth confirms that she, in fact, is last in the queue and briefly exchanges a greeting with the Canterbury sisters. She knows that Elizabeth carries an almost obsessive concern about being openly denounced for her tribady, and this is perfectly understandable. But she is still deeply hurt by the knowledge that Elizabeth would see her wedded to a life of misery as a means of retaining her own respectability at the expense of Rosina's happiness. And then there has been this meeting at Ancoats Hall about which she has given Elizabeth the thinnest of details. She had thought to mock her mother for her tale that Prince Charles Edward had also been present, but she has been sworn to secrecy on the matter and, for once, she is happy to comply. *Mama talks stuff, of course,* she thinks, *but this is a conversation that I could not share with Elizabeth in any case. It would be I who should be mocked, and the Cause too.*

She occupies herself with an exploration of the hats, shirts, ruffles, kerchiefs and gown trims that Brimstone has crafted for sale from her merchandise, while Elizabeth asks whether the imported pinners have arrived from Milan. And indeed they have! A large box is produced. Such choice. Such workmanship. But one in particular has caught Elizabeth's eye. The finest lace, she believes, that she has ever seen. The body of the cap in buckram, dressed with the lace, that rises high at the crown almost like a fan, gathered at the top in imitation of an open flower, held intact by a yellow gemstone. A garnet? Yes, a garnet. Unusual. May she try? Yes, of course. So Elizabeth removes her own cap and carefully sets the pinner upon her head. It is large, as modesty demands of a lady in her position, covering most of her flaxen hair. She jests with Brimstone. It would not answer to inflame the passions of gentlemen in the coffee house by a simple failure to cover herself properly. *Hypocrite*, thinks Rosina. But the matter is settled, and Elizabeth sets down four silver shillings and six copper pennies for the bonnet, while Brimstone wraps the cap carefully. They leave the shop and return to the street.

'La! Do you think that the thing was over-priced?' says Elizabeth.

'Oh, hardly any price to pay at all for the maintenance of your modesty, my dear,' Rosina replies, the sarcasm harsh and her humour low.

'I think that *somebody* needs a draught of Sydenham's!' And Rosina can feel her body responding even to this mere suggestion on Elizabeth's part. She has felt herself somehow more anxious, more agitated, more prone to her mother's megrims, whenever she is deprived of the tonic for too long.

'Ah, that has brightened your mood, I see,' Elizabeth continues. 'But it must wait a while, until we have been to the bookshop. Though, since this is your Saint's Day, perhaps you deserve an additional cup. We shall see. And you still owe me a proper account of this mysterious meeting at Ancoats Hall that so encouraged your father to his unexpected conclusion.'

'There is little to tell. And, besides, whenever I speak of the Jacobite Cause it always seems to distance us.' The prospect troubles her for, on more than one occasion, they have quarrelled violently about their political beliefs and Rosina does not relish this at any time, but particularly when it might spoil an otherwise pleasurable day with her lover. Particularly when it might deprive her of the laudanum.

'But on this occasion,' says Elizabeth, 'it seems to concern us each equally. Pray tell! My imagination has been running positively wild. I even imagined that the Young Pretender himself must have been present and instructed your parents that you must be married. La! *Santa Rosina deve essere sposati.*'

'Prince Charles Edward is neither Pretender *nor* Italian, my dear. And, for your information, Mama believes that she did, indeed, see him at Sir Oswald's.' Damn. She had not intended to say that. But it has been dismissed by Elizabeth as swiftly as Rosina herself had scorned the idea. 'And it was the older Townley, the French Captain, who carried the message that a successful Stuart bid for the throne might be imminent. You may discount the possibility as much as you like but I tell you, Elizabeth, that the Jacobites will not be thwarted on this occasion.'

'Oh, I tremble in my bed each night at the mere thought. La, Rosina! Your mother has infected you with her own fantasies, I fear. Yet how did it set with her that this message was conveyed, as you say, by a *French* Captain. She has such a distaste for their entire nation. I wonder that she did not baulk at the thought of their hordes inflicting murder, pillage and rapine across our homeland in the name of your Sacred Stuarts.'

'Ah, but the gleam in Mama's eye as she recounted her conversations with this *particular* French Captain lead me to believe that she found him attractive. If she can be brought to believe that John Townley is a typical specimen of their army, I suspect that her entire view of France may change in good time, though perhaps *after* the rapine rather than before! And so far as Captain Townley's message is concerned, why, I should have expected you to welcome his exhortation that good order might be restored in our town.'

Rosina can read the temptation in Elizabeth to debate the issue further but it is also clear that she has chosen not to do so. Instead, she jests only that here is yet another justification for Rosina to be married but, yes, she agrees, it is a worthy objective even if it should be for entirely inappropriate reason and even if it has taken a servant of King Louis to deliver the ultimatum.

But they are arrived at the establishment of Mister Wilding who greets them on the lane, dressed in his finest, according to his custom, and acting as his own barker. Wilding's is the largest bookshop in town and is generally busy, today being no exception. Books are in high demand and Wilding conducts a brisk business, both here and also through trade by post with respectable customers in the country. He is a close associate of Adam Scatterbuck, naturally, so there is a warm welcome to both Elizabeth *and* Rosina. They make their way inside, steering a path between the stools that Wilding supplies, most of them occupied by ladies and the occasional gentleman sampling the loose sheets from the many unbound volumes that will be finished to order if they find favour with the readers. There are title pages everywhere, fixed to shelves and walls, and advertising the works of Defoe, Congreve, Rowe, Steele, Swift and Dennis.

And there are stacks of second-hand books and dramatic plays too – Galland's translation of the *Nights*, Ockley's translation of Ibn Tufail, Defoe's *Captain Singleton*, Swift's *Modest Proposal*, a Chambers *Cyclopaedia*, Lillo's *London Merchant*, and Penelope Aubin's *Lady Lucy*.

'You see, Rosina,' says Elizabeth. 'The very thing! Eliza Haywood. *Love in Excess.*'

Rosina responds only with an icy stare, knowing that the book deals with the themes of marriage and education, the interplay between each. 'What are you looking for?' she says. 'Not Eliza Haywood I assume.'

'No, indeed, yet you will think that I am still practising upon you if I say that I read some pages of *Pamela* when I was last here. To be honest, it had caused such a commotion that I believe myself deterred from finding anything of value in it. I had attended the various readings at the Exchange, of course, but I could not really understand all the stir until I read the thing itself. Naturally I could not afford a bound copy so promised myself that I should try to find a used edition, if only I can find one in good health.'

'I have a copy myself, at home,' says Rosina. 'You could borrow it. Keep it, should you choose. I have little time for Richardson and soon tired of his device. La! An entire book, two volumes indeed, devoted to the letters of an enslaved serving girl. And such an ending, that her wealthy captor should finally reward her virtue by marriage and an introduction to polite society.'

'Oh, a fie upon it! There is that word *marriage* again. I apologise, yet I think that you do the work little justice, my dear. I am a great convert to Richardson. One of the very few men who has troubled himself to fully understand the female mind. And if you should not mind lending me your copy, I should enjoy it of all things!'

'No,' says Rosina. 'I have a better idea, despite the cruelty you have shown me.' And she calls to Mister Wilding, enquires whether he has a copy of *Pamela* ready for binding. Why, naturally, he replies. Still selling better than any other. He shows her to the unbound stacks, the novel printed entire on three different qualities of paper.

'Oh, the best, of course, sir. This, with the Turkish marbling. And now the binding. Well, Mistress Cooper? Which should you choose?'

She enjoys Elizabeth's confusion for a moment.

'You are ordering a second copy, my dear?' says Elizabeth.

'A gift for your birthday,' Rosina replies, as Wilding raises his hand to his mouth, coughs discreetly against the knuckles, and suggests that he may leave them to their deliberations. Elizabeth protests. It should be Rosina who is receiving gifts, this being her Saint's Day. Not her own birthday for almost a month and, in any case, it is too expensive. But Rosina sees the temptation in her. Nonsense, she says. Call it an early birthday gift, perhaps. And she still has the prize-money from her good fortune at the Kersal Races. So Elizabeth is persuaded to accept and they thumb through the available bindings, settling finally on a natural calf-skin, its borders to be gold-tooled in the French style, and with a marker ribbon of red silk. As it happens, according to Mister Wilding's estimates, Scatterbuck should be able to complete the work within two weeks, a happy coincidence so far as Rosina is concerned since this will chime nicely with Elizabeth's birthing day on the twentieth of next month. They are almost done when she sees that Beppy Byrom has entered the shop. She has not seen Beppy for some months and is unsure of the reception that she might receive since the Byroms are certain to have heard the rumours too. But she calls to her all the same and is pleased to receive an excited and warm greeting in return, although Beppy is positively frigid in her manner towards Elizabeth. She has come, she says, to see whether she might order a copy of Pope's *Dunciad*. Her father has so many of the various editions, of course, but not the final revision of the entire poem. Poor man. At least he completed it before his tragic death. Such a loss.

'Yes,' says Elizabeth, touching the calf-skin again. 'So few Catholic writers of note, I find. Or, at least, few of any quality.'

'Yes, I suppose so. But what are *you* purchasing, Mistress?' Beppy says. 'Oh, Richardson. *Pamela*. Well, I should not have thought you a follower of romantic fictions. But each to their own taste, I suppose.'

'You should not wrinkle your nose so at Richardson,' says Rosina. 'I admire his style greatly. And writing by epistle is not so very different, surely, from the way that we script our journals?' Rosina sees Elizabeth stiffen at the mention of her diary since it still vexes her. She fears that, in the wrong hands, it would provide an irrefutable confession of their sin.

'Then you still maintain one!' says Beppy with delight. 'La! But such an addiction, are they not? And, as it happens, I have been writing a detailed account of thy Mister Owen's visit to the house last night.'

'He is studying shorthand with your father?' asks Rosina, though the question seems foolish as soon as it is spoken. She has a brief image of Aran, the charming Mister Bradstreet, Byrom's shorthand book, and her mother's description of the militia officer who had disrupted the gathering at Ancoats Hall, the cold fury he had displayed at finding only Sir Oswald, Aran and

Mama within his net. And Aran's silence during her mother's account of the incident…

'My dear, why should you think so?' says Beppy. 'Shorthand? No, Papa has commissioned Aran to complete a portrait for him. Rather, for Reverend Clayton, to be exact. Mister Devis had undertaken some initial outline sketches but it shall be Aran Owen who has the honour of finishing.'

And, suddenly, Rosina feels fatigued. Perhaps this mention of Aran Owen again, such an obvious candidate within her father's circle to whom she might be bequeathed. Or perhaps her body's increasing agitation at the imminent prospect of the prophylactic bottle. In either case, she makes her excuses to Beppy, who belatedly recalls that this is her Saint's Day, offers felicitations and a fare thee well.

'That was such a low comment!' says Rosina as they leave Wildings for the short step to the coffee house. 'Catholic writers indeed. You are ungrateful, upon my word, madam.'

'Ungrateful? I did not seek any gift from you, Rosina. Yet it was more than generous. A great kindness. More than I deserve from you. But I cannot abide that strumpet. She is infatuated with you! It is plain as Beppy Byrom herself. La! To remember your Saint's Day. *Thee* and *thou* at every turn. Plain as day I tell you.'

'What stuff! You cannot mean that Beppy is also… Well, I cannot bear to use the word when it has been hurled so disparagingly at myself. But jealousy does not become you and I cannot conceive that you could show such envy at the friendly attentions of another woman yet so willingly see me married to some brute of a man!'

'Exactly the point,' says Elizabeth. 'I should not *wish* to see you married to a man, but at least I would have the benefit of knowing that his affections were not reciprocated. And I hardly think that your father would set you in the clutches of a brute. There can be few possibilities, after all. Aran Owen, perhaps. Jacob Driscoll. Neither would expect anything but the outward pretence of a blissful marriage whilst we, my dear, could continue this happy state without any fear of denunciation. Perhaps your father's proposal is not such a bad one, when all is said and done.'

'Then why do *you* not marry, Elizabeth? It is such a splendid concept, to be sure.'

Rosina's mood remains sour even when they have reached Elizabeth's rooms and each taken a measure of Sydenham's. But it mellows to some extent while Elizabeth is below, ensuring that Crableck is managing properly in her absence, and when she returns it is with news of s surprise.

'I have told Crableck to run to the Swan and ask them to send a carriage, as soon as possible,' says Elizabeth. 'It is such a beautiful day and I do not wish to waste a moment more in argument with you. And you are so very pleasing to the eye, Miss Redmond, with those fiery ringlets piled high in that way. See how they spill around your pretty face!' And she takes Rosina in her arms, kisses her, presses her tongue between those gentle lips. 'But for the rest of your Saint's Day gift, you must wait until later.'

Rosina makes some mewling half-protest but the laudanum has sunk her into complacency through which she observes herself, in some second-person dream, conveyed by the Swan's carriage south to the Pleasure Garden at Old Man Castle. The ruins sit in fields owned by the Mosleys, and Lady Bland had cleared some of the ground within the walls to establish public pathways, with an entrance ticket price of tuppence. She had even organised Midsummer dancing and other entertainments here, though these ended with her death. They are not elaborate but an improvement on those that Sir Holland Egerton had tried to establish at Heaton House on the outskirts of Prestwich. They are certainly not Spring Gardens in London, or Ranelagh Gardens in Liverpool, or Sydney Gardens in Bath. But there are promenades, arbours, flower beds. And all set magnificently within the crumbling walls and turf ramparts of the Roman fortress. A stall near the entrance sells sweet pastries and negus, but this concoction serves only to dull Rosina's senses still further.

It is Thursday, so there are few people in the gardens, and they stroll and chat through the herb patches, edged with low box and filling the air with scent, bee and butterfly, that heady mix of sunlight, heat and background insect aria from a fine English summer afternoon that even Rosina's inebriation cannot fail to appreciate. They stroll but, Rosina notices, with some determination on Elizabeth's part, straight to the far corner of the castle where some hornbeam arches form secluded bowers, each with a stone bench. Still, her cares seem distant now and she sets them aside as, alone in all the world, they kiss again, partially undress each other, slowly appreciating every newly exposed area of warm flesh. They whisper together, words that Rosina would not even have known just six months earlier, and they ask whether *this* is good, whether *that* feels fine. Their kisses, the warm zephyrs of their breath, touch fingers, neck, ear and slender forearm. Their fingers, moving through clothing with the experience of previous encounters, find buttocks, belly, and breast. And they have all the time they need, Elizabeth first straddling Rosina's knee, grinding herself against the hardness of her leg while she reaches down through the younger woman's petticoats, bringing them each quickly to a climax.

They jump in alarm when they fear themselves discovered but collapse in laughter when they realise that it is merely two young men, themselves in search of seclusion, and more afraid than the two women as they hurry off to another spot. But the laughter subsides, by degrees, and Elizabeth becomes more urgent, her lips on Rosina's before moving down her body, pushing her back onto the bench, kneeling before her, brushing her tongue along Rosina's thighs, using her mouth to explore each part, opening her with her fingers, pausing to tell Rosina how very beautiful it looks. And then Elizabeth's tongue is inside her, licking, flicking at the wings of her soul. Wicked tongue. Wicked,

wicked. Rosina feels the waves begin. She can never think of another way to describe them. But they are there, like a series of tiny shocks that build, forcing her to raise her hips against the pressure of Elizabeth's lips as she becomes wet, swells, breathing hard and clasping her hands around the back of her lover's head. The waves build and they finally break. Spasms shake her whole lower body, her legs, and she is spent. But not entirely. For they are both damp now. Hot and damp. Enough to allow each to explore the other with fingers, slowly at first, gently, then cupping fingers around thumb and turning. Slow, upwards, turning. Elizabeth has taught her well, likes to act out some fantasy while they perform. But Rosina can barely hear her. And this time it lasts and lasts. By the Mass, how it lasts!

So how can anything be wrong with this relationship? They lie exhausted on the grass beneath the hornbeams a while, staring up at the clear blue of the August sky, watching the birds dance above them. The lazy hum of bees in the distance. An occasional exchange of comment. A touch of hands. Merriment as they recall the expression on the faces of the two young sodomites. And the slow recollection that Rosina has promised to return home for a Saint's Day supper with her family. But there is no carriage now, so they must walk the half-mile back along the lane, then Deansgate, to town.

'You knew that those bowers were there then?' asks Rosina as her head begins to clear of the Sydenham's and negus but leave in their place a dull ache.

'Why no!' says Elizabeth. 'I saw the trees and simply thought that they might offer some shelter. I had no idea that they would be so commodious. But it was a wonderful afternoon, was it not?'

And Rosina agrees, of course, that it was, indeed. The very finest. Such a time. Wishes that she might never be separated in life from Elizabeth. Wishes all their days could be as sweet as this one. For she does not relish its end, wishes now that she had found the determination to tell Mama that she wanted no part of the Saint's Day supper. But they are near the corner with Market Street Lane, too late for a change of heart, though Rosina has come to a halt at Apsley's, the tobacconist. The window is full of jars, loose tobaccos, as well as pipes in every variety and, of course, trade bills for each popular brand of snuff.

They part at the Commodities Exchange and Rosina crosses to her house. Not the end to their afternoon that she would have wished but she is quickly swept back into the turmoil of family life when O'Farrell opens the front door and is almost knocked aside by her sisters, showering her with congratulations, Maeve pulling at her arm to deliver a small gift, a wooden trinket box that she has decorated herself. Then the fore-parlour where Katherine applies the few chords that she has learned on the harpsichord, an accompaniment for Anna-Marie who performs a song of her own invention, celebrating the slightly lewd adventures of a certain Saint Rosina. They laugh together. Thank Our Lady for the girls, she thinks. She had missed them so badly when they were in Southport. Though how they have grown to their respective ages without suffering any obvious ill-effect from the peculiarities of her parents she will never understand. And such news, they say, since Father Cuthbert has arrived to share supper with them. Rosina's heart sinks, for she is sure that there will be lectures about her failure to attend the makeshift chapel at Roman Entry for Confession.

But the supper passes, after all, without any major discomfort – at least, so far as Rosina is concerned. She suffers slightly from the effects of the Sydenham's and the negus, of course. And she finds herself frequently distracted by images of Elizabeth. Such images!

For her own part, when the priest blesses the meal, Rosina says a small prayer for Anna-Marie, Katherine and Maeve. Poor Maeve, she thinks. The subject of filthy rumour too by that vile man. Bradley's daughter indeed! How dare he? Not a mention of Confession though, as Rosina has feared, but rather an outpouring of woes from the old priest, counter-pointed by the efforts of Maria-Louise to turn the conversation to more pleasant matters. Popery mobs, he says, everywhere except Lancashire doing great damage to the property of Catholics as scare-mongering spreads about the possible return of the Stuarts. How good of him, then, says Maria-Louise, to find time to join them for Rosina's Naming Day. Ah, yes, he remembers. Santa Rosa of Lima. The first person born in the Western Hemisphere to be canonized. Did they know? 1671. He had enquired. Though little time, these days, for study and investigation.

Father Cuthbert finally offers his apologies. An early start on the morrow. So he is escorted below by the whole family. There are farewells and, yes, he can find his way to the rooming house quite adequately. The younger girls are sent to their beds, and Rosina is summoned to join her parents in the sitting room, they ensconced on the walnut settee with the needlework tapestry, she on an occasional chair near the chimney-piece.

'You have been with that woman all day, I expect?' says her mother, but without the ire that she normally reserves for references to Elizabeth, an unaccustomed tremble to her voice.

'I cannot tell you how low I feel when you try to make me express a preference between Jacob and Aran in that way. I love neither of them and you know fine well that I have been with Elizabeth, Mama. We were shopping. I told you before I left the house yet you chose to ignore me.'

'You will not use that tone to your mother, Rosina,' says Titus, tugging left-handed at the right side of his moustache, the creases of his face seeming deeper in the gathering twilight. He seems less than comfortable in his role tonight. 'And I have told you before that *love* is no more than an illusion. Companionship is the thing that makes a marriage. And the ability to harmoniously accommodate each other's bodily functions. It is not *love* that binds people for a lifetime, and you should not trust any cunny-licker who tells you otherwise.'

'Romance is not entirely dead between you then?' says Rosina. 'The intimate discussions about your respective *bodily functions* must be a joy to behold. Yet whether for love or any other purpose, I will not make a choice between Jacob Driscoll and Aran Owen.'

'And nor would we expect such a choice to be made,' says Titus. 'For you need to understand that a decision upon your future must be determined by the circumstances that we face. And due to those circumstances, my dear, you may of course have the ability to fashion your own life in the manner that you choose, but only so far as it can be agreed between yourself and your husband.'

'You mean that I could cuckold him so long as I am discreet, Papa? So long as he is a willing party to the deception? It seems that there is no respect in this house for the sanctity of marriage. And have you discussed the matter with Father Cuthbert?'

'It did not seem relevant,' says Maria-Louise.

La! thinks Rosina. *I have never seen her so distraught.* 'Then I have to assume that you have already discounted a marriage with Jacob since a ceremony within our Faith would then have been obvious. It is Aran Owen then!' She stands and walks towards the door, fighting back tears, fists clenched but, at the same time, recognising that if marriage is indeed inevitable, Aran may be the most amenable of the two possibilities so far as reaching an amicable arrangement might be concerned. Rosina returns to her chair.

'Yes,' says Titus, 'we have indeed discounted poor Jacob, though only with some difficulty on my part.' He turns to his wife. 'By the Mass, your father has much for which to answer that he cursed me so!' He makes a sign of the Cross. 'Fucking lick-spittle. I hope that he is rotting in Hell. But there are things that I needed to consider, Rosina. And your mother's attendance at Ancoats Hall with Aran made their solution clear to me. First, the Subscription that I announced earlier in the year must now proceed with urgency and unhindered for it will answer Captain Townley's concerns that His Royal Highness may have revenue on which he can call almost immediately. Second, the rumours, these vile fucking rumours, must be closed at once, not only for the family's sake but also because their continuance offers a lasting source of conflict that will distract us from our greater purpose. Third, we must all learn now that, when we have struggled so hard to set the Stuarts back on the throne of England, as God has surely ordained, we cannot simply ignore a royal edict when one is issued. And Captain Townley's message cannot have been plainer. Bridges must be built. Wounds healed for the benefit of the common well-being.'

The lion-headed knocker on the front door sounds loud, echoes through the entrance hall. Rosina can hear O'Farrell, but the exchange is indistinct. He is come then, she thinks. Though how Aran Owen might play a part in resolving the various matters that her father has outlined is still difficult to grasp. And her mother's chin has sunk into her bosom.

'Our Lady be praised!' says Titus. 'Just like the cunny-sucker to be late.'

'And was there ever a fourth consideration, Papa? Please tell me that you at least considered the possibility. That from whatever options might have been available to you, Aran Owen seemed to be the one person with whom I could reach an accommodation. Just the slightest chance that some happiness might yet be achievable within this dishonest and ungodly match-making that my dear parents have undertaken?'

She sees her mother's hand go to Papa's arm, tears now rolling freely down her cheeks. 'For pity's sake, Titus,' says Maria-Louise. 'You must tell her! Rosina, you assume too much. We discounted Jacob, yes. But we discounted Aran also.'

There is a gentle rapping at the door, and O'Farrell opens slowly to admit their visitor.

Not Aran Owen, Rosina sees, disbelief strangling her with wracking spasms of revulsion. It is James Bradley, smiling at her lasciviously, sucking at his teeth, and dressed in a suit of green that almost matches the verditer of the walls.

Chapter Twenty-Four

Tarquin the Pig must today perform his civic duty. He is the very stuff of legend, named for the giant who, according to legend itself, once occupied Old Man Castle. It is said that his sire had been brought all the way from Canton with one of the earliest tea cargoes and that, bred with a Lancashire White, this accounts for his offspring's strangely oriental features, the upturned muzzle, short head and almond-shaped eyes. He has been cleaning the streets of Manchester for at least twenty years past and exasperated mothers will often warn their children that, unless their behaviour improves, Old Tarquin will come for them. Indeed, there are tales of families that have left their recently deceased unattended for a while and returned to find the corpse disappeared, the house disturbed, and Tarquin usually somewhere in the vicinity, more heavy-set even than usual. He is not the only pig roaming the streets of the town, but he is unique in having the distinction of belonging officially to the Court Leet, gifted to them from his sire's first litter by a grateful local farmer. Sadly, the remainder were purchased at market by a Keswick man so that the new breed would forever be known as Cumberlands.

Still, if Tarquin can be claimed by any one individual, it would be Sir Oswald as Lord of the Manor. In his absence, the honour would fall to James Bradley, senior member of the Court Leet, and it is Bradley who now supervises Tarquin's handlers in the narrow confines of Acres Court, the passage leading to Acres Field, recently enclosed by new building but retained as a significant open space stretching north from Saint Ann's Church. And retained particularly for the Annual Fair, this strange event that is supposed to celebrate the Feast of Saint Matthew but which Mosley has brought forward to avoid being over-burdened when Michaelmas falls, with its Quarter Day responsibilities at the end of this month, or when the Michaelmas Court Leet meeting occurs, the most important of the year, at the beginning of October. So Sir Oswald insists that the Fair, their Harvest Fair, should be set up each year on the Nineteenth Day of September, and conducted over the following three days, despite, in bad seasons, the harvest often not being ready at this time. Fortunately, '44 has gifted them with an excellent summer, a plentiful and early crop.

First light on this Wednesday morning, the Twentieth of September, therefore shines forth with optimism, giving the signal for Bradley's men to drive Tarquin, whips cracking, through the still darkened Acres Court to the square beyond. They drive him as fast as they are able so that he seems catapulted into the open space, pauses a moment, adjusts his watery eyes to the sudden glare, baulks when the waiting crowd erupts into a raucous cheer as they get first sight of him. Without instruction, the spectators open a passage down the centre of the square, the whips crack once more, and Tarquin is driven forward again, now pelted also with acorns by the townsfolk, his white belly and pendulous ears dragging on the ground. The symbolism is lost in time, of course, the ancient protest against their Lord's imposition of the Fair onto their common grazing land now become a popular spectacle, attracting buyers, sellers and pleasure-seekers from across the County.

And any symbolism is certainly lost on poor Tarquin. Twisting and turning so far as his bulk will allow, jowls shaking, screeching with rage as only a pig is able at each sting of the whip, with each acorn that smacks his hide, he finally reaches the far end of the square, is turned down another alley and, thankfully, finds his duties completed. He will doubtless wander back into the area later, or over the coming days, all insult apparently forgotten, to consume the rubbish left behind by the Fair-goers, but the observant will note a more malicious turn to the pig's eye and tales will be told of the revenge he has taken on the unwary, a vicious bite here, a trodden foot there.

But, meanwhile, Sir Oswald has mounted a wooden podium, a small stage outside Saint Ann's in company with the town's religious leaders. And since the Fair takes place outside his own church, it is the Presbyterian Reverend Hoole who opens with a blessing, though strongly supported of course by his Episcopalian friend, Doctor Clayton.

'God of Mercy,' he shouts, 'you chose a tax collector, Saint Matthew, to share the dignity of the apostles. By his example and prayers help us to follow the path of righteousness, and remain faithful in Your service. Help us also to appreciate the beneficence bestowed upon us at this season by Your grace and favour. We ask this through our Lord, Jesus Christ, your Son, who lives and reigns with you and the Holy Spirit, one God, forever and ever. Amen.'

At the foot of the steps leading to the podium, while the Bellman recites the times of each entertainment to take place during the Fair, Bradley has joined the other members of the Court Leet and the gathered dignitaries of the town. Yet their customary composure is disturbed this year for there are two additions to their ranks – and neither has any right to be present. There are mutterings, muted naturally, but mutterings none the less. Though neither Bradley nor his guests seem especially disturbed.

'Well, the blessing was mercifully short this year, at least,' says Titus.

'Apposite too,' says James Bradley. 'For if the Good Lord could reconcile himself to Saint Matthew, a tax collector, there must *surely* be hope for you and me, sirrah.'

'It is Mistress Cooper who collects the taxes here,' says Aran, 'and

I doubt that even the Lord could bring about a reconciliation to our problem in that direction.'

It had been Aran Owen, in fact, who had first suggested this monstrously public display of the new easing of tensions between Redmond and Bradley, no formal treaty yet, certainly far from harmony, but a truce of sorts. He had been shocked, naturally, when the news had first come to him, though *shock* barely delivers justice to the sentiments that roiled within him. He had not seen Rosina on her Naming Day. He had visited, of course but on discovering that she was spending the day with Elizabeth Cooper he had sunk into ill-humour. He chooses to believe that it was then he had finally surrendered any illusion of a possible future with Rosina, even though he had received the strongest possible inference from Titus that he may be a leading contender in a marriage arranged for his daughter. But the inference had, in any case, been a poisoned chalice. Rosina was a prize to be valued, that much was certain. Yet how much value to a prize awarded solely that the donor might be rid of it? A marriage based on avoiding rumour might breed a cold and solitary state. And all that without the added complication of Rosina's strange inclinations. Oh, he had for a while harboured the popular belief that a woman might be turned from tribady if only the right man could be found for her although, in his depths, the ashes of this belief had long been scattered to the wind. He had, in truth, been angered by Rosina's absence on her Saint's Day and, if he had received the news about she and Bradley at any other time than on the morrow of that anger, it might have been different. But on *that* day, shocked though he may initially have been, his overwhelming sentiment was one of sanctimonious gratification. He may have relented later, softened when she came to him in such distress to seek his help, his advice, though not to a degree that might have prevented Aran from bestowing on her a lecture about loyalty and respect for her father. And barely a recognition on his part that it was perhaps he, rather than Rosina, who might benefit from such a lecture. No recognition that, though hidden behind his pompous sanctimony, there was still a part of him that felt bitter because Titus had not chosen *him* for Rosina's husband.

'It is nothing to concern us,' says Titus. 'My daughter has a mere infatuation with the Cooper woman. She will grow beyond it.'

'I have known Mistress Cooper a long time,' says Bradley. 'And despite any inadvertent culpability on my own part for the notoriety that seems to have attached to her, I am pleased to take your word, sir, that my dear Rosina has not been infected by Elizabeth's enthusiasms. Such an excellent suggestion, too, that we might present the fruits of this *armistice* that we currently enjoy to the people in this way.'

'It serves each of us equally, I think,' says Titus. 'Though I cannot imagine how Sir Edward must view the prospect of an alliance between us. That cunny-licker!'

'Oh, you must not judge Sir Edward too harshly. He is a Tory at heart when all is said and done. The Lord knows that he has been trying to convert me from Whiggery long enough. He may simply see our accord as a step in that direction. In any case, I am not alone in needing some contingency should my current allegiance to the Hanovers come under scrutiny at some point. And even the Earl of Derby cannot have failed to notice how badly goes the Hanovers' war with France.' Badly indeed, thinks Aran. For the English and their allies have tried to outflank Marshal Saxe, moved south to the plains of Lille to threaten French fortified towns there. But then realised that they are without siege artillery. So they have marched north again, preparing their winter quarters even though it is still September. All London is demoralised, they say. Initiative lost and the threat of a French victory more likely. The wheel turning slowly in favour of the Jacobites once more. 'In any case,' Bradley continues, 'I never truly saw the sense in animosity between us. Not from a business viewpoint, at least.'

'Nor any other,' says Titus. It scrupled neither of us that you fucked my wife with such alacrity. Yet we troubled each other so with vanities political and financial.'

And here is the very issue that troubles Aran *almost* more than anything else. That Rosina may be betrothed to an entirely inappropriate suitor might cause some minor disturbance to him, yet he feels that she deserves whatever miseries may ensue simply because she has rejected *him*. But that she should be betrothed to the one man in all Manchester with the capacity to steal the affections of Maria-Louise is a noisome canker that eats his vitals.

'Why, sir,' says Bradley, 'are finance and politics not the themes that cause the world to revolve? For pity's sake, we shall never be remembered nor immortalised for the condition of our marriages. Such things account for little, if anything at all. For what other reason could we so readily have settled our differences than by the simple expedient of my wedding your daughter? And similar examples dominate the pages of our history. It is unthinkable that so many marriages of convenience could have taken place if men of prominence had set any genuine store or value in the matrimonial state. If the price of alliance was land or treasure, any item of meaningful value, you can be assured that the negotiation would have failed!'

'By the Mass, sir,' says Titus, 'I trust that you will not speak thus in the company of Maria-Louise. She believes so devoutly that Rosina's hand is worth a veritable King's Ransom. And you shall pay my daughter the respect that she deserves. I hope we understand each other, Mister Bradley. I hope so indeed.'

'You need have no concern, Titus, I assure you. Ah, God's Hooks, the damn'd fellow has finished at last!' And the Bellman has, indeed, completed his list of announcements, allowing Sir Oswald to finally declare the Fair in session. 'And shall the ladies join us, d'you imagine?' Perhaps later, says Titus, for Maria-Louise has apparently promised to bring the girls in time to see the Harvest Queen crowned at noon. So talk moves to trade as they pass to a nearby stall and partake of mulled wine. Aran is praised for helping to oversee the various threads of the Redmond empire while Titus recovered from his injury. And, no, of course he never truly believed that James could be responsible for the act. No more than Bradley could have believed Titus guilty of arson. But there have been some strange incidents. Driscoll has been set to investigate. And Aran offers his apologies, leaves them to their discussion. On the one hand, he cannot avoid a certain amount of further jealousy arising from Titus seeming recently to have rejected Aran's companionship in favour of Bradley. It is a nonsense, he knows, for Titus is acting a part, evidently shares with Bradley only so much as he absolutely needs. Yet he cannot help feeling somewhat discarded. And, on the other, he does not care to hear more about the investigation since this is the singular matter that concerns him even more than his jealousy of the link between Maria-Louise and Bradley.

He wanders between the boxes, baskets and barrows of those merchants who have paid stallage tolls for the privilege of selling their wares at the Fair, and through the awnings erected by those sufficiently wealthy to pay pickage for the right to set up their tent poles. This is primarily Traders' Day and some of those present are the same that frequent the weekly market. But there are others here with produce direct from harvest and the fruits of their labour over the past month, honey in all its variety, fresh cheeses, hops, seed for the following year's planting, turnips for winter feed, onions and legumes in every colour and size, and the first delicious roast pork of the season. Displays of wheat, barley, flax and mustards, naturally, but also vendors of cloth, leather goods, iron-mongery. And amongst the larger items for sale, seed drills, horse-drawn hoes, Rotherham ploughs, all the mechanical novelty that has done so much to change the face of farming these thirty years past. All the novelty, thinks Aran, against which Maria-Louise has sometimes railed, decrying the way that their development has driven women from equal standing with their menfolk, no longer sharing work upon the land, but now to a subservient role, unable any longer to handle the heavy machinery and therefore consigned to cottage industry, to service, to lower worth, to even worse.

Aran is drawn by the scent of the roasting pork, stops to buy a slice, with a cup of small beer to wash it down, but he casts a careful eye about him as he does so. Since the incident at Ancoats Hall he has frequently had the sense of being followed. Indeed, he has sometimes seen an ill-looking cove in his vicinity, always the same fellow, a man who seems as though his narrow head has been twisted to one side from the mouth upwards. A most particular cove, yet he has never approached too closely and has always slipped away as soon as Aran shows any sign of having noticed him. Some creature of Striker's, he is sure. Yet Striker himself has been nowhere in evidence, not since the evening in question. Captain Townley and his companions had taken themselves to the

Priest Hole and thence, he assumes, to the ice-house and escape. Maria-Louise had played her own part admirably, raising Sir Oswald to his feet and steadying him as the Captain had requested, instructing a manservant to open the door when the militia had come hammering at its timbers. Red uniform coats had filled the Great Hall, firearms at the ready, and Sir Oswald had finally had the presence to demand an explanation. They were led by Striker, of course, now sporting an officer's uniform and a warrant to confirm his authority. Yet Aran could discern from his expression that Striker knew himself foiled, that he was come too late. And he felt the threat from that expression when, after no more than a cursory search, he called off his men, delivered some barbed apology to Sir Oswald, and left. But Maria-Louise had also noticed the exchange between them and had queried Aran about it. His warning to be cautious, too. What had he meant? Not mere premonition, surely. She would have pressed him further, he believed, if she had not been so certain of only recently having stood in the presence of her true sovereign or, at least, the Royal Prince, his son. Thus Aran, far from certain that Townley's companion had indeed *been* Charles Edward, has encouraged her self-deception. It seems to have answered, too, for Titus – whilst having questioned him time and again about the night's events, and particularly his wife's insistence on having seen the Prince – has never once asked about his warning to Maria-Louise.

But Jacob Driscoll and his damn'd investigation! Now, that is another matter. Driscoll had shown particular interest in this militia officer. Clearly informed about the meeting as, of course, everybody else had assumed. Yet the information could have come from a dozen sources. It had been secretive but not entirely clandestine, after all. Then why should it have attracted such a display of force on the part of the militia? Secretive meetings of one sort or another could be uncovered within the County almost every day of the week. So why *this* meeting? Something concerning John Townley, perhaps? Sensitivity about the war in Flanders? Or something else? And there was the description that Maria-Louise had offered. The militia officer. Remarkably similar to Rosina's account of Aran's friend, Mister Bradstreet. Or the fellow at Mother Blossom's in the Monmouth cap, perhaps. A final thing, too. For Titus had written long since to the family of the Dublin man involved in their failed attempt on the Excise duty back in March. He had felt that it was his duty to explain that, though he could offer no certainty, Titus feared that some accident of fate may have befallen their son. He had received no response initially but this was no surprise since the young man had, he recalled, been all but disowned by them. It was therefore a surprise to receive an express from the MacLaines, during August, confirming that whilst they had not the slightest interest in the fate of the boy, their affection for Maria-Louise and her family had prompted them to set all fears at ease, since they had reports, several of them, from acquaintances who had sighted young James in London during the summer. There were other details, about the disreputable nature of his lifestyle and the like, but Driscoll had been especially taken with the idea that, if the Dubliner had been released on Chat Moss, and could be traced, he might yet shed some light on the identity of the mysterious agent who seems to dog them.

Aran fears that the closer Driscoll might come to discovering Striker's identity, the more he himself is likely to be exposed. So he has been driven on so many occasions to confess, and the sooner the better, of course. For would anybody condemn him for the minor information that he may have divulged when he has suffered such duress? But the further he gets from his nightmare at Lancaster, the harder seems a confession.

And, now, the hurdy gurdy beckons, as it does every year. Tomorrow will be Gentlefolk's Day at the Fair, given over largely to entertainment rather than trade, but there is a significant number of jugglers and musicians already performing, and most have gathered around the red-striped tents belonging to the Grotesque Show where the barrel organ player cranks his handle to summon the faithful. Thruppence to enter, the barker tells him. But worth each of them, sir. See the King of Lilliput. See the Horse of Knowledge. See the Two-Headed Albino. See the Invisible Girl – ah, perhaps not, sir. So Aran reaches for his purse, hidden deep against the pickpockets who gather here like flies, and passes across the three pennies, ducking within the flap, letting his eyes adjust to the gloom within and joining a few other *voyeurs*. Through a second opening to a darkened enclosure, suddenly illuminated by lamplight to reveal Gulliver, an impossibly tall Gulliver, a giant who would stand at eight feet or more if he were given the chance, but stretched now upon his back and struggling against a spider's web of cordage thrown about him by a veritable army of minute dwarves and secured to the earth by a score of wooden pegs. The dwarves, male and female alike, some barely clothed, climb upon the giant's legs, dance on his belly, make lewd gestures at the gasping spectators.

The lights go down. Another room. Darkness again. The disembodied voice of a woman presents the Man of Stone, a living Lithophagus. Room Three. Fully lit and occupied by the Horse of Knowledge, a tiny and perfectly formed beast. A Sapient Stallion, claims its handler, standing before a curved hoarding on which are painted each letter of the alphabet and numerals, one to nought. And the audience are invited to test the creature, allowing it to spell chosen words, to guess the speaker's age and sundry other wonders, in each of which the pony succeeds without effort.

In Room Four, an oriental magician creates a Phantasmagoria, arcane symbols set upon the floor and a half-light through which he eventually produces the life-size and almost transparent image of a young woman, the Invisible Girl, of course.

Aran is shaken, almost stumbles into Room Five, for the Two-Headed Albino. The light comes up to reveal a cage in the corner, and within the cage is a boy of perhaps ten years old. He is slumped against the rear bars, moving with feeble gestures, his skin the colour of soured milk. His hair and eyelashes are purest white and his eyes, peering from half-closed lids, are pink. But the child does not possess two eyes. He has four since, from his unnaturally wide shoulders, a monstrous head has sprung. In truth two heads joined at the cheek. Like the others who accompany him, Aran waits for the illusion to reveal itself, for somebody to explain the trickery at play here. Yet they wait in vain until, at last, silent and shocked, somebody ushers them from the tent. What do they expect for thruppence? To stand here all bloody day? There are others waiting to see the show, after all. But they could return in the afternoon if they choose, for there will be more to see. Painted savages. A talking sheep. A living statue.

'You seem pale, Mister Owen,' says Elizabeth Cooper as Aran almost collides with her. 'Was the display not to your taste?'

'Mistress Cooper! Such an aberration I have rarely seen.'

'You are referring to the Grotesque Show, I trust? Perhaps you should sit a while, until you have composed yourself once more. Though I appreciate that you would not wish to do so in *my* company. How was it, now, that you described me to Rosina? Ah, yes. An error of nature, I collect. Then it would be fitting, do you not think, that I should be inside the tent rather than without?'

Aran may be taken aback by the direct nature of Elizabeth's assault upon him, and it is certainly his nature to be polite whenever chance allows, but he is still shaken by the sight to which he has so recently been subjected. He is angered, too, that Rosina should have shared his comments so. They were spoken in private, were they not? There, another reason that Rosina was not worthy of him. Good riddance to her. 'Since you mention it, madam,' says Aran, 'then I must allow that you are correct. I cannot deny believing that your particular predilections disturb me indeed. I do not doubt that they result from some process of nature, but an error none the less, not a part of God's plan.'

'And you went still further, I believe. Some theory that the fault might rest with my father. That he had ill-treated me perhaps. An absence of maternal affection. And a similar situation causing Rosina's own *predilection*, as you call it. Is that your belief, sir? You are something of a philosopher, I find. Though you may find that your views are somewhat outmoded. It is some time now, you must realise, since Plato considered and then dismissed the very views that you have so recently discovered.'

'I have read Plato, Mistress. It was his conclusion, as I recall, that love between two men – and he wrote *only* of men, I think – is almost an ideal state, especially where such desires are encouraged and espoused by the civilisation within which they live. Our *own* civilisation sees its morality a little differently, I find.'

'It is *your* morality that should concern us, Mister Owen, rather than any other. It was *you*, I think, who chose to use my honest establishment as a base from which to organise a theft of the Crown's revenue. Oh, you need not scruple to deny it. Lancaster may have set you at liberty once more yet you remain guilty in the eyes of the Lord, sir. And when dear Rosina was fearful in the face of marriage to James Bradley, she came to you for support, believing that you were her friend. Yet you rejected her like a scrub. She had some notion that you might represent a better prospect. That if you went jointly to her Papa and proposed an alternative, you might collectively overcome Mister Redmond's lack of trust sufficiently to honour you, rather than Bradley, with her hand. Well, I tell you, sir, that Rosina will be infinitely better served in marriage to James Bradley that ever she would be in *your* careless company. Now I give you good morning, Mister Owen!'

And she was gone, Aran still reeling from her words. Could it be true, he wonders, that Rosina had conceived such a plan and that he had denied her the chance to elucidate? This with Titus, too. Mistress Cooper had said that Titus did not *trust* him enough. Yet surely the decision had been made on the basis that Rosina's marriage to Bradley would help create less friction in the town, allow a state in which the Jacobite Cause can more easily be propagated. No, it must have been that Rosina had used the word in a different context, that Elizabeth has simply adopted this to sting him still further. Damn the woman. To preach thus on morality!

He spends the morning touring the rest of the Fair. More trader stalls. Musicians. Jugglers. A theatrical booth preparing for the following day. And a puppet show, until the crowd slowly shifts and comes together again before the church with its temporary podium. In such densely packed conditions, the thieves' work is made easy and the proceedings are frequently interrupted as some other innocent finds that they have become a victim. But Sir Oswald perseveres and, to general acclaim by the citizens of Manchester, their Harvest Queen is paraded through the grounds to a musical accompaniment.

Aran sees Maria-Louise with the three younger girls and makes his way to join them.

'What think you of this year's Earth Mother, Aran?' says Maria-Louise. 'Is she not the most comely girl that they could possibly have found for the honour!' And she is correct, for the young woman's jowls would not have disgraced Old Tarquin. 'Katherine is perfectly green, though they would never have selected a Papist, of course. Yet the Fair has grown tired now. Simply cannot compare with the *Samhain* festivals back home in Ireland. Maeve! Here, stay by Mama. She *will* go wandering off, so.'

'You must not take them to the Grotesque Show this year, neither,' says Aran. 'There is a terrible monstrosity. A boy child. Bloodless. Deathly white. And two heads. No, I swear that it is the truth!'

But the Harvest Queen is now upon the podium, closely followed by other young maidens bearing the Corn Doll. It is fashioned, as always, from the last sheaf of grain to be cut on Sir Oswald's lands, then woven to represent human form and richly decorated with ribbon and flower. It will be paraded continually through the streets throughout the period of the Fair until, on the final day, it will be carried in great procession to Christ's Church, the Collegiate Church, where it will remain in reverence until Harvest Sunday.

So, the Harvest Queen is crowned, and Aran's troubled thoughts return to Rosina.

'I spent some time earlier in company of Mister Bradley and your husband. It seemed so very rare.'

'We must all accustom ourselves to Mister Bradley's company, I collect. Each in our own way. It may seem strange to you, Aran, but I assure you that the thing will be as nothing compared to my own discomfort.'

'And plans for the wedding?' says Aran. 'Shall there be banns read?'

'Titus and Mister Bradley will apply for a licence. It is, at once, both more discreet and more prestigious. A special licence, in this case, due to the differences. Their religions. Their ages. That sort of thing. Five guineas. There must be a bond too, of course, and the amount has still to be settled. But my husband believes that it will be a significant sum, in the circumstances. Yet once it is agreed, a date can be set. In December, naturally. It cannot be a grand affair, but Rosina will not have it so in any case.'

'And she is now resigned to the matter?'

'Her main concern seems to be that the ceremony cannot be sanctified within our own Faith. But Mister Bradley would never agree it. They are settled on almost every other point but this particular. My poor Rosina. It would have been so very different if only...' She touches Aran lightly on the arm and he relives Elizabeth Cooper's outburst. Yes, if only! 'But where *is* that girl? Katherine. Anna-Marie. Have you seen where Maeve has gone?'

She will not be far, Aran assures her. Most likely gone to find her father. He will seek Titus and meet here again shortly. So he searches the stalls, the tents, any that Titus would be likely to frequent. But there is no sign of either Titus nor Maeve. And he is delayed, of course, with each enquiry to those who know Titus best. George Fletcher, the linen draper. William Fowden, the tin man. Abraham Howarth, the joiner. No, they have not seen Titus. But is it true about the wedding? Rosina and that Whiggish fucker, Bradley? They could hardly credit it. Thirty minutes pass, and Aran begins to suspect that Titus may be sufficiently recovered to have renewed his visits to the bawdy-house, though Mother Blossom herself is no longer there. One of the younger harlots seeking to run the place, restore its damaged reputation. But he does not trouble about tarrying, convinced that Maeve will already be united with her mother.

Yet when he reaches the podium, Maria-Louise has still not found the girl. She is distraught, being consoled by Jacob Driscoll who has assured her, he is certain, that Mister Owen will have discovered Maeve at the Puppet Show or such like.

'Tha've searched everywhere?' he says to Aran. 'Th'art sure? Nothin' to fret about, Mistress. She would not 'ave left the Field. She'd need to pass one or other o' the toll booths. A sensible girl too, for all her madcap japes.'

But Maria-Louise is now gripped by that panic which ensues whenever a child is unaccountably missing. It is unlike Maeve, and there are so many strange folk at the Fair! They agree to search again. The two older girls will remain here, in the hope that either Maeve or their father will return. Maria-Louise and Driscoll will search along the west side of the Field, the Deansgate side, while Aran will take the opposite route. To be honest, he has given this side only the most cursory of inspections since it contains most of the craft stalls and food merchants, neither likely to be greatly attractive to the girl. So he now searches more diligently. More enquiries. More delays, until the possibilities are all but exhausted. He stops, turns near a group of clergymen to look back down the length of the Fair towards Saint Ann's.

'Ah, such an elegant sight,' says one of the clergymen, but the voice is familiar. Striker, peering at him with that awful smile from beneath the broad brim of his ecclesiastical black hat, and then back at the church, drawing Aran's gaze like a magnet too. Just thirty years old, the pink sandstone remains fresh and sharp. Six double tiers of round-headed windows return his gaze, and the western end is finished with a tower, tall and square, crowned by a three-stage wooden spire and vane. 'They tell me,' says Striker, 'that the best pews can demand a price of one hundred pounds. And the view from the tower quite the best!' Aran returns his attention to the tower, up past the louvred belfry window to the balustraded parapet, perhaps eighty or a hundred feet above the ground. But what is he looking for? He takes a step forward. A second pace, straining his eyes, for the September sun now frames the building in a bright glow. Somebody at the parapet itself. No, two people. He walks slowly down through the centre of the Fair, fear rising in his gorge. A young woman, he can now discern, a girl. And another clergyman. Is it Lewthwaite, one of the Assistant Curates? It looks very like him. Yet… 'You know, Mister Owen, that I am so *very* disappointed in you,' and he grips Aran's elbow, preventing him from going further.

'Striker!' says Aran. 'Yet I sent you intelligence as you requested. I could not know that Captain Townley and his companions would have an escape planned so well.'

'You have spent too much time with these Manchester dissemblers, I see. You delayed sending that intelligence until the eleventh hour, sir. So late that I could scarce have prevented an escape even had I known that one was planned. And I have asked myself this question a thousand times without a satisfactory answer, for why should such a well-planned escape have even been necessary? For Townley? For whichever *chevaliers* of France had accompanied him? Hardly a catch that would have created any great stir. Do you not agree, Mister Owen? Or am I missing the point?'

So, thinks Aran, *he does not know about the Prince. If, indeed, it was he. But should I tell him?* And his gaze returns to the parapet of the church tower, trepidation gripping his heart.

'I sense,' Striker continues, 'that this is another point in our relationship where tokens must be exchanged. What if I were to promise that the girl should be immediately returned to her mother?'

Aran maintains his silence, for he has played this game with Striker once before. And lost. What does he mean? The spectre of little Maeve hurled down to the square below rushes to meet him, Striker smiling that he had done no more than fulfil his part of the bargain, returned the girl immediately to Marie-Louise. 'No,' he says. 'No tokens. Not this time. Mistress Redmond believes that one of Townley's companions was the Royal Prince, Charles Edward, though I did not see him personally.'

'So the rumours were correct,' says Striker. 'The cub has left his lair. But why risk such an adventure at this time? We know that he plans a rising within the year. So to hazard his plans now! And no tokens, friend Aran? I thought you should have welcomed such an exchange. Ah, but I see. A fie upon you, sir. You do not trust me. Very well, tell me more of this famous meeting and we shall see. You must have gleaned some sense of the Pretender's purpose, even if you were not in his presence. Else why should Townley have required the Redmonds to be present at all?'

He knows already, thinks Aran. *He knows and he baits a trap for me.* 'He needs help with the silver,' he says, simply. 'Now let the girl go, I beg you.'

'Of course! The Vatican silver. And should you truly want my companion to release the child? It can be so easily arranged. The merest signal...' And he begins to raise his arm.

'No, stop!' shouts Aran. 'In the name of God, I have given you the token you sought. Do not toy further with me, nor that hapless child neither.'

'A token? That? I think not, Mister Owen. You have simply returned that which was due to me already. And you will keep me informed, sir, about this Jacobite silver. You need not trouble me with details of the illicit ways in which the Redmonds shall help them to convert the currency. The Redmonds ably assisted by your good self, of course, their Jacobites' apprentice. It is all perfectly predictable. But intelligence of shipment, sirrah. That manner of thing. You will keep me informed or I swear that, next time you cause me disappointment, there will be a death on your hands. Either *that* child or another of the Redmonds' spawn. No, sir. Your token shall be quite different. For I need to know about this other Redmond, the Squire of Llanffynon. He has contact with the Jacobites himself, I collect, in Wales?'

'First, you shall promise that no harm will befall the girl. Swear it!'

'I swear, but you must tell me all you know about Josiah Redmond. And quick about it, for I cannot answer if my associate, the holy Mister Lewthwaite, should be disturbed at his work. He has strict instructions,

I am afraid. Come. Speak.'

So Aran tells Striker about the letter he had received from old Josiah, the news of the approach made to him by the Rector of Hawarden, Richard Williams. But the Squire will have no involvement with the Jacobite Cause, Aran stresses. None whatsoever. He carefully explains Josiah's antipathy towards the entire matter. Striker says that he understands, simply needs the intelligence to confirm that they have nothing to fear from the older Redmond. Yet this about Williams is useful. It will help. Aye, another Minister of the Church, thinks Aran. This disguise of Striker's, too. Was this the same black garb that he wore to murder Sir Peter Leighton? But, as Striker relishes the information about Llanffynon, he lifts his left arm high to signal the tower, Aran has a different question. 'Is it truly necessary to have me followed?' he asks.

'Why, bless you, friend Aran! Not necessary in the slightest. For I know exactly how to find you at any time. What purpose would it serve to waste good money having you followed. La! How amusing.'

And suddenly he is gone, leaving Aran to wonder whether it has now been Striker's turn to dissemble. Perhaps, after all, Aran has been mistaken, that the cove he has seen so many times may not have been following him as he had believed. But he hurries back towards Saint Ann's, to find mother and daughter already reunited, Maeve being soundly scolded for her trouble while protesting that she had been perfectly safe and in company with Mister Lewthwaite all the time. He had shown her the church. Shown her the whole Fair laid out below them from the tower.

Driscoll, too, is relieved to see the girl safely back with her mother, but he is angered at the news of Rosina's forthcoming marriage, demanding to know why he might not have been eligible as her husband. Has he not worked faithfully for the family all these years?

Maria-Louise attempts to pacify him. He should speak with Titus on the matter, she suggests, but Jacob should know that there was little choice in the matter. They are all subject to a higher authority here, instructed by royal decree to find any means possible to bring an end to the unrest that has plagued the town. Does he think that the matter is easy for *her*? Rosina's mother? Yet they have one aim now. All of them. Think of it, Jacob. The return, finally, of the Stuart line. An end to all the injustices that they have suffered as Roman Catholics. The sacrifice is unthinkable but necessary. And made more so by the mischief stirred up in their town. Find the perpetrator of that mischief, Jacob, and vent your anger on that creature. Is that not the point of his investigation?

And Lewthwaite himself arrives on the scene. An unlikely associate for Striker, thinks Aran. No true agent, surely, but under Striker's control, to be sure. Frightened too, as Maria-Louise berates him for his irresponsibility, his failure to take the obvious step of informing before taking the girl off on some escapade. Though she supposes that he intended no harm. Of course not, madam, he agrees. Apologies, naturally.

But Maria-Louise regards him quizzically as he leaves them. 'You know, Aran,' she says, 'that Lewthwaite has always seemed a man so much at peace with himself. Yet now, why, he wears the same haunted expression that I have seen so many times on your own face.'

Chapter Twenty-Five

The condums still flutter at the bawdy-house windows though Mother Blossom is no longer there to oversee the business. Susannah Cole has been given that responsibility, the four-shilling piece who may now be past her prime but who, as Titus has discovered, has fulfilled her reputation wonderfully. By the Mass, how she had helped him recover! But she has brought him problems too. For one thing, she lacks Blossom's skills in maintaining equanimity amongst the drabs for, despite the pleasurable natures that they display for customers, they are a wicked bunch of bitches when left to their own devices. And Susannah's manner of dealing with their individuality relies too much on either putting the most unruly on the street or plying them with ever greater quantities of laudanum and geneva, each solution costly in its different way. And Titus can scarce afford the additional expense, for trade has fallen noticeably since the attack.

But the latest problem which Susannah has created is her insistence that she should have her own Flash-Man. Oh, George Blossom may have served well enough as the establishment's cock-pimp in his day, but she needs somebody younger and, of course, she knows the very fellow. And George? Well, he had been little enough use to his own wife, let alone the other doxies, when push had come to shove. Why, the blind fiddler had shown more spirit! Yet Titus, knowing that she is correct, cannot quite bring himself to dispense so readily with the Blossoms. Bad enough that he had to insist on Mother Blossom leaving the place but the Lord knows that she is healing badly. She could easily have taken her place amongst the Fair's Grotesques, so disfigured that the children might have employed her to ward off Stingy Jack on All Hallows' Eve. It has thus been a matter of minor charity to assist her with a few guineas, helping her repair to one of the hovels near the Irk, her fortune lost in the robbery. It might have been a fortune stolen from Titus in the first place, but business is business. You have to expect and allow for these things.

'So, George!' he says. 'Sit down, I beg, and tell me what grieves you.'

George Blossom resembles a pug, his eyes just too large for his small, wrinkled head, his snout flattened through the damage inflicted by the strong-box, and his cheeks, chin and mouth darkened by a perpetual black stubble. He barks, too, in staccato bursts, yapping at those around him through lips and teeth also irredeemably ravaged in the attack. 'Which it won't answer,

221

sir,' says George, turning his felt hat between his hands and accepting the chair that Jacob Driscoll has so recently vacated in his favour. 'Which it won't answer at all. My wife an' me now in that evil-smellin' place. An' this doxy which you 'as made madam, sir. Wants me out. She does so. Billy Bender, she says. Wants 'im for 'er Flash-Man, sir. No mistake. An' what for, eh? Which she 'as no need for a Flash-Man, sir. I can still do my job.'

As it happens, they both agree with him. Bender is one of the town's worst rogues and Titus would not see the cove within a hundred yards of the bawdy-house. But neither Titus nor Jacob say so.

'I will speak with Mistress Cole, George, have no fear,' says Titus. 'Now be about your business and make sure that there is gin a-plenty for tonight.' Blossom tries to make some further protest but Driscoll has ushered him through the door before he can complete another half-formed sentence. 'So, Jacob, you were saying about these Manxmen of yours?'

The salon outside is, it seems, full of the fellows. A good boost for the bawdy-house at least, whenever the *Swift* is in port. And the skipper, Angus Christian, has developed his trade well. He had begun by shipping cargoes of foreign goods on behalf of Manx merchants from England to the island. Since the price of these goods included the import duties levied on them when they were first brought to Britain, and since the island was exempt from such duties, the merchants were entitled to reclaim that portion of the cost that equated to the tax. Once that was done, Christian would accommodate the merchants by shipping the same goods back to the English coast where they would sell for a tidy profit. But Christian had been amongst the first to realise that the process was more efficient if the merchants simply arranged for the goods to be shipped direct to the island in the first place and later smuggled straight into England. Hence, the Swedish East India Company delivered tea and other free-trade commodities to the island so that Angus Christian, amongst others, could deliver them onwards to their respective networks of buyers like Titus Redmond.

'Christian brings a message, sir. A strange one,' says Driscoll.

How very dramatic, thinks Titus. 'And will you share it with me, pray? Fie, Jacob, it is not like you to be so mysterious. Perhaps we should bring the cunny-licker hence and hear it from his own lips.'

Driscoll agrees that this might be best and leaves Titus alone while he goes to find the Manx skipper.

'Likely up to his balls in one of my doxies by now,' says Titus Redmond as Driscoll leaves, and he wonders what message can possibly have been entrusted to Christian. Like most of his breed, the skipper fancies that he might have been able to fashion a more handsome living, an honest one as he puts it, were it not for the all these bad folk from beyond the island, Liverpool and Manchester merchants, Irish bankrupts, fugitives and the like, who had lured the decent people of Mannin to their disreputable trades. But the skipper is affable enough when he enters, moments later, carrying a rolled chart, adjusting his dress, and offering Titus a rare smile.

'Give you good afternoon, Captain,' says Titus, rising from the couch, bowing politely and offering him the chair near the lacquered cabinet. 'I trust that the seas were not unkind to you. Such winds, these days past.'

'Middlin', I thank thee. Nothin' that'd stop the *Swift*, that's certain. An' you, boy? All better now, I see, though not yet caught the jiggler as laid you low, I gather.'

'Our good friend Driscoll is working on the matter, sir. We will find the lick-spittle, never fear. But he tells me that you have received news that may be of interest?'

Christian looks to Jacob, who responds only with the briefest nod of his head, long arms folded across his chest in the customary fashion. Yet they both seem uncomfortable, Titus thinks.

'Aye,' says the Captain. 'Picked up some skeet in Douglas two weeks done. French privateer in the bay, bold as brass. 'E 'as some neck, I thought, when I sees 'im. Put a boat ashore an' all. Feller finds me an' says he speaks for some'n called Townley.'

'Captain John Townley?' says Titus. 'Why in the name of Our Lady should Townley send a message to the island? No offence to yourself, Captain Christian, but we have our own lines of communication with Townley. Is he in trouble?'

'I don't offend easy, boy. Not easy at all. An' I cannot answer for 'em. Just promised to pass on the skeet when next I saw thee. But this feller says you'll understand. After last time, 'e says. An' they need a gatherin' to talk about a special delivery in the spring or summer. Somewhere a bit more private, that was 'is words. An' asked 'specially for friend Driscoll 'ere. To be at the gatherin'. Says that a skutch of us need to come across too, bringin' some Frenchie with us. Sounds like a big'n, though I'd not trouble to ask what it might be.'

Titus studies the Manxman a moment. Then Driscoll too. He has discussed the Ancoats Hall meeting with Jacob, naturally. It had been essential simply because the smugglers would be vital to their success in safely bringing ashore whatever portion of the Jacobite treasury might be allotted here, to Manchester. But the operation must surely be some time away and he is surprised that they have received news so soon and in such an unaccustomed fashion.

'Is there more, Captain?' he asks. 'Do we have a date, a time, a location for this gathering?'

'That's all that's in, boy, just about. But, aye, we know the wheres and whens. If I may...?' He gestures for permission to join Titus on the settee and spreads the chart across his knees. It details the familiar outline of the North West coast, and the Captain's finger traces a line down into the Mersey

223

Estuary, across the many soundings, to a point on the rugged coast of the peninsula that separates Mersey from Dee. The peninsula seems like familiar territory to Titus since, while he has never been there, he has seen it laid out before him from the hills at Llanffynon on those rare occasions when he has visited his brother's Flintshire home.

'Here,' says the Captain. 'We've got a good little place at us. Just up from the rock. An' we must just pray for decent weather, for they've chosen a rare date to gather. December, boy. Little more than a se'nnight afore Christmas-tide. The fifteenth or as near as we can get.'

'The date of my daughter's wedding,' says Titus. 'And what? Five weeks hence? Are you certain this was the date they set? Well, sir, it is damn'd inconvenient.' Christian makes a small movement with his chin, indicating that the matter is beyond his control but, at the same time, Titus sees that the fellow's eyes meet those of Jacob Driscoll. 'Fucking cunny-suckers!' he says, to nobody in particular, but he gestures for Driscoll to proceed. So details are taken of the meeting place, signals to be given in the event of danger, steps to be taken if the weather turns too foul for the crossing to be made, and when all is done, Christian begs leave to return to his drab. Titus thanks him, leads him to the door and wishes him well of the doxy. But there is something about this that makes Titus uneasy.

'Convenient for *you* though, Jacob! That you shall not now be able to attend Rosina's wedding. For I assume that you are willing to make this journey? To attend this mysterious gathering?' he says when they are alone once more. 'Though I must allow that this hardly seems like any enterprise that Captain Townley might have planned.'

'I don't expect anybody to mind my absence, beggin' your pardon. I should 'ardly 'ave felt any comfort from t' occasion. It better suits my position to be an agent for t' family, sir, than a part of it, when all is said an' done. Mysterious it may be, but what else might we expect from the French?'

By the Mass, thinks Titus, *how long will Driscoll bear this grievance?* For Jacob rarely allows a meeting between them to pass without some reference to his hurt that the Redmonds should have chosen Bradley rather than himself. And no amount of discussion about the reason, the logic, the difficulty of the situation has helped to assuage Driscoll's bitterness.

'Yet I should add a further burden to you, Jacob, since it would be useful if Mister Owen should join you. Once the silver eventually arrives, it will be Aran's part to ensure that profits are turned quickly from it.'

A snort of derision from Driscoll. 'Should you choose to 'ave Mister Owen, sir, it is no concern o' mine. But I shall travel alone. 'E shall 'ave none o' my company. Not until I know that 'e can be trusted.'

'You will trust Aran Owen, Jacob, until I tell you otherwise or until this damn'd investigation that you have undertaken is complete. Yet how long must we wait? Your associates in London have not been able to locate

MacLaine. Though, even if he lives, and I am doubtful of it, I do not see what he might add to our knowledge. Another description that leads us nowhere, perhaps? And I still do not understand how Mister Owen is implicated in any of this.' But, of course, Titus understands very well. He had discounted all Jacob's preoccupation with the Birmingham fellow that Rosina had met in company with Aran, this despite Phelim O'Farrell having sensed something amiss with the cove. And O'Farrell's senses are rarely wrong. Yet he cannot entirely ignore the strange circumstance of the meeting at Ancoats Hall. Maria-Louise had recounted the events most carefully for him, including the warning that Aran had given her to be careful. Could he have known that the meeting would be disrupted? And, if so, how? Aran had been badly used in Lancaster Gaol, of course. But could there be some association between these things? If so, he wonders whether he might best keep word of Captain Christian's news to himself. But, naturally, this is impossible. He hopes that he is mistaken, and particularly since Aran's efforts on behalf of the family seem to increase with each month that passes. The new Fly Wagon routes, the picking system at the warehouses, their encroachment into the more legitimate tea trade. All goes well. And the fustian trade too, expanding rapidly through a significantly better local supply chain for ticking, tapes, filleting and linen cloth. Even the *Journal* is beginning to show some modest return on their investment. Everything running smoothly excepting the bawdy-house and the geneva consumption, but neither of these problems can be laid at Aran Owen's feet. So it is unthinkable that he should deny Aran knowledge of the gathering and its possible implications for the business.

'Well, we shall see!' says Driscoll. 'But I tell you this, sir. That all my enquiries in Birmingham 'ave turned up no purveyor of pastries named Bradstreet. Not a one. An' if we can find t' Dubliner, why, it is still possible that 'e can tell us somethin' to our advantage. But until I know one way or the other, sir, I prefer to reserve my judgement on Mister Owen. Yet I shall not brook his interference with my associates.'

'Christian and his coves are a rare breed, I will grant you that, Jacob. It would not answer if they should be made uneasy by the presence of anybody other than yourself. Very well, you shall go alone. And Our Lady speed you back to us for the festive season. In any case, I suspect that Mister Owen, at least, might want to dance at my daughter's wedding. Not that he is lacking a certain disappointment himself, mind, in that direction. Yet so far as your investigation is concerned, it has occurred to me that there might be some slight possibility of expediting matters. I had forgotten that Byrom is so well connected in London. Perhaps not so well as when he was supposed to be fucking old Queen Caroline, and I cannot abide the lick-spittle, but he may be useful. I have arranged to speak with him later though and, as you say, we shall see! I have a strange day ahead of me, to be sure.'

Strange indeed, and his visit to the Byrom household not the least of it.

Titus may be the owner of one of Manchester's finest houses, but he is not beyond some envy in relation to Byrom's palatial home on Hanging Ditch. Its thirty rooms exceed his own eighteen, of course, but their floor space is nearly thrice that of the Redmonds'. And these double front doors, set in the broad, paved terrace raised almost a storey above street level, must carry more weight of oak than all the panelling within his Market Street Lane property. But his arrival causes some stir. Byrom's manservant is astonished for, while Titus Redmond is known by sight to all within Manchester, he rarely departs from the strictly observed circuit around his various business interests. It is an almost exotic occurrence for him to call unannounced at another's threshold. So, yes sir, Mister Byrom is indeed within. And receiving visitors, yes sir. Please, sir, be so good...

John Byrom seems almost more surprised than his manservant. Flustered even. He makes some excuse that he is only recently returned from Matlock Bath and Chesterfield. His good friend Wesley has been preaching there, it seems. But please, let him offer some refreshment. Mister Redmond's health much improved, Byrom hopes. Such a pleasure to see him. *Fucking hypocrite*, thinks Titus. *He can no more tolerate my presence that I can stand to be in his.* The house is quite empty, Byrom fears. The girls all gone with their mother to visit his sister. The boys at Saint Cyprian's, of course. Ah, and speaking of the school, he should come this way. He will be quite delighted. So Titus is escorted through the entrance hall to the large rooms that Byrom has set aside for use by his Academy, to an easel on which sits a painting, six feet long by four feet high, a huge thing.

'Mister Owen's work, d'you see! And almost complete. It was Devis, of course, who did the initial outline, and, in truth, our young friend has put quite his own mark, do you not think?'

Titus has known for a long time that Aran possesses many talents, but he seems to be alone in thinking that painting is not amongst them. He accepts, however, that he has no time for this particular exercise of passion. In truth, he cannot think of an occasion when he has *ever* seen a work of art and considered its value as more than the constituent elements of canvass and pigment.

'Ah, nice!' he says. The figures seem flat, lifeless, the portrait of Doctor Clayton in his Salford school yard flattering, his scabrous skin miraculously smoothed and youthful, though the folds of his blue velvet gown and its white silk lining are well-executed, Titus will allow.

'Nice, sir?' says Byrom. 'Well, upon my soul. I have never understood how a word that has, at turns, been used to mean foolish, fastidious, delicate or precise is now fallen to imply mere mediocrity. The most worthless adjective in our language, surely. For my own part, I find the picture quite remarkable. The boys deliver their pieces for Clayton before they break up for the holidays. Here is my own dear Ted, seated on the steps. A good likeness. Here is Billie

Brettargh. Reciting my *Black Crows*, apparently. Ashton Lever here, poor boy. His father was a dear friend, you know. Doctor Clayton himself, of course, but see this detail. The scroll. The quotation from Horace, the *Exhortation to the Young Lollius*. Perfectly apt! The sun-dial stroking the hour of four. Exquisite. Young Assheton, here. And little Charlie Deacon too, next to my own modest appearance beneath the tree. Why, he has captured the entire flowering youth of our Manchester Jacobites, would you not allow?'

'And thus the point of my visit, perhaps, if you will allow me, sir?' says Titus. 'For Mister Owen has been pleased to remind me lately of the words you spoke during the Town Meeting back in June. The words of the one cautious Trojan upon seeing the wooden horse of the Greeks. A machine *contrived against our liberties*, if I have it right?'

'Indeed, sir. Virgil's Laocoon. And it has delighted me, Mister Redmond, that you should have shared my opinion on the need to settle tranquillity upon our town, thus better to prevent the external interference with our affairs that might surely have followed had we not done so. Yet I find that you, sir, have paid a heavy price to deliver us from the threat posed by the Earl of Derby's militia. A heavy price indeed. My family will be delighted to accept, of course. And, while I thank you for the invitation, if I may speak frankly, it was a most surprising announcement. My dearest Beppy, I understand, has had quite some discussion with Rosina on the matter though I have cautioned that she should not be so free with her opinions at this time. She has the unfortunate habit of speaking without first the benefit of objective consideration.'

'My own daughter suffers a similar affliction, I find,' says Titus. 'And the question of her marriage may certainly have surprised the town. Yet you are correct, of course. It is a matter for her family, though we shall be equally delighted that your own can help us mark it. But if I might return to brave-hearted Laocoon, Mister Byrom? This is a delicate subject, and I speak to you in utmost confidence here. So if I told you that there may be an entirely distinct Trojan Horse at play in our town, and one that may be responsible for much of our mischief, might I call upon your good offices for some assistance?'

'If I take your point, sir, you believe that one of Newcastle's agents may be operating here? Ah, Titus, you seem surprised in turn. Yet there is no need, I assure you. I spend so much of my time in London's corrupt streets that I betimes forget how seldom its daily tattle succeeds in reaching extremities of the country like our own. In the capital, our good Jacobite folk see agents at every turn of the thoroughfare and, to some extent, with just cause. Their imaginations may sometimes feed them a diet too rich for their good, but the simple truth is that Newcastle has apparently hundreds of these skulkers at his command. It would be strange indeed should he have chosen to ignore dear Manchester for their attentions, would it not? Hence, if I may speak openly once more, I applaud the sacrifice that you are making to help lessen those attentions. A family matter, you will say to me again. But a sacrifice all the same, and one for which God will thank you, I am certain, once Charles Edward sits safe upon the throne. Yet, while I should be cheerfully disposed towards easing your burden with any assistance that you might seek, I do not fully understand what this might be!'

And neither, in truth, does Titus. It had seemed like a possibility when the thought had first occurred to him, but the chance that Byrom, through the strange miscellany of notable misfits with which he associates, might be able to find the identity of his assailant now appears to him absurd in the extreme. But he poses the question all the same and Byrom agrees to make his own discreet enquiries, flattered that Titus Redmond should consider him so potentially well equipped for this task on behalf of their Cause. He thanks Titus for his visit, will see him at the wedding if not before, and bids him maintain a cheerful frame of mind in the face of his adversities. The surest way, he says, of showing our appreciation for God's love.

It is difficult to feel the warmth of divine affection, however, when your next appointment must needs be with the very source of a grievous wound, and also at a location where that wound will be chafed raw by the addition of salt in prodigious quantity. *It is not the thanks of God I seek*, thinks Titus, *for my efforts, but rather that of Charles Edward himself!* And if God had any true affection for him, He should not now have required Titus to attend a meeting the main purpose of which is to finalise the sale of his daughter to a lick-spittle like Bradley nor, worse, that it should be taking place in the very house where Maria-Louise has trysted so long with that cunny-sucking fucker. Yet this God, he recalls, has a certain level of experience so far as the sacrifice of offspring is concerned, making it unreasonable, he supposes, to expect any real measure of sympathy.

It is some slight consolation, though, that Bradley's house stands so near to Byrom's and almost matches its magnificence. The interior is well-apportioned too and Titus momentarily wonders whether his wife's relationship with this man might have extended beyond the simply physical. *By the Mass*, he thinks. *Might she have helped the cove select his furnishings?* But he dismisses the thought. Foolish. That truly *would* be the act of a whore!

'Why, Mister Redmond. Sirrah!' says Bradley. 'Give you joy of my humble home. I am so entirely overcome. Please, your coat, sir. It may be temperate for the season but still cold, I find. A cup of mulled wine with you, perhaps. And Liptrott already here.'

Liptrott is the Attorney most commonly serving the needs of the town's Whigs and is still relatively young, having served his apprenticeship under Isaac Greene of Liverpool. One hundred and fifty guineas, so they say, for the five-year term. Yet he has affected an unnatural maturity far beyond his actual years, a permanently austere manner, a full-bodied peruke long out of fashion amongst his peers, and a permanent adherence to black court coats for his everyday attire.

'The final draft, I hope?' says Titus, indicating the document bundles set around the table in Bradley's drawing room. 'This must constitute the most protracted negotiation of my career! Which owes much, I suppose, to my eldest daughter being the object of our transactions. But an equal amount, we must collect, to the petty-fogging practices of lawyers like Mister Liptrott.' The cunny-licker has driven a hard bargain in the process of arranging the Marriage Settlement. It has been almost finalised during the previous month and now needs only to be read afresh, then signed before witnesses. Each document covers no less than four sheets of parchment, joined by pink tape threaded through holes at the bottom and the whole sealed with wax. The Settlement provides a Marriage Portion of two hundred pounds as Rosina's dowry to her new husband, hedged around with the normal conditions for all possible eventualities. The sum is indemnified, for example, by a clause making it clear that, should Rosina survive her husband, his Executors will return to her the sum of this Portion within six months of his death.

Bradley, however, has concerns about property implications, for the Portion is not particularly generous and, for merchant families like their own, it would not be unusual to also include some further gift of real estate. Titus has resisted the suggestion strongly since the matter is complicated by his other daughters and they have finally settled on an additional Jointure of three hundred pounds, as compensation for the lack of such property element, to be paid to Bradley immediately after the wedding ceremony has taken place but only so long as it is a competent arrangement. Put simply, Bradley has been forced to agree that, in exchange, the Settlement will include a contract covering any sale of his own present properties while he yet lives. By law, Rosina will of course, in any case, be entitled to her Third of Bradley's estate should she survive him. But this additional clause commits Bradley to an arrangement by which, whenever he sells property owned by him at the date of marriage, he will require the buyer to retain one-third of the purchase price, to be paid to Rosina at her husband's death, or to Bradley if he survives her. Meanwhile, the buyer will pay them interest at four per cent each year while they both live.

'It was by mutual agreement, Mister Redmond,' says a sour Liptrott, 'that you, lay gentlemen both, decided to source this Settlement with my good self. It will not answer, sir, if I do not enjoy the trust of each party. And the petty-fogging in Manchester I may safely leave in the hands of Todd.' Titus studies the re-drafted clauses closely. They seem fine and he cannot truly dispute Liptrott's retort, since he would not trust the Tory Attorney, Todd, so long as he had breath in his lungs. But it does not make him like this lick-spittle lawyer any better, nor his entire profession neither. 'Now, sirs,' Liptrott continues. 'Shall we discuss a possible date on which the Settlement might be signed and witnessed?'

'And the Bond, Mister Liptrott. Have you forgotten the Bond?' says

Titus. The Special License has already been issued, of course, by the Collegiate Church at a cost of five guineas but, following normal practice, they also require the applicant to sign a Bond, by which he will suffer financial penalty if it should be found that there is any legal impediment to the marriage. And the Bond has been the subject of continuous heated debate between Titus and Bradley, both now thankfully exhausted of argument. For Titus, the issue has revolved around fears that his daughter may not be well-treated by her new husband while Bradley has contended that it is she who is likely to breach the terms first, through her affection for tribady.

'It is set at two hundred pounds, sir,' says Liptrott. 'Upon my word! We agreed the sum at our previous encounter. And, so far as I am aware, Mister Bradley has completed a Bond to this effect that is now in the hands of the licensing authority. Is that not correct, Mister Bradley.' Indeed, it is! Bradley sucks at his teeth, produces a copy of the Bond in evidence. 'And the Special License, I should remind you, gentlemen, was necessary due to your daughter's faith, Mister Redmond, and to the great disparity in your ages, Mister Bradley. Now, sirrah! A date and the witnesses perhaps? Ah, though I understand that Mister Bradley wishes to discuss a witness privately. I shall wait in the reception hall.' He bows low and leaves them.

'Witness?' says Titus. 'What is this? There should be no complication in the matter, surely.'

'Hardly a complication, sir,' says Bradley. 'More a pleasant surprise, I trust you will find. For I have another visitor, Titus, who wishes a word. His Lordship, the Earl of Derby.'

'Stanley, here? What trickery is this, Bradley? And why should he have any interest in my daughter's wedding?'

'I shall quickly tire of this game, sir, if you continue to accuse me of trickery each time I make genuine effort to augment our relationship. His Lordship has offered to sign the Settlement as a witness today and also appears on this very document as second bondsman.' He flourishes the completed Bond once again. 'It is not necessary to agree with his politics. Simply to accept that we could have no better hand underwriting our agreement.'

Titus applies a dozen different suspicions to this sudden involvement of Lancashire's Lord Lieutenant but none of them result in any intelligent outcome. Very well. Then let them be about it, he says. And Liptrott is called back to the room, the documents gathered, carried carefully to Bradley's study where Sir Edward Stanley is immersed in several papers recently produced by the Royal Society, one by James Parsons, for this year's Crounian Lecture, on the effect of air upon muscular movement in animals. A second detailing the results of Magnetical Experiments conducted by Mister Knight.

'Such an extraordinary age, gentlemen, d'you not agree?' he says, setting down the pamphlets and rising to greet Titus. 'Ah, Mister Redmond. We have not had the pleasure, I think.' No, they have certainly not, thinks

Titus. And extraordinary indeed. For here is the very fellow who, he is sure, would be able to instantly provide the information that he has set John Byrom to uncovering, though he is naturally unable to put the question. He offers the Earl his most formal greeting, however. 'And a Marriage Settlement to be signed and witnessed, if you will allow me the honour, sir?' Sir Edward continues. The honour, says Titus, is all his, and the documents are all quickly affirmed, Mister Liptrott dismissed. Titus, however, cannot so readily avoid his suspicions.

'You will forgive me, Lordship,' he says. 'But the last thing that I had expected from this day was to find myself a co-signatory to the Earl of Derby. And I cannot believe that your interest in my daughter's wedding may be a mere act of charity towards one of Manchester's lowlier families.'

'Oh, a fie upon you, Redmond,' says the Earl. 'You have a propensity for coming it the jester, I see. How delicious. A lowly family, says you. Why, sir, the entire County stands in awe of you. And this wedding of which you speak as though it was some any day occurrence! Well, I can barely contain my excitement. I had quite forsaken the likelihood that we should ever bring any sense to this town. And you need not think that your hand in this is not appreciated, sir. But you would perhaps allow me a possible further service? For Mister Bradley tells me that the conduct of the service itself remains in some doubt. Well, gentlemen, without putting too fine a point on the matter, I have spoke just two days past with Bishop Peploe and, with your agreement, of course, he will make himself available on the fifteenth day of December. I have the date correct, I hope?'

Oh, correct indeed. And Samuel Peploe, Bishop of Chester, is also Warden of Manchester's Collegiate Church, Christ's Church.

Another argument had raged for a while, since Bradley would have preferred the ceremony to be conducted at Saint Ann's where, as a Presbyterian, he chooses to worship. Yet, since only the Collegiate Church is authorised for the issuing of Special Licenses, its choice is more obvious. Besides, since this is a temple to High Church Anglicanism, it provides the closest alternative that the Redmond family will find to a Roman Catholic wedding. The obvious person to preside would be Doctor Clayton, most prominent of the Chaplains at the Collegiate Church although, since he so staunchly advocates the Jacobites' cause, Bradley will not entertain the idea. Thomas Deacon has been discounted for the same reason since, though he styles himself Bishop of Manchester, this is a title only bestowed on him by his own Non-Juror colleagues and Bradley will have nothing to do with those who have made themselves ineligible to hold official positions in the church due to their refusal of a loyalty oath to the current monarchy. There are Chaplains and Ministers at the Collegiate Church apart from Clayton, of course, but none on which the two parties have been able to agree. Peploe had not even been considered since both Titus and Bradley had thought him unattainable. He has held the Chester Diocese since '38 when he succeeded his unpopular father as Bishop. The younger Peploe has, at least, brought some diplomacy to the post and has done much to bring together the various factions within his Manchester wardenship. He may be High Church, but he is broadly respected by the Presbyterians too.

'A commendable choice, Sir Edward, and I am sure we both thank you for the intervention with My Lord Bishop,' says Bradley. 'Yet perhaps this means that we need to be more precise about invitations to the ceremony, Mister Redmond. Would you agree? It cannot be a grand affair, as we have already decided, but it would also be unfortunate if our respective guest lists should create any conflict with the Bishop present. And you will appreciate the value, I am certain, of ensuring that as many of the new Court Leet Officers and Jurors as possible might attend. You should feel pleased with your efforts, Titus. The first time that we have elected your Jacobite friends to such positions. Tipping as one of the Constables. John Clough amongst the Jurors. Yet they must work together now!'

'They can do little worse than the fools elected last year,' says Sir Edward. And Titus secretly agrees with him. John Hawkswell had been chosen last month to replace Bower as the Borough Reeve. John Upton and Thomas Tipping significant improvements on Miles Bower and Robert Hibbert as Constables. The new Jurors an acceptable group for the most part. And, so far as invitations are concerned, there is simply Francis Townley and his associates to exclude. It is hardly payment enough for Townley's insult against Maria-Louise, but it is a beginning. 'But there is a price to be paid,' continues the Earl of Derby. 'This Subscription of yours must be terminated, Mister Redmond. Your *Journal* carry no further attack on the Government. A small price compared to others that you seem prepared to pay!' *What,* thinks Titus, *that I should have chosen this cunny-sucker Bradley for my daughter's husband, rather than Jacob Driscoll or Aran Owen?* Whether he has had doubts about Jacob's suitability, doubts about whether Aran may somehow have been inadvertently used by Newcastle's agents, the fact is that only Bradley matches all the criteria that Titus and Maria-Louise have set as a reasonable justification for arranging Rosina's marriage. 'Yet shall we enjoy some refreshments, Mister Bradley?' says Sir Edward.

Bradley leaves the room, calls to his manservant from the entrance hall.

'Now, Mister Redmond,' whispers the Earl of Derby, 'I hope that we may enjoy a mutually satisfactory future. The war in France goes badly. Our allies retired early to their winter quarters. The French have gained the respite they sought. There is no money to pay our Austrian friends, while the Austrian Netherlands can no longer provide our armies with forage. Then there is General Wade. Sick in mind and body. Sick of the Austrians. This is not yet known, Mister Redmond, but Wade has resigned his command. Resigned. You take my meaning, sir? If matters should develop in a certain way. If Prince Charles Edward is successful, I trust you will remember your friends!'

Chapter Twenty-Six

It is Saturday, the fifteenth day of December in the Year 1744. Elizabeth Cooper is thirty-one years old and feels a certain degree of accomplishment within her life. The coffee house is a success. It could be the foundation for some greater enterprise, yet still a success. She has status and position within the town. She enjoys the love and adoration of Rosina Redmond. And, now, with Rosina's marriage, she can continue to savour that adoration without any further risk to her reputation. For who will now be able to cast the allegation of tribady against Rosina once she has become James Bradley's wife? Oh, there have been times when she could scarce believe that the marriage would occur. Times when she was so softened by Rosina's distress that she had almost dissuaded the girl from continuing. It would have been easy enough, for Rosina had argued day after day, week after week with her parents on the matter. But slowly, weakened by the futility of her position, Rosina had succumbed to the situation. She had been assisted in this surrender primarily by Elizabeth herself. Elizabeth who had persuaded Rosina of Bradley's assurance that he required no more than the outward appearance of marriage, a mere political charade. Merely accept and they will be able to continue enjoying each other for as long as they might choose. So Rosina had accepted and, today, she will sanctify her acceptance in this Collegiate Church of Manchester.

Elizabeth awaits her lover's arrival now, seated in the pews allocated to the Groom. Yet Bradley has no family, so far as she is aware. He has spoken of his father at times, but she has assumed that he is no longer living. Simply this collection of Whig merchants, their associates and their families. John Clowes, breeches maker. Thomas Walley, clock maker. James Tomlinson, miller. Joseph Bancroft, smallware manufacturer. The new Jurors, Allen, Ayrton, Bancroft and Woolmer. A dozen others that she does not know by name. The recently elected Borough Reeve, John Hawkswell. Matthew Liptrott, Attorney. The Presbyterians, Benjamin Nichols and Thomas Lewthwaite. The Dissenter, Joseph Mottershead. Bradley himself, waiting nervously near the altar with his Groom's Man, Robert Jobb. They are, collectively, her most regular customers.

Across the aisle are Rosina's people. More properly, they are Titus Redmond's people. Adam Scatterbuck, the printer. Father Peter Scobie, the family's Catholic Confessor, risen from his sick-bed. The clergy with

Non-Jurist principles, John Clayton, Joseph Hoole, Thomas Deacon with his wife, Sarah, and their various offspring. Redmond's merchant allies. George Fletcher, linen draper, with his wife, Susanna. Robert Gartside, fustian manufacturer, with his wife, Alice. Peter Moss, linen draper, and his wife, Mary. Thomas Tipping, yarn merchant. William Fowden, tin man. John Clough, yarn merchant. Abraham Howarth, joiner. The Byrom family, John and Elisabeth, their children, Beppy, Molly, Doll and Ted. Their cousins, James Dawson and John Beswicke. The servants, Mudge and O'Farrell. Aran Owen, of course. But no Jacob Driscoll, Elizabeth notes. And at least none of the *banditti* who attach themselves to young Townley. Why, she had half-expected the church to be filled with those Manx wreckers who perform so much of the Redmonds' illicit undertaking.

She laughs. Such a wedding, she thinks. Strange enough to begin any normal marriage by dividing the couple's family and friends into such distinct factions. But here! One half of the Church filled by Hanoverian loyalists, Whigs and Presbyterians. The other half by Jacobites, Papists, Tories and High Anglicans. And the women wear their respective beauty patches to declare their own affiliations. Yet there is one thing that binds this gathering today, at least, for they are all layered against the cold. So Elizabeth swaddles herself more deeply within her shawl, wondering at those few who cannot so easily decide where to position themselves. Sir Oswald Mosley and Lady Anne, for example. Francis Reynolds from Strangeways. They move to one side, then the other, unable to bring themselves so openly to declare an allegiance. Incongruous, given that this whole affair is supposed to signal a new beginning for the town. They should have joined the whores, of course. For the doxies, strictly speaking not invited, have turned out in force, a colourful addition to the congregation, though they remain standing near the font.

Finally, Rosina is here.

The parish organ in the Collegiate Church is nothing short of a mechanical miracle – but it had been a Redmond family riches miracle that saw its completion in time for the wedding. It is a very grand affair, with its towering wooden case panels intricately carved to show King David playing his harp, whilst the case itself frames the instrument's thirty wood and metal pipes. At the keyboard, in the organ loft, sits Mrs Starkey, for Rosina would agree to no other, manipulating the stops to give full vent to the instrument's Nason, its Sesqualtera, its Vox Humana and its Great Cornet. So there she now sits, thundering out the opening bars to Purcell's *Trumpet Tune and Air* as Rosina walks purposefully down the aisle, in blue silk, upon her father's arm, each treading the diamond-pattern tiles that stretch from tower to altar between arched pillars. And behind, the sisters, her Bride-Maids. Anna-Marie, Katherine and Maeve, dressed respectively in ivory, apricot and apple-green. Rosina is beautiful, dried orange blossom in her hair to symbolise her virginity. But today a stone virgin, expressionless. *And truly a virgin?* thinks

Elizabeth. *La! If only they knew. And how I should love to be amongst her petticoats at this moment.*

The Collegiate Church is renowned, of course, for its carpentry, mostly the product of the famed Ripon Carvers who had worked their magic upon the choir stalls and choir seats; the carved bosses on the nave ceilings; the miserichord, with its depictions of Reynold the Fox; and the quire screen, with its double doors intricately fashioned from solid oak and topped by the pulpit, its *façade* painted with the likeness of saints and embellished with gold leaf. Elizabeth is no admirer of church painting, by and large, and these vivid images, with their equally vivid pastoral backgrounds are no exception. It had been the Spaniard, Cervantes, she thinks, who said, 'Good painters imitate nature. Bad ones spew it up.' It is an ancient church though and, frankly, deserves better from the journeymen who had inflicted such poor painting on such fine woodwork. Bishop Peploe seems to think so too, scratching at some chipped enamel from a hand-rail while he waits for the Bride and her father to reach him. He is resplendent in purple cassock. Over this, he wears his white *rochet* reaching almost to the cassock's hem, with a black *chimere* sleeveless gown, and a red academic hood.

Bradley stands before him, sporting a new and expensive tie wig, a suit of silk in palest grey, buff waistcoat embroidered with red. He blows upon his numbed fingers, turns to watch his prospective bride take the final few steps of her freedom, looks to her for some sign of recognition. But there is nothing. Rosina is impassive and Elizabeth wonders, suddenly, whether she might have dosed herself with Sydenham's. She wonders, too, whether Rosina and Bradley may even have spoken with each other in the days before the wedding. Yet she doubts it. And so, Titus Redmond hands his daughter forward to the altar of sacrifice, a modern Jacob, the muscles in his lined face flickering as he fingers the moustache. He looks about him as though the Lord may, at last, intervene and Elizabeth recalls some nonsense told to her by Rosina, that Titus has pledged to shave the unsightly thing only when he is accepted by the town's Whigs as an equal. *Does he believe that this shall be the day?* she wonders. *If so, how little he knows his enemies.* For there is a visible stir on this side of the church, a mounting self-satisfied excitement whilst, on the other, all is muted, silent. Elizabeth looks to the foremost pew of Rosina's clan, where Maria-Louise stands stiffly, joined now by her other girls, each of them with expressions more apt for a funeral than a family wedding.

And, suddenly, Bishop Peploe is begun.

They are all, seemingly, dearly beloved, come together in the presence of God to witness and bless the joining together of this man and this woman in Holy Matrimony. The bond and covenant of marriage, he says, was established by God in creation, and our Lord Jesus Christ adorned this manner of life by his presence and first miracle at a wedding in Cana of Galilee. It signifies the mystery of the union between Christ and his Church, and Holy Scripture

235

commends it to be honoured among all people. The union of husband and wife in heart, body and mind is intended by God, he intones, for their mutual joy, for the help and comfort given one another in property and adversity and, when it is God's will, for the procreation of children and their nurture in the knowledge and love of the Lord.

Now that would simply not answer! thinks Elizabeth. Children had not entered her calculation and, when she had spoken with Bradley on the matter, whilst he had not seemed greatly interested in the carnal aspect of the marriage, she had perhaps not been entirely truthful with Rosina when she had assured her that a charade might be the extent of her obligations. For marriage, as the good Bishop is just confirming, is not to be entered into unadvisedly or lightly. But, rather, reverently, deliberately, and in accordance with the purposes for which it was instituted by God.

Amen!

And into this holy union, James and Rosina now come to be joined. If any can show just cause why they may not lawfully be married, they should speak now, or else forever hold their peace. Silence. Astonishing silence. So Bishop Peploe proceeds with readings that will serve to confirm the Lord's view on the sanctity of the moment.

From Genesis, Proverbs, Ecclesiastes, Isaiah.

And, finally, Revelation.

Let us be glad and rejoice and give Him glory, for the marriage of the Lamb has come, and His wife has made herself ready. And to her it was granted to be arrayed in fine linen, clean and bright, for the fine linen is the righteous acts of the saints. Then he said to me, 'Write: Blessed are those who are called to the marriage supper of the Lamb!' And he said to me, 'These are the true sayings of God.'

Amen! Though Elizabeth must admit that she has never quite understood Revelation as well as she might.

But, in the presence of God and these their friends, Rosina Redmond and James Bradley take each other to be husband and wife, promising with Divine assistance to be faithful so long as they both shall live. They promise to mutually love and to cherish, while Rosina alone must also promise to obey, though she sounds less than convincing. Sickness and health are mentioned, God's holy ordinance. Troth is plighted by the groom, given by the bride. And then Bradley is required to place the ring on Rosina's finger. With this Ring I thee wed. With my body I thee worship. And with all my worldly goods I thee endow. In the name of the Father, and of the Son, and of the Holy Ghost. Amen.

Amen!

Thus, at last, the wedding reaches its inevitable conclusion. But there is no embarrassed kiss to seal their affection, just the signatures in the vestry before they file out, showered with grains of wheat for their fertility, the church bells in competition to the strains of Mrs Starkey performing a version of the madrigal by Antonio Lotti – the very same tune that had caused such a bitter dispute between the composer and his rival, Bononcini, who had claimed the madrigal as his own. So Rosina's choice of music had been interesting, carefully avoiding all of the Lutheran tunes that are generally popular now for marriage ceremonies – and studiously avoiding anything by Handel, whom she has dismissed as 'that Hanoverian puppet'.

Out into the cold December morning, and now to the White Lion on Parsonage Lane, neutral ground and with a good reputation for Wedding Breakfasts served in the extensive upstairs room towards the rear of the establishment, a welcome log fire at each end. And the White Lion does not disappoint. A modest but well-presented selection of hot rolls, pink tongues, honey-scented hams, sizzling eggs, smoking beef, brown ale and steaming punch, with the centre-piece an enormous Bride's Pie, deliciously filled with minced mutton and sweet breads. The pie contains a glass ring too which, according to tradition, of course, if discovered by a woman would indicate that she should be the next to marry.

They sit at long tables, each faction to its own, and there are speeches. But they are brief. Titus Redmond as the father of the bride, Robert Jobb as the Groom's Man, and Bradley himself with some short words of thanks to the Bride's family and, naturally, to the beautiful Bride herself. Beautiful and remote, Rosina spends most of the meal darting glances in Elizabeth's direction, but Elizabeth manages to deflect a few with reassuring smile and to ignore the rest by engaging in deep conversation with her neighbours, Nichols and Lewthwaite. A story-teller is summoned. O'Farrell, the Redmond's manservant. More desiccated than she could have imagined. Rosina has described him as taciturn, but such a voice now. A blessing upon the house, then launches forth with, 'One day the amorous Lysander...' Aphra Behn. She might have known. And nothing more suitable than *The Disappointment* for introducing some harmless ribaldry to the proceedings through its fourteen long, lewd verses. There are some amongst the guests who are less than happy with the selection but any discomfort on Elizabeth's part owes more to her attire, and she shifts uncomfortably on the bench.

'Ah, Mister Lewthwaite,' she says. 'How I envy you your breeches this day!'

'Indeed,' replies Lewthwaite. 'It will take some time to recover from this morning's chill. Our own Saint Ann's is so much more agreeable, I find. And Bishop Peploe's words did little, I must confess, to add any warmth. It being so near Christmas-tide one may have assumed that he would take his texts from the appropriate Gospels. Saint Matthew is most edifying on the matter. The trials that Mary and Joseph had to endure to maintain their marriage. Most edifying. And yet, whilst you were contemplating my breeches, Elizabeth, I was admiring your own brocades for the same reason. I have rarely seen such a fine, warm weave.'

'A fie upon you, Tom! Admiring my brocades indeed. Why, I had not thought that you were so inclined.' It is an obvious jest, yet she sees that it strikes a nerve. And poor Ben Nichols has all but choked on a sliver of beef. *Goodness, beneath my very nose and never noticed*, she thinks. But why not? The world knows that sodomy is rife amongst the clergy, though many a year has passed since any were hung for the offence. 'Yet you must know sir,' she says, 'that your secret is safe with me. Safe, indeed!' She laughs. 'But I did not refer to your breeches for any want of warmth. It is these damn'd hoops. Difficult enough to manoeuvre upon a chair, but these benches. La!' They exchange comment about their own church, the problems with Reverend Hoole and his continuing support for the Non-Jurors, but the conversation is stilted now. She tries to lighten the situation. 'Ah look, Tom, you have yet another admirer, I see. Mister Owen can barely take his eyes from you. Another surprise!'

Yet she sees, when Lewthwaite returns Aran's gaze, that there is neither lust nor affection between them. On the contrary, just the cold stare of two men who, she imagines, may be afraid of each other. Meanwhile, O'Farrell has reached the end of his recital, succeeded in breaking the ice of this winter's afternoon, and sits to rapturous applause while Bradley is subjected to a string of raucous comparisons with the unfortunate Lysander. And, the meal now over, tables and benches are moved back against the wall, a fiddler comes forward to scratch his jigs for their entertainment and dancing, while Bradley himself serves punch to each of the guests.

'I had thought it obligatory,' Elizabeth says to him, at last able to stand, 'for the Groom to dance each of the women around the room, beginning with his new wife?'

'Dance, Mistress Cooper?' replies Bradley. 'I cannot secure even a smile from the girl and I realise now that the Marriage Settlement may have needed some additional clauses, though that fucking Attorney never troubled himself to advise me of the fact.'

'Is Rosina's Marriage Portion insufficient then, sir? The Bride weeps before her marriage, the Groom for its duration, is that not so? But a dowry of two hundred pounds is a significant amount. The additional Jointure a princely sum. Though you cannot purchase your wife's soul, James. You must know this. Far more could be gained by reaching your own separate accord with her. Allow her sufficient freedom, her harpsichord, her pleasures. For I see that Rosina's dear Mama still views you with passion, regardless of any earlier difference between you. How easy it would be, now, to resume your tryst with her. I had thought your strategy of circulating those damnable rumours a foolish one, but look where it has brought us. La! I bow to

238

your wisdom, Mister Bradley.'

'There is no wisdom in this,' he says. 'And you simply wish to start fingering the girl again as soon as you may be able. It was good advice that you gave me, Elizabeth. Prestigious marriage to a beautiful young woman. Peace achieved between myself and Redmond. Permanent and easy access to Maria-Louise. Perspective maintained for Good King George on the Jacobite activity within the town. How perfect! But I had not then given any thought to Rosina herself. You have good taste, my dear. For she is lovely. I wonder that I had not seen it before. So she shall have her harpsichord – and more besides!'

He moves on with the punch bowl, and she wonders at his meaning, determines to pursue the matter. For they had an agreement, Bradley and herself. Does he mean, now, to revoke it? She must follow him. But, as she steps aside to avoid the dancers, she meets Aran Owen head-on. She has spoken to him only ever once before. That time at the Fair. Once, despite all the times that Rosina has mentioned him.

'We seem to have a flair for collision, Mister Owen. Yet give you joy of this day, sir. I trust you are now better reconciled to the recognition that dear Rosina has made such an admirable marriage?'

'I recall,' says Aran, 'that during our previous encounter you rather implied that I was responsible for the fact. A scrub, you called me, for rejecting her. For my failure to put some joint alternative to her father. For Titus not trusting me with her hand. For the careless company that I could offer her. Better, you thought, with James Bradley. Yet it was not myself, madam, who made the bed in which Rosina must now lie. For my part I must confess a certain bitterness that her father did not see fit to choose me, and I was indeed something of a scrub towards Rosina. So yes, I am so reconciled and wish her every happiness. And I may yet make amends, I think. Whereas you, Mistress Cooper...'

His words hang in the air as Maria-Louise joins them. Elizabeth would have avoided her if it had been possible. Indeed, she had been surprised to even receive an invitation to attend. But Rosina apparently insisted upon it.

'Mister Owen,' says Maria-Louise, 'you have been neglecting me!' And she folds herself around Aran's arm. *God's Hooks,* thinks Elizabeth. *She has taken too much of the punch!* 'And here I find you in company with this woman – though I have never been certain whether a Myra may be comfortable with describing herself so. You should be careful lest her appetites are contagious. Come tip a stave with me, sir. We could join the girls, perhaps. La! But I forget myself. As the Bride's mother, I collect that I should bid you welcome to our family celebration, Mistress Cooper.' She attempts a curtsy but must needs rely on Aran to prevent her falling.

'Your hospitality overwhelms me, madam,' says Elizabeth, returning the bob with perfect balance. She exaggerates the grace of it, almost a mockery in itself. 'Yet I do not think that Mister Owen has anything to fear from *my* company. He has his own fancies, it seems. For I saw him exchange the most exquisite glance with Tom Lewthwaite some little time ago. I assume that, with your daughter now wed to Bradley, you must look elsewhere for your own satisfactions but I do not think that Mister Owen is man enough for that task. Ah, your daughters come to take you dancing, I see. Sweet girls, all three. But please excuse me.'

And she steps past them, plunges herself amongst a group of Bradley's associates to escape. Damnable woman, she thinks. To call her a Myra to her face. She weaves her way between the harlots, also the worse for punch, as they step a lively reel, Mag Mudge at their centre, back amongst old friends and dribbling spittle to the floor with each step that she makes. Through the whores and across to the table where Rosina has now been joined by Katherine and a serving girl from the White Lion who has brought a knife to cut the Bride's Pie. But, at Elizabeth's approach, Katherine lowers her eyes, whispers a brief word to her sister and moves away.

'I see that your Mama has been instructing her remaining daughters on the dangers of my proximity,' says Elizabeth. 'Why, she paled significantly when I commented on their sweetness just now, and that despite her being barely able to stand unassisted. She is fucking Mister Owen now, I assume? How fickle a suitor *he* would have made. And Jacob Driscoll too. Could not be bothered even to drag his knuckles along the ground to be here!'

'Do you not consider this day already sufficiently dark that you must needs daub it with an even thicker layer of gloom, my dear?' says Rosina. 'Such an image! Mama and Aran Owen. You are quite scandalous. And poor Jacob has business elsewhere. But how I admire your dress, madam. You found brocade in blue to match my own. How clever!'

'You are the second to have admired it in only a short time. Oh, *how* I love to see that flash of jealousy in those emerald eyes, Mistress. Yet it was merely Mister Lewthwaite. A wondrous revelation, too, but we shall speak of that later. For now, I wanted only to know that you are coping with this strangest of days, that you do not feel its darkness too deeply since that would wound me so. And to offer a word of advice from one who loves you without reservation. For you should know, Rosina, that we must allow Mister Bradley at least the appearance that you have pleasure in being his spouse. Else how other might we persuade him to allow you the freedom we need to spend our days together?'

'La! I am merchandise this day as surely as though it were myself tied with pink ribbon and delivered to James Bradley. How else would you have me feel? And those vows! I had thought them only words before this morning. But the weight of them, every one, now presses on my bosom, pierces my heart. The Marriage Settlement too. Those clauses about the Jointure, the clauses dealing with which of us may survive the other. It could be twenty years, more even, before I am rid of him. Twenty years, Elizabeth. And what shall become of you and me meanwhile? We could have fled, my love. Just we two. Posed as man and wife, as others have done. You would have made such a fine husband. It is not too late, even now!'

'My sweet, Rosina,' says Elizabeth. 'How many times have we had this discussion? You know that it is impossible. And, in any case, we shall be perfectly happy here. You must simply act the wife to Bradley in public. Apart from that, I am sure that he will not trouble us.'

She does not believe this, naturally, and the serving girl moves among the guests, distributing the Bride's Pie. But Rosina and Elizabeth barely notice as they receive their own portions.

'Yet a marriage so arranged,' says Rosina. 'The entire world knows that it cannot succeed. And how shall I deal with this wedding night nonsense? At least we shall not have to suffer any foolish tradition. The very idea of James Bradley and myself appearing in our night-shirts so that Mama and my sisters might fling their stockings over our heads! But my father has still arranged for a great bonfire, for bell-ringing. I shall never be able to show my face on the street again.'

'A fie upon you, Rosina. Marriages are arranged this way almost daily, my dear. Why, they are the very thing! And look. How amusing. It seems that I have the glass ring.' Elizabeth carefully extracts it from the plate, licks it clean of minced mutton and holds it to the light. 'Perhaps you were correct, and we *shall* be married after all.'

'For pity's sake,' says Rosina, 'put that trinket away. How foolish we shall look if anybody notices. And see, that awful lecher Robert Jobb is watching us. I cannot imagine why Bradley should have chosen the cove as his Groom's Man. Detestable fellow. At least I shall not suffer the indignity of having him remove my garter and delivering it to my husband.'

Oh, my dear! thinks Elizabeth. For she fears that this will be the very least of the indignities that Rosina must face this night.

Chapter Twenty-Seven

'Stolen sweets are best,' Colley Cibber had said in *The Rival Fools*. And what theft can be sweeter, thinks Striker, than that of another's identity?

He had come tapping up the lane to Llanffynon Old Hall, early in October, and found Josiah Redmond, as Aran had predicted, busy in his gardens, with a battered red felt hat, barely distinguishable from the fellows he employs and feeding a fire to dispose of their fallen leaves in great clouds of bitter-scented woodsmoke. In the guise of a half-starved vagrant seeking work, Striker had carelessly allowed the old man to draw forth his tale, piece by gruelling piece, confidence by grudging confidence. He had been a soldier, William Owen by name. It had struck a chord, of course, as Striker had known it must. Owen, Josiah had said. Such coincidence, for he himself had a friend, a *protégé* almost, Aran Owen by name. Now in Manchester. *Oh, how delicious!* Striker had thought. But this *William* Owen, it seemed, had served with the Twenty-Third of Foot. Yes, the Royal Welsh Fusiliers. At Dettingen, his eyes half-blinded by smoke and powder burns. His mother still in Aberystwyth, though English by birth, that might account for the strangeness of his accent. That and having run away from the local lead mines to join the army at the age of fifteen. With most of his life spent outside Wales, he had lost much of his native tongue. Yet it was returning quickly now that he had come home at last. Well, as near to home as he dared. And, at the third or fourth time of asking, William Owen had finally been persuaded to admit that he was a deserter. Not uncommon, of course. There were many on the byways either damaged by the war or fleeing from it. But he had nothing to fear at Llanffynon. Josiah would provide work for a while, some shelter too, though he seemed anxious to reconsider when, days later, William Owen had confessed that his situation was perhaps more acute than he had given the good gentlemen to understand. For his desertion had been particularly occasioned when his sergeant had marked him for a Jacobite sympathiser.

Newcastle had been very helpful, naturally, in identifying this William Owen, who had died on the field at Dettingen, as a possible counterpart. Owen's family had been regrettably notified of his demise but it was a simple matter to delude them into thinking that he is alive after all, and Striker had been forced to spend some of his hard-earned silver to grease their credulity. The family is, indeed, in Aberystwyth but the part about an English mother, the escape from the lead mines, is purest fiction though he doubts that there is any real chance of any investigation at such depth.

The Welsh tongue had posed a problem, however. Gifted a linguist as he might be, even the Siouan dialect of the Catawba had made more sense to him, had sounded less foreign, than the twisted perversity that passes for *Cymraeg*. And this despite his decent grasp of the Gaelic. He will manage though. The myth of years spent without the language, its use heavily discouraged within the ranks, will serve him well, and he has the skill of faltering English grammar at times, lapsing into well-rehearsed snatches of Welsh whenever he needs them. And the further east he is able to locate his *alter ego*, the less he will have to depend on its use.

He had slowly let Josiah come to recognise that, although he might be without formal education, William Owen is not entirely lacking some innate academic talent and, both wishing to help the fellow and, at the same time, be rid of any further connection to the Jacobite Cause, the Squire had effected an introduction to none other than the Rector of Hawarden, Richard Williams. The Rector had been desperately seeking a secretary to assist him in his efforts to establish his own library. A modest affair. But he has assumed some responsibility for record-keeping on behalf of the village industries. Coal is dug there, iron smelted and bricks fired. A thriving corn mill too. And Hawarden sits, of course, on the post road from Chester to Holyhead. So there is much to be done, though Mister Owen shall not be burdened with anything beyond his ability. But help to catalogue the books and ledgers perhaps? Perchance the occasional excursion to Chester or beyond when the Rector wishes to purchase additional volumes from book-vendors. And, within a month of his first appearance at the gates of Llanffynon Hall, Striker's cuckoo is safely ensconced within its nest.

And such a nest he might never have expected, for the rectory is an impressive brick-built manse, standing next to Saint Deiniol's Church. It is warm and comfortable, and Striker now simply needs to await some contact between the Rector and Sir Watkin Williams Wynn. Or with his associate, the lawyer David Morgan, perhaps. It will not be long in coming, he is certain, before he can implement the next stage of Newcastle's plan for infiltration of the Jacobite high command. And no better way to do so than through this Welsh connection with which Aran has provided him. Meanwhile, William Owen has made it clear, of course, that his mother is unwell and may rely on him for assistance, though his visits to Aberystwyth must be clandestine in nature. But this, along with the book-buying, should give him good cause to be absent whenever he needs.

Yet he had not expected to need it so quickly.

Barely a month in Mister Williams's service and, during the second week of December, he had been instructed away from the companionable glow of the Rectory to brave the winter road to Chester for the purchase of accompting books, quantities of parchment, and the collection of three tomes from Mistress Adams, who owns the book emporium. He had thought himself quite able to become accustomed to this casual lifestyle, and the scholar within had turned its thoughts once more to the compilation of his *opus magnus*, that Book of Receipts for Pastry, Cakes, Biscuits and Sweetmeats. Yes, the Biscuits should definitely be included. He had considered this during the icy seven mile journey to town in the Rector's closed chariot but, having previously left instructions with his various couriers to forward any message to him at the Feathers on Bridge Street, where his own bay mare is stabled, duty had overcome him and caused him to visit the inn. There, he had been surprised to find a note from Aran, that other Mister Owen. At least, he assumes that it is so for it has occurred to him lately that he has no way of discerning the source of one message from another, apart from familiarity with the hand. And because his various informants all use the Byrom shorthand, they each seem devilishly similar. He must devise some better system!

Still, the message had said that an important meeting is due to take place at a house on Liskard Moor, just above the Mersey's high water mark. *Where is that?* he had wondered. Then this mysterious Frenchman who would be in attendance. *And when?* The fifteenth day of December. Only two days away and hardly worth returning to Hawarden. He had sent the carriage back with a note that he suffered a minor ague and would remain in Chester until he is cured. But he had lifted Aran Owen's message to his nose, smelled it for suspicion, checked the Byrom envelope with its single letter 'S'. He had known the truth, that he should have sought help. For Aran had warned him that a group of Manx smugglers would be there too, as well as Jacob Driscoll. And it was Driscoll who had sealed the matter. Unfinished business. Had not the simian fellow promised him a reckoning, according to Aran? Then a reckoning there will be!

So he has visited Cooke the Cartographer, studied the maps and found a traveller's description for the peninsular Hundred of Wirral that he needs to traverse. Geometrically, a rhomboid, a parallelogram in which adjacent sides are of unequal lengths and angles are oblique, as Euclid might have described it. Yet irregular, since the long sides, following the litoral of the Mersey on its east side and the Dee on its west, are not quite straight lines, and neither are its opposite ends quite equal, the longer northern edge bordering the Irish Sea and the narrower southern neck joining the mainland at the Chester marches. He has noted the principal settlements, Burton, Oldfield, Raby with its significant mere, Bebington, Birken's Head and Stanney. Good farming land, for the most part, it seemed. The description recounted that the fields are well-ditched, and generally, the land is undulating, with few hills of any considerable height. But there are two ranges, one from Shotwick to West Kirby, having its highest elevation at Heswall, and the other from Spital to Bidston. He has traced the course of its main waterways too. The excavated line of the New Cut at the base of the Dee Estuary, opened just seven years ago to improve access with Chester but, in so doing, diverted the course of the Dee proper away from the ports on the Wirral coastline. And there are smaller rivers. The Fender rising north-west of Barnston, where it is known as Prenton Brook, and flowing hard by Thingwall, passing under Prenton Bridge, by Woodchurch, to join its waters with the Birken, close to Bidston Moss. And the Birken itself, rising in the neighbourhood of Grange, an apparently meagre stream at this stretch, making its slow progress across the plains to Moreton, whence it empties itself into the Wallasey Pool. And it is here that Striker has come for his *rendezvous*.

A pre-dawn start and a solitary lunch at Thurstaston, where he has gathered his first decent intelligence about the house called Seabank Nook. Discreetly sought, discreetly given, it seems that, though it changes hand with remarkable frequency, the land is currently owned by one Martin Figgis, a Liverpool merchant. Rumour of his links with certain questionable activity but nothing definite, and the house seemingly unoccupied at the moment, used as a warehouse, more or less. Then another two hours in the saddle have brought him to Liskard Moor with enough light left to reconnoitre the ground. He has made a long sweep past the neglected Mockbeggar Hall, along the shoreline, to approach from the north, past the Black Skerry, that infamous outcrop on which a modest, perch-green tower has been erected as a daylight aid to navigation. The tide is low at this hour, but there are still many vessels and a veritable shoal of fishing boats plying the sand-dark waves of the central channel. From this river, Liverpool has developed a rich, growing trade to the Colonies, to all other parts of the British coast, to Norway, to the Baltic. And the wind that would carry them there whips at the map, hand-drawn, showing him the location of Seabank Nook, the house now before him. But it is a strange moment. One of those when time seems frozen, when you cannot imagine any event beyond the one that now binds you. It must be like this at the moment of death, he thinks. Immeasurably sad. Yet it will not pass, not for several minutes at least until, finally, Striker is able to drag attention back to his goal.

The house itself is two-storey, white-washed, with tall chimneys at each end, but set against a background of dark woodland. A small coppice stands on this northern side and, behind, some form of outbuilding, quite large. A broken fence surrounds the front, terminating in a ship's mast, a signalling device, and he notes with satisfaction that the spar is topped by a lanthorn, slung from a halyard. Aran's note tells him that, when the lamp is lit, all will be safe for a landing, but with picquets posted. Beyond the house, to the south, stand three cottages, and this whole cluster of dwellings, the Nook included, is protected from encroachment by the sea with a stout stone wall, descending perhaps five or six feet to the sand and shingle below. He studies it a while, hidden from the house itself by a great willow, calculating his approach, learning the ground so that he will find his footing even in the dark and, once

245

satisfied, he turns the mare inland to check for possible escape routes.

But he cannot easily find one. To the south, and accurately portrayed on his map, the Wallasey Pool is impassable for a mile inland, with the small village of Poulton hugging its banks while, to the west, in order to reach the hamlet of Liskard and the meagre lane that leads away to Bidston, he would need to cross Liskard Moor itself. He explores this carefully, encounters nobody in the process, and soon finds himself meandering through a veritable labyrinth of pools, quagmires, and winding waters with no obvious path to follow. Finally, however, he comes to a strange place where the jawbones of a leviathan have been laid across the water, with sturdy cross-beams forming a crude but effective bridge. The beast must have been enormous, he thinks, and imagines how the feeble-minded would be afraid of the site. For it is bleak and forbidding. Yet from this landmark he is now able to discern the damp path between Liskard inland and Seabank Nook back in the direction from which he has come. It is less than ideal but probably better than trying to pick his way along the shoreline, that had been difficult enough earlier in the day. He takes a bearing from the trees behind him and, satisfied that he will be able to retrace the track later, he follows it.

He does not expect much from Liskard and perhaps it looks better when the sun is shining. Maybe in summer it is vibrant, a good place to be, but in the gathering early dark of a December evening, with a cold frost settling and its few windows unlit, it is a godless and unwelcoming prospect. Yet Striker must rest and eat, and its only tavern, the Boot Inn, will have to suffice.

A boy sees his arrival and rushes out to greet him, anxious to secure his trade. *God's Hooks*, thinks Striker, *the lad smells of shit.* 'Here,' he says. 'Take good care of her and there shall be a penny for your trouble.' And Striker dismounts, hands him the reins.

The boy spits on the ground, looks at Striker as though it is, rather, *he* who stinks. He mumbles some insolence but takes the horse to the back of the inn.

Inside, the Boot offers even less than he could have imagined, not even warm, forcing Striker to pull the folds of his redingote closer about him. By his Graham timepiece, previously the property of Sir Peter Leighton, he sees that it is barely five o' the clock. Three more hours, but only of course if the landing is being made tonight. According to Aran Owen, if it is not tonight then it could be on either of the two succeeding evenings. He hopes that this is not some fool's errand, certainly hopes that he should not have to spend even more time here, but he finds an unoccupied corner and calls for sustenance.

He must suffer enquiry in exchange, naturally. Suspicion, rather than hospitality, must be the mainstay of *this* fellow's stock and trade. 'Servant for the Rector of Hawarden, I am.' he says, relishing the Welsh accent that he has come to adopt almost without thinking this month gone. 'On my way to Liverpool, d'you see, and looking for one of the ferries but lost my bearings and come too far north now. Must wait for morning, I s'ppose.'

The innkeeper laughs at him, features like a pink porker. 'Not done too bad, not for a Welshy,' he says, in a tone so coarse that Striker can barely understand him. 'Wilson runs a boat most days. Early and late. From the Point, just along the lane. It's the quickest crossin' anyhow. Lucky accident, eh? 'E can do it in an hour at slack an' if there's not too much wind. Should be alright on the morrow. Room 'ere if y'need one. Stablin' too, Cheap. Think on it and I'll fetch food.' And he does. Thin gruel, watery cabbage and potato, shredded meat of some sort, impossible to identify. He manages to eat only a small portion, washes it down with some ale, and drifts into thoughts of his family. He sees the Valley of Virginia again, contrasts its beauty to this dismal location. He sees his mother and brothers, driven from their land by Lord Fairfax, wonders what has become of them. And the drift of his thoughts lapses into a fitful, inexcusable sleep.

But he is jolted awake, cursing his stupidity. Somebody has banged into the table on which Striker has laid his slumbering head, though his instincts at least force him to maintain the pretence of slumber. He hears the stamping of boots on the stone floor slabs as newcomers try to warm the blood in their toes. 'What I needs is a bonnag o' bread, boy. Some decent rum too. Think he'll come tonight then?' says a voice, Manx by its sound.

Striker half-opens an eye, and sees the small room now occupied by six evil-looking coves but, worse he finds Jacob Driscoll staring back at him. The unmistakeable Jacob Driscoll. The brace of martial flintlocks is still within the valise on his mare's rump. He has his paring knife, Striker recalls, but this is within his waistcoat. A third pistol, too, lies deep within a pocket of his redingote yet it is only his turn-off piece, palm-sized and usually more trouble than it is worth with its screw-on barrel. A weapon of last resort, which his present predicament may, of course, constitute. But to reach either of them will give these fellows the chance to have his hide, and he suffers that same sensation again. Time stands still. 'Oh, 'e'll come,' says Driscoll, and his gaze passes on to one of the others in the room. 'Maybe already 'ere.'

The men shout for ale and the innkeeper, no hint of suspicion with these coves, grovels obsequiously to their needs.

'Any strangers tonight?' demands Driscoll. 'And that one, t' sleepin' fellow, who's 'e?' The stale stench of the gruel seeps into Striker's nostrils from the wooden bowl by his face. This game could well be run, he thinks. Yet he should not care to die with this foul essence in his nose. He snorts, starts with a short cry as though he has woken himself by his own commotion, and his left hand spasms as he does so, sending bowl and contents to the floor. Heads spin, smugglers jerk upright from their benches.

'*Cach!*' says Striker, the strongest word he has yet learned in Welsh, but his right hand has, at least, dropped unseen to the pistol pocket. *With any luck, Driscoll shall accompany me on the long ride to oblivion*, he thinks.

'Easy, gents,' says the innkeeper. 'Just a lost Welshy. But ain't they all, eh? Poor fuckers. Hey, Billy' he shouts to the boy out at the back, 'bring some cloths, eh? Clean up this mess! You want some more stew, Welshy?' Striker shakes his head, a pretence of continued drowsiness.

Driscoll walks deliberately back to Striker's table, glowers down at him. And Striker avoids his eyes, enacting soldierly subservience to a superior. 'Welshman, eh?' says Driscoll. 'Where from?'

'Says 'e come from 'Awarden or some such,' says the innkeeper while the boy, Billy, soaks up the slops at Driscoll's feet. 'Never 'eard o' the fuckin' place meself, though!'

'Aberystwyth,' says Striker. 'But working in Hawarden now, d'you see? For the Rector. Mister Williams.' And Striker sees recognition dawn on Driscoll's horse face. *Oh yes*, he thinks, *you know that name, Mister Driscoll Another of your Jacobite traitors.*

Driscoll looks at him afresh, considers and then dismisses him as a possible threat. It is a difficult role that Striker has chosen, this William Owen. Former soldier who has seen action. A man hardened by his experiences. Yet now a fugitive, a deserter. A wary man who must avoid confrontations and attention. Yes, an interesting role indeed. Perhaps he should think of the stage as a future career? For life now stretches out before him again. But will Driscoll question him further about the Williams connection? Striker thinks not. He no more needs unwarranted attention than Striker himself. And he is correct.

'Maybe a flagon of ale with thee then, sir?' says Driscoll. 'For tha' trouble?'

'*Dim diolch*,' Striker replies. No, I thank you. It has been a long day and another on the morrow, so he will take the innkeeper's offer of a bed for the night and retire early. Billy is sent for the valise. There is discussion about a key, but apparently none of the rooms has a lock. Safe as houses here though, sir. Safe as houses. He can sleep easy in *this* establishment. And having taken his leave, smattered liberally with more Welsh barbarity, Striker climbs to the filthy garret allocated to him on the first floor. Thank the Lord that he does not have to sleep here – or, at least he hopes not!

He keeps the door slightly open, partly to help him keep track of what is happening below, partly because the damn'd thing would not shut properly even if he so wished it. Thus he has time to consider Newcastle's most recent instruction to him. Infiltration of the Jacobite leadership is now paramount, and gathering intelligence about the Stuarts' silver, held all this time by the Vatican bankers, is the most crucial tactical aim within the overall Hanoverian strategy. And why? Because Pelham's Government now sees that it can use the silver, the very purposes to which it has been put, to generate revenue for itself. A fie upon it, Newcastle has said, we could remain at war with France for the next twenty years, more even, if we possessed such resources. Imagine, just imagine, the damage that could be done to their economy over such a period.

Well, given sufficient time, we could topple the very Throne of France itself! Striker had not troubled to ask his master about the possible consequences of such a success but he doubts that the Pelhams even care.

And, while considering these affairs of state, he prepares in his own modest manner. He spreads a small set of tools on the bed, then removes each of the pistols from the valise, checks that the flints are still sharp and firmly seated, uses the vent prick to clear touch-holes, a spot of oil on the locks and then a tow worm employed to make sure that both lock and bore are free of oil and any other moisture, brings the lock to half-cock and, opening the frizzen, measures ten grains of powder from a silver horn into the outer half of the pan, before closing it again. He has performed the operation so often that the measure is met precisely without any deliberate concentration so Striker completes the process rapidly, turning the barrel mouth upwards, pouring the rest of the charge down the bore, ramming home a ball half-wrapped in wadding patch to keep the whole arrangement in place until it might be needed. A beautiful matched pair of weapons, one with its lock on the right side, as is normal, the other with its lock on the left. For Striker prefers to keep his pistols concealed, whenever possible, in leather holsters worn outside his vest and, having one of them a left-handed piece, he is able to draw them at will without too much chance of the mechanism snagging his clothing. So he holsters them, half-cocked in the safety position, makes sure that they can be drawn smoothly. And, naturally, he checks that he has some of the ready-made *cartouches* with which to re-load the Queen Anne's turn-off gun, though he has never before found a circumstance in which the diminutive object might be at all helpful. Finally, he attaches powder horn to belt, wraps some dried beef from the valise in linen, to curb the hunger that this damn'd innkeeper's gruel has failed to assuage, and sets it within a coat pocket along with a small flask of brandy, his tinder-box, the powder horn, a dozen bullets wrapped tight to prevent noise, and spare patches of wadding.

After a while, he hears Driscoll and his men leaving the inn, checks the Graham again. It is thirty minutes after the hour of seven or thereabouts, and he moves as silently as possible down the stairs. Then to the stable with tools and valise, readies the bay mare for later. He is unseen, steps out into the night, fastening the redingote and tying a kerchief around his head for extra warmth, knot to the back, before pulling the tricorne hat down to his ears, a muffler about his face. The smugglers are away in the distance now, out of the hamlet and, Striker guesses, off the lane on the path across the Moor. He finds it easily, follows it back to whalebone bridge, sees a window lit at the house but, with no signal set, and no other sign of life, he skulks carefully back to his former vantage point at the willow.

It is numbingly cold now and almost impossible to remain still when you are freezing. He takes a sip of brandy, looks up at the clear night sky. Sirius, brightest of the stars, just emerged in the south-east. Further north shine

Betelgeuse and Rigel, brilliant protectors of Orion's Belt and Sword. Even further to the north-west, the Seven Sisters of the Pleiades, a bright cluster of nestling diamonds. Then the easily identified 'w' of Cassiopeia and, finally, in the south-west, beautiful Andromeda. The moon is waning gibbous, with decent light to see and plenty of shadows cast within which to hide.

Across the river, huge lanterns glow. They mark the floodgates, he imagines, that give entrance to the Liver's wet dock, a modern wonder, Striker has been told. Far down the river, flames flicker in the dark to unmask some navigational hazard and, to the north, similar lights glow on the eastern shoreline. More closely, a small beacon glimmers on the Black Skerry's green tower.

After perhaps fifteen minutes, another light in the darkness, this time as the front door of the Nook opens and one of the smugglers goes casually to the signal mast, lets down the lantern, sets taper to its wick and then hauls it upwards again. He returns to the house and the door is closed.

How strange! thinks Striker. According to the note, the signal means that a landing is safe. But there is no obvious vessel standing off-shore. No picquets set. And little about the house that might suggest that a clandestine meeting is due to occur. He can hear their noise even from this distance. Even above the noise of the waves as the incoming tide breaks against the shingle. Perhaps not tonight then but, if so, why the signal light?

He breaks from the willow, steals along to the sea wall, uses it to provide cover from the house and edges along, sand beneath his boots, towards the steps that lead up from beach to front door, perhaps twenty feet away. The salt smell of the river is strong here, the coldness of the night slipping from his bones as the promise of imminent action warms him. *I really should have a plan*, he thinks, not for the first time today. And he probably could have secured some assistance from Chester's excellent militia. But his new guise, as William Owen, is just too fresh. Too soon to risk it with introductions to folk with whom he is not acquainted. In any case, this might be an entirely wasted venture. A fool's errand as he had thought earlier. So long as he is careful, there can be little danger, though the inn had been a close thing. Yet Driscoll has never set eyes on him, so why did he feel so much at risk there?

Striker ducks low, passes the steps and creeps to the shadows before one of the smaller cottages at the far side of Seabank Nook. He raises his head above the parapet, slowly, carefully. The noise from the house is even louder, a scent of manure on the offshore breeze. Still no sign of an approaching boat. *What then?* he wonders. *A quick look at the back?*

He hauls himself to the top of the wall, checks his pockets, checks that the pistols are still sitting comfortably in their holsters. All fine. And he is at the cottage wall, shadow-hidden, looking across the palisade that separates the properties. Sure enough, there is the manure heap just to the rear of the Nook. *I imagine that Billy, the innkeeper's boy, must venture here to bathe himself in the ordure,* thinks Striker, as he moves around to the yard.

But suddenly there are the dogs. Two of them, snarling, barking and stretching at their ropes to reach him. One so close to him that he can feel the heat of its breath. Its slaver splashes him and shock grips his heart. There had been no sign of the beasts from his observation post on the opposite side of the house. No sound from them either. *Good hounds,* he thinks. *The Lenape would have valued such as these!*

The door to Seabank Nook is thrown open. A head appears. He hears a weapon cocked. Voices within. *And the Lenape would know how to handle the creatures,* he thinks.

He drops to his knees in the gloom, careful to keep his head above those of the dogs and slightly beyond the range of their jaws. He emits a low growl, bares his own upper teeth but not in a snarl, more like a lunatic grin, reaches in his pocket for the pieces of dried meat and offers one, then the other, with the tips of his fingers, all the while making snuffling sounds that resemble nothing more closely than a low, barking laughter. Sometimes there is nothing so helpful as acting the fool. For they instantly subside, become playful too, though silenced again so that, within a few minutes, Driscoll's men have returned to the house, apparently satisfied.

But Striker, still playing quietly with the hounds, is also transported back to the Shenandoah River, so very many miles from the Mersey. He had been raiding with his Lenape brothers, returning to their own territory and camped at a place where the streams forked, settled for the night, tales of the day's exploits being told and told again. Two of the warriors professed themselves Christians, converted by the Jesuit Priests, so they wore the Crucifix amongst their beads and feathers, carried bibles amongst their possessions. Then suddenly the Catawba had sprung their ambush. The Lenape died one by one until only Striker was left, using anything at hand to keep at bay the slowly tightening circle of his enemies. And he had seen the bible, drenched in its former owner's blood but with the Sign of God still shining gold on its cover. He had crouched, seized it and howled at *that* night's gibbous moon with all the power in his lungs, then taken his knife and begun to scalp each of the Lenape dead, holding the bible aloft and singing every hymn that he had ever learned at the top of his voice. Acting the fool, playing the madman. Yet it had saved his life, for the Catawba, had been amused. Superstitious too, but basically amused. Taken the scalps he offered and left him there.

So, the bible had been his salvation. Ha! Religion. And he spares a passing thought for the sodomite Lewthwaite, now firmly within Striker's web. *Would he, in truth, have let the Redmond girl fall, that day at the Fair, if I had given him the signal? I suppose not.* Then he gives a final, playful tug on the dogs' ears, makes his way back to the fence and follows it to its end, where it meets a stream winding along the rear boundary of the house and cottages. He swings around the final fence-post, careful to avoid the freezing water and into the Nook's yard. There is light in the rear windows, a kitchen he imagines. So he skirts the manure heap, crosses to the large outbuilding – a brew-house by its smell – and thence to the back door. He crouches below the lit window. The timepiece again. Ten o' the clock. And still no landing.

But the men inside are arguing. Why can they not return to the inn? At least there is ale. Either that or back to the *Swift*. And how much longer must they wait here?

Their vessel must by lying in the Wallasey Pool, Striker imagines.

Driscoll's voice, loud above the others.

'Tha've been well-paid for this night's work, Captain. An' next two also, if needed. Now earn tha' silver an' tell these men they can have all the ale they need when t' job's done!'

'Easy, boy. Easy!' says the other. 'Can't blame the lads for bein' a bit touched. It's one thing chancin' an arm with the Excise man an' runnin' your blasted tea, but this feller we's waitin' for, why'd you need such a skutch on us any'ow?'

'Precautions, Captain. Just precautions,' says Driscoll. 'A slippery customer this one. An' a shooter too. Thought I was done for on Chat Moss. But 'e 'as caused us grief, this year, so I owe 'im!'

Striker instinctively sinks lower to the ground. A trap? And set by Aran Owen, it seems. Well, he has had his warning. This time the bastard shall pay with more than a finger! And he will need no skirted curate to perform the task on his behalf. He will choose one of the Redmond girls carefully, delight in taking his token. He will curdle Aran Owen's blood with the price he shall extract. But for now? The intelligent course, he knows, would be to slip away, settle his score with Driscoll another day. Yet he knows that, tonight, he will not take the intelligent course.

'This customer o' your'n might not even come 'ere,' says the one who Driscoll has addressed as Captain. 'Why not let some o' the lads go yonder for their ale? They can get back sharp enough if trouble brews. An' three or four of us should be more'n enough no matter how slippery 'e might be!'

'Tha' doesn't know 'im,' Driscoll says. 'But I supposed 'e would be 'ere by now. Fine, Captain. Three to the inn, but they get themselves back within an hour. Bolt the doors when they're gone an' let go the watcher!'

The Captain relays the instructions, calls out names of the three who will head back to the Boot. Kelly, Cain, Watterson. But which door will they use? And the watcher? Another hound, he assumes, though he had heard no response of one within when the others had been barking earlier. Striker glides from below the window, to a corner of the abandoned brew-house, watches the men come around from the front, cross the patch of light spilling from the kitchen until the moon briefly illuminates their precarious passage of a narrow bridge, no more than a long plank. He had not seen it earlier but it sits over the stream, leads directly to the Moor, and the men are soon lost to sight, only their chatter carrying back through the darkness.

Striker waits. He hears bolts slid closed on the doors. *The odds are lessened*, he thinks, *but only so long as they remain at the inn.* Time is short, but he must be patient too, Any premature commotion might bring them scurrying home.

Back to the seaward side now, careful to avoid too much noise though, inside, voices are raised once more. *I doubt they would hear me even should I choose to sing.* But not yet. He will need their attention soon enough, however.

He is at the steps again. The tide almost full now, lapping at the very base of the wall. Yet still enough dry stairs to accommodate him, crouching out of sight. He takes the brace of pistols, cocks them fully, lays them at the top of the stair. Then he waits, counting the minutes in his mind to allow the three who have left plenty of space to reach the hamlet, and thinking through a plan. At last, a plan. *But I need some help*, he thinks. And who better than his newest acquaintances?

Striker takes a stone from the top of the wall and throws it to the place where the dogs are hidden. Nothing. A second, and this one must find its mark, for the dogs take up a deafening chorus of roaring, snarling anger. No answering bark from the house, but the front door opens once again, as it had done earlier. A figure is silhouetted against the dim light of the interior, takes a long stride over the threshold and, Striker notes, apparently also over some other obstacle that he cannot see properly. A step? If so then the door would not close. The man has a firearm, points it gingerly in the direction of the dogs and peers into the gloom.

The pistols are in Striker's own hands now. He levels the left, sights along the barrel and squeezes the trigger. Flint strikes frizzen. Its spark meets the ten grains in the pan. Flash leaps through touch-hole. And the ignited charge in the barrel sends ball and wadding straight to the smuggler's throat. He slams back against the door-post, hands grasping vainly at the pumping wound. A thrill of excitement replaces tension as Striker sees the man slide to the ground, though he had not aimed quite so high.

'Lights!' Driscoll's voice, shouting, urgent. And the house is plunged into darkness.

It is Striker who might now be caught against the glow from the signal lamp. He should have thought of it earlier. Worth the chance though. So he keeps low, scurries right, to the mast. Quickly releases the halyard turns on the cleat and lets the lanthorn's own weight bring it smashing to the ground. In the intervening seconds he has reached the fallen smuggler, dead already, the sticky mess of his life spread down his chest.

Striker risks a glance into the hallway. Nothing. No sound. Deep shadows with just the image of a staircase to his front. He looks up its length but can see no evidence of anybody on the stairs themselves or at their top. No evidence of anybody at all!

He moves forward in a squatting position, carefully, avoiding entanglement in the folds of his redingote, the remaining loaded pistol extended in his outstretched right hand. One step to straddle the dead man's legs. A second to reach the threshold. Nothing. Silence. Dark upon shadow. A third into the doorway.

And falling. Falling. Sideways. Down. Confusion. Crashing to a floor. Explosion as the pistol discharges itself. An instant of light in the blackness. Crates and boxes. Big room, cellar. Blackness again. The pain begins but he has the presence to roll quickly away from where he has landed. Anywhere to escape the vulnerability of his position below the trap. The watcher.

'Well!' Driscoll laughs. 'A rat in the 'ole, that's what we've got my lads. Rat in a fuckin' 'ole! 'Ere's tha' jiggler, Angus. No, don't go near,' he shouts. 'I told thee 'e's slippery. Just slam t' door an' check on poor Kewley. We'll deal with our rat when t' other lads get back.'

'But the fall might o' killed 'im,' says another, the captain again, Striker thinks, pulling down the muffler to feel his lip, which he has bitten through in the fall. It is already swelling, blood trickling to his chin and into his mouth.

'Does tha' hear that, Ratty?' Driscoll calls out. 'Tha' dead, then? No, Captain, 'e's not dead. Not yet. An' I've got some interestin' questions to ask 'im later. About precious Mister Aran Owen amongst other things. 'E'll see some fun before 'e dies, will our Ratty!'

And the trap door slams shut, so that now the darkness is complete.

Striker takes a kerchief, uses it to staunch the flow from his lip while he checks himself for damage. His head hurts like the devil, the left temple badly grazed and the eye beginning to close. His left shoulder too. It pains when moved but does not seem broken. No dislocation, at least.

He feels his way on hands and knees to a wall, beneath the frontage of the house he imagines and just a little north from the trap. It is wet with damp. Cold. Smells of mildew. But he stands, sets his back to it and takes steps, toe to heal, heal to toe, away from the wall. A gap of six feet and he touches a wooden crate. Two crates, in fact, one atop the other. Reaches left and finds a single box, a little lower. He moves in front of this case, takes the tinder-box from his pocket, along with a few of the spare wadding patches, and sets them on the flat surface, carefully removing the lid from the box. There is only a small quantity of tinder inside and he must not waste it. He divides the contents into two portions, sets half on the lid of the crate, leaves the rest within the box, then uses the mechanism to grate against flint and fire the tinder. It flares nicely and he adds the patches to create a meagre flame. But it suffices. For, just a few crates away, he has seen a lanthorn. Filled, he hopes, and his faith is justified when, having moved to his new location, he is able to light the lamp with his remaining tinder.

His surroundings revealed. A large cellar, brick arches above him. And the space all but filled with crates, boxes and barrels. Hundreds of them. The illicit merchandise of Mister Figgis, he supposes. And the Manx smugglers, of course. But time is too pressing for an investigation. He re-loads the pistols, now recovered from the floor. Two minutes a-piece. He holsters them. And he must find a way out of this hole before either the other men return, or before Driscoll sends for them.

Nothing to the north side of the cellar. Then must he die here, as Driscoll has said, like a rat in a trap? He has left instructions, of course. Trusts that Newcastle, politician though he is, might carry them through. Payments due from Government, the pouches of silver and gold that he has garnered from raids like that on Redmond's bawdy-house. Newcastle to find his mother. Any of his surviving family. Let them have his fortune. *But we're not done yet, Striker!* For, at the opposite end, the cave turns right, an L-shape and, at its end, a ladder.

Striker climbs, pulls aside a wooden latch, puts shoulders to the door above. Pain shoots through his left side but he pushes all the same. Yet it gives. Not much, but it gives. Something is weighting it down from the outside. He pushes again, sweat breaking on his forehead. And such a stench. He ignores it, braces his feet on the ladder step and puts both hands flat on the under-surface of the trap door. Heaving, straining himself upright, arms at full stretch until...

The door goes up, crashing backwards. And the shit comes down!

The trap door had been hidden by the manure heap and he is now showered in the ordure. His hat might have deflected some of the mess but it remains below and no time now to fetch it.

Commotion within the house, lamps lit afresh. Driscoll and his crew alerted by the sound of the trap door, he guesses.

Bolts drawn, the back door smashes open. Two men spill into the yard. One with pistol, the other with short cutlass. No sign of Driscoll though. And these two cannot see him properly. They stop, look about, for Striker is only half-emerged from the cellar, part-hidden by this heaven-sent manure heap.

The shorter man, no natural pistoleer, fumbles his piece while Striker, with right hand, draws and cocks his own weapon. Flash from the pan. Sharp. The short man, bullet-headed, takes one step forward. The last of his life. Thunder-clap retort. Flame in the dark. Acrid sulphur stink of powder. And the fellow leaps backward, shot through the heart.

Striker draws his second while Mister Cutlass makes his own mistake. He should charge now, while he has the chance. Running, perhaps side to side, perhaps more difficult to hit. But he chooses instead to step back, looks to his fallen companion, probably his skipper, glances to the house, finds himself alone, and dies in his turn. An easy head-shot.

Still no noise from the Nook, so Striker lifts himself clear of the cellar ladder, sits on the edge of the open trap, remains alert whilst he re-loads one of the pistols. *Just one. It will suffice!* For the second he now hefts by its barrel, as lethal a clubbing weapon as anything used by the Lenape.

He creeps towards the door, gaze moving from one corner of the house to the other. Nothing. *So how intent may the fellow be on his reckoning, I wonder?* 'Well, Jacob! Just thee and myself now. Give you joy of this fine night, sir, though it may have ended differently than you had supposed.'

No response. The back door open, Striker pokes the pistol inside. No answering movement. *What am I facing here? Another pistol? Did he possess such a piece at Chat Moss? I cannot recall!* 'Dammit, Driscoll. Can we reach no accommodation, you and me? You seem a fine fellow, for all your Jacobite ways. And I rather think we have a shared purpose. Am I not correct?'

Nobody in the kitchen, Striker moves quickly to an opposite doorway, that leading into a passage behind the stairs and thence to the front door. *So where is he? Round to the left or up the stairs? Though I have not heard any sound from above. Or maybe gone out to the fore-shore? No, the room to the left then. I am certain of it!* 'Well, Jacob? You want to know about Aran Owen, I collect. A traitor to your noble Cause, sir, as you will have guessed. And, for my part, the same toe-rag has lured me here so that you may kill me. Is that not so?'

Out from the doorway and into cover beneath the stairs. Forward, along the passage. A glance up into the stair-well. He waits. Three seconds. Four. Then levels the piece towards the open door to his left, readies the pistol-cum-cudgel in his right hand and straightens himself against the open front door, standing now on top of the trap though which he had fallen earlier. The door behind him is oak, inches thick, and square-headed studs press into his back. Difficult now to keep his piece pointed for his arm and shoulder are stiffening. His lip throbs. Sweat runs unhindered down his face. *How much time do I have before the others return?* 'Well, you need not fear, Driscoll. You may meet your Papist Maker secure in the knowledge that Mister Owen shall receive just dessert for his treachery. After I have delighted myself with those sweet Redmond girls, naturally!'

Yet if there is a room there, on the north side of the house…

The force of the front door slamming against his back catapults him out onto the path. His finger inadvertently squeezes the trigger. One pistol fires into the night and the other flies from his grip. *Christ in Heaven. Not twice, surely!*

Striker tries to reverse the discharged gun but Driscoll has moved quickly, emerging from hiding in the Nook's southern room, previously masked by the open outside door. Driscoll's boot kicks savagely at his wrist, sending the second pistol rattling across the dirt too. So Striker rolls on his back, reaches for the paring knife.

Driscoll drops astride him though, sitting on his chest, left knee pinioning Striker's right arm. His fist drives into Striker's face. Jarring pain as the bones crack in his cheek. 'I need no weapons t' take thee down, Mister Rat! I'm goin' to kill thee with my bare 'ands. An' enjoy every second of it.'

Striker threshes beneath him, tries to use his feet and legs. But Driscoll's height and build make it impossible. He manages to flail at him with his free left hand but it has been badly damaged by the kick and, anyway, the length of Driscoll's arms allow the cove to keep well out of range yet still punish Striker with impunity.

Driscoll has him by the throat, one massive hand choking Striker through his muffler while the other lands punch after punch on his face. The already damaged eye now feels like it must soon burst from its socket. The nose is pummelled and gushing gore. *Thank God I shall not survive to see the mess he has made of me!* And he begins to sink into stupor. The blows happening to somebody else. That feeling again, like before. The wheel of life stopped in its tracks. Nothing beyond this moment.

Driscoll's grip tightens, both hands now on Striker's wind-pipe, squeezing the last vestige of existence from him. 'So that's *thee* gone, Ratty!' Driscoll grunts with his efforts, perspiration glistening in the moonlight. 'I only wish I knew tha' true name so's I could take it back to Manchester with me. Not Bradstreet, I'll be bound. Nor Rector's man, neither.' *He does not know my name! I shall die nameless.* And Striker's feeble left hand moves to the pocket of his coat, finds the turn-off pistol. He makes one final, choked cry of pain as his thumb pulls back the hammer.

Driscoll's mouth is open in a grimace of effort, almost in his face as Striker brings up the tiny piece, pushes it between Jacob's teeth. Driscoll gags, shifts his hands quickly to Striker's wrist, his eyes wide. 'Dudley Striker, sir!' he manages to croak, drowned by the percussion, and too late for Driscoll to hear since the ball has, by now, torn through his brain.

Chapter Twenty-Eight

Winter had taken Manchester by the throat too. Or, at least, it had done so by Christmas-tide.

Blankets of snow had begun to fall, threatening to choke off supplies, with the Irwell, Irk, Medlock and Tib all freezing fast. Like her heart, Maria-Louise had thought, chilling a little more with each day's passing since Rosina's wedding. She had imagined so much for her girls. Such ambition. Such futures. She had imagined other things too. That the marriage might somehow heal the rift between mother and daughter. Fie upon it! Would Rosina not set about changing matters in Bradley's home to help make it her own? Call upon her Mama to help her do so? She could surely not long continue the silence that she seems to have taken upon herself as protest at the thing! Yet there would perhaps have been disagreement even about so trivial a matter as the choice of new *décor*.

But Christmas may change matters, though Rosina cannot join them for dinner. Her new husband has insisted that they spend the day with Robert Jobb and his family. Maria-Louise fears the outcome however. For Bradley will be sadly disappointed if he expects that Rosina might conform to any normality of social intercourse.

Still, the day has given Maria-Louise herself much to occupy her mind, to distract her from her routine preoccupations. And how she enjoys this celebration of Our Lord's birth. But imagine all those years when Cromwell's regicides and puritans had prohibited the festival! Claimed it to be a Papist confection. And then this nonsense about the date. Newton, naturally. Always at some mischief, at least until his death, in Winchester, two decades past. But such an invention, that the twenty-fifth day of December had been selected by an early Pope to conveniently correspond with the winter solstice. Now this Lutheran, another German, Jablonski, also says that the date had been picked because it is the one on which a pagan Roman holiday had fallen. Are they mad? To think that the Church would simply have *invented* such a thing merely to distract heathens from their idolatry? *They should do well to read Saint Matthew*, she thinks – but then recalls that the Gospel according to this most noble Apostle does not actually give any indication of Christ's birthing day either. Indeed, it is the only one of the Gospels that describes the Nativity at all. *Strange that such an important element of our Christian Faith should not have been noteworthy for the others!*

All this commerce, too. Why, December hardly arrives these days without a seemingly endless stream of beggars hammering at the door to sell hollies, ivy, bay and the rest. Vendors on every street corner as well.

So last night she had ventured to the Collegiate Church once more, taking comfort and warmth from the Eucharist Midnight Mass. It had presented her with a chance to escape, both from thoughts of Rosina and Bradley, but also from the vexed concerns of her husband, who has become morose once more, sunk again almost to that level which had followed the attack upon his person. He is worried mostly about Jacob Driscoll from whom nothing has been heard since he set off for some secret gathering near Liverpool. Yet he has confided in her that an even greater worry stems from Titus himself having passed on information about the gathering to Aran. There was something not quite right about the thing. When he had considered it later, the whole idea that the French would land some agent to meet with Jacob in this way seemed entirely unrealistic. And then Jacob had been at such pains to explain every fine detail of the arrangement to Titus who, in turn, and though he had no real need to do so, had relayed them to Aran Owen. And what? she had said. That Aran had relayed them to somebody else? To what purpose? To whom? But she had discovered herself a dissembler. For had the same thoughts not passed through her own mind since that fateful night at Ancoats Hall? Aran's warning to her. Then the intrusion of the militia. And their captain, such evil eyes. Aran himself, of course. His humours erratic, troubled.

He will be here today though. For Christmas dinner, since she had persuaded Titus that Aran should join them. Scatterbuck too. The three girls.

There are vases in each room, along every mantle, filled to overflowing with mistletoe, every other manner of evergreen. Yew and fir. Green. Deepest green. Scents of resin and cedar. And while the town's poor must rely on Sir Oswald's charity this day, the Redmonds have the finest goose, exquisite wines, but a poverty of discourse.

'Dammit!' says Titus. 'Jacob should be here. Where *is* the fellow?'

'I have told you, my dear, that he is likely gone direct to his family for the festivities. And you know very well that he remains aggrieved about Rosina's marriage. I declare that it has affected him more than I could have imagined.'

'To Ormschurch?' says her husband, wiping gravy sauce from his moustache. 'Perhaps. But I shall not have the cunny-sucker behaving so.' Katherine, Anna-Marie and Maeve develop an attack of giggling. 'We have businesses to run,' Titus continues. 'Aran, you have nothing to say on the matter?'

'What *can* I say? You told me that Jacob would not have me accompany him to the meeting so I do not know how I may now be expected to define whatever has become of him. Yet this goose, madam, is exquisite. Quite the best I have ever eaten.'

'Oh, bravo!' says Maria-Louise. 'For this is Christmas-tide, a time of good will. And I shall not have it spoiled by harsh words.' Though, in truth, she believes that Aran may have changed the subject just a little too quickly.

'Kind words can warm for three winters, while harsh words can chill even in the heat of summer,' Scatterbuck says. He is at least free of printing ink today, though his face seems even more troubled by eruptions than normally. And she dare not *think* how any self-respecting tailor could have sent him forth in those clothes.

Titus mutters some profanity into his napkin but peace seems restored, for a while anyway, and Scatterbuck succeeds in soliciting some exchange from Aran about his completion of the painting for Byrom. Then a discussion about the *Journal* until Maeve insists that they should all play Straight Face. She instantly sports her most bizarre smile in an effort to make the others grin too, though this is not the object of the game since, to succeed in passing the turn to somebody else, she must switch quickly to her most serious frown and make one of them laugh as a result. The turn passes backwards and forwards mainly between the girls, though Scatterbuck is once persuaded to play a part.

Then riddles, Maeve suggests when they have exhausted the game. What kind of room is not in a house? What can be seen falling down but never crying? What has three feet but cannot run? And the tongue-twisters. Blackbirds bring bright berries.

And, all the time, Maria-Louise, quite affected by the wine, has slipped off her shoe, stretches her leg carefully under the table, and strokes Aran's shin with her toes. *Well, at least that seems to have brought a smile to his face.* Until the brandied peaches arrive, and also the remains of the plum pottage, carefully preserved by Mudge from their Harvest Supper, with its suet and dried fruits. A successful meal on balance, she thinks, though thank Our Lady that she had dissuaded Titus from inviting the Blossoms, as he had suggested. Fie upon it, the very thought!

O'Farrell and Mudge are thanked for their efforts, permitted to take a glass of sherry with the family, but they are barely done when there is a knock, a hammering rather, at the front door. An express boy, it seems. On Christmas Day, quite extraordinary. Frozen to the marrow, of course. Yet ridden by stages from Warrington. The roads 'a real dog's bollocks' apparently. Mudge called upon to show him the kitchen, feed him, warm him through. And, meanwhile, Titus has examined the envelope. *Mister Redmond, Manchester.* Ripped it open and studied the note within. Solemnly sends the girls to amuse themselves in the fore-parlour, then reads from the sheet of paper, actually the reverse of a small trade bill for some lincture or other. An illiterate scrawl but the message plain enough.

Fifteenth. December. Liskard Moor. Beg to inform death of Mister Driscoll, Captain Christian and two hands. Attacked this night

*at Seabank Nook. Attackers unknown. Sailing with ebb tide for
Douglas. Will bury at sea and ask innkeeper, Boot Inn, to forward
note by express. Regrets. Robert Quirk, First Mate, Swift.*

'The fifteenth,' says Titus. 'Express? Ten days ago! Those lick-spittles...'
And he gazes wildly to the door, as though he will have the boy's hide for this.
But Maria-Louise sees the tear start in her husband's eye. He may be harsh,
resilient, but he has had a relationship with Driscoll deeper than anybody
might have guessed. When the five-year old had watched his father hang, it
had been Titus, ten years his senior, who had stood alongside him, initially
just another witless spectator but later catching young Jacob in his arms when
the boy swooned. The Crown had taken Driscoll's father, taken the modest
means of his merchant enterprise too. Dispossessed the whole family while
Titus, whose own father had also been tried for treason in the Year '15, yet
been acquitted, was at least left with a business to inherit, damaged though it
might have been. Thus it had seemed natural to him that he should share some
of his relatively better fortune with Driscoll so that, within five more years,
the lad was regularly running errands for him, and had done so ever since, in
one way or another.

'My dear sir,' says Scatterbuck. 'Words can barely express my extreme
sorrow at your news. My condolences, sirrah!' Titus seems, at first, not to
hear though he finally makes some cursory acknowledgement of Scatterbuck's
comment. He will be recalling, she thinks, all those times when Jacob had
queried the reason for their association with this verbose little man for he
could never truly understand why Titus treated the printer as though he were
some official mentor to the family. And Scatterbuck himself will already be
composing an obituary, she imagines, for the *Journal* and its front page. It will
be more dramatic than anything appearing in the *Gentleman's Magazine*, she
predicts.

> *To those who have sympathy with our true Jacobite Cause and
> those who so nobly defend it, the following notice is addressed. Few
> persons in this town will remain unacquainted with the dedication
> and endeavour of Mister Jacob Driscoll, Esq, whose soul departed
> our world, this Fifteenth Day of December past, at the age of
> thirty-four. Our dear son, struck down in his prime by person or
> persons unknown, will be sorely missed and the proprietors of this
> humble publication convey their deepest sympathies to those of
> his family who survive him.*

'Oh God in Heaven,' says Aran, slumping back in his chair and burying
his head in hands. *Well,* she thinks, *I hope that He is heeding your prayer, my
dear, for I fear that you know more about this than you have yet allowed.* And

what is he thinking? About the times when he had described Jacob as no more than the Redmonds' pit-dog? About the occasion when he had apparently accused Driscoll of some involvement in young Sourwood's suicide? About the jealousy of which he had spoken to her in relation to Jacob's fondness for Rosina – a fondness that had never abated, of course, unlike Aran's own fickle sentiment, so easily overturned when he thought himself rejected in favour of Elizabeth Cooper?

'I should like to offer a prayer,' she says. 'On this most sacred of days, it seems most fitting.' And she moves to the small cabinet where her rosary is kept. She touches the Crucifix. 'Hail, Mary, full of grace, the Lord is with thee. Blessed art thou among women, and blessed is the fruit of thy womb, Jesus. Holy Mary, Mother of God, pray for us sinners. Now, and at the hour of our death. Amen.' Amen, they say. Then the large beads. 'Eternal rest grant unto thy servant, Jacob Driscoll, O Lord. And let perpetual light shine upon him' Amen. 'My God, I believe in Thee, because Thou art Truth itself; I firmly believe the truths revealed to the Church.' Amen. 'My God, I hope in Thee, because Thou art infinitely good.' Amen. 'My God, I love Thee with all my heart, and above all things, because Thou art infinitely perfect; and I love my neighbour as myself, for the love of Thee.' Amen. And the small beads, last of all. 'Sweet Heart of Jesus, be my love. Sweet Heart of Mary, be our salvation.' Again and again, while she recalls the many kindnesses that this rough-hewn man, this long-limbed, horse-faced fellow, this Jacob Driscoll has shown to her and the girls.

'We must send word to Ormschurch,' says Titus at last. 'And arrange some manner of Memorial Service, I collect. I wonder, Adam, would you be so kind? As soon as we may be able, perhaps, after the close of this festive season. Jacob would not, I think, have wished to detract from anybody's enjoyment.'

Scatterbuck will, of course, be delighted. Anything to assist, my dear fellow. And, having discussed some small matters of detail, he leaves them. Yet no sooner gone than Titus is waving the express at Aran.

'I could never have been appointed as a lick-spittle diplomat, sir,' he says. 'And it grieves me more than I can say to put the point. But I must know. I must *know*, sir. Whether you spoke with anybody about the Liskard Moor meeting. Anybody, mind!'

'Ah!' says Aran. 'So now we are about it! I see, sir. Not trusted enough to wed your daughter. Set aside without a by-your-leave the moment that James Bradley looks set to become Rosina's husband. And now accused of... Well, I do not know exactly *what* accusation I face. But I can tell you, sir, on my mother's memory, by everything that I hold dear, that I spoke with *nobody* about the matter.'

Another man than her husband might be taken aback by Aran's indignation but Titus has never been one who can be easily impressed by such performance. He takes another glance at the note, then back at Aran Owen before walking slowly to the dining room door and holding it open. 'It seems that dinner is over,' he says. 'I bid you good day, sir.' Titus waits until Aran has left. 'Well, I suppose you believe the cunny-sucker?'

'My dear,' says Maria-Louise. 'I have no doubt about the matter. Aran Owen would not lie to you, Titus. You should know that! Yet he perceives matters somewhat differently from ourselves at times and I should like to ask him how *he* considers Jacob to have met this untimely death. A terrible day, husband, I protest.'

'One of my worst, I think. Your father's curse sits heavily on this house, fuck him. Mudge!' he bellows. 'Mudge there! Bring the geneva, woman. My best, if you please.' He sits, runs fingers and thumb down his jaw-line, then the edges of his moustache, the permanent lines on his face even deeper now. 'But you know, dearest, that I cannot help the basic belief that I should have kept Jacob's news from Aran. It is not even a matter of trust. Just some supernatural sense that I cannot properly define. Well, madam, you must work your charms on the fellow. I cannot abide petulance and I cannot afford to be without his skills. In the meanwhile, we must cross the express boy's palm with silver for his troubles and then begin the task of discovering how poor Driscoll met his fate. That and how it has taken ten days for word to reach us. Yet the matter confounds me.'

But they receive something of an explanation when, mid-way between Christmas Day and the end of the month, there is a visit by the Borough Reeve, John Hawkswell, in company with a Waterguard Officer from the Excise Service at Chester. Yes, says the Officer, a most difficult journey. But urgent enough, he feels, to warrant the discomfort of road and weather alike. He shows Titus a note. Yet another damn'd note. Written in a coarse script.

Be pleased to find the mortal remains of a Manchester man, Jacob Driscoll, and sundry Manx wreckers at Seabank Nook, Liskard.

Nothing more, and left on the Excise office door. When? Let him think, now. It must have been the seventeenth of this month. He had taken a party to investigate on the following day, found signs of carnage, blood and such a-plenty, but no mortal remains. Considerable quantities of contraband though. Property of a Liverpool merchant, Figgis, it transpired. Enquiries at the local inn, of course, but discovered little of value. Yes, there had been some sailors. A Welshman too, who had left without paying. Nothing more. So they have followed the Driscoll lead here to Manchester and Mister Hawkswell has told him that the fellow had been in the Redmonds' employ. Moreover, that this Driscoll is, indeed, deceased. For a Memorial Service is arranged in the fellow's honour. Drowned in some boating accident, he understands?

Well, says Titus. He doubts that this can be the same man. They had not seen Jacob for several weeks, as he had set off early in December to undertake some business on his own behalf. For he has never, strictly speaking, been in the family's employ. Rather, he has fulfilled various contracts from time to time. Relating to the fustian trade, the Officer will understand. Perfectly legitimate. And, oh my dear, smugglers! Not Jacob Driscoll, surely. Hawkswell is certain to have given this Waterguard his own briefing on their activities but Titus has not flinched and, yes, of course, Officer, he has been instrumental in arranging the Memorial Service, but simply on behalf of Jacob's family in Ormschurch. He had been visiting there, it seemed. Drowned indeed near Southport. They have no details either, but such a tragedy! Naturally, if they learn anything further...

But they do not. The old year passes, although it will not officially end, of course, until Lady Day on the twenty-fifth day of March. And, by Twelfth Night, they are no further forward with their speculations. Four men dead. Attackers unknown, Yet not Excise men nor Militia, else the Waterguard Officer would surely have known. His involvement, however, may explain the delay in receiving the express, and Maria-Louise has imagined an innkeeper at Liskard – he is a rotund, jovial fellow in her reveries – waiting anxiously for the opportunity to forward the message, then confronted by this gentleman of the Crown, realising that he might be implicated in some illicit activity and subsequently having to allow time to pass before ensuring its delivery to Manchester. The thought that the innkeeper may be some careless cove who could not be bothered to find a rider until almost Christmas Eve would not occur to her. So who *were* the attackers. And how many?

'D'you know, my dear,' she says, as she cuts the first slice, 'that this Epiphany Cake has cost twenty shillings? La! Such expense. I wonder that we needed one so large. There shall be twenty slices at least. What, in the name of Heaven, do you intend to do with them all?'

'The guests will each expect a slice, will they not?'

'But there shall be no more than a dozen even if we include Mudge and O'Farrell. And how delightful that Rosina shall be here! Delightful indeed.' She has spent the past two days ensuring that Aran will also attend, feels perfectly gratified at her success in that regard. Though, goodness, such a trial. And it is clearly far more than simple bitterness resulting from their selection of Bradley for Rosina's husband. Why, she has discerned that he is, well, afraid. Yes, afraid.

'I had thought that we might distribute some of the remainder,' says Titus. 'To the Blossoms, for example.'

'And your *whores*, I suppose! A fie upon you, Titus Redmond.'

Yet the guests arrive, few though they may be. Scatterbuck again, and Aran Owen. James Bradley and Rosina. Nobody expects that this evening will have the same sense of celebration that one would expect normally from Epiphany Eve, for Jacob Driscoll's ghost haunts all those in the house, with the possible exception of Bradley. And he has kept things moving at a lively pace, a veritable Lord of Misrule, throughout the meal and, now, as they divide the cake. Maria-Louise feels strangely about his presence in her house, however. Feels strangely about him suddenly becoming her son-in-law, for Heaven's sake! Feels something stir inside her again at the sight of him. But he has perhaps taken more than his fair share of the punch.

'Why do you not play the harpsichord for us, my sweet one?' he says to Rosina. 'What? Timid dearest? Why not play that... That *thing*!'

'Were I to perform a piece, then the *thing* would have been my Couperin, *Les Barricades Mystérieuses*, and I would have played it in tribute to poor Jacob Driscoll. Yet you will recall, sir, that I have been unable to practise, these weeks past, since your promise that we should have an instrument at home has not been fulfilled.'

'Ah, fulfilment! Perhaps something that neither of us should expect from this marriage. Yet the morrow being Twelfth Day, perhaps there shall be an epiphany for each of us. And the girls, what gifts may the Three Kings leave for them, do you imagine?'

'Mama has promised that I shall have a new spinning top,' says Maeve.

'Indeed I have, miss,' says Maria-Louise, who has found herself quite bemused by the affection that her youngest has come to demonstrate towards Bradley. Yet Maeve treats him as though he were some wounded animal. Perceptive, she thinks. 'Though the Kings shall leave nothing unless you eat every morsel of your cake.'

'Then shall I find the pea in my portion, mother? For I should dearly love to be this year's Queen.'

But the honour falls, on this occasion, to Mag Mudge. And the guest who discovers the cake's hidden dried bean? He that shall become Mudge's Bean King for the night? Why, Aran Owen, of course. So this Royal Couple become entitled to fealty from all others until midnight. To be waited upon. Served anything for which they may call. King Aran and Queen Mudge, the one playing his role with reluctance, the other hers with relish.

'So, my dear,' says Maria-Louise when the others are diverted by Her Majesty's antics, securing a few moments of modest privacy with Rosina. 'You have survived your wedding night, I see.'

'No thanks to my Mama, I think. Oh, it was *so* delightful! I had to endure that buffoon, Robert Jobb, claiming that, as the Groom's Man, he had some *droit de seigneur*. And then that dear man, my new husband, wishing to know whether I was still a virgin. I had believed that we had an arrangement. Yet to avoid the worst, I must needs perform an unspeakable act. Unspeakable, Mama. Though at least it kept him from my cunny. There, does *that* suffice? You are quite welcome to the creature, you know. Perhaps if he had something else to occupy his mind, he may be more inclined to leave me in peace.'

'Rosina, my heart. You must believe that, while I might wish it otherwise, if I could have my time again, I would not make any different decision on this matter. Your Papa, this town, our entire Cause, required this marriage. But it is sealed and done, and shall there be no peace between us, no respite. If not for your mother's sake, perhaps in memory of poor Jacob. He would not wish us so divided.'

'Oh, a fie upon you, Mama. To abuse Driscoll's memory thus. Do you think me such a cull? I shall honour *poor Jacob* in the proper way, next Sunday, at the same heretic temple where you sold me to James Bradley!'

So, on the day prior to the Memorial Service, late on the Saturday, with snow sweeping once again through the town, they are called to the front door by O'Farrell and there, up the Lane, ride the spectral figures of Driscoll's remaining family, and his friends, from Ormschurch. They appear, one by one, from the curtain of snow flakes, silent, shrouded white in wrapping blankets, or redingotes, each leaning at his or her own peculiar angle from the saddle, upwards of a dozen in total. Titus has arranged stabling for them at the closest inns, some accommodation too, though Driscoll's cousin, Peter Kenyon, and his wife Mary will lodge with them. And in the evening, over a simple meal, Kenyon thanks them for their kindness.

'Yet 'tis a terrible thing,' he says. 'And this with the funeral – or, rather, without one. Th'art sure that Jacob 'as been properly buried, sir?'

'We have heard no more from the Manxmen so must assume that, as their note implied, Jacob is buried at sea,' says Titus. 'And I cannot help but think that he would not have been too distressed at that.'

'Jacob would be pleased that 'e died for t' Cause though maybe not the way 'e would 'ave expected,' says Kenyon. 'But at least not at th' end of a rope neither, like 'is father, 'ung for a traitor when all 'e had done was fought for t' True King. An' Jacob made to watch it all. Nothin' more than a small boy, eh?'

'Another sample of Hanoverian justice,' says Maria-Louise. 'Yet I confess, Mister Kenyon, that we remain troubled by the manner of Jacob's death. There are so many mysteries here. And the note from Mister Quirk makes no mention of any Frenchman. It was our understanding that the Manxmen were landing a messenger of some sort. I suppose that Jacob may not have shared any more detail with your good self?'

'No, Mistress, 'e did not. 'E visited, as tha' knows, early December. Told us that there was some agent of Newcastle at work in town. This town, of course. According to Jacob, 'e 'ad some plan to flush the fellow out. A trap, or some such. But more than that 'e would not say. No mention of any meeting, though perhaps 'e would not 'ave shared such with ourselves. Not that 'e didn't trust us, mind. But 'e could be a close cove could our cousin!'

Close indeed, she thinks. *Is it possible that there was no meeting arranged at all then?* If so, then it followed that Jacob had given false information to Titus. Was it possible? That he had lied to her husband? Well, there seems little doubt about that. Jacob, the Manxmen, the *Swift*, had all clearly been

266

at Liskard as planned, but no French messenger. And then Kenyon's words, repeated more than once, that Jacob had been setting a trap. So the promised meeting must therefore simply have been bait. No more than bait. But how far had this bait been cast, and for what end? Surely only so that it would be relayed to this agent whose activities he had blamed for the past year's reverses. To draw him out. *So relayed by which of us, did Jacob imagine? By me? By Titus himself? By somebody else? After all, we cannot be sure that he told only ourselves about this. Or by Aran Owen?* And, yes, she thinks. He had never liked Aran. Never altogether trusted him. Yet the sentiment was mutual and no reason to believe that either was justified in his suspicion of the other. Jacob had seen Aran as a rival in his quest for Rosina, apart from anything else. But there is a credibility about this that feels correct. That Jacob had invented the importance of the meeting, persuaded Captain Christian to support it. Not difficult considering the closeness between the two of them. And then shared it with Titus in the knowledge, the almost certain knowledge, that Titus would share it in turn with Aran. *He was banking on a repeat of Ancoats Hall*, she thinks. *That after Aran had received news of that gathering, the militia had arrived. Possibly this agent too, in the guise of their captain maybe. So another meeting, but this time with Driscoll waiting in the wings.*

But why Aran Owen? There must have been a dozen others, in the end, who had known about Ancoats Hall, though Aran's behaviour had been strange, that much is certain. And she lies awake most of the night, discusses some of her thoughts with Titus who, predictably, has come to exactly the same conclusions.

The thoughts preoccupy them on the morrow, too. Sunday, the thirteenth day of January.

The snow has stopped falling again but still lies in great drifts everywhere, and must be negotiated with care as they make their way to the Collegiate Church where the Reverend Doctor John Clayton has arranged the Service and will conduct it in person. But the congregation today will be quite different from that at Rosina's wedding, or even the one that had packed the Midnight Mass, for this service will attract only the town's Jacobites, numerous though they might be. Pattens protect shoe and boot, heavy coats help keep out the cold. And so they meet, in the name of our Lord, Jesus Christ, who died and was raised to the glory of God the Father. Grace and mercy are bestowed upon them.

'We look not to the things that are seen but to the things that are unseen. For the things that are seen are transient but the things that are unseen are eternal. Today we come together to remember before God our brother Jacob Driscoll, to give thanks for his life and to comfort one another in our grief.'

There is a canticle, but not especially apt since it refers so frequently to dry land. Readings and a sermon. Scorn heaped on Pharisees, Lawyers and Tax-Gatherers. Faith affirmed. Prayers of penitence. Absolution. Prayers of intercession and thanksgiving. For God has created all things, and by His will they have their being. *Te Deum*. Incense. The Commendation. The Lord's Prayer. The Peace of the Risen Christ be with them always. And with *you* brother. And you! Then the Dismissal.

They gather at the Bull's Head, so that they may toast the journey of poor Jacob's soul. For Maria-Louise, like all Catholics, understands this truth very well. Jacob's mortal remains may have sunk within the Irish Sea but they will be resurrected and reunited with his spirit at the coming of Our Lord and the Last Judgement. Corinthians, she knows, holds the secret. 'Behold, I tell you a mystery. We shall all indeed rise again. But we shall not all be changed. In a moment, in the twinkling of an eye, at the last trumpet. For the trumpet shall sound and the dead shall rise again incorruptible.' But she worries, for the absence of Jacob's corpse, their inability to hold a wake, to keep vigil before burial, surely means that his soul may easily have found the road to Hell.

Still, perhaps this belated ceremony will suffice.

Some of those present sit in one corner, smoking clay pipes and telling tales of Driscoll's life while others, the younger people mostly, once the ale and mulled wine have begun to flow more freely, begin to undertake those amusements that would have graced a wake proper. Townley's men, of course, well-acquainted with the Ormschurch folk. Feats of strength and arm-wrestling. Shaving the Friar. And the Cockfight, where two opponents are trussed, squatting, with sharp sticks gripped in tied hands. They stab at each other, try to overbalance their enemy. Fill the room with laughter and merriment.

And Maria-Louise recalls her father's wake. The arrival of a stranger bearing the Fey Rod, according to custom. That ghastly measuring stick with its Ogham script, to ensure that the dead will fit correctly within his or her final resting place. A thing of terror, that all seek to avoid, to keep at a distance. For should it accidentally take your measure, rather than that of the deceased, then your own doom will surely follow soon. But it had touched *her*. And she has ever since believed herself fated to meet an early end, surprised to survive each year that passes.

Yet no Fey Rod for Jacob Driscoll. No need. Simply his family discussing the distribution of his meagre possessions. At least, those that are still available. His horse, for example, must presumably be reclaimed from that jovial innkeeper on Liskard Moor.

And Townley's men, a different discussion.

'Driscoll shall have his reward soon enough,' she hears him say. 'Though perhaps not in the manner that he would have chosen. For Charles Edward will surely come this year, and the French will march with him. My brother has assured me. All is sealed. The Stuarts' silver will purchase a mighty host. More than this feeble English army might resist!'

Can this be true? she wonders. For had she not spoken directly with John

Townley on the matter? She had his assurance, or so she has imagined, that the forces of the Prince would come from Connaught or some such. Anywhere but France. Intolerable! And Francis Townley relishing the prospect. Townley, whom Titus had overheard calling her a whore. Townley, who had written off her husband as a spent force. *Well, Mister Townley, we shall see!*

But there are matters of more immediate concern, for Driscoll's Ormschurch people, Peter Kenyon amongst them, have confronted Aran.

'So *thou* art Mister Owen,' he says. 'I am surprised t' find thee 'ere, sir. For I 'ad gathered there was little love lost between thee and our cousin, Jacob.'

'It is true that there may have been some personal animosity between us. Yet I think that the time for such concerns must now be passed, do you not think? And a great blow has been struck against our Cause. For Jacob was crucial to these noble endeavours. Our link to the Manxmen.'

'Jacob did not trust thee, sir. That much I know. I may not understand the why, the wherefore, but 'e did not trust thee. And Jacob Driscoll was a good judge of character, I always found. So 'ear this well, Mister Owen. For we shall one day discover those who betrayed 'im. Those that led Jacob to 'is murder. And when we do, 'e shall be sweetly revenged. Tha' may count on it, Mister Owen.'

By the Mass, thinks Maria-Louise. *Poor Aran looks frightened from his wits.*

So she attempts a rescue, begs forgiveness of Kenyon, but may she borrow Mister Owen? For her husband has sent for him. Some problem to be resolved. And on such a day! Then hurries Aran out of the room, though the eyes of the two men remain locked for as long as they are able. Aran is shaking, febrile, distraught. So what is it, she asks, that troubles him in such a way? Time for some honesty between them, perhaps. For he has had some part in Jacob's demise, is that not so?

'You want to know what troubles me? Then look at this!' Aran holds up his left hand with its mutilated index finger. He is angry. More than she has ever seen before. 'No, my dear. Look at it *properly*. Look at it differently, I beg you. This *agent* that we discuss so comfortably, so anonymously, took my finger. He took it with a pair of blacksmith's pincers, Maria-Louise. His name is Striker. Dudley Striker. What is that look? Pity?' And he laughs.

'Call it pity if you wish, Aran. Yet I had thought it an expression of sympathy. Will you tell me now that I should not show you sympathy? And nobody would criticise you for actions that you may have taken as a result of torture. Such brutality. From an agent of government. La! It is beyond belief.'

'Oh, the torture? No, sweet lady. It had little to do with the torture itself. You see, Striker made it clear that this was simply a token between us. A mere exchange. My shackles for this finger. Mister Striker is a man who trades in tokens of this sort, you see. There was a different price paid *entirely* for my betrayal of our Cause. You cannot guess? Well, the price has been safety for yourself and the girls. Oh yes, Striker would not scruple for one moment and you have seen the evidence for yourself. You remember the Annual Fair? Maeve's disappearance? *That* was Striker!'

'But she was with Lewthwaite. Perfectly safe, as you assured me. Even so, if you truly believed that we were at risk and took steps to protect us, why should we have blamed you? And for what? Providing this Striker with information about a meeting at Ancoats Hall that a dozen others already knew about? And no harm done, I think, from that. We should tell my husband, I believe. He would applaud your protection of his family, not condemn you for it!'

'I do not fully understand Striker's hold on Lewthwaite but our good Assistant Curate is certainly under his control, you can be sure of it. He had instruction from Striker to let Maeve fall from the tower simply because I had failed to inform him about the meeting until the eleventh hour. He is no stranger either. You have met him already. The militia captain at the Hall. Rosina too. That fellow Bradstreet. Yet you must attach no nobility to my actions, my dear. I care deeply about yourself, the girls too, naturally, but the truth is that ultimately it was fear for my own life that drove me. I have spent night after lonely night imagining the pain-riven death that Striker would inflict upon me should I fail him in any significant way. And I cannot bear the thought. I am afraid.'

'And with that fear, when my husband told you about Jacob's meeting on Liskard Moor, you passed the information to this Striker. Oh, I read your expression carefully, my sweet, when you replied to my husband's question. For indeed you had not *spoken* with anybody about the arrangements. You had no need, for there is some other method of communication between yourself and Newcastle's creature. But you see where this leads us, Aran, my love? For Jacob had lied to my husband. Pretended that there was a gathering of some importance. My husband advised you of the detail and you, in your turn, sent some message to Striker. It was indeed a trap. Driscoll's trap! But Striker has survived it, so it seems. And he will believe that you, too, were complicit in its execution. How, now, do you think he will react? We are all in danger together, I think.'

'Then perhaps we should tell Titus, as you suggest. God knows, I should be relieved to have this damn'd weight off my shoulders at last, danger or no danger! Though I think that you overestimate your husband's affection for me and I fear that I will lose his trust forever.'

'Perhaps. But in any case *now* I think that we should delay a while. I have quite changed my opinion. He will listen to me. He always does. So I shall convince him that his suspicions about you are wrong. I will speak with O'Farrell too, however. Let him know that the girls will need special care over the next few months. A cautious word to Bradley as well, maybe. And who knows? It is still just possible that we might turn this matter to our mutual advantage.'

Chapter Twenty-Nine

As always, the severity of the weather had caught everybody unawares but, as the bitter chill began to grip, there had been a real threat that the grain supplies would be exhausted. The stores of vegetables had already become corrupted and blackened by frost, while the chickens and pigs that normally roamed so freely around the lanes and market square soon began to disappear. It seemed that even Old Tarquin might be at risk, as fishing holes were hacked through the deepening ice of the Irwell, and the short-sighted began to slaughter their breeding stock. Foraging trips for firewood ranged further and further from the town and there were violent clashes between Manchester's own people and those from Beswick, or Newton or Cheetham. Indeed, from almost *any* of the neighbouring towns within the Salford Hundred.

But by Saint Valentine's Day much of the snow has disappeared, to be replaced by a further cycle of frosts and a seemingly permanent coating of diamantine rime on tree and hedge, on house and highway. Biting cold, but clear enough for a journey to be safely ventured beyond the town's limits.

So James Bradley takes his wife, reluctant bride now reluctant traveller, and ensures that she is wrapped tight within rug and blanket, sat comfortably within the carriage that his footman has spent all morning preparing with warming pans. Bradley himself joins her and they begin the two-hour drive to the township of Droylsden, an inconvenient route, south of the Medlock and then east by lanes that take them through Openshaw and the road towards Ashton.

For this is also his birthday and the occasion for an annual pilgrimage. To visit his family. Yes, his family.

'Your parents must be delighted that you can afford them so much of your time,' says Rosina. 'Or that you are willing to take such risk, to travel so far, for the simple pleasure of their company.'

He *could* declaim her for a hypocrite, of course, given the condition of relationships between Rosina and her mother. *Her dear mother. How I miss her sweet ministrations!* And scarce much better with Titus. But he does not care for another confrontation and remains fatigued from the protracted negotiation that needed to be undertaken simply to ensure that she accompanies him on the trip. Everything in his life, it seems, has now become a negotiation. And for what? To make a journey the mere prospect

271

of which usually disquiets him for the whole of January and this first half of February too. So he ignores her comment, rubs at the gathering glaciation of the carriage window with the knuckles of his gloved hand, trying to clear some small aperture through which the world might be perceived. *At least today*, he thinks, *she does not seem so badly under the influence of that damn'd cordial that she favours so much.*

'And will they not take it amiss that you should arrive with a shining new bride when you did not even trouble to invite them to the wedding? La! Elizabeth, who counts herself your friend, did not even know that you *have* a family.'

Oh yes, his good friend Elizabeth who has never even *asked* whether he has a family. And, whilst it is hardly unusual for a fellow to be cuckolded by a so-called friend, his must surely be a unique situation. Friend, indeed. Well, they say that arranged marriages cause the couple to devote more time to learning the character of their respective spouse. For when people profess themselves in love, they put on a persona that they think will be attractive to their opposite number and, it being rarely their true self, once doffed in marriage, disappointment results. Resentment even. So, Rosina must put some effort into understanding him. Including this issue with his family.

It might seem unnatural to others but the fact is that he has never had *any* affection for them. Never. He does not despise them as Rosina seems to despise her Mama. There is simply, well, nothing. Ambivalence would be the kindest way to describe it. He is grateful to them, in his way. To his mother for helping him survive childhood. To his father, for introducing him to his trade. But no more than that. And hence the odyssey each year upon his birthday. An unspoken thing. Yet they will expect him. And beyond that? To be frank, he is surprised that they have survived so long. They *should* have been dead long since yet they continue to thrive.

'Do I now not even merit a response? And did you not justify the journey to Droylsden, only this morning, by reminding me that this marriage represents a coming together not of two people but, rather, of two families? Some nonsense, I recall, that the fact would make our union stronger. Based upon a belief that blood is thicker than water, I assume.'

'My dear, I am reluctant to reply only because, it seems, every time I enter a discussion with you, there is a cost involved. I recall being turned over for the price of a new harpsichord simply so that I might have you join me today. And blood is only thicker than water in the literal sense. We choose our friends and, in my case at least, I have had the fortune to be able to pick a wife too. But relatives are forced upon us, their characters randomly selected from the chaotic assortment of whims and humours exhibited from the many dozens of folk who make up their fore-bears.'

'Then I do not see how the bringing together of two such families can possibly create a stronger marriage or assist in any way. The fact is, Mister

Bradley, that a marriage arranged like our own is no more than a device to help *my* parents and *your* business interests protect their status. A fie upon it! What else is the dowry, the Marriage Portion, the Jointure, unless they are all elements in a commodity exchange. And the commodity in question happens to be myself. Where is *my* right to choose, sir?'

'Ah, and so many wonderful examples where lovers have chosen each other for marriage, are there not? They confuse affection with fucking for the most part and then, when the passion has run its course, find themselves left with nothing. Well, nobody could ever accuse *this* marriage of having its base in physical passion. At least, not between bride and groom. But you barter well, Rosina, I will give you that much. I realise now that Titus can have no concerns about a successor to operate his various enterprises after he is gone. Which reminds me. I must ask him whether there is any reduction for family members at his bawdy-house. No, my dear, I prefer a marriage nurtured here on earth to one created in Heaven.'

The lane runs through Openshaw, across Skerrat's Brook, and along Edge Lane, a thoroughfare in such poor fettle that they are lucky it has frozen hard, for it is not uncommon to see wagons and carts sunk in mud to their axle-trees along this stretch. But they pass safely to Lane Head and Droylsden itself, where the carriage turns left towards Greenside, halting in front of a row of cottages, and drawing attention from a ragged assortment of neighbours.

As always, Bradley casts a professional eye over the property as he steps down. The row is all post and pane construction, the timber framing of the cottages filled with brickwork and each house having a single lath and plaster dormer in the roof. But the condition still looks good despite, by now, having stood here for a century and a half.

He hands Rosina down and takes a hamper from the coachman, dismissing him for two hours but not one minute longer while, behind him, his mother wrestles with the winter-warped door, forcing it open just enough to allow entry.

'Jim?' she shouts, thin-voiced and peering out to the lane. And how he *hates* being called Jim. 'That you, Jim? Oh, goodness. Glory. I told Pa you'd be here. But he went off to the bakery anyhow. It's Thursday, you know. Thursday? Glory, I forget. Well, come in. Come in!'

She beckons Bradley to follow, so he puts his back to the door, opening it further so that he can get through with the hamper, and Rosina follows him into the house-place, a kitchen with enough room for a stout dining table and assorted chairs, a decent hearth to the right that boasts a welcome fire. And hanging above the fire, his mother's blackened kettle.

'Close the door, Jim,' she says. 'Close the door, boy. And who's that with you, eh?'

He sets down the hamper, forces the door back into its frame, closing its latch while Rosina waits for her introduction, looking from mother to son as though she expects to find some similarity, some likeness. But there is none. His mother is bird-like, small and thin, her head constantly in movement upon her narrow neck, framed by wisps of white down.

'This?' says Bradley. 'Ah, my wife, Ma.'

'Wife? You have one? I'd forgot. I'm sorry, dear,' she says to Rosina. 'You must remind me. I can't remember your name. Oh, glory!'

'Rosina, Mistress Bradley. Rosina Redmond that was.'

'Rosina? Ah, yes, of course. I remember now. Glory, what it is to grow old, my dear! Come and sit by the fire. Warm yourself. The kettle will soon be boiled. And, Jim! Did you bring anything special for your Ma? Oh, but what am I thinking? Your birthing day, and not even a kiss yet from your own mother. Your Pa told me. Made me say it over and over. So's I wouldn't forget. Come. Kiss me.'

He bends almost double to receive a peck from his mother's cold beak, wonders whether he should tell her about the wedding but knows that he would be wasting the effort. Travelling clothes are removed and he collects the hamper, sets it near the fire and opens it for her.

'Here, Ma!' he says. 'Some bottles of best porter for Pa. Some of that Italian sausage that he likes so much. Crab-apple cider from France. Cheeses and macaroni too. You recall how to cook it, Ma? Mango pickle. Jars of preserved turtle. His favourite black pudding. And two pounds of tea.'

'Tea, Jim? Oh, bless you. We can't afford tea in this house, Rosie. You would not believe the price!'

He catches the disapproving look that Rosina has cast in his direction. *She thinks I keep them in penury. Yet I furnish them with a pension of forty guineas each year. It is hardly my fault that Ma will not spend above the half of it!* But he does not feel inclined to correct her.

'Well, you have some now, Ma. The finest too. Why, I purchased it from a dear friend of Rosina. From Mistress Cooper herself. Is that not right, my sweet? I imagine that we should all enjoy a saucer.'

'And the children,' his mother continues. 'How are they, Rosie? You do *have* children, Jim, do you not?'

'No, Ma. Rosina and I are only recently wed. No children yet.'

Nor none likely, if the best I can achieve on my own wedding night is a hand-job. And even that with a price to be paid. Some agreement that he must not press her on this matter, that he must give her time, in return for some conjugal civilities while they are in public together. *But not too much time. No Mistress Valentine, you shall feel the length of my pricker before too long! Either that or the comforts of your dear Mama once more.*

'No children? Glory! And a Redmond did you say?'

'Yes, Mistress. My father is Titus Redmond. A fustian manufacturer in Manchester itself.'

A fustian manufacturer and far more besides.

'Why, I know him!' says Mrs Bradley. 'A true supporter of Good King James. I know him, Jim.'

'No, Ma, you knew Redmond's father.' And he wishes that they could have avoided this subject. Dammit, he can see the gleam in Rosina's eye when she realises that here might be a political ally. It is three decades since old Redmond died and she must have been, perhaps, fifty years old at the time. A totemic age, by which many will be dead. But those who survive it, like his father and mother, seem able to continue forever. Why, the broadsheets are full of longevity tales, it seems.

'You follow the Cause, ma'am,' says Rosina. 'And knew my Grandfather Redmond, too. La!'

'Did I, Rosie? I don't remember. Now, shall you take tea, my dear? One of my oat cakes perhaps?'

Rosina tries hard to draw further comment about her grandfather from Mrs Bradley but is treated, instead, to an inspection of the property. This house-place, of course. The parlour too. Tiny and only opened on very special occasions, cold enough at the moment for a meat larder. And the stair, no more than a broad ladder in truth, from the kitchen up to the sleeping-space in the rafters, with just the dormer for light and a heavy drape that must once have served to partition the area. A moist, mildew aroma to the place despite the blaze that seems adequate for keeping the cottage warm.

The tour takes three, perhaps four minutes and terminates with a further viewing of the dresser's contents, by which time Bradley's father has returned, a patched blanket wound about his workman's coat and thick canvas spatterdashes lashed around his trousers. He seems hardly bigger than Ma Bradley though James remembers him as a strong fellow. To see him struggling merely with loaves fetched from the bakery, you would hardly credit the prodigious reputation he had once enjoyed, first as a bricklayer, then as a bricklayers' gaffer.

'Pa!' says Bradley. 'Let me take those from you. And keeping well, I see?' But he instantly curses himself for the enquiry as he sets the bread down and his father begins to struggle free of his wrappings.

'Well? Me?' His voice is reedy, though remains strong despite the frailty of his form. 'I have not enjoyed a day's good health since I married your mother. Those bloody oat cakes, I swear. I have been often tempted to haul her on a halter to the market place and chance that I might get a decent guinea for her. Is it still lawful to do so?'

'Perfectly lawful, sir. Yet I understand that it has become the custom to base such auctions upon the weight of the wife for sale.'

'God's Teeth, I shall be lucky to fetch a florin!' says his father, shaking his head sorrowfully as he appraises Ma Bradley on imaginary scales. 'Yet this one looks more promising. You've married at last? I doubt that you would have brought some doxy here. Or, at least, no self-respecting doxy would trouble to make the journey. Must be a wife then. Though she doesn't *look* like a wife.'

'This is Rosie, Pa. Jim's wife, Rosie. Don't you remember? Oh, and give you joy of your birthing day, Jim. Or did I say that already? Glory. Such a day!'

'A good day to *you*, sir,' says Rosina.

'Good day? Hardly that, I think. My knees, my elbows, all ache as though they have been beat with hammers. I return home to find my prodigal son here for his annual visit and my wife still breathing. I should marry again though, if only she would shuffle off and leave me to it! And if I could find myself a flame-haired beauty like you, my dear. Here! Help me off with these leggings.' He sets his boot on the bench alongside Rosina so that she can unfasten the ties around the muddied canvas.

'You do not seem so infirm that you may not deal with your own shanks, sir,' says Rosina. 'Though I should not wish to appear lacking the attributes of a dutiful daughter lest you encourage James to sell me at market also. Ah, yet the Marriage Settlement will, at least, protect me from *that* fate, I fancy. Now, my dear husband, your Pa's leggings if you please, while he tells me a little of my grandfather.'

His father's turn to chortle now. *Well, he appreciates her fire it seems. Though the damn'd woman treats me at times like a common servant. It will not answer.* Yet he bends to the lashings that fasten canvas to his father's shins.

'She's Amos Redmond's girl, Pa. Rosie Redmond. Glory!' says his mother.

'His grand-daughter, Pa,' Bradley corrects her, and his father explains how old Amos, a good man, had been associated with the fustian trade here in Droylsden. It is not simply a town of weavers, of course. There are bleachers here, too. And hatters, shoemakers, blacksmiths, crofters, colliers. But fustian manufacture had been its core for many years.

'Yes, good man,' says Pa Bradley. 'Broken by the trial, though. Never the same after. We would have been the same age, I think. And you, my dear. What trial has brought you to marriage with my Whiggish son, I wonder?'

'Why, sir, the trial of fortune and finance, naturally. James and my father deemed the arrangement profitable to their respective business. Yet I am not broke by it, as you may well allow.'

Oh, not yet, my sweet. But you shall take to the halter soon enough, I protest. Bradley finishes with the spatterdashes, throws them in a corner near the hearth, wondering how much of his two hours here are already spent. He must return as soon as possible for he has associates to meet this evening. The last of his fellow-Jurors whose votes he needs so that he can become Clerk of the Town Works. A costly investment at one hundred guineas for the position itself, but considerably more when he has finished gifting his various colleagues appropriately. But Clough is posing a problem for him. He had known it was a mistake, allowing a Tory Jacobite to join the Court Leet. It will all be worthwhile, though, once the post is in his hands.

'Glory! I told her already, Pa. There's worse ways to start a marriage. They need to take their time, I said. Learn each other's habits. Friends first, lovers later. That's the road.'

'La! Such ambition,' says Rosina. 'Yet there are so many other ways to bind a couple, do you not think? To share a faith, for example, or a cause, perhaps. Support for the Stuarts, maybe. Am I correct in thinking that you are both also followers of King James?'

'You *must* remind me how many of those matters you share in common with your good friend, Mistress Cooper, my dear,' says Bradley.

'And dangerous days for wearing loyalties too plain upon our sleeves, my girl,' says Bradley senior.

But the coachman is at the door.

'Ah, so soon!' says James, retrieving his riding cloak and taking from its pocket a small purse of coins. 'Here, Pa. Forty guineas. Are you certain it is sufficient.?'

Of course, says his father. More than enough. They are fortunate. There are many who must rely on Parish and Poor Law here. And not just old folk. Hand-outs of food and fuel. But not for them. And never once to the Worshipful Company, neither, for their Charity Shillings. Wishes him joy of his birthday. Next year, if God spares them...

Oh, Glory!

Hurried farewells and back to the carriage. Rug and blanket once more.

'They are perfectly charming,' says Rosina. 'I had thought myself immune from all manner of shameful behaviour on your part, Mister Bradley. Yet to abandon those dear people with no more than a bag of gold and a curtailed annual visit. Well, a fie upon you, sir!'

'They have all the charm of a millstone, my sweet. And there are many in this pretty town of Droylsden who would gladly exchange places with them for the gold alone, never mind the pleasure of my company each year. And if you think so highly of them, why, it can become a part of your wifely duties to visit them in my stead.'

'I should like to do so, of all things. Indeed. Yet we shall need to discuss the terms for such a development, do you not agree?'

'If they are so charming, I should have thought that you would visit for affection's sake. Please do not trouble to do so on *my* account. I must say, my dear, that I weary of this constant bartering. The Marriage Settlement is at least clear. Written. Ink upon paper. Yet the more subtle accord between us does not seem to function as Mistress Cooper had led me to expect!'

'We are two months married, sir, and subtlety I have yet to discover in this relationship. I do not see how you contrive to involve Elizabeth in the matter. We discussed the thing at length and, at her persuasion, I finally agreed this damnable marriage on the accord that I should have the freedom to pursue my own life when we are not in public. And it is I who should complain at sundry breaches to *those* terms.'

'Oh, my dear,' laughs Bradley, then sucks at his teeth while he clears another loophole in the frosted window. 'I could not have made the point better about lovers and blinkered affections! Elizabeth seems so righteous, yet such a rogue. Do you not know that she told me the very reverse? That if I allowed your sapphic liberties, then you should act the compliant wife in all other matters, in all other ways? *All* of them, mind.'

Chapter Thirty

'Walpole is dead!' cries Sir Watkin Williams Wynn, stabbing his pudding finger against the front page. 'Lord in Heaven, there is justice in the world after all. At least this levels the score for Scudamore. The effects of his urinary gravel, it seems. Though I shall have to wait until my return to London before I can discover the full details. This rag of his own invention is riddled with eulogy and nothing more.' He passes the *Daily Gazetteer* to Sir John Glynne, his fellow Parliamentarian and Member for Flintshire. 'I wish I could have been there to see his pain. They say that Ranby drew from his penis a stone the size of a kidney bean, last month I think. God, how he must have suffered.' And he smiles with contentment, leans back in his seat and takes another sugared almond.

David Morgan, the gentleman barrister, draws on his long-stemmed pipe, blows the smoke carefully away from Sir John, peers over his shoulder so that he may read the text. He might be wealthy, but his patched, brown coat contrasts strongly with the immaculate clothes of his companions, including the clerical grey of Richard Williams. As a matter of fact, even the Rector's Secretary, William Owen by name, seems less shabby than Morgan.

Striker has never met Walpole, of course, but the man's character has always intrigued him. He has never understood how one person could be so reviled by half of the population, so revered by the other. It is natural, he supposes, that Tories like Sir Watkin should despise him so, for Sir Robert had almost single-handedly driven their faction from supremacy to impotence yet, at the same time, made his own Whig Party a byword for corruption. He had been responsible for keeping Britain free of involvement with the continental carnage for twenty years until his fall from grace but only, they say, due to his strange partnership with the former French *Premier*, Cardinal Fleury. A peculiar twist of fate, though, that he had died within weeks of his most bitter opponent, Henry Scudamore, the third Duke of Beaufort.

'He died at Arlington Street, it seems,' says Sir John. 'Alone, apart from Ranby. I have several friends who suffer from the gravel, d'you know. They swear by Jurin's lixivium. Claim that it dissolves the stones quite away. Yet it *is* the end of an era, as they say. And for all the moral turpitude of the Fat Squire, I should prefer him any day to these damn'd Pelhams. And you did not find him so ill, I collect, when you were neighbours, Watkin?'

'Ah! The difference is that I procured Number Fourteen by honest means, whilst Bob Bluestring received Number Ten as a grace and favour, another reward for selling his country to the Hanover crowd! I met with him there often enough. I had to do so on Party business. Yet I was always careful to count my fingers at the end.'

Striker hides a smile. Walpole had become Leader of the House and First Lord of the Treasury in '21, appointed then of course by the Sovereign specifically to act as his or her intermediary with Parliament. The entire country, knows that the Monarch appoints Ministers so that they will present the royal will, to negotiate with Members of each House, persuading, coercing, bribing so that the King may enjoy the support of a majority in all matters crucial to him. It might even be necessary, at times, to explain the Crown's financial needs and, God forbid, occasionally to account for the way in which taxes have been spent. To do so, it has become increasingly necessary for these Chief Ministers of the King to attend sessions of the Commons and, these days, they attend so frequently that they have been allocated their own seats on a particular bench, the Treasury Bench, the front bench, as it happens.

It is obviously necessary for the Monarch to ensure that his Ministers fully understand the royal prerogative before they attend sessions of Parliament, so he organises regular meetings of his appointed Ministers, his Cabinet, to brief them. And in '21, with Walpole appointed Leader and First Lord, George the First had diligently continued to participate fully in these meetings. Difficult, since he had not possessed a word of English but relied on his son, now George the Second, to provide a frequently inadequate translation. When the king had finally tired of this nonsense, it had become easier to meet simply with Walpole alone, so that Sir Robert had become 'the Great Man', no longer simply a Chief Minister but taking upon himself the role of *Prime* Minister. It is a term that may have been used in earlier administrations, but it is Walpole who takes the role and makes it his own. And rewards from a grateful Monarch are showered upon his head. A fine house in Downing Street. The Order of the Garter, never previously bestowed upon a commoner and earning him the nickname, Sir Bob Bluestring.

And what a gift for the satirist! Swift in *Gulliver's Travels*. Fielding's *Life and Death of Jonathan Wild*. John Gay and his *Beggar's Opera*. A dozen more of similar renown. A score of prints. A hundred street ballads. A thousand pamphlets. Oh, and the efforts to repress them, to keep plays like *Polly* from the stage. Well, the Great Man had fallen from power, and now he is dead.

'Yet rewards come in many forms, it seems,' says David Morgan. 'According to this, with Wade resigned, Cumberland is made Captain-General of the army in Flanders. Why, the French shall have nothing to fear from *that* young pup!' The Duke of Cumberland, Prince William Augustus, and second surviving son to King George.

'He should not be under-estimated, I think,' says Richard Williams. 'He acquitted himself well at Dettingen, I understand. With the Dutch cowering in their garrisons and the Austrians half-starved, a Royal Prince may be just what they need to re-unite Hanover's allies.'

'So, Richard!' sneers Sir Watkin, his mouth stuffed with more sugared almonds. 'You have become a military strategist, I see. William must be stocking your library with a very distinct category of literature these days, eh William?'

I do not know which of us this sanguine fellow despises most, thinks Striker.

'Strange that you should say so, Sir Watkin,' he says, at his obsequious best. 'For I have only recently acquired for the Rector an administrative document, written, signed and sealed by a certain Monsieur Pattyn. Administrative, as I say, but a most illuminating account of the Siege of Ypres. Vellum, you know. The finest, sir.'

Sir Watkin, it seems, has taken a dislike to William Owen from their first meeting.

Striker had under-estimated the extent of the damage suffered to his own person on Liskard Moor, but such things are not unusual. He had left the bodies of those who had sought *his* death where they had fallen and made his way back to the whale-jaw bridge. There he had hidden himself, and just in time, for the remaining three Manxmen had come bustling across in the opposite direction only minutes later. It had been all muttered, *Damn the fucking Skipper for landin' us wi' this!* And, *Watch where you're goin', Kelly, for Christ's sake!* Or, *It's too bloody quiet for my likin'.* But once gone, Striker had himself passed over the brook and thence to the inn, recovering the bay mare as silently as he was able and trotting back towards Thurstaston. He had stopped where the road crosses the Birken to wash the worst of the blood from his face, muffled himself again to cover some of the injury, and found himself a decent hostelry where he took to his room for a day and a night before returning to Chester. There, a hastily scribbled note left on the door of the Excise Office and then a visit to the Constables, telling them that he had been attacked and robbed in town on the previous night. Probably Welshmen, they had said. And he Welsh too? Well…

Another day's rest, then back to Hawarden on a Fly-Wagon. Richard Williams relieved to see him, concerned for his welfare. And only his welfare, Striker had wondered? Yet he had faithfully described the mythical attack upon him in Chester. Apologies too since, whilst he had been able to collect the three tomes from Mistress Adams, the robbery had happened before he had purchased the accompting books and parchment supplies. The associated silver had, at least, defrayed some of Striker's disbursements over the past few days and, whilst he had thought seriously about applying the same principle to the new acquisitions, he had finally decided to collect them so that he might have something for his own entertainment during a convalescence.

The latest four-book, single volume edition of Pope's *Dunciad*, printed according to the complete copy found in '42. A translation from Philadelphia of Cicero's *Cato Major*, a real beauty, green crushed Levant Morocco, the covers gilt-tooled in a panel design, and the contents printed on finest Genoese paper. Well, according to the Widow Adams, at least. A fine-looking woman, too. And, third, a first English translation of Jean de la Fontaine's *Loves of Cupid and Psyche*, calf-skin, richly decorated spine, but not Striker's thing at all.

Pope and Cicero he had enjoyed, however, relishing the tender ministrations of the Rector throughout Christmas-tide, each of them dismayed at the anti-Welsh sentiment so prevalent in Chester Town, the ineptitude of the Constables. Yet what else could you expect with the Whigs in power, the country gone to wrack and ruin? They had shared confidences too, Jacobite aspirations, for Squire Redmond had already told Richard that William might have similar sentiment. Yes, it is Richard now. And William's woeful tales, of campaign chaos, of friends fallen, of battles braved, of punishments imposed. Incentives, too, for all those willing to denounce comrades as Jacobite, as friend to the vile Pretender. All told between readings from Richard's Welsh Bible. All told against the dark winter fireside of the Hawarden manse.

And to the manse, at the end of January, had come Sir Watkin Williams Wynn himself, making the road from his home in Ruabon with a small retinue so that he might perhaps break a journey to visit with Sir John. He carried news, but had been careful to impart this only to the Rector and had paid only the slightest attention to Richard's new Secretary, while Striker had reprised his William Owen performance, deferential yet slightly disdainful, as reluctant to share his past with this gentleman as Sir Watkin might be to share pleasantries and trust with a serving person. But the fellow's face, Richard? Looks like he has been beaten to within an inch of his life. Explanations, but distances maintained, while Striker makes his own assessment of this rubicund Parliamentarian Baronet, critic of corruption but too corpulent himself to have entirely eschewed the cash cow of political patronage. The corpulence, the suet-fisted obesity of great wealth.

Striker's initial assessment may be faulty. And, God knows, our first impressions of people are invariably lacking. But he believes that he has the fundamentals. Men of wealth thrive generally on the creation of further fortune, an end in itself. Other Jacobites will support their Cause for Faith. Some for a notion of liberty, like David Morgan's belief that the Stuarts might free Wales from an English yoke. Some in hope that their respective woes and disaffections might be corrected by whatever promises of reform they have heard whispered by surrogates of the Pretenders. And some, Sir Watkin Williams Wynn and Sir John Glynne amongst them, because there is a collective memory of the era, not so long ago, when a Stuart Monarchy implied a level of opulence to which they, for all their current riches, can barely aspire.

'Well, I'll be damn'd!' says Sir Watkin. 'Ypres, you say. A long way from Wrecsam, William, eh? What think you of the place. Not like Aberystwyth, I should hazard?'

'No, indeed,' says Striker, glancing out the window of the Eagles Hotel to the town's High Street where endless strings of ponies are being led towards their destination at the Beast Market. His first visit to Wrecsam, yet he is struck by the opulence of the place, its plethora of horologists, perukers, hatters, tobacco-cutters and spectacle-makers, its fine houses on Priory Lane, Tuttle Street and the Mount. 'It is prodigious, sir. Quite prodigious. Yet only we Welsh, I think, could so arrange matters that an Annual Fair might fall in the middle of Lent.'

'It would not happen in the south, Mister Owen,' says David Morgan. 'Enjoy our creature comforts too much in Merthyr! But are we agreed, Sir Watkin? I am for Connaught then? Or should we need another course before the thing is settled?'

Morgan has been irascible throughout the meal, though Striker knows that this is the fellow's normal demeanour. *Why, he would complain of cold breakfast even if he faced the hangman.*

'To Galway Town itself,' says Sir Watkin. 'Within the month, David. If this Gordon has the following that he claims within the five counties of the Province, we must consolidate as soon as possible. The message from the Duke of Perth is clear. He is sending an entire entourage of Catholic agents to meet with Gordon at the end of April, and begs us to send our own embassy, to persuade those who do not share his Faith that this is not some Papist invention.'

In truth, Striker doubts that there is much veracity to these claims about Connaught. He has heard them before. And now a new Messiah arisen there. Edward Gordon, a former Ensign of the Thirty-Ninth, garrisoned in Ireland until the unit's recall last year and, strongly Jacobite in his views they say, elected not to accompany the Regiment when it returned to England for service overseas. Yet one more deserter. Yet one more divided family since, according to Sir Watkin, the man has a brother still serving as a Captain in Lord Loudon's. *Well, we shall see how far loyalty may stretch if the Young Pretender makes his landing.* But this Connaught business. There is disaffection there, he knows, but these past few years have been difficult for his homeland. Crop failures and the like.

If it had only been Connaught, he should certainly have dismissed it. But, over the expansive dinner, a patchwork of conversations, quite open conversations, have woven themselves into a colourful quilt of significant proportion. The Earl of Cork working mischief elsewhere in Ireland itself. Growing support for the Jacobites in London through Sir Watkin's own Independent Electors' Club. Strong contacts made in the North East, at Scarborough, Whitby, Hull and Sunderland. The Duke of Beaufort's initiative, prior to his death, in South Wales and Cornwall. The Earl of Barrymore in neighbouring Cheshire, persuaded finally to take up the mantle so cruelly fallen when Sir Peter Leighton was murdered at Higher Poynton. *Oh, that exquisite cheese! I must remember to return there.* And the Scots, of course. The Duke of Perth still busy as a beaver.

'It would be easier to do so, 'says Sir John Glynne, 'if we enjoyed more support here. I am still confounded that Barrymore did not attend, after all his promises.'

James Barry is the Fourth Earl of Barrymore, from Marbury Hall in Cheshire. Striker has heard different tales of the man, ostensibly a strong supporter of the Stuarts but another of these phenomenally wealthy landowners, unlikely to risk his comforts unless he is certain beyond doubt that their Cause will triumph. And he has failed to join them, not for the first time, apparently. These Gentleman Jacobites, thinks Striker, may not have the stomach for it. Oh, they have stomach a-plenty for plotting over dinners of this White Rose Circle, this political dining club of Sir Watkin's. And such a dinner!

The Eagles Hotel has served them with royal splendour in a private room. Sir Watkin, as senior, had taken the head of the table. Next, Sir John Glynne. Then the remaining guests according to their status. George Shakerley of Gwersyllt and uncle to the Shakerleys of Somerford in Cheshire. The two Catholic Vaughan brothers, travelled from Courtfield, and related to Sir Watkin through his marriage to Ann Vaughan. Wilson, the artist. Henry Lloyd, born here and travelled to France seeking a Commission, but presently serving as a Jesuit lay brother. Morgan, of course. Richard Williams. And Striker himself, wondering at the strange dichotomy that brings these influential folk together, planning sedition over a meal that could have fed much of starving Connaught.

The bumpers of fine wine, and toasting the True King. Then the meal. Three simple courses but balanced so that each would contain the same number of dishes, ten to complement the number of diners.

The first course of Pigeon Bisque, Boiled Rabbit, Beef Stew, Cod's Head, Quaking Pudding, Johnson Pie, Creamed Marrow, Rice Florentine, Collared Eels, and a centre-piece of Bombarded Veal, each sliver of tender meat wrapped in bacon, seasoned, coated in bread-crumb and served with a fine *ragoût*.

Discussion around the table throughout this part of the meal had been mostly about property, a singular preoccupation for them, it had seemed to Striker. Sir Watkin's plans to develop Wynnstay. Sir John's intention to flatten Broadlane House in Hawarden and build a modern castle there. Richard and William Vaughan on their family's problems with drainage on their estate at Bicknor.

A second course, somewhat lighter than the first, with Scotched Collops of Veal, Pigeon Pears, Hashed Calves' Head, Buttered Lobster, Sliced Pheasant,

Potato Pudding, Stewed Soul, *Oeufs au Miroir*, Regalia of Cowcumbers, Quince Jellies.

And now, at last, with this selection of dainties, had come the substance of the gathering. Reports from *this* contact, from *that* source, about the state of readiness of friends around the country. General excitement, possibly fuelled by the claret, at prospect of Charles Edward's imminent return. Welsh spoken more frequently. But an overall sense of unease arising from Scudamore's death. The Duke of Beaufort had, after all, not yet reached thirty-eight years of age and there are rumours about the circumstances of his death. It is claimed that he was simply worn out by a complication of disorders and, God knows, he had been a sickly man. But as the major English sponsor of Stuart Restoration, they had speculated, he would have been a prime target for one of Newcastle's agents. Striker had felt a moment of jealousy but consoled himself with the thought that this *is* no more than speculation.

Dessert course. Peach Fritters, Whipped Syllabub, Portugal Cake, Wiggs, Sugar Plums, Ginger Bread, three varieties of cheese and, of course, the Sugared Almonds. The sugared almonds and inevitable disputation about the French.

It had been clear to Striker that many of these Welshmen still held to their original insistence that they would only come out if the Stuarts were backed by a strong French army. And Sir Watkin had been in Versailles once again to receive further assurances on this matter. But they had also mellowed somewhat on the point. They could not fail to have done so, he supposed, if support was, indeed, growing at such a rate across England and Scotland. The Duke of Beaufort is a set-back but there will be others who can rally the West Country. Why, Scudamore's nephew, Charles Noel Somerset, will inherit, so it is likely that the incoming Duke may be more Jacobite even than his predecessor. And Sir Watkin's latest news, about this fellow Gordon in Connaught, had brought them near to ecstasy. Speculation is a wonderful thing after so much food and fine wine, and it had not taken the diners long to imagine an entire fleet of French transports landing a legion of Connaught men along the coast. A glorious march of Irish and Welsh across the border into England to meet up with a Franco-Scottish army coming south. A *rendezvous*. But where? Chester, perhaps. Or Manchester.

Ah, Manchester! Mention of the town had brought new and more sober direction. Well, Sir Watkin had said, perhaps the involvement of the Irish might at least help resolve their *problem* with Manchester. For while the rest of them had taken the stance that there could be no repeat of the failures in 'Fifteen, and that only a fitting French presence might assure victory, those fine Manchester merchants had adopted quite the contrary measure. Stuff! It is Redmond, of course. And his wife. A real beauty though. Why, had this been the Kit-Cat Club they could have toasted her looks! Beautiful but dangerous. For they need Manchester. They need blades like young Townley.

Yes, Henry Lloyd had said. He has met the elder Townley. A fine soldier. Believes his brother will raise a regiment for them. But only if they may by-pass the negative influence of the merchants, those deluded into thinking that the French will demand some undefined 'pound of flesh' for their involvement, and that this is somehow a price too high to pay for liberty from Hanover.

Well, Sir Watkin had said, the Redmonds may have had their uses. And none can deny that they have raised gold a-plenty for the Cause through their activities. But Titus does not seem the same man as he used to be. Too occupied now, it seems, with his bawdy-house and his gin. His value to the Cause is diminished, surely. Why, he has lost Jacob Driscoll, lost his links with the Manxmen too, it seems! And how will smuggling tea serve them further in any case, when Pelham has announced that the import duties on that commodity will be slashed? For Heaven's sake, it will be more profitable to import the damn'd stuff legally. Yet, Striker had thought, these Redmonds may still have a part to play.

The thought had kept him amused as the port had been served and, one by one, Sir Watkin's guests had given apology and dispersed until only himself, Richard Williams, David Morgan and Sir John Glynne remain.

'Confound Barrymore!' says Morgan. 'We do not need him and, by the time our forces arrive in Cheshire, the thing will be already decided. But we do need Manchester. Connaught too. Though I expect there will be questions about gold?'

And Striker has his own problems with Manchester. There is Lewthwaite, the Assistant Curate of Saint Ann's to consider. His hold on Lewthwaite is tenuous at best. Aran Owen too, naturally. He had recalled Aran Owen's question about whether Striker had arranged for him to be followed. He had dismissed the thing as a foolishness. But if he really *had* been followed, then by whom? Yes, the Aran Owen situation troubles him. His passing reference on an earlier encounter to Leighton's execution. His involvement with Driscoll's trap. By God's Hooks, if he had been capable on that day after Liskard Moor, Manchester would have known the true meaning of retribution. He would have wreaked such havoc upon the Redmond girls that Aran Owen would live the remainder of his miserable existence in such a Hell that even Dante could not have conjured. The early days of Striker's recovery were full of it, the cold, careful planning. Yet, as the winter weeks crept by, doubts had occurred. He had put the matter straight enough to Driscoll, peering into that darkened passage-way at the Nook. Aran Owen had lured him there, had he not? No denial, but there were other things on Driscoll's mind that night and Striker has learned by now that nothing is quite the way it seems at first glance. In any case, as Striker had pictured the torments that he would inflict on saintly Anna-Marie, on long-limbed Katherine, on sweet little Maeve, he found himself quite incapable of including red-headed Rosina in his calculation. His meeting with her in the Market Square. It had been June? Surely not.

Nine months gone? She had *liked* him, he thought. Or, at least, she had liked Bradstreet. The same thing.

'Gold, Mister Morgan?' says Sir Watkin. 'I am sure that you can deal with any such questions, sir, given your profession. In any case, there may be further news on the matter of resource for our enterprise by the time you sail for Ireland.'

He is clearly reluctant to say anything further in present company, suggests that they should take a turn around the town, perhaps the Horse Auction. And it is Pack and Penny Day, after all, the final day of the Annual Fair. Some wonderful bargains to be had when the traders reduce their prices.

I wonder whether Sir Watkin has news of the Vatican silver? thinks Striker. *If they want it here in time to signify, they must make plans for its safe delivery soon. But little chance that he will share intelligence with myself or the good Rector.*

Yet it is crucial to Newcastle, this cache of treasure that the Stuarts have set aside for their future treasury, invested with the Papal bankers and soon to form an instant Exchequer. And such a plan! To sequester the Jacobite coffers and use the contents as investment capital for the same business enterprises that have so successfully raised revenue for the Stuarts. A hostile Hanoverian acquisition of the Stuart corporation. And perhaps a merest portion of the returns paid to faithful agents who may have assisted in its successful conclusion?

Outside, it is a fine afternoon. Small clouds scurry across an otherwise clear sky, driven by a fresh south-westerly. Wrecsam all a-bustle, an ebb and flow of local citizen, of outside visitor, 'twixt shop and Market Fair. White cottage wall and thatch. New red-brick. Ruabon brick, of course, Sir Watkin boasts. Narrow thoroughfare from High Street to Beast Market. The vendors' cries. The auctioneers. Warm waft of manure, mingled with the scent of cooking stalls, of the bake-house ovens.

Sir Watkin cannot help himself. For despite the scope of their recent dinner, he is drawn to the bakery door. There is no place on earth, fine day or foul, more welcoming than a bake-house porch and they have passed this low, squat building, with its large window looking out over the acres of animal pens, at the precise moment when Baker Bevan has thrown open the iron door of his cavernous oven and begun to bring forth his final batch of cottage loaves and ginger-bread. This latter he presents, with a satisfied smile, on the broad blade of his long-handled spatula for the inspection of those awaiting his wares.

'I salute you, Bevan,' says Sir Watkin, blustering his way through the customers, entirely oblivious to the scornful looks that he receives in return. *Not the sort of deference that the Baronet would expect, I collect.* 'This is the finest ginger-bread outside London, I protest! Five shilling-worth of your best, if you please.' And the baker makes his bow, offers regrets to the queue, begins to wrap the purchase.

But something has caught Striker's eye. A woman, more acid than insolent, has lowered her gaze and edged back through the other shoppers. Dressed in Lenten Black, she does not seem hurried, as though her place in line, now lost, may have been critical. She does not move in a way that would suggest protest at Sir Watkin's rudeness. In fact, she displays a certain deliberation. *Perhaps nothing, but worth a check.*

Striker follows the woman, until he stands once again in the porch, sees her edge through the crowd, occasional backward glances, until she reaches the pens. He instinctively keeps himself hidden behind the porch-post, observes her speaking, agitated now, to a group of men who had previously been watching the Auctioneer at his work. The men look towards the bake-house. They call to others, and to one in particular. *I should take them for farm-hands*, thinks Striker, *though it is damnably difficult to say when the whole world sports its finest for a day at the Fair. But this cove is no labouring fellow, methinks. A gentleman to match Sir Watkin unless I am mistaken!*

And Sir Watkin is engaged in a dispute with Bevan. David Morgan and Richard Williams have left the shop as a result, while Sir John Glynne has turned his attention to the customers, threatening to horse-whip a complainant, though he has no such weapon to-hand. 'Damn your eyes, sir! You think I do not know the weight of five shilling of biscuit?' shouts Sir Watkin.

The dandy at the pen fences is now difficult to see, for he has gathered upwards of a dozen men about him, but Striker gestures towards him in any case, inviting both Morgan and the Rector to follow his gaze. 'Do either of you know that coxcomb?' he asks.

The group is assuming that hive quality, each individual infecting another with sense of enraged invasion, while one or two fly through the crowd in different directions to gather others. 'I have never seen the man in person,' says Richard Williams, 'but if I should hazard a guess, I would say that he must be Myddleton.'

The Myddletons are, indeed, almost a match for Sir Watkin, since they are the other major land-owners locally, and John Myddleton of Chirk Castle had challenged the Baronet for the Denbighshire seat in the '41 General Election. Myddleton had duly been declared the winner by the Accounting Officer with just over nine hundred votes against Sir Watkin's seven hundred and fifty. This could not be right, of course, since Sir Watkin had paid handsomely for a considerably greater number. At least five hundred more. So he had sent out his factors to gather signatures from those who had promised their support and received his silver in return, then challenged the result. It had been difficult since the Accounting Officer was also High Sheriff of the County and Receiver of the Crown Revenues for North Wales. In addition, he was Myddleton's cousin. William Myddleton. But Sir Watkin had, by circuitous means gained the support of the Parliamentary Commissioner in first investigating and then overturning the result in July of the following year. William Myddleton had been stripped of his positions and sent to prison. And John Myddleton, it seems, has not forgotten the affair. He has now disappeared entirely, however, but his supporters have not.

A line of men is approaching the bake-house, several fellows armed with staves or cudgels and others with stones in hand. *This looks devilish,* thinks Striker. *I wonder whether His Grace would pay handsomely to have Sir Watkin and his friends out of the way?* 'Where is he?' shouts one of the men. 'The Great Devil of Wynnstay! Come forth, sir.' And the cry is taken up by others.

A crowd of spectators begins to gather, though at a respectful distance, and Bevan's customers either move deeper into the shop or make their escape while the baker himself, eager to avoid involvement, presses one of the shillings back into Sir Watkin's fist, apologises for mistaking his weights. A foolish error, lordship, but with his permission the shop must now close. And he ushers both Sir Watkin and Sir John through the door.

The first stone is hurled, falls short at their feet, so that these gentlemen are finally aware of the mob outside. 'There's the Devil himself!' Striker steps behind Sir Watkin, while Sir John Glynne announces that he, himself, shall bring the Constables. And he is gone.

'Why,' calls Sir Watkin, 'these fellows are Dissenter dogs unless I am much mistaken. I fancy I have seen *that* fellow before!'

The seemingly most assertive of the rioters, a willowy fellow with a crooked face and few teeth, shakes a cudgel. 'Dogs are we? Then I expect we'll end up chained in your bloody kennels like that poor fucking Preacher, eh?' Another stone, nearer the mark this time, and a chorus of curses.

Whether these are Whigs or Methodist Dissenters, Sir Watkin is clearly not lacking in enemies. And he had, indeed, reacted violently only two years ago to the news of a Revivalist Preacher peddling his trade at the Cross in Ruabon, dragged the poor man by his collar all the way back to Wynnstay and, yes, he had tied him up with his hounds for punishment.

Richard Williams steps into the breach, imploring Sir Watkin not to inflame matters, then standing forth in front of the crowd. 'Now see,' he shouts. 'Some of you know me. I am Rector of Hawarden and a man of God. If you have grievances with Sir Watkin, this is not the way to resolve them.' David Morgan joins him, invokes the law, threatens the Riot Act. More curses, but no more stones at least. *Yet I do not think that these two have much experience in this field. The fools shall get themselves killed.* And Striker casts about for a likely weapon. Perhaps he should leave the three of them to their fate, and bad luck that Sir John Glynne is not amongst them, but he has decided that he does not care for this mob. If he had arranged the thing himself, he might have felt differently perhaps. But he at least owes Sir Watkin a debt for today's fine meal. And there may be a higher purpose for which to play here. Let this settle their account then.

Sir Watkin's own blood is up. 'Kennels, you say? My kennels are too good for the likes of you, fellow! Seward's would be a more fitting end for scum of *your* sort.'

There is stunned silence. William Seward had been a Revivalist preaching in South Wales in '40, and stoned to death by an aggressive crowd. *A particularly inappropriate taunt in the circumstances, perhaps,* thinks Striker as the small mob surges forward at last. For the stones fly free and fast now, several hitting Sir Watkin while Richard Williams and David Morgan are attacked with cudgels and fists. They defend themselves as best they can, but Striker is back in the bake-house for, on the wall, where the spatulas and rakes are hung, he has also seen Bevan's other implements, including the douter, that peculiar chain flail with an eight-foot handle used for cleaning the oven of ash. The baker himself has retreated up the stair to his flour store so Striker helps himself to the heavy weapon, struggles a moment to get it out of the door while, at the same time, pulling Sir Watkin back to greater safety.

He runs forward, hefting the cumbersome flail above his head. A small rock hits his chest as he kicks, high, into the stomach of one of Morgan's assailants. *The petty-fogger knows how to fight, too,* he thinks, for the barrister has already downed a rioter. And rage takes him. A step forward, the douter swung in a long arc that takes it over the heads of Morgan and Williams, then whistling downwards towards the crowd, its long chain loop slicing the top of one man's head, the left eye of a second, the arm of a third and wrapping itself around the knee of a fourth, tangling there.

Striker heaves to free it, succeeds only in dragging the cove to the ground while the apparent ring-leader, the crook-faced fellow, jumps towards him, arm back to strike with his club. 'Get the Devil! Get Wynnstay!' yells the man. But Striker switches his grip on the handle, takes it mid-shaft, swings its free end to block the incoming blow, then follows through with a vicious quarter-staff upper-cut that removes his attacker's remaining teeth, leaving one of them incongruously embedded within the wood and its former owner sprawled senseless in a mess of gore, his upper jaw smashed.

And, suddenly, it is over. Striker keeps the douter poised while the hale amongst their assailants collect the wounded. Morgan and Williams help each other to the bake-house porch while Sir Watkin, blood seeping from beneath the edge of his wig, calls down curses on their attackers for the cowards that they are! The implement is returned to Bevan, an incisor still dug into the handle, with some quip from Striker that this is twice in one day that the baker has been bit.

Townspeople join them, offer consolation. Such ruffians. Disgrace, honest folk unable to go about their business these days. A dwindling escort of the concerned and the inquisitive back to the Eagles Hotel. The proprietor shocked to see them treated so. Please permit him to offer some comfort. Water to bathe their injuries and a physician sent for. Sir John returning, breathless, with Gwilym Roberts, the Constable. Questions, descriptions, promises. And Striker's standing raised beyond measure. Compliments from Sir Watkin, grudging respect from David Morgan, open adulation from Rector Williams. The story re-told for Glynne's benefit. Oh, how he wishes he might have been there to deliver his own chastisement!

'It occurs to me, Mister Owen,' says Sir Watkin when the five of them are settled and alone again once more, 'that perhaps we should not send our good barrister alone into the wilds of Connaught. You have proved yourself a useful fellow. Can never repay you for your service today. What say you? Will you join him on his trip to Ireland. I am sure that the Rector might spare you for a few weeks and David would appreciate the company, I think?'

Striker weighs the possibilities. *You cannot know how close you came today,* thinks Striker, *or you might not be so gracious with your praise.* And Sir Watkin *could* repay him easily. *Does he think me too noble to accept monetary reward? The fool.* And while Richard seems willing to release him for the journey to Connaught, David Morgan does not seem quite so convinced. Ireland is a tempting possibility though. A diversion to Tipperary, too, perhaps. Tempting indeed. Newcastle would need to be informed, naturally. But he would not object for Striker would, without doubt, be able to find some contrivance to thwart the plans of this new Messiah, Edward Gordon. Yet he thinks not. He doubts whether Gordon, or anybody else for that matter, can deliver any meaningful fighting force for the Jacobites at this time. The doubts must show on his normally impassive features.

'You seem unsure, William,' says Sir Watkin. 'Is it the expense perhaps? If so, you should have no fear on that score. All costs would be met from the funds of this Circle, sir, I protest. And think of the glory, Mister Owen. The possible patronage of a grateful Monarch. Or is it the venture itself that gives you pause? A shrewd fellow, I see. Ah, I collect that I am near the mark. You doubt success, sir! Well, I think it is safe to share our news with William, Sir John, do you not say so?'

'Sir Watkin...' begins David Morgan, a note of caution in his voice.

'No, David,' says Sir John Glynne, 'I agree with Watkin. Mister Owen has shown his mettle. We should now show him our own.'

'Indeed,' Sir Watkin continues. 'And the news is good. We are assured that the Connaught men will come out. But, just in case, it seems that we shall be able to offer them considerable inducement.' *So,* thinks Striker. *The Stuart coffers after all.* David Morgan's obvious exasperation. *Yes, Sir Watkin is not a man to guard his tongue too closely.* 'It is not common knowledge but King James has been able to maintain his own treasury while he has been in exile. Some of that treasury, Mister Owen, has been set aside for just such a purpose as our project in Connaught. There will be finance a-plenty for our Irish friends. And within the month, we shall have the dates and details by which it shall be available. What say you now, William?'

'I am grateful for the confidence that you have shown in me, Sir Watkin,' says Striker. 'Yet I believe that Mister Morgan is the correct choice for this task and does not need to be encumbered with unnecessary baggage on his journey. And I have no doubt that his venture shall be successful. No, sir. If I showed concern, it was simple guilt on my part that I have not done more to speed our Cause. So let Mister Morgan bring us a Connaught Legion and give him joy of his task. For my part, I should be willing to undertake whatever work may be set for me here, in Wales or in England, that you may deem appropriate to my humble skills.'

For they are correct, he thinks. *This Jacobite silver could just tip the balance and bring the Connaught men aboard. More reason, then, to stay close to Sir Watkin and further both Newcastle's ends and my own.*

Chapter Thirty-One

After the solemnity of Palm Sunday and Holy Friday comes the relative levity of Easter Sunday, this year falling on the fourteenth day in April. There has been spiced bread King's Crown with sugared fruits, Cross Buns, and the lanes alive with children all a'Pace-Egging.

It is a custom of which Aran has never grown tired, since it does not exist in Llanffynon. Pace-Egging is common enough in Lancashire towns and villages, of course, but in Manchester it has grown to quite a spectacle. There is not just one team of Jolly Boys here but five or six, each group wandering the streets while performing their traditional drama. Saint George in battle with the Mahometan, Bold Slasher, but strung out with a lengthy series of lesser comedies involving the other players. Betty Brownbags, the Lady Gay, the Fool. The whole thing set to preposterous rhyme. And, at the rear, Old Tosspot, his face blackened, his exotic costume varying from one group of Jolly Boys to another, but each similar in the item of his tail, a long straw affair set through with sharp pins or thorns.

Here cometh the Jolly Boys, all of one mind
We've come a Pace-Egging, and hope you'll prove kind
We hope you'll prove kind with your eggs and strong beer
And we'll come no more nigh thee until it's next year.

The song is sung, the tail is swung. The foolish try to grab it. But thorns cut deep and victims weep. A very silly habit. Or so say the girls, since Aran has joined Anna-Marie, Katherine and Maeve, accompanying them to the Market Place to watch the fun. It sounds like a piece of Byrom's doggerel but they insist that it is their own invention. He has been warned, of course, by their Mama to keep each of them constantly under his supervision but he does not sense any danger to them here. Indeed, he does not feel any threat from Striker at all now. His hand troubles him no longer and he has not received contact from Striker since the business with Jacob. It seems that he must have escaped from whatever took place at Liskard since who else but Striker could have alerted the Excise Service officers in Chester? But there is just a chance, he supposes, that the fellow may have been wounded in the affray. And perhaps mortally wounded. Still, it is reasonable to remain vigilant. Though his immediate concern is to avoid the barbed swinging tail of a particularly athletic Old Tosser who leaps and cavorts at the edge of the watchers, proffering his basket and calling for coins, cakes and ale, or the Pace Eggs themselves as payment for their efforts.

The girls are disappointed since their own supply is long-since exhausted, despite having spent most of yesterday in the kitchen with Mag Mudge, wrapping eggs in layers of onion skin and boiling them until they are quite hard but also until they have assumed that wonderful gold mottle. And Pace Eggs, Katherine has responded to Maeve's question, from the Latin word for Easter. *Pascha*. They have given quite a few to the various Jolly Boys, naturally, but others they have eaten themselves, careful to crush the empty shells for fear that, otherwise, Lancashire's witches, vividly real in the girls' minds, will take them, as is their wont, for boats from which they might haunt the local rivers. But Aran gives them a few farthings and ha'pennies so that they can contribute to this particular Old Tosser's collection. A worthy enough contribution since the Jolly Boys, in turn, will distribute the eggs and any other food donations to those many amongst the crowd whom they deem deserving of some charity.

'You know, Aran,' says Katherine, 'that we have never seen your lodgings. Are you ashamed of them, sir? And so close. Which room is yours? I should so like to see it.' She looks up at the half-timbered building behind them.

'Katherine!' scolds her older sister. 'La, but you are such a flirt. It would be perfectly improper for Aran to be alone in his room with any one of us. But all three!'

'It is the second window. There, just above the Punch House,' says Aran. 'And perhaps we could employ O'Farrell as *chaperon* if you should care to visit, Miss Katherine. It is a humble dwelling but comfortable enough in its way.' Katherine favours her mother's features that are small and dark, though the girl herself is much taller, becoming a real beauty while Anna-Marie, now nineteen years old, seems suited only to a nunnery. Her face has become plain and she has a tendency to plumpness, not unfashionable but not attractive either.

'What kind of eggs does a wicked hen lay?' asks Maeve, the youngest.

'I imagine that they must be devill'd eggs, my dear,' he replies, as her beaming face collapses to a frown of feigned disappointment. She is still the child of the family, despite her fourteen years but it is a role that she seems to cherish. And, strangely, this role seems to have also constrained her growth. She is tiny for her age, with Rosina's emerald eyes. Ringlets too, though Maeve's are burnt umber to Rosina's Indian red.

Insults develop between the various teams of Jolly Boys. Blows are exchanged. Wooden swords and walking staves.

Katherine moves closer to Aran, grips his arm. 'Oh, my goodness!' she whispers, and presses herself against him. He cannot claim to be dispassionate about this giddy girl's attentions, and he recalls an admonishment from

Titus, some time since, regarding Aran's failure to pursue either Anna-Marie or Katherine as an alternative to Rosina. But there are sufficient Redmond women complications in his life already, so he carefully extricates himself from her embrace while, at the same time, an urchin comes running to find him. 'Beggin' pardon, sir, but thee is wanted at t' warehouse.'

'Very well,' says Aran. 'I shall be there directly.' The three girls express their disappointment, pleading that he should stay a while longer.

Maeve seeks to distract him with her favourite riddle. 'I saw Humpty-Dumpty asleep on a wall,' she says. 'I saw Humpty-Dumpty a'having his fall. Three score of King's Horses, three score of King's Men, they could not heal Humpty, not ever again. Who is Humpty?'

'A fie upon it,' Aran replies after a moment's concentrated effort, and greatly to Maeve's satisfaction. 'I am entirely confounded, my dear. Totally ditched. But we must needs return to the house and find O'Farrell or your Mama.' For while he does not sense any immediate danger from Striker, he cannot entirely discount the possibility. Maria-Louise had been right. Titus had told Aran about the meeting at Seabank Nook, and Aran had dutifully sent the message to Striker. He had not known, of course, that the meeting was an invention, a trap set by Jacob Driscoll. Oh, it must have been easy enough, he now supposes. He had thought that Striker had arranged for him to be followed but it is clear that this was all Jacob's doing. It is unlikely that Striker should see it thus, however, and will now feel himself betrayed. Betrayed by Aran Owen. And Striker had made the price of such betrayal plain enough.

He leaves the girls at Market Street Lane in O'Farrell's cautious charge. Katherine has stolen a flighty coquette's kiss, of course, and he smiles at the recollection. He is sorry that he has not seen Maria-Louise but somewhat relieved at the same time. Aran had initially experienced great comfort from his confession to her but, with time, it seems to have become a further barrier between them. And a similar barrier has developed 'twixt himself and Titus too. It is not a tangible thing, and Maria-Louise has evidently maintained her silence about his dealings with Striker, but a barrier all the same.

It had been evident at the birthday rout held eight days previously. Why, it is hard to credit that, only a year ago, Titus had paraded him around the gathering like some latter-day hero escaped from his tribulations at Lancaster. But on *this* occasion barely a word had passed between them, despite the general air of levity amongst the guests arising from their expectations of a Stuart Restoration within the present year. A levity reflected as well in Titus Redmond's renewal of his Subscription. At the end of last year's collection, Titus had gathered a little less than two thousand pounds, only half the amount that he had expected and barely a quarter of that which would have accumulated through their acquisition of the Excise duties. Francis Townley had urged a similar venture this Lady Day too, but the idea had been properly considered reckless and flying in the face of the admonitions they had received from Sir Oswald and, indeed, from envoys of the Prince himself. In any case, the prevalent air of optimism amongst every shade of Tory and Jacobite in the town, as well as a significant increase in the profits of many, had resulted in *this* year's Subscription raising three thousand guineas.

'There can be no other part of England, Wales or Ireland,' says Titus after Aran has entered the small warehouse office, 'in which such a Subscription could have been raised. Those cunny-suckers in Northumberland enjoy the pretence that their fervour is stronger than our own. But it is weight of gold that measures a man's loyalty.' He picks a purse from his table, measures the worth of the coin within. 'Cunny-suckers!' he says again, almost wistfully. 'Good pickings for our fat Welsh friend. And apparently I must also hand over to him the proceeds from the tea sales, now that Beaufort has passed on.'

Aran says nothing, nodding merely as Titus draws his finger down the columns of the Waste Book, occasionally pausing to examine a corresponding entry in the Letter and Bill Book. It is the most that Titus has said to him in two months. But Aran notices that he has also brought his personal accounts ledger with him today. He has only ever seen it once before since it usually remains concealed within his private closet at the house. On that occasion, Titus had met with the Chief Factor of the Duke of Beaufort, receiving his signature for the margins generated by the Jacobite investments. The Stuarts' agents arrange transaction with the Swedish Company. The Company delivers cargo of tea and other commodities through their various outlets in England. Profits recorded. Handling charges retained to cover disbursements and modest reward. And the rest returned to the Stuarts through their agents once more. But with the death of Henry Scudamore, Third Duke of Beaufort, Sir Watkin Williams Wynn has been appointed to act as agent for the Manchester business pending any other arrangement.

'I expect that our next shipments from Captain Eriksson,' says Aran, 'may contain some of the Japanese steam-dried leaves. They are now available in Canton, I understand, though the Chinese are unhappy about the trade.'

'It will be September at the earliest before we receive any new shipment. And we have to repair our links with those lick-spittle Manxmen by then. At least the *Swift* now has a new Master. Though I wish that poor Jacob could so easily be replaced.'

'I am surprised that you have not chosen Bradley for the task. He is so much involved in our enterprise these days that he might as well attend our planning meetings.'

Titus Redmond's gyrfalcon eyes measure him. 'You have become a man overburdened by grievances, Aran. What eats you now? You still believe I should have chosen you for Rosina's husband? You perceive yourself lacking my trust? Or is it Driscoll himself – that you still hold some absurd opinion about his responsibility for Sourwood's suicide? And now this with Bradley. Do you not realise, sir, that James Bradley is no more than a commercial and political expedient? That he will learn only so much about our affairs as we should choose to gift him?'

'Grievances? I have *none*. How could I truly feel aggrieved when I owe this family so much? And more than you can imagine, sirrah. No, not grievances. Yet I certainly grieve. Not for the want of selection as your daughter's groom but, rather, that I acted the scrub towards her when she so needed a friend. Nor for any moderation in our own relationship but, instead, because by word or deed I may have earned your displeasure. Neither for the harsh words that I exchanged at times with Jacob Driscoll yet, in truth, so many of them remaining unsaid at his end. And more, for the loss of his skills that you feel so keenly. But, of all things, I grieve not for Bradley's insinuation into the family but, at the final count, because he is a cuckoo in our nest. Derby's man. And Derby is Newcastle's own!'

'Grief is no manly occupation, sir. It is for lick-spittles! At least the pursuit of grievance requires some bottom. James Bradley cannot have been responsible for such fortuitous appearance of the militia at Ancoats Hall. Nor for Jacob's death. But the net draws tighter on a solution to these mysteries, my friend, for I know now the name of the cove who may have been their engineer.' Aran's blood chills. 'I asked Byrom to use his contacts,' Titus continues. 'I might despise the cunny-sucker but I cannot fault his connections. Sir Edward Stanley may be Newcastle's man yet he is not above seeking to protect his own arse against the eventuality of a Stuart Restoration. And Newcastle himself? Why, the fellow seems to have struck his finest blow against us by persuading his brother to drop the Excise duty on tea imports! What use the finest network of Manx smugglers now, when we might as easily ask the Swedish Company to deliver the stuff direct to Manchester itself as legal cargo?'

Aran tries to avoid any hint of anxiety in his voice. No unseemly haste to share the name that Byrom may have discovered. 'The fact, sir' he says, 'is that the business could now run almost as easily from the legitimate sale of tea as we have previously done from our illicit trade. The profits to the Cause might not be so great but it would turn a decent penny, to be sure. Our Fly Wagons compete equally with some of the finest in town and the new routes, to the north, remain largely unchallenged. The truth is that, with the further investment promised by Captain Townley, the tea trade could soon be producing greater margins than your fustian manufacture. And still no news, sir, of the silver that is promised to the Company for that purpose?'

'The silver is a matter between the Stuarts and the Swedes. You need not concern yourself with *that* detail, Aran.' Titus rapidly swats away the matter, perhaps *too* rapidly, and returns to a study of his ledgers. 'Yet I am certain they will appreciate the efforts you have made on their behalf. If the price of tea now falls due to the cut in duty, there may be a further increase in demand, and the changes that you have made should guarantee that we are able to maximise the benefits. For His Royal Highness, naturally.'

Aran notes the sardonic smile, knowing that Titus has never truly been content with the modest rewards received by the family for the trade that they run on the Stuarts' behalf. 'Yet once returned to power,' Aran says, 'they will not have any long-term interest in the business, surely. Will they not wish to dispose of their association with it? And are you not best placed to assist them in that regard? Why, with the Stuarts safely on the throne once more, and with both the fustian trade *and* the tea business under your own control, there would be no other merchant in Manchester to match you, sir.'

Titus fingers his moustache. 'You think I do not see the possibilities myself? There are few who can match us even now, though the cunny-suckers do not accept me as an equal. But they shall!' There is a small jug and a cup on the counting table. Gin, Aran assumes, as Titus pours a measure, throwing back the liquor with a single swallow. It has become a more frequent habit with him since the attack on his bawdy-house and Aran has seen him under the ill effects of the beverage on more than one occasion. 'And you have no curiosity, my friend, about the identity of this cove uncovered by Byrom? You continue to surprise me, Aran. By the Mass, you do!'

Aran assumes an air of nonchalance that is far distant from his true feelings. 'I had assumed that this, too, might be a matter of detail which does not concern me,' he says, 'though I must confess to having felt myself guilty, at times, by mere association with Mister Bradstreet of Birmingham. Yet I am certain that *he* cannot be your man.' He has thought a great deal, lately, about the Jacobite silver, and Striker's instruction that he should be appraised of any intelligence regarding its transportation. But, to all intents and purposes, Striker has vanished from the face of the earth. And the silver is a potent matter for his Jacobite friends. There might be some risk involved but Aran has decided that, even should knowledge of the Stuarts' coffers come his way, he will keep it to himself. For he has reasoned that, should Maria-Louise be correct, and Striker believes him to have been complicit in Driscoll's trap, the fellow is likely to be suspicious of further communications from him in any case.

Titus closes the Waste Book, sets it aside with the Letter and Bill Book, but pockets the smaller private accounts ledger. 'Perhaps you are right,' he says. 'In any case, I am away to meet Scatterbuck at the Cockpit. Will you join us, sir? Or does the spectacle still offend your latent Welsh sensibilities?'

It may be England's national sport but, in truth , the ancient art of cockfighting has never been his favoured way of passing an afternoon or evening, though Aran has executed some fine sketches of proceedings at the pit itself. All levels of Manchester society gather there for its regular blood-soaked bouts, packed inside the circular arena built for the purpose in the small alley of steps leading north from the further end of Market Street Lane, east of the Market Place and close to Old Millgate. In any case, his priority now is to find Maria-Louise, for he must surely be able to discover from her whatever knowledge Titus may have gained from John Byrom.

'No, I thank you, sir,' says Aran. 'As you suggest, I have no stomach for the thing. And I enjoyed the pleasure of Mister Scatterbuck's company throughout the better part of yesterday. He has written a fine piece for the *Journal* about Walpole's funeral. A wonderful, whimsical thing in which he ponders a great conundrum. How can such a high and mighty fellow, he asks, end his days in some obscure Norfolk grave-yard without even a memorial to his name, unless the entire nation has come to recognise the evil and corruption that marked his career? We tempered elements of his prose, naturally, but you will enjoy reading it, to be sure. For my own part, I have some minor commissions to complete. But may I enquire, sir, whether you have plans to resolve the matter of Jacob's replacement in your dealings with the Manxmen?'

Titus locks the small office, turns to survey the mound of yarn within the half-empty warehouse. The crates of tea behind are now but thinly disguised and the mark of the Swedish East India Company, that red octagon framing a stencilled monkey and Chinese character, shows clearly between the bales. 'Stocks are dwindling,' he says. 'Let us hope that we have sufficient to meet demand until the next shipment arrives.'

Aran does not press his question any further. Instead, he will return to the Redmonds' house but, since he does not particularly wish Titus to know his plan, and because the route from warehouse to Cockpit would otherwise take them in the same direction, he decides to make a detour to his own lodgings. Yet, when he arrives there, he finds his humour so low that he thinks better of his intention to seek out Maria-Louise. His confession to her has not been the only barrier between them for, since Christmas-tide, her attentions towards him have become increasingly amorous and, at the birthday rout, Mag Mudge had almost discovered them in a most compromising embrace. At one level, he would happily consummate their relationship, for Maria-Louise has the power to inflame him in a way that no other woman has ever done but, at another, he fears the vortex of unknown eddies into which such lustful veniality might plunge them.

So, knowing that Titus will be engaged elsewhere, and to appease both hungering and humour alike, he pays a visit to Mother Blossom's. He sets down a shilling with Susannah Cole for an Earl's Protector and bids good afternoon to George Blossom, as ill-mannered as ever but still sheltered by Titus from the bawd's attempts to replace him as the establishment's Flash-Man. All the same, Susannah has managed after all to find a role in the place for her own cock-pimp, Billy Bender, since he has joined the blind fiddler in a rendition of *My Thing is My Own*, though it is hardly a virtuoso performance of the tin whistle. Titus will be furious but Susannah must also have known that he would not visit today or she should not have risked Billy's presence. Blossom will inform his master, naturally, but Susannah Cole knows the tricks of her profession sufficiently well that she will find ways to appease him.

Despite the music, the salon does not seem especially animated today, the effects of gin and laudanum weighing heavily upon many of the doxies, and the room particularly heavy with pipe smoke. Aran weaves between various couplings and joins two of the newer bunters on a settee for the usual banal chatter before settling a sovereign upon the youngest, following her to an upstairs room where the condum goes unused as he sucks on country pleasures while she plays the fellatrice.

Predictably, though, their activities assist him but marginally and his blue mood persists throughout the following days until, mid-week when, with payment received for a portrait commissioned by the Moss family and fresh coin in his purse, he passes Wilding's book emporium. He sees Rosina within. Beppy Byrom too. Yet he cannot bring himself to enter. He continues, then stops, so abruptly that a woman shopper behind walks into him. She damns him for a fool and he curses himself for a coward. Muttered apologies and doffing of his hat. And he steps briskly back to the shop, pushes open the door with such force that the artificial breeze created by his action causes each loose leaf to seek simultaneous escape from the wall or shelf at which it is fixed. The nostalgic odour of print and parchment fill his senses. Customers look in his direction as though directed by a single purpose but Rosina is the first, he perceives, to avert her gaze once more, ignoring him entirely. Wilding himself, it seems, is at least pleased to see him, though in truth Aran is rarely a visitor to the establishment. All the same, the proprietor greets him as a valued client, promises to find him a stool, an offer politely declined as Aran crosses to those occupied by the two young women.

'Mister Owen,' says Beppy. 'How delightful to see you, sir. I bid you good morning.'

Aran has not seen Rosina since Twelfth Night and is surprised at the dull languor of her eyes. It almost reminds him of the haunted expression that he has seen so often on the faces at Mother Blossoms. 'And give you joy of it also, Beppy Byrom. Rosina too. I am so very pleased to find you in such apparent good looks, my dear. Positively blooming.'

'You have come to purchase some treatise on the efficient propagation of *camellia sinensis*, I fancy,' says Rosina. 'Else a history of Gutenburg perhaps. Or an instructive upon the proper use of *aquarelle* amongst the Flemish School. The latter might be the most appropriate if you find my colour to your taste, sirrah. Mister Owen is such a polymath. A true prodigy. Yet a dissembler, I fear.'

'La, Rosina!' Beppy says. 'I have never before heard the word polymath used with such barbarity. And is it really so long since you sang Mister Owen's praises to me for defending your own and your family's honour against Francis Townley's comments. Comments which, I collect, you took so unkindly as insults?'

'There was no mistaking Townley's intent, I think, though it seems like a lifetime ago,' says Aran. 'Yet it remains in those halcyon days before my brutal and boorish behaviour towards Miss Rosina so squandered our former friendship.'

'Oh poor Alcyone!' Rosina cries. 'To throw herself into the sea thus at news of her husband's shipwreck. And blessed gods to transform the devoted couple as kingfishers, protecting their nest and fledgling young for seven days each year when storms may not occur. I am certain that Wilding must have a copy of the Marais *libretto* somewhere. Or perhaps you prefer Ovid's account of the thing. Stuff! Halcyon days indeed.'

'Yet I do not think that Mister Owen intended to offend thee, my dear,' says Beppy. 'And *halcyon* is indeed a modest way to describe those summer months whose passing, in truth, we should welcome. There shall be no more calm awhile, now. Not until a Stuart King sits properly once more upon the throne of England.' Some of the more Whiggish ladies amongst Wilding's clients turn anguished heads. 'We do not have long to wait, I think, and we three should all sup from the same cup of pleasure in this matter. Loyal Jacobites, each of us, methinks. But *you*, Rosina?' she whispers. 'How difficult to share your home with one so bitterly opposed to our Cause.'

'And though I risk setting yet further distance between us,' Aran says, 'I cannot imagine that Mistress Cooper will share your passions in *this* peculiar, at least.'

'You are impertinent, sir,' says Rosina. 'Yet it is true that I must needs defend my beliefs almost daily against the criticisms of both Elizabeth and Mister Bradley alike. He raves so about Mister Clough's role in the Court Leet. Jacobite conspiracy, he cries. But, so far as I can discern, they have done no more than impose the usual fines for bad beef and cockles. Another for Contempt when some fellow fails to attend the meeting itself. I have every word recorded in my journal, naturally. He says the most outrageous things about the Stuarts. You cannot imagine, dear Beppy.'

'Indeed, I may imagine it all too clearly,' Beppy says. 'I maintain careful account in my own journal, you may be sure, of each perfidious remark to reach my ears, against that day when accounts may be settled. And tell me, Rosina, how matters stand these days with your Mama. Or perhaps Aran may enlighten me. For I understand that she, too, is wavering in her support for the Cause?'

'Mistress Redmond's support,' says Aran, bristling, 'is staunch as ever. And I trust that your respective journals will carry true account in this regard. I cannot imagine where you may have heard such a thing. Though she holds firm to her belief that French involvement is a thing accursed, a true anathema.'

'So you believe that your talents now extend to an understanding of Mama's sentiments also. And how quick to defend her virtue! A pity that you could not have done me the same courtesy. Yet my mother's hatred for the French may have abated now that poor Jacob is no longer here to help nurture it, and it is certainly tempered since she encountered Captain John Townley. '

'A fie upon you, Rosina,' Beppy says. 'How positively indelicate! Though Captain Townley shows a certain dash, does he not? A quality quite lacking in his poor brother. Yet I can find no fault in Francis Townley's vigour for our endeavour, at least. He will answer very well, I think. And if the French can help deliver us from those Hanoverian jackals, well, strike on, I say!' More heads are turned and two women leave the shop in evident disgust, making some passing comment to an apologetic Wilding as they go.

'As it happens,' Aran says, 'I share your mother's concern about the French, and there are many more with similar views besides. For my own part, I believe that we should be suitably grateful for the shelter that they have provided to the Stuarts yet take advantage of those many areas of England, Wales and Ireland willing to raise forces, alongside the Scots, for the purpose of restoring them. But doing so as an independent act, forsooth! I see this as a noble aim. And, so far as Francis Townley is concerned, I must disagree with you, Beppy. He is a rash cove, to say the least.'

'Ah, nobility!' says Rosina. 'Another subject on which Mister Owen is well-versed it seems. And these *many others* of whom you speak – can you name them I wonder? Yet do you not know, sir, that Mama is more concerned these days about whether or not I shall produce babes? Yes, children. Mewling infants. She is insufferable. And I must endure the same from my husband's parents too.'

'You visit them in Droylsden, I collect,' says Beppy. 'And did you know, Aran, that Mister Bradley furnishes them with a comfortable pension each month. La, I was perfectly surprised. And you have learned to call him *husband* I see, Rosina? How sweetly domestic! Though I cannot imagine you with child. The very thought! But I must chide you, sir, for your comments about Mister Townley. He may not have his brother's dash, but I count him a particular friend. And as loyal a Jacobite as we will find in this town.'

Aran makes his bow to her. 'My apologies if I have offended you, yet I think we may need to diverge amicably on the point.' He turns to Rosina. 'I think you will find, my dear, that most of your father's associates share concerns about the French. And I am perfectly certain that you, as it happens, would make a remarkable mother. I had not considered the matter before, yet...'

'I have not the slightest intention of becoming a mother, sirrah. Not the slightest. And I am sure that we must distract you from more profitable enterprise, Mister Owen. It was delightful to see you, I am sure, but I assume that you entered the emporium for the purpose of perusing Wilding's considerable stock. I apologise if we have detained you.'

Beppy Byrom flusters, embarrassed, at her friend's shrewish behaviour, then finds herself relieved as the shop door opens once more and the various cover pages flutter again in unison. 'Ah, Mister Lewthwaite. Mister Nichols.

Good day, gentlemen!' The Assistant Curates nod their greetings, kiss Beppy's hand.

And Aran, uncomfortable now in Lewthwaite's company, speaks quickly, quietly, to Rosina. 'In truth, my dear, I entered only because I saw you within. I have so little time for reading these days and hoped for a chance that I might say this more privately. But you must be assured that I will one day make amends for my scrubbish behaviour towards you and would like nothing better, of all things, than to resume our friendship.'

'Then I shall note your assurance in my journal, sir, and await with interest the manner of its fulfilment.' She says no more, offers no fare-thee-well and returns her attention to Beppy's conversation with Nichols and Lewthwaite.

Aran, for his part, bids them a pleasant forenoon, begs that Beppy should pass his best regards to her father, and is swiftly back on the street. He supposes that he can expect no more from Rosina at this point, but he had hoped that there might be some melting of the ice between them. He is disappointed at her lack of warmth, but remains sanguine. He has made a beginning, at least. In truth, he had intended some of his newly-earned guineas for the tailor, but he has spent so long at Wilding's that he is now late for his work.

His various *devoirs* allow him considerable freedom, for he has no fixed hours such as may bind a shopkeeper, a warehouseman, a clerk, a builder. But neither is there regularity in his salary. This is Wednesday, the day on which the Redmond Fly Wagon departs for Carlisle from the Pack-Horse Inn, whilst a second leaves for London, so it is also the day that Aran devotes to the tasks set him by Titus. As a result, Titus rewards him with payment of three shillings weekly from the handling charges that he is allowed to retain by the Stuarts' agents. On Saturdays, he works with Scatterbuck, helping to draft copy for the coming week's two pages of the *Journal,* which has successfully avoided the damnable Stamp Duty as they intended, but he accepts no payment for this work 'bating recompense in kind, in the manner of a country doctor, so that he has unlimited column space for his own announcements that call attention to his trade. Mondays and Tuesdays are spent in his lodging or at Mister Byrom's Academy rooms, scripting and finishing the various trade bills, cards, flyers and occasional ballad sheets which, he considers, put the bread and meat upon his table, generating three or four shillings each and every week. Thursdays and Fridays allow him sufficient hours to work on the artistic commissions that have now begun to come his way more regularly, and the recent portrait of Peter Moss, wife Mary, and their children will itself attract further similar work. He calculates, therefore, that he will this year earn in excess of forty pounds, an amount approximating that which any other independent journeyman or artisan might enjoy.

He oversees the Fly Wagon's loading at the warehouse, a slow process today, undertaken amidst the stench of wet horses and their wastes, then accompanies the vehicle to the Pack-Horse where other cargo and a couple of passengers are stowed on board. And, as he works, he ponders Beppy's recent defence of Francis Townley. Does she have some affection for the fellow? He is so much older than she. And then there is the matter of Nichols and Lewthwaite to consider. For whilst Aran may be aware that Striker has some hold over Lewthwaite, is the Assistant Curate also sensible of Striker's grip upon Aran himself? He thinks not, but difficult to be certain.

April drizzle has begun to dilute the Lane's excrement, household dust, ash, cinder, cabbage leaf and a thousand other items of discarded decay, while Old Tarquin and his companions who survived the winter grunt and nuzzle, disposing of rubbish and occasional dead rodent alike. And Aran, returning to his room in the gathering twilight, pauses outside the Redmonds' house, sees O'Farrell lighting the lamps and candles, so that a soft amber glow beckons from the windows. He is tempted by that light, flutters a while near the edge of its influence but finally decides that he should spend the evening writing to Josiah. The old gentleman's own had arrived two weeks earlier but there has yet been no opportunity to respond. And Aran has been intrigued by a particular paragraph.

> *You may recall the visit paid to me by the Rector of Hawarden, Richard Williams, in which he sought my support for the cause of which I spoke. Well, my boy, I have to tell you about a remarkable coincidence for I have met here a man who shares your name. He is William Owen and, while I am not at liberty to detail the fellow's background, I was able to offer him some small charity and, later, to place him in service with the good Rector himself. This was fortuitous since they seem well-suited both in temperament and belief yet, above all other things, Owen's arrival appears to have dispelled all interest on the part of Mister Williams in my own modest affairs.*

Intriguing simply because he recalls Striker's enquiry about Josiah at the Annual Fair. He attempts to make connections but they evade him. So he restricts his missive to limited news about the business, about his own enterprise, and about the girls, including a few words about Rosina. In the morning, he reviews the letter, line by line, makes some minor corrections and, having broken his fast, he repairs to the Bull's Head busy post office to pay for its dispatch – only to find Maria-Louise engaged in the same purpose.

'A fine early start to your day, Mister Owen,' she says, and he can see that he must suffer a difficult encounter. 'Yet too early for your customary visit to Mother Blossom's, I collect. Or is it Mistress Cole's these days? I forget.'

'Mother Blossom's? Why...' Aran struggles for a reply that will shout his innocence of the allegation, wondering how she can possibly have known so soon about his recent visit to the establishment. But, in a manner designed to make clear that subterfuge is impossible, Maria-Louise smiles wistfully at him and gestures to a small stool near the front of the room where Mag Mudge is safely seated. He should have known, for Mudge often maintains contact between Titus and George Blossom whenever Mister Redmond is unable to visit the bawdy-house in person.

Mudge offers him her most lopsided grin, lifts her one good arm and extends a gnarled finger. 'Cunny-sucker!' she drools, and almost falls from the stool as she collapses into cackling laughter. Customers turn to stare at him.

'Madam,' he says, as quietly as possible. 'Have I *no* privacy? Pursued by that rascal Striker. Then followed by Driscoll's man, it seems. And now spied upon by this misshapen creature!'

'It is no less than you deserve, sir. In any case, Mudge simply relayed a message from George Blossom to my husband about Billy Bender's presence at the place. It was Blossom himself who mentioned that you had also been in attendance. Titus was quite enraged that you had neither acted on his behalf nor, at least, advised him of the matter. Had you visited, I might have warned you.'

'I am no Flash-Man that I have responsibility for his bawdy-den. Though it would be some relief, I think, to know that I enjoyed his confidence in *some* regard. But I had hoped to see you on Sunday when I returned with the girls after the Pace-Egging.'

'You hoped to see me, yet hoped too that you might not, I think.' They move forward in the queue and Maria-Louise sets down two shillings for the brace of letters bound, on her husband's behalf, for London. 'And yesterday evening I looked from my window and saw you, my dear. You gazed at the house so dolefully yet did not approach. I fear that I must have set some barrier between us.'

'There! My movements observed once more.' He breaks off for a moment to argue with the post-master. 'No, sir,' says Aran. 'It is a *local* post. And a single page, as you can plainly see. Yes, Llanffynon is a Welsh direction though it is within the eighty-mile limit, I assure you. Thruppence, sir, is the price that I have previously paid. No more.' Maria-Louise confirms that she has never spent more than three pennies for her husband's own letters to his brother, and the post-master reluctantly concedes.

'It pleasures me to observe you in motion, young man,' she says when they have left the Bull's Head. 'But would you oblige me with a promenade along the river? There is something that I would discuss with you. A matter of some delicacy, I find.' Aran searches for a reason to decline but Maria-Louise is already issuing brief instructions to Mag Mudge, duties to undertake on her return to the house, and he knows that it will be fruitless to resist. 'So,' she says, as they begin their perambulation, 'first you must tell me why you felt unable to knock upon my door. And why, sir, the comment about not enjoying my husband's confidence?'

They cross Deansgate and into Saint Mary's Gate. 'I had much to concern me yesterday and did not consider myself fit company by evening. I had seen Rosina at Wilding's and the encounter had left me low.'

'The girl is now quite beyond my reach too. And when she is in company with that Myra. La! I fancy that I shall die before I am reconciled with my daughter.'

'You must not speak so, madam. She had Beppy Byrom for company as it happens, yet matters did not proceed as I should have liked. And the encounter was somewhat curtailed by the arrival of Lewthwaite and Nichols, that naturally brought back memories of less happy days.'

'Upon my soul. Do you truly think that they are sodomites? Fie upon them. For all we know, there may be a Mollies Club here in Manchester itself. I have heard of such things in London, and they were rife in Paris, of course. But here? I cannot think so.'

They cross Parsonage Walk also, then take the alley that cuts between its row of very fine houses so recently erected. Their rear elevations and gardens overlook the river itself. The alley leads to a narrow path running atop the low, sandstone cliffs on which the houses stand.

'I have no inclination on the matter,' says Aran, gazing across to Salford and the open fields of adjoining Ordsall.

'I should hope not, indeed. Though had you some inclination towards sodomy it might, at least, explain your cool reception of my advances. No, do not look so! It was a jest, no more, and I am anxious to hear about your meeting with my husband.'

She takes his arm, and they begin to follow the path southwards. The river is alive with activity today, seems more so as several vessels crowd sail to take advantage of the favourable wind.

'He was distant, my dear. As if he knows...'

'What, sir? About your confession to me? I shall be vexed indeed if you seek to imply that I may have broken your confidence, Aran. We share a certain intimacy, you and I, and it is not your first confession to me, after all. You confessed that you considered yourself in competition with James Bradley for my affections. Do you recall? And you confessed to me your premonition about the Ancoats Hall affair. I naturally shared neither with Titus. And, of course, you confessed to me that the loss of your poor finger had been no accident after all.'

'My point exactly, madam! The words barely from my lips and you had run to Titus with the news. But no. This was something else entirely. He was distant, as I have said. But less so than during his birthing-day. He has received intelligence from John Byrom though he would not share it with me. Indeed, he almost challenged me to press him on the point, though I resisted. It seemed the proper thing. To pretend indifference. Likewise on the matter of Jacob's replacement, though I angered him without warrant by suggesting that Bradley might now enjoy such favour with him that it would make him a candidate.'

'It is foolish to provoke him so. He has a name from Byrom. No more. And that name is Striker, as you will have guessed. But a name conveys nothing in itself. There is no connection between Striker's name and your own. In truth, he knows nothing of the fellow.'

'Yet nor do I! Here is a cove who seems to know the most profound secrets of my soul, yet I still know nothing about *him* except his name. And to now hear that name upon your own sweet tongue seems most unnatural.'

Several clinker-built wherries ply the water here, carrying passengers and goods between each bank and down as far as the Quay.

'At least it seems to have satisfied his need for investigation. Titus has quite abandoned any hope of finding young MacLaine. And, so far as a replacement for Jacob in our dealings with the Manxmen, why, my husband *has* no plan. But did he not speak to you of the silver? The Stuarts' revenue?'

'He told me that I need not concern myself with that detail. It is a matter for the Stuarts and the Swedes, he said.'

'Indeed, he is correct. A matter for the Swedish Company indeed. Their investment when all is said and done. Yet it has significance, does it not? For there are those amongst our ranks – those lacking confidence in our own ability to overturn the Hanover pack – who will see the silver as a tangible sign of foreign support. They will thirst for news of it, hoping that the French will execute the deed that, in truth, honest Englishmen should perform. They will see only the Frenchmen that it may purchase, as the weak may come to rely on a crutch, growing weaker still simply by its use. And to quench that thirst, Sir Watkin sends Titus word of Charles Edward's intentions. So that the implications might be disseminated. Tell all our friends, he says, that a French army comes to deliver us. Well, sir, I for one seek no deliverance at French hands.'

'You are sensible that I share your views. But Captain Townley was explicit on the matter, was he not?' says Aran. 'The French Declaration that they have no design upon us. And, in any case, whilst the Stuarts' silver may in part be intended to raise arms and men, the greater part is destined for commercial investment and the provision of an Exchequer independent of the Hanovers. Is that not so?'

'Yes, my sweet, and welcome it shall be. But this particular shipment is destined for the French. Why, I heard Townley's crook-tooth'd brother say as much. And now this message from the Welsh. Not that Titus is well pleased at having Sir Watkin foisted upon him as the bonnie Prince's agent.'

'Titus has news of the shipment itself, then?'

'He knows only that two French privateers are tasked with loading a portion of the silver in Rome around the twenty-fifth day of June. The overland route is less secure, they fear, with the Continent's campaign season begun

307

again in earnest. And the privateers are not bound for Sweden, Aran, but for one of the French Atlantic ports. My husband suspects Nantes or Brest. Imagine such a fortune in the hands of the French. Imagine the invasion force that the French might assemble on Charles Edward's behalf? And how could he refuse? Such temptation is beyond endurance. Yet if we cannot rid *ourselves* of the Hanovers, we shall simply replace *their* sequestration of these islands with some measure of French dominion. For all their Declarations, how in the name of the Holy Sacrament could they resist *that* temptation in turn? Like England, they are a nation intent on Empire. At one stroke they might resolve their rivalry with our nation and take Britain itself into their sphere.'

They have reached the extremity of the clifftop path, and here it joins the lower end of Dole Field Lane, heading inland once more to meet Deansgate. But Maria-Louise shows no urgency in returning to town.

'Such matters are beyond our control, are they not?' Aran says to her. 'Our loyalties, surely, are to the Cause and we must place our trust in God Almighty that we may have sufficient sway to resist such intentions, if indeed they exist, once the country is restored to its rightful rulers.'

'You do not know the French, my dear. They are an evil breed. Or those who lead them, at least. Why, the Scots may talk of Old Alliance but that convenience only exists at times of benefit to the French. I spent two years in Paris. I told you, did I not? My father sent me there at the age of fifteen to study with the children of an uncle. He was an officer of the French army's Irish Brigade. My Papa believed that the experience would broaden me. Natural philosophy, literature, bible studies. French and English. Some Italian, too, though I have lost every word. And tuition in the arts, naturally.'

'The very place to be for such tuition. How I envy you!'

'You do? Well, it was not the best of times to arrive. The Banque Royale had collapsed just weeks before. The fault of the Scotsman, John Law, of course. Hard to find any French feeling for the Old Alliance when so many thousands of Parisians had lost their life's savings through his speculation. And this on top of the South Sea affair. Another evil inflicted by perfidious Albion, seemed to be the general sentiment. Yet the thing that surprised me was the way in which these matters had no impact whatsoever on any level of society beyond the *bourgeoisie*. The merchant classes left to suffer horribly, as were the honest workmen of the city. And the conditions of the poor, my dear, I cannot bring myself to describe.'

Aran has an image of the legendary Court of Miracles, those slums of Paris that are the disgrace of Europe, far worse than anything that exists even in London's most impoverished areas. 'Yet might the same condition not apply here in similar circumstances? I have heard Mister Byrom and Reverend Clayton rail often enough about the iniquities of the poor and the need to leave them to their own devices.'

'It is not the same thing. No, indeed. In France, Aran, there are ten thousand noble families. Ten thousand *families*. Our Lady alone knows how many individual members of that class. Yet it is not truly a class either, for they themselves are divided into a dozen different strata. The only thing that unites them is their genuine belief that they are a race apart. It is true. The French nobility considers itself descended from a superior breed of mankind quite distinct from their fellows. And they enjoy a strange relationship with the Monarchy. It is *laissez-faire* in the true sense of the expression. They have surrendered to the Crown all vestige of their own responsibilities. Despite the flaws that we might associate with our own institutions, there is no Parliament in France. An Estates General, perhaps, but it has not sat in a hundred years! So they allow the King to function as he pleases, supported by the most bloated bureaucracy imaginable. And, as reward, the nobility, those hundreds of thousands, find themselves beyond reproach, beyond the law.'

They turn slowly along Deansgate Street, then cut through the thoroughfares to Acres Field and Saint Ann's Church, and Aran begins to sense, for the first time, that Maria-Louise has some first-hand experience of this injustice. They pause close to the very spot where he had last encountered Striker. Yet it is neither Newcastle's agent, nor little Maeve in danger that he pictures but, instead, the hapless Double-Headed Albino. The child cannot still be alive surely. And were those who had exhibited his deformity not beyond the law also? Or those responsible for Semple's killing? Striker himself and his assassination of Sir Peter Leighton? The entire world, it seems, is these days beyond the law. And has it not always been so?

'And does this fully explain your hatred for the French?' says Aran. 'Or is there more? Some personal tragedy perhaps?'

'Ah, my dearest, you have smoked me! How clever. Yes, of course I was violated in the most despicable manner by a French *Milord*. Several of them. An entire host. Would that make it more intelligible? But the truth is perhaps worse. For there *was* no such single tragedy. Rather an entire succession of them, Aran. Almost weekly for two whole years. A child playing in the street outside our apartments and run down by the carriage of a *Vicomte* and his family. They did not even stop. The child's body left where she fell. The local baker dragged to his death behind a nobleman's horse because he had splashed mud on the gentleman's shoes. A woman burned for witchcraft upon the word of some *Seigneur* when the entire *arrondissement* knew that he had accused her from malice after she had slighted him. Elderly estate workers left to starve during that terrible famine of '21.'

'Yet there must be exceptions. I cannot believe that the entire structure of French aristocracy can stand condemned.'

'There are exceptions to every measure, Aran Owen, yet the measure still remains. I met some *fine* exceptions. Of course I did! Why, I had the honour of meeting Rosalba Carriera when she visited the salon of the Marquise d'Alincourt in the Rue de Fleurus. I could recount a hundred stories of French culture and their astonishing achievements in the natural sciences, yet collectively they would not eradicate even one of those crimes that I saw perpetrated with complete impunity by so many members of that corrupt nobility. And *that* is the France which would pretend to deliver us on behalf of Good King James. Yet we have it in our hands to change matters.'

'Change matters? You speak the words so lightly but, if I understand your meaning, madam, you contemplate an intervention which, from our Jacobite viewpoint, is pure sedition. And if we are so at risk from the French as you suppose, would King James and Prince Charles Edward not see this danger also. Being *good*, would they not protect the very nation for which they are prepared to sacrifice so much?'

'I suspect that they only see as much as the times allow. The Prince has made a commitment and must fulfil it. Yet if he comes, and the commitment is fulfilled, but he comes without the French at his back, why, it is obvious that his supporters in England, in Wales, in Ireland, will have no choice except to come out in support of the Prince and those of his wild clansmen on whom he can so naturally depend. So let us suppose that your Mister Striker should receive news of the silver. He would inform his masters, would he not? And there is every chance that the payment might be intercepted.'

'But the silver destined for the Swedish Company. What of that? The Stuarts need the investments for their future Exchequer, do they not?'

'According to my husband, Sir Watkin has assured him that this is simply the portion of their silver destined for the French. But a fie upon you, sir. Do you waver?'

'I trust you without question, my dear. But the thing seems momentous to me. How if the shipment is lost and King James simply arranges another? How if the silver falls into Hanoverian hands and simply supplements the coffers of our enemies? How if Striker does not take such a message seriously? How if he is no longer even alive? How if the shipment evades all obstacles and reaches its destination as intended?'

'If the shipment is lost there will be no opportunity to send another in time to precede Charles Edward's arrival and, by that time, our supporters will be out and no need of the French. If, however, the silver is after all delivered to the French then we shall have to live with the consequences I suppose. But then our circumstances shall be no worse than at present, and we will have the satisfaction of knowing that we tried. So far as the Hanoverians are concerned, this amount will hardly plug a single hole in the leaking bucket of their finances. And Striker? Well, there is not simply Striker, but my husband also. Let us consider. Titus has told you nothing about the silver and, should anything happen to it, he can certainly not blame you on *this* occasion. Striker, on the other hand, if he lives, cannot afford to ignore such a message, do you not agree, my sweet? If he does not, again, we have lost nothing by the attempt. Now, tell me. How do you contact him?'

Aran knows that this is wrong. He dreads renewing any form of contact with Striker, particularly when he has so recently determined not to inform the fellow of any knowledge he might gather on this very matter. He knows that, despite her reasoning, this act must be a profound betrayal of the Cause for which they have worked so diligently. So long. But he is swept along by the conviction of this woman. Maria-Louise assures him that, together, they have the ability to strike a blow that will change the course of history. To ensure that, when the Stuarts are restored, when so many other liberties are restored also, their victory shall not be endangered by French involvement and that England shall remain a sovereign nation in a new and glorious age of enlightenment.

So he shares Striker's instructions. The message to be disguised using Byrom's shorthand, then sealed in a special envelope, and this latter marked with a single letter 'S' before delivering it to an express courier, contacted through the Star Inn. The courier must have particular directions for Striker himself, though he supposes that this will be no more than a deposit box, some secure point from which the agent may collect his messages in safety.

They have slowly walked the length of Acres Field, stand once again in Market Street Lane.

'You must have no fear in this thing, my dear,' she says. 'Trust me, I pray. Let me find a reason to leave the house this evening and I will come to your lodgings, discreetly, of course, so that we may compose the note to Striker. And perhaps I shall also find a way to play upon your flute in a way that would shame even Susannah's doxies!'

Chapter Thirty-Two

'In the name of God, gentlemen,' cries James Bradley, 'let us try to be composed!'

News of the disaster had reached them three days ago but, as so frequently with these things, the full import of the matter had insinuated itself into the town less slowly.

The Duke of Cumberland had crossed to Flanders at the end of March, taken command of the allied forces, marching them south to prevent Marshal Saxe from besieging Mons or Tournai, and encountering the French army near the village of Fontenoy. Battle had ensued on Tuesday, the thirtieth day of April, and the outcome, according to that first intelligence, had been indecisive.

In truth, it had not been a single piece of intelligence but, rather, several gentlemen of the town had each separately received an express from respective friends or colleagues in London on the eleventh of May, details being scant at that point and only arriving in substance a little later, filling the various broadsheets of the capital over the ensuing week and finally finding their way northwards.

Even then, the news had initially been contradictory, for the *Daily Gazetteer*, that organ of the Pelhams' Administration, had still implied victory for Cumberland's troops. So it was the arrival of the *London Gazette*, swiftly followed by the *Daily Courant*, with their first-hand accounts of the *débacle*, that had sealed matters. This copy had, in turn, been seized upon by Adam Scatterbuck, and the *Journal* had finally turned the episode into the worst feat of English arms since the Battle of Hastings.

Copies of these various publications, along with several maps, now litter the tables, chairs and benches of the Angel Inn, where Bradley is attempting to restore order. Its interior is commodious, almost luxuriant, and contrasting strongly with its outside appearance, the herringbone brickwork and half-timber frames of which glower sullenly across the Market Place towards the Bull's Head and John Shaw's Punch House where, today, surely the Jacobites must gloat.

'I do not understand how they account for this discrepancy,' says Liptrott, the attorney. The *Gazette* claims less than two thousand losses in its eleventh of May edition but the *Courant*, only two days later, puts the figure amongst the Foot alone at six thousand, including four thousand Englishmen.

The *Journal* says that, by French accounts, the dead and wounded amongst our allies number fully ten thousand.'

'A fie upon them!' Robert Jobb insists. 'They are broadsheets. Do they not exaggerate as a matter of commerce. They seek sensation, sir. We should trust only the *Gazetteer*. It puts our losses far lower than those of the French, which is entirely credible. And insists that Cumberland has accomplished a most notable tactical withdrawal. He lives to fight another day.'

'The *Gazetteer*?' says James Tomlinson, the miller. 'Why, only two days earlier they were claiming that Cumberland had *won* the damn'd battle. But look at this list. The names of officers killed or injured. Brigadiers. Colonels. Lieutenant-Colonels. Majors. Captains and Subalterns. Such a list! Why, from the Generals of Foot, it says, only Skelton, Ligonier and the Duke himself escaped unhurt. Those figures do not tally with modest losses gentlemen.'

John Clowes, the breeches maker, insists on reading again the *Courant* account of the opening dispositions.

The French drawn up along a dog-leg ridge, pictures Bradley, their left pointing east and protected by a formidable redoubt, as well as woodland, and opposed by the Duke of Cumberland's English and Hanoverians. The French right points north-west, to be confronted by Königseck and the Austrians, while the village of Fontenoy is itself a strongpoint at the line's central joint, an objective to be taken by our Dutch allies, commanded by the Prince of Waldeck. An allied army of fifty thousand, facing fifty-six thousand Frenchmen, under the command of Marshal Saxe and King Louis himself, in defensive positions on higher ground. *I do not believe I would have taken those odds*, he thinks.

'And have you seen Sir Oswald, sir?' asks the clock-maker, Thomas Walley. 'I am m-m-most concerned that he has not joined us at this m-m-momentous hour. He is Lord of the M-m-manor when all is said and done. A few words of reassurance would not have gone amiss.'

'There is nothing from Sir Oswald,' Bradley replies. 'But, as his representative within the Court Leet, I can tell you that there is no cause for alarm, sir. He is at Rolleston, I understand. Engaged on business. Yet if there was any threat, he would be here in Manchester, I am certain.' In truth, he is certain of no such thing. *The damn'd Jacobite would be as far from any danger as his fortune might allow.*

'Staffordshire, sir?' says Walley. 'His property m-m-might be there, but his responsibility is *here*, Mister Bradley. Here, sir. I shall t-t-tell him so should the opportunity present.'

He might, too, for Thomas Walley is not without some mettle of his own, despite his speech problem. *I wonder whether I could persuade him to stand as Constable this year? That is, if we have not all been destroyed by then!*

Joseph Bancroft, one of the town's many smallware manufacturers, is clamouring for news of the engagement itself, and Clowes is persuaded to take up the *Courant* again.

'What a monstrous blunder,' says Matthew Liptrott. 'To leave a heavily-armed redoubt on our flank. Ingoldsby should be court-martialled. Cashiered from the army!'

'A court-martial there shall be without doubt, yet I see that Ingoldsby has already given account of himself in the *Gazette*,' says Thomas Fielden, the present Borough Reeve. He reads ponderously. Ingoldsby's own account. Conflicting instructions.

'The fellow has added his name,' says Fielden. 'Richard Ingoldsby. Such nerve! To represent himself so, in a broadsheet. Forsooth!'

Indeed, thinks Bradley. But what will a court-martial decide in this case? That Ingoldsby was singularly responsible for the way in which the English flank was shredded from the redoubt as they executed their subsequent advance? Or that there was confusion in his orders, despite which he played a noble part in the advance itself, being seriously wounded during its course? The latter, surely. A censure, perhaps, for his error judgement.

A pity though, for Bradley has recently used his position as Clerk of the Town Works to push through agreement for the redecoration of the Commerce Exchange, and had set his heart upon the main hall being adorned with murals of military tenacity. Contemporary tenacity, he had imagined. Something that would portray support for the Monarchy. There is still Dettingen, he supposes. But King George the Second's victory must now be over-shadowed by his son's defeat. Glorious defeat as it will now be portrayed, a defeat all the same. And then there has been Rosina's proposition. Extraordinary. That the murals should be undertaken by Titus Redmond's spaniel, this Aran Owen. It is bizarre. Yet, if there was some way to find a margin for himself in the thing…

'By the Mass,' cries John Clowes, 'they must have been cut to pieces. Caught in crossed fires, gentlemen. Listen to this!'

The differing accounts all agree on this point, at least, that the English regiments, with parade ground precision, marched in their now traditional slow time, measured pace, punished unmercifully by the guns of the redoubt, mounted the ridge and pushed the French back by a considerable distance, only retiring – and still in perfect order – once it became clear that they were now taking fire from three sides, not only from their front but also from the redoubt on their right and from Fontenoy on their left, Prince Waldeck having failed to take it.

'There,' says Jobb. 'Retired in good order. Cumberland lives to fight another day.'

'With w-w-what?' shouts Thomas. 'He has lost one-fifth of our entire army. What stands now between the French and complete victory? Between this country and a French invasion?'

'And how those Jacobite rabble will stream from their middens to support them,' says Joseph Bancroft. 'We will be overwhelmed!'

'I beg you once more, gentlemen, to compose yourselves,' Bradley insists. 'We are being premature I think.'

'I expect that it may not be such a crucial issue for *you*, Mister Bradley,' Bancroft says. 'You will doubtless be protected by your new *family*, sir.'

Bradley presses his tongue against the back of his teeth, makes a low whistling noise as he meets Bancroft's eyes, holding them until the smallware manufacturer is finally forced to avert his gaze, muttering a modest apology.

'There is mention here of the Irish, gentlemen,' says Liptrott. For the *Journal* has carried a particularly lurid account. Scatterbuck had taken up the history at the point where the English had rallied and made their second assault on the French ridge.

Though the DUKE OF CUMBERLAND's position was precarious, in fact King Louis was about to leave the field, believing himself defeated. In this juncture, Saxe order'd up his last reserve, their Irish Brigade. It consisted that day of the Regiments of Clare, Lally, Dillon, Berwick, Roth, and Buckley, with FitzJames' Horse. Aided by two French regiments, they were order'd to charge upon the flank of our badly-led Englishmen with fixed bayonets and without firing.

Upon the approach of this splendid body of men, our battalions were halted on the slope of a hill, and up that slope the brigade rushed rapidly, with 'Remember Limerick and Saxon Perfidy' being re-echoed from man to man. The fortune of the field was no longer doubtful. Our poor English were weary with a long day's fighting, cut up by cannon, charge, and musketry, and dispirited by the appearance of the Brigade. Still they gave their fire well and fatally. But they were literally stunned by the shout, and shattered by the Irish charge. They broke before the Irish bayonets, and tumbl'd down the far side of the hill disorganiz'd, hopeless, and falling by hundreds. The victory was bloody and complete. Louis is said to have ridden down to the Irish bivouac, and personally thanked them.

'It is merely Adam Scatterbuck's rambling,' says Bradley. 'There is no mention of such a thing in the *Courant* or the *Gazette*.'

'I beg to differ, sir,' Bancroft says, taking courage once more. 'You see, gentlemen? The *Gazetteer* has a similar account. Less colourful, perhaps, and still claiming that the withdrawal was orderly yet still confirming that it was the damn'd Irish Brigade that turned the tide. And what next, gentlemen? The French will unleash these Irish fiends on *us*, I tell you.'

Maria-Louise, at least, may take some satisfaction from this apparent Irish feat of arms, Bradley assumes, though he remains certain that the accounts must be heavily embellished. *On the other hand, she despises the French so much that it would be difficult to know how she would react at all to this news of Fontenoy!* In any case, when he pictures her, his imagination does not see her entwined in political debate but, rather, in his arms. He can almost catch the scent of her. He regularly lives again the moments of passion that they had enjoyed. He misses her. He relishes the occasional family gatherings when he can once again be in her company. But the frustration of those gatherings is also quite unbearable. They are becoming less frequent, too, as the gulf between mother and daughter grows.

Liptrott picks up the latest of the *Courant* editions. 'And this, gentlemen, I suspect,' he says, 'is the true cost. Lieutenant-General Campbell had his leg shot off, and is since dead. Major-General Ponsonby killed upon the spot. Lord Albemarle and Major-General Howard, along with Brigadiers Churchill and Ingoldsby are sorely wounded, General Howard in four places. So many of our best cut down.'

Yes, so many. And what delight it must inspire in their enemies. So James Bradley has a vision, too, of Titus. He has shaved his moustache in this vision, no longer needs it since a new Monarch will sit on the throne, the rights of Papists restored, and Redmond himself in the ascendancy, deposing Bradley within the Court Leet. Perhaps with power that James cannot yet imagine. But for the nonce a vision only it remains. And the Whigs are not defeated yet.

'A bloodbath it may have been, gentlemen,' he says. 'But we must not be cast down. Why, should we not take a leaf from the *banditti* themselves? When matters seemed dark for them, Titus Redmond was raising subscription to help restore their fortunes. I suggest, gentlemen, that we should consider no less a possibility ourselves.'

'Subscription, sir?' says John Clowes. 'It will take more than our meagre guineas to replace the men squandered by the young Duke. He may be the King's son but at the age of twenty-four it is sheer folly to have given him such responsibility. Marshal Saxe has been fighting battles for the past thirty years and more.'

'Cumberland has a reputation for being overly headstrong,' Bradley agrees. 'And, like yourselves, I recall the days when it was customary to win our wars against the French. Perhaps those days may return once more. But meanwhile a subscription will do more than finance recruitment. It will give us a goal of our own and help to maintain morale at this evil hour. Let us think on it, gentlemen, and speak again when matters are more clear. And do we know where the Duke has now gone?'

'This latest edition of the *Gazetteer*,' says Liptrott, 'places them at Ath, and falling back towards Brussels. Tournai will be lost, I fear. Ghent too. The whole of Flanders perhaps.'

A grim position, and Bradley ponders its implications as he leaves the Angel and makes his way to the coffee house, for there is business to discuss with Elizabeth Cooper. He must wait awhile, however, for she has left the premises to pursue some enterprise of her own, so he hands a penny to crippled Crableck, dismisses both coffee and chocolate from the hearth, and demands tea, duly served in a small pot. He is assailed with questions here too, of course, the mood of panic amongst its customers as palpable as that in the Angel. Only the tobacco smoke is thicker, so that he is eventually able to extricate himself from Allen, Ayrton, Woolmer, Nichols, Lewthwaite and the rest, finding a small booth near a window from which he can see the Exchange.

'Ah!' cries Elizabeth Cooper, some ten minutes later. 'I perceive that your loyalties have veered. A family matter, I collect.'

'You have me at a disadvantage, Mistress. Loyalties, you say. I am not sensible of any change in my loyalties else why should I still take beverage in your establishment when you have treated me so ill?'

'Your tea, sir. I refer to your tea. You have always been a coffee man. An occasional chocolate, perhaps. But here I find you taking tea. In the very week that I have changed supplier to accommodate that rogue Redmond.'

'This?' he says, looking quickly to the remains of his amber liquid. 'It is a very fine *Assam*, my dear. Much to my liking but the flavour might have been affected had I known that I was supping an illicit brew. And the rogue to whom you refer. Not my beloved I trust?'

'Why, James, if I had spoken of dear Rosina, I should have most dutifully described her as *Mistress Bradley* or some such. You cannot assume me so fro'ward, surely, to define your spouse in derogatory terms. I know my duty, sir. And all duty paid on your purchase, too, I am pleased to say. I prefer the *Twankay* or the *Souchong* myself but the *Assam* is perfectly acceptable. I like to pretend that the leaf is fresher, travelling overland only from the Quay rather than from Liverpool, but it is a foolish deceit.'

'If your supplier is now Titus Redmond, I hope that you have seen some proof of taxation. And what says Mister Rivers about the matter?'

'He took my decision manfully enough. He has supplied me all these years yet he cannot deny the financial advantage to myself if I no longer have to pay carriage costs from Liverpool to Manchester. Redmond sent young Mister Owen to see me. He is a pompous prig, I find, though he was civil enough on this occasion. He brought all the necessary accompts and ledgers, paid me upon the spot for the outstanding Customs Duties. A formal apology, too, that payment had not been made on Lady Day. I could not be sure whether this was intended as jibe or jest. The fellow should be upon the stage, I protest! But I could hardly ignore a legitimate supplier of tea here upon my own threshold. And Mister Rivers shall still supply my chocolates and coffees. At least, so long as the Redmonds do not encroach in that direction also.'

'It was, in part, about Mister Owen that I needed to speak with you, my dear. If I might seek your confidence, that is? Well, that and another matter. A more private matter. But Mister Owen first, I think. You see, Elizabeth, that my sweet Rosina has put to me a certain proposition concerning the young gentleman. That he should be given the opportunity to complete a certain contract, for mural painting within the Exchange.'

Elizabeth sits, joining him in the booth and glancing involuntarily at the side of the brick and stone temple that overlooks them.

'La! You do say? And you wanted to know, sir, whether *sweet Rosina* has spoken to *me* on the matter? Yet I wonder what the other half of such a bargain may have been, for Rosina would not expect reward unless she believed it fair exchange for favour rendered. Something grander than a hand-job, I warrant.'

'Please, *cara mia*! Such images of intimacy are not to be borne in polite company. Yet I see that you, too, must have suffered this strange mercantile obsession of Rosina's. Why, I sometimes find myself thinking twice before I ask her to pass the salt. But I perceive that you also remain ignorant of her suggestion about Aran Owen and the murals.'

'Indeed. Though she does seem to consider him greatly of late. I had accused him of acting the scrub towards her and he told me of his intention to make amends. He repeated the same to Rosina not a month since and, while she scoffed and derided him when we spoke, I could see that she was somewhat touched by his endeavour. They have enjoyed a strange relationship, I think. Like rival siblings, competing for her father's favour. I know nothing of murals, however. And your second matter, James? More delicate, I think. Though I shall not assist you unless you apologise for your claim that I have treated you ill!'

'*They* enjoy a strange relationship? You say so? Fie upon you, Elizabeth Cooper. Such wit! That you can describe a thing thus when we speak here, myself the husband cuckolded by a breeches-bawd and you, the tribade enamoured of a sapphist shrew. God's Hooks, it is a comedy that even the Bard himself could not have conceived. A fine couple. And this matter between us, the way in which you practised upon both myself and Rosina, allowing each of us to believe that neither would levy demands on the other from our marriage. I doubt that I owe *you* apology, madam. Quite the reverse!'

'Yet it was never as you describe, James Bradley. Rosina drew her own conclusion that you would not make any venial claim upon her and you, on the other hand, had made some foolish assumption that Rosina would surrender to your will on the basis that she could maintain her liaison with myself. The fault is hardly mine if you did not clarify these details face to face. But the fact is, James, that neither you nor I now seem wholly satisfied with the outcome. So let us come to your second matter, my friend.'

'Any assumption that I may have made was based entirely on that which

318

you specifically told me, madam. You have more guile than a vixen before the hounds. But correct, I suppose, that the finer detail should have been more thoroughly confirmed. And so with this matter. For I have begun to discover, sequestered about the house, bottles of a certain lincture. A prophylactic cordial, I understand. And Rosina herself, when she is neither bargaining for some advantage, nor pressing her Jacobite sympathies upon me, seems otherwise listless. I have seen the symptoms before amongst others, I collect. In certain low establishments. You understand me, I think?'

'Rosina has an affection for the Sydenham's, I must allow, though I am sure I do not know how she procures such quantities. It makes me quite low to see her. Yet I think she may have inherited the weakness from her Papa who is, she tells me, especially attached to his own geneva. I am surprised, however, that you have not seen a certain advantage here.'

'Advantage? How so? It seems to me that we shared a certain expectation, Mistress Cooper. An expectation that we would each benefit from my marriage. And so it may eventually transpire if recent news of Fontenoy truly heralds a Jacobite supremacy. Yet meanwhile, in place of profit, we are both reviled, lectured upon our politics, our religion. How can it be that we each achieved exactly the thing which we wanted but now find that it is *we* who must pay the price of our success?'

'For you the Marriage Settlement, James, for me the Bride's Pie glass ring. But what do we each *seek*, Mister Bradley? For you, the proper consummation of your marriage. Your rights as a husband. Why, children, I imagine. And me? I long for the Rosina Redmond that I once knew. The nymph. The enchantress. But, that creature no longer existing, I would have my freedom, sir. And the Sydenham's my friend, might provide the advantage to us both. I have noticed that, when she is under its influence, the dear girl is so much more...'

'Compliant?'

Elizabeth Cooper thinks carefully for a moment.

'Why, yes, sir. An excellent choice of word. Compliant indeed!"

Chapter Thirty-Three

Maria-Louise had been raised on tales about 'The Flight of the Wild Geese.' Sometimes at her father's knee, other times that of O'Farrell, in English or in Gaelic, the tale had assumed epic proportion in her mind.

Twenty years before her birth, and following their defeat at the Boyne, the Irish Jacobite army had been given the chance to leave their native soil as part of the Treaty of Limerick, signed when the Williamite War drew to its sad close. With James the Second exiled, fourteen thousand soldiers, and another ten thousand women and children, had left their homes in Ireland to take up service with various European nations. Those of the Wild Geese who had flown to France had formed the nucleus of the French Irish Brigade, and this had been supplemented over the years through the recruitment to its ranks by Catholic Irish gentry. The practice had been encouraged by the Authorities in Ireland since Catholics were still banned from the military there, and it was preferable to have young and excitable Papists safely away in France than unemployed on the streets at home.

Her father, however, had chosen a different path, determined that he could remain in Ireland and rebuild the life they had previously enjoyed. But he had been wrong. As an officer veteran of the losing side, he had fallen from one misfortune to another until, finally, he had sold some of their more valuable possessions and made the move to England, taking O'Farrell with them, for the fellow had himself fought for King James and served the family with loyal distinction.

So celebration in the Redmonds' home has almost reached excess.

The English defeated at Fontenoy, and their defeat achieved at the point of Irish, rather than French bayonets. The Regiments of Dillon, Buckley, Roth, Berwick, Lally and Clare, the Squadrons of FitzJames, each toasted and then toasted yet again. The Wild Geese had carried the day, and the Redmonds' normally muted homage to Restoration Day, the twenty-ninth of May, had turned without any true planning into a very different sort of rout. Restoration Day itself denotes simply the date on which Charles the Second had been brought back to the throne in 1660 but it is noted now only by those who retain strong anti-Cromwellian sentiment. Yet this year, for supporters of the Stuarts, and following Fontenoy, it has had a peculiar significance.

And in Manchester, almost unbidden, they had gathered at the Redmond house, causing Maria-Louise to send Mudge and Anna-Marie in search of dainties and cold meats, though in the end she had no reason to trouble herself for it developed in a form that she remembered from Paris as something of a *pique-nique*. Susannah Fletcher and her husband had arrived with a game pie, the Byroms with an enormous ham borne by two of their manservants, Mary Moss fetched a round of cold boiled beef. Even Francis Townley and his friends had arrived with flagons of strong ale, as well as a letter from his brother.

Francis had been pressed to reading it.

Captain Townley's regiment had acquitted itself well, it seemed, though the French Horse badly mauled in the final stages of the battle. A strange find amongst the prisoners though for, despite the normal proscriptions of their faith, there had been some Methodist Dissenters. They had all heard John Wesley speak at various times but one of them was also familiar with Mister Byrom, had met him along with Reverend Clayton.

Both men had preened themselves at mention of their names. Yet read on, sir, please!

A reference also to some Welsh Jacobites in French service. An associate of Sir Watkin, Mister Lloyd. It seemed that he might be presented with a Commission for some technical work that he had undertaken, engineering sketches and the like.

And great praise for the Irish Brigade, naturally. Though terrible losses suffered. No less than seven hundred casualties from fewer than four thousand men who had taken the field that day. A great victory all the same. He had given his friends in Manchester joy of it, bidden them remain staunch for, he had assured them, the day was fast approaching that they had all anticipated so eagerly.

'God praise the fellow,' Reverend Clayton had cried.

The blind fiddler from Mother Blossom's had been fetched and O'Farrell persuaded to lead them in a creaky jig, despite his considerable age, before being also persuaded to a recitation. A haunting epic by the ancient bard O'Dubhagain in praise of the Lally family, alongside whom O'Farrell himself had once fought. Maria-Louise had remembered it, could follow much of the genealogy and some of the Gaelic. But even those who had not shared the language had been held spell-bound by the lilting beauty of the poem's form.

Songs had been sung, though no Rosina to lead them, and Maria-Louise had at once felt the loss of her presence in equal measure with anger that her daughter remained so estranged from her. Estranged too from these young blades who would have shared her joint fervour for the Stuarts and the French alike. The Deacon boys. Chaddock. Holker. Whitlock. Collow. Dawson. Beswicke. Francis Townley himself.

'Mistress, do you now think better of the French, I wonder?' he had said to her.

'Why, Mister Townley, I think no more nor less of them than I have always done. Your Frenchman will answer perfectly well as an individual, yet set a few of them together and they will assume an air of superiority that is entirely overwhelming. And when led by scoundrels, as they are so often, they develop tendencies that lend them no credit. Yet I do not grudge them their victories. Indeed, I applaud them so long as they will confine them to foreign soil. But I should not like to see them practise so upon our own domain.'

'Fie, madam, I cannot discern whether that response was yay or nay.'

'A question with a single-word response, sir, was never worth the asking. Do you not find, Mister Townley, that a one-word answer does nothing but dishonour the questioner, implying lack of true worth in the query? Indeed, it belies the complex nature of the universe, I find, where nothing is either totally black nor completely white.'

Townley laughs, his crooked teeth causing the effort to emit a fine spray of spittle. 'By the Mass, lady,' he says, 'you should have been a politician.'

'I am pleased to have risen so in your opinion. You once described me as a whore, I understand. Though, upon reflection, perhaps I should have been better pleased with your first assessment. Politician indeed. La!'

'I cannot imagine who could possibly have attributed such indecent words to me, madam. I hold yourself, your family, your husband in highest esteem. Titus Redmond's subscription for our Cause this year is renowned amongst our friends, the envy of our enemies, across the nation.'

'So you no longer consider him a spent force then? I am pleased to hear it. And do you have news from Connaught, sir? For Titus had word from Sir Watkin that his associate, Mister Morgan, was hopeful of encouraging support there.'

'I know only that he has repaired to Ireland for that very purpose, Mistress. But he could not enjoy a more favourable climate in which to undertake his venture than one in which the Irish Brigade has garnered such acclaim. And your husband, madam? It is true that I believed him sore-affected by the attack upon him. He seems, at times, not quite himself. He has seemed even less so since Jacob Driscoll's demise. Yet still a gentleman of considerable substance in our ranks, naturally.'

Yet my husband shall one day seek retribution on you for those slights, sir, she had thought. *And on Striker, too, for poor Jacob, I imagine.*

And the following weeks had passed in a succession of events, some high, some low, but each affected in its way by that single event at Fontenoy, so far distant on the fields of Flanders. The birthday of exiled King James the Third, the tenth of June, had been more exuberant than normal whilst the anniversary bonfire to celebrate the inauguration of George the Second, on the very day afterwards, had been dampened by a Whiggish lack of enthusiasm on the one hand, and a torrential downpour on the other. More gloating amongst both Tory and Jacobite. An omen surely.

Then Aran Owen's own birthing day, on the twelfth, had gone almost entirely unremarked by everybody apart from Maria-Louise herself and, she was surprised to note, by Katherine. *My God, could the girl be interested in him?* Well, Mama wished her good luck for she, Maria-Louise, had certainly enjoyed little success in bedding the fellow. She had shared with him the intimacy of scripting a secret message to Striker but no more than that. In truth, she could not properly recall how Aran had managed to deflect her advances but the message, at least, had been sent.

She had experienced relief, deep relief, at her actions and that was even before news of Fontenoy had arrived. For with Cumberland defeated, what now would stand between England and a French invasion except the small matter of finance? And the other side of this silver coin, naturally, had been the significance of the Irish Brigade's charge. The lesson learned that the defeat of an English Hanoverian army need not depend upon the French. It had lit a beacon for *all* opponents of the Hanoverians, be they Scots or Irish, English or Welsh, that the thing could be done!

Her decision seems to have been timed to perfection and her feeling of achievement, of having done the correct thing, remains with her throughout the month, burning brightly still today, as the annual race meeting takes place at Kersal Moor to mark Midsummer. Its sponsors include almost every peer of the County, though it is bitterly opposed by Mister Byrom who owns another property here, and the meeting attracts thousands, blocking lane and byway for miles around with carriage and cart, drawn towards the rainbow flags and sparkling tents that mark the presence of temporary tavern, gambling sideshow and fortune-teller.

The Moor itself stretches upwards across the higher ground north of Salford and that long horse-shoe meander in the Irwell, ground that is partially wooded and scattered with knolls upon which crowds gather to gain the best views of the roughly oval course itself. On the highest, a wooden structure is erected to allow an even better perspective for those prepared to pay an extra shilling. There are few big purses to be won, such as might be had at Newmarket or Epsom, but there is a fair mix of races over four miles for thoroughbreds and geldings, or over two miles for race colts and fillies, and the stakes are always reasonable. Besides, it has become a major fixture in the town's social calendar, to rival only the Annual Fair so that, like a magnet, it draws almost as many traders as it does gamblers. Pudding men with their heating stoves on barrows. Ballad sellers chanting the week's best satirical gems. Pie vendors with their kit-cats piping hot. Flagon jennies selling jugs of geneva. Lottery touts fobbing off as many blanks as possible on each passing cull. And every other available grade and status of harlot that Manchester has to hand. Expensive ladies of pleasure, standard-priced whores, part-time park walkers, sixpenny bunters, and the penny-a-throw bulk mongers.

In fact, such is the significance of the three-day event that it occasions even a rare public appearance by her husband and she takes his arm affectionately, pleased to be seen in his company even though they must also share the moment with Adam Scatterbuck.

'Well, sir,' says Titus, 'do you have any advice? Any intelligence gained for an appropriate wager?'

Scatterbuck wipes sweat from the undulating terrain of his cheeks and neck, dabs at his pimpled brow with yet another ink-stained kerchief. 'The matter creates a difficulty of considerable magnitude, I find. For I have been entirely inculcated with the commandment forbidding me to unjustly take or retain the wealth of my neighbours. Mister Wesley may describe the article more succinctly, for he expressly prohibits the act of gambling for a device to gain fortune at the expense and harm of others, a belief that melds well with our own Catholic Catechism. Yet here I find myself gathering copy to fill the pages of the *Journal* with news of the very act itself and to produce profit therefrom. A sufficiently sinful act, would you not agree, without making the thing worse by taking part in the process itself?'

'By the Mass, Adam,' Titus says, 'I never suggested that you should *place* the wager for me! You have grown sanctimonious, sir. Like my wife. I collect that the Holy Father must have deemed her a suitable candidate for beatification and she has been awaiting the appropriate moment to share the joyous tidings with her husband. Is that not so, my dear? I can think of little else that may have caused this air of contentment. There has been the ghost of a smile playing upon your lips permanently for many weeks now.'

She supposes that this must be true. Her humour has certainly been raised since the message to Striker was sent, though there have been other factors at play, too. Amongst other things, her monthly problem has been made exquisitely more comfortable by the Catamenic Napkins that Mistress Brimstone has been able to import tactfully from Milan. No trade bill for *this* product, naturally. Simple word of mouth. But such an improvement on fashioning one's own and they are quite the thing, with their ribboned loops and waist-ties. Why, she could almost have taken to wearing one as a regular nether-garment. How useful such a thing might be during the winter months. How much more modest than going permanently bare-arsed!

'I cannot grasp why you might imagine such a thing,' she replies. 'For Our Lady knows that I have little enough to lighten me with my eldest daughter now almost a stranger. Yet Fontenoy lifted me, to be sure. And anything more than this I must attribute to the ineffable enjoyment of my husband's company. That and the general good fortune of the Cause to which we aspire.'

'Good fortune indeed!' says Scatterbuck. 'Sir Watkin must have been perfectly green that we were able to raise three thousand guineas. From this one humble town, sir. It shames the rest of them, forsooth.'

'That *we* raised, you say? I think you are mistaken for it was I, dear Scatterbuck, that raised the Subscription. Yourself and others undoubtedly contributed to its success but the concept was my own. But see, the first race is due to begin and I have still not placed my wager. Since my wife takes such delight in my company, we shall leave you to your scribbling and endeavour to defy the Catechism a little more.'

They find a stewards' tent, recording in the Promissory Book her husband's one guinea wager on the bay owned by the Duke of Bolton and which that gentleman intends to ride himself. But this three o'clock race is a disappointment. Spectacular enough, with the hired jockey and gentlemen competitor each vivid in his red or blue, green or purple, yellow or black, the all-powerful essences of the equine world, the thunder of hooves, the flying sand and clods of earth. Yet, in the end, the Duke and *Little John* come a poor and unexpected second to the chestnut, *Diamond*, that earns its owner, Henry Curwen, a very reasonable fifty guinea purse.

'Well, that was a guinea poorly spent,' says Titus, 'but I should happily part with fifty if I might only know your secret, my dear. For a secret you surely possess!'

'Oh, a dozen at the least. La! I should have thought you would be pleased to see me content. And content I am, indeed. Apart from Rosina, matters are progressing well, I protest. Our enterprises each profitable and your relationship with Aran now improved.'

'You still believe me wrong to have mistrusted him? I must confess that I remain uncertain. But at least I now have the name of this cove Striker and, by the Mass, I shall find some method of repaying the cunny-sucker for Driscoll's murder – though I still cannot imagine what must have come over Jacob to have driven him thus. And if you have truly found such contentment, why then do you cast about so, my dear? As though searching for some lost thing or person?'

She wonders whether she has, indeed, developed such a habit. If so, she has not remarked the fact but it would be understandable. For some weeks following Aran's confession about Striker she imagined everywhere the face of that militia captain who had interrupted the meeting at Ancoats Hall. Everywhere. But the months had passed and O'Farrell had successfully kept the girls protected. Safe. Bless his noble soul. Almost eighty years of age. Too old to carry such responsibility, but kept them safe. So she has stopped thinking about Striker except as the recipient of her note. Or so she had believed.

'I think you are mistaken, Mister Redmond,' she says. 'Yet if I *should* have a secret? Let us suppose that I found myself in a position to act on behalf of us both, of many others also, but could not share the matter with you for fear that it may put you in harm's way. Or that it might have an outcome with dubious implications? What then? Would you think the less of me?'

'You encourage me to thoughts more appropriate to a romantic *novella*, yet I cannot imagine any circumstance,' says Titus, 'in which the value I place upon you could diminish by a featherweight. There are lick-spittles who might look at our lives and fail to understand them but I have told you before, my dear, that our relationship is beyond normal measure. We might each take some action of which the other would be better unapprised. But *that* will never diminish us. Then guard your secret, madam, and share with me its outcome only when you feel able. But perhaps we may need to continue this another day, for I perceive that Mistress Cole has some business to pursue.'

And so she does. Concerns about the number of bulk-mongers at the Course. How can honest whores be expected to turn a profit? Of course, if they had a more competent Flash-Man – Billy Bender, for example. He is here, naturally. And could throw a few frights up those part-time punks if only Mister Redmond will agree. But he will not. If his wife will excuse him, he must attend to the matter in person. So, once again, his bawd and his whores come first. Well…

She decides to find O'Farrell, check on the girls herself. And Aran is here, too. She has seen him at a distance. But she encounters none of these at the tavern tent. Only James Bradley, in company with Thomas Walley, Robert Jobb, Matthew Liptrott and a few others. He excuses himself and she chooses to ignore the knowing glances exchanged between the men as Bradley comes to join her.

'*Cara mia*,' he says. 'I am overwhelmed to find you alone and unattended in this den of thieves. The poor Constables have been busy all day. Yet might I offer you some refreshment? You could help to share my good fortune for that dear horse has earned me ten shillings. Two whole sovereigns, my dear. Does that not seem prophetic at this time?'

'To take refreshment here? With you, sir? I see that Mister Jobb's tongue has not ceased wagging since I entered. I can scarce imagine the loathsome direction of his thoughts. No, I thank you. I prefer to wander the Moor alone than suffer the fellow's licentious gaze. Besides, I will be perfectly safe. The world knows me for Titus Redmond's wife and there is not a nipper, bully ruffian, buzz-man, cloak twitcher nor forker who would set hands on me without knowing the cost of their deed. In any case, I have not altogether forgotten your sordid attempt to blackmail my family.'

'Then since I would take the air also, and would see the next race without fear of theft, perhaps you would do the honour of escorting *me*, Mistress? And perhaps I shall be allowed to make amends for my indiscretion,' Bradley replies.

And she feels again the thrill of his charms. He presents quite a figure too, lost a little weight since she saw him last. Past crimes less corpulent also. His own powdered hair is tied back with ribbon, according to his custom, and his knee-breeches, jacket and waistcoat are cut from silk of the deepest burgundy, his stockings fashionable. Such a contrast to the drab shades preferred by her husband.

'If you need my protection, sir, I should be pleased to provide it. Though I see that you have brought your weapon.'

He extends a polite hand, providing a resting place for her own, as though they might dance a *quadrille*. On his right, of course, away from the offending blade.

'I am surprised that you should find it worthy of note, my dear. For there are few gentlemen who would venture to Kersal Moor without such protection. Your husband may be the exception, naturally, having a reputation that precedes him like a *vedette*. I am pleased to say, however, that I have never needed to draw the thing in anger.'

They climb the path from the tented area to the top of the nearest hillock, seeking a vantage point from which they may view the Kersal Moor Great Stakes, the main event of the afternoon.

'My daughter is not with you, I assume?'

'No, she chose to make another journey to Droylsden, her regular visit now to Ma and Pa.'

'Ah, it is so often easier to care for another's kin than one's own.'

'In my case, I should happily allow that it is so. Whenever was a man blessed with such a mother-in-law? I have prayed for the day when you might tire of your husband and return to me. So that I might make amends for past misdeeds at least.'

'Mister Bradley! You are quite improper, sirrah. Such a thing might almost seem an incest and I shall never tire of my husband. Whatever pleasures I may have found upon your cock should not be mistaken for affection. And can you truly contemplate such infidelity so soon within your marriage?'

'My marriage, madam, is a model for many things. For my wife's devotion towards my parents. For the sharpness of its conversation on all matters from politics, to religion, to commerce. For the musical enchantment that it has brought to my dull existence. For the condescension that your daughter displays towards her poor husband. Yet I must allow that it is lacking a certain refinement. A quality that is difficult to adequately describe!'

'She still does not permit you to fuck her?'

'*Per piacere, bambina!* This is your daughter that we discuss. But you have touched the essence of the matter. She continues to find her comforts with Mistress Cooper but these exceed the merely venial, I think. She suffers badly with the megrims and I fear that they share a certain enjoyment of Morphean reveries.'

'You say? But, if so, the fault may be mine also for I have frequently resorted to such linctures and cordials myself. Yet it has not dulled her wit, I perceive, nor her musical ability.'

'Indeed not. In fact she has resumed her Wednesday morning lessons with Mrs Starkey. The good lady has been providing tuition at our house since your daughter extorted from me her own harpsichord. Another damn'd Jacobite, of course. But Rosina now finds it necessary to receive two lessons each week, one at home and one at Mrs Starkey's. And her negotiating skills

327

are not blunted, for this double cost was also a price I paid for some concession on Rosina's part, though I can no longer remember whatever profit I may have made from the bargain.'

The crowd erupts with excitement as the Great Stakes One Hundred Guineas is run over four miles for geldings, with Richard Harrison's *Fearnought*, carrying off the prize ahead of more famous contenders like John Turner's *Lath*, another bay from the Duke of Bolton's stables, *Quiet Cuddy*, and the Irish grey, *Potatoe*.

'One hundred guineas for Harrison and at least five for me!' says Bradley. 'How shall we spend it, do you think?'

'I have no suggestions, though I *do* have a question.'

'Then ask away, my dear. You know that I can refuse you very little.'

'Titus has been informed by John Clough that you may be awarding a contract for murals to be painted at the Exchange. Is it true, sir?'

'Oh, a fie upon you, Mistress Redmond. Not such a difference 'twixt mother and daughter after all.'

'You must explain yourself, Mister Bradley. It was a simple enough question.'

'And the very same that Rosina put to me so very recently. If I was a suspicious man, I might wonder at the fascination that you each share for Aran Owen.'

'She asked you to award the commission to Aran?'

'Of course! And were you not intent on adding weight to her proposal?'

'I knew nothing about her proposal, sir. Yet they have become like brother and sister, though Aran has not always behaved well towards her and now seeks to make amends. I assume that her proposition is simply Rosina's way of acknowledging his efforts. Though how should I know, being simply her mother?'

'And your own reason, Mistress?'

'My own, Mister Bradley, as you say. But I have not heard your response.'

'You may be certain that I would not give him the work to please Rosina, my dear, though I have to confess a certain degree of curiosity about how much I could gain in return. But, on reflection, for the sweet pleasures of your cunny again perhaps I might be persuaded.'

'And you say that Rosina has resumed her weekly lessons with Mrs Starkey?'

'Indeed, my dear.'

'Then you may offer Mister Owen the commission, sirrah!'

And she turns so that he may not see the smile that she cannot hide, leaves him so she may share the good news with Aran, if only she can find him. It takes almost ten minutes but she finally sees him, his back turned towards her as he looks down upon the Course.

'Aran, my dear,' she calls as she approaches him. 'I have some excellent…'

He turns and she sees that his face is pale as bleached linen. 'You look as though you have seen a ghost.'

'And so I have! I had hoped that he was gone from my life forever, but I was wrong.'

'Striker?'

'None other.'

'But the message. He received it? And Jacob Driscoll...'

'Yes, it was received. But he had come here intent on mayhem. Mayhem, I tell you. I feared for the girls. He threatened such things that you would not believe yet, in the end, I believe I managed to persuade him that his suspicion was groundless – that I had no part in Driscoll's plan. Yet nothing is ever quite so simple with Striker. He has given me only the benefit of his doubts. But I have to tell you, madam, that he has demanded yet another token from me.'

Chapter Thirty-Four

'God blind me!' says Thomas Pelham-Holles, the Duke of Newcastle, as Sir Edward enters the room. 'Good news at last. Come, sir. Join us, I pray.' Pelham's private library in Newcastle House seems smaller than he remembers, but it is also busier. 'Let me name these gentlemen,' the Duke continues. 'Bedford you already know.'

Sir Edward Stanley offers a bow, so far as his girth will permit, to John Russell, the Fourth Duke of Bedford, thirty-five years old, medium build with dark eyes, straight-mouthed and a distinctly protruding lower lip. He sports a short wig and is dressed in russet. He has sat in the House of Lords for twelve years already and is not greatly in favour with the King. Yet despite this the present Administration had seen fit to give him the post as First Lord of the Admiralty in the previous November. He may have been promoted by Pelham's brother, the Prime Minister, but there is often friction between Newcastle and Bedford. The main source of such friction rests in Bedford being a civilian, and Newcastle had firmly believed that, at this time, the post requires an incumbent with at least *some* military or naval experience.

'Anson too. Acquainted, I assume?' says Pelham.

'Naturally, Your Grace,' replies Sir Edward, exchanging deferences with the austere Commodore, a fine-looking fellow with long scarlet waistcoat, gold-trimmed, beneath his blue naval coat. Not quite fifty, George Anson is something of a legend. A navy man from the age of fifteen, he had risen to his present rank in the Year '40, taking command of a squadron charged with harrying Spanish possessions in South America. His subsequent difficulties with the voyage are familiar to the entire nation and yet, reduced to a single vessel, the *Centurion*, and enduring great hardships, Anson had completed a significant circumnavigation and, in the bargain, captured a Spanish galleon carrying more than one million pieces of eight. He had returned in the previous year, been elected as the Honourable Member for Hedon, in Yorkshire, and joined the Admiralty Board this past December. At Newcastle's insistence, he is now Bedford's principal advisor.

'Sir Richard?' asks Pelham.

'Delighted, as always, sir,' Sir Edward says, shaking hands with the similarly rotund Sir Richard Hoare, grandson and namesake of the renowned gentleman who had founded Hoare's Bank, of which Sir Richard is now himself a partner and also recently elected Lord Mayor of London.

'These other two gentlemen. Not known to you, however,' says Pelham. 'Mister Corbet. Admiralty Office.' A senior clerk, perhaps, from his garb, though with a significant air of superiority about him. 'And Edward Masterson. First Lieutenant Masterson, I should say. Of the *Prince Frederick*. Gentlemen, Sir Edward Stanley. Eleventh Earl of Derby. Lord Lieutenant of Lancashire. *Et cetera*.' Corbet and Masterson show due courtesy towards His Lordship.

Masterson is the anomaly amongst the group. His blue coat is not quite naval but it is crusted with salt and threadbare. Indeed, the fellow looks as though he has hardly slept and, under Sir Edward's severe gaze, becomes almost self-conscious, straightening the broad pockets and making a visible effort to hold himself more erect.

'Must forgive Masterson's appearance, Sir Edward,' Pelham says. 'Difficult journey, Lieutenant. Would you not say so?'

'Thirteen days at sea, sir. That is, thirteen since the battle itself. Landed at Plymouth three days ago.'

'And made remarkable progress reaching London from there, Lieutenant, if I may congratulate you?' says Sir Richard Hoare.

'Battle, you say?' enquires Sir Edward, feeling as though he has missed something crucial.

'Indeed, sir. A battle,' says Pelham. 'More of that *anon*. First, refreshments. Eh, Lieutenant? Seat perhaps, also?'

'Most welcome, Your Grace,' Masterson replies, accepting a glass of cordial from Pelham's servant. 'Yet I would prefer to stand, sir, if it's all the same with you. Sea legs still, if you catch my drift.'

'As you wish, sir,' says Pelham. 'Understandable. Perfectly. And when you are composed, we shall hear your tale. Eh, gentlemen? But Sir Edward has been staying in London, I collect. Have you not, sir?'

'Indeed, Your Grace. Taking treatment for my bile.'

'And the fair Lady Elizabeth with you also?'

Mention of his wife provokes Sir Edward to a defiant pinch of snuff. 'We have been residing with her cousin, at their house in Brook Street, Your Grace.' And indeed they have. Treatment for the gravel but also escape from the County, for Lancashire has been gripped by Jacobite fever since news arrived of Cumberland's defeat at Fontenoy.

'Brook Street, you say? Neighbours of Mister Handel then?'

'The adjacent house, sir.'

'Admire him greatly,' says Pelham. 'Greatly! Yet had we better explain our presence here, Sir Edward? What say you, sir? But where to start? With Sir Richard perhaps?' And Sir Richard gestures with his right hand, a casual gesture of consent. 'Now, sir, you are familiar with Sir Richard. The illustrious bank in which he is a distinguished partner. Yet did you know, Sir Edward, that he enjoys another career? Entirely separate, you know.'

'A mere investor in the enterprise, Your Grace,' says Sir Richard.

'Principal investor, sir. Principal. You have heard of the Royal Family I suppose, Sir Edward?'

Not the kin of His Highness, naturally, but rather a well-known consortium of privateers, owned by some of London's wealthiest, including the present Lord Mayor, it seems, and so called because each of their vessels bears the name of a prince or princess of the royal blood. Yet the term *privateer* is one to be used with care. It is not even used in the contracts issued to their proprietors. They may be a necessary part of warfare and have remained so for two centuries, but the word carries unseemly connotations. Privateers are commerce raiders, pirates, licensed buccaneers. Thus, alternative terminology has been devised.

'Ah!' says Sir Edward, turning to Masterson. 'Then the *Prince Frederick* is a letter of marque?'

'Why, bless you, no sir,' Masterson replies. 'We are private ships of war, our sole purpose to capture prizes. We carry no cargo for trade overseas, and the men who joined us know that our only objective is to find enemy ships and bring them back. Or sink them.'

'Perhaps I should elucidate,' says Anson. 'Letters of marque are outfitted primarily for commercial trading ventures. The owners of these vessels are simple merchants who, during times of war, take out privateering commissions as both a safeguard and an investment opportunity. Thus, even though letters of marque are primarily merchant trading vessels, they carry privateering commissions in case they encounter the enemy at sea. Yet, because their primary purpose remains commerce, they offer wages to their crews in the normal way. Any prize money is therefore a happy supplement. Ships of war, on the other hand, as Lieutenant Masterson confirms, are employed only to destroy and capture our enemies. The rewards for crews of such vessels stem entirely from the prizes that they harvest. Though, God knows, the distinction between private ships of war and letters of marque is often poorly enough drawn in their respective contracts. I am sure that the First Lord may agree?'

But John Russell, Duke of Bedford, defers immediately to Corbet on the matter.

'A problem that we seem to have inherited from previous Administrations,' says Corbet. 'But we are in the process of drafting new forms of contract that will correct the matter. Although – present company excluded, Sir Richard, naturally – there have been issues with both sides at times. Failure to undertake the specified objectives and the like. Parliament has therefore deemed it appropriate that owners will subsequently be required to post bonds, dependent upon the size of the venture, against the contract's fulfilment.'

'It should assist us in weeding out the very few less reputable owners,' says Bedford, 'without damaging the worthy majority of whom the Royal

Family is such a fine example and upon whom we rely so heavily at present times to supplement the navy itself. We would be entirely ditched without them, gentlemen.'

Indeed, thinks Sir Edward, *and they also would be similarly ditched without the profits that war may bring them*. Fabulous wealth for all concerned, so that the three thousand pound bond that Sir Richard may be expected to post for a normal privateering venture will seem the merest trifle by comparison. And Bedford, as First Lord, will not be without his own percentage. A strange choice for the post, too, Sir Edward believes, for there had been rumours about Russell's own leaning towards the Jacobites at times. Still, his coat seems firmly turned towards Hanover for now, at least.

'Indeed, Your Grace,' says Anson. 'With the war turned so badly in Flanders, our domination of the seas may be the only thing that can save us from French invasion. Which brings us, once again, to the Royal Family and my good friend, Commodore Walker, I think.' George Walker had come to prominence during the previous autumn and his gallant action aboard the privateer *Boscawen*. 'You sailed with him, I collect, Masterson?'

'I had that privilege, sir. A most remarkable officer. He promoted me to First when that scoundrel Kennedy deserted, before I transferred to the *Prince Frederick* to fill a vacancy there.'

'Yet it is Mister Corbet,' says the First Lord, 'who has had particular dealings with him. Perhaps, Mister Corbet, you might complete some of the background for Sir Edward. I assume that everybody is familiar with the generalities yet the details are extraordinary, Corbet, are they not?'

'A remarkable fellow indeed,' says Sir Richard Hoare. 'Myself and a few associates had already commissioned those vessels that have now become known as the Royal Family. *King George*, *Prince Frederick*, the *Duke* and *Princess Amelia*. We had no hesitation whatsoever in offering the command of this fine squadron to Commodore Walker. Why, the old *Boscawens* rolled up with hundreds of other prime seamen to join Walker's flag at Bristol. It was most edifying.'

'Edifying and timely,' says Bedford. 'For we needed to disrupt our enemies' trade with New France, and therefore contracted with the Royal Family that they might undertake a cruise between the Azores and the Newfoundland Banks.'

'And Commodore Walker no sooner departed upon this venture,' says Newcastle, 'than we received intelligence. Interesting intelligence. From an agent.. You met the fellow, Sir Edward. Here, in this very room. The Stuarts' plan. To convey a considerable amount of their silver from Rome aboard French privateers. Then to a *rendezvous* point on the west coast of France. Finance for a French invasion, gentlemen. Nothing less than a French invasion. And insufficient vessels of our own available to ensure that the plan might be thwarted. Turned, naturally, to Sir Richard. Hoped that he might assist.'

'And, by a stroke of good fortune,' says Sir Richard, 'the *Prince Frederick* had been late joining the squadron, having been left in dock at Bristol in May. Fortuitous, since we were able to send sealed instructions with her when she sailed. We could not risk all, however, so we agreed with the Admiralty that the squadron should divide, half searching for the silver and the rest continuing their allotted cruise towards the Banks. Lieutenant Masterson, it might be appropriate if you take up the tale at this point, I think.'

Masterson holds himself a little straighter, grins wide and proud. 'Well, gentlemen, we joined the squadron at the island of Terceira. Shall I say a word about the squadron, Your Grace?' Newcastle affirms. 'In total, sirs, we are the *King George*, under the command of Commodore Walker himself. She's a thirty-two and carries three hundred men. Then the *Princess Amelia*, of twenty-four guns and one hundred and fifty men. Captain Denham. The *Duke*, commanded by Captain Morecock. Twenty guns and a crew of two hundred and sixty. Finally, our own *Prince Frederick* of twenty-six guns and two hundred and sixty men. Captain James Talbot in command, as you may know.

'And by the time that we reached Terceira, why bless me, if Commodore Walker hadn't already managed to take prizes. Including the French *Postillion*, gentlemen. The neatest little polacre I ever did see. We renamed her *Prince George* and she was attached to the *Prince Frederick* and *Duke* as tender, for it had been agreed that this smaller squadron should be left behind to seek out these privateers that Your Grace has mentioned. A fine prize in her own right too. Cargo of beeswax and other goods. Expected to raise fifteen hundred guineas. And an old French lady on board, too, the Marquise de Saint-Antoine.'

'You will forgive my ignorance, Lieutenant,' says Sir Edward. 'But a polacre?'

'Why, sir, she's a rig usually peculiar to the Mediterranean. Some have two masts and others have three, and the *Prince George* is of the latter variety. She's lateen-rigged on her fore-mast and mizzen-mast, and square-rigged on the mainmast. She looks a bit odd to most eyes for she has pole masts with neither tops nor cross-trees. This, and the arrangement for staying her masts means the yards can be braced much closer to the centre-line than in any normal square-rigger. This makes her extremely weatherly, Lordship. Why, we are able to trim her yards fifteen degrees to the centreline. Fifteen! There are no footropes to the yards, so the crew stand on the topsail yards to loose, or furl, the topgallant sails. And on the lower yards to loose, reef, or furl the topsails, the yards themselves being lowered sufficiently for that purpose. You follow, sir?'

'I am certain of it, Lieutenant,' says Newcastle. 'Yet received an entirely separate account. Amusing. About Commodore Walker's visit to Terceira. Old dog devoted a small fortune to the entertainment of the Marquise, too. She, in turn, being formerly a facetious and bitter witch, was entirely taken with the attentions lavished upon her. Part of those attentions included the hire of a carriage. So that Walker could show her the island. But no sooner had they set out upon the road than there fell in behind them his entire band of musicians. And a whole cavalcade of our honest tars and their harlots. To do the thing in style, they had hired every kind of horse, ass and vehicle in Terceira. Dressed them with all the coloured ribbon they could find. Decorated their own hats, the rumps of their horses, and even the teats of their women.'

'Oh indeed, sirs,' Masterson cries. 'And, sure, never were horses, whores and ribbons all so dear in one day upon Terceira! Oh, beg pardon, gentlemen. But there were such huzzahs across the island.'

'Yet did Commodore Walker not consider that such frivolity were a dereliction of his duties. Lieutenant?' says Sir Edward.

Masterson seems shocked at the suggestion. 'Why, no sir. Bless you, Lordship, but this whole thing took no more time than that required for taking on fresh water and additional powder. Then the squadrons sailed, Commodore Walker to the west and ourselves to the north. So just a few days later, we had taken up station off Cape Saint Vincent. Then, on the ninth day of July, just after two bells of the forenoon watch... That's nine o' the clock, in the morning, sirs. The man at the masthead called down, that he saw a sail in the offing, upon which Captain Talbot signalled to Captain Morecock, desiring that he should make all possible sail and investigate.

'But no sooner was the *Duke* about her business than a second sail was espied by the man at the masthead, and at half-past eleven Captain Morecock sent back that they were enemies. Naturally, gentlemen, they also did at the same time with respect to us, making all sail and bearing away southwards, with top-gallant royals, lower, top-mast, and top-gallant steering sails, keeping all as full they were able.

'For our own part, we left the *Prince George* to follow as best she could and set everything aloft too. The *Prince Frederick* being a right handy craft, and Captain Talbot a fine sailor, we bent our will to trimming sail and brace, spread every possible inch of canvas. Mainsail and forecourse drew fully, night and day, with the wind on her best point of sail, just abaft the beam. Hands were piped to supper, breakfast and dinner, watch by watch, and the chase was on, sirs. Day after day.'

Sir Edward listens to Masterson's deferential tones, the mariner's voice slightly raised in order to aid the understanding of the landsmen in his audience as he describes the intricacies of the scene. The Earl sees himself at the starboard rail, the weather rail, holding himself against the gentle pitch of deck over swell as a steady north-westerly drives them second by second, minute upon minute, degree past degree, down through the more southerly latitudes of the North Atlantic.

Clear, starlit nights, Antares low above the south-eastern horizon,

Altair, Aquila, Aquarius and Cygnus overhead. Cassiopeia, Cepheus and Draco away to the north, beyond their wake. The log heaved. Seven knots. Eight, but never more than that. Steady as you like. The glass holding too. The hour-timer turned. The bell struck. The lookouts cry 'All's well!' The wind changes from time to time but never enough to make any real alteration to trim or course. The smell of tar and cordage, brine and must, smoke from the galley fire. Cream-coloured canvas. Small white-caps break the sea's grey-green surface for hours on end but never build to anything significant. The Captain turning in only for an hour at a time. Eight bells of the middle watch, four o'the clock, and the morning watch raised from their hammocks. The decks swabbed. There is urgency but the casual observer would hardly know it. Neither pursuers nor quarry start their water overboard nor anything else that might lighten ship. Roundshot is chipped clean and smooth. They press on more sail.

The wind holds unnaturally steady, though it picks up a little on the following day. The gap is closed until they can plainly see the name on the stern of each enemy ship. The *Louis Erasmé* and the *Marquis d'Antin*. But that is as close as they come. It is the damn'dest thing, for the *Louis Erasmé* is a good match for the privateers, she also being a twenty-six, while the *Marquis d'Antin* is a thirty. Smaller guns, of course, they being John Frenchmen. But thirty eight-pounders on her gun deck, fifteen on each side, with four six-pounders on her quarter deck.

Yet the enemy does not offer battle. A simple matter of arithmetic. The English squadron carries a total broadside of three hundred and three pounds, against the Frenchman's two hundred and thirty-six. They could not prevail without some advantage. And, as Captain Talbot is fond of reminding them, John Frenchman is always so intent upon his mission that he will avoid battle at all costs. Oh, and how he loves his leeward gauge too! He believes that it will leave him free to break off as he chooses and flee before the wind. But it gives him a tendency to fire his broadsides on the upward roll, trying for his enemy's rigging, though he rarely shoots well enough to disable them completely.

By the twelfth, the wind has shifted into the south-west and the ships are once more in sight of the Azores, now sailing on the larboard tack. All that time just out of each other's range but close enough that the French cannot lose their pursuers, even during the hours of darkness. Then, as the sun gets up, there is another sail on the horizon and coming up fast, going large. By noon, and the end of the morning watch, it is clear she is another Frenchman, the *Notre Dame de la Délivrance* and a big bugger too. A sixty-four. The other two must think it their lucky day for they beat to quarters and shorten sail, hoping to catch their attackers between two fires.

But to the Englishmen's surprise, the *Délivrance* stands off again, crowds sail and chases away eastwards. There is no obvious reason but, by this time, they have closed the gap. The wind has slackened but still in Talbot's favour so that the Frenchmen, having the lee gauge, are each heeled over, exposing part of their bottoms to shot from both of the privateers on occasion. Yet they still lead them a merry dance, allowing them all the time to get to windward, seemingly surrendering the weather gauge but then, every time the raiders begin to draw alongside, and just as they bear up before the wind to take them, the devils use the leeward gauge to pull ahead again.

The *Prince Frederick* has overhauled the *Duke* some time since but she is coming up steady and, by three o'clock, they are able to open fire on the *Marquis d'Antin* with their larboard battery. The action is so hot that, after ten minutes, the Frenchman cannot see a thing for the smoke blown down upon her. A good wind but the weather not so heavy that it hinders the privateers in any way. For the Frenchie's part, there are a great number of men at small arms in her tops, poop, quarter deck and forecastle, while the *Prince Frederick* has a clear ship fore and aft, the galley fires extinguished, and everything ready for action, with colours flying, her people in great spirits and giving three cheers. The fellows on the *Duke* do likewise, from astern.

The Frenchmen are cheering too, though faintly, and giving reply of their own broadsides, playing havoc with the privateers below and aloft.

Then the *Louis Erasmé* hauls her wind, bearing up and then away again so that they might fall upon the *Prince Frederick*'s starboard side, trapping her between their two ships. But they time the thing badly. Captain Talbot has already run out his starboard battery guns. The crews are ready for them, and they are still presenting their stern as they begin to fall off.

So the *Prince Frederick* rakes her. End to end. By God, she does!

Ball after ball slices along the length of the Frenchman's deck, cutting through seamen, dismounting guns from their carriages, hacking into her masts, a fury of iron, splinters and blood, while a second lethal broadside cuts their tiller rope, along with a great part of her wheel, so that she luffs up entirely into the wind, leaving her at the mercy of the fast-approaching *Duke*.

They try to get tackles upon their tiller below, shivering their after-falls and working hard to turn her bow a-port to catch the wind again. But it is too late for them. Captain Morecock lays the *Duke* alongside her, pouring in one broadside after another, their yards touching until, one by one, the masts of the *Louis Erasmé* are all shot to hell and, at last the Frenchman finally falls silent.

Prince Frederick is left free to practise entirely upon the *Marquis d'Antin*, her gun crews all now working the larboard battery. They hull her several times between wind and water. And then her ensign comes down. There are cries that she has struck. But it seems that her ensign has simply fouled, for the Frenchman suddenly puts her helm a-lee and begins to fire again, always on the upward roll and throwing great quantities of shot, bar and chain into her enemy's sails and rigging. The men are hard pressed to reeve and splice sufficient to keep braces and bowlines all intact, yet still they lose the mizzen topsail. In short, everything is so torn and cut to pieces that, had the weather not been so fine, the privateer must surely have lost all her masts too, for she has scarce a whole shroud left intact.

'We kept our pace all the same,' says Masterson, 'putting shot into her all the time. It was late afternoon by now and several of her gun ports had been beat into one, and she was wracked by two explosions. Then her main came down. Burning wads fell upon us, setting fire to our hammocks in the poop, though we soon extinguished them. But still she fought and her captain there on the quarter deck of the *Marquis d'Antin*, as cool as might be in the midst of all that slaughter. Yet it could not continue and, finally, that brave captain himself fell, taken by a pistol shot. Yes sirs, we were that close. And so she struck.'

'By God, gentlemen,' says Newcastle. 'Such an action!'

Sir Edward blinks, the scene dissolving behind his eyes, for a brief moment surprised to find his feet planted on the floor of Pelham's library and not on the shifting deck of the *Prince Frederick*.

'Though you know not the half of it,' Bedford replies. 'For we have here the inventory taken of the French cargoes by good Captain Talbot. Give you joy of it, my friends. Eight hundred thousand sterling in silver, much of it coin. A Count of France too, as well as an abundance of Papist friars. Such a catch!'

'Almost beyond belief,' Newcastle says. 'Yet we will not see our treasure this side of September, I collect. That not correct, Mister Masterson?'

'Why, yes sir. Captain Talbot had a difficult choice. Repairs. The dead and wounded, of course. Yet we had to resolve their inventories, too. Not just the silver, gentlemen, but eight hundred tons of cocoa besides. Cocoa, sirs, you see? They had put into Cartagena, as we had been informed they might. Letters of marque always put commerce before prizes, else they might have succeeded in slipping past us. Or escaping us. But the Frenchmen, for their part, now have barely a mast left between them and need towing all the way home, gentlemen. A cruel, slow journey if they're not to put into Gibraltar.'

'If I know Captain Talbot he will not do so,' says Sir Richard. 'Though, if not, he must run the gauntlet of Jack Spaniard and John Frenchman for many weeks to come. If he brings them home, we shall not see them before the end of August, I fear.'

'A whole month,' says Bedford, 'yet we shall put the Channel squadrons at their disposal, send them out to help bring Talbot in, if they are able.'

'Naturally,' says Newcastle. 'And, meanwhile, you were dispatched in the *Prince George* to bring us the news, Masterson?'

'Yes, sir. Like I said, the neatest little polacre I ever did see.'

'Well then,' says Sir Edward, 'all credit to Sir Richard and his sea-dogs. Give you joy of your victory, Lieutenant. And your fellow-proprietors their prizes, Sir Richard, eh?'

338

Sir Richard smiles politely. 'We have already pledged the owners' portion to the King, Sir Edward. Though the crew shall enjoy a fine slice. One hundred pounds each for the ordinary hands, over twelve thousand to Captain Talbot and twice that amount to Commodore Walker. And some of the praise must go, besides, to those informants who first provided the intelligence.'

'Indeed, Sir Richard,' says Newcastle. 'Intelligence from Manchester, gentlemen. According to my agent.' *But they will not see fit*, thinks the Earl of Derby, *to share with me the identity of these contacts. My own County, forsooth!* 'Yet we have a problem,' Newcastle continues. 'News brought by Lieutenant Masterson may be excellent from our viewpoint. Yet it may be construed differently amongst the general public.'

'How so, sir?' asks Bedford. 'A sure sign that the Jacobites are spent, surely? Invasion averted.'

'Will put to you a hypothesis, gentlemen,' Newcastle replies. 'In June, a certain Alasdair McDonald of Glengarry observed by our agents, recruiting for a regiment in Scotland. Royal Écossais Regiment. Formation of which approved by King Louis last August. Specifically to support a Jacobite insurrection. In Ireland, some fellow called Gordon. Been trying to raise forces in Connaught. May not have been successful but that is almost an irrelevance. In Wales, Sir Watkin Williams Wynn has considerable support. And in England, we should look no further than Sir Edward's Lancashire. For the length of the Jacobites' reach. What say you, Sir Edward?'

'Well, Your Grace, there are many Lancashire Protestants and Loyalists who are well-disposed towards the Crown. I should not like to give a contrary view. We are certain to raise a subscription of thirteen thousand pounds over the next two months. Firm pledges, every one. And militia too. Yet we will struggle to find sufficient officers for even seven companies. And herein lies the unhappy condition of Lancashire, gentlemen, where so many fine estates are in Popish hands. Jacobite recruits a-plenty, too, in towns like Preston, Ormschurch, Manchester itself. Only Liverpool and Warrington wholly reliable, it seems. And so few young fellows of quality amongst our Protestant families. Why, was you to press me, I know only one within a radius of ten miles who would answer.'

'Very succinct, Sir Edward,' says Newcastle. 'Finely put. Jacobites so very deeply rooted within our society. And news that they might have eight hundred thousand pounds to invest in their Cause may be subject to some misinterpretation.'

'Yet they have lost it,' says Bedford. 'Thanks to Sir Richard and young Masterson.'

'Yes, gentlemen,' says Newcastle. 'Though perhaps we have already detained the good Lieutenant and Mister Corbet too long.' He thanks them both profusely for their attendance, trusts that he can rely on their discretion. Farewells are exchanged, and the two men are ushered from the office. 'Now, my friends,' he continues, 'the Stuarts may have lost their silver. But the public is likely to believe that they have yet more still in their possession. They will think this simply a token amount. And, for all we know, they may be correct.'

'Our agents cannot verify the depths of the Pretender's pockets, Your Grace?' says Sir Edward.

'Must confess, Sir Edward, that it shall please me to be rid of these agents. One or two exceptions, but their intelligence frequently imprecise. Grasping fellows, all of them. Expect the Crown to pay them every five minutes. Well enough, in their way. Awkward necessity at this time. And some I would never trust not to be employed equally by the Jacobites themselves. Playing each end of the same game, so to speak.' *An endeavour for which they could hardly be blamed*, thinks Sir Edward, *given the uncertainty of the outcome*. And he ponders his own link with Titus Redmond, the favour done by persuading Bishop Peploe to officiate at his daughter's wedding to Bradley. A strange affair, he now considers, since there are rumours that Bradley's bride is a tribade. Perhaps, if matters with the Jacobites proceed badly, he may need to give and receive further favours yet. 'In any case,' Newcastle continues, 'I simply believe it expedient that we should exult in the news of our success yet be conservative in the nature of its source.'

'Then perhaps,' says Anson, 'I might make a suggestion. For we know that the *Notre Dame de la Délivrance* had been in Callao as late as November. If we confuse the stories somewhat, it should be no great difficulty to suggest that the treasure we intercepted had, in fact, originated in Peru. What do you say, Your Grace? We could even draft a letter for Lieutenant Masterson, to be published in the *Gentlemen's Magazine*, confirming that the proprietors have waited upon the King and offered seven hundred thousand pounds, their share of the prizes, to be immediately employed for His Majesty's service. He would be willing, I am sure. It will seem, therefore, that the silver had belonged to Jack Spaniard. It will finally be minted afresh, I assume?'

'Then we shall ask Corbet and the Admiralty,' says Bedford, 'to suggest some suitable inscription for the new coinage when it comes into circulation.'

'Yes,' says Newcastle. 'Seems entirely appropriate. But one final piece of news, gentlemen. Or perhaps I should leave it to Bedford. For there has been another action this month. Another engagement altogether, but this time involving His Majesty's Navy.'

'His Grace refers to the action that took place off the Lizard,' says the First Lord, 'on the ninth of this month. Captain Brett's frigate, the *Lion*, a sixty-four, intercepted two French vessels, which he took to be making for the Americas. The vessels in question were the *Doutelle* and *L'Elisabeth*. The engagement lasted almost five hours and, at its close, Brett was so badly damaged that he was forced to put back into port. The *Elisabeth* was similarly forced to withdraw towards the French coast. It is the action of the *Doutelle*, however, that has given us pause for concern.'

'How so, Your Grace?' enquires Sir Edward.

Yet it is Commodore Anson who replies. 'For one thing,' he says, 'although she took part in the opening shots of the engagement, she spent the remainder of the action entirely apart from the fight, when she could so clearly have decided the matter in John Frenchman's favour. And then, when the fight was done, she neither sailed south nor west but, rather, northwards, making for Ireland or Scotland.'

'In short, Sir Edward,' says Newcastle, 'the need for some perspicacity in relation to the Jacobite silver may be augmented by another likelihood. That the cargo carried by *L'Elisabeth* might have been even more valuable. We believe, sir, that the *Chevalier*, the Young Pretender, may have slipped through our fingers. And, by now, be landed upon our shores.'

Chapter Thirty-Five

'I thought that you should have seemed happier,' says Rosina, her voice echoing around the walls of the almost empty main hall in the Commodities Exchange.

'Then you must forgive me, my dear,' replies Aran Owen. 'I have been somewhat distracted of late. And I must confess a certain surprise that your husband has not seen fit to confirm in person his award of this commission. Your mother mentioned the matter to me some weeks ago.'

'A fie upon you, sir! You are an ingrate. And Mama? My mother cannot possibly know anything of this. Mister Bradley only decided the thing last Wednesday. He asked me particularly to inform you and intends to invite you to dine with us, so that he can consider any views that you might have about possible subjects. La! I had so hoped that you would be pleased.'

'And so I am, Rosina. Of all things. Humbled too, I must confess, for I cannot believe that your husband should offer me such a chance without some considerable influence and, perhaps, also cost on your part. Much more than a scrub like myself should deserve. Yet I can furnish proposals a-plenty and the prospect of dining with you fills me with childish anticipation. I am less certain about your husband's company, however, for he has never shown any slight regard for me. Quite the contrary, my dear. Nor I for him, in truth. Yet you are mistaken about your Mama. Why, she hinted at the thing weeks ago, upon Kersal Moor. I recall the moment quite precisely. I have good reason to do so.'

'Then I shall confront him, sirrah. Though I am certain that you are wrong. And you must not concern yourself about the dinner. Mister Bradley is capable of exhibiting charm whenever he cares to make the attempt, and I shall make sure that he does so on this occasion. In any case, it shall be in his interest, for he must be able to supervise the work, must he not? He will require good relations with you.'

'The history of art is littered with tales of patrons who enjoyed the most appalling relations with the artists they employed. Treated them as little better than serfs. Much depends upon the fee set for the commission, naturally, yet I should count myself sufficiently rewarded simply by your generosity and forgiveness, my dear.'

'You cannot live on forgiveness, Mister Owen. And, anyway, did I say that you are forgiven? I think not. No, sir, you must set the fee appropriately. For my own part, I have no concept of the thing. The duration of the work, nor the manner of its execution.'

'You seem weary, Rosina. Shall I fetch a chair? Or should you prefer to leave this for another day?'

'No, Aran. If I might sit a moment, I should enjoy hearing your intentions.' He offers her a polite bow, then brings a seat from the table at the other side of the hall.

'There, my dear, but you must tell me when you are tired of my prattle. For I estimate that, maintaining the minimum amount of time that I need each week for other duties, the work will take me two years to complete. Yet if it can be accomplished satisfactorily, it may establish my reputation, and thus have a value far exceeding the fee itself. The scale of each panel is my main concern and whilst I have learned much from those who have addressed us at Mister Byrom's Academy, my knowledge of such large pieces is essentially theoretical.'

'Yet are there not examples that you could study?'

'Of course, my dear. If only I had the means to travel freely within Italy or France. But here in England the art of the mural-painter is sadly neglected. There are notable exceptions, and I have seen illustrations of the wall paintings attributed to Benedictine monks at churches like Ashampstead, or the Chapter House in Westminster Abbey. But so far as more contemporary accomplishments are concerned, only those of Rubens or Thornhill might give me any true inspiration. And, likewise, I have never seen any of their masterpieces with my own eye.'

'I am sure that you will bring your own style to the thing. Scientifically philosophical, as befits the age. Alive with *le goût*. And images to reflect the changes still to come in our society.'

'Well, I shall be restricted by certain elements, of course. I cannot work here in the Exchange, for the building is so much in use. I must take the example of Master Rubens and work on canvas elsewhere. This in itself will limit the size of each panel according to the place in which I may be permitted to store them – though the Academy rooms seem the most logical choice. Each canvas perhaps twenty feet by eight feet. You see? So that they will fit perfectly within those spaces. Three on each side of the hall. So far as the subjects are concerned, I expect that your husband will seek depictions of martial valour. Allegories extolling the virtues of the Court Leet, the Lord of the Manor, the Lord Lieutenant, perhaps.'

'La! Whigs, every one of them. Though Sir Edward may once have pretended otherwise. Elizabeth says that neither Sir Oswald *nor* Sir Edward is to be wholly trusted, that each of them would turn his coat at a moment's notice depending upon how the wind finally blows. Especially now, with the Prince apparently home at last. Yet Our Lady alone knows what might have become of him.'

The stories had circulated in the first days of August. Prince Charles Edward Stuart landed at Eriskay. Then tale and counter-tale. He has an army at his back, many thousands strong. No, he is alone and lacking support. Another French invasion fleet in the Channel. No Frenchmen, just a few Connaught fellows and a rabble of heathen Highlanders. And finally – nothing. No further word of any sort.

'Elizabeth is a woman of strong opinions, my dear, now a customer of your father, I declare. And I expect that we shall hear favourable news of His Royal Highness soon. No need to fear for his safety, I am sure. But tell me, the dinner of which you spoke?'

'You truly think the Prince is safe? My father says that, if the news were bad, the Hanover pack would be shouting the news from our rooftops. But, yes, the dinner! You may not recall but tomorrow is my birthing day. My husband wished to celebrate in some manner but I have persuaded him that I should rather mark my Name Day. It is only two weeks hence, the thirtieth. A Friday.'

She sees Aran reach into the large side-pocket of his waistcoat, from which he withdraws a small bag, deep crimson and fastened with gilded ribbon.

'You imagine that I should forget your birthday,' he says. 'A scrub I should certainly be were I to do so. Here, a small gift. No, please accept it, my dear. Partly to commemorate your twenty-first year, partly in gratitude for your intervention in this commission and partly, I hope, to confirm our renewed friendship. The friendship I so carelessly cast aside when it was already only in its infancy.'

'Why, Mister Owen, I cannot accept, sir. It would be quite churlish. I had chosen not to be reminded that so many years of my life have already passed. And the commission you owe to my husband, rather than myself, when all is said and done – though I must allow some small part in its *dénouement*. So far as our friendship is concerned, I may have accused you of some recent scrubbery yet the silence between us caused me to recall those many years, eight or nine if I am not mistaken, during which my behaviour towards yourself, as a stranger in a strange land, was perfectly intolerable.'

'Then please accept it as a premature gift for your Name Day and also as a sign that I am, after all, forgiven.'

Rosina unfastens the slender ribbon, opens the moleskin bag and tips the content into her palm. A slender gold chain and locket, the latter opening to reveal the most tiny and perfect miniature of her own features. She bites back a tear.

'Oh, my dear,' she whispers. 'I shall treasure it always. Quite exquisite.' She reaches up and kisses his cheek. *I wonder if my life might have been different.*

'And the dinner?' he says. 'Not simply we three, I assume?'

'Indeed not. That should have been perfectly dull. Well, perhaps dull is not the correct word, but it seems that we are to be honoured with the company of Sir Edward himself. It was that which caused my discussion of the fellow with Elizabeth. Though he shall not be accompanied by his wife, I gather, and I have no intention of being the only woman present at table. I had hoped that Beppy might join us but she is already gone to visit family. A grand tour, to Preston, Blackpool, Ormschurch and Liverpool. We shall not see her until the middle of September it seems. My own dearest Elizabeth is out of the question, of course. Yet I have persuaded Mister Bradley that Mrs Starkey might join us. Which means, Aran Owen, that you must also choose a companion to bring with you. Female, naturally. I place no stipulation on the thing 'bating that you may not select Mama, nor any harlot, nor any child under the age of sixteen.'

'So it is Anna-Marie or Katherine then?'

'Except that Anna-Marie is such dull company.'

Very well, he promises, it shall be Katherine, though he might surprise her with some other companion, and they part on the best of terms.

Later in the evening, she describes their meeting to her husband, explains Aran's initial plans, which he accepts happily enough, confirming that the dinner will provide a good opportunity to formalise the thing.

'Yet Mister Owen told me a strange thing, sir,' she says. 'That Mama made some passing reference to the commission some weeks ago, during the Kersal Races. I know that we had already discussed the matter but you did not mention talking to my mother also. It is your own concern, naturally. Though he seemed to have drawn the inference that the thing was decided so long ago when, to my recollection, you were only resolved upon it last Wednesday. It *was* Wednesday, sir, was it not? I seem to recall that you regaled me with the news on my return from Mrs Starkey's.'

'The fellow must be mistaken, my dear. Why, I see so little of my in-laws these days, Mama and Papa alike, that I should scarcely waste such precious moments with debate about Mister Owen or this commission, important though the work itself may be. I would remind you that I awarded the work to him very much at your own insistence, yet if I am to be confronted at every turn with accusations about mere trivialities, or be presented with examples of the cove's confusion, I am certain that I could find another artist more suited to the work.'

Accusations, indeed. A strange choice of words. And his insistence on referring to her parents as the *in-laws*. Mama this. Papa that. When Bradley and her father are the same age and *Mama* is merely six years his junior. How vexing. But she allows the moment to pass, fortifying herself later with a considerable measure of the Sydenham's.

Her birthing day passes with a visit by her sisters, bearing a posy that they have gathered themselves, and a parcel of fine lace from mother and father. She half expects that Mama will visit but she is damn'd if she will show *her* forgiveness though, in any event, no such visit takes place. She meets Papa, however, while he is undertaking his regular hour at the warehouse but, once again, she resists his brief attempt at a suggested reconciliation between mother and daughter. Perhaps she might dine with them on her naming day, he proposes? Ah, such a shame, but her husband has already arranged a dinner at their house. Mister Owen will attend and she has reason to believe that he might invite Katherine to be his companion. Mama and Papa would be welcome to attend too, naturally, but she knows that the uneasy peace her father has established with Mister Bradley since the wedding can only be borne by either party in small doses. It is hardly her father's custom to dine in the homes of other folk, in any case, and Mama would certainly not wish to spend an evening in company with Mrs Starkey. La! How the fur would fly.

Yet she misses her mother in one regard, at least, for Mama is so organised when it comes to social occasions. Rosina, on the other hand, has little experience of such things. In the early months of her marriage, she had made it clear to Bradley that she interpreted any form of responsibility for his household as a subjugation to his will, a thing that she considered quite beyond the requirements of the Marriage Settlement. She had imagined, anyhow, that his existing housekeeper and servants might prefer to be allowed continuity in their routines, that they might even admire her for allowing them the liberty of proceeding exactly as they had always done. They might not be Mudge or O'Farrell but she knew that they, at least, would have resisted any attempt to change their established practices. But she had been wrong. Quite the reverse. She had been surprised to find that they were surly towards her, which she had initially taken as some form of prejudice. Arising from rumour, she supposed. Spread by Bradley himself in the first place, she had railed. Yet he had taken pains to explain that, on the contrary, his household expected to be managed, believed that this was her duty as their Mistress, saw it as a weakness on her part that she showed no interest in them. And while she had initially resisted the thing, she had eventually seen an advantage, negotiated yet another clause to their arrangement by which she would learn this duty, as he wished, but in exchange for the resumption of her lessons with Mrs Starkey.

It has been a road fraught with problems but a rapport has been established between herself and the domestic staff, though not sufficient to trust herself with a dinner to be attended by the Lord Lieutenant of Lancashire, regardless of the fellow's loyalties to the Pelhams. So she has engaged Mistress Hepple, remembering the fine spread that she normally arranges for Papa's birthday routs. They spend time together, calculating symmetry between the courses, quantities to be purchased.

And they are thus engaged on Saturday, the twenty-fourth of August, with six days to run before the dinner itself, when their trip to the Shambles is interrupted by the boy employed by Scatterbuck to distribute the *Journal*.

But he has no broadsheet to sell today, running hither and thither in a state of great excitement.

'The Prince!' he shouts. 'The Prince! Glory be. He has raised his standard at Glenfinnan. The Scots are out. The Scots are out.'

Folk around the stalls gather in small groups, friends, or political allies, sometimes simply strangers needing somebody, anybody, with whom to share the moment.

At last, she thinks. So the news of the landing at Eriskay had been accurate after all. And perhaps no army of Frenchmen but a host of faithful Highlanders at his heel. Just imagine the way that Scottish associates must be acclaiming his return. The pipers, the bards, the harpers!

Men emerge from the Market Square's two main hostelries, Francis Townley and his crowd from the Bull's Head, Robert Jobb and many of the Whiggish faction from the Angel.

Townley sees her from the inn steps. 'What news, Mistress?' he cries.

'The best, Mister Townley. The boy says that the Royal Prince has arrived at a place called Glenfinnan, raised the Stuart standard there. Do you know the place, sir? Is it near or far?'

He crosses to her, sending some of his fellows to check the news.

'I know not,' he says. 'But the news is welcome in any case. We had received such confused tales of his landing, and those almost a month ago. He had a lucky escape though, by all accounts. Almost intercepted by an English frigate, they say. And lost the vessel sent to accompany him bearing arms and men, it seems. Yet look. There can be little doubt about the thing. Mind how crestfallen are Jobb's comforters there!' The group outside the Angel are studying a note, an express by its appearance. Heads are shaken, disbelief shown plain upon their faces as they slowly disperse, either returning inside or away to home and business. 'They had convinced themselves that it was all up for us. In Jesu's name, we have had to endure their taunts enough these past weeks. Well, Mistress, there is interest now to be paid upon that loan!'

By the following day, the thing is all confirmed. The express riders are busy, coming in from all directions with letters from one town or another. The Prince has, indeed, raised his standard, the Royal Standard of King James the Third of England, James the Eighth of Scotland. But the Whigs have news too, fortified and restored since an English army, six thousand strong is under the command of the Earl of Stair, while Sir John Cope is already in Scotland with a further four thousand.

And the Prince, they say, had no more than fifteen hundred clansmen at the gathering where the red silk banner, with its white square inset, was blessed by Catholic Bishop Hugh MacDonald.

On the twenty-sixth, the Bellman is about the town. His Majesty, King George the Second now returned from his excursion to Hanover, it seems. All is well. And the Whigs take heart though, in truth, nobody in the town had realised that King George was anywhere except where they thought he belonged, safely ensconced in his favourite royal residence at Kensington Palace.

Throughout the next three days, the Bellman is particularly busy. Sir John Cope set to intercept the insurrectionists. At the direction of Parliament, a bounty of thirty thousand pounds upon the head of the outlaw, Charles Edward Stuart.

'I should have thought that, in the circumstances, you might have considered abandoning the dinner, my sweet,' says Elizabeth Cooper as they lie together during the morning of the thirtieth. Rosina touches Elizabeth's nipple, feels it tighten and swell before moving the tips of her fingers down to the spot immediately below her breast which, she knows, will arouse her afresh.

'Do you know,' she says, 'that an entire year has flown since you first took me in the Pleasure Garden at Old Man Castle? How properly that place is named. Yet a whole year. Can you believe it?'

They have each fisted the other already this day, turn by turn, while Crableck attends to business in the coffee house, but now they begin again, sweat glistening on neck, belly and thigh.

'And you acting the jealous whore,' murmurs Elizabeth, 'convinced that I had taken other lovers to the Hornbeam bower before you.'

She throws Rosina on her back, grasps the back of her knees and thrusts her legs upwards, spreading them so that she can gain easy access for tongue-tip to the roseate delights of the younger woman's clitoris and Mound of Venus.

'So had you not?' says Rosina, though it is now some ten minutes later, while they are dressing again. 'Taken other lovers in that place, I mean. I should not mind too much. And I am no fool, Elizabeth. You have such art in these matters. Delightful art, too. I still know so very little of your past life.'

'What, you require a list, madam? You find it difficult to believe that there are not others in this town who share our passion. La, my dear! How surprised you should be. Yet you are not without your own admirers, I find. That Byrom person fawning upon you whenever she is given the chance. I am surprised that she is not invited to your precious dinner. She would make *such* an acceptable companion. You could finger her beneath the table and nobody the wiser, forsooth.'

It would be less than discreet, thinks Rosina, *to admit that I had considered an invitation for Beppy but could not proceed since she is out of town. On reflection, how fortunate!*

'The very idea!' she says. 'Beppy Byrom indeed. And she has been nothing but a good friend. Why, we have known each other since we were very small. And never a hint of impropriety. You cannot imagine...'

'I really do not care. But I tell you, my sweet, as one who has more experience than you, that innocent Miss Byrom has as much tendency towards sapphism as we two combined.'

'It remains possible that you are mistaken, Elizabeth. Indeed, I am perfectly certain that there is something between Beppy and Francis Townley. She dotes upon him so. Attentive to his every word and will not tolerate the slightest criticism of him.'

'That will be the Jacobite in her and, God knows, it can only become worse until this traitor that you all support is finally brought to justice. A fie upon it! Such a dinner it shall be. Yourself, Mister Owen and the Starkey woman on one side of the table, I assume. And your husband supporting the fat Earl of Derby on the other. Your sister swooning at every word passing from Mister Owen's lips. Another foolish girl trying to catch a man to whom she can dedicate the rest of her life in bondage for his whims.'

'It need not be so, I imagine. I have often wondered at the possibilities open to a young woman who both marries for love *and* is able to establish her own parameters for the marriage, in the manner that I have achieved, for the most part, with Mister Bradley.'

'Oh, my girl! You do not imagine that there is anything normal about your Settlement with James, surely? Hoity! Toity! You are too much your own person, these days. Quite inflated with the bargains that you have secured from the poor fellow. He is a perfectly decent man, I find. A good friend to me, and simply a want of children between himself and perfect happiness. I am amazed that he has not forced upon you a fulfilment of the bargain you reached in that regard.'

'There *was* no such bargain. And you know it perfectly well. We have already had this conversation, Elizabeth, and I am astonished that you deny your proper part in the thing. I was tricked into this marriage, yet intend to make the best of it for my own ends. For our *mutual* ends, I had imagined. That we might be together, you and I. It is less than perfect, I must allow, but better than I had once feared.'

'For the marriage of the Lamb has come, and His wife has made herself ready,' quotes Elizabeth. 'Is that how you now see yourself, my dear? Arrayed in fine linen, clean and bright? Blessed are those who are called to the marriage supper of the Lamb?'

'I thought that you had no love for the Book of Revelation? So how do you see *me*, I wonder? The Great Harlot Babylon, perhaps, associated with the Jacobite Beast? The Counterfeit Bride?'

'Why no, Rosina. We Protestants leave such interpretation of Revelation to Jesuits and Papists. For our part we are instructed to see it simply as a prediction of the apocalypse currently playing itself out in the history of the Church itself, one in which the idolatry of your own Faith will be cast down. Though I am tempted to see parallels between the King Conqueror who shall ride forth on a white horse and our own noble George the Second, while your

Pretender, this *chevalier* Charles Stuart, is undoubtedly mounted upon the red steed of war, and shall visit both famine *and* death upon our land in due course.'

Rosina detests these increasingly frequent acrimonies between herself and Elizabeth. She blames herself for the most part, so often drifting from a state of deep contentment at one hour to a peak of acute agitation the next. Beppy says that it is the effect of the Sydenham's. And perhaps she is correct. Though it is inexcusable that Elizabeth should so often resort to attacking her Catholicism whenever tempers become frayed.

'Stuff!' she says. 'I shall not permit you to spoil my Name Day. Famine and death indeed. We shall see a Golden Age and very soon, my dear. One in which I shall be free to worship as I see fit. And famine? Well, none in *my* household if the bill for tonight's dinner is anything by which to judge.'

'And I am sure that the Earl of Derby will eat his fill, though quite how you shall sate that girth is beyond me. Still, word at the tables below says that he goes from one faction to another, seeking accommodation from each to protect his position, whatever the outcome.'

Their parting is thin on affection, but Rosina has little time to concern herself with the exchange as she hurries to meet Mistress Hepple, completing preparations for the evening and allowing adequate time for her journal. Her husband is engaged elsewhere during the afternoon and she hears him return at around six o'the clock while she is beginning to dress for her guests. He raps quietly upon her door, begs for a word, and is rewarded with the most polite of rejections. She is busy with her creams and powders, she says, and would not have him see her in such a condition. Let him return within the hour and she will be happy to discourse with him then.

But he does not return until their guests have begun to arrive and now only to escort her down the elegant stairs, with no more than a starched and cursory compliment on her attire. The reception hall in the Bradley house is akin to that of the Byrom's, almost wide enough for a rout, although Bradley's is a modern affair. A similar design to her father's but considerably larger. Solid brick, all of it.

Introductions are completed and the pleasant murmur of polite conversation begun as her husband offers his arm to Mrs Starkey, pleased to find herself senior lady among the guests, and leads her through to the dining room. Sir Edward follows, escorting an excitable Katherine and, finally, Rosina herself with Mister Owen.

The dining room is a joy, set at the rear of the house but enjoying views of the formal garden that her husband has been at such pains to develop.

'A fine house, Mister Bradley,' says Sir Edward once he is seated to her husband's right, at the foot of the table, with Mrs Starkey facing him. She has powdered her face until it is almost perfectly white, a style that Rosina herself has only adopted since her marriage, shoulders and breasts similarly lightened, lips and cheeks rouged, and each of them wearing a decorative patch near the corner of the left eye to highlight their political leanings. Rosina, taking her place at the table's head, smoothes a crease from her best green satin, settles the hoops.

'I am glad you think well of it, My Lord,' Bradley replies. 'I bless the age in which we live that a bricklayer's son is able to better himself, to enjoy such relative comforts. Hard work, of course. Constant hard work. Yet, in earlier times, the lowliness of my birth would have consigned me to a life of servitude, and crippling hard work simply the price expected of me for the right merely to exist.'

Discussion ensues between the two men about ambition and fulfilment in which Mrs Starkey also becomes engaged.

'And you, my sweet,' Rosina says to her sister, as the first course is laid, 'how did Mama receive news of your invitation to dine?'

This being Friday, Rosina had deemed it proper that fish should form the staple of the meal, although Mistress Hepple has wisely insisted on some meat dishes for those who might not be partial to *fruits de mer*. So the table quickly fills with a tureen of fish soup, a potato pudding, trout with bacon and almonds, a *cassoulet* of haricot beans, with a chyne of mutton.

'She refused to discuss the event,' replies Katherine. 'It was *so* difficult. How I wish that things were resolved between you.'

Bradley begins to serve the soup.

'A glass of wine with you, sir,' calls Sir Edward, disrupting the process and raising his glass, as soon as the manservant has filled it, to toast his host's health. The process is repeated until each guest has been similarly honoured.

'I shall never forgive her,' says Rosina.

'You are too harsh, Rosina,' says Aran. 'But give you joy of your sister's presence. Does she not look elegant, my dear?'

Katherine colours, having spurned all but the merest hint of leaded powder and Rosina notices, for the first time, the red leather heart-shaped patch at her cheek. Seventeen and a woman grown.

'Joy indeed,' she says, 'yet I hope you display that *mouche* with Papa's concurrence, you flighty girl. And Mister Owen, I assume, is the *amour* to whom it is dedicated?'

'Mistress!' cries Aran, as Katherine's fingers involuntarily touch the patch and her eyes are cast down. 'How fro'ward you are. Katherine, my dear, you must ignore her, I implore you.'

The raised voices, Rosina's own laughter, draw Sir Edward's attention.

'Ah, Mister Owen. Our good host were telling me that you are awarded a commission at the Commodity Exchange. Murals, I understand?'

Aran looks uncertainly towards Bradley.

'Murals, yes,' says Bradley. 'The Court Leet have approved the contract and Mister Owen will receive a fine purse for the work. We agreed one hundred guineas, I believe. Did we not, Mister Owen?'

Rosina sees the surprise on Aran's face. No such fee, she knows has ever been even discussed and, besides, she is also aware that the Court Leet have set aside twice that amount, vesting in her husband the authority, as Clerk of the Town Works, to have the contract executed.

'I thought that you spoke of one hundred and fifty, husband. Or am I mistaken?'

Bradley looks up with surprise. 'One hundred and fifty?' he says. 'My dear...'

'And Mister Owen told me such a strange tale about Mama having mentioned the commission herself.'

'Your Mama?'. He blusters, she sees. 'I am sure that Mister Owen must be confused, Rosina. But one hundred and fifty guineas? Yes, I stand corrected. Of course. Though that price includes the materials and any related costs, naturally.'

'A handsome purse indeed, sir,' says Sir Edward. 'And what may we expect in return, Mister Owen?'

Aran remains momentarily stunned by the unexpected manner of the agreement and Rosina feels the need to intercede once more while the poor man coughs soup into his napkin.

'Mister Owen described it to me only recently,' she says. 'Six canvas panels, each twenty feet by eight feet, to be mounted in the hall, one for each of the most central alcoves between the pillars. I imagine that it will be quite an improvement on those drab lozenges that now fill the space.'

'Then shall they match the quality of the Banqueting House ceiling, I wonder, or Thornhill's Painted Hall at the Greenwich Hospital?' says Sir Edward. 'Was you to match Thornhill, sir, that would be an achievement, eh? I counted him a friend, Mister Bradley. A fine fellow. Met him often at meetings of the Royal Society. A great loss to us.'

'He was a great inspiration to me, My Lord,' Aran replies, having now settled himself once more. 'I admire many of the great Italian, French and Dutch mural painters, yet Sir James proved beyond a doubt that we could be a match for them here in England too. You are fortunate, Sir Edward, to have seen the Painted Hall in all its glory. My own knowledge of it comes only from illustrations in the Chetham's library. Yet I will do credit to this commission, sir, I am certain. And I thank the Court Leet for the commission, Mister Bradley. I may not have served my apprenticeship as a decorative painter, nor yet be a Freeman of the Painter-Stainers' Company, but see myself as you do, sir, a self-made man.'

'I certainly hope so, Mister Owen,' says Bradley. 'For the Court Leet shall pursue you, sir, if the work is less than satisfactory. Yet, in all your shared fervour for the rising eminence of English wall-painters, I am damn'd if I know how we shall explain that our own were completed by a Welshman.

Eh, Sir Edward?' And both men subside into unrestrained mirth.

'And the theme of these panels, Mister Owen?' asks Mrs Starkey.

'I have some preparatory sketches. One for a panorama of the town, featuring the Commodities Exchange itself in the centre. For the opposite alcove, a portrait of the hall's interior, with the panels *in situ* – a slight conceit that I hope might be forgiven – but essentially a depiction of the Court Leet members themselves. The other four will show, at each of the corners I hope, some of the great moments of our age. An allegory, with each of the century's greatest writers and pictorial references to their work. Another with the achievements of natural philosophy. One depicting our trade routes across the globe. And, finally, another giving thanks and praise to God for the bounty that He has bestowed upon our town and its people.'

'What, sir,' says Sir Edward, 'no mention of martial prowess? Ah, perhaps not.' But he lapses into a long discussion with Bradley and Mrs Starkey about some of the latest papers delivered at the Society and that might be appropriate for the Natural Philosophy Panel, as it now seems to have become accepted. New agricultural machinery and such.

'You know, my dear,' says Aran, sampling the trout, 'that this *brithyll* is excellent. My mother used to cook it exactly so. One of your uncle's favourites, I collect.'

'Do you miss your Mama, Mister Owen?' asks Katherine. 'I cannot imagine life without my own, though they say that we never truly appreciates our parents until they are no longer with us. Do you think that true?'

'I am ashamed to say that I rather resented my own for many years after they had died,' he says. 'I blamed them for deserting me, I think. How foolish. As though they had somehow chosen to abandon me.'

'And when shall the work progress, Mister Owen?' says Sir Edward. 'Or must we wait for Sir Oswald to confirm the thing? Though, was that the case we might wait forever. Have you heard the rumour, Mister Bradley, that he seeks disposal of the Manor? To sell his title, indeed. I have never heard the like.'

'We live in strange times, My Lord,' Bradley replies. 'Though it should not surprise me. The family spends so much of its time in Staffordshire now. Yet I have full authority, on behalf of the Court Leet, to complete this particular transaction and Mister Owen may commence at his own convenience, his small conceit accepted as an addendum to the fee.'

'Then I should like to begin at once,' says Aran. 'For there is much initial preparation to undertake and I should wish the Court Leet to see my sketches as soon as possible. Perhaps at the October meeting. I should then be able to commence the actual painting in the following month, God willing.'

The table is cleared, its dirtied linen removed and a fresh cloth, plates and cutlery set, along with the second course. Savouried eels, fresh from the Irk. Basil salmon terrine. Soused mackerel with rhubarb. Buttered artichokes.

Snipe and partridge pie. The haricot beans, potato and artichokes are a luxury with which Bradley is keen to demonstrate their affluence for, Rosina knows, he has frequently been critical of dinner parties arranged by the rich and powerful at which the vegetables have been a bitter disappointment. But, with Mistress Hepple's assistance, tonight's have been purchased and prepared with perfection. She shall present it as her own contribution to the agreement on the commission and her husband will be given, tacitly of course, to understand that she will make no further reference to whatever may have transpired between himself and Mama on the matter.

The Earl of Derby requests the pie. A manservant moves to hand him the plate. And the moment she has dreaded must finally arrive, for Sir Edward has decided to broach the subject that has properly brought him to dinner – though she had assumed that he would wait until the meal was finished and discuss the matter privately with her husband. The question of a Whig Subscription to the Hanoverian muster.

'So, Mister Bradley, what reckons the Court Leet on the crisis, sir? They say that the *Chevalier* has four hundred MacDonalds of Clanranald at his back. A thousand Camerons too, Lochiels for the most part. That he has already captured some of the companies sent to intercept him. Though Cope should stop him once he has a chance to consolidate his forces, I think.'

So it is 'Chevalier' now, Rosina thinks. *Too polite to say 'Pretender' at my table at least.* And she does not flinch from debating these matters. Indeed, Beppy Byrom has frequently assured her that it is the duty of every Jacobite woman to do so. But she should so have preferred to finish dinner in some tranquillity.

'I imagine,' says Mrs Starkey, 'that it can be no minor matter to track a relatively small force in such wild terrain as the Scottish Highlands. And Cope's soldiers are largely untrained, are they not?'

'A small force indeed, madam,' Bradley says, 'yet grown considerably since this Pretender landed with seven rag-tag companions and no troops at all. He had to be carried ashore pick-a-pack, we are told. And these Highlanders, no more than barbarians. No match for our battalions, trained or otherwise.'

The claret causes him to be abrupt, thinks Rosina. *That must be the second bottle of Margaux that he has consumed already.* And she feels her megrims begin. Oh, for the Sydenham's.

'Though the state of readiness of our forces, Mrs Starkey,' says Sir Edward, 'is indeed a matter of concern. The campaign in Flanders, too, naturally. Ghent now captured by the French. Both the Royal Scots and the Twenty-Third captured with it. The Duke of Cumberland forced back on Antwerp. All in all, the very reasons for my visit, eh, Mister Bradley? Subscription, sir, that is the order of the day. Finances needed to help raise new regiments for His Majesty. But you must forgive me, gentlemen, ladies. This damn'd bile, you know. I assume...?' He gestures towards the screens at the farther end of the room.

'Of course, sir,' Bradley replies, and the Earl of Derby shifts himself with difficulty from his dining chair, makes his way behind the lacquered panels that hide the chamber pots. 'And you will be pleased to learn, My Lord,' Bradley continues, shouting slightly to counter the noise of Sir Edward's preparations, 'that my colleagues have now confirmed the result of our endeavours. One thousand nine hundred and sixty-six pounds, plus three shillings, sir.' Sir Edward groans for several seconds, hidden by the screens, before a low murmur coincides with the stream of his relief hitting ceramic bowl.

Katherine suppresses her amusement, chided silently by Aran.

'And were the thing well supported?' says the Earl, adjusting his attire, and still hidden from view. 'Bishop Peploe promised to give it his blessing, I collect.'

'In truth, sir,' Bradley replies, 'he was alone in making a contribution from all those associated with the Collegiate Church, though we enjoyed more success at Saint Ann's, as you might expect. And a significant sum, I hope you will agree. Sufficient, at least, to raise a troop for the militia, we trust.'

Less than two thousand pounds, thinks Rosina. *La! What a pittance.* Her Papa has raised considerably more for the Cause. And she exchanges a glance with her husband, tilts her head to one side, mouths a single silent word. A question. Two? 'You know, my dear,' she says, 'that I have been considering the purchase of new drapes for this room. These are so drab. Do you not agree?'

James Bradley touches a finger to his lips, narrows his eyes, an admonishment to remain silent on the matter of Subscriptions. 'Of course, wife,' he says, though slurring badly. 'New drapes it shall be! And a glass with you, my sweet, to toast your Name Day.'

A reasonable bargain struck, all things considered.

'Ah, yes,' says Sir Edward, returning to his place, while yet another table cloth is fetched, fresh settings for dessert – cheddar cheese, stewed apple and nutmeg, sugared apricot, pickled walnuts and a compote of summer fruits. Port for the gentlemen and sweet wine for the ladies. 'Yet you must tell me, my dear. Rosina is an unusual name. And today marks the holy day for *which* of the Saints, precisely?'

'Saint Rose of Lima, My Lord. An obscure beatification, I fear.'

'Lima, you say? Peru once more. Extraordinary coincidence, eh? Reminds me, too. My thanks to you, Mister Bradley,' says Sir Edward, 'and those of a grateful monarch also, to be sure. Manchester has shown its mettle once more, I am pleased to say.'

'Once more, My Lord?' Bradley replies. 'The entire town is a veritable nest of Jacobites, as you well know. In my own home, too, sirrah. We are positively surrounded, at least for the moment.'

'But not for long, I think,' Sir Edward says. He gazes around the table, nervous but insistent on his message. 'Since the game is now changed. And I would urge all those – some good friends included – who may previously have taken the thing lightly, to now see it through the eyes of the State. Sedition. Yes, and sedition failed. For the Jacobite Cause is now entirely ditched. Ditched, sir. And it seems that we have friends here in Manchester to thank, though none of us yet aware of their efforts. They have done for the young *Chevalier*, however, that much is certain. Ah, but I am in danger of breaking a confidence. Damn'd indiscreet, eh?'

Ditched? Whatever can he mean? Prince Charles Edward is hardly begun. And with the Hanoverian army all tatterdemalion in Flanders, precious little real opposition here in England, his success must certainly be assured. She sees that Mrs Starkey, even young Katherine, share her own confusion. But Aran Owen, she notes, appears to be choking on a pickled walnut and in a state of some distress.

Chapter Thirty-Six

'Lost, sir?' says Titus, as quietly as he is able, given the level of his incredulity. 'The entire Exchequer of the Stuart Royal House?'

'Gone, sir,' replies Sir Watkin, grief etched upon his features. 'Saving some mere thousands of pounds, I understand.'

The two men have taken an early evening table at John Shaw's Punch House, having agreed the meeting place originally so that Titus could transfer the Subscription and some proceeds of the business into the Welshman's own keeping.

'What sort of cunny-suckers have allowed this to happen? The work, all these years of toil. Hazard too. By the Mass, the risks that we have run to supplement His Majesty's treasury.'

'Buccaneers, my friend. In the pay of the Pelhams, naturally. An outrage. Intercepted honest merchantmen on the high seas. An act of piracy that Teach, Morgan, Roberts or Bonnet could barely have surpassed.'

'You mean that the vessels of which you spoke to me were no more than merchantmen? This must have been a *French* plan, I assume.'

'Letters of marque, Mister Redmond. Armed and capable, yet chosen rather for their speed. And the details were known only to a few of us, as you are aware. It had to be thus since the timing was arranged to coincide with the plans of the Prince himself – and to *that* matter, his intended expedition to regain his realm, not even his own father was privy.'

'Timing, you say? I recall that you mentioned some *rendezvous* for these vessels. At one of the French Atlantic ports. A *rendezvous* with Charles Edward, then?'

'Not precisely. Rather, with the Prince's Parisian banker, Mister Walters, who had advanced His Royal Highness a considerable sum and was, in exchange, to oversee the safe deposit, investment and subsequent availability of the silver, But there was certainly a connection, for the shipment was due to arrive in Nantes within weeks of the Prince himself departing that same port. To ensure that it might follow him swiftly.'

'But half the world must have known. King James may not have been aware of the Prince's intentions – though I find that hard to believe – but he must clearly have approved the silver's shipment. So his intermediaries, the representatives of the French Government, the Vatican bankers, the owners of the vessels, the Swedish Bank itself...'

'But the chosen dates, sir, were selected by the Prince alone. To fit his own timetable. It was the Prince who, through Lord Clare, had undertaken the negotiations personally with the shipping owners. Two gentlemen of Irish extraction, *Messieurs* Walsh and Ruttledge. It was they who arranged the vessels dispatched to convey the silver and also those on which His Royal Highness would sail for Scotland. As I say, the dates were known only to the Prince himself, his closest advisers in France, the ship owners. And ourselves, naturally, since so much of the investment plans involved your own operations. The plan was perfectly sound but it seems that, once again, we were betrayed. For word from the Admiralty indicates that these pirates were clearly lying in wait for the Frenchmen. A maritime ambuscade, sir!'

Titus leans across the table, his lips almost to Sir Watkin's ear. 'But there is no implication, I trust,' he hisses, 'that this betrayal has any connection to Manchester?'

He knows, of course, that it may well do so. For Aran Owen has already shared with him the strange comment by the Earl of Derby at his daughter's naming day dinner. Three days previous. Three days to turn over the information in his mind. The Jacobite Cause entirely ditched, he had said. And *friends here in Manchester to thank*, though Sir Edward had seemingly not known their identity. Nor expanded on his reference. He had pressed Aran over again, but he was quite positive. His Lordship had subsequently refrained from imbibing anything more and could not be drawn further on the matter. Bradley, meanwhile, had later managed to drink himself almost to a stupor. Now the news brought by this lick-spittle, Sir Watkin Williams Wynn. *Damn his accusatory tongue. I shall cut it from his throat if he dares...*

'My dear sir! Yourself, your family. Beyond reproach, my good fellow.'
But he sounds hardly convincing.
'And this lost fortune,' says Titus, 'where is it now?'

'Landed at Bristol three days since. Some tale invented that it was taken from a Spanish galleon *en route* from Peru. But there is no doubt that it is the same. Seventy-eight tons, now loaded on forty-five wagons and travelling overland to the Tower under heavy guard. More than two and a half million silver dollars, pieces of eight, the equivalent of eight hundred thousand pounds sterling, along with gold doubloons and *pistoles*, gold bars, plus eight hundred tons of cocoa. Cocoa, sir!'

Three days. The thirtieth. Rosina's Name Day once more.

'And is it true, Sir Watkin, that the Prince himself was also intercepted? Betrayed too, do you think?'

'Intercepted, sir, yes. Embarked upon one vessel from Nantes, as intended, whilst the second was laden with two thousand muskets, five hundred broadswords and one hundred marines raised by Lord Clare. A personal bodyguard. An advance party of those that the Prince hoped to purchase with the silver. His Royal Highness himself sailed only with selected friends and advisors. His former tutor and veteran of the Boyne, Sir Thomas Sheridan. The Duke of Atholl – the *second* Duke of Atholl, naturally. Sir John MacDonald, who has seen considerable service with the Spanish. Colonel Francis Strickland of Westmorland. Let me see. Yes, George Kelly, a clergyman of some repute. Aeneas MacDonald, another financier. And Colonel O'Sullivan, a true soldier. Some few servants, but none others. Both ships set sail for Scotland. Almost the same day that the silver shipment was being attacked further south. But intercepted, as you say. West of the Lizard. Simple mischance, by all accounts. In any case, the second vessel, the *Elizabeth*, was badly mauled in the engagement whilst the captain of the Prince's ship refused to endanger his charge, remained aloof from the fight, though His Royal Highness tried to insist that they should join the battle, I hear. The Captain would not be gainsaid, however, and the poor *Elizabeth* was left to her own fate, but fought the Englishman to a standstill, despite all. With no opportunity to transfer the precious cargo from their unfortunate companion, the Prince was left with little option except to continue alone.'

'By the Mass!' says Titus. 'A dog's arse. And also not three days since, I am told, the Earl of Derby was in town claiming that the entire Cause is ditched. That was his word, Sir Watkin. Ditched! And it seems he was correct.'

Titus waits upon the other man's reaction. *Is it possible that this cunny-sucker has knowledge of the Earl's assertion about Manchester informants?* But there *is* no reaction except that which he might have expected.

'Ditched?' Sir Watkin looks crumpled, belittled. 'No French army, and now no prospect of one. No men of Connaught neither, as you have heard.' Sir Watkin's travelling companion, the lawyer Morgan, had earlier given them an account of his unsuccessful attempts to contact groups of Irish Jacobites. 'I fear for the outcome, Mister Redmond, if I am honest. Yet here we are. The Prince in Scotland and only those now prepared to declare for him along the road upon whom he can rely to bear arms.'

And exactly as Maria-Louise has always believed proper. Myself too, at heart. But it is a vision of Kersal Moor that dominates his thoughts. 'Yet if I should have a secret?' he hears her say. 'Let us suppose that I found myself in a position to act on behalf of us both, of many others also, but could not share the matter with you for fear that it may put you in harm's way. Or that it might have an outcome with dubious implications? What then? Would you think the less of me?' Yet how had he answered? *Damn'd if I can recall. Some flattery to be sure.*

'Yet without knowledge of these disasters,' says Titus, 'there is more heart in our supporters than I have seen for many years. It is remarkable that the Pelhams have not shouted the news from the roof-tops, in order to lay low our morale.'

'They seem to believe that the news may have worked against them.

Been taken by the *mobile vulgus* as simply showing the extent of resources available to the Stuarts. As things stand, the truth is known only to those few of us who shared knowledge of this plan in the first place. And amongst ourselves, I fear, its effect might be truly damaging.'

'All the same, my associate, Mister Scatterbuck – he prints a local broadsheet for us – is carrying a piece about Admiral Vernon being transferred to the Downs. Against the possibility of a French invasion still, across the Channel.'

'True enough,' Sir Edward says. 'I think that Government itself, particularly the King, by all accounts, is far from certain that the threat is removed. Ah, but Mister Morgan has returned.' Titus sees the lawyer mounting the steps to the Punch House in company with Aran Owen, the latter carrying the principal ledgers for the business beneath his arm. 'Mister Owen too. He is an amiable fellow, is he not? And did I tell you, sir, that I now have my *own* Mister Owen?' He calls to John Shaw while Aran and Morgan join them at the table. 'You, sir! Four more bumpers of your finest, prithee.' Sir Watkin turns to the newcomers. 'I was just explaining, Mister Owen, that we now have your namesake as a valued associate. Mister William Owen. Remarkable fellow. Previously secretary to the Rector of Hawarden and, before that, in the army.' He whispers. 'Unfortunate circumstances, however.'

'Yes, I know of him,' says Aran. 'The Squire, Mister Redmond's brother, wrote to me about him.'

'And is he with you, Sir Watkin?' Titus asks. 'It would be interesting to calculate whether there is any familial likeness between himself and young Aran.'

'A fie upon you, sir. How amusing! Why, the whole of Wales is awash with Owens. But you shall be denied the pleasure in any case. For I have sent him north to see whether he might locate the Prince. Some dispatches from myself and, I fancy, with all the fellow's knowledge, His Royal Highness may find him useful.'

'Let us hope so,' says Titus. 'If my brother, Josiah, perceived value in the man then you may rely on his judgement. I myself was fortunate to be blessed with *this* Mister Owen from the same source.' *Aran would normally colour at such a compliment, yet today he blanches. How strange.* 'But now to business. Perhaps the Subscription first?'

'Every penny is needed, sir, as you are now aware,' Sir Edward says. 'Ah, Mister Owen. I have recently shared some intelligence with Mister Redmond. The details must remain confidential but suffice it to say that the finances available to His Royal Highness have suffered something of a reverse. The importance of your efforts here in Manchester are therefore now heightened even beyond their earlier significance.'

Aran makes no comment but sets the ledgers on the table for Titus to consult, observing Sir Watkin intently as the Welshman takes his own account book from the satchel at the side of his bench and John Shaw arrives with the refreshments, the Captain Radcliffe's, heavily laced with brandy and nutmeg.

'And, John,' says Titus, 'I have asked our friend, Mister Clough, as you requested, to raise within the Court Leet the possibility of extending your licensed hours. The cunny-suckers will probably deny the request, but we shall see!' Shaw murmurs his thanks and leaves them. 'Then here, sir,' Titus continues. 'My promissory note for three thousand guineas. You may redeem the amount at any time from Mister Dickenson's house, a little further up the Lane. Mister Owen will show you the place. Perhaps best to collect it as you leave town. And I assume that you have taken steps to guard the gold upon the road? If not, we can assist you in that regards also.'

'Admirable, Mister Redmond. Perfectly so. I thank you, sir!' And Sir Watkin signs the receipt that Titus slides across the table to him with the note, before entering the amount in his own ledger. 'And the proceeds from our investments?'

'Indeed, Sir Watkin,' Titus replies. 'You should know that the Duke of Beaufort's Factor had not collected for some months before His Grace's death. On the other hand, our business has fallen off a little these past few months and the effect of the reduction in Duty has done little to assist us. Aran, have you anything to add on the matter? What keeps you so mumchance there?'

Aran responds as though slapped from a waking dream.

'My apologies,' he says. 'I was digesting Sir Watkin's words. Thinking about...'

'The Earl of Derby's assertion that we are *ditched*?' says Titus. 'Yes, I have told him. And yes, too, it seems that he may have been referring to the same reverse in the Stuart finances. But you will say nothing to any other living soul on the subject, naturally.'

Did I choose my words correctly? he wonders, as Aran begins a more detailed account of the tea business. Not so brisk as previously, and stocks running low. New shipments on their way, though.

For I asked him on a previous occasion whether he had spoken to anybody about the meeting at Liskard Moor at which poor Jacob died, and he told me nay quite unequivocally. Yet it has haunted me since that the question was badly phrased, though too late to press the thing further.

Expecting to hear from the Swedish Company, Captain Eriksson, their Manx contacts too, within the month, Aran is explaining.

And then that damn'd business at Ancoats Hall. All my instincts tell me that the arrival of the militia could not have been an accident.

Meanwhile, says Aran, with the Duty lowered, and prices reduced as a result, some customers lost who are no longer willing to accept illicit merchandise when a legitimate supply brings almost the same margin. Their own profits reduced, naturally.

Yet Maria-Louise was adamant that I was wrong to be suspicious.

Insistent that I had wronged him by thinking Aran implicated. So what was she telling me? Not Aran Owen, but perhaps herself...?

'I have shown the details to Mister Morgan,' says Aran. 'And I think that he is satisfied?'

'Indeed, gentlemen,' Morgan replies. 'A most remarkable enterprise. For Manchester, at least. Significantly better than I should have expected.'

'Truly?' says Titus. 'How gratifying to enjoy your good opinion, sir. Yet here is the agreed portion. A further promissory note. Four thousand, one hundred and sixteen pounds, four shillings and sevenpence, to be precise. This note to be drawn on Mister Childers the goldsmith, however. It never helps to keep all one's eggs in a single basket, I find.'

Another receipt, another entry in Sir Watkin's ledger, Aran all attention now.

How carefully he studies the thing. Why, Mister Owen trusts this lick-spittle no more than I do!

'Well, Mister Redmond,' says Sir Watkin. 'Remarkable indeed, as David says. Just over seven thousand guineas from Manchester's efforts alone. If only we could rely on other towns in the same way!'

'If only we were in charge of silver shipments, Sir Watkin!' whispers Titus. 'But now, gentlemen, with that concluded I trust you will allow me to provide some entertainment at the Cockpit this evening. Then supper at the Bull's Head? Mister Owen has no taste for cockfighting but may perhaps join us later.'

'Indeed, I shall be delighted,' says Aran. 'Yet you have rooms at the Bull's Head too, I collect. They are comfortable, I trust? Such mixed quality at the Bull.'

'They are perfectly admirable,' David Morgan replies. 'Their two largest, I think. At the front, overlooking the Market Square. Not the most quiet of accommodations but well-appointed.'

'By Manchester standards, I assume. Then give you joy of them, gentlemen,' says Titus, 'and I shall meet you there in, say, one hour – after Mister Owen and myself have attended to another matter.'

They leave Sir Watkin and his companion outside the Punch House and make their way towards the bawdy-den, for Titus had already shared with Aran the task that they must undertake.

'So what do you make of Sir Watkin's lawyer?' says Titus. 'He thinks highly of himself, does he not?'

'He has an abrasive temperament, to be sure. And for a lawyer, he frequently employs a poor choice of words. Yet he is keen enough to see action. A true passion for the Cause, I think. But are you at liberty, sir, to tell me the extent of the reverse suffered by good King James?'

Titus senses the implication beneath the question. *Or is this a matter which does not concern me? That is his meaning, though he does not speak the words.*

'You are changed, Aran, are you not? New skills upon which to rely, I perceive. Do you know that you have never once asked me to tell you the name of Newcastle's agent? He who has caused us so much trouble. The fellow who, in all likelihood, lured poor Jacob to his death. A simple lack of curiosity? Or something besides?'

'It may be that I simply wheedled the information from Mister Byrom himself, might it not? I have been accused so frequently this past year of dissembling that it should have been easy enough to accomplish.'

'I think not,' says Titus. 'I still recall the land of which you spoke in which all are either rogues or righteous. It was quite meaningless to me yet, if such a place existed, you would surely be amongst the latter rather than the former. A dissembler you might sometimes need to be, though it would always be a poor one. Well then, sir, you will recall the silver that John Townley promised when you met him at Ancoats Hall. Additional silver that we might invest on behalf of His Majesty? Funds to help raise arms and men, too. Indeed, you do. As you know, we had been given to believe that this would be a particular portion of the Stuart Exchequer, whilst the balance was destined elsewhere. You will not know, however, that arrangements were subsequently made for the entire treasury to be shipped from Rome. And that treasury, my friend, is now lost. Taken by the Pelhams' pirates.'

'The *entire* treasury? And this, then, was Sir Edward's meaning. Yet you are certain, sir? The entire treasury. It cannot be, surely?'

'Almost every last shilling. But intelligence that must remain amongst ourselves. There may be no widespread circulation of this news or we shall, indeed, be ditched. We need time, now. To think. To consider, Aran. Though I suspect that others in the town will have this news also. Meanwhile, did you do as I asked?'

'The entire treasury,' says Aran, still unable to grasp the magnitude of this news. 'But yes, sir. I have checked the lists that Blossom has given us. If George is correct, and even allowing for Mistress Cole to take considerably more than her agreed share, you should be able to collect an absolute minimum of thirty-four guineas at Quarter Day. And that without the proceeds of the gin sales.'

'In the previous two quarters we have taken less than half that amount. I had thought that our custom might have declined since the attack but now I am not so sure. If Susannah has been taking more than her allotted slice, by the Mass, she will regret it. And I have no intention of waiting until Michaelmas before finding out. Now, how was the rest of my daughter's dinner?'

Aran gives him a brief summary of the meal. The murals. The fee involved. Rosina's part in its settlement. Katherine – who has naturally already given Papa her own account. *She is quite smitten with the fellow*, thinks Titus. *They will make a good match. Poor Anna-Marie, however!* Mister Bradley's behaviour. And, of course, regrets that matters have reached such a pass between Rosina and her mother.

'They shall be reconciled in due course, I am certain,' says Titus, stopping in front of the bawdy-house. 'Yet here we are. You need say nothing unless I ask you. Now come.' He steps over the threshold and crosses himself at the very spot on which he had been assaulted, yet he also touches the wooden frame against fortune and, for good measure, makes the sign of the horns to ward off further evil. 'Striker!' he says suddenly and sharply.

He sees his companion start, recoil and look quickly about him. 'Your pardon, sir?' says Aran.

'The name of Newcastle's agent,' Titus replies. 'Most likely the blackguard who came here with his ruffians. Ah, Susannah! Give you joy of this fine evening.'

Susannah Cole is seated at the table in the antechamber, just as Mother Blossom was once wont to do. The same powder, scent and silks too. But there the similarity ends. *How old is she, I wonder. Forty? Forty-five?* Slender as a willow, though. Sharp features, prominent cheekbones. And she is momentarily placed at a disadvantage by his appearance.

'Titus, darling. I'd not expected you today.'

'So I see, my dear,' he says, looking through the double doors to the long salon. 'For that is Billy Bender, I perceive. Supping my gin and looking as though he may be in his own home. Or am I mistaken?'

'Yet he don't do harm, sirrah. None at all. An' the geneva is all paid for. Straight and square.'

'Harm, Mistress? "Once harm has been done, even a fool might understand it." Eh, Mister Owen? Who says that?'

'Homer, sir.'

'Homer indeed! And the harm is done, Susannah, simply by that fellow's presence here. Now go tell him to leave.'

'He'll take it amiss, sir.'

'Yet take it he will! He has two choices, my dear. To leave either whole and hearty. Or to leave a cripple.' The woman makes to protest, yet sees in his eyes that Titus is not to be crossed. Not today, at least. So she moves elegantly through the doxies and their customers, sets a hand upon the shoulder of the blind fiddler and whispers in Bender's ear. He looks towards the antechamber, insolence then acquiescence, while Titus leads Aran into the drawing room that serves as the bawd's inner sanctum. *A cornered rat and his bolt hole,* thinks Titus. *Best to allow it escape with dignity.* But he calls for George Blossom all the same.

'So, George, you have your own list?'

This Flash-Man with the pug's face has nothing but the rudiments of writing yet they suffice for the needs of his profession and he takes from his coat a small, well-worn journal from which, Titus knows, he had previously made a copy for Aran's examination.

'Which it is here, sir,' Blossom barks.

And Titus watches for Billy Bender's departure before calling Susannah Cole back into the room.

'Why, we are doing excellent trade, my dear. And this only a Monday.'

'Most unusual,' she says. 'We don't do this much normal, like.'

'Truly? Yet George tells me different. He says that evening business is brisk. Better than ever, he thinks. You have a tally, do you not?'

'Darling Titus, you think I keep a list of every Jack-trick provender who comes through the door?'

'Mother Blossom did so,' says Titus. 'And George still does, it seems. Even Mister Owen has learned to keep me informed about anything that may interest me from his occasional visits.'

'You set these coves to spy on us? God blind me! I've nothing to hide from *you*, Titus dear. When have I ever held anything back so far as you're concerned, eh?'

And Titus recalls some memorable moments spent in Susannah's embrace.

'Then you shall not hold back from sharing with me the contents of our strong-box?' he says.

'Why, the payments fall due on Quarter Day, sweet man. Yet if you wish them early...'

Titus watches as she takes a small key from around her neck, carefully opens the ancient lacquered cabinet. Susannah searches within for a larger key, hidden beneath a shelf, and takes this to the couch, kneeling to pull out the iron-bound chest that it conceals. It is absurd, he knows, that they have kept precisely the same arrangement as existed when those bastards stole his gold from Mother Blossom and so mutilated her face. But lightning, he believes, will never strike the same tree twice.

'There,' she says, taking a large purse from within and counting the contents on the floor. 'Twelve guinea pieces. Twenty-four sovereigns. Eighteen shillings. Not a bad take, I reckon.' She smiles at him. A saintly smile.

'Nineteen pounds and ten shillings,' says Titus. 'Handsome. Yet, from George's list, I think I am owed thirty-four guineas, my dear. And the gin money too, naturally. Mister Owen has studied the accompts most carefully, doxy by doxy, totalled each individual price, calculated your fifth, summed my own share. Thirty-four guineas, and you show me less than nineteen.'

'Titus, my darling,' says Susannah. 'I've told you before. Poor George's brains are in his bollocks now.'

'I know what I sees,' yaps Blossom. 'Wants me out. Wants that Bender as 'er Flash-Man, sir. So she does. Ask 'er about the second purse, then. The one in that dresser.'

'Yes, George,' Titus says. 'A fine suggestion.' And he steps forward to intercept Susannah as she attempts to also reach the cabinet, pushes her back onto the settee. 'Mister Owen, if you please!'

Aran throws open the still unlocked doors of the dresser while Mistress Cole utters oaths and imprecations that Titus chooses to ignore, waiting while drawers and shelves alike are emptied until, finally, triumphantly, a leather bag is produced. At his bidding, Aran empties this pouch also. A little over forty guineas.

'George,' says Titus, 'you may run and tell Mother Blossom that I have work for her again. Though the arrangement may be temporary and she will need to remain veiled. While you, Mistress, shall pack whatever belongings may truly be yours and leave. In that regard, you have the same choice as your cock-pimp, Bender.' A staccato stream of thanks from the Flash-Man.

'But my gold!' says Susannah. 'I wouldn't steal from you, my handsome. Some of that purse is my own and the rest I was just keeping safe.'

He tosses her a guinea. 'It is a bawd's duty to steal at least a little, Susannah. In your own case, you have simply been too ambitious. Now take this for your troubles, Mistress Cole. You were only ever a four-shilling piece, after all.'

'Yet good enough for *you*, Titus Redmond. May you rot in Hell for today's work. You and the whore you call wife. The breeches-bawd you call daughter!'

'Oh, I have been cursed by professionals, my dear. And George,' Titus says, as an afterthought, 'before you go, please put this garbage out upon the nearest midden.'

Blossom hauls the woman roughly from the couch, drags her screeching out through the vestibule and from the house.

'Well, Mister Owen,' says Titus, 'with your assistance I now find myself considerably enriched. Will you not help me to invest some of this fortune at the Cockpit after all? I suppose that I should declare it to Sir Watkin. Increase my own portion of the Subscription. But perhaps not. You will join us, my friend?'

'I should prefer to see this gold, or at least the major part of it, safely with Mister Childers. For there has been a shocking increase in theft about the town lately, I am told. And then I must finish some of the sketches for Mister Bradley's murals. I thank you though, for your confidence, sir. Oh, and watch for Bender. He is the vengeful sort.'

A sensible warning, but unnecessary. For Titus has already taken steps to deal with Billy Bender and, by the end of the week, the cove will have provided an interesting alternative to Old Tarquin's normal diet. Yet, speaking of alternatives, Titus must give some thought to the bawdy-house. Mother Blossom may manage its affairs adequately enough in the short-term. But beyond? Regardless of the outcome to the gathering conflict, he knows that acceptance by the town's burgesses will never accrue to the proprietor of Manchester's most celebrated bawdy-den. He strokes his moustache a moment, then leaves for his further appointment with Sir Watkin.

A good night, too, at the Cockpit. Blood flows freely in bout after bout, while the crowd presses against the wall surrounding the small arena, yelling encouragements or screaming in outrage as their wagers flounder. Titus, Sir Watkin and David Morgan discuss the congenital aggression that each cock possesses towards every other male of its species, as well as other matters pertinent to this noble entertainment. The events are carefully regulated, naturally, the rules complex and the theme of so many books that Wilding has an entire section on the subject. The birds carefully weighed, matched, fought in the proper succession. The only sport in the entire country with any restrictions whatsoever until Jack Broughton had borrowed extensively from them for his own fist-fighting rules now adopted by adherents of pugilation almost everywhere.

An evening marred only by the attendance of Francis Townley and his friends, though the fellow shows considerable respect towards Sir Watkin. He lets them know, privately, that he too is aware of the disaster befallen the Jacobite Exchequer. An express from his brother, along with an exhortation that he should seize the moment, begin mustering volunteers who might form at least a company, a regiment perhaps, in the Prince's name. So the Subscription, he suggests. If Bradley and his Whiggish friends have raised two thousand pounds to furnish a militia troop for the Earl of Derby, how many foot might they raise with three? And he has a contact who can arrange the purchase of muskets from Birmingham. Not too many, but enough.

Titus is unhappy with the plan. Many of the subscribers will not take kindly to the perception that their donations are being utilised in a manner different from that which they might have imagined. Yet it is difficult to avoid Townley's logic. And His Royal Highness has hardly shown great aptitude in fiduciary duties and the proper care for his own finances. Sir Watkin is persuaded and, so they are agreed, the promissory note for the Subscription shall be transferred to Townley. But perhaps it may be better to leave the subscribers in ignorance of the change. Safer for Mister Townley and the transactions he must undertake. He will keep accounts, naturally, with any balance to be collected in due course.

Is this the way of it? Titus thinks. *That I am now to play second fiddle to this crook-tooth'd cove? This cunny-sucker who thinks himself at liberty to insult my wife in our own home?* And he exchanges barely a word with the Welshmen as they eventually make their way back to the lodgings at the Bull's Head. But Titus is still encouraged to wait, to take a final cup of wine together, while Sir Watkin climbs to his room so that he may return the promissory note now intended for Townley.

But when he descends again, it is in a state of considerable distress.

'My book of accompts, sir!' he cries. 'It is gone. Stolen.'

Chapter Thirty-Seven

Idle hands are the Devil's plaything, they say. So why has hard work not kept him from sin, Aran wonders. He has followed all normal convention on the matter. Each biblical wisdom. Every relevant literary reference from Seneca to Aesop, Aristotle to Shakespeare. That one might work hard and become a leader, yet remain lazy and succeed at nothing. That whatever measure one might deal out to others, the same shall be dealt to you in return. That six days we should labour and do all our work, yet the seventh day is a Sabbath upon which to rest. That he who works his land shall enjoy abundance whilst the fellow who chases fantasies is lacking in judgement. That we have to toil a while, endure a while, believe always, and never turn back. That little by little does the trick. That we are what we repeatedly perform. That where joy is, there should be our work. And that opportunity always comes disguised as hard effort.

Well, he has seen enough of it already today. A Wednesday again, the Fly Wagon to be loaded for Carlisle, but such chaos in town, tomorrow being the start of this year's Acres Field Fair. So an early start has seen the cart loaded at the warehouse. McClellands in Edinburgh need twenty pounds of *Souchong* and it has reduced the cost considerably for the Redmonds to arrange transport of half the distance. Scarrow in Carlisle wants ten one-pound caddies of Twankay as well as fifteen pounds of *Singo* – a handsome order for such a small borough. But the orders will exhaust the very final supplies of those precious varieties. Thank God for the imminent return of Captain Eriksson and the Götheburg with the replenishment of their stocks. Then the Fly Wagon escorted, as normal, to the Pack-Horse Inn, other cargoes and travellers set on board before Aran returns to the warehouse to fill requirements for the Punch Bowl in York. It is a strongly Whiggish establishment but they seem untroubled at the prospect of trading with Titus the Jacobite so long as it helps them profit.

Hard work a-plenty, therefore, but any reward for this day's labour will be overshadowed by the wages to be received for his crimes, since tonight he must travel to Salford, to the Ship, and Striker's lodgings.

Still, it is difficult for anything to cloud the news from the north. The Irwell sparkles with it. The sandstone bluffs along the river's margent smile pink and warm at its reception. The bells of the Collegiate Church still chime a greeting to the intelligence. And the very air carries scent of Jacobite heather or broom. For His Royal Highness is well upon the road, arrived in Edinburgh at five o'the morning on the seventeenth, initially opposed by the superior numbers of the Hanoverian garrison, yet the gates accidentally left open so that some enterprising fellows of the Prince were able to rush inside and seize the town.

A piece of good fortune, but one that is hardly likely to compensate for news of the Stuart Exchequer's demise. There seems to have been reasonable success, locally, in keeping a shroud wrapped tight about the mortal remains, yet neither Titus nor Aran had found themselves capable of keeping the thing from Maria-Louise and she, poor dear, has had chance a-plenty to dissect the corpse.

'What does this mean?' she had said to him, suffering visibly from the blue devils after her husband had told her of Sir Watkin's account. 'The Prince is ordained by God and Our Lady to become King. It is his Divine Right. And I have tampered with that divinity, have I not? I shall be damn'd for this. Damn'd for eternity.'

'It is a bitter development,' Aran had replied, 'but you must keep the matter confined to its true proportion, my dear. First, your intentions were noble and you acted only on the assumption that a mere portion of the coffers were destined to finance a French invasion. Second, it was the decision of Their Majesties to transport the entire amount in such a hazardous manner. Why, it is almost beyond comprehension. And, third, we still do not know how the matter will end. After all, the Prince is already at Perth, silver or no, and Cope marching hither and thither, it seems, unable to deny his passage to the Lowlands.'

'These are fine words, Aran Owen. Yet I know myself a transgressor. A miscreant who must confess herself. Though each time that I have attended upon Father Peter I have been unable to speak the words, so heinous is my iniquity.'

'But is it not possible that this apparent happenstance may be a part of God's design entire? How could Father Peter Scobie say otherwise? I think that no end of confessional at Roman Entry might resolve this for you. You were convinced, I recall, that Our Lady had given you guidance, and from such direction no priest may grant you absolution. Is that not so? Have faith, madam!'

'I shall offer the Rosary to God and Our Lady so that I might receive guidance. So that this particular mystery may be revealed. It is a bold and brazen proposal, yet I believe that Our Lady will sometimes answer seemingly impossible requests to those praying their first Rosary, or to those who face a particular trial. And I shall ask Her to heal your own troubled mind as well, dear Aran.'

'My mind is filled with recollections of Sir Edward's knowledge about unknown friends in Manchester. Informants. The Cause ditched by their actions. I saw myself through his eyes. Some sneaking, skulking fellow. A spy. It caused me to almost choke upon a pickled walnut at your daughter's dinner. And Rosina knows me too well, as you do also. For she has pressed me on the thing three times in this past week alone.'

'You have a certain transparency. A charming though dangerous attribute, which my daughter would seek to exploit as she does so many other situations, so many of those around her.'

'I sense that she is unhappy. Her dealings with Mistress Cooper no longer bring her the joy that once they might have done. There are matters, too, from her Marriage Settlement that vex her. And both of these combine to prevent a reconciliation with her Mama.'

'Though none of these are issues that need concern you, sir. You feel some guilt that, for one moment, you acted the scrub towards her and now seek to make amends by taking upon yourself the entire burden of those matters that my daughter has simply brought upon herself. And I tell you, Aran, that my daughter shall wound you.'

'Well, I must do as my conscience dictates. Though it, too, has served me ill of late.'

'Sir Watkin's ledger?'

He had looked at her in surprise, recalling his further confession to her, at Kersal Moor Races, about Striker's latest demand. Evidence of Sir Watkin's complicity in the planned insurrection. His involvement as a principal for the Jacobite Cause. Yet he had never subsequently mentioned the thing to her again. Not once in the intervening three months. Indeed, he had again determined to ignore his instruction, to claim that no such opportunity had presented itself. But he had then found himself in the Punch House, alongside Sir Watkin as he transacted business with Titus, the small ledger there on the table before him, the entries and signatures clear for all to see.

'As I say, you know me too well, my dear.'

With the business at the bawdy-den completed, the idea of theft had been sufficiently upon his mind that Aran had warned Titus about the need to protect the gold so recently secured from Mistress Cole. And, with Titus now gone to the Cockpit in company of Sir Watkin and David Morgan, he had made his way to the Bull's Head. Aran frequents the place almost daily, of course, so his first difficulty had been whether he might enter unseen, though this had not been such a challenge as he had imagined for, the parlour being full and the smoke especially thick, he had turned straight to the stairs where tremulous legs carried him to the first floor. The doors had been unlocked, as he had supposed, for Sir Watkin was unlikely to have paid the additional charge for a key unless leaving coin within. Only two of the rooms seemed occupied and one of them he had identified as Sir Watkin's from the gentleman's valise packed ready for the morrow's travel and happily containing the ledger, along with the promissory notes, some letters, an elegant mahogany writing box and Sir Watkin's dirty linen. Aran had made a pretence of ransacking both rooms as though this were some random search for easy pickings, finding nothing worthy even of the most desperate dubber amongst Morgan's belongings, but taking the writing box and a fine though soiled shirt from Sir Watkin, along with the ledger, naturally. The ledger had been sequestered in a secure location at the warehouse whilst the writing box, wrapped in the shirt, and with some chagrin, for it was a remarkable piece of craftsmanship, had ended in the Irwell.

'I recalled your agitation upon Kersal Moor,' Maria-Louise had said. 'And though you gave me only the merest detail of Striker's instruction to you, when my husband told me of the dosing that had taken place in the Bull, I thought of you at once. Sir Watkin, it seems, was quite enraged. No, more than that. Titus spoke of fear. But he suspects nothing except that this were the work of some petty pilferer. And Our Lady knows, there are enough of them about!'

In fact, Aran had only this week removed the ledger and hidden it within his own lodgings following receipt of an express from Striker that set their meeting for this night. And, throughout the subsequent days, each waking thought, every element of his labours, has been overcast by Striker's shadow.

Still, Monday and Tuesday had seen him successfully negotiate construction of the frames on which his mural canvas will be mounted and, since the Byroms have recently returned from visiting their various Lancashire relatives, Aran has also been able to confirm permission from Mister Byrom himself that the work might proceed at the Academy rooms. The ninety-six inch height of the panels will, it seems, just allow their passage through the Hanging Ditch entrance and, diagonally, through the doorway leading to the workshops. So Herringbone, the carpenter, has been contracted to build them, using native fir in the stretcher bars themselves and the joints left with neither glue nor other fastening so that the canvas can be tensioned, periodically, using the frame's key wedges.

The canvas, too, is ordered from the ship's chandlery at the Quay and will be delivered from Liverpool shortly, leaving Aran sufficient time to begin preparation of the gesso with which the fabric must be coated. A rabbit-skin glue first, of course, spread over the fibres and then the compound of linseed oil and white lead. But there is a problem, for the Flemish and Dutch Masters, he knows, would spend many months in layering their canvas, polishing its surface, repeating the process, until not a trace of the original texture remained – and this is a luxury that he cannot afford. So he has settled on a single layer and will attempt to use the resultant imperfections to his own advantage.

And thus, with his labours at the warehouse finished, the Fly Wagon safely dispatched towards Carlisle, and thoughts of the murals running chaotically through his mind, he sets off for Salford. He crosses the Irwell bridge with its dank and largely unused dungeon and walks to the junction with Chapel Street, the Ship Inn facing him. But there is no sign of Striker within. He makes enquiry of the innkeeper. A travelling gentleman? No, sir, there are no strangers here tonight. From Birmingham, perhaps. A Mister Bradstreet? Nobody of that name. Most people upon the road making direct for Manchester and tomorrow's Fair.

So he takes supper alone, a hearty stew and thin beer. A pipe of tobacco too, for he has recently begun to foster the habit. It soothes him, he finds. Helps give free rein to his imagination. And he spends some pleasant moments conjuring ideas for the mural designs until, at last, a darker thought crosses his mind. That Striker has never previously arranged a meeting with him in this way. No. He has, rather, always appeared at times when Aran was not particularly expecting him. Indeed, the only occasion on which any formal encounter has been part of a specific plan was that on which Jacob had used him for luring Striker to Seabank Nook. And Striker had been clear on Kersal Moor that Aran's innocence was still strongly in doubt on that score. So why would Striker have set such a meeting if there is any likelihood that Aran might spring another trap? Of course, he would not. Which means that Striker is either watching the place or waiting to intercept Aran on his return to Manchester. And what better vantage point for both purposes than the bridge?

Well, I shall disappoint him. So he settles his account, bids the innkeeper a good night and leaves the Ship once more. Instead of retracing his steps, however, he walks down Chapel Street, past the Sacred Trinity, and then the narrow lanes that lead to the Salford bank of the Irwell. He follows the river path south for a quarter-mile until he reaches the cluster of houses and a small jetty from which the wherries ply back and forth, persuading the boatman to make one final crossing for the evening, returning him finally to the Manchester Quay.

He will have seen me leave and will now be waiting at my lodgings, he thinks, amused by this childish evasion, and spending the next ten minutes returning to the Market Square and the Bull's Head. The inn is truly a house of good cheer tonight, with Francis Townley entertaining in lavish style.

'Ah, Mister Owen!' he cries, spraying a fine drizzle of spittle in Aran's direction. 'You will volunteer to fight in the Cause, will you not, sirrah?'

And there are clearly a good number who have already signed the pledge. Collow, Dawson, Beswicke, Chaddock, the Deacon boys. All now deeply in their cups.

'Time a-plenty for that, I fancy,' Aran replies. 'And good news on the Prince Regent's progress, I gather?'

'Edinburgh taken,' says Townley. 'Yet we have some warm-weather friends, I think. Tom Deacon was just telling me that even his father has doubts now. He has told the lads that he will support the rising only under duress, for he sees no material gain for himself from the enterprise. Material gain, sir! His very words. Then for what reason has the fellow maintained his Non-Juror principles?'

'I imagine it may be possible to reject the Hanoverian usurpers yet not welcome the internecine strife that their removal may occasion. And for a man of God, like Bishop Deacon, it must be a sore trial.'

'All the same, the time is coming when sides must be chosen. For you, too, Aran Owen. You shall not have the luxury of daubing paint on canvas once the thing is on our own doorstep. And a careful hand on your purse in this place! You heard about the burglary?'

'Indeed!' Aran replies. 'Yet the Constables unable to find the culprit.'

'Constables!' spits Townley. 'A pox upon them. Yet the whole town knows the cove responsible. That fool Bender, for he has not been seen from that day to this.'

No, not Billy Bender, thinks Aran, bidding Townley a good night and leaving the Bull for his own rooms above the Punch House, climbing the stairs as quietly as possible, convinced that Striker will have found some way to enter the lodging and be waiting to accost him. So he lights his candles, finds himself foolishly checking under the bed and anywhere else that might hide somebody in this tiny cell. Nothing. He slides the latch, checks that the ledger remains safe, wonders whether he might turn its possession to some advantage of his own if it is not, after all, collected. And, as the bells of Saint Ann's and the Collegiate Church each chime eleven, he snuffs out the candles and takes to his bed.

Sleep escapes him, however, as effectively as he, apparently, has escaped Striker, though he suffers those waking dreams that so often fill the vacancy 'twixt sheet and slumber. He finds himself painting Striker's features into a mural allegory, but a canvas that fills the entire length of Market Street Lane with images of the town's glories. Two-headed albino children. Maria-Louise's quim. Ice-bound esquimeaux – surely some strange word association of his mind. A blind harpsichord player. Old Tarquin chewing on something that remains just beyond Aran's vision. The Duke of Bolton's stable entire competing at Kersal Moor, yet every jockey dressed in darkest sable and their apocalyptic mounts, white, red, black, and phantom pale. A naked, cherubic and winged Elizabeth Cooper. Jacob Driscoll's headstone, washed by the darkest green flood of the Irish Sea. An endlessly revolving circle of warships, their broadsides ablaze. The shattered ruin of Mother Blossom's face. And a pair of blackened pincers – the sort with which one might snip the fingers from a sleeping man. Why, he can almost feel the cold grip of their jaws on his own hand.

Cold.

Yet some token I still desire, he hears Striker say. A point to be made, so that you shall understand Dudley Striker more fully.

He feels again the Gaoler's grip.

Castigo te non quod odio habeum, sed quod amem. I chastise thee not out of hatred, but out of love.

And, as he feels the pincers biting once more into his flesh, he emits another scream as intense as that which once shook the walls of Lancaster Castle.

But this time it is a scream stifled by a powerful hand clamped about his jaws.

'Quiet, you damn'd fool!' whispers Striker. 'Else you shall rouse the entire town.' Aran finds himself awake, safe in his lodgings, yet staring wide-eyed at Striker's cynical smile, illuminated by milky moonlight. 'And what, prithee, was all that harlequinade that you forced me to endure earlier? You thought, Ah! I shall make poor Striker dance to my tune for once. Is that not so, my dear? You said to yourself, Oh, poor Striker has not shown himself because he fears another ambush. Well, it was a merry dance, to be sure. But you see, friend Aran, how I have come to trust you once more? For I never considered that you might fail me. Not after the astonishing intelligence that you gifted me about the Stuarts' silver. La! How astonished I was to find that you had told me true at Kersal Moor. I said to myself, Dudley, are you certain that this emanates from Mister Owen? What if he takes credit for another's work? But the message was contained in a Byrom's envelope. Unique. So there was really no doubt about its sender. Ah, but I see you are now composed once more.' And he removes his hand, at last, from Aran's mouth, shifting himself from the cot. 'Yet is there any food in this accursed place? It seems that I missed my supper.'

Aran struggles to sit, reaching for tinder-box and lighting his candle afresh. 'Food?' he says. 'It must be three in the morning. Do you imagine that I have some hidden larder, sir? It is the meanest of lodgings and I may not keep food here lest it should attract vermin. Though it seems that I am prone to infestation regardless. And how did you get in? No, never mind. It was a foolish question. I have a confession though. For whilst the hand on the message was certainly mine, the sentiment behind it was another's. I should want to know that, if matters end badly for the Prince Regent – indeed, perhaps even if they end well – that this person shall be protected.'

'A fie upon you, sir! Perhaps I have jiggered the wrong door. This cannot be the same Aran Owen who cowered so at my approach not three months since. Why, friend, I find you quite changed. And this other person cannot be a man else you would have said so. Who, then? Such a dainty would have been known to very few in Manchester. Townley perhaps. Redmond almost certainly. And not the daughter, I collect. Not now. Sweet Rosina! How I have craved for her, dear fellow. But then to find her a tribade. And worse, a tribade wed to James Bradley. La! How I laughed. So the wife, the elegant Maria-Louise. Sly dog you are, sir. Yet she is rabid as the rest of them in your Jacobite camp. What then has caused her change of allegiance, I wonder?'

'She is more the patriot than any of us, I think. For she wishes to see the Elector of Hanover removed and the True King restored, yet will not see us under the heel of John Frenchman in the process. She knew that the shipment, part of it at least, was intended to purchase a French army, and she could not bear the thought. And yes, I think you find me changed. At Kersal Moor, you took me by surprise. Those threats you made, too, upon the lives of her daughters. I could not believe that anybody might even imagine such depravities, let alone speak them.'

'We each possess the mind of an artist, Mister Owen. It is the reason for our friendship, I find. Its very strength. The thing that binds us. My own may have its private peculiarities, yet I am an artist none-the-less. On occasion my designs may shock a little, yet what is art if it does not extend our horizons from time to time? And you must know that I intended none of those things in truth. I practised upon you a little, no more than that. Yet such words you employ. Elector of Hanover, indeed. You have fallen too far into this Jacobite midden, dear fellow. King George the Second is true ruler of these lands. Anointed so in the eyes of God! And why should you imagine that your fair Titania, Mistress Redmond, should be imperilled by the outcome of this insurrection? An outcome no longer in any doubt, I should add. Or perhaps I should phrase the thing differently. For the envelope was Byrom's. The hand was thine – and how is your poor hand, by the way? Yet the sentiment belonged to Maria-Louise. So how, prithee, did the good lady even know of my existence?'

'It was following the memorial service for Jacob Driscoll. I feared your reprisal so greatly. For it was clear to me that you should assume me guilty of leading you to a trap when I, myself, Titus Redmond too, had merely been duped by him. And you may say, now, that you intended none of the threats you made against the girls yet, had you the opportunity back then, and without receipt of Mistress Redmond's intelligence to stay your hand, I think you should have carried out those evil designs, Striker. By God, I do! So I confessed myself to Maria-Louise, partly in fear for my own life, I must allow, but also that we might place some protection around her daughters. Yes, sir. You find me changed. Though I fear you still, if that is any comfort to you. For at Seabank Nook there were four men dead. All at your hand, I assume? And you have influence, it seems. Enough to place a shield around this good lady, perhaps, should she need one. As, indeed, she might if the Earl of Derby remains so free with his tongue.'

'Derby, you say? And you are certain that there is no food, no morsel of cheese perhaps? No, I see that you have none. But what has Sir Edward been saying? He has met me, of course. Knows that I have informants here in town. But nothing else. No names. And I assure you, my friend, that her secret is safe with me. Ah! But I see. How very amusing. Mistress Redmond could not have known, of course, that the entire Jacobite Exchequer had been entrusted to those unfortunate letters of marque. Well, she has done me a great service, Aran. For I have awaited a commission such a long time, and now it is almost within my grasp. Yes, a commission. His Grace, the Duke of Newcastle, has finally agreed to act as my patron in the matter. The thing to be arranged as soon as possible. Though I suspect that he finds skulkers like myself something of an embarrassment. So back to the Colonies I shall go, though bearing the King's Commission as reward from a grateful monarch. You know, I have a fancy to reclaim the lands from which my family was dispossessed. Perhaps you shall come with me, my dear. What a formidable pair we should make!'

'The idea is perfectly preposterous. But Seabank Nook, sirrah? And tell me, I must ask you, Striker. Sir Watkin Williams Wynn mentioned another fellow called Owen.'

Striker's smile widens, inane pleasure etched on his face. 'You see, friend Aran, how much you have changed? Why, you have pieced together the whole affair in such few words. Yes, Seabank Nook. I truly believed that the game was up for me. The brutes had me trapped in a cellar. Caught like the rodent that you seemingly imagine me to be. And he was a strong fellow, your Jacob Driscoll. But, yes, I dispatched all four in the end, though I was grievous wounded in the process. And had it not been for my new-found comrades in Wales! Ah, but I have you to thank for them. The Rector of Hawarden. A charming gentleman. Your good Squire Redmond, too. Though he is tuppence short of the whole shilling, I find. Sir Watkin, on the other hand, is a dangerous insurrectionist. But one, I think, who will not hazard his own skin when it comes time to toss the bones. You have something for me, I suppose, concerning Sir Watkin?' He looks around the room, eyes settling upon the chest that bears Aran's belongings. 'May I?' Aran nods, and Striker lifts the lid, removing the ledger. He carries it to the candle, turns the pages, murmuring appreciatively as he does so.

'Titus Redmond has sworn revenge upon you, Striker, for Jacob's death. For Jacob, and for your mutilation of Mother Blossom, too. He has your name also. From Mister Byrom, I think. And he, in turn, from some person at Newcastle House who also frequents the Royal Academy. Though I suppose that a person who hopes to bear the King's Commission, even one from he who should not truly style himself King, may think himself immune from such simple dangers.'

'Revenge? When I merely defended myself against Driscoll's infamy? Or for crafting a message upon the face of that scented bawd? Ah, but I shall deal with Redmond when I must! Either myself or this William Owen that you mentioned. No matter. William Owen. Dudley Striker. We are one, after all. For William Owen, once a loyal soldier for King George, is now a trusted adherent of the Welsh Jacobites. And you see how much I revere you, dear friend? For I chose your name through my respect for you. Nothing else. Why, it makes us almost brothers, does it not? And how proud you would have been to see this sweet brother presented to your own bonnie Prince. Yes, the bold Chevalier himself. Sir Watkin believed that I might be useful to him and sent me north with promises of Welshmen by the thousand, if only he will march on England. I met up with them just before they reached Perth though, days before, I had almost run into General Cope's men. I was nearly captured by them. Yet there they were, marching northwards, and must have passed within an ace of the Chevalier heading south. Though pass each other they did, sir! And I was able to bring the news of Cope's whereabouts to Charles Edward myself. He was delighted. The Irishman, O'Sullivan, is his Adjutant-General. Interesting fellow. A man who understands the value of irregular warfare and good intelligence too. Insisted on creating a corps of picquets for that purpose. Though it displeases Murray a great deal. Why, I fancy that I may even find myself serving within it.'

'Lord George Murray? I had though him a traitor to the Stuarts. I recall Townley reporting that he had rejected the Duke of Perth's overtures that he might come out on the Prince Regent's behalf?'

'Prince Regent? What titles you bestow upon seditionists, my friend. La! Bless you. But you are correct. Little more than a month has passed since Lord George was swearing allegiance to General Cope and was made Deputy-Sheriff of Perthshire for his pains. Then turns up at the camp of the Chevalier only a se'nnight later and becomes a Lieutenant-General.'

'Then I do not follow how you can say that the outcome of the expedition is no longer in doubt. You speak as though the Cause is lost. Yet Edinburgh is taken. General Cope an incompetent, not capable of even locating the Prince's army. And great men now flocking to the Royal Standard. Even without the Exchequer, the Stuart star is in the ascendancy, Striker. And Maria-Louise was correct. It will all be achieved without French involvement.'

'You have been suckling too long on that beauty's fulsome teats, I think. Edinburgh, my dear one, was taken by the merest fortune. I was with the *banditti* when they passed Stirling and had to leave the whole town unmolested. The garrison fired upon us from the ramparts with the utmost derision. And Cope is no more than a makeweight, thrown upon the balance until the full strength of the English army – the Hanoverian army, as you would have it – can be brought to bear against this treacherous rabble. And great men, you say. Flocking to the Stuart Standard. I should hardly give Lord George Murray such credit, sirrah. For he was either playing Cope false in August, or your Chevalier in September. Hardly a man of integrity. And then our good Duke of Newcastle has been receiving deputations, swearing loyalty to the Hanoverian Crown, almost daily from the very English Papists – Sir William Gage and others – on whom Charles Stuart thinks he may himself depend. No, Mister Owen, I doubt that your Prince shall ever leave Scotland and may, I fear, die there. The sooner the better too, for this double life is exceeding hard. I was still in Edinburgh until the eighteenth, sent back to confirm arrangements for the Welsh to join this stupidity. And just as well since His Grace also requires duties of me here in Lancashire. Though I must ride like the Devil to complete my business. Sleeping in hedge-rows for the most part, dear heart. Poor Striker, you will say. I may not give him food yet I shall not deny him a bed.'

'At such an hour, Mister Striker, I should grant you almost anything so long as I am allowed to sleep myself. I am therefore happy to provide you with a bed, though you should note that you are presently standing upon it. But you may advise the Pelhams that they should not mistake the oaths of a few like Sir William Gage for a general desertion of the Stuarts by those of the Jacobite Faith. I know not, in truth, whether God may be on one side or the other in this thing. Yet if matters for our Jacobite Cause are so parlous, why should the Pelhams' Government have decreed that those iniquitous Catholic Penal Laws should be both strengthened and fully enforced. I suspect that these are the duties that bring you back to Lancashire, sirrah. And hardly a worthy occupation for one who seeks to present himself as an officer and a gentleman. Still, yesterday was tiresome. Mister Redmond's enterprise makes considerable demands upon me, as you might imagine. So now, sir, if you wish to sleep upon my floor, you are reluctantly welcome since I perceive that I have but little choice in the matter.'

Striker weighs Sir Watkin's ledger in his hand. He looks thoughtful. 'Well, I had at least expected that, as brothers, we might be allowed to share the cot. But so be it! The road from Edinburgh to Wales was a long one and I do have business in Lancashire to which I must attend before returning north. We must all accept the duties that fall upon us, Mister Owen, lowly or otherwise. Yet I owe you some reward for this tome, my dear. So I am happy to relieve some of life's other burdens from you, sir. For you shall need to labour no more in that tumbling ruin of a warehouse. Why, I am amazed that you have not suffered some serious injury there. Though it no longer presents a risk for you.'

Aran finds himself leaping from the bed, peering through the window and expecting to see flames rising from the distant Quay. But there is nothing.

'What mischief now, Striker? What have you done, sir?'

'Oh, such gratitude! I have done nothing, dear one. Except to bring news, for I know how anxiously you have awaited all those crates of Tippy Pekoe, that wonderful Bobea, the Singo, the Hyson, the Twankay. And how they have helped to support those troublesome Stuarts. But no more, brother Aran. For the Götheburg, that fine Swedish East Indiaman, is no more. Sunk with her entire cargo before even a single caddy could be transferred to your Manx smuggler friends. I thought it only just, considering their willingness to assist Driscoll with my demise. So no further tea trade for the Redmonds. The crew mercifully escaped, however, though the bold Captain Eriksson, it seems, has gone down with his vessel!'

Chapter Thirty-Eight

Later in the same week, Elizabeth Cooper has also suffered sleeplessness, lying awake on two consecutive nights as she contemplates a particularly distressing turn of events. Normally, it is her custom to slumber without disturbance, blissfully ignorant of the symphony that, beyond her rooms, fills Manchester's hours of darkness. But on *these* nights she hears every note. The church bells, of course, marking the passing of endless hours. The Night Watch, crying his painful reminder of the bells' recent announcements. *Past three o'clock and a clear night!* The Lamplighter, paying his regular visits to the nearest of the town's two public lanthorns, just along the street at the Cross, but making such a commotion with his ladder and oil-can that he might waken even the dead. The occasional late reveller, naturally. The snorting, snuffling sounds of Old Tarquin and his fellow-pigs. A periodic cow bell. And then the Midnight Mechanics, though they might attend at any hour until sunrise. This small army of black-coated Night Soil Men, hired by the Court Leet to empty the chamber pots, privies and cesspits from private house or public establishment. Contractors, of course, and well-esteemed. They will empty excrement into tubs, urine into casks, then transport the former beyond the town boundaries for sale as manure, or the latter to the mills for fulling processes. Somebody needs to grant them entry to the particular source of their business, though, and in Elizabeth's case it is Crableck, roused from his palliasse behind the high entrance desk in the coffee house. But she can hear them at every other dwelling in Market Street Lane too, hammering for access, carrying out their trade. She remembers the riddle. *What has four legs, a wheel, and flies?* Answer, the Night Soil Men and their barrow. And, to irritate still further, she can hear them pause periodically to admire some treasure that they might have discovered amongst their wares. A gold coin, a silver button, fallen or lost in an over-hasty dropping of breeches. 'It may be shit to them,' she hears one say, laughing loud, 'but it's bread and butter to us, eh Tom?' And no sooner are these honey-pot men gone than the Scavengers have arrived with the first light of day. More bells rung, and citizens exhorted to bring out their rubbish for the collecting cart.

Then what is this thing that has caused Elizabeth such a lack of repose? And not Elizabeth alone. For half the townsfolk or more lay awake these nights. Not from an excess of excitement at the pleasures to be found at the

379

Acres Field Fair. Not from a surfeit of good food and fine wine. But from fear. From the news that arrived early on Thursday and has continued to run through the town like flood water.

It is best summarised, perhaps, by the pamphlet that has circulated, written by a certain gentlemen, a witness to the late bloody and desperate battle fought at Gladsmuir betwixt the army under the command of His Royal Highness, Prince Charles Edward Stuart, and that commanded by Lieutenant General John Cope on Saturday, the twenty-first of September, this year of Our Lord, 1745.

The gentleman in question makes it clear that he has no Party rage, has taken no side in the conflict, yet finds himself an admirer of the Prince, a direct descendant from the ancient line of Scottish Kings, after all, and one who might have chosen to spend his years in ease, safety and splendour abroad, rather than risk his very life in the rescue from ruin of these precious islands. Entirely impartial, therefore. And notes that, the Prince having liberated Edinburgh from the Hanoverian yoke, Lieutenant General Cope had transferred his army by ship to Dunbar, then marched to attack the Highlanders. An account of Sir John's speech to his forces at Preston Grange, six miles east of Edinburgh town. They would pose no threat, naturally, this parcel of rabble, this pack of brutes, to his own professional battalions. Yet his soldiers could expect no booty from such a despicable breed, so the good Lieutenant General had pledged to them eight full hours of freedom to plunder and pillage the town and its suburbs.

That same day, the twentieth, the Prince had put himself at the head of his own forces, presented his sword. 'My friends,' he had cried, 'I have flung away the scabbard!' then marched them to the brow of Carberry Hill, to find Cope moved down to the lower ground, east of Prestonpans. The Highlanders had followed them until they were barely a half-mile from the English forces, the latter four thousand strong and discharging their artillery at the Prince's men during the evening. Both sides, reports the gentleman, had lain under arms that night but, at three in the morning of the twenty-first, the Highlanders were raised from the ground and marched silently to the rear of their enemies' lines. The signals were given to form and attack, manoeuvres that they performed with the utmost celerity, although Cope's picquets were alerted and, being called to arms, the English succeeded in turning about and discharging a ragged volley that did little damage. The Scots, on the other hand, fired their own muskets in good order and then, throwing down their firearms, drew swords to sweep down from the morning mist, many wearing no more than their shirts, and giving a most frightful and hideous howl, to carry all before them like a torrent, killing or making prisoner almost every officer of infantry so that, in seven or eight minutes, both horse and foot were totally routed and driven from the field of battle.

So it had been that the Prince's force, only fifteen hundred Highland irregulars, had obtained a most signal and complete victory over a trained army, with infantry, cavalry and artillery, more than four thousand strong. And from that force, it is computed, five hundred lay slain, nine hundred are wounded, and one thousand four hundred are captured, along with their cannon, mortars, regimental standards, and an abundance of horses, arms, baggage, equipment, five thousand pounds in gold.

Initial reaction to the pamphlet has been honest disbelief. A propaganda, surely. Yet with the arrival of this express and that, or the London broadsheets, it is all so horribly confirmed. It may not have been an engagement on the scale of Fontenoy but its repercussions are so much more profound. That the achievements of such a momentous event as the Glorious Revolution, sixty years before, should now be threatened by a storm cloud that had initially seemed so insignificant.

Inconceivable! That this fellow, this self-styled Prince of Wales, Prince Regent indeed, a man of no acknowledged character or skill, they say, should have so recently landed without friends or finance but accomplished thus quickly the defeat of an English army. *Their* English army, think the town's Whigs. And what next? What now may prevent this band of brigands, this barbarian horde from sweeping down upon them at any minute. Why, there are tales. Miller Tomlinson claims that a cousin was found amongst the dead, butchered like a beast, hands and feet removed, his innards opened to invite the attention of carrion. Reports, too, from Berwick, Carlisle, Scarborough, that witnesses have seen the Jacobite army passing south at speed, already across the English border, wraith-like, on the high moorlands. Hardly an hour passes without some new development, some refinement of the terror.

And for Mistress Cooper the news of Gladsmuir has come so rapidly on the heels of another. Less catastrophic, perhaps, but linked and still significant. For Rosina had paid her a visit early on the twenty-sixth, saying that her father's enterprise, or at least that part of it that related to the trade in tea, illicit and otherwise, was ruined. The Swedish vessel carrying their precious cargo from Canton now sunk though whether this was accident or the work of privateer remains unknown. The damn'd girl had expected sympathy, it seemed. La! There had never been a secret made of the purpose for which this business was begun. To raise gold for the Stuart Cause. And Elizabeth had little enough regard for the Redmonds' loss even before pamphlet or word of Cope's defeat had begun to arrive later that same morning. Beforehand, the whole matter of money-raising amongst the Jacobite merchants had seemed like nothing but a foolish vanity, a matter of manly pride, of politics. Yet from the moment of this knowledge of Gladsmuir, the world had assumed a different shape. Each penny they had raised poured blood of English soldiers upon the hands of every Tory, High Churchman and Catholic in the town – including dear, sweet Rosina.

But it had not taken Elizabeth long to sense an opportunity, so notes had been written, delicate inquiries set in motion. Today will see the meetings take place at which this opportunity may be refined.

She prepares carefully, washing and drying, brushing and dressing her pale hair before applying the white leader powder to face, shoulder and bosom. Rouge as necessary. A simple black *mouche* high on her right cheek, for on this, of all days, she must declare her Whiggish allegiance plain for all to see. The dress she chooses is modest, a simple grey silk, and finally the buckram and lace Milanese pinner for which she had paid four shillings and sixpence from Mistress Brimstone.

The glass shows that although her thirty-second birthday turned this past week, Elizabeth Cooper remains a handsome woman, her cheek-bones prominent and exaggerated by the rouge, her mouth a trifle hard perhaps, her chin strong. A woman who has made her way in the world, in this man's world of commerce and natural philosophies.

She hears Crableck upon the stairs, unmistakeable as the restrictions of his crook-back and shrunken leg cause him to mount each riser in turn and to halt, his usual custom, no more than half-way to the top and calling out whatever message he may bear.

Elizabeth opens her door. 'What is it, Crableck?'

'Mistress Bradley to see you!' he cries. 'Waiting below, she is.'

Rosina again. To sustain our disagreement? Or to offer some simpering repair? I neither know nor care. Yet in the circumstance of her impending encounter, Elizabeth feels obliged to reject the girl gently.

'Please offer my most profound apologies, Crableck, yet explain that I must complete the preparation of my accounts for this morning's meeting. Please tell her that I must focus all my attentions upon them, yet I shall meet with her later. I am sure she will understand.'

The coffee house is not so large, and customers not so numerous at this hour, that Rosina will have failed to hear the exchange for herself, so Elizabeth has been careful to insert the necessary quantity of care and regret into her words.

'Indeed, Mistress. Meeting it shall be. Indeed.'

And faithful Crableck descends once more. He has been with her almost as long as the coffee house itself, formerly a clerk for Mister Liptrott's father, also an attorney, until some dispute had cost him the position. Yet he works diligently, clears his palliasse each morning before the opening hour, and apparently survives tolerably on the few shillings that she pays him weekly, supplemented by the occasional gratuity bestowed upon him by a grateful customer. He has entirely ignored her sapphic tendencies whilst, with utmost subtlety, permitting her to know that her secret is safe with him as, indeed, it has always been.

She pauses with the door open, listening until her door-keeper has delivered the message to Rosina, unable to precisely hear details but sufficient of the tone to know that her young friend has not taken the rejection well. Her gaze turns to the mantle-shelf where the Bride's Pie glass ring sits as a remembrance of better days amongst other mementoes. But lately there are so many disagreements, at times bitter, frequently stemming from Rosina's Jacobite fervour and, oh, good gracious, how much worse shall they be now. She has calculated quite incorrectly, of course, for she had assumed that their relationship would have reached a natural conclusion by this point. Well, the *most* natural, in fact, since she had taken for granted that James Bradley would, by now, have Rosina with child. God's Hooks, does the fellow have no balls? Still, on this most strange of days, it is not Rosina that she must entertain – but the girl's father.

And two hours later, Titus Redmond steps over the threshold of her coffee house for the first time. *How does the fellow succeed in seeming as though he is master of all that surrounds him?* she wonders. His full-bodied coat, high-collared waistcoat and knee breeches are each a matching shade of deep chestnut, his stockings the lightest shade of cream, his wig freshly powdered. He doffs his hat as he sees her, bends the knee, transfers his tricorne to the hand that holds his walking cane, strokes his moustache thoughtfully with the other, while the many creases of his face resolve themselves to a broad smile.

'Give you joy of the morning, Mistress Cooper,' he cries, while several astonished customers spill chocolate from their saucers, the entire assembly falling mute at Redmond's presence among them. 'And *such* an establishment. Delightful!'

'I am honoured that you have ventured such a distance to see it for yourself, sir.' And she takes pleasure that, almost involuntarily, Titus has turned his head back to the door, reviewing the hundred paces or so that he has travelled to get here. She changes to a conspiratorial whisper. 'Yet little joy within these walls today, as you may imagine.' He casts an eye over her Whiggish clients, their discourse slowly returning to its earlier level as they compare broadsheets, the *Gazetteer*, the *Courant*, the *Gazette* and several others each presenting its own version of the events at Gladsmuir, or Prestonpans as one of them now prefers, but there is not a word of encouragement in any of them.

'If your customers are low in spirit now, madam,' he says, radiantly, 'you will not wish to see them when friend Scatterbuck has completed this latest edition of the *Journal*, I think. He has acquired an eye-witness account that tells how the lick-spittle officers of the English army were the first to flee the field, the men being left to their own device and ruin. I have reminded him, naturally, that he must also print the text of our Prince Regent's proclamation forbidding any to gloat at the defeat of his father's subjects.'

'That would be salt in our wounds indeed, sir. Yet I hazard that you should not have agreed to this meeting were you entirely sanguine about the manner in which the wheels are turning. And perhaps we should join Mister

Rivers? He has been waiting some time and wishes to make the journey back to Liverpool today. It will be arduous yet he should reach his bed before midnight if we do not detain him over-long.' Titus bends his knee once again. He has a certain grace, she finds, for his forty-five years. Quite recovered from the attack upon him last year. Almost *more* than recovered. Rejuvenated, she might say. 'And I trust that you will not object to conducting our discussion here, rather than in my rooms. It would...'

She had intended to say that it would attract more attention from her customers if their gathering seemed too private, but the inner voice of the Sydenham's speaks rather that it would hardly be appropriate to meet in the very room where she has so frequently fucked his daughter. So she leads him to the booth-like corner, just away from the hearth, where Mister Rivers is already seated. They have earlier spent a half-hour in their own debate about the proposal, and broadly agree its efficacy. But will Redmond share their vision? Well, he is come at least.

'Mister Redmond,' she says, 'allow me to name Mister Rivers of Liverpool. Mister Rivers, this is Mister Titus Redmond, of whom I have spoken to you previously. A gentleman of very considerable influence in our town.'

The two men greet each other cordially enough as Crableck hobbles to the table for their orders, chocolate for Rivers and coffee for Redmond.

'Well,' says Titus, while Crableck pours their portions at the hearth, 'your note indicated that you have a proposal by which my tea business may be saved, Mistress. I must assume that a member of my family has shared with you the tragic loss of the *Götheburg*, though Our Lady be praised that the crew was largely spared. So while I thank you for your considerations, if such they were, it is hard to see how a business can be saved when it is, quite literally, entirely sunk. And Mister Rivers, I collect, could be nothing but delighted that a competitor within his trade has been so effectively removed.'

'I have always welcomed competition, sir,' Rivers replies, as their beverages are set before them. Crableck offers them each a pipe, and the Liverpool merchant accepts, asking whether they have a blend of curly cut and dark-fired. He is older than Titus, but slight of build, many of his teeth blackened, and an unpleasant breath even by general standards. 'I am an admirer of Hulme, sir. Agree with his *Treatise* entire. Free will and competition. Inextricably linked.' He spends a moment on his theme as Crableck returns once more with a pewter pot of weed and a clay, one of the house specials in its mahogany pipe-box. A tamper too, so that Rivers might begin the elaborate ritual of filling the bowl, adding a pinch of snuff from his own container. It is larger than a gentleman would normally carry in his coat and Elizabeth cannot avoid touching the thing as he sets it back upon the table. Such a handsome object. It is no *carillon à musique,* of course. But handsome, all the same.

'And your supply, Mister Redmond, may be sunk,' says Elizabeth, 'but the business itself most certainly yet floats. I beg you to hear our proposition, sir, and then judge whether it might be to our mutual benefit. As I have already said, the wheels of the world are turning in strange fashion – for all of us, I collect.'

'I may have lost the means of my enterprise, Mistress, yet this apart, and from my own viewpoint, the world seems to possess a remarkable equilibrium. The Prince Regent victorious. Cope's forces scattered to the winds. General Wade a mere relic of his former self and incapable of intervening, I imagine, to restore Hanoverian fortunes. And no other significant force able to stand in the Highlanders' path. The future appears bright, madam. And those of the Roman Faith look forward to our freedom once more.'

'The future, sir,' Elizabeth says, 'merely seems uncertain for us all. The thing may turn differently once the Duke of Cumberland and all his army return from Flanders. They are recalled, I gather.' She lowers her voice to a whisper. 'And not so bright, I think, for those many of your Faith from Whitby so recently hacked and hewn to death by their neighbours after rejoicing for the defeat of the King's foes.'

'This is not Whitby, madam,' says Titus. 'Yet I will hear the proposition.'

'Well, sir, I am not a political man,' Rivers replies, setting down the long clay pipe a moment. 'A no-faction sort of fellow. But the proposition is simple and obvious. As things stand, I trade currently through a Bristol merchant, purchasing tea supplied diligently by the India Company. Our *own* India Company. The tea is shipped from Bristol to Liverpool on coastal vessels. My coffees and cocoas, my chocolates, come direct to Liverpool from the New World, arriving in the holds of dependable ship-owners returning from their voyages to Africa and thence to the Americas before journeying home. There is now an opportunity for my own expansion, filling demand in the market that your late misfortune will soon leave unsatisfied. Mistress Cooper, meanwhile, has aspiration to expand also and, as you know, has a fine head for business. Why, such is her acumen that she might almost have been a man, sirrah!' He hoots with laughter, stopping quickly when he sees that neither Titus nor Elizabeth have shared his mirth. 'Well, as I say. Acumen, sir. Since she already purchases her other commodities,' he lifts his saucer of chocolate in salute to her, 'from myself, her plan is simply to resume supply of tea for this fine establishment from my warehouses, yet reach an understanding with yourself so that she may deliver to your own considerable list of customers also.'

'And Mistress Cooper,' says Titus, 'will then persuade my customers that they should purchase their coffee and chocolate from a single source, reduce supply costs and increase their margins. For your own part, you acquire a score of the additional outlets for your goods that include many of the best coffee houses outside London itself. Yet am I missing the two most obvious flaws in your proposal, madam?'

'Only two, Mister Redmond?' she says. 'La! Then I assume you mean, first, the reason that Mister Rivers does not prosecute this opportunity without my own modest involvement and, second, the less than obvious benefit that might accrue to your good self and, therefore, cause you to even consider enabling us to access your customers. For I am certain, sir, knowing the manner of many of them, that they will not transfer their allegiance to another supplier without some strong recommendation or cause.' Indeed not. For she has tested this possibility already, some little time since. From the moment that the Redmonds had begun to pay their Excise duties – or, at least, sufficient of them to create a more respectable and legitimate air for their enterprise – she had wondered about the future for her own enterprise. And she had imagined a dozen situations in which she might persuade Titus to either sell or share this side of his business. Yet it was clear from her own knowledge that those owning the coffee houses that Titus supplies, those in Edinburgh, Carlisle, Harrogate, Bristol and others, are themselves staunch Jacobites or, at least, strong Tories, happy to support their Cause whilst turning a tidy profit too. 'Mister Rivers may account for his own part in the thing,' she continues, whilst the second point I am happy to set before you. Effectively, I would purchase supplies of tea from Mister Rivers, supply my own needs and those of your previous customers, and persuade them to deal with him for their other merchandise, myself acting as his agent. To do so, I shall need warehouse space, sir. My proposal is, therefore, that I should contract with *you* for that space, the use of your Fly Wagon too, naturally, paying the commercial rate currently applicable in town. In addition, I would purchase the *good will* of your business and, thereby, a list of your customers as well as a letter of recommendation from you, urging that they now trade with myself.'

'For my part,' says Rivers, 'whilst I should welcome the opportunity to develop without Mistress Cooper's participation, I am unable to do so from my existing facility and, in any case, I am given to believe that you would have been unlikely to receive such an approach from myself in any amicable fashion. Besides, I have ambition elsewhere, Mister Redmond. I have been contemplating the thing for some time and unless I make incursions at this point, I fear I shall miss the opportunity altogether. The Cunliffes, the ship-owners of whom I spoke, can barely meet the requirements of their particular trade, one in which Liverpool has already outstripped both London and Bristol, yet still with no more than twenty ships each year bound for the Africa trade. Some financier friends of mine estimate that the town could support perhaps twice that number over the next ten years, demand being so great. And new opportunities, they say, along the Bight of Benin. Demand opening, too, in the Carolinas and beyond. No, sir, this modest proposal of which we speak shall do no more than keep the butter spread thin upon my loaf.'

Elizabeth recalls the Night Soil Men, their own comment about bread and butter.

'You mean the trade in slavery, Mister Rivers?' Titus says. 'I have to say that I find the thing abhorrent.'

'Abhorrent, sir? Why, there is a natural order between master and servant, Mister Redmond, established by the decree of God Almighty. It is sanctioned and endorsed in the Bible, is it not? Both Old Testament and New. Genesis to Revelation.' *Ah, Revelation once more!* 'It is an order existing through the ages, in every advanced civilisation,' Rivers continues. 'Besides, what better way to free the heathen from his heresy and bring him to the Word of God? And better, surely, to bring these fellows safe to the well-organised sanctuary of plantations under European ownership than leave them to the mercy of Mahometans who would see them treated very differently indeed.'

'I hear tales, Mister Rivers,' says Titus, 'of families indiscriminately separated. Of brutal treatment towards those taken aboard the slave ships. Of inhuman conditions to be endured during the voyages and beyond. And none of these justified, I think, by the practise of slavery being equally practised amongst their own African races or, indeed, amongst the Mahometans. No, sir, if you must make profit in such a way then say as much honestly and without invoking the good name of Our Lord.'

'Yet such profit indeed, sir,' says Rivers. 'Why, the Cunliffes are making regular profit in excess of three hundred per cent on each voyage. And the value of the trade to our nation's economy, my friend! You cannot dispute this, surely, regardless of the name under which the country is governed? Think about guns alone. Tens of thousands exported as trade goods to Africa each year, the benefits all accruing to the manufacturers in Birmingham. But do you know the principal item with which the Cunliffe's are able to purchase their goods, sir? Why, it is fustian, Mister Redmond. Good fustian, manufactured by gentlemen like yourself. And you may not simply dismiss the Lord's blessing on this trade when the Church is such a beneficiary, at the Codrington Plantation in Barbados, for example. No, Mister Redmond, it will not answer. And do you not know that Liverpool town has only recently equipped a regiment of militia on the proceeds? Eight hundred blue-coats already under arms and... Oh, my goodness!'

Elizabeth has kicked him sharply under the table.

'It is a fortunate thing, Mister Rivers,' says Titus, 'that Mistress Cooper has not suggested a formal partnership arrangement between us, since I should have to decline. But as I understand matters, Elizabeth, you propose simply to be my tenant in regard to the warehouse and to pay me appropriately for the right to assume my business and its customers. So, how *appropriately*, I wonder?'

'I think that it will serve neither of us to haggle over the matter, Mister Redmond,' she says, 'so I shall come immediately to the point. My offer, sir, is four hundred guineas.'

'Four hundred, you say? But my business generates considerably more than that!'

'Tea brings you four thousand pounds each year, I understand,' says Elizabeth, while Titus makes a theatrical display of banging the tip of his walking cane loudly on the floor. He looks to the door again, shakes his head sadly as if smoked. 'Most of that amount destined for Jacobite coffers, and I assure you that every customer in this room finds the fact equally abhorrent. Yet you can only create such an amount by using your own existing warehouse and workers. You incur no overheads in its operation, while I would need to pay those costs, transport too, and employ a Factor and labourers who can operate the business on my behalf. I estimate that five hundred guineas would be the effective gain from the enterprise during its first year at least. I shall receive no return until considerably later. In any case, your business may have generated such amounts previously, yet they shall not do so in future, given the predicament of your supplies. But there are less obvious benefits to each of us, I think?'

'I could find an alternative supplier, and the *Götheburg* was not the only Swedish Company vessel due to complete its return trip from Canton. We could wait. Yet I am intrigued by these other benefits of which you speak.'

'By the time that any alternatives become available, sir, your customers will have been pressed, regardless of their loyalties, to find their own. And I doubt, sir,' says Elizabeth, 'that you would have entered my establishment if you had not already considered the other benefits open to us. You seek… How shall we name it? Acceptance? Yet you shall never achieve it while operating an enterprise so clearly linked to the seditious traditions of the town, and this is regardless of whoever may claim the throne. Rights you may undoubtedly acquire yet the new ruling class, those wielding mercantile power, will rest unchanged. They sit around you, suffering every manner of fear for their future. But the fact remains that, while the current disturbance may create some momentary imbalance in their lives, when it is done they will be as necessary to the nation as now.' She whispers again. 'While you, Mister Redmond, after the first flush of back-slapping is done, may simply be an embarrassment.'

Titus spreads his hands wide, warding off further assault upon his sensibilities.

'You see how it is, Mister Rivers?' he says. 'We fellows have been raised to believe women the weaker sex. Decorative yet crucial to the process of begetting our heirs. How duped we are! What culls! And so, Mistress Cooper, I am provided with the means to shed my association honourably. After all, I cannot be blamed for the loss of the *Götheburg* and my precious cargo, can I? And I am offered a degree of compensation. A small degree but compensation none-the-less. Rentals to collect, besides. Sums that could, if I chose, and depending upon your turning wheel, still be used to show my loyalty in this direction or that. For your own part, and that of Mister Rivers, you are able to grow your commercial ambitions whilst, dependent upon the outcome, to also either claim credit for closing down sedition's wet-nurse or, alternatively, for saving one of the faithful enterprises that have helped restore the Stuart line.'

'It is a reasonable summary, Mister Redmond,' says Rivers. 'Do you need time to consider, sir? For my own is pressing, I am afraid, and I must be upon the road. As you say, I am only a third party in this venture. The thing is, quite properly, between yourself and Mistress Cooper. Though I should like to know how the land may lie before setting out, if that is possible.'

'Then, on the assumption that Mistress Cooper and myself may reach an accommodation on the sums involved, you may take it, sir, that we have an agreement. We may not wish each other well, however, since I would not invite ill-fortune by blessing such an enterprise as that which you now contemplate, regardless of whether my own fustian trade may be an incidental beneficiary of it. And nor can I expect that a Liverpool man could tolerate the thought of success in my own Jacobite pursuits. But I may bid you a safe journey with open heart, all the same, Mister Rivers.'

It is another ten minutes before Rivers finally departs, however. Crableck finds a boy who may run to the inn and have the gentleman's horse brought around. Lengthy farewells are exchanged and advice given on how to avoid the crowds in town for Pack and Penny Day at the Fair. An article in one of the broadsheets catches his eye and he enters a short dialogue with two of the Whig merchants on the subject. But at last he has gone and Elizabeth joins Titus Redmond in the box once more.

'So, Mister Redmond, are we settled on four hundred guineas? It seems a modest enough sum to seal negotiations when it is still little more than a year since you conspired to ruin my reputation as a Collector of Excise.'

'Madam, such an accusation! Yet, when it comes to the matter of which of us has inflicted the greater pain on the other, I believe the scales might weigh heavily against you. My dear wife tells me that, in Ireland, it is still the custom to settle matters of honour, even murder, by bestowing a financial arrangement upon the offended family. She calls it *enech-lann*, I think. Perhaps we should discuss the value that we would respectively set upon my family's loss of a daughter and take account of this within our haggling.'

'It is Pack and Penny Day here, as well as the Fair, I collect! But the bid is with you, sir. I have named my price. If you believe that my association with Rosina should have some impact on the sum, then you must say so. What do you think, Mister Redmond? That I might pay some reparation to supplement the four hundred guineas? To five hundred perhaps? Or six?'

'Six hundred guineas would, I believe, be acceptable, madam.'

'Yet six has not been offered. I did not arrange your daughter's wedding, nor cause your wife's disaffection from Rosina. My offer stands at four hundred guineas, and I shall not offer a penny more. Nor can I spend all day on this issue for Michaelmas approaches and I must prepare for Quarter Day.

Besides, I might have insisted on some consideration towards that bawdy-den which adjoins the warehouse for I am not happy that an enterprise in which I am engaged should so closely be associated with such a place. But I shall have to tolerate that inconvenience whilst you, Mister Redmond, must also accept a settlement that, though less than you might wish, is the best that can be achieved.'

'Quarter Day, you say? But no quarter for Titus Redmond, I see. Cursed I am, yet know a limit when I see it. Well, Mistress Cooper, it seems that we have an agreement so I assume that you will ask Mister Liptrott to draw up the papers and I look forward to receiving your promissory note. We shall hardly be partners though perhaps, with time...'

Chapter Thirty-Nine

Striker has travelled these ruined roads between Chester and the Scottish capital three times in little over a month. But he is impressed, as always, by the prospect of this unusual town, stretching along the ridge that rises from the east, upwards towards the castle on its rocky precipice at the western extremity, streets and houses spilling steeply down the southern flank. But as he approaches Edinburgh, on this lane from Kelso, Striker realises that much has changed over the past weeks. He knows the way in which Lochiel's men had taken the gate and entered the upper districts but he had assumed that, somehow, an accommodation would by now be reached between the garrison and the Jacobite intruders. There had been much speculation on the road from Perth and Stirling about one of the castle's commanders being himself a Jacobite. So the cannon fire, the crackle of musketry and the pall of pale smoke that drifts towards him from the still distant town are unexpected. He sets his horse to a canter, presenting his credentials to the Highlanders guarding the Cowgate Port and rides up between the tall buildings of Saint Mary's Wynde to reach the Nether Bow, the very portal that the Camerons had seized while the Prince's main force was approaching the town and trying to keep from the reach of the Castle's guns. Lochiel himself, it is said, who seized the sentinel's musket with his bare hands while the townsfolk watched from open windows in the early light of dawn.

And here, this afternoon, he is met by scenes of complete chaos. He halts in the main thoroughfare, looking to his left through the town's central gatehouse, more like a small fortress with its flanking towers, crenellated battlements and square central keep of dark stone. It rises four storeys above the raised portcullis through which, fleeing towards him from the High Street, comes a desperate procession of fugitives. Women carry babes in arms, or bundles of possessions. Others townsfolk are seriously injured and collapse in small clusters as soon as they reach the sanctuary on this eastern side of the Nether Bow Port. A physician and some assistants staunch wounds, apply dressings, carry away the dead while, from away up the slope, from beyond the Church of Saint Giles, from the far side of Lawnmarket, comes the regular thunder of thirty-two pounder cannons, the intermittent crack of lighter field pieces, the rattle of small arms, and the unmistakeable crash of masonry. The stench of burning timber too, thickening smoke drifting down in acrid clouds.

Striker follows a party of clansmen, each one carrying a full array of weapons. Broadswords and studded targes, pistols, dirks, all with army muskets, presumably taken from the town's arsenal, and the further up the High Street they travel, the more Highlanders he encounters. *They must have been arriving thick and fast since I left*, he thinks. And not just Highlanders but equal numbers, it seems, from the Lowlands now, Scots still, and most sporting some token of tartan but their clothing distinct, coats and breeches.

'What is it, man?' he calls to one of them as the throng is pressed together where the Luckenbooths and the solid bulk of the Tolbooth narrow the thoroughfare past Saint Giles.

'Thae loons fra' the castle ha' fired the James's Court,' says the fellow, his accent heavy and coarse compared to the musical lilt of the Highlanders' Gaelic. And, sure enough, as they pass into the Lawnmarket, flames are licking above the roofs of the high and overcrowded tenements that enclose the square behind. But a bucket-chain has been organised from the well and reservoir, through the entrance close.

To their front, the Weigh House is also under fire from the Castle's battlements while, beyond the Weigh House itself and half-way up Castle Hill, the garrison has established some form of redoubt from which they maintain a murderous fire of musket and field-piece.

Another roundshot screeches through the air, crashing into stone-work on the other side of the tenements, unseen but deadly.

What are they doing? thinks Striker, who himself has no qualm about inflicting pain on woman or child whenever he feels the need but who still recoils from the scale of *this* barbarity.

The Prince's men who have recently arrived in the Lawnmarket make their way past the permanent stalls and take cover in and around the Weigh House or wherever opportunity presents, returning a ragged but ineffective fire upon the redoubt, while still more families flee the area.

It seems that aged General Preston is now commander of the garrison, and certainly no Jacobite. The Highlanders had cut off communication and all supplies to the Castle and Preston had threatened reprisals, a bombardment of the town. Then, in the previous week, the Prince had apparently promised to destroy the house of Preston's brother if any such attack should take place. Preston had responded by promising some additional escalation but, in the end, agreed to wait for further instructions from London before taking any other action. The townsfolk had breathed a sigh of relief but, the next day, some of those wild Highlanders had randomly fired upon the Castle and seemingly sparked all the subsequent tragedy. The Weigh House enfiladed, that building acting as a base for the Jacobite picquets. Some people killed in the street. Sallies by the garrison into the town. Twice, the fellow thinks. Some Jacobites captured. Then, last night, a sally in force, hundreds of redcoats and a wide trench dug across the Castle Hill to form the redoubt from which

392

they have kept up a steady fire ever since on anything that moves. But all the while, cannon-fire upon the easiest targets in town, the highest buildings and, therefore, the dwellings of James's Court prominent amongst them. And this afternoon, an even greater bombardment.

But Striker is aware of cannons from another direction too. He had initially thought that the grim confines of the streets were distorting reports from the Castle but now he knows that this is entirely distinct, a regular rolling fire followed by a short silence before commencing again, and coming from the direction of Leith, a couple of miles away.

Striker, however, rides out to Duddingston, near the Jacobites' main encampment, where he finds stable and lodging for the night at the Sheep Heid, though the price is excessive, accommodation now being at a premium and this particular inn having gained some celebrity since housing the Prince Regent himself on the eve of Gladsmuir.

It is too late on a long day to argue, however, so he sets down his shillings and pays for a stew, begging the innkeeper to spend a few minutes at his table.

'Is there news from Leith, Mister Sibbald?' he asks. 'It sounded like a second bombardment.'

'English frigates, sir. A fair few dead, they say,' replies the innkeeper. 'Two o' them. Opened fire on the town when they heard the garrison guns. The *Fox* and the *Ludlow Castle*, they say! Pish on the bloody English. No offence, sir.'

'I am Welsh, Mister Sibbald. But I need to see Colonel O'Sullivan. Do you know where he is now quartered?'

'Aye, at Holyrood, wi' the Prince. But he's here each mornin', sir. Bright an' early. For the review, ye understand?'

And from Sibbald he learns about the new recruits who have joined the *Chevalier* over the past two weeks. Lord David Ogilvy from Angus with six hundred men. Sir John Gordon of Glenbucket with four hundred. Four hundred and eighty more from the Gordon country of Strathbogie and Enzie. Lowlanders from the east coast, as numerous as those from the Highland Clans. Highlanders and bagpipes have replaced drums and dragoons. In total, one thousand within Edinburgh's walls, five thousand more here at Duddingston, and more expected every day.

Striker persuades the innkeeper to raise him at first light, sleeps soundly and, by seven o'the clock, he has ridden in a misty drizzle to the east of the village, the dark bulk of Arthur's Seat at his back, towards the wide area of flat common land that overlooks Duddingston Loch. The innkeeper's call had been unnecessary, of course, for the sound of an army being roused from its own slumbers can be heard from some distance under normal circumstances but, here, with the echoes of skirling pipes against the volcanic slopes and crags to the west, it is quite unmistakeable.

The camp itself is arranged around a hollow square, with some sections occupied by neatly spaced white tents and others simply scattered with carts, wagons and cooking fires, but the various regiments are uniformly assembled around the edges of the square itself, facing inwards. Striker cannot yet distinguish one regiment from another but it is not difficult to make some intelligent assumptions from his own knowledge, supplemented by the news he has gathered from Innkeeper Sibbald. In the first place, more than half of the units are not clansmen, their attire showing them to be from the Lowland areas, plain coats with breeches or leggings, a variety of headgear but many with tartan sash or blue bonnet, and even the occasional scarlet jacket, presumably taken from the field of Gladsmuir. And there are seven such units gathered here, three of them close together, so presumably the battalions of the Atholl Brigade. The others therefore the separate regiments commanded respectively by Lord Ogilvy, the Duke of Perth, Gordon of Glenbucket and John Roy Stuart, though some of these seem badly under-strength.

Then the clan regiments. There are five present today and, though he cannot tell them apart, he knows that these are led by Cameron of Lochiel, the MacDonalds of Clanranald, Glengarry and Keppoch, and Stewart of Appin. But these five men now stand, each before his own regiment, surrounded by their own henchmen and pipers, an elite bodyguard formed by the two finest warriors in each of their companies, the *leine chrios*, those who in earlier times would have been honoured and distinguished by their mail shirts, who will sacrifice their lives to protect him. Behind their chief, the clan companies stand in line, each with its own captain, every one the son of the Chieftain, or a close relative, or the chief of a smaller clan sept – for all clans are also composed of smaller sub-clans. And each company has two lieutenants with two ensigns, again, every one himself a chief's son or grandson. The companies divided into ranks, and each rank with its own status, the foremost composed of those within the clan who own land or can at least be classed as gentlemen, all decently dressed, most with tartan jackets, trews or hose. Then those with successively less claim to status so that the rear ranks are composed of the wilder folk, bearded, the tenants, the servants. Kilted, with the upper part of their drab belted plaid today pulled up and fastened about shoulders against the thin rain. But even these, Striker knows, are arranged by family, sons and brothers gathered around fathers so that the oldest and most revered will always be closest to the enemy. And here there are more ancient weapons alongside the modern muskets. Two-handed broadswords and those vicious Lochaber axes, the long pole-arm so favoured by many clansmen.

He had come to know some of these men on the march from Perth, surprised to learn how few of them were Papists, as the Government would have everybody believe, and just how many were Episcopalian. On the other hand, far more of the Clans were opposed to the Jacobites than had come out on their behalf. So the Pretender's army was then small, better organised than Cope's Englishmen perhaps, but lacking a scale to make them seem a serious threat.

Well, he thinks, *Gladsmuir has changed all that! And five thousand here, not including the men stationed in town. They are becoming formidable despite their lack of gold and silver. I must advise Newcastle as soon as possible.*

The review is already under way, the Prince and his generals riding from regiment to regiment, company to company, pausing often to exchange a greeting, to seek an opinion. Colonel O'Sullivan and Lord George Murray are with him, a small mounted escort too, though there is yet no evidence of other cavalry amongst the Jacobite forces. Several small field-pieces, however, line the square's centre, also *souvenirs* of the victory at Gladsmuir.

Striker maintains his distance while, the review complete, one of the Prince's entourage, an equerry, rides forward to read several proclamations, only one of which seems to have much significance and that the announcement that Colonel O'Sullivan, in recognition for his gallant service and his fervour, along with Lochiel, in seizing the Nether Bow Port, shall be made Quartermaster-General to the Royal Army in addition to his duties as Adjutant to His Highness. All Colonels of Regiments and Battalion Commanders to meet as customary in Council at ten o'clock. And the assembly dismissed. But there seem very few who receive news of O'Sullivan's promotion with good grace and Lord George Murray seems positively outraged. Some of the clan chiefs join him and appear to be remonstrating with Charles Edward while O'Sullivan receives some sparse congratulations.

'Give you joy of your promotion, Colonel,' says Striker as he edges his mount alongside the Irishman. They had met when Striker first discovered the Prince's column near Perth three weeks previously. 'And my apologies, sir, for failing to report last evening when I arrived in town. But there was such commotion and the journey north had been tiresome.'

'Ah! Mister Owen, is it not? Bid you good morning, and I thank you for your congratulations, right enough,' says the Irishman. 'Though there seem to be few who share your felicitation. And yesterday evening? Sure, the bombardment. Of course. Well, at least the fires were all extinguished. You delivered the instructions to Sir Watkin, I gather?'

'Indeed, sir, and he will report as you require. Meanwhile, he has begun to plan for an advance on Chester in the event that he is called upon to undertake such action. But does that signify, Colonel, that His Royal Highness is now determined on an invasion of England?'

'It is too early to speculate, Mister Owen. And there are many about us who seek to persuade him that he should merely consolidate his position here, claiming only the throne of Scotland. But we shall see! Meanwhile, we must put your skills to better use, sir. We are building an intelligence service that, I hope, shall rival that of the French. In any case, we must be more than a match for Newcastle, eh?' *Oh, I am certain that we can manage that,* thinks Striker, while O'Sullivan turns in his saddle towards the Prince's party. 'Sir John.

A moment if you please.' O'Sullivan is a handsome fellow for his forty-five years, dressed plainly with a tricorne sat neatly upon a short wig. He is rubicund, and made more so by the reddened nostrils and thick voice that mark him as suffering presently from a constipation of the head. Indeed, as Sir John brings his horse about to join them, the Irishmen places a finger to his nose and hawks a thick gobbet of phlegm to the ground. 'Feckless English weather,' he says, seemingly oblivious of his actual location. 'Sir John, allow me to name Mister Owen, the Welshman of whom I spoke. A gentleman volunteer. Indeed he is! Mister Owen, I have the pleasure of naming Sir John McDonald who shall command a significant squadron of horse for us – if only they can find their way from France, eh, Sir John?'

Striker knows there have been large numbers of the French Irish Brigade attempting to arrange passage and join the Prince from the day they took news of his landing at Eriskay. But, so far, few have materialised.

'The Wild Geese shall wing their way home in due course, sir, never fear!' says Sir John, a slender man, weather-beaten with a liverish scar on his left cheek, who shares none of O'Sullivan's jocosity. His accent is a curious mixture of Scots, Irish and French. 'So you are to join my picquets, Mister Owen? More precisely, Colonel O'Sullivan has requested that you should join our Company of Rangers. It is a privilege, sir, to be so nominated, for they are all Chosen Men.'

'Then I hope I shall not disappoint, Sir John,' says Striker. He has seen French rangers at work in the Colonies, the *coureurs des bois*, sometimes fur trapping down far into the south and, though not loved by the Montreal authorities, often also acting as unofficial surveyors and agents for them. He understands at once the source from which O'Sullivan and Sir John have drawn inspiration for their new company.

'Oh, I do not brook disappointments, Mister Owen. *Trooper* Owen, I should say. The accurate gathering of intelligence for His Royal Highness is worth a dozen battalions. And you have joined us at a propitious moment, sir, for this evening we have a peculiar duty to perform.'

'Trooper Owen has been upon the road for some weeks about our business, Sir John,' says O'Sullivan. 'Might I suggest that we allow him today so that he can refresh himself?' The beginnings of a sneeze disrupt his flow and he reaches to his coat pocket for a kerchief, releasing the repressed expulsion with a violence that almost causes him to fall from his mount. 'Shall he be quartered here or in the town?' he asks, recovering himself.

'Here, Colonel, I think! The town is already full to overflowing.' MacDonald gestures to a small knot of dismounted riders, variously clothed and combining dragoon and clansman both, in their dress. 'Angus Mór,' he shouts, 'so that the youngest but tallest of the fellows mounts and trots to join them. 'This is *Lieutenant* McDonald. He will show you to your quarters and you may then pass the day as you please, but you shall join us at four, sharp, in the Abbey Close.' He turns to the young man. 'This is Trooper Owen, Lieutenant. He joins your company though he is a Welshman. Make sure that he is quartered and provision made for his beast. Introduce him to the others. Gentlemen, you are dismissed!'

And Sir John, in company with O'Sullivan, wheels his horse to re-join the Prince.

'Come!' says Angus Mór MacDonald. 'I will show you to your mess.' But he pauses when huzzahs, an outburst of cheering from the western edge of the encampment heralds the arrival of further clansmen. 'More of Lochiel's men. And MacDonalds of Keppoch.'

'Yet more MacDonalds, Lieutenant. You are a numerous clan, indeed. And Sir John…?'

'My father, Mister Owen. And not truly one clan, but several. Now, this way.' He leads Striker to the farther end of the camp, where horse lines are prepared and, close to these, a cluster of standard-issue tents, each seven feet long and six feet in height. 'Here,' he says, indicating one of the tents. 'This mess needs a fifth man. There are three of my kinsmen here, and a Northumbrian, Radcliffe by name. He will show you what is expected and arrange any equipment that you might need, though I expect you already have blanket roll and forage bags. We have no farrier but you will find the army's blacksmiths easily enough. And remember! Four o'the clock at Abbey Close.'

Striker thanks the Lieutenant, who returns to his own duties, but finding none of his mess-mates within the tent, he makes the short ride back into town, stabling his horse near Holyrood and taking from his portmanteau only those items that he needs for the day.

A short walk up the High Street brings him near the Physicians' Hall of the College and the famous Musaeum of Rarities, Doctor Balfour's remarkable collection of scientific and medical books, curiosities and instruments, the like of which is not matched anywhere else in Europe – at least, not according to the sign near the entrance. Within, Striker finds an almost deserted reading room where he is able to compose a lengthy dispatch to Newcastle. He uses a code, also based on shorthand, but the Timothy Bright system, so much older than Byrom's. A brief account of his travels. Confirmation that he has collected the article from Manchester. Confirmation, too, that he has fulfilled his tasks in Lancashire and arranged for any significant discoveries to be conveyed to Sir Edward. Then details of the Jacobite forces, their disposition at Duddingston. A second letter, to Chester, with instructions that any correspondence arriving there by the fifteenth instant should be forwarded to the post office in Edinburgh, ensconced within the White Hart. He folds his dispatch inside the letter, sets both into an envelope addressed to his contact, and conveys this to the White Hart itself. There are risks, but he should be able to overcome them and he doubts that O'Sullivan's team of intelligence gatherers is yet sufficiently sophisticated to spy upon itself.

The day passes quickly, and he returns, as ordered, to the Abbey Close at around a quarter to four o'the clock noticing, as he does so, that Jacobite picquets are gathered near the Nether Bow, where the smell of woodsmoke is still heavy, keeping the area clear of townsfolk despite their complaints. In the Close itself, a crowd of spectators has assembled, aware that matters are afoot, since eight small companies of heavily armed troops have been paraded, half of them Highlanders, and the whole numbering perhaps two hundred. In the centre, their officers are being briefed by two obviously more senior commanders whilst, away to one side, stand O'Sullivan, Sir John MacDonald with Angus Mór and a dozen others.

'Owen,' says the Irishman, 'fall in with these other gentlemen, if you please.' His eyes look heavy with the ague that plagues him, and Striker pushes himself between his new comrades, many dressed in civilian attire but a few, like Angus, in the uniform of dragoons to which tartan jacket or trews have been added. 'Yet we are all assembled, I collect,' O'Sullivan continues. '*Ça va!* Let me outline our intentions, for this afternoon we must take that damnable redoubt. Or rather, Lochiel and Glenbucket shall take it.' He nods in the direction of the two senior officers, still occupied with instructions to their captains and lieutenants. Donald Cameron of Lochiel seems a similar age to O'Sullivan, short-browed and with a harsh mouth despite his reputation as a kindly leader. He wears a full black coat, trews and his own hair tied back with dark ribbon. He could be mistaken for the Lowland gentleman while John Gordon of Glenbucket, by comparison, is bent with the rheumatic weight of his seventy-three years and swathed entirely in belted plaid, his wild grey mane hanging in damp tangles around his grizzled face. 'Your task, gentlemen,' continues O'Sullivan, when he has outlined the rest of the plan, 'is to follow behind the main assault and ensure that we have a considerable number of prisoners, some of whom we may wish to interrogate.'

'Lord George shall not be joining us, I collect?' says Sir John.

'No, sir. He believes the operation to be foolhardy, like most of my proposals. Now, are there questions?'

Striker looks around his companions, all of whom remain perfectly mute. 'And after the trench, Colonel?' he asks, emphasising his Welsh accent. 'What then? Might we not be able to force the Castle itself?'

'Indeed not! We take the trench and no more. I admire your spirit, Owen, but such an action *would* be foolhardy. The cost would be considerable. No, His Royal Highness wants an end to the misery being inflicted on the townsfolk but General Preston shall insist, we think, on the blockade of the Castle being lifted before he will terminate the bombardment. We therefore need a small victory that will allow the Prince to show some magnanimity in the affair. Perhaps an exchange of prisoners to sweeten the negotiation too.'

And to save his face, thinks Striker. O'Sullivan studies his time-piece, sees that Lochiel and Glenbucket have finished addressing their subordinates and that these, in turn, are now issuing a summary of the instructions to their respective companies.

They wait in silence while O'Sullivan inspects his dozen men once more, his eyes finally alighting on Striker. 'Why, Mister Owen,' he cries, '*je suis désolé!* We have not troubled to arm you, I see.'

Striker has his paring knife, naturally, and that wicked little turn-off piece that so admirably dispatched Driscoll, but these are well-hidden, while his brace of fine pistols remain deep within his portmanteau. 'No, Colonel,' he says, drawing himself to some form of attention.

'Then, Lieutenant MacDonald, if you please,' says the Irishman, causing Angus Mór to draw one of the long and ornate guns from his own belt and hand it to Striker. O'Sullivan checks his time-piece once more, signals to Glenbucket and Lochiel, who set their companies to trotting up the hill. '*Carpe diem*, gentlemen,' O'Sullivan cries, when the others are all on the move. '*Carpe diem*. And good fortune, Sir John!' He stands aside as Sir John MacDonald leads the dozen picquets into the High Street some little distance behind the main body, and they are soon at the round towers of the Nether Bow, smoke visible in profusion on the far side but more spectators also, leaning from upstairs windows and variously shouting either words of encouragement or thinly veiled abuse.

Delay, as the companies are led through the gate and Striker has the chance to take stock of his position. He had not expected to face such clear danger so soon in his mission but there can be little threat from the task of collecting prisoners and, anyway, he has this fine pistol of Angus Mór's to protect him, though it is no use without powder and shot to load it.

'I expect that you shall return my weapon in good order once the quartermaster has issued your own,' says the Lieutenant, passing him a pouch and horn, spare equipment it seems from another amongst these Chosen Men. 'Radcliffe! Owen joins your mess. Make sure that he is prepared.'

He means, make sure that I know how to load the thing. So he removes his hat, clutching it between his knees, and pulls his coat up, over his head, to provide temporary shelter from the damp, checks flint and touch-hole, sets the lock to half-cock, opens frizzen. Ten grains in the pan, no more, no less. Frizzen closed. Barrel upwards, charge, ball and wadding, all rammed home. He hefts the loaded weapon. A heavy Dragoon pistol, probably four pounds in weight, well-balanced for its twenty inch length. A whimsical affair with raised and engraved carving around lock and trigger guard, its butt cap large enough to act as a skull-breaker and the long ears serving as reinforcement for the stock.

'Ye' have done this before then,' remarks the man, Radcliffe, a Northumbrian, as Angus Mór had earlier told him but now confirmed by his accent.

'A few times,' Striker replies, pushing the pistol back into his belt and easing the coat back onto his shoulders.

'Aye, and not much to say for yersel'. Why, man, they say that ye'r from Wales. Gi' me thy hand then. I'm Radcliffe. Charlie Radcliffe.' The fellow extends a hand but Striker chooses to ignore it. In any case, it is time for Sir John's small band to follow the last of Glenbucket's men as they disappear through the Nether Bow Port. They run up the High Street, between the grey gloom of the tenements, past the Fountain Close well, the Tron Kirk with its wooden spire, the closes to Fleshmarket and Fishmarket, the Cross. More delays as the companies are restricted by the Luckenbooths and the Tolbooth, before emptying into the Lawnmarket near the first of its square stone well-heads. The smoke is thicker here, pouring from a close at the upper end of the space and supplemented by the gunfire that plays back and forth between Weigh House, trench and Castle. Musketry and the heavy roar of cannon from the battlements.

Angus Mór takes a glass from his pocket, a slender thing of brass and leather. He snaps it open and peers through the pale clouds. 'Auch, the old devil himself,' he cries. 'Preston! Why, the fellow is eighty-seven, they say. And needs to be wheeled about in a bath chair. But there he is, plain as day.'

And Lochiel's men are now forming against the right side of the Lawnmarket, one behind the other in extended line, taking whatever cover the buildings will afford, while Glenbucket's fellows do the same on this left side. Muskets are slung across backs for the most part, for this attack will be a hand-to-hand engagement with sword and pole-arms, though some of the Lowlanders have bayonets screwed to guns and many have pistol at the ready.

More waiting, the crash and whine of gunnery increasing until, at last, Lochiel raises his broadsword, yells a war cry taken up by his followers.

It is a bloody business, brisk and brutal.

At the stroke of five, on Donald Cameron's signal, the Highlanders furthest back from the Weigh House begin to break from the cover of alley and doorway, wall and window, slanting diagonally across the thoroughfare, followed by those progressively nearer the enemy redoubt. The effect is that of a door, swinging to close the street but then, once shut, gathering pace in a wild charge towards the English line. And, once moving, they are followed by Glenbucket's Lowlanders, the old fellow himself hobbling at their head. They hinge outwards too, forming a second wave just behind the clansmen.

The manoeuvres are well-executed but do not altogether allow for the narrowing of their approach as they squeeze past the Weigh House into the lower end of Castle Hill so that Highlander and Lowlander alike become bunched, their momentum slowed.

Striker's companions, a thin third wave, do not share this problem being so few in number, and he can see tolerably well the progress made by the leading ranks. For the first fifty yards of their advance they are protected by friendly fire from the upper stories of tall houses to left and right but, for the second, as these volleys slacken to avoid hitting their comrades below, the trench ahead becomes suddenly alive with scarlet coats and well-directed musketry brings down a dozen or more kilted Jacobites.

Within minutes, Striker and Angus Mór's men are stepping over their bodies but, by now, Lochiel has reached the trench. The musketry ceases almost entirely, the occasional shot, pistols discharged, but mostly replaced by the clash of steel on steel. Thrust and hack. Cut, slice and bludgeon. The Englishmen at a serious disadvantage, butchered where they stand, initially too tight-packed in the trench to escape its confines, their blood pooling almost ankle-deep in its lowest levels. Several more of the Jacobites dead also, but now the officer commanding the redoubt is surrendering his sword to Lochiel.

It seems to be a complete and speedy victory, as Sir John MacDonald moves forward, motioning for his scouts to begin gathering their captives, calling his congratulations to Glenbucket.

Yet, suddenly, the Castle gate is thrown open and a company of redcoats sallies forth while the cannons upon the walls fire both round-shot and grape, though this inflicts damage only upon their own men, currently trying to climb from the back of the trench at the same time as Striker and his companions reach the front.

The more immediate danger, however, comes from the Jacobites' left flank where another group of English soldiers, who must have earlier sequestered themselves in the tenement alongside the redoubt, suddenly appear at windows and lay down a volley into the Scotsmen.

Angus Mór is thrown backwards from the parapet and straight into Striker's arms and he, Striker, drags the Lieutenant towards the rear seeing, at the same moment, the English officer renouncing his parole by seizing his sword afresh from Lochiel's surprised hands and aiming a treacherous blow at the Camerons' Chieftain. Lochiel parries, turns the fellow's blade, and they are pushed apart as the trench becomes a heaving mass of confusion, some of the redcoats following their officer's bellicose example, while others still try to escape.

Striker sets Angus Mór upon the ground as gently as possible, noting that the young man is gut-shot, with both plaid and dragoon jacket already showing a darkening stain around the upper part of his abdomen. The Lieutenant grasps his hand, mutters some indistinct words, thanks perhaps, before Striker is pushed aside by the man's kinsmen.

Firing has now commenced once more from those tenements occupied by the Jacobites while some of Glenbucket's men, having cleared their own section of the trench, have established a defensive line along its rear edge so that, between these two sources, the sally is stalled, disrupted too by the steady stream of Englishmen running back to the Castle's protection.

Fighting in the trench continues, though it is an uneven contest with a desperate and outnumbered group of soldiers rallied around the same officer, his only advantage now being the redcoats still holding the adjacent building and maintaining a steady fire on the Jacobites below. And the Jacobites, Striker notes while crouching low to avoid the randomly flying musket balls, can do little about this particular menace from within the trench itself. But there are still men here, around its edges, most tending fallen friends or simply sheltering from the musketry. Well, he is damn'd if he will stay here to be shot like a duck in a barrel and he cannot, in all conscience, simply slide away, much as he may prefer to do so. Anyway, there is always some hidden advantage to be gained from the occasional rash act.

Striker stands, draws Angus Mór's pistol from his belt, raises it high.

'Angus Mór!' he cries, so that those around the fallen Lieutenant look up in surprise. 'MacDonald's Rangers!' he cries once more, feeling foolish and wishing that he could have conjured something more imaginative.

And then, not knowing whether he is followed or not, he pounds across the lane, along the parapet edge and, still unscathed, skirts the side of the trench onto the narrow section of street-level paving that separates tenement from redoubt.

He ducks instinctively beneath the first window although, in truth, this is just above the height of his head in any case and, pushing the pistol back into his belt, he reaches up to grasp the barrel of a musket that has just appeared above him. He does not succeed in taking it, however, although the soldier inside applies so much effort in pulling the weapon from Striker's grasp that it discharges harmlessly into the air.

Drawing the pistol once again, he turns his back to the wall and is gratified to see that he is steadily being joined by others from his company, including the Northumbrian, Radcliffe. 'Mind yersel'!' shouts the fellow, pointing to the window.

Striker looks upwards, sees a soldier's head and shoulders above him, a musket being brought to bear. But before he can use his own weapon, a shot from elsewhere has shattered the top of the redcoat's head, splashing gore and the mess of his brain down upon Striker's upturned face. He wipes a sleeve across his nose and mouth, then reaches the few steps leading up to the building's front door. But he gets no further. for the other Rangers are now clustered about him, rushing the steps and entering the house to clear it while Sir John, obviously believing Striker wounded, takes his arm and urges him to sit.

'Nobly done, Owen,' MacDonald says to him. 'Nobly done indeed!'

Sir John leaves him there, leaps down into the trench where Lochiel has now, for the second time, received the English officer's surrender.

The rest, as Striker would say, is mere history.

The prisoners are taken, a score of them including their Captain. Twice this number dead or seriously wounded, while a further forty have escaped back to the Castle. From the dozen who had hidden themselves in the tenement, not one survives.

Amongst the Jacobites, thirty are dead or wounded. Angus Mór still lives but his friends have no faith that he will last the night, and only then in the greatest agony.

There are congratulations from O'Sullivan, quickly upon the scene and writing a hasty note for General Preston's attention, to be delivered by one of the prisoners, offering a truce of one hour so that the English may collect their fallen.

Meanwhile, the two light field pieces, which had served no real purpose in the struggle, are taken from the redoubt and removed to Duddingston, while the trench itself is freshly garrisoned by a company of Glenbucket's men.

Later in the day, the Pretender issues a formal proclamation, proposing that the blockade of the Castle shall be lifted on condition that there shall be no further belligerent acts on the part of either party and the redoubt on Castle Hill to be demolished, the thoroughfare returned to its original condition. The eighty-seven year old General Preston graciously accepts the conditions, having gained from the negotiation precisely that which he desired.

The Welshman, William Owen, returns to Duddingston camp and the five-man mess tent that he must now share with Radcliffe, a troublesome cove, one of those who takes rejection of proffered friendship merely as a challenge to renewed effort. He insists on relieving Striker from the tedium of preparing the mess kettle whenever it is William Owen's turn at that duty. He sees it as his personal responsibility to familiarise Owen with every detail of camp life, accompanies him to the quartermaster and ensures that he is well-equipped with musket, pistols and hanger.

So Radcliffe has his uses. And, from him, Striker learns a great deal about the army's leaders. O'Sullivan, for example. A native of County Kerry it seems, and sent abroad at the age of fifteen to be educated for the priesthood. Yet chose a military life instead, becoming secretary to the French Marshal Maillabois, whose son he also tutored. He had seen active service in Corsica and elsewhere, gaining a reputation as an expert in irregular warfare, the use of surprise and ambuscade in which small bodies of men might hold down entire battalions.

'They say that Maillabois was in his cups most o' the day and night,' Radcliffe tells him, 'while wor' bonnie lad, O'Sullivan, had to take up most o' his duties!'

In the course of his service, the Irishman had been introduced to Charles Edward's father and so impressed him with his skills that O'Sullivan had later been asked to join the Young Pretender's household as his Adjutant.

Radcliffe, however, seems to have little regard for Lord George Murray, six years older than O'Sullivan and had served as an ensign with the Royal Scots though, according to the Northumbrian, never seen action with them. Then he had come out for the Jacobites in the Year '15 but had been busy gathering his taxes during the main engagement at Sheriffmuir. Out again four years later and taken part in the scuffle at Glenshiel though Radcliffe has never met anybody who could tell him whether His Lordship had actually struck a blow in anger.

'Aye, and some blither about service with the army o' Sardinia, though it's all in his mind, I reckon. Been farming his estates in Atholl ever since and hoying himself at the Hanover pack every chance he gets. Too prone to turning his coat for my likin', man!'

But he seems to have a genuine admiration for the Prince, admits that Charles Edward may have only seen action at the Siege of Geta and then at Dettingen, but the military life comes naturally to him, says Radcliffe. To the manor born, you might say.

'An' ye know the main thing?' No, says Striker, tell him. 'He's lucky!'

Well, there can be no denying the fellow on that score. Radcliffe may be showing a certain bias, but he firmly believes that it will be O'Sullivan and the Prince who will lead them to victory, supported by the Duke of Perth, of course. James Drummond, the third Earl of Perth, had been named as joint commander of the army alongside Lord George Murray, partly in recognition for the work he had undertaken on behalf of the Stuart Cause in mobilising support within Scotland.

And that work continues to pay dividends for, over the coming week, eighty light cavalry are raised in Edinburgh itself, and put under the command of John Murray of Broughton. Then Lord Pitsligo arrives, on the ninth, a fervent Episcopalian, with over one hundred horse and three hundred foot from Aberdeen, to be attached to the Duke of Perth's Regiment.

Two days later, and the arrival of both Gordon of Aberlour and Stuart of Tinninnar, bringing with them two companies of foot from Banffshire.

On the thirteenth, McKinnon and his Clan, with one hundred and twenty more, and followed by a stream of deserters from Johnny Cope's defeated army.

And all this while, Angus Mór still lives. A surgeon has removed the ball, satisfied that it appears to have damaged no vital organs but also that he had been able to extract the pieces of clothing carried into the wound by the bullet's entry. But the Lieutenant remains cruelly weak. Striker has returned the pistol to him, in good order as the Scot had demanded, and received a whispered rebuke for 'tipping it the hero' but he finds his hand taken once more, William Owen thanked for his care.

The daily inspection of the army continues, although the Rangers are frequently absent from the ranks, being dispatched to gather intelligence. There is a growing anxiety within the encampment about this long delay at Edinburgh. Views are divided on whether the Prince should march at once on England or whether he should, at the very least, secure the borders of Scotland itself. But, in either case, knowledge about the movement of Hanoverian forces is paramount in importance.

So William Owen is variously engaged on a raid into Berwickshire to capture horses from some notable Whiggish families, on a survey of Berwick itself to assess the town's state of readiness and defence against possible Jacobite incursion, and on a covert assignment to Newcastle-upon-Tyne where he gathers intelligence about the remnants of Cope's army gathered there to lick its wounds. And, with every successful mission, Sir John MacDonald's confidence in his abilities is enhanced.

Then, on the fourteenth day of October, with the weather turning distinctly towards winter, there is significant news at Duddingston. For an entourage has arrived at Holyrood, no less a personage than the personal representative of Louis the Fifteenth, the Marquis d'Eguilles, Alexandre de Boyer. He had landed at Montrose during the previous week and made the journey to Edinburgh unheralded but he brings news of other vessels, privateers, two already in Montrose itself and two more with instructions to land at Peterhead, between them carrying four thousand guineas in gold, twelve hundred muskets, six field pieces and a dozen French artillerymen.

And there is more. King Louis apparently due to sign a treaty by which the French will no longer recognise Hanoverian George as King of England but acknowledging James the Eighth as ruler of Scotland and England both, so long as Parliament should accept the restoration. In addition, France would send further elements of the Irish Brigade for Charles Edward's assistance. Plans, too, for a French invasion. Ten thousand men, they say, being readied to sail for the English channel ports.

The news trickles into camp though it is impossible to tell the extent of speculation, exaggeration or simple fabrication in its telling.

Other intelligence seems more reliable, however.

The Earl of Stoneywood has captured Aberdeen for the Jacobites.

The encampment itself to be disbanded, with most of the army removed to billets within the town, though whether this will dissuade the Highlanders from their deplorable habit of sleeping on open ground wrapped in their plaids is another matter.

Reports of a Hanoverian Council of War. Field Marshal Wade, now in his seventy-second year, given eleven thousand men to confront the Jacobite army here in the north. Lieutenant General Sir John Ligonier to assemble a further eleven thousand at either Chester or Nottingham. Dutch and Swiss reinforcements brought from Flanders along with all of Cumberland's battalions not needed on the Continent.

Further arrivals to bolster the Jacobite ranks too. Lord Lewis Gordon and the Master of Strathallan with three hundred Balquhidder men, Lord Lewis himself appointed to the Prince's Privy Council, made Lord Lieutenant of Aberdeenshire and Banffshire and sent north again almost immediately to recruit and to raise finances.

Striker is there to watch him ride out again, for the mess that he shares with Radcliffe and the other men is being broken up, allocated to lodgings in the town.

Colonel O'Sullivan is there also.

'Well, Trooper Owen,' he says. 'What think you? German George has his armies on the march. King Louis stirring finally to our needs. Men still gathering to our standards. *Le Prince Edouard* almost persuaded at last to advance on England. And the Irish Brigade on their way to help us. The Wild Geese are winging home at last! The Lord praise them. And what more could the world offer us, d'you think? Well, one more thing perhaps.' He holds in his hand a scrolled document that he opens carefully. 'This is a Royal Warrant, sir, signed by Charles, Prince of Wales, Regent of the Kingdoms of England, Scotland, France and Ireland, and the Dominions thereunto belonging. It is dated this sixteenth day of October in the Year of Our Lord 1745, and the document, in summary, you understand, confirms that His Highness's loyal servant, one William Owen Esquire, is hereby granted a commission, with the rank of Lieutenant, within His Majesty's forces.'

Chapter Forty

A few Days since, died in Ireland Doctor Jonathan Swift, Dean of Saint Patrick's in Dublin. A genius who deserves to be ranked among the first whom the World ever saw. He possessed the talents of a Lucian, a Rabelais and a Cervantes, and in his Works exceeded them all.

Maria-Louise folds her copy of the *Journal*. Such an obituary that Mister Fielding has written, and Adam Scatterbuck has obtained a version while it is still fresh, including it as part of a special edition.

'You see, Mudge?' she says, as the damaged housekeeper clumsily clears the breakfast plates. 'Dean Swift is deceased.'

'Seedy beast,' slurs Mudge, using her sleeve to wipe some drool from her chin and displaying a crooked smirk.

'No,' says Maria-Louise. *Did the woman not attend me correctly?* 'Never mind. Are the girls ready? We must not be late.'

'Bloody housekeeper, not bastard wet-nurse!' And she is gone, dropping some of the plates as she fumbles with the door.

Why *does* she put up with Mag Mudge? It was her husband's guilt, not her own, after all, that had brought her to work for them. She has never challenged him about the thing but the story still rankles. *Damn'd bulk-mongers.*

Titus himself has left the house at first light, for this is a Wednesday, when the Fly Wagon begins its journey to Carlisle, though this week the arrangement is very different for there is no Redmond tea cargo to be loaded or dispatched. This week it will be Elizabeth Cooper's goods that fill the orders in distant coffee houses. *By the Mass, Elizabeth Cooper!* And Aran has been clear that, since she now has the trade, she can also have the labour associated with it. Yet Titus feels some obligation to assist the woman. He claims that it will fetch bad luck if he fails to do so, though he was suffering the ill-effects of gin when he told her so.

She calls the girls, for it *is* Wednesday, one of the mornings each week when her daughters now join the Byrom children at their house for private tuition with Doctor Clayton, himself taking time from his duties at Saint Cyprian's. It will not answer for much longer, of course, for they are quite grown. Still there is always her cousin in Geneva. The *other* Geneva. She might assist in finishing their education. Either that or the possibility of suitable marriage. It is an admirable arrangement for the nonce however since, of course, Wednesday morning is also the time when Rosina is away from home, at one of her harpsichord lessons with Mrs Starkey. And, since the end of July, *that* has provided Maria-Louise with the opportunity to resume her trysts with James Bradley.

So she gathers Anna-Marie, Katherine and Maeve together, checks that each of them has fastened pattens to their shoes and, having clattered down the front steps balanced upon the flat metal rings, she leads them to Hanging Ditch like a gaggle of geese, weaving and teetering their way through the mud, puddles, wind and driven autumn leaves. But Our Lady knows that she feels her age today, now in her fortieth year.

They gain admittance to the Byrom's house, having removed their pattens in the entrance hall. *Such an admirable residence.* She leaves the girls with young Dolly and enquires from the manservant whether Mister Owen is at work within the Academy. Indeed he is, madam, and would she care to visit him? He leads her down the passage and into the large room, that now seems strangely to have grown, since the six enormous wood and canvas frames have illustrated its true scale. Being at the rear of the house, it is south-facing and, despite the weather outside, the room is filled with light.

'You have seen Scatterbuck's piece on Dean Swift, I collect?' she asks as Aran turns from the furthest frame to greet her.

'Why, yes. I helped him to compose the thing. He had intended to include the entire obituary. I persuaded him to use only the least ambiguous sections. This being Fielding, he had chosen to make some odd remarks about superstition within religion, praising the good Dean for their exposure. Such a curious claim to make about so devout a Man of God. And might I now be permitted to bid you good morning, my dear?'

'Oh, give you joy, sir! I had quite forgot myself. And such boards. They are complete, I see. Yet you shall forgive me if I comment on their pungency, I trust. For I assume that their treatment is somehow the cause of these foul odours?'

'I am very much afraid that you are correct. Herringbone completed the stretcher bars, the frames, a week since and then employed a whole team of upholsterers to help with the canvas. They have been here four days now and I have attended upon them ever since, applying the *gesso* that, as you may observe has now dried. Your culprit, I fear, must be the rabbit-skin glue within the compound though I swear that the odour is positively inert compared to its heated state. But allow me to adjust this final wedge. There, all done!' He crosses the room, kisses the proffered cheek, careful not to disturb her powder and rouge. 'Whereas you, Mistress,' he says, 'have a quite distinct fragrance. Some special occasion? Not your birthing day for that was three weeks ago. Nor your name day, which is July as I collect. Ah, no. Of course! It is *Wednesday*, and you are scheduled for your weekly fuck with your son-in-law.'

'I should infinitely prefer to be fucked by an artist but none has yet offered himself to the task, though I remain confident that my ambition shall one day be fulfilled. My ambition and my appetites both. But, for now, I must seemingly content myself with an appreciation of your other talents. Doctor Swift, I believe, said that we are limited, not by our abilities, but by our vision. You certainly have the *ability* to fuck me, opportunity too, yet you lack the vision to seize the day.'

'I lack a certain courage in that direction, *cariad*, and frequently find myself overcome by an unaccountable fear of the consequences. Not fear of your husband, you understand, nor even of the scandal, but an insatiable concern that I might, on the one hand, lose respect for Titus, whom I esteem greatly, whilst on the other be entirely swept away by my devotion to *you*. I have explained this to you before. I am quite devoted to you, my dearest, but could not bear it if the floodgates of my emotions were opened and then, so to speak, left half-ajar.'

'You are a gentleman of a different epoch, Aran Owen. My father should have liked you, methinks. And I see that I must bridle my frustrations once again. But tell me, have you heard from that fellow Striker?'

'Not a word. He took Sir Watkin's ledger from me, as you know, and disappeared about his strange business. It still concerns me, though, that the Earl of Derby is so free with his comments about informants in Manchester. I do not sleep well, thinking on it.'

Aran moves to the table on which his satchel lies, removing from its folds a clay pipe that he fills with tobacco from a leather pouch. *He has become quite taken with the weed*, she thinks, though she has nothing against the habit.

'Yet you must surely know whether His Lordship continues with his rantings in that regard,' she says, 'you being such an intimate of Sir Edward's, his regular dinner companion.'

'We ate dinner once only, as you are fully aware. At your daughter's house and... Ah, Beppy my dear!'

Maria-Louise turns to find the Byrom's eldest girl in the doorway. 'Beppy, you are safe returned from your travels, I see. And such a pretty dress. It is new, is it not? Come, have you ever witnessed such grandeur as these frames upon which Aran will paint his murals?'

Beppy enters, takes the older woman's hands in greeting and offers a curtsey to Aran, who returns the gesture with a polite bow.

'Indeed not!' she says. 'La, but their odour is quite preposterous. Mama says that she should have preferred to extend our visit to Liverpool, if she had known, despite it being such a devilish Whig-ridden enclave. A good place for dress-makers, all the same. I paid twelve shillings for it But they have raised a full regiment of militia against us. Five hundred men, they say, and now rigged out in blue coats, hats and stockings. A different shade from my dress, naturally. Yet I am sure that Francis Townley cannot achieve so much here, despite his efforts. They drill the fellows every day in the town.'

'And poor Manchester little better,' says Maria-Louise, 'with redcoat companies marched almost daily through our streets. And the Presbyterians sending away everything that they hold valuable. Even their wives and children. All this and the Jacobite army still in Edinburgh. Still, I admire your new dress greatly.'

'All shall be well, I am certain,' Aran assures them. 'But shall you not view my sketches, given that the Court Leet have finally approved them. They made some extraordinary suggestions for alternatives. But Mister Bradley made great speech upon the fee of one hundred and fifty guineas, so that they could not expect to dictate the matter. Indeed, he called several of them buffoons.'

'When a true genius appears in this world,' quotes Beppy, 'you may know him by this sign. That the dunces are all in confederacy against him.'

'Dean Swift once more,' says Aran. 'I fear that he plays upon *all* our minds this day. But see…'

He leads them to a corner of the room, behind one of the frames, where a brace of stout boards protects a sheaf of papers. He unfastens the ribbon from the boards and leans the nearest against his knee so that they can view the sketches within.

'It was strange to return home and find so many things changed,' says Beppy. 'The soldiers passing through. The strange news about Mistress Cooper having taken over your husband's tea trade. And Aran awarded this wonderful commission. I give thee joy of it, friend Aran. Of all things, I do! And look. How prophetic. For here is Jonathan Swift himself, unless I am mistaken, against a depiction of Lilliput. It is not my favourite work but easily recognised, I collect.'

'I had already determined upon an allegory to display the century's great writers. Here, on another, I have Defoe. But Dean Swift shall have prominence, I think. And I may now include an extract from the verses that he wrote on the subject of his own death, though he penned them so long ago. Still, they are poignant now.'

Footsteps along the corridor and within the Academy room itself. John Byrom and Reverend Clayton, the latter dressed almost exactly as Aran had depicted him, a long scholar's gown of blue, his flaking face framed by a full-bodied wig.

'And what have we, Mister Owen?' asks Clayton, imperiously. Maria-Louise does not enjoy Clayton's company and is always surprised that he should appear to suffer such decrepitude, for he is younger than she by several years. He is also verbose, one of the few men in town who can exceed even Adam Scatterbuck for tautology. And she must not allow herself to be detained beyond ten o'clock. 'A very good morning to you, ladies,' Clayton continues. 'Ah, Swift! You shall not include him amongst the town's murals, to be sure? A profligate and unprincipled man. Hateful fellow.'

'He may not be amongst my favourite writers, Reverend,' says Beppy, 'but he has been a fine satirist. Perhaps the best in the world.'

'I am surprised to hear you say so, my dear,' John Byrom says. He stoops more with each year that passes, as though to deliberately reduce his extraordinary height to that of other mortals. She conjures a picture of that strange beast the camelopard, legs apart and long neck bent to reach its fodder. 'He speaks of women with unvaried rudeness and contempt. And they say that he caused the deaths of two, perhaps three, of the women with whom he had relationships. I had reason to study his piece entitled *A Beautiful Young Nymph*. Ghastly thing. And entirely dismissive of my friends at the Royal Society. Why, his Flying Island, this Laputa, is so obviously intended to stand for the Society and its endeavours, mocking the experiments of its members, claiming that they serve only to turn useful items into their banal and eccentric opposites.'

'I have always taken Swift's work,' says Maria-Louise, 'as setting a helpful looking-glass on the evident weakness in human nature. And you would not deny, Doctor Byrom, that some, at least, of the experiments conducted in the Society's name, are intended for any other purpose than to deceive the spectator or to promote the interests of those who present them. To inflate a dog with bellows, or to attempt the extraction of sunbeams from cowcumbers, these are simple parodies of that process, are they not? It is these, surely, that Dean Swift had sought to expose as the deception of charlatans. And I find it difficult to find fault with a man who, himself a High Anglican, has done so much to defend the Catholic Church in Ireland.'

'You deceive yourself, madam,' Clayton says. 'He has been no friend of the Catholic Faith or its practitioners, I think. Why, was it not Swift who proposed that, in order to ease poverty amongst families of Irish Catholics, their children should be sold for meat – to be stewed, roasted, baked or boiled, fricasseed or served with a *ragoût*? Outrageous. No, Mistress Redmond. The fellow was a Whig turned Tory and then back again. The type who rails against the whole of humanity, dismissing each of us as a wretch, making no distinction between the classes, between the successful and the parish-gathering pariah. He views us all the same and thinks it an indignity to share a common nature.'

'Well, sir,' says Aran, 'I had the chance to read *A Modest Proposal* for myself. If you should care to do likewise, Reverend, I think you may find that the work is intended as a satire. It is, after all, the thing for which Dean Swift is famed. And his actions show that he *has* done much to defend Catholics from those iniquities so often inflicted upon them in Ireland. I had cause to collect his words only recently, those which remind us that we have just enough religion to make us hate, but not enough to make us love one another. It seemed entirely relevant to the current unrest.'

The rebuke, she sees, has stung Clayton, a man who does not take kindly to correction.

'A sentiment,' says John Byrom, hastily, with the obvious intention of preventing a riposte from his friend, 'that our good friend Wesley would describe as an atheism, I am sure. Yet there is no denying that, with the Assistant Curates at Saint Ann's preaching so regularly against the Jacobite Cause, the Hanoverian pack have enlisted Presbyterianism to stir up the very hatred that you describe, Mister Owen. It will be the death of Hoole, I swear, for he is so opposed to the rantings of Nichols and Lewthwaite.'

A knock on the door, and Maria-Louise sees that it is Katherine.

'Pray forgive me, gentlemen,' her daughter says, 'but I am sent to say, Reverend, that we have completed the tasks you set us.'

'Is that so, my dear?' Clayton replies, testily. 'Then I had best discover some greater challenges to set before you, else I am accused of neglect as well as *naïveté*. But have you seen these sketches undertaken by knowledgeable Mister Owen, Katherine. Come, what say you of their execution? Does he himself intend some satire here, d'you think?'

And Maria-Louise takes this opportunity to leave them, while Katherine is explaining just how much she has come to admire Mister Owen and his artistry. *If I am not careful, she will have young Aran ahead of me.*

Outside, she is faced with another dilemma, for the lane is busy today and she runs a serious risk of being seen entering Bradley's house by prying eyes. So, as she ties her pattens once more, she is pleased when yet another company of redcoats come marching around the corner from Deansgate and Cateaton Street. General Cholmondeley himself was here two weeks previously, with recruits for his new Seventy-Third Regiment. A se'nnight later and it was troops from Blakeney's Twenty-Seventh. And now these young boys and ruffians from Gower's, another recently created battalion. But all of them *en route* from Chester to join the army now assigned to General Wade at Newcastle-upon-Tyne. With all eyes turned upon the shambling and badly disciplined soldiers, she descends from the paved terrace outside the Byroms' double front doors, the noise of her pattens mingling with the metallic clatter of fresh army boots, and keeps pace with their ranks until she is able to slip across to the north side of Hanging Ditch and Bradley's house.

The manservant bids her enter as he has done for so many years, taking her coat and waiting patiently for the pattens. He ushers her to the library, without expression or hint of reproach, leaving Maria-Louise to adjust the hair that she has piled and powdered so carefully.

A moment of apprehension. Her daughter's house now, when all is said and done. But she feels comparatively secure, here in the room which her restored *inamorato* has retained as his own private sanctum and office-space. She studies the leather-bound books, many of them technical treatises, but her eye settles inevitably on the ochres, olives and crimsons that bind Bradley's collection of Dean Swift. *A Tale of a Tub. The Battle of the Books. A Modest Proposal. Drapier's Letters.* And, of course, the *Travels.*

What, I wonder, shall history make of my own deeds, dear Doctor? For am I not also a Lemuel, faced with the chance to save the Lilliputian Palace and its rulers by urinating upon them but knowing that, in doing so, I may earn the enmity of the small-minded for having acted so profanely? There would be few amongst my Jacobite comrades, I collect, who would judge my actions as good intent undertaken in an unfortunate manner, rather than a damnable heresy.

'What price shall I pay?' she asks herself aloud.

'Price, my dear?' says Bradley, making her spin from the shelves, having failed to hear him enter.

'I was musing about Swift. His views about infidelity.'

'As I recall, the fellow railed about that over-stated failing only so far as it relates to matters of religion. The growing lack of Faith within our society. Though I must confess that I had not prepared myself for a morning of intellectual and philosophical debate. It would be such a waste when, if I may say so, you appear in such fine blossom for an autumn day.'

He makes that soft sibilant sound with his teeth, evidently relishing the effort she has made, for it is difficult to be alluring when she must dress in daily attire.

'And you, sir? Satisfied with the new Court Leet, I trust.'

A polite tapping on the library door before the manservant enters, a discreet cough, bearing a silver tray, two glasses and a bottle of the topaz-coloured Tokaji that Bradley favours so much.

'Extremely satisfied. Thomas Fielden elected as Borough Reeve. Fowden and Walley elected Constables. Fowden is another of your Jacobite sympathisers, of course, but Thomas Walley shall do well enough. He still maintains that he will confront Sir Oswald about his regular absence from the Manor. Little change in the Jurors themselves, however, which is a blessing. My thanks, Merriman,' he says, as the manservant hands a glass of the sweet wine to each of them and leaves the room.

Bradley sets his own glass upon the desk, once they are alone, and Maria-Louise takes a sip before doing likewise, feeling the heat rise in her. It is an animal thing, she knows, emanating from his proximity, something in his scent, the tangible taste of his breath whenever he is close to her. And she can see his arousal already. So she leans back against the desk, beginning to raise the linsey-woolsey of her red dress, the hoops beneath, that he might take her as he has done in every recent week.

But on this occasion he caresses her hands, holds them in his own, letting the fabric fall back while he kisses her thin lips with delicate passion. He continues to kiss her when he finally releases her fingers so that his own may begin to unfasten the laces of her bodice.

She leans backwards from him. 'Do we have time for this?' she says, for he has never before sought to undress her. But, still, she plays her own part by reaching for the drawstrings about her waist, loosing each side in turn.

'This may be all the time that God shall allow us,' he whispers, lifting both skirt and bodice over her head as she raises her arms to facilitate the thing, 'and I no longer wish to waste it on some rutting fumble with you, Maria-Louise.'

He steps away from her, seemingly to admire the fine veil of black lace covering her petticoat hoops but she quickly leads his fingers to the ribbons that fasten the whalebone *panier* above her hips, helping him with the ties and letting it collapse to the floor, along with the pocket in which she carries her powders and creams.

'Why now, sir? After so many years.' And her lips brush his neck, her hands working the buttons of his waistcoat, feeling the hardness of him though the thin fabric of her chemise, while he runs fingers around her shoulders, down the smooth flesh of her upper back, exploring the cords that close her stays.

'Now? Because the world is turning upside down once again, my dear. And my years weigh upon me with the guilt of wasted opportunity.'

He bends to kiss her throat, turns her around slowly, touches her breasts through the fabric of the stays, runs a hand down across the russet satin of her stomacher, then deftly unties the tightly drawn strings that hold the garment in place, cupping her breasts and teasing her nipples once more as it falls away.

'I could wish for more romantic reasoning than your guilt and advancing years, James Bradley,' she says, slipping the embroidered straps of her chemise and letting this, too, drop to the floor, shrugging herself free of its short sleeves, trembling as he touches her buttocks, reaches around to find her bush.

'I am afraid, *cara mia*, that anything else would be wasted effort and certain to meet with your rejection. For, whatever may be between us, I know that I could not take you from your husband.'

She turns about, displaying herself to him, holding her own small breasts towards him, wearing only her stockings, garters and shoes.

'But you *will* take me now, James, will you not?' she whispers.

'Oh yes, my dear. For you are beautiful beyond compare!' And he does indeed take her, free now from his own breeches, lifting her onto the desk's edge and filling her. In fact, he fills some part of her that she had not previously realised was empty and, as the spasms and pleasures of her wet climax shudder through her, Maria-Louise Redmond finds that tears are running down her cheeks, silent wracking sobs that make Bradley hold her closer, spurring him to renewed vigour and a second, more prolonged fulfilment.

Later, he carries her to the small library sofa, remembers that he should have locked the door and does so belatedly, then settles beside her.

'I must not become too comfortable,' she says. 'It would not answer should Rosina return home. And might the servants not confide in her, James? After all, she is mistress of this house now.'

'My servants are discreet, sweet joy. And I doubt that Rosina would display either surprise or concern were we discovered. But best to avoid the issue, I suppose. Neither she nor myself could, in truth, claim that our Marriage Settlement is fully discharged. I had thought, at one time, that she might soften towards me, and I regret to some extent that this has not transpired. But she is rarely herself these days. The Sydenham's, I think. Why, I might even drag her to the Market Cross and see whether she might fetch a price! Yet you are correct. It would not answer to be found in such a compromise.'

'Then I must dress and be gone,' she says. 'But I would crave your indulgence on two matters, Mister Bradley. The first is this. You mentioned the world turned upside down and I have been considering the same matter. So, tell me, do you think that we shall be affected directly by its meanderings, you and I? And second, you should know, whatever happens, that I have enjoyed our time together. I would not have it otherwise and, should we resume our more normal trysting next week, or whenever time allows, I should not be distressed.'

'So far as the second is concerned, having now suffered the exquisite pain of your naked charms, I intend to ensure that every one of our subsequent assignations shall meet or exceed the standard set today. As for the first, why, you must be better placed than myself to gauge the future. We must not spoil this precious day with political rant but an express this morning informs me that privateers have landed at Peterhead with five thousand in gold pieces for your *Chevalier*. This, along with the Stuart Exchequer, their recent successes, it cannot but mean one thing. That we shall soon be over-run by the French, regardless of the Pretender's progress.'

'Not by the French after all, I think,' she whispers. 'And the Stuart Exchequer? Why, you overheard my ramblings about a price that I may have to pay. I have something, James, that I must needs confide to you.'

Chapter Forty-One

'Mister King seems to possess a very narrow view of Lesbian Love, does he not?' says Rosina, setting down the book and pulling her feet further into the lavender fabric and cushions of Elizabeth Cooper's settee to keep them from the cold. Even the lincture cannot keep it at bay tonight and has served to simply sink her spirits.

Elizabeth continues with her writing, does not even look up from the growing mound of letters upon her writing table. Flowing black script upon ghostly ground.

'He is an Oxford Don, my dear,' she replies, flatly. 'Principal of Saint Mary Hall, as I collect. An academic fellow. What would *he* know of the world? Anyway, I told you. It is a smutty little work.'

But Rosina had intended to read it ever since Mama's reference, and Mister Wilding had finally acquired a copy for her at a price of two shillings. It is worn, its green leather faded, but it has generally amused her, smutty or not. It is the second edition. *The Toast, an Heroic Poem in Four Books, Written in Latin by Frederick Schaffer.* A clever ruse, of course. A mere pretence on the part of King to protect himself as a satirist, the entire text being his own work. But his mock translator's preface, his notes and observations are all so sharply observed. It is a cruel attack upon the Duchess of Newborough, however.

'And is this the way that the world perceives us, do you think? That we are all to be compared with hirsute wrestlers? Strong enough to carry a full-grown oxen, is the way that he describes his heroine.'

The quill scratches upon another sheet.

'You will learn, Rosina, that there are as many different shades of lesbiana and tribady as there are variations in venereal practise between the sexes, or even amongst those strange hermaphroditic creatures. The Duchess, I perceive, may well have fallen into that category commonly defined as *bull-and-bear*, where each partner has a disposition towards the manly. We are something of a rarity, you and me, being rather *femme-et-femme*.'

Elizabeth has talked of this before, claiming the more usual form of sapphic passion to involve that which she describes as *homme-et-femme*.

But you are not above acting the bear yourself, Elizabeth Cooper, when the humour takes you. And here she is, dressed once more in heavy workman's shirt and dark trousers.

'A rarity in many other particulars too, my dear,' says Rosina, almost in a whisper.

'Oh, let me count the ways!' Elizabeth replies, a note of sarcasm in her voice.

'Then should you not care to show me some novelty, sweet nymph? Teach me some daring new way to pleasure you, I beg.'

'You know, Rosina, that I must prepare for tomorrow. The Fly Wagon leaves early and I must have letters prepared to accompany each delivery, else I shall never acquire the necessary orders for coffee and chocolate in addition to supplying simply their teas. And Heaven knows whether my goods shall even reach Carlisle and beyond now that your wild Scotsmen have finally crossed the Solway. I durst suppose that we shall all be murdered in our beds before too long, in any case.'

She blows upon her fingers, the meagre fire deficient in defence against this spectacularly bitter mid-November evening.

'You sound like a disciple of Doctor Hall,' says Rosina, 'going about the town and frightening the feeble. You have nothing to fear from our good Prince, my dearest. And Papa is almost your business associate these days. So you may even stand amongst the honoured when the town is finally set at liberty.'

'Without your father's help, I doubt that I could have survived these past weeks. I did not imagine that Mister Owen would be *so* capable of scrubbery that he would abandon the enterprise so readily. Perhaps you should ask *him* to entertain your needs. Though I expect that you will leap to his part, that you will tell me he is required to complete those damn'd murals for your husband. But liberty, you say? Some French fashion, I assume. Though the nation whose virtues you too frequently extol seems so sadly lacking in that estimable quality itself, do you not find? In France, I am told, women like ourselves are still regularly burned for witches. Unless they belong to the aristocracy, of course. Is that the form of liberty which you shall gift me, my love?'

Rosina feels the familiar tightening around her neck, the beginnings of yellow light darting before her eyes. The certain start of another megrim.

'Our loyal Scots are managing perfectly well without French assistance so far, though I am sure that King Louis shall provide support whenever it is needed. No, it shall be noble Highlanders who will free us from the Hanover chains. They are simple, honest folk from mountain and forest, not the savages that Doctor Hall might pretend. But if I tire you, perhaps I had better leave. Why, I should receive more attention from Mister Bradley, methinks.'

And, since Elizabeth does not attempt to dissuade her, she returns to her own house. For she now considers it such.

Her husband has already taken himself to bed which, for some reason, irritates her this night, along with the growing pain behind her eyes. She finds her *tresor trové* of Sydenham's and doses herself, gaining some temporary relief but knowing that she will suffer for it later. Such goblins and demons will fill her dreams.

She dismisses the servants, then sits alone in the salon for a long time, still wrapped in her coat, until their sounds have finally died away. The pain slackens too, for a while, and her mind is filled with many fleeting images, pleasant thoughts of Aran Owen, though some jealousy at the linked recollection of her sister's fondness for him. Thoughts of her father, generally positive. Confused meanderings about James. The angry upsurge of rancour against Mama. And the constantly returning recollections of frustrated hours with Elizabeth.

Finally, with the megrim and the opiate taking hold again, she lights the stairs to her room, her unsteady legs betraying her more than once so that, before she has reached the first landing, Bradley himself has emerged above her, his own candle held high above his head, his velvet-capped head, and the flame's guttering gleam creates a halo reflected from the white linen of his nightgown.

'What o'clock is it, my dear?' he asks. 'And you are unwell, I see.'

'Ah, Saint James!' she says. 'First amongst Apostles. What miracles shall you perform for me, my dear?'

'You mistake my taper for the Santiago Star, I collect. Yet this is no *campo stella* and the only miracle that I might weave shall be to see you safely abed.'

He descends the few treads to where she leans heavily against the baluster. Bradley relieves her of the silver sconce, snuffs the wick and sets it down upon the staircase, then takes her arm, supports her weight and helps her up the remaining steps.

'And have you heard the news, sir? That our own *Caballeros Santiaguistas* are come to drive the Mahometans from this land? Give you joy, husband.'

Yet she does not feel an excess of joy. Indeed, she may vomit. But a vision spins in her brain of a thousand Charles Edwards, each sporting upon his white cloak the elaborate red cross with its down-pointed blade, more dagger than crucifix.

'If you speak of the Jacobite *banditti* then, yes, I have indeed heard the news. Six thousand of the devils encamped at Carlisle, I gather. I imagine that it will cry havoc for Mistress Cooper's new enterprise.'

The recollection of Elizabeth Cooper's sarcasms serves to disperse the royal crusaders. Nausea again.

'I fear that I may be sick, Mister Bradley.'

'Then please wait until we reach the sanctity of your chambers, I beg you. And did you visit Ma and Pa today, as you promised? Or were you overly occupied by thoughts of your bold *Chevalier*?'

But, yes, she had made the journey to Droylsden. Nothing out of the ordinary. The old lady barely able to recollect her name or the reason for

418

her presence but lifted by the package of dainties put together by her Jim. Though, in truth, it was Rosina who had prepared the contents. Porter for Pa Bradley, as usual, and he complaining of his aches and pains. Each of them seeming frail to her now. And more home-spun philosophy from Ma about the blessings of children. The thought presses upon her as they finally reach the door to her room.

'And shall you now attempt to take advantage of my weakened condition in order to vent your passions upon me, sir?'

'I had thought, rather, to set the pot alongside your bed to comfort you, dear wife. Any passions that I might otherwise have experienced would be quite dampened, I assure you, by the possibility of your regurgitation.'

'Yet might you assist me to undress?'

'Indeed not! I have had an excessively tedious evening with the new members of the Court Leet and must be fresh for tomorrow's duties while you, dear lady, have to face Mrs Starkey for your lesson. No, Rosina, you must either divest yourself alone or lie abed fully clothed. The choice is your own.'

In the morning, she is woken by her maidservant, the megrim returned with all its brutal malevolence. She attempts breakfast with her husband but cannot face the food. It truth, she can barely face *him* for she recalls that she may have said some things during the previous night whose meanings may have been ambiguous. And does she also feel some sense of rejection? If so, she buries it deep. Yet he seems ineffably cheerful today, making not the slightest reference to the episode. Indeed, she begins to wonder whether the Sydenham's has practised upon her memory.

'You must know, my dear, that the Jacobites are now at Carlisle?' he says, holding out his plate so that their manservant can fetch some more of the grilled kidney from the serpentine-fronted sideboard. 'Yes, of course. But I have a letter from Sir Edward, too. No reference to it in the broadsheets but he tells me that Cumberland is returned from Flanders. Arrived in London on the twenty-eighth. Twenty-five battalions of infantry with him and a dozen squadrons of horse. Your self-styled Prince will be caught like a rat in a trap, I fear.'

'I see that you are elegantly dressed and *parfumé*, Mister Bradley. Some significant meeting perhaps? It cannot be simply to celebrate the Duke of Cumberland's return, I think, for if that pompous fellow has left Flanders, you may be sure that the French army shall be close upon his heels. And the English battalions, we may assume, shall be in a parlous state after their experience this summer.'

'Do you say so, wife? Well, you may be correct. Though the French may not be so anxious to intervene as you believe.'

'How so, sir? Does the Earl of Derby tell you so? It is not long since he tried to persuade us that the Jacobite Cause was ditched. Yet here we are. Across the border. Has he now expounded on his theory perhaps? Spread more mystery concerning his *friends here in Manchester*? More feigned indiscretions?'

'I fear not, Rosina. And His Lordship may be more sincere than you can credit. His warning against sedition was timely. Well-intentioned. Still, I think that I have now plumbed the mystery of which you speak.'

'How so?'

'Oh, nought of significance, my dear. Nothing at all! But perhaps you should care to rest today? To forsake your lesson. To spend the day with your husband. No? Then I shall bid you a good morning and return to my study.'

But his perfume lingers after he has left the room and it remains in her nostrils even an hour later when she arrives at Mrs Starkey's at Pool Fold. It takes the sharper tang of blazing logs from the music room hearth to finally dispel it.

'You do not look your best today,' says the music teacher, 'if you will forgive me for saying so. A megrim once more?'

Rosina looks at herself in the gilt-framed mirror above the mantel.

'Indeed. My husband insisted that I should see Doctor Hall, though the fellow is more concerned with phantasms just now. He sees wild Highlanders at every corner. He speculated that there are merely two forms of this complaint. One that afflicts sufferers in the evening and seems to arise from a flux occasioned by certain substances. The other occurring in the morning hours and resulting from a muscular distortion of the face during sleep. He has made a study of the thing. Demanded to know whether my own affliction is evident in the evening or in the morning. He was quite put about when I told him that I seem to be suffering both forms at the same time. But I feel a little easier than at breakfast, I thank you. And perhaps we might finish the lesson somewhat earlier than usual?'

So Mrs Starkey does not tax her too much. Dandrieu's *Carillon*. The style is almost that of Couperin but the counterpoint is quite distinct, and the composer's imitation of peeling bells, the joyous second movement, the dancing ecstasy of its third, all serve to lighten Rosina's humour enormously. The *clavecin* responds well to her touch and, rather than the lesson being curtailed, she finds that she has rather exceeded her allotted time.

They reserve some moments, naturally, for sharing news about the Prince Regent's progress but Rosina declines the offer of a dish of tea since she has arranged to meet at Beppy Byrom's house for that same purpose. Yet when she arrives at Hanging Ditch, she finds that her friend is already entertaining Francis Townley in the spacious drawing room.

His ill-formed teeth form a smile of sorts but he does not stir from the divan, nor show her any proper courtesy. His dress, always extravagant, today has a distinctly military cut, a coat of blue satin, his waistcoat and breeches white and his tricorne, laid upon the seat beside him, sporting a white cockade. He is now in his thirty-seventh year, dashing enough in his own way despite

420

the clumsy set of his jaw.

'Mistress Bradley,' he says, 'give you joy of this propitious day! And see?' He holds up his hat. 'Miss Byrom has been kind enough to fashion my cockade.'

'Indeed I did!' says Beppy, embracing her warmly. 'And welcome, dearest Rosina. As Mister Townley has already declared, a most propitious day.'

Rosina quickly recalls her reasons for disliking the fellow. The disagreeable exchanges between Townley and Aran Owen. Townley's incitement of the mob responsible for Dissenter Semple's death. Papa's vexation at his attempts to interfere with the conduct of the *Journal*.

'And is it safe, might we consider,' she says, 'to sport the white cockade so openly just now? There are those who cry sedition at lesser symbols of our Cause.' She recalls, too, Aran's strange behaviour during her Name Day dinner following Sir Edward's obtuse comments on the subject.

'Thy concerns are certainly astute,' says Beppy. 'For I fear that we Lancashire Jacobites are quite surrounded. We are hemmed by the Pennines in the east, the Mersey marshes to the south. In the south-west, the Whiggish towns of Warrington and Liverpool. The Irish Sea beyond and, to the north, the mountains of Westmorland and Cumberland. To the north-east, those fanatics of Rossendale who would see good Catholics like yourselves hung for heretics. Or worse. I pray to Our Lord that He shall clear a path so that the bold Prince might reach us before our enemies close about us. In the meanwhile, I think that we *should* sport our favours openly, as Mister Townley has chosen to do. We must each lead by example.' She touches a hand to her own blue and white dress, almost matching Townley's own attire. 'And he has received a letter from his brother. From Captain Townley. Shalt thou share it with us, sir?'

'The contents contain no secret, my dear. And I should be pleased to divulge its significant points. But were we not promised a dish of tea, Miss Byrom?' An apology from Beppy and she goes to the door, summons one of the servants to fetch tea while Townley takes his dispatch from an inside coat pocket. 'Now,' he continues, 'you will have collected that the Prince Regent's Grand Council met at the end of October and agreed the invasion of England. My brother sends details of its deliberations, for His Highness had insisted that he could only legitimately claim the throne for his noble father through a conquest of this country. And his preferred option for doing so had been an incursion through Northumberland and down the east coast to Yorkshire.'

'The *east* coast?' cries Beppy. 'La! Yet the strength of his support amongst the English lies here, in Lancashire.'

'I fear, Miss Byrom, that the choice was not so simple. For my brother tells me that the Clan Chieftains did not favour an invasion in *any* form, preferring to remain in Scotland. To strengthen the Stuarts' hold on that Kingdom. John tells me that the Highlanders are stout fellows but prone to pursuing their own ends, returning to their crofts whenever they are not fully occupied. They therefore agreed a compromise, do you see? To keep the army in active campaign by moving on London, yet to do so by marching the western route. Even so, the thing was only decided by a single vote. But they are on the move at last, dear ladies. Five thousand foot and five hundred horse.'

'Yet it would be a grave mistake,' says Rosina, 'should His Royal Highness believe that, even here, he is entirely with friends. We are beset by foes of our own in Manchester, sir.'

'And your husband principal amongst them, madam. For the Subscription that he has helped to raise will put a troop of militia in the field against us under the Earl of Derby. And your *friend*, Mistress Cooper,' he sneers, 'now reaping the benefits from your father's tea trade that should, more properly, belong to our Cause. Or your dear Mama, still speaking openly against our French allies. How amused she must now be that, for the nonce at least, we seem to stand alone. Those sodomite clergymen too, at Saint Ann's, preaching sermons against us, crying perfidy, rebellion, treason. Lewthwaite calls us Shechemites, while Nichols cites the Book of Jeremiah to condemn our actions. Even Hoole himself, that faithless Rector, that supposed Non-Juror, draws parallels between the Jacobite nobles and the disciples who abandoned Our Lord, claiming that their sworn duty, above all others, is to protect the King already anointed in the Name of God Almighty. He reserves for Charles Edward, naturally, the role of Iscariot, though it is a feeble comparison. And your father, Miss Byrom, there to hear him, I understand.'

It is a comprehensive assault, bitter, underscored by the fine spray of spittle that accompanies Townley's diatribe. But the tea service has arrived and Beppy unlocks the mahogany chest containing the caddies, to begin the ritual by which the beverage is brewed and served.

'My father, sir,' she says, 'shall not be listed amongst the enemies of our Cause. It is a gross abuse that you should call upon me and then slander him thus in his own home. Heaven knows, I have disagreements with him a-plenty on the matter for he has an honest antipathy to violence in all its forms. Yet that hardly makes him less a Jacobite. Nor my friend's Mama neither. Above all, Mister Townley, I blush to hear you cite the most heinous of sins in such polite company. A fie upon you, sir. It simply will not answer!'

It is well that my father cannot hear him, for I fear that he is adding greatly to the grievances already outstanding you, Francis Townley! But what has he meant about standing alone? And does he truly have evidence of sodomy on the part of Joseph Hoole's Assistant Curates?

'I fear that my passions may have got the better of me, my dear ladies, and I humbly crave forgiveness. But this is no time, Miss Byrom, for equivocation. Some life must, inevitably, be sacrificed in this Cause.'

'Yet you fear, sir,' says Rosina, 'that we now stand alone. Can you explain, Mister Townley?'

She sees him hesitate before responding. 'I simply referred, Mistresses, to the dice now being cast. French assistance will, I am sure, follow soon. My brother is certain of the fact. Some of it already arrived. Gold, muskets, field pieces and such. The French Ambassador and my brother landed with him. But the Prince is already upon the road and little more can reach him, I fear, before he must confront Wade and the Hanoverian army. And, in order to liberate England, he has been forced to a difficult choice. For, in Scotland itself, forces are gathering against us. That treacherous dog Loudon has landed at Inverness and raises the Presbyterian Clans against us.'

'Then thou art right to remind us of the sacrifices we must make,' says Beppy, 'for there can be no greater sacrifice to be made than that of the Prince Regent in leaving his father's most loyal fiefdom to such iniquities. Yet perhaps it is an error, after all, this invasion of England? To abandon Edinburgh and the Lothians so readily?'

'At such times, my dear, difficult choices must be made. And John tells me that His Royal Highness has been driven, amongst other things, by the need to recognise the sacrifices made by others. Those here in England, for example, who have risked so much, who have shown the True King such devotion. Your father's tireless endeavours, Mistress Bradley. Our own Subscription here in Manchester, for example, which I am already using to furnish men for his forces, an entire regiment, no less. We shall be in good order, I believe, to support him when he reaches Lancashire. And reach this County he must soon, to be sure, while he still has finance for the venture.'

'Finance?' says Rosina, her head now feeling dull and heavy, the normal aftermath of the megrim. And how she now craves some more of her lincture. 'You have spoken already, sir, of gold from the French. Yet the Stuarts have their own Exchequer surely? I have heard my father speak of it so many times. The source from which the tea trade has been fed and nurtured, turned to greater profit.'

Townley regards her quizzically, his head turned slightly to one side as though, somehow, he does not trust her words. *Is there something that he thinks I should know?*

'John tells me that the *Louis d'Or* sent by the French are already spent. He has Cope's coffers, of course. But a mere three thousand guineas. Though the Bank of Scotland has been helpful and the Prince Regent has sent to all the boroughs of Scotland, especially perfidious Glasgow and Dumfries, demanding payment of their taxes to the True Crown on pain of being branded traitors.'

'And the Exchequer?' asks Rosina.

'Some delay in its delivery, I understand,' replies Townley, yet she senses that he is being disingenuous. 'Nothing of significance, I am sure.'

My husband used almost those same words this morning. Am I the only one who does not share their respective secrets?

423

And her disquiet is not assuaged when, finally, she must leave them. Beppy escorts her to the front door, apologising for Aran not being currently in the Academy to meet her, expressing anxiety at the pallor of her complexion today. Rosina, not for the first time, whispers her own surprise at Beppy's apparent attachment to Townley.

'Why, my dearest, he is merely a companionable fellow,' says her friend, 'and Francis shall have some prominent part to play before long, I am certain. But at least I collect that matters must now be improved with your Mama,' Yet how so? 'For did I not see her earlier this morning in the lane. Visiting your home, it seemed.'

Chapter Forty-Two

Sir Edward Stanley holds the hymnal between thumb and thick fingers. His deep but tuneless baritone reverberates around the church, though always one beat too early or too late, as if his weight somehow prevents him from quite keeping pace with the rest of the congregation.

Our God, our help in ages past,
Our hope for years to come...

How very suitable, he thinks, and turns an affectionate smile upon his wife as they stand in the gallery above the aisle of Saint Ann's. He had not immediately taken to the place for he does not greatly admire the Baroque style but, with time, he has come to appreciate its simple interior, its plain glass windows, the chequer-board of its floor tiles, the white-washed upper walls above their lower panelling.

Beneath the shadow of Thy throne...

A good choice, to use Saint Ann's for the celebration, rather than the Collegiate Church. Poor Bishop Peploe will barely venture near the place, Warden or not, since the Jacobites have become so much more strident. And Heaven knows, they were always strident enough in this detestable town. He somehow cannot quite avoid associating the *banditti* with the livestock that they allow so freely to roam their streets. Although some of them not entirely unpleasant. The Reverend Doctor Clayton, now taken over Peploe's duties almost permanently. He may be a Jacobite but at least he shares an interest in the natural philosophies. All the same, it would not have answered to have the fellow officiate today. After all, the dedication of Manchester's own Company within the Lancashire Regiment of Militia!

Before the hills in order stood...

The Earl of Derby's frame does not altogether lend itself to the King's uniform, however, and he shuffles frequently in the tight breeches, the military boots that pinch just too tight upon his toes. But it is a noble attire and, as

Colonel of the Regiment, he must learn to wear it with pride. For the Militia has a modestly glorious history, originated by King William the Third at the outset of his reign and fought for him with distinction at Carrickfergus, at the Boyne and at Athlone. Disbanded, naturally, once the threat from William's enemies was passed but embodied again in the Year '15 to counter the Old Pretender's insurrection. The Regiment had fought at Preston, endured great hardship there and suffered heavy loss before the Jacobites were finally defeated. And disbanded, once again, in the following year.

...Short as the watch that ends the night
Before the rising sun.

He would welcome some small degree of sunshine at this moment for the church, with all its simple comforts, is like an ice-house. Perhaps he could persuade them to a circulating stove such as that which he has finally installed at Bickerstaffe. He will speak with Reynolds about the matter when this damnably unpleasant business is finished. And Francis Reynolds, their host once more, gives him a reassuring smile. *Why, I think he were properly sold, yesterday evening, on my insistence that he should come to Parliament. He has all the necessary bottom, to be sure!* And if Sir Edward must come to Manchester, well, there is no finer place to stay than Strangeways Hall. He had been so pleased to escape the County for a while, their sojourn with Elizabeth's cousin at Brook Street so very pleasant. But now duty beckons, and he peers over the edge of the gallery, down into the pews below where his officers mingle amongst the more loyal of the townsfolk. Well, with the exception of that cove Byrom, naturally. What *is* the man doing here? And unpleasant recollections of the Workhouse affair cause him to falter at the start of the next verse.

...Are carried downward by the flood,
And lost in following years.

He never can quite catch that *following* as he might like. But the *busy tribe* of his Defensive Association is now mustered at least, embodied at Bury on the fifth though, in doing so, he had pre-empted parliamentary approval to raise the Militia by more than a week. Still, cometh the hour, as Saint John might say. And nobody will censure him, surely, for taking this initiative without waiting for the written authority that the Mutiny Act requires.

'Thy Word commands our flesh to dust...'

It is his favourite hymn, though this is the shortened version, he notes.. And the music – Croft's *Saint Anne* – well, he could not have chosen better had he tried. But all this dust and earth, he thinks. Is bloodshed now inevitable? *I suppose it must be so. I fear it, though it is a necessary evil if, in the end, we can finally bring a close to this nation's endless history of civil strife. And did the Lord not regale Mankind with the dubious gift of warfare so that we might cleanse the detritus from within our society?*

> *Time, like an ever rolling stream,*
> *Bears all its sons away;*
> *They fly forgotten as a dream*
> *Dies at the opening day.*

Forgotten dreams? An image of Newcastle's agent. *What* was *his name and where is the cove?* he wonders. *Damn his eyes.* Those strange impenetrable eyes. Off on some errand for His Grace, though never a word to Sir Edward. Why no, *he* is merely Lord Lieutenant of Lancashire. So Newcastle is not the only one who will be pleased to see the back of his spy. But God knows, the man is knowledgeable. He had shown such concern for the Earl's bile too. Stung him with his criticisms though. And the Earl never *has* been able to fulfil his promise to Newcastle that he would leave no stone unturned in the search for Dissenter Semple's killer. But how could you discover *any* truth in this town of rogues?

> *...Be Thou our guard while life shall last,*
> *And our eternal home.*

Such a rousing finish. Inspirational! He beams, despite the discomfort in his groin, throughout the entire progress of Reverend Hoole's final reading. Psalm Number Ninety, to be sure. The clergyman looks barely capable of the part, however. So slender and pale, cadaverous. But he is there at the church door to bestow blessings upon each parishioner as they all file out into Acres Field and another dull November morning, fog still clinging around the base of the hornbeams that line the open space, though currently a space occupied by the ranks of his Militia. Such a pleasurable sight!

Yet a pleasure short-lived, for here comes his Adjutant, Captain-Lieutenant James Sergeant, leading Sir Edward's horse to the mounting stone.

Dammit! he thinks, handing Lady Elizabeth to Reynolds. *How preferable it would be was I able to review my boys from the John Tull chaise.* For neither his age, nor his bulk, nor his ailments any longer lend themselves to equestrian comfort.

But he tackles the duty manfully enough, even managing a pretence of expertise as the large roan jogs across the soft ground, receiving the salute from his own Colonel's Company, properly the Blackburn Company, formed to his left. His young Ensign, Robert Richmond, barks orders to the scarlet-coated militiamen as Sir Edward moves on to the second Company, lined in front of him. These are the newest of his recruits, recently formed as the Manchester

Company under the captaincy of Humphrey Trafford whose Lieutenant and Ensign are the sons of local Whiggish merchants, strongly recommended by James Bradley.

He still finds Bradley to be an insolent wretch but, until he can establish some non-Jacobite Tories in the town, he supposes that he must tolerate him. A rum type, however, to suffer tribady on the part of his wife. He has never heard such a thing before! Though she was perfectly charming during the dinner at their house. Remove after remove of fine food, too. *I were almost indiscreet about that skulker though. Lord, I shall needs be more careful tonight!*

The new Company hardly appears impressive though for, whilst the entire Regiment may not have benefited from any training these thirty years past, the Manchester men have only been under arms for three days and have not inspired much confidence during their time on Camp Field.

But the Warrington Company, at least, shows more promise. For these are under the command of Patten, the oldest of his captains, now in his fifty-fifth year but at least with military experience under his belt. And they are brought to the *present arms* now by their Ensign, an exceptionally dashing fellow called Tobin. Sir Edward wheels right, passes their front on his return to the church, and suffering a grimace of remorse as, finally in the review, he must bear an indignity to his Regiment's good name. For his authority from Parliament also permits him to raise a troop of horse from amongst the County's loyal gentlemen. And here they sit. Every last one that he has been able to muster. All six of them.

Thank God for the Foot! he thinks, swiftly passing the horsemen since, besides the three Companies gathered here, he has five others dispersed amongst the towns that have subscribed for them, one each in Preston, Bury, Ormschurch, Rochdale and Lancaster. A significant achievement, he thinks, since virtually no other English County has received such authority. *And then, we had but twenty muskets to begin!*

Once returned to the church, dismounted and climbed upon the dais normally reserved for the opening of the Annual Fair, he is joined by Sir Oswald, by Reynolds, by High Sheriff William Shawe, by Bradley, and by Reverend Hoole, while Ensign Richmond calls his Company to order and marches them forward towards their Colonel and his waiting dignitaries. The men come to a shambling, ragged halt in front of the platform.

Sir Edward gestures to his Adjutant. 'Lieutenant Sergeant, if you please!' he cries, and the young officer reaches into his pouch, drawing forth a sheaf of ballad sheets, hastily produced for them by that notable artist, Mister Owen. The ballad itself is entitled *The Gunpowder Plot*, the sheets illustrated with Aran's simple sketches of Westminster's Palace.

True Protestants, I pray you do draw near,
Unto this story lend attentive ear,

The lines are few, although the subject's old,
Likewise it is true as e'er 'twas told.
The tale of wretched Papists, all agreed
Which way to make the King and Nation bleed.
By powder all did try with joint consent,
To blow up both the King and Parliament.

And each man is gifted with a copy of this ancient, wretched but still powerful propaganda. Then the Oath of Association to be sworn, Reverend Hoole reading out each line, the men attempting to repeat the difficult phrases, some of which Sir Edward has amended, ever so marginally, so that they no longer promise to defend King George but, rather, 'to protect this present and most happy Establishment.' Why, how pleased he is! Such penmanship. La, when this is all over...

A blessing, finally, and the troops are marched back by Companies to Camp Field.

'Well, gentlemen,' cries Sir Edward, stepping down once more from the dais. 'There we have it. The town's own Company of Militia. You were pleased with the ceremony, I trust? A fine job, too, Lieutenant,' he says to Mister Sergeant. 'Find Owen for me, if you please. I must thank him for his efforts.'

'It was handsomely done,' says Francis Reynolds, whose footman now returns Lady Elizabeth to their company, 'and all credit to Mister Bradley for his part in raising the Subscription. Two thousand guineas is an admirable sum.'

'Yet barely half of that raised by the Jacobites, I fear,' Bradley replies. 'And begun too late, for the *banditti* have been raising funds these years past, have they not, Sir Oswald?'

Bradley's implication is clear. And indeed he is correct. For they have been allowed excessive leeway for too long by a Lord of the Manor either ambivalent to their activities or, perhaps, even complicit in them.

'Heh? What's that you say, sir?' says the aged Mosley, still trying to descend the podium steps. 'All over now. Redmond out of business, I understand.'

'Yet all credit to Mister Bradley, sir, in that regard,' insists Sir Edward. 'Still, we have the High Sheriff of Lancashire with us now. What say you, Shawe? Shall we finally set some of these rogues by the heel?'

William Shawe has only recently been confirmed in his post and will serve for the coming year. Sir Edward likes young Shawe, thinks him an admirable fellow too. From Preston, and well-connected by his marriage to Anne Cunliffe. Fine woman.

'I am certain of the thing, Lordship,' Shawe replies. 'And we shall start with the case of John Semple, perhaps. I hope that Mister Bradley, or Reverend

Hoole, can steer us towards possible witnesses.'

'Oh, I am rather afraid that I know nothing of the matter, sir,' says Hoole. 'Nothing factual, you understand.'

'The whole town,' Bradley says, 'knows the culprits, Sir Edward. It was Townley's young blades, to be sure. Yet we shall never succeed in producing a witness to the deed itself. To whoever struck the guilty blow. And it is Townley who now goes freely about the streets raising volunteers for the Pretender. They speak of a complete regiment, I gather.'

'Fiddlestick, my dear fellow! And a pox on them. They shall be no match for my Militia, I can assure you. Ah, but here is Mister Owen himself. The good Lieutenant has found him. And not alone, I see. Your Pa-in-Law too, Mister Bradley.'

The Earl of Derby considers his reference jocose and his face assumes a self-congratulatory grin. Still, Bradley's comment about a whole regiment of Manchester Jacobites is worrying. And, yes, he supposes that he does, after all, have Titus Redmond to blame for this embarrassment. If only Manchester had raised the same amounts for King George. If only many of the other Lancashire towns had raised *anything*! But just look at this Redmond, strutting about the place as though *he* were Lord of the Manor, with Lady Maria-Louise upon his arm. *I wonder if she and Bradley are still…*

'Well, give you joy of this fine Sunday, Mister Redmond,' he says, then a slight bow to the woman. 'Madam, good morning. And Mister Owen. Where should we be without you, sir? To have completed the ballad sheets so swiftly. Remarkable.'

'Perhaps I might name Mister Scatterbuck, Lordship?' says Aran. 'For it was Mister Scatterbuck's printing press, in truth, that accounted for their rapid production.'

'Though with little say in the matter!' says the Scatterbuck person, a man in the most ill-fitting clothes that Sir Edward has ever seen, his face covered with as many lumpen blemishes as Redmond's has creases. 'Are we to suffer such despotism, sir, that a man may be roused from his slumbers, in his private abode, and subjected to intimidations, to menacing invective, to the evil blast of coercion? And to what purpose, sir? I shall tell you. For the purpose of producing items offensive to my Faith, sir. Libellous items, intended to stir bigotry and intolerance.'

'Why, bless my soul!' says Sir Edward. 'I had quite forgot. This accounts for not seeing you during the service, Mister Redmond. I had thought you at the Collegiate Church, rather than here at this fine temple. Yet you are Romans, are you not? And this, dear Scatterbuck, is a time of national crisis. We cannot set our private concerns above the needs of the state, surely. And libellous, you say? Why, 'tis nothing but a ballad sheet. It does not preach sedition. Nor defame any honest individual. Nor blaspheme against the Church of England. They are the only libels recognised in law, methinks. Whereas, gentlemen, the

430

town's *Journal*, as your magazine is styled, has breached all three at one time or another. Now, tell me, Lieutenant,' he calls to his Adjutant, 'is it true that that Mister Scatterbuck were threatened?'

'Not directly, sir. Though I had cause to advise Mister Owen that the presses would be smashed if they should fail to cooperate.'

'Quite so, Lieutenant. My precise instruction.' He gestures to the Adjutant, who takes Scatterbuck's arm and drags him away, with some commotion and protest, the fellow invoking the names of that Whig, Locke; the disgraced Bacon; the French libertarian, Voltaire. How extraordinary. 'Such a small thing too, Mister Redmond, to return my favour in arranging Bishop Peploe's performance at Rosina's wedding. And may I say, sir, how handsomely I were entertained by your daughter when I had cause to visit Mister Bradley in August. She is, indeed, most *handsome*, eh Bradley?'

La! What a merry jest.

'My daughter may not have performed thus, Sir Edward,' says Maria-Louise, with venom in her emerald eyes, 'had she known that you would return so soon for the purpose of disseminating such malicious incitement against the Faith that she, like ourselves and many others in this town, holds true above all others. By Our Lady, may our good Prince Regent arrive soon for our deliverance!'

'And Adam Scatterbuck, for all his many faults,' adds Titus, 'is a particular friend of this family, sir. To see him pulled about the streets like a common felon is beyond forbearance. You will ensure that he is released at once, prithee?'

'Released, Mister Redmond? God's Hooks, he is not confined, sir. My Adjutant merely removed him from our company lest he should say something regrettable in his fury. Understandable, I suppose. And I apologise if our pamphlet should have caused offence. But the new recruits, I find, frequently need something to inspire their loyalty once the shilling is spent, you understand. This is, after all, and with no further disrespect intended, yet another Popish Plot, is it not? This *Prince Regent*, as you call him, sent here to restore a line of Papists to the throne. But he shall get no further, I think. He shall find Carlisle an impossible nut to crack and Wade shall also come up with him soon. Yet let us end this rancour, I beg you. Will you not attend as my guests at tonight's rout? It shall be the very thing, I understand. Eh, Bradley?'

Redmond, he sees, sets a finger to that damnably unfashionable moustache, strokes it twice, while his whore of a wife turns her head in exasperation towards Aran Owen.

'I think, Sir Edward,' says Titus, slowly, 'that you must excuse our non-attendance. Some family constraints as I am sure my son-in-law will understand. And you will forgive *us*, I hope, if we do not share your enthusiasm for this Hanoverian soldiery that you have raised.'

431

'Then you must beware that you do not fall foul of the Mutiny Act yourself, Mister Redmond. Yet so be it! And Mister Owen, at least, shall join us at the Court Leet. I expect a glittering affair, Mister Bradley. No less. No less, sir!'

'I fear, sir,' says Aran Owen, 'that I must also decline, since...'

Damn'd insolent dog!

'You mistake me, Mister Owen, for I issued no polite invitation in your *own* case. An instruction, sir. You shall dance attendance to explain your murals for my officers and their ladies, else Sir Oswald will ensure that the Court Leet appoints some other painter to the task. Is that not so, Mosley?'

And, with an imperious toss of his head, he provides an arm for his wife's hand once more to lead his party from the Square.

By evening, he has almost forgotten his displeasure with the Redmonds and is gratified to see that Aran Owen is, indeed, present when he enters the upstairs hall at the Commodities Exchange with his Elizabeth, delighted to hear that the small orchestra is already about its business. And it is, indeed, a glittering occasion. Bradley has ensured that every possible Whig merchant, even those few Tories who do not actively support the Jacobites, has turned out in their finest to help celebrate the Company's embodiment. Silks and satins. Greens, blues, burgundies. The scarlet, yellows and precious metals of the officers' uniforms.

So here is Bradley and, surprisingly, his young wife to greet him. Introductions are effected since Rosina has never formally met Lady Elizabeth, but their greetings are stiff, almost hostile.

'And shall there be some special entertainment to supplement the dancing, Sir Edward?' Rosina enquires. 'A heretic to be burned, perhaps? A Papist to be stoned? For I am given to understand that you may now be wanting a sufficient supply of ballad sheets.'

'You will forgive my wife's acerbic wit I trust, Lordship.'

'I have already apologised to your parents, my dear,' says Sir Edward. 'And I am happy to repeat same to your good self, madam. But should you not care to dance, my dear? Such a waste otherwise.'

The musicians are working hard, a few simple Sixes to stimulate the event. *The Beggar Boy.* Then *Kemp's Jegg.* Two fiddlers, one of them a vast wart-strewn woman who also acts the caller. The second violin a green-clad weasel. A bearded bass player. A youthful serpentist. Two flutes, each the middle-aged twin of the other.

'I should rather dance the *Gavotte*, a *Menuet*, or the *Sarabande*, Sir Edward,' Rosina replies. 'For French dance is so superior to our own.'

'My husband particularly required that there should be nothing of perfidious France about this evening, Mistress Bradley. A fie upon you to praise our enemies in any form.'

'At least we no longer need fear invasion, my dear. But come, there are others that we must greet. My thanks to you, however, Mister Bradley. And to the Court Leet also. Perhaps we shall speak again later.'

The orchestra has struck up *Tom Tinker*, a Longways, for there are now many dancers lining the hall and waiting to stretch a leg.

'That contemptible tribade and her French ways!' says Elizabeth Stanley.

'I am amazed that Bradley agreed to marry the girl,' Sir Edward replies, 'though I feel in some small part responsible since it were I that insisted on the fellow finding some way of bringing order to the town. Ah, Sir Oswald. Lady Anne. Delighted.'

And Sir Edward's duties at the rout continue in this fashion. A discussion with Mosley about refinements made to Manchester's fire carriage. Polite enquiries about the improvements made to their Staffordshire property, while the orchestra plays *Bobbing Joe*.

Then Doctor Hall, the Earl attempting a sensible discussion about his latest symptoms but the physician almost beside himself with fear of the Highlanders' imminent arrival.

Skellamesago.

Mister Owen again, this time successfully persuaded to explain his intended murals to Lady Elizabeth and also to Captain Trafford and Ensign Richmond too, both of whom appear to have attached themselves permanently to their Colonel.

The musicians have moved on to perform Roundels, though the chamber is, in truth, over-narrow to permit them. *Chirping of the Nightingale.*

The members of the Court Leet to be congratulated. Clowes, Allen and Ayrton. The attorney, Liptrott. The Borough Reeve, Fielden. The new Constables, Fowden and Walley, the former clearly a Jacobite sympathiser.

Pepper's Black.

And a clutch of his officers. The Surgeon-Lieutenant, William Leigh. Lieutenant Bradshaw. Ensign Bayley. That charming fellow Tobin, the Warrington Company's Ensign. Completely smitten with the Cooper woman, it seems, she standing in the midst of their small circle, her laughter melding with the orchestra's music.

How shocked young Tobin would be, if only he knew!

But here comes his Adjutant, and looking anxious. What can be the matter with him now? He has a dispatch, a letter from Colonel Durand, the garrison commander at Carlisle. *Such coincidence, for I only spoke of that place this half-hour past. So what can he need of me?* He breaks the seal, holds the parchment to the light, reads its short message line by line. Then again. It cannot be!

Durand has sent his detailed *communiqués* to the appropriate quarters but has taken the trouble to alert Sir Edward since it is likely that Lancashire shall shortly suffer the Jacobites' attentions. For, incredibly, Carlisle is fallen. Durand forced to surrender since General Wade, marching to his relief, had been halted by early snows in the Tyne Gap, turned back to Newcastle. And the musicians play *Drive the Cold Winter Away*, a tune that he will now always associate with disasters. But his face betrays him. Elizabeth's own fear, too, when she has read the dispatch. Bradley has noticed. Others beside. A growing flock gathers about him.

'What is it, Sir Edward?' says Bradley.

The Earl of Derby hands him the letter.

'Here, look for yourself. Those damn'd rebels have taken Carlisle.'

Rosina, he sees, standing behind her husband, has assumed an air of hubris but at least has the grace to remain silent.

'Now what shall become of us?' cries a hysterical Doctor Hall. 'Shall there be Papists, priests, debauchers of morality flocking our streets? Perhaps already here. Lord protect and save us!'

And Sir Edward is trying to calculate the thing. How long will it take them to march south? And which route shall they take? Perhaps some of them already upon the move. *But how soon? In the Name of God, how soon?*

An anxious Ensign Richmond runs breathless at his side, having earlier stepped out for a pipe.

'No time for panic, Richmond,' he says. 'Must remain calm, sir. 'Tis our duty.'

'No, sir,' says Richmond. 'There is something else. Firing from the camp. I fear that we are under attack.'

The Jacobites here so soon? Townley risen with his regiment and caught us in a trap?

'Lancashire Militia,' he cries. 'To *me*, gentlemen!' And he strides from the hall, down the steps, Bradley at his heels. 'So, here we are again, Mister Bradley. What say you, sir? It feels familiar, does it not?' He is reminded of the Pantomime, the fire at Bradley's terrace. *This pox'd town.* But tonight his chaise is waiting for him, the postillion at the ready and, though the carriage is really too small to accommodate them, he brings on board as many of the Regiment's officers as may be managed, though urging caution with his gleaming yellow paintwork. 'To the sound of the guns, good Hector!' he cries, as the vehicle steers through the dark streets, along Deansgate and down to the Camp Field.

The Colonel's Adjutant advises Sir Edward to remain with the chaise, runs with the others to ascertain the scale of the threat, but they are not gone long.

'It seems safe, sir,' says the Adjutant when he returns. 'The picquets heard a disturbance. Some noise that they describe as *heathen gallic*, sir. They called the camp to arms and shots were exchanged. Yet they think the intruders slain, Lordship. All appears quiet enough now. Should you care to inspect, sir?'

Lanthorns are brought, the ground searched, expectations high that the corpses of kilted Highlanders shall soon be discovered. Excitement at so early and honourable an action fought and won. But there are no dead Scotsmen. Simply the mortal remains of a hog, the most enormous and ugly brute that Sir Edward has ever seen. For Tarquin the Pig shall perform no further civic duties in Manchester.

Chapter Forty-Three

The Fire Bell had peeled several times through the previous day, disturbing the Sunday peace and acting as alarm against militiamen sent to destroy the bridge to Salford. Not Sir Edward's recruits, naturally, since those honest fellows, whilst lacking any form of martial tendency, now paid their shilling, supplied with good warm coats, and received the elegant blue cockades manufactured for them by Miss Clegg, at the cost of four shillings from the Earl of Derby's purse, had drawn a line at the instruction that *they* might sever the link between their own bank of the Irwell and that of the neighbouring borough. They had rebelled, mutinied and, finally, been disbanded again almost as swiftly as they were raised, their weapons sent to Liverpool that they might not be left for Townley's folk.

Exeunt Sir Edward, to join those other Companies still left him. Enter Lord Cholmondeley. Such insult added to injury! The Lord Lieutenant of their *own* County superseded by that of Cheshire in this vandals' endeavour.

He had arrived with companies of Cheshire Blues to begin the deed. Yet he could not have expected the response. For it had been Beppy Byrom, that plainest of women, who had first alerted the citizens of Manchester, rushing to the Cross and heaving on the bell rope for all that she was worth, imploring those who ran to discover the emergency's source that they should go at once to prevent this calumny. And they had done so, gathering in an angry swarm. Not merely Jacobites but all those worthy townsfolk who relied upon the bridge for their livelihood or communication with the rest of Lancashire. So the Blues, believing discretion to be the better part of valour, had decided to withdraw. There were other bridges to break, after all, and news came in regularly during the day of their destruction at Stretford, Carrington, Barton and Stockport, measures designed to impede any southward march of the Scots, to show that action was being taken. Decisive action. But action taken to reassure can often serve simply to confirm worst fears. So the morning's righteous anger had later been replaced by panic, many of those who had earlier helped to save the bridge now using it to flee with their families, carts piled high with their possessions. Even the postmaster from the Bull's Head, flown to London, they said, and all the post money gone with him.

The new Constables, Walley and Fowden, had therefore been seen at

436

every meeting place and watering hole, calling for calm, with the Day and Night Bellman paid to cry about the streets.

Then shall it be known that the honourable members of the Court Leet consider it contrary to the common wealth of this town for its warehouses to be depleted or its provisions and bedding removed. Notice is therefore given that prosecutions shall be commenced against any person offending in like fashion. God save the King and the Lord of our Manor!

Francis Townley had taken advantage of the day by recruiting some additional volunteers for a potential regiment, and Titus had been surprised by the way in which the various events had also created such a clamouring for the Cause, the reverse face of the hysteria coin. He had been doubly shocked when Townley had suggested that they might journey together to Ormschurch on the morrow, for the purpose of raising more men and to display some leadership for their loyal friends in those parts. But Titus is persuaded more by the overdue need to pay renewed respects to Driscoll's kin. Perhaps, too, after visiting Ormschurch itself, he will travel on, to Preston in time to meet the Fly Wagon when it arrives there and, hopefully, to catch his first glimpse of the Jacobite army.

Thus, on Monday the twenty-fifth of November, he hires a sure-footed mount from the Livery and bids an early morning farewell to Maria-Louise and the three girls. His wife is barely recovered from her anger about Sir Edward's anti-Catholic propaganda and, for the first time that he can recall, she has vented her ire against Aran Owen since, while there could have been no real prospect of avoiding cooperation with printing the ballad sheets, she had believed it inexcusable for him to so willingly illustrate the things. She would not have risked his friendship so readily, however, he thinks, if she did not have Bradley to entertain her once more. But it does not trouble him. For they understand each other well enough after so many years. He has his whores for comfort, after all. Yet his wife's liaison with Bradley still gives him pause. For he has shared with her the entire truth learned from Sir Watkin about the Stuarts' Exchequer and now fears that he may have erred in doing so. It was a difficult enough matter already, for she had initially been badly shaken by the news. Excessively so, he had considered. Almost as though their shared antipathy toward French involvement had, in itself, brought down disaster upon the very coffers that could have funded such an intervention. Catholic guilt, of course – that deeply inculcated superstition that, he supposes, is the bedrock of all faiths but which, in their own, is polished to such extreme. But it did not seem that Bradley or his faction were yet aware of the Treasury's entire loss and it would not answer if he should learn of it through some careless chatter.

'I understand that your son-in-law has arranged for the Court Leet to agree an extension to Shaw's hours?' says Townley as they head across the Irwell Bridge, so recently saved from destruction.

'There is likely to be great demand for the Punch House facilities when the Prince and his army reach us.' And Titus knows that their arrival is now imminent, regular reports being received of their progress south, seemingly in three columns, Lord Elcho scouting ahead with the cavalry, Lord George Murray with the Lowland Division, and Charles Edward himself with the Highlanders and rest of the cavalry.

The journey passes easily enough so that they reach Wigan after noon when they rest and feed on Wallgate. The discussion, never quite companionable between these two, has ranged from gossip about the Jacobite prospects to the success or failure of their latest wagers in the Cockpit. Townley has received word, though not from his brother, that the Duke of Perth has been given a less prominent role in the army due to his strong Catholic Faith and the Prince's obsession with presenting himself as leader of a broader kirk. Then on the road once more, now cloaked against an insistent rain, driven to a sullen silence in which Titus broods on the many causes of his dislike for Townley while they pass through Upholland, Skelmersdale, Westhead and into Ormschurch itself climbing the eastern slope of the ridge on which the town is balanced, passing Crosse Hall, home of the Earl of Derby's cousins, along the main thoroughfare and, finally, dismounting at the Brewer's Arms in Aughton Street where they arrange accommodation for the night.

But there is little chance for rest since, Townley having sent ahead his intention of visiting the town, a gathering has been arranged at the Mass House, the dwelling adjoining the inn and used by local Roman Catholics for their worship. Still, the two men take a bowl of stew, some small beer, until they are disturbed both by the growing clamour outside and also by the excited entry of Jacob's cousin, Peter Kenyon.

'Give thee joy o' this night, gentlemen,' cries Kenyon. 'Such a sight I never would 'ave thought to see. No, finish tha' food, I beg!'

'Kenyon,' says Titus. 'It is good to see you again. But such a tumult. What is it, man?'

Kenyon gestures for them to look themselves, so Titus and Townley set down a few coins, gather their coats and step out into the wind-swept slope of the lane, just below the Cross that marks the junction of roads to Preston in the north, Liverpool in the south, and Wigan in the east, the area in which the town's famous Thursday market takes place. To their right, the neighbouring house, a simple brick dwelling, has every window ablaze, its rooms obviously full, its occupants spilling into the street and forming a crowd more than one hundred strong.

'Word is out, Mister Townley,' shouts Kenyon, above the surrounding clamour. 'And these good folk come, every one, to sign for tha' regiment. But come. Will tha' not say a word or two?'

He calls for passage without even waiting to see if they follow. But, of course, they do so, jostled by these glovers, foundrymen, brewers, ropers, farm labourers and watch-makers. Titus Redmond's own pocket-piece was made here, fitted with its reliable Ormschurch Mechanism. The clock in his reception hall, too, a Taylor longcase.

Through the house, pushing their way up the stairs and into a front room, its large window now thrown open. Kenyon thrusts his head and shoulders outside, holds up his hands for silence as torches flare and gutter below him.

'Good citizens of Ormschurch,' he says. 'Such generosity of spirit! Such loyalty to our King over the water!' Huzzahs and cries of *Hear him!* Titus pushed forwards, close behind Kenyon. 'How long have we awaited this day? His Royal Highness at Lancaster, they say. Preston by tomorrow's night. Manchester this week. And the Hanoverian pack all distressed. All a-panic. My Lord Warrington, we hear, fled from his roost with twenty thousand ounces of silver plate from his own town, and blew their fine Mersey bridge behind him! And here in our midst we have two of t' gentlemen who worked so long for this night. For our deliverance! Good people of Ormschurch, allow me to name Mister Titus Redmond, esquire of Manchester.'

More huzzahs, as Kenyon pulls himself from the window and Titus, his modest reluctance flattened, is thrust into the aperture, struggling for appropriate words. *Esquire, indeed!*

'Friends of freedom!' he says, at last. 'Peter Kenyon does me too much honour, for I am only one of many in this County who have subscribed for His Majesty's return. There are plenty here tonight who have done likewise. And such a response! Myself and our associates in Manchester had known that your town would rise to this occasion as it has done throughout the ages. But this is beyond our dreams. Yet Mister Kenyon is only partly correct about the Earl of Warrington. Do we not, at times, find friends in strange places? For it was this same George Booth who helped to finance the very turnpikes down which our Prince Regent now hastens to us.' Huzzahs and laughter both. 'A man after my own heart, who puts the efforts of Hanover to the profit of Stuart' Cheers and applause. 'Yet we must not forget the purpose for which we are here, and so I give you Mister Francis Townley.'

Titus is rescued from the window. *Hear him! Hear him!* And Townley is pushed forward in his place.

'So,' he cries, 'Jacobites they name us and Jacobites we are proud to be! United now, at last. And I am joyous to bring greetings of this fraternity from your brothers in Manchester town. Not Manchester alone, mind. But from every town and hamlet of the Salford Hundred. We do not seek war for, by the Mass, these lands have been ravaged enough by conflict both abroad and here, on our own soil. Yet if it is war that Hanover and German George desire then, in the name of Our Lord, war they shall have! Let them learn the lesson of Gladsmuir Field. For they cannot stand against honest folk, fighting to restore the True King of this Realm. They say that we covenant with the Pope, you and I, mistaking us all for believers in the Church of Rome. But I know, as you do, that there are many in our midst with a different faith.' The huzzahs are more muted here. Men in the room with Titus look to each other. 'Yet all of us,' Townley continues, 'share a faith in Good King James.' The applause more certain again now. 'And if any would take up arms on his behalf, if any are willing to join us in His Majesty's defence, then you may sign your names below. Mister Kenyon shall set a table in this house, and you may make your mark. We do not stand alone, gentlemen, for my brother, who rides with the noble Prince, sends word that the Scottish Host, the warriors of Our Lady, shall reach Manchester in a matter of days. Those that sign tonight shall join them there, for I shall lead you. A mighty army and one that, my brother tells me, shall soon be supported by our friends from France. Hunger and death await our foes, while glory and freedom await our allies. The day is near, good people, when those who are Catholic among you shall not be forced to worship in a Mass House such as this, nor in the secret rooms of Catholic Lords, yet shall have the right once more to build your own churches, that we may receive the Word of our Lord, that we may find Salvation through the Holy Sacraments, in the way that God intended. So bless King James the Third! And bless the Prince of Wales, Regent of these lands!'

There is a great deal of back-slapping as Townley is helped from the window, begging them, prithee, to be careful with his fine blue coat. Titus, too, finds himself quite carried away by the moment as the people outside, those on the stairs and elsewhere within the Mass house as well, continue their loud endorsement.

He answers questions to the best of his ability, but evading any explicit answers, as they are led downstairs once more. How many are already signed for the Manchester Regiment? What manner of arms shall they bear? Are there uniforms? Pay? Not an important matter, naturally, but one likes to know these things. Will there be fighting, or shall the army of King George turn its tail again?

In a room on the ground floor, a table has indeed been positioned, a thin line of fellows waiting impatiently to sign or mark their names while pen and paper are found so that the thing may be made official. Townley, it seems, is now very much the man of the hour, making arrangements to join Kenyon and a few others in going about the town later and beating up for more volunteers. A drum has even been fetched to give the thing some military *gravitas*. But Titus declines the invitation to accompany them. No, he will stay at the Brewer's Arms and rest a while for, though Townley shall return tomorrow to Manchester with as many as will join him, Titus himself has determined on an early start to Preston and, yes, he is happy to convey a brief note from Francis to his brother with the latest news.

Yet there is no rest, for many of the men follow him into the inn, their questions endless, and when he finally believes that he might escape to his bed, some bloody-pated cove comes stumbling through the door to tell them that mayhem has broken out near the Parish Church. Mayhem indeed. For as Titus comes out onto a cold and draughty Aughton Street, he and his fellows from the tavern, like stopper from the bottle, there are men running in all directions, a few women too, but most of the activity is up near the Cross, to his left.

'What is happening?' he shouts.

The cove with a kerchief pressed to his bleeding skull is at his side.

'They caught your friend, sir,' he says, 'and Kenyon, too. Top end o' Church Street. Whiggish bastards. Damn'd Presbyterians. They give us 'ard knocks, sir.'

So, Townley in trouble. Well, we shall see how he handles himself! There is a moment's temptation to leave him stew, but it quickly passes.

'Shall we go to their aid, gentlemen?' he cries. And yes, sir, lead on, they reply. 'Then, in the name of Our Lady, keep together,' Titus warns them and leads off up the lane at the head of twenty others. More men join them as they near the Cross, turning back rallied from inglorious flight.

Left into narrow Church Street, winding up to the highest western point of the town's ridge and the open space before Saint Peter and Saint Paul's, dominated by the bulk of its large tower and a rarity in also having a steeple, though this latter largely in ruin, blown down some years before. This, Titus knows, is the resting place for so many of Sir Edward Stanley's ancestors. *Damn him and his Popish Plots!*

The small green resembles a battlefield, dozens injured while, at the farther edge, against the wall, a knot of men, Townley at their centre, is surrounded by a much larger group, striking at them with any makeshift weapon but being held mostly at bay, it seems, by Townley himself. For this is a Francis Townley that he has rarely seen. Townley, formerly of the French army. Townley the cudgeller. Oh, he has seen him fight his share of bouts in *canne de combat*. But that is an entirely different environment. Here, he is pitting his skills as a singlestick fighter against a score of opponents at the same time. And enjoying the game, it seems, as he spews profanities against them.

Titus halts his followers a moment since, to their left, another scuffle is taking place. More of their Jacobite friends, he assumes, but this dozen entirely overwhelmed by a gang significantly more numerous than themselves. Papist scum, shout the attackers, along with similar insults and led, it seems, by two men who must surely be the Town Constables, each sporting a long staff, tipped with silver. One of them notices the newcomers, pulls at his companion, looks from Titus to Townley's *mêlée*.

'You gentlemen, go about your business, if you know what's good for you!' shouts this crow-faced fellow, as they begin to drag their captives back along the street towards the town centre.

A woman appears, distressed and frightened. She sees a man that she is plainly seeking amongst the prisoners. Husband or brother, perhaps.

'William, in God's name...' But she is knocked aside.

'Where are they taking them?' says Titus, though already knowing that they are bound for the House of Correction. Should they engage the Constables? Try to release those already taken? But he knows that they could not prevail over so large a force. 'Come,' he shouts. 'Let us help those that we may!' And he leads them against Townley's attackers, using his fists like hammers to strike one of the dogs about the neck, felling him and stamping on his back for good measure once he is down. He grasps another's stick from behind, kicks him in the arse to send him scuttling until, at last, the mob melts away, leaving only the battered defenders of Jacobite honour and their thinly-populated relief force.

Kenyon is amongst the fallen, his face badly beaten and, it seems, a leg broken. They send word for Mary, his wife, trying to make him comfortable against the wall, while Townley checks for damage to coat, his person being entirely unscathed.

'Well, that warmed the evening,' he says, tossing aside the cudgel with which he has conducted the defence. He picks up the drum, trampled and broken, then throws it aside again. 'Such a mess of our rowdy-dowdy. Yet a timely intervention, friend Titus. If you had not arrived, I suspect those Constables and their ruffians would have turned the balance against us. Perhaps we should consider a commission for you in the Regiment.'

'Me?' says Titus. 'I think not. I am a spent force, after all. Am I not?' And, as the fellow that he had struck down begins to raise himself on tender elbows, Redmond turns to him, aiming a vicious kick against the side of his head.

Next morning, the town is remarkably quiet, much to Townley's annoyance. Most of those who had signed the list as volunteers do not appear, and there are fewer than thirty who finally muster for the journey to Manchester. Oh, there are messages sent from others, of course. Fathers, husbands, sons, who will follow later, when order is restored, when their friends are released, when their affairs are put in order. Annoyed perhaps, but never dejected, it seems. For his bearing could be that of a Marshal in the service of King Louis, thinks Titus, as Townley proudly leads his mixed force, some mounted, a few afoot, others crowded in a cart, from the Mass House, past the jeering spectators at the Cross, and off towards the Wigan Road.

For his own part, an aching Titus Redmond packs his valise, including the note to Townley's brother, and spurs his horse northwards, ignored by the anti-Catholic crowd. They have been fired, the innkeeper had told him, by tales that the Jacobites had taken women and children, during their siege of Carlisle, bound and chained them to use as human shields against the garrison's cannon. Other stories, predictable he supposes, about the Highlanders' fondness for spitting and roasting babies. Has there ever been a war, he wonders, in which one side has not levelled that ridiculous charge against the other? So down Burscough Street towards the village for which that thoroughfare is named, and thence onto the Roman Way that leads through Rufford and beyond, the long, straight route over heath and moss to Preston, where it meanders across the Ribble, between the market gardens, fields and orchards which surround that place.

It is night again when he arrives, but the weather turned milder once more, the town like a celestial chart, glistening with a thousand lanthorns, pulsating with the tramp of marching feet as the last of the Scottish regiments come in, keening with the drone of pipers somewhere in the distance, licking at the darkness with the smoke from cook fires and the dripped juices of roast meat. The town is crowded, though he eventually finds lodging at the Mitre on Fishergate, where he takes a late mutton supper in company with another fellow also recently arrived, sharing a bottle with him.

He introduces himself as Grant, James Grant, lately in the army of King Louis but now proud to be representing His Majesty by serving the artillery train of the Prince Regent. An Irishman, of course, as his accent will betray.

'I have heard,' says Titus 'that there is a gentleman of that name who not only serves but commands the train. Do I have the honour to be addressing Lieutenant-Colonel Grant, sir?'

'You are well-informed, friend. Not another spy, I trust? We seem to have been plagued by them. I mean no offence, sir, but you are...?'

Titus gives a brief account of himself. A fustian manufacturer from Manchester. But a loyal servant of the Cause and married to the daughter of James FitzWilliams, who fought at the Boyne. His wife has spoken frequently about the Grants of Iverk. Neighbours, he thinks, though perhaps there is no connection here. But connection there *is*, and the door to informality opened. For Grant recalls the FitzWilliams family very well. He himself, like so many of his countrymen, had left Ireland to seek fortune in France, studied mathematics there, worked for a while as assistant to the great Cassini in the Paris Observatory and eventually enticed to join Lally's Regiment as a Lieutenant, using his skills to assist the military engineers. He had fought at Fontenoy and not hesitated a moment, not a single moment, when he had heard of the Prince's expedition. And, yes, now finds himself a Lieutenant-Colonel, to be sure. Such a thing!

'Give you joy of your success, sir,' Titus says. 'Then you must have been with His Highness since Edinburgh, I collect. And is he already arrived in Preston then? I must confess myself abhorrent to this modern obsession with celebrity of the individual, for the reality is so often a disappointment, do you not find? Yet I should like to have seen this Stuart Prince for whom we have waited so long.'

'You have no great faith in the human spirit then Mister Redmond? But, yes, the Prince is here, just along by the court to the Shamble. Came in this afternoon. White charger and pipers at his tail. The townsfolk all a'cheering and tossing their bonnets. And a true leader, sir. You would not find disappointment with *that* gentleman, I think. Never a river to cross that he is not first to leap in and show the way. Never a road to be trod that he is not at the head, and always walking like his men, though it has near killed him, I fear, on occasion.'

'Then he must be a rare specimen indeed. And a miracle from Our Lady that he is sent to us. There are so few, I fear, with true sagacity. And those, for the most part, simply folk with sufficient intelligence to understand their own fallibility. The genuinely wise man is he who understands his own propensity for foolishness, is he not? If His Royal Highness displays no more than *that* quality, it marks him for distinction.'

'You shall not be disappointed, Mister Redmond, I believe. Why, sir, there was nobody more astonished than myself to find that our three separate columns, following quite distinct paths from the north, should have united again here in Preston at the precise hour appointed by our Royal Commander. And his plan alone that brought us here. Yet it is not the place I had imagined. Do you know the town, sir?'

Two fiddlers have appeared, and Titus smiles as they strike up *The King Shall Play His Own Again*.

'I do indeed, though not well. A pretty enough place, not Manchester, nor Liverpool, but well enough in its way, sitting as it does on the main thoroughfare between north and south. I know many of the merchants here, traders in linen yarn and cloth, like myself. Good trade, too, if you can ever establish yourself. The Guilds Merchant control things tightly here, and meet only once in a generation to consider new admissions. But I have never known a borough, neither, so full of attorneys, notaries and proctors. Petty-foggers, all of them, naturally. But your journey south, sir, it was difficult? And we hear so many rumours about the size of your forces. Yet perhaps you shall fear that I am spying once more?'

'So far as our army is concerned, I suspect that the time for concealment is well passed. We are five thousand now, so far as I can tell. Less than when we started from Edinburgh for the Scots have a tendency to drift away, so. The Highlanders, the best of them at least, are well enough. Lord Kilmarnock came in before we left the town. Then more MacGregors. Ewan MacPherson of Cluny with four hundred, though the rogue had already changed sides twice previously. Six hundred raised by Tullibardine. And then, at last, my own sweet darlings. Our pieces brought from Montrose. Six four-pounders that we took at Fontenoy. Light barrels in the old Swedish style. Six curricles taken from Cope at Gladsmuir, or Prestonpans as they now prefer. Each throwing only a one and a half-pound shot, but mobile, by God. And my

444

pretty Octagon. A long brassy wench but older than my grandsires. Ah, here come my captains, Mister Redmond. Please allow me to name Du Saussey...' *Enchanté*, says an absurdly tall cove in French uniform. 'And Burnet.' A polite greeting from the latter, burdened with the broad dialect of Aberdeenshire, unless Titus is mistaken. 'I was just explaining to Mister Redmond, one of our honest Manchester Jacobites, gentlemen, about our significant artillery train. Not quite the scale to which Du Saussey is accustomed, I fear. He likes his siege guns, you see. But he commands a company of his own here. Burnet too. Fine fellows. But thank Heaven for the gunners, eh? We brought twelve of our own from France with us. A brace of lieutenants besides. D'Andrion and Bodin. Good men both.'

'Yet will you join us gentlemen?' asks Titus. 'With the Colonel's permission of course?' Freely given. 'And a glass of wine with you both. A difficult journey, I gather?'

'There was snow on the high fells,' says Burnet, a stocky and pugnacious man, recently come from some hard labour by the dirt on his hands and under his nails. 'Oh, you will forgive me, sir,' he says, noticing the direction of Redmond's gaze. 'I am literally just returned from our positions. His Royal Highness is always insistent on our readiness for action and, while our gunners know their trade, we are sadly lacking a company of pioneers. They will insist on sending us gardeners and any others who they cannot easily turn to soldiery, believing that they will suffice.' The Frenchman, Du Saussey, nods in agreement though Titus suspects that he can barely follow a word of the conversation. 'But here is the thing, Mister Redmond. The question on all our lips, sir. Will the English Jacobites come out now? For we have seen no evidence of it thus far.'

'I can promise you, Captain,' says Titus, 'that when you reach Manchester, matters will be different. Why, sir, we were all caught by surprise. One minute at Edinburgh and every indication that the Prince would stay in Scotland a while longer, to secure his Kingdom there, naturally. And the next moment, we hear that he is reached Carlisle. You must forgive us for being ill-prepared, I think. Yet only last evening we were about the towns of Lancashire drumming for supporters. To supplement those waiting to take up arms in Manchester itself. Myself and Mister Townley, brother to a French Captain of that name. You know him?'

'Captain Townley?' says Grant. 'Naturally. He is with the good Prince now, I think. And one of those responsible for your apparent lack of preparation then, I might add. For the debate in Edinburgh was endless. Townley was amongst those supporting the Prince in his view that further delay in Scotland would only serve to help the Hanoverians rally, that a speedy descent into England would prevent the army drifting apart and more speedily attract a French invasion.'

'Still talk of invasion then?' Titus says. 'We were given to understand that circumstances would not now be considered… How shall I put this? Appropriate?'

Grant shrugs his shoulders. 'Ça va! It is all a matter of finances, I suppose, eh? But the Prince has assured his Council that he has absolute letters of support, pledges of assistance, from King Louis. But I am for my bed, gentlemen, if you will excuse me.'

They all stand. A bow from Burnet and 'Goodnight, Colonel'. A snapping to attention from Du Saussey and '*Monsieur le Baron*'. A polite 'Great pleasure, sir' from Titus who, with Grant retired now offers his own apologies to the two officers.

'But Captain Du Saussey,' he says, 'referred to Colonel Grant as *Monsieur le Baron*? Or did I not attend him correctly?'

'No, Mister Redmond,' says Burnet. 'You attended perfectly well. For the Prince has this week conferred a peerage upon our noble Lieutenant-Colonel. For his part at the siege of Carlisle. He is now Baron of Iverk. *Le Baron d'Iverque*.'

The following day, Wednesday the twenty-seventh of November, dawns mild and clear. A pleasant day, unseasonal. and in prosperous Preston, proud Preston, a day of rest has been declared. A holiday, almost. So Titus sends a boy from the inn for John Townley at the army's headquarters in Church Street, suggesting that, should he be at liberty, Mister Redmond would be pleased if they might break their fast together at the Mitre, and he is taken somewhat by surprise when the good Captain himself arrives within ten minutes to accept his offer.

'My dear fellow,' says Titus, 'I am so very pleased to see you again. And in such circumstances. By the Mass, how long is it since we met at Townley Hall to speculate about this day? It must be eighteen months. Longer perhaps. And Mistress Cecilia? Still in mourning?'

'I doubt that she will ever recover from my nephew's death. But it is nearer twenty months since we met, Mister Redmond, and much has passed for each of us, I think.'

'Francis will have kept you abreast of matters in Manchester, I collect. Ah, and while I recall, I have a note from him. He left it with me when we parted in Ormschurch yesterday morning. Both he and our friend, Peter Kenyon, were attacked quite shamelessly by a damn'd Whiggish mob. Kenyon's leg is broken, I fear. And many of the better townsfolk deterred from joining our Cause.'

He passes the letter to Townley. It is not sealed and he opens it quickly, scanning the lines.

'Yes,' he says. 'He makes reference here, says that you came to his rescue, sir. A fie upon him, he was always prone to finding trouble. Tilts headlong at everything in his path. Impatience. It will be the death of him, I swear! But he hopes to join us here tonight.'

'I must confess, Captain, that I had imagined you would be much in demand today.'

'Well, I have the honour to act as guard for the Marquis d'Eguilles. You know that the Marquis serves as Ambassador to the Stuart Court here? Yes, of course. And I am normally required to accompany him for the Prince Regent's Council Meetings. But not today. A private discussion in attempt to break their deadlock. For the Prince is set on moving quickly on London, and the Marquis supports him in the matter. But the others – well, I cannot speak for them. It is certainly true that they have lost some heart by the lack of English support. Not only its lack but, at times, open hostility. The attack on Kilmarnock's son at Lowther Hall. The men of Whitehaven risen against us while we were at Carlisle. Our Lord be praised that we are now on more friendly territory. But will our good Lancastrians come out, Mister Redmond? That is the question, sir.'

They take breakfast at the Mitre, with Titus updating the Captain on the Subscription, his brother's work in raising volunteers while John Townley, for his part, gives a lively account of his past year with the Black Musketeers, their actions in Flanders, at Fontenoy, his pride at the heroism of the Irish Brigade. They agree to take a turn around the town but they are no sooner on Fishergate than a ragged band of recruiters comes beating up the street.

'Sergeant Dickson and his crew,' says Townley.

'Dickson?'

'The fellow with the English uniform and the plaid. He was taken at Prestonpans and turned his coat. It seems that he is now our most fervent advocate, though I do not believe that he has brought us many people.'

'And the woman? Not one of our sergeants, surely.'

'Some whore that he has found along the way. They call her Long Preston Peggy. It seems that she has the gift of prophecy'

'And have we dared ask her how this thing will end?'

'I fear that none of us have been so bold. Yet we should not delay. Do you know that the King shall be proclaimed at noon? We must away to the Cross, my friend.'

They arrive at the Moot Hall, turning left into Cheapside and the Market Square, already crowded with a gathering throng, noisy townsfolk leaning from every window of its perimeter dwellings, its timbered houses, large and small, its inns and taverns. They find a gin-house where Titus indulges his habit, fetching a cup out to the street so that he see the regiments arrive, though it is difficult with so many already here before them. And they can hear them, of course, long before they come into sight. Bagpipes, drumming too, a tremor in the paving slabs, growing stronger over five minutes, maybe ten, and then the clatter of hooves, the jingle of harness until the Prince's Lifeguards trot around the corner and into view, Lord Elcho at their head, says Townley, his men resplendent in blue jackets with red facings, their waistcoats scarlet and trimmed with gold lace, tricorne hats each bearing a white cockade.

A pause, while the skirling echoes louder, and Titus is finally able to see the Highlanders about whom he has heard so much. A small banner first, followed by a line of pipers, and then a fine-looking fellow in dark coat, tartan trousers. Donald Cameron of Lochiel, his clan regiment behind him, rank upon rank of warrior Scots, the first groups finely attired. Officers and gentlemen, Titus assumes, in their colourful chequered jackets and trews, their polished weaponry while, to their rear march three hundred more, their drab-patterned plaids belted at the waist, the upper parts rolled and slung across chest and shoulder, or bound about the stomach. Young men already bearded, old fellows with white hair streaming from their bonnets, some armed with broadsword and studded wooden shield, but the majority bearing modern muskets.

Behind the Camerons, the Prince himself. Charles Edward Louis John Casimir Silvester Severino Maria Stuart. Tall in his saddle. Blue coarse-spun grogram and gold lacing. Red waistcoat and breeches. Star and garter on his left side, and a fine basket-hilted sword hanging from a baldric over his shoulder. Three-cornered hat with white feathers and a white cockade. Handsome enough, Titus supposes, and the women in the crowd certainly seem to agree, but his pouting lips seem to set the Prince apart from the men about him, his features owing more, perhaps, to his Polish ancestry than to the Stuart bloodline. He seems languid too, almost melancholy, more a man of fashion than the conquering hero that Titus had expected. *Well, there you have it! Set some cunny-sucker on a pedestal and you deserve disappointment.*

Another regiment, the Lowlanders of John Roy Stuart, uniformed in dark browns, greys and ochres, and then a procession of the town's Guildsmen before, finally, the last of the units on parade for this occasion, the Stewarts of Appin.

They form up around the sides of the Square, the Prince taking station with his Lifeguards. Somebody calls for three huzzahs, but it is a feeble attempt, lost in the overall cheering that does not abate throughout the short proceedings. An equerry, at the Prince Regent's command, rides forward to the Cross and, still mounted, unfurls a parchment, reading out the contents with grandiose theatricality. Wasted talent, of course, since nobody but himself can actually hear the words that King James the Third hereby proclaims... Well, whatever is written. But the general tenor is understood and the crowd's inability to hear the fellow does nothing to dampen their ardour when he is finished, the scroll tied once more for another day.

Townley suggests that, if they wish to dine, they should escape before the crowds and, since it will be impossible to find a table in the immediate vicinity, perhaps they might repair to the Joiner's Arms, for he understands that David Morgan is also in town and lodging there. It is a tidy step away from the square, in North Street, but the Captain has correctly calculated that it will be easier to find space there and, as it happens, Morgan has had the same idea, already enjoying a plate of beef, a dish of kidneys and a good stout.

'Mister Redmond!' cries the Welsh lawyer. 'And Captain Townley. We are met again, good sirs. William,' he says to his companion, 'this is the Manchester gentleman of whom we have spoke so often. A prodigious fund-raiser. And, Mister Redmond, allow me to name William Vaughan, of Courtfield.' Titus bows to each in turn. Townley too. 'And the good Captain has the distinction to serve with the French Horse Guards. A Black Musketeer no less. How is your brother, sir? I have not seen him since September, that unfortunate evening when Sir Watkins's ledger was stolen. Unfortunate, too, since your brother bested me in several wagers at the Cockpit, Captain Townley.'

Sir Watkin sends his warmest greetings, naturally. But such a pleasure to meet again. They share the table, call for bread, one of the inn's famous meat puddings, more ale. Morgan dominates the discussion, as usual, ascertains that Townley is presently performing duties for the French Ambassador here. He, himself, is due to meet Lord Elcho, to confirm Sir Watkin's plans for a march on Chester, to offer his humble talents, to place them at the disposal of His Royal Highness. Vaughan also, for *his* brother is already an officer in the Duke of Perth's Regiment. How strange to be here in Preston, however. After all this time. And he recalls their conversations at Townley Hall, about the Captain's elder brother, Richard Townley, the manner of his legal defence against charges of sedition for his part in the Rising of the Year '15. He had been on his way north, to join Forster and the army. Just turned twenty and eager for the fight. But all over before he even reached England.

'Aye,' says Titus, 'I remember our meeting too, Mister Morgan. I feared that the Prince might raise no more than ten thousand Scots for our Cause, and you reminded me that, even in '15, twice that number had come out. And now, here he is with only five thousand.' But Titus recalls other things too. His concerns about Sir Watkin and the motivation behind his support for the Jacobites. *You still plan to buy the Throne, Sir Watkin? And where are the rest of your rich Tory Remitters now? The Duke of Beaufort dead. The Earls of Barrymore and Cork gone to ground. The Stuart Exchequer lost. Do you yet believe that you can purchase the influence with King James that you have been denied by Turnip George?*

'Still,' says Morgan, 'we are here in Preston. Several marches ahead of General Wade and in fine order to defeat Ligonier should we come up with him. And your Manchester fellows not yet joined us, nor Sir John Glynne's Flintshiremen. Hundreds of them, Mister Redmond.'

'And London, sir?' asks Townley. 'What news of London?'

'As I have always maintained, Captain, the matter will be settled long before we reach London. But we have sufficient supporters there, also, to defend the Capital.'

Townley hopes that he is correct, but is reminded that the Prince intends to review the disposition of his forces later in the afternoon and, while the Captain must attend upon the Ambassador, they would all be welcome to join him. Morgan and Vaughan will meet them at three o'clock outside the Mitre so long as the meeting with Lord Elcho concludes early enough.

'You do not like Lawyer Morgan, I gather?' says Townley as they walk back towards Fishergate.

'He is a lick-spittle Petty-Fogger,' Titus replies. 'What is there *not* to find objectionable? Yet, in truth, he does not trouble me greatly, though he is a prickly character.'

They part in good spirits, Townley heading off to meet the Marquis but promising to return, if he is able, at three.

The appointed hour arrives, and the four men meet again, mounted, at the Mitre, all of them surprised to find that Francis Townley has also arrived, ridden like the devil to reach them. He had made the return journey from Ormschurch to Manchester in time to find billets for his new charges that night, and left at first light this morning, travelling almost without rest to reach Preston. His horse is spent, however, so he spends some time at the Livery, paying for the care of his own beast and hiring another for this evening. He brings news, too, that many of the Mersey bridges have now been completely destroyed by the various groups of Militia, including those companies remaining to Sir Edward.

Morgan assures them, however, that Lord Elcho already possesses this intelligence, so they ride back to the Cross, meet with the Marquis d'Eguilles and his party. Introductions again. *Votre serviteur, Monsieur*, this to Titus. Polite greetings to the others also. *Now this French fellow would charm even Maria-Louise.* He chats amiably, a good grasp of the English language, professes himself in difficulty with the idiom adopted by the east coast Scotsmen, hopes that he shall fare better here in Lancashire. Good progress being made, too, now that they are finally marching south. Such limited opportunities for success in Scotland. And have they heard that his peculiar friend, the *Comte de Maurepas*, had suggested that they might help the Scots establish a republic in that country. The very idea, *Messieurs*. A republic! And proposed by France. It is… Perhaps they have the word in English also. *Risible!*

The small cavalcade passes out into Fishergate, east into Church Street, past the much decayed and frequently repaired squat shape of Saint John the Divine, and out to the junction with Ribchester Road where they catch the Lifeguards at the rear of the Prince's own party as it swings south, down across the Swill Brook and through the small township of Fishwick before crossing the Ribble to the open heath flanking the new turnpike road to Standish, Chorley and Wigan. There is a northwards bend in that eminently navigable river here, and the Jacobite forces have thrown up a series of earthworks between the lower ends of the meander, forming an almost impregnable semi-circle in which their camp is protected.

It is a significant location for the Scots, for when their Covenanter Army had marched on England during the Great Civil War, it was on the northern side of the Ribble that they had been caught and destroyed by Cromwell's Ironsides. Likewise, in the Year '15, the Jacobite army had found itself trapped in Preston town itself and been defeated there. And thus, according to Townley, there had been great fear within the Prince's regiments, amongst people with superstition bred in the bone, that the Ribble would once again be their nemesis, a barrier that they would not succeed in passing. So, for this reason alone, Lord George Murray having reached Preston, he simply continued onwards, riding over the Ribble Bridge and planting their standard on the ground beyond. 'There, good fellows!' he had cried. 'We are now deeper into England than any Scots army has ever trod before us.'

Lord George rides to join the Prince now, Murray a colourful figure in the brightest tartans and trews that Titus has yet seen, vivid orange and blues, his round face placid, intelligent. They ride together along the forward defences, pausing at any significant emplacement, and Titus is able to see Lieutenant-Colonel Grant and his officers responding to whatever questions the Prince may have chosen to cast them. The inspection lasts perhaps twenty minutes until, after a few moments of final conversation, Murray stands in his stirrups and turns to point back across the river. He calls instructions, too, for some of his officers, and there is a flurry of activity as several of the oldest amongst them also take horse to fall in beside their Commander-in-Chief.

'What is this?' Titus asks, but nobody seems to know.

Charles Edward and his extended escort break into a fast trot, cross the bridge again and, once more on the Fishwick side, they turn slightly left, off the road itself and towards a line of trees. As they approach, the whole group now spreads along the southern margent of the Swill Brook so that they can see, on the farther ground, the shallow grass-grown remains of a ditch and low embankment, stretching along their front.

The older men who have so recently accompanied the Prince are now pointing in this direction and that, to the road away to their right and also up the rising terrain before them and the buildings which, at the crown of the ridge, form the outskirts of the town centre, only a quarter-mile away. So it becomes clear, from their descriptions, their gestures, their emotion, that they stand on the scene of fighting in which they took part here, in the name of Charles Edward's father, veterans of that other struggle, lost thirty years earlier.

'It shall not be so on this occasion, loyal friends,' they hear the Prince say, and he sits a moment, quietly surveying the scene.

Captain Townley turns to the Ambassador.

'*Monsieur le Marquis,*' he says, '*je tiens à présenter mes compagnons du Monseigneur. C'est possible?*'

451

But of course it is possible, and de Boyer urges his mount alongside His Royal Highness, all graceful diplomacy, apologies for the intrusion, until Charles Edward glances in their direction, a faint smile parting his plump lips, and the Marquis gestures for them to join him.

'*Le Capitaine* Townley is already known to us, of course' says the Prince, his accent a curious mixture of the continental and Irish, it seems to Titus. He seems almost nervous at the encounter, too, his brown eyes flicking from one to the other of his subjects, wisps of his own red hair poking from beneath the powdered peruke. *So young! Though he does not appear so from a distance.*

Francis Townley presented next. The good Captain's brother, previously in French service also. And both of *them* brothers to the former Squire of Townley Hall, who had fought for His Majesty here at Preston. Of course, says the Prince, who hears that the gentleman has been prodigious successful in raising volunteers in Lancashire. Efforts that shall not go unrewarded, he promises.

Morgan and Vaughan, the latter due to join the ranks, the former an envoy from Sir Watkin Williams Wynn and those loyal servants in Charles Edward's own Principality of Wales. Mister Morgan an Attorney of some note.

'If so, Mister Morgan,' replies the Prince, 'we should be pleased to have you join our person for we have sore need of a legal voice within the Privy Council.'

'You do me too much honour, Your Highness,' says Morgan, while the Prince whispers some instruction to his secretary.

And, finally, Mister Titus Redmond, also from Manchester, a merchant of those parts and one of His Majesty's most faithful adherents. The Prince seems almost surprised, fixes Titus with a penetrating gaze that belies his youthful appearance. But he says nothing, turns instead to some of the officers at a little distance from him, seems as though he will send his secretary with a message but then changes his mind.

'Colonel!' he calls, seeming embarrassed, breaking some protocol perhaps by raising his voice to such a pitch in public. 'Colonel O'Sullivan!'

This fellow, Titus knows, must be John William O'Sullivan, the Prince's Adjutant and now Quartermaster-General, though you might not know it from his plain dress, and he looks far from well, sneezing and clapping a kerchief to his face.

'Your Highness will forgive me, I trust,' says the Irishman, 'if I maintain a respectful distance. For this damn'd cold, this constipation, refuses to dissipate.'

'It has plagued you since Edinburgh, one collects,' the Prince replies, seeming angered by the fact. 'Still, Colonel, allow us to name Mister Redmond, sir. Mister Titus Redmond.'

'The same, sir?' says O'Sullivan. 'Why, your reputation and good name precede you, Mister Redmond. Yet we had not hoped to make your acquaintance until we reached Manchester itself. And these gentlemen with you? Captain Townley, I know, but...'

So Titus, surprised to find himself thus renowned, makes the introductions yet again while O'Sullivan begs him to meet later, for a private discussion, at his quarters in town.

They are dismissed by a gesture of the royal hand and ride back up the hill, past the House of Correction where, just as they turn along Church Street, Titus catches sight of his own Fly Wagon on the last few hundred yards of its journey from Manchester. He falls in alongside the wagon-master, a decent fellow whose tongue is too large for his mouth, excited almost beyond clumsy words to be here amongst the Jacobite army but bringing news that Reverend Hoole has died. He does not have the detail and Titus is not greatly concerned, one way or the other. He may be a Non-Juror but he has proven to be no friend to the Jacobite Cause. *Another cunny-sucker!* Titus sees the cart to its destination, its Preston goods safely unloaded and several passengers disembarked, including two friends of Francis Townley, unable to contain themselves until the Prince reaches Manchester and anxious to enlist immediately. The wagoner is quartered for the night and reassured that he will meet no more than the normal perils for his onward journey to Carlisle.

Thus, by seven o' the clock, with yet more bonfires being lit about the town and the bells ringing from several of Preston's churches, Titus is standing in line within the reception hall of Mister Astenbury's fine house on Friargate, where Colonel O'Sullivan has made his headquarters, some distance from the rest of the senior officers but with sufficient space here to manage his diverse responsibilities. He is flanked by a pair of clerks, dictates notes to them at the conclusion of each interview with those awaiting an audience and, while the queue is not long, Titus feels as though his status is now returned to that of some common supplicant. It is not the *private discussion* that he had expected and, frankly, he is tiring after such strenuous days.

But his attention is focused, once more, when he hears a familiar name.

'Here,' says O'Sullivan to a dark-coated fop sat resting casually against the corner of his table, 'deliver this quickly to Sir Watkin. Two of his fellows have arrived today but they do not seem to attend the urgency in the matter. I want you to impress upon the gentleman that it is crucial he should act immediately. To join us in Macclesfield at the latest. Take this. An instruction, signed by His Royal Highness.'

He hands a richly sealed dispatch to the man who turns and walks hurriedly back down the line, passing Titus so that, briefly, their eyes meet. Strange, disturbing and oddly familiar eyes. But where...?

At that moment, O'Sullivan also looks up at the queue, observes Titus Redmond and instantly calls for his clerks to dismiss the rest of the line until later in the evening.

'My good fellow,' says the Colonel, 'I had not intended that *you* should wait upon me so!' And Titus is led to a private room, served with a fine bumper of claret. More apologies. Forgiveness begged for the Irishman's ague, this chill occasioned by the damp vapours of Edinburgh, he thinks. And these lozenges, Spanish liquorice and anise-seed, perfectly useless. But perhaps he would be kind enough to help with one or two matters? For the whole Court knows of Mister Redmond's part in raising Subscription for the Cause. And he knows about the Exchequer, one assumes? It would have been a costly mistake indeed had it not been for the monies raised by their good friends in Manchester and elsewhere. The very reason for following this particular route. The potential regiment raised in his town also. Might Captain Townley's brother be capable of leading it, does he think? And what of the sixty who have volunteered in Preston? Would there be animosity if these were added to its ranks? Oh, the bridges too. They have received word that the militia have been destroying them all along the Mersey? But the bridge into Manchester? Fording places beyond? Any word of Ligonier's forces. A few final points. Foolish, he knows. But exactly how far *are* they now... from the sea? From Wales? From London?

Titus answers each of them with weary patience, hinting discreetly at caution so far as Francis Townley is concerned. Other candidates too, perhaps. Attorney Morgan, for example. The Welsh interests to be considered. But most of his responses seem to satisfy O'Sullivan who, at last, pours them each another bumper.

'I fear that I have tired you, Mister Redmond,' he says. 'But I have one further boon to crave of you, sir. For we shall arrive in Manchester within the next couple of days and not yet arranged accommodation for His Royal Highness. Might I ask you, if it does not impose too greatly on the novelty of our acquaintance, whether your own home might be put at his disposal.'

Titus imagines that, in all circumstances except those in which he now finds himself, his response would be entirely unequivocal. He imagines the reaction that he might expect from Maria-Louise, ponders a moment on whether he has time to feed Mag Mudge to old Tarquin before the royal party arrives, recalls that the poor hog is slain by Sir Edward's fools. But, above all, he is haunted by the eyes of the cove to whom O'Sullivan had entrusted his missive out in the reception hall.

'Colonel,' he says, 'it would do the greatest honour to my family that you should even consider the thing and I am happy to agree. I shall return forthwith to Manchester and ensure that everything is set in hand. But might I ask one question in return, though it bears no relation to your own request in any form. Yet the fellow outside, in the hall while I was waiting, the fellow who takes your message to Sir Watkin, might I know his name?'

O'Sullivan considers a moment, weighs the matter, but finally shrugs away any concern.

'You mean Lieutenant Owen, I collect.'

Chapter Forty-Four

It is not today's thick frost that causes Elizabeth Cooper to quake so, but this strange tale of ghosts and goblins.

'You do not mean to tell me, sir,' she says to Benjamin Nichols, 'that you truly believe Reverend Hoole to have been killed by a boggart?' she says. 'I have scarce heard anything more ludicrous. Except, perhaps, for the news that our poor town is likely to be taken by barbarian savages within the next few hours!'

There had been the normal late-morning panic earlier. Strangers seen at the Salford Bridge. Rumours of the Jacobite army almost upon them. Estimates that they have twenty-five thousand men under arms, though the more optimistic amongst the Tories put the figure at half that number. A steady trickle of people still leaving, too, despite the instructions of the Court Leet. And then this uncanny stillness, far more fearsome than the commotion it had replaced.

'We had the tale from the Rector himself,' Nichols insists. 'It seems that, when he was Vicar of Haxey, his neighbour at the Rectory of Epworth was Samuel Wesley.'

'The father of Mister John Wesley, of course,' adds Tom Lewthwaite.

'Mistress Wesley, for *her* part, was a staunch Jacobite and, in the wake of the rebellion in '15, her husband had cast her from the house until such time as she might recant. And it was about this time that the sprite first appeared. Blood-curdling groans from deep within the house, hammering upon the internal doors and on the walls, pots and plates left smashed in the otherwise deserted kitchen, their huge mastiff whining in terror at every manifestation'

'And why, prithee,' says Elizabeth, 'should this have any relevance to Mister Hoole? Except that the Wesleys were neighbours, of course.'

'It was rather by way of a professional relevance than gregarious sociability that caused him to become embroiled,' Lewthwaite tells her. They are sitting at the normal table, having taken a dish of chocolate almost an hour since and now toying with the empty porcelain though, as always, unwilling to set down a second penny.

'Would you care for a refill, gentlemen?' she asks, breaking a strict rule of her own. 'A small gratuity for the entertainment that you provide me on this strange and doleful day.' The clergymen are suitably grateful and she calls for Crableck to replenish them. 'You were saying, Mister Lewthwaite, that there was some ecclesiastical link to the Wesleys' sprite, sir? Mister Hoole was required to exorcise the demon, I assume.'

'Precisely, Mistress. He told us that he visited the Epworth Rectory with a team of investigators and, Reverend Wesley being induced to intone some imprecations against the Jacobites in general and his wife in peculiar, to pray also for the health of King George, an especially violent visitation ensued. All manner of howling, vibrations, a portrait of Samuel Wesley cast to the floor, doors held against them as they attempted to move from room to room.'

Suddenly, something thumps against the window where they are sat, and a long, ghastly face appears against the clouded glass. Lewthwaite leaps from his seat, an ungodly oath upon his lips, as the cow moves off down the lane, itself startled by the sudden movement within.

'Oh, my dear fellow!' says Nichols, touching his associate's hand, she notices, with a mixture of admonition and affection. Lewthwaite sits once more. 'Well,' Nichols continues, 'he finally ventured alone into that chamber which seemed worst affected by the impish activity and performed all the normal exhortations and litanies, or so many as our Faith will allow. How one envies the Popish attention to detail when one must deal with devils. Yet he told us that, as the commotion grew increasingly violent about him, he experienced an overwhelming urge to run from that accursed place.'

'And run he did!' says Lewthwaite, now composed again and settled by the fresh chocolate that Crableck has set before him. 'Yet he recalled nothing of the thing itself, merely finding himself, much later, on the road back to Haxey. He remained Vicar there for almost thirty-five years, did you know? In any case, Reverend Wesley was greatly pleased for, he claimed, the goblin never more returned to Epworth.'

'But it *did* appear at Haxey, I must assume?' says Elizabeth, now seeing where the story must unfold.

'A fie upon you, Mistress,' Nichols protests, 'you steal my thunder!'

'Perhaps, though unlike John Dennis your own play is allowed to run a little longer, sir. And the boggart appeared not only in Haxey but here too, perhaps?'

'Well indeed! There was little reason for the Jacobite Cause ever to be mentioned in that quiet Lincolnshire backwater and yet Mister Hoole, like many others, had himself adopted Non-Juror principles by that time, feeling himself unable to take the oath of allegiance to King George the First who, he felt, had acceded to the throne purely on the grounds of his Protestantism and to the exclusion of all other creeds. Yet the Vicar was never a supporter of the Stuarts and it was during a moment of reflection on this fact, he claimed, that the goblin began to haunt his own home. He had not exorcised the demon, it seemed, but rather adopted the thing! And it followed him here, when he replaced the first Rector of Saint Ann's nine years ago. He placated it by never

456

allowing thought or word of Jacobitism to prosper in his home. But lately…'

'The subject has been difficult to avoid. Yes, sir, I perceive the process and drift of your course. So the recent sermons from your pulpit have caused the demon to rise in defence of the Jacobites whose spawn it must definitely be…'

'And the shock has killed him, madam. A terrible dilemma, however, since Mistress Hoole fears that either the imp or its Jacobite masters may seek to disrupt the good Rector's interment and wishes to have him buried forthwith. Yet we cannot pay proper respect to his memory without due ceremony and it has proved impossible to make any arrangements earlier than tomorrow noon'

'A dilemma indeed,' says Elizabeth. 'And you are certain that it was the demon that caused his demise?'

'There can be no other explanation, madam,' says Lewthwaite, 'for he was hale and hearty beforehand.'

Elizabeth muses about the thing. The truth is that Mister Hoole has looked increasingly ill for the past year.

'Well,' she says, 'there is at least *one* other explanation.' She leans closer to the clergyman, whispers in his ear. 'For it seems that I am not the only one who trysts in the Pleasure Garden at Old Man Castle. It is hardly the most discreet of venues, Mister Lewthwaite. I trust that the Rector did not also discover your guilty secret?'

She leaves them, red-faced and silent, to attend her other customers, though they are few in number today, their tobacco smoke hanging thinly from the beams. The attorney, Matthew Liptrott, sitting alone and attempting to study recent editions of the London broadsheets but with that distracted air of somebody awaiting the arrival of bad news about which they have already received premonition. Last year's Borough Reeve, John Hawkswell, in company with the two former Constables, Bower and Hibbert, still suffering from the disgrace of their failure to protect the Excise convoy and now arguing loudly with Hawkswell that the thing has somehow endangered them still further with the imminent arrival of the very fiends from whom they had sought to protect it. And the miller, Tomlinson, in negotiation with one of the carters in a belated effort to arrange for his family and belongings to be sent from the town.

Elizabeth instructs Crableck, an increasingly insubordinate Crableck, she has noticed, to set some more logs on the fire and also in the oven at the rear of the premises so that they might roast another quantity of coffee beans.

But, as the door-keeper hobbles away to undertake these tasks, the already muted atmosphere within the establishment is silenced entirely by the noise outside. A drum in the distance. The unmistakeable ratter-tat-tat of a military drum. The men leave their tables, crowd to the window, press faces against the panes, can see nothing but will not venture to the street.

It must be near three o'the clock and Market Street Lane, normally so busy at this hour, is almost deserted. *How strange that even the town's Jacobites are not here to welcome their bestial friends. Have they been advised to remain indoors while the monsters commit rapine only upon those loyal to His Majesty?*

The drumming louder now, incessant. Ratter-tat-tat. Ratter-tat-tat

And where is Rosina on the one occasion, these days, that she needs her? For surely the girl would speak for her. Prevent any excess, she being the daughter of so prominent a fellow as Titus Redmond. And, forsooth, he is almost her business partner. It must count for *something*, to be sure.

The tone of the drum changes, echoing more strongly as it turns from Deansgate into the narrower confines of the Lane itself, mingling now with the clatter of horses, and Elizabeth's lasting memory of the moment will be linked to the aroma of roasting coffee, a smell that she has always adored but one that will now forever conjure a sense of opprobrium.

For the horses are only two in number. *Two!* They peer down the road behind the brace of steeds, expecting to hear bagpipes, to see serried ranks of marching men. But there is nothing. So their eyes attempt to catch the fleeting spectacle that has already passed, riding in front of the Commodities Exchange, pausing for a moment. The drummer mounted on one pony, a bedraggled, short-legged beast, and two people on the other, a cob in slightly better condition than the first. Its riders are a fellow all swaddled in dirty chequered cloth, looking like a bundle of dirty washing, and a woman, sideways behind him. An absurdly tall woman with tangles of long hair, singing something entirely indistinguishable and drowning whatever her companion may be shouting to the empty windows of houses on either side, for both of them are muted in turn by the cherry-faced drummer.

'Is that it?' says Hawkswell as the procession finally disappears from their view when the horses turn left at the farther end of the Exchange towards the Cross. Silence. Stunned silence. Then he takes Hibbert by the shoulder. 'Quickly,' he says, 'find the Constables this instant. Bring them here with some men, for we can stop this rebellion before it is begun. And you, good Bower. Back to the Salford Bridge, fellow, and bring us word if there are more of them.'

Are they quite mad? thinks Elizabeth. *They imagine that the Jacobites have come with no more than two ruffians on hempen haltered horses? Yet I could put that rope to better use just now, methinks.* But look at Bower and Hibbert, a blaze of excitement in their eyes. *This pair of fools who think they can redeem themselves by capturing two coves and a whore!*

The two men run from the coffee house as they are bid. The drumming recedes away towards the Market Square and, like rodents after cheese, townsfolk slowly begin to follow the noise. Hawkswell steps outside to meet Thomas Walley and William Fowden when they arrive ten minutes later,

458

a small *posse comitatus* of fellows armed with cudgels at their back. There is a disagreement, however, Fowden arguing that Hawkswell is no longer Reeve and has no jurisdiction here. *But what do they expect? For his sympathies have always tended towards the Jacobite.*

Despite Fowden's objections, the small force sets off towards the Shambles and, for a while, peace descends again on the coffee house, with only Liptrott, Lewthwaite and Nichols left inside. Yet it cannot last and, before long, Hawkswell is returned, dragged along by some local men, Francis Townley's friends, the barber Tom Sydall and the checkman George Fletcher. The door is thrown open and Hawkswell pushed inside, colliding heavily with the high chair in which Crableck normally takes station. Sydall grabs his leg and hauls him along the floor to one of the tables, where Fletcher helps him to heave the prisoner up onto a chair.

'Damn'd treacherous dog,' snarls Sydall. 'Tried to assault the official representative of His Royal Highness. And came from this establishment, we understand, Mistress Cooper!'

The place is filling now. More of their associates. Tom Chaddock. The Deacon boys. And, pushing through their midst, the wash-bag that she had last seen on the cob, his harlot hag alongside him and the drummer peering over his shoulder.

'I neither know nor care what Mister Hawkswell may have done since he left this place,' she says, 'yet he departed of his own volition and without a word from myself or any other within these walls. Now I would ask you all to leave my coffee house, gentlemen, if you please.'

'What Hawkswell 'as *done*,' says Chaddock, 'is to set 'ands on one of His Majesty's officers. Sergeant Dickson, 'ere, is on military business. And attacked in a most cowardly way. It is sedition, madam. Our Lady be praised that we came along in time to break a few crowns o' those who committed the crime. They shall think twice afore they try the likes again.'

'And what, pray, has this to do with me? I have already said…'

'It has *this* to do with you, madam,' says the badly bundled Scotsman who is apparently a sergeant, though he looks like no army officer that she has ever seen before. He wears a scarlet tunic, English pattern unless she is mistaken, but faded and dirtied, the whole thing covered almost entirely by that strange form of dress that they call a kilt, that seems to be no more than a mass of coarse homespun wound in untidy skirts around and around his waist and thighs with a considerable amount of the remainder rolled and bound about his chest. He has a bonnet, large and blue, a blunderbuss upon the crook of his arm. 'That I have been set upon and, had it not been for this beauty…' He pats the blunderbuss. '…And the help of these loyal fellows here, your town might now be facing serious retribution. As it stands, my masters shall be pleased that we have so quickly found such volunteers. Aye, and a few folk to be pressed besides.' He lifts a foot against Hawkswell's chest and propels him backwards, toppling over, chair as well, so that the poor fellow crashes to the floor, taking a table with him as he goes. Hawkswell mumbles something about refusing the press, though his comments are ignored and he is left tangled in her furniture, a netted fish. 'But I need a base, Mistress,' Dickson continues, his Scots accent difficult for Elizabeth to follow at times. 'A headquarters for the recruitment with which I am charged and, since the Bull and most other fine places seem to already be promised away for the Colonels, the Majors, the Captains an' all, well, this seems the very place!'

'Will none of you help Mister Hawkswell?' she says, casting about for support but meeting only animosity in the eyes of those around her. Crableck is nowhere to be seen and the two Assistant Curates also seem to have disappeared. 'For you shall not bring your mayhem and barbarity across my threshold, sir.' And she bends to help Hawkswell herself, assisting him to his feet and then righting chair and table, so that he may be seated again. 'And *this*, gentlemen, is no garrison bivouac!'

'I think you mistake your place, Mistress,' snarls barber Sydall. 'For this place that you have used for the collection of the Hanovers' Excise duty must class as an office of government, may it not? And, government now being in the hands of good King James and the Prince Regent, his royal son, all such offices now behove to His Majesty.'

'Excise, is it?' says Sergeant Dickson. 'Then there should be a pretty penny or two for the coffers, eh?' But his pocked bluff face shows no sign of good humour.

'There has been no collection of taxes since Michaelmas, Sergeant. Yet perhaps if you wait until the next Quarter Day? Ah, but I forget myself, for you shall swing from a gibbet long before Christmas!'

'There are Whigs a-plenty in this town that shall swing before John Dickson,' he replies. 'Yet stay in this fine shop we will, madam.' And he begins to issue his instructions. Hawkswell to be bound. Gagged too, for good measure. The woman, Peg he calls her, sent to look for victuals for, he says, they have been on the road since the middle of the night to reach Manchester early. Sydall and Fletcher to set up some tables so that the enlistments may be done properly.

And Elizabeth, forgotten for a while, escapes to her room where she weeps bitter tears of frustration and anger, a taste or two of the Sydenham's to settle her.

It is a half-hour later when she descends again to find Crableck dispensing beverages freely to Dickson's growing cohort of assistants. She cannot tell whether the old crook-back has been instructed to do so or whether he acts through some latent love of Jacobites, for she has never troubled, she realises, to test the fellow's politics. Still, she is hardly in a position to raise objection and perhaps she, too, had underestimated the strength of feeling in the town for the Stuart Cause, for she is astonished at the number of men waiting to volunteer. Excitable men, noisy and exuberant, in numbers that stretch from her door and away along cold Market Street Lane. A sense of menace in the smoky winter air also, as happens when menfolk arouse themselves to strife.

'How fare you, Mistress?' says Aran Owen, standing near her but previously unseen by Elizabeth.

'Mister Owen,' she says. 'Come to gloat, I imagine. And you must not pretend to any real concern for how I am faring. Nor any polite enquiry about my health. Yet you see, sir, where your own and others' support for the Jacobites has brought us?'

'I must suppose that I put the question from respect to Rosina and, because, just though I believe the Jacobite Cause to be, I understand how noxious this must seem from your own perspective. For *my* part, I see only loyal supporters of the True King, anxious to serve him. Look, there are the Deacon brothers. Every one of them.'

But the Deacon brothers are not without problems of their own, she perceives. For, as they move forward in the queue to reach the tables, their father has also arrived. Thomas Deacon may be a Presbyterian, but he is also a dissident Non-Juror, more Jacobite than even the High Churchmen, though apparently not so fervent that he wishes to see each of his three sons enter military service. He has evidently already argued unsuccessfully with the boys themselves, now turning his pleas to Sergeant Dickson himself.

'Yet surely they cannot *all* be needed? And Charles is barely turned fifteen!'

Not just Charles, either, for the next in line is young William Brettargh. They are in school together at Saint Cyprian's. *Both sent by that hypocrite Clayton*, she imagines.

'Old enough to take the shilling, sir, if they so choose,' says Dickson. 'And a handsome five guineas to also be paid when the bold Prince arrives.'

And Deacon is pushed aside so that the boys can sign. Charles, fifteen. Robert, nineteen. And Thomas, the eldest of them, twenty-two. *I spend my days praying that our loyal army shall catch the rebels and destroy them. Yet I should not wish harm on those young men. And how clearly I perceive their end. Neither have I love of Deacon, yet his pain must be unbearable. And the fellow only recently lost his wife besides. Seven daughters still to be raised.*

'So I must assume that you have already volunteered, Mister Owen? For otherwise you would be in the line, I collect. Or have you turned your coat at last, now being a purveyor of artistic ballad sheets for Sir Edward Stanley's Militia, I understand?'

And, oh, Sir Edward's Militia! The very words set her pulse a-racing. But she receives no more response from Aran Owen than a muted excuse that he has other duties to perform. The enlistment process, however, is interrupted once more as Thomas Walley is brought into the coffee house by another of the ruffians.

461

The clock maker has not picked the best of times to be elected Constable, she thinks, as Dickson tells the fellow that he must take Hawkswell to the House of Correction until he may be required to answer for his actions. The Constable himself graciously forgiven for his own part in the attack upon the Sergeant, though he must identify and similarly apprehend any others involved. Walley attempts to stammer a defiance, a protest that such work does not fall within…

'But you are the C-c-c-constable, are you not?' cries Dickson, to the crowd's general amusement. 'Then about your b-b-business, sir.' And he dispatches Sydall with Walley and Hawkswell to ensure that his orders are followed.

Meanwhile, a fiddler has been fetched. The blind fiddler, from Redmond's bawdy-house, she thinks. Some jugs of porter too. And the woman, Peg, is induced to sing for her Sergeant, beating a rhythm on the drum as the signings persist and the shillings dispensed. The candles all lit, too, in their sconces.

Adam Scatterbuck arrives, joining Aran Owen, delight on the fellow's blotched and blistered face. A temporary break in the proceedings called while Dickson is interviewed for the *Journal*. Yes, the main army coming along the turnpike from Standish to Wigan. The Prince due to stay in that town tonight but arrive in Manchester on the morrow. And Dickson himself? Why, a humble Lowlander pressed to service in the Forty-Seventh Foot and forced to take part with Johnny Cope's army at Prestonpans. Yet always a true believer in the King Over the Water and pleased to be liberated on that field, offering himself for duty with the Duke of Perth's Regiment. Now servant and sergeant to that brave *Chevalier* Johnstone and sent ahead to scout the ground. His intrepid companions? Mister Hamilton, from Halifax, formerly also an unwilling guest of Hanover George, but with a sister here at Slade Hall, and related by marriage to Mister Sydall. The lady? Travelled from Settle, from Long Preston to be precise, to show her support for the Prince. Peggy Marshall by name. Such a singer!

And then Beppy Byrom with her father, come to join the event. Greetings exchanged with Aran Owen, now in company with Scatterbuck.

I am surprised that she was not here ahead of them. Seditious bitch!

'So, Mistress Cooper,' says the young woman, 'I had never imagined that your coffee house should play host to such events. Give you joy of this alchemical conversion, madam.'

'It is always a mistake, I find, to confuse alchemy with the natural physics of life, the latter being employed to conjure solutions to practical problems, the former merely to assuage self-interest.'

'Yet we saw Mister Hawkswell,' says John Byrom, 'apparently a prisoner, bound and shackled, under guard to the House of Correction. Do you know the circumstances, my dear?'

'The circumstances, sir, seem self-evident. The Vandals are not merely at the gates of Rome, yet settled themselves and taking tea in the very Forum itself. And none to stop them since your daughter so bravely prevented the bridge from destruction. I should have thought, Mister Byrom, that a man of your learning would be less concerned with the circumstance and more with the consequences. Just a singular sample of which you have already witnessed. An innocent citizen taken to be pressed, and none here to help him. Our bold Assistant Curates were present a while but seem to have been the victims of a heavenly miracle, taken up and vanished at the moment when they might have assisted poor Hawkswell.'

'La!' says Beppy. 'Nichols and Lewthwaite? Papa tells me that the theme of last Sunday's sermon was *He that has no sword, let him sell his garment and buy one.* Perhaps they are, this very moment, at Mistress Brimstone's in an effort to heed their own admonition. And now, what is this?'

Another rumour, apparently, that the town's Whiggish faction is planning to take back the town.

'Take it back?' says Byrom. 'Why, it is only seized in the first place by two men and a half!'

But more orders are issued, and Samuel Dickenson steps forward from the waiting line, another boy little more than sixteen years old, volunteering to go about town and identify the leaders amongst their enemies, for they must be taken before they can combine. He is the son of John Dickenson, of course, that linen draper who also acts as banker for so many in the town.

His father would be shamed by him, she thinks. *The worthless weasel!*

And it is not long before further prisoners are brought to the coffee house.

First, Robert Jobb, accused of paying ten pounds to the Hanoverian Subscription.

'So, sir, we shall have the same amount for His Royal Highness, if you please!' demands the Sergeant.

'Yet I have no more upon my person than four pounds and fifteen shillings,' Jobb protests, unable to keep the fear from his voice.

'Liar!' cries young Samuel the Prosecutor. 'He is worth ten thousand at the least!'

'Then he shall be detained until his fine is redeemed!' And Jobb is bundled away to the rear tables, bound to a chair near the hearth. 'Next!'

Next is John Taylor, a citizen of the town though not fully in possession of all his faculties, who had volunteered for Sir Edward's Manchester Militia Company, the same that had so quickly been disembodied again. Taylor is a good example of the reason.

But those other companies, thinks Elizabeth. *Oh, passion! Yet where are they in our hour of need?*

Sentence passed on Taylor too. Fitting justice, according to Dickson. If the fellow was happy to fight then let him do so for a more noble purpose.

463

'To be pressed,' the Sergeant pronounces, and the fellow is dragged off to accompany Robert Jobb.

Others too. John Clowes, the breeches maker. Joseph Bancroft, the smallware manufacturer. Mister Allen. Mister Ayrton. Each of their donations to the Subscription detailed by Samuel Dickenson. Fines set against their good behaviour. Hibbert and Bower brought in by Constable Fowden, both bloodied from their scuffle in the Market Square, both terrified. The seats for the sentenced filling rapidly in Elizabeth Cooper's transformed premises until the last prisoner is brought forward. James Bradley, of course, and pushed to his knees before the Sergeant's table.

'And this one?' says Dickson.

'This one,' says Beppy Byrom, stepping forward, 'is the Master of Manchester Whiggery. The man who believed that the election of a mere Tory to the Court Leet constituted a Jacobite conspiracy. The man who has singularly raised such a Subscription for the Hanover pack that it has financed an entire company of militiamen – though none of them worth a damn. The man who purchased a wife as a political expedient. But what good has it done you, Mister Bradley? All that control and never a hint of true opposition to our noble Cause!'

'Beppy, my sweet,' says John Byrom, 'I do not think...'

'What, Papa? Does it offend your morality that I speak these truths? You profess yourself a Jacobite. Or at least you do so when not composing your poems. Those amusing allegorical poems. But sometimes, Papa, choosing sides may mean that we must act. And, sometimes, our actions will inflict pain. They may cause conflict. But without conflict in a just cause, there can be no resolution. And so, Sergeant, what will you do with this wretch who raised two thousand guineas against us?'

But it is James Bradley, not Sergeant Dickson, who answers her, raising his head for the first time.

'Rosina believes you to be her friend,' he says, his voice barely a whisper. 'Do you truly believe that she would wish you to denounce me in this way? Though, in all honesty, I should happily have confessed myself guilty of every word that you have spoken. And proud to do so. For I would see you hanged, sir,' he says to Dickson, 'along with every traitor who has taken your shilling.'

'Take this fool away,' says the Sergeant. 'Fined one hundred guineas against his immediate behaviour and to be held in custody pending the Prince Regent's pleasure. Somebody take word to the families of these men that their fines must be paid in full.'

So Bradley, too, is dragged towards the other prisoners, poison in his eyes as he passes Beppy Byrom.

'And so many other loathsome treacheries,' she says, intended as a whisper, but spoken loud enough for Bradley to hear over the room's clamour, 'that I would spare my dear friend Rosina from mentioning.' But, though

Beppy may have intended them as a private exchange, these latter words have dropped into a sudden silence in the coffee house occasioned by Rosina Redmond's own arrival at the door.

She is flushed with excitement and Elizabeth feels a rush of her early passion for the girl, but Rosina's excitement turns quickly to confusion as the quiet deepens, looks enquiringly at Beppy. *Oh, that angelic smile.*

'You would spare me?' says Rosina. 'What, pray?'

And, as Beppy averts her gaze, Rosina looks about the room, hoping for an answer perhaps from those on whom her eyes rest momentarily in turn. Adam Scatterbuck. Aran Owen, of course. Elizabeth herself. She takes an expectant step forward towards her lover and, in that moment, sees her husband also, forced upon a chair amongst all the others.

'What is this?' she says, addressing herself finally to Dickson. William Fowden whispers in his ear, a lengthy briefing.

'My thanks, Constable,' says the Sergeant. 'And I apologise, madam, that you should have been occasioned to witness this scene. Though, given the eminence of your family in this burgh, as I understand, I am sure you will appreciate the need to protect against any mischief, any insurgency which these rabid Whigs may seek to arrange against His Royal Highness.'

'I could scarce fail to appreciate such a thing, sir,' Rosina replies, 'since I have recently learned that the Prince himself shall be a guest in my father's house tomorrow night. Yet you are...?'

A gasp from the assembly at Rosina's news and Aran steps to her side.

'Allow me to name Sergeant John Dickson,' he says. 'From the Duke of Perth's Regiment, yet here under instruction from Lord George Murray's *Aide-de-Camp* for the purpose of raising volunteers.

'Then you seem to have exceeded your orders, Sergeant. And I guarantee that His Royal Highness shall hear of it directly unless these men are treated with dignity. Mister Bradley may have no love for our Cause yet he is no insurrectionist. I am sure that he shall pledge his *parole d'honneur* in exchange for these gentlemen being freed from the bonds of criminals.' Bradley shrugs his agreement. 'Now impose your fines as you wish, sirs, but let us remember the noble nature of our enterprise!'

Dickson signals for the prisoners to be untied.

'Let it be so,' he says. 'But know, madam, that your husband will still go to the House of Correction until His Royal Highness determines his fate.'

The noise builds again and the enlistments resume as Rosina presses deeper among the thronging mass.

'So,' says Elizabeth, 'Sergeant Dickson is a fine example of the noble Highlanders about whom you have spoken so passionately?'

'I think you must find,' Rosina replies, 'that he is a Lowlander, my dear. He has his duties to perform, I am sure. And I am certain that I should feel some sense of childish delight at Mister Bradley being treated so. Yet I cannot find it

465

in my heart.' She looks towards her husband but he is engaged in some covert discussion with his fellow-prisoners. 'Now, friend Beppy,' Rosina continues, 'you were in the act of sparing me some painful experience, I collect.'

But Beppy is spared in turn by her father.

'You will forgive me, ladies,' he says. 'But I fear that I must find the Borough Reeve and ensure that peace is maintained throughout the town.'

And, with a final glare of rebuke towards his outspoken daughter, he leaves them while, on the other side of the room, Dickson's drab is singing again. To the tune of *Chevy Chase* that Elizabeth has heard Rosina perform so often.

Long Preston Peggy to Proud Preston went,

A roar of approval from the men surrounding her.

To see the Scotch Rebels it was her intent,

Rosina comments that the woman has a surprisingly fine voice.

For in brave deeds of arms she did take much delight,

Hear her. Hear her.

And therefore she went with the Rebels to fight.

Rebels indeed, thinks Elizabeth. *And good that one of them should finally have recognised the thing.*

But, at the back of the room, a very different patriotism is stirring and James Bradley's fine tenor, tremulous in the first few lines but growing stronger as he picks up his own refrain, inspires his fellow-prisoners to join him in a defiance. 'The Roast Beef of Old England.'

There is not a soul in the place, of course, who does not know Fielding's lyrics, or Leveridge's fine music. Indeed, on almost any other occasion they would have sung along. It was a favourite of audiences everywhere and frequently given an impromptu rendition before the opening of any new play. And Bradley seems to have endowed the thing with this quality now, as though the very act of its performance by these Whiggish fellows has factionalised the thing.

Dickson calls for them to be silenced but none seem willing to interfere.

When good Queen Elizabeth sat on the throne,
'Ere coffee, or tea, or such slip-slops were known,
The world was in terror if e'er she did frown.

Oh! The Roast Beef of Old England,
And old English Roast Beef!

*Slip-slops indeed! But, Mister Bradley. La! I find myself moved to tears
by your bravado.*

Yet, outside, there are new developments that cause Bradley's choir
to gradually desist. Dickson's long-awaited reinforcements and, Elizabeth
knows, the end now for any hopes that their own Hanoverian forces might
rescue them. *But how I had yearned…*

A squadron of Horse in Market Street Lane under the command,
according to the Sergeant, of the venerable Alexander Forbes, Lord of Pitsligo.
Folk spill into the street, watching the old fellow dismount at the stone, assisted
by a young trooper from the ranks.

'Why, it is Hugh!' cries Beppy. 'Hugh Stirling, Rosina. You remember
him? From Calderbank and apprenticed here in town. His mother had told
me that he had gone to join the Prince but I never imagined seeing him again
so soon.'

The troopers' commander pushes his way through the spectators, enters
the coffee house, and Sergeant Dickson springs to attention.

'What is the meaning of this assembly?' says the old fellow.

'Why, My Lord,' Dickson replies, 'we have been beating up for volunteers
as we were ordered. For the Manchester Regiment, sir.'

And a fine regiment indeed, thinks Elizabeth, *begun with the town's
lowest orders and those of the vilest principles.*

'Well that may be, Sergeant,' says Pitsligo. 'Yet we need quarters, good
fellow. Billets for six thousand. Decent billets too. Is there no town elder who
can arrange the thing?'

'We have the foremost member of their Court Leet, My Lord. Though he
is a treacherous Whig. And the town's Constable.' He pulls Fowden forward
by his arm.

'Excellent,' says Lord Forbes. 'Then the Constable it shall be. You have
a Bellman, I assume? Then have him cry about the town with instruction that
all citizens are to provide quarters for the Prince's army. We shall allocate
them by regiment as they arrive. And every householder loyal to King James
shall illuminate their windows!'

'And by what authority shall the Bellman inform them that he acts?' says
Fowden, timidly.

'Authority, sir?' bellows Pitsligo, pulling his broadsword from its
scabbard. 'By God, sir. Damn you. By this!' He brandishes the blade in
Fowden's face until the Constable, looking as though he will faint quite away,
mutters his understanding and flees into the night to carry out his instruction.
Hugh Stirling approaches his Colonel, speaks softly to him. 'Yet we will brook
no nonsense, Sergeant,' he says to Dickson. 'Now continue with your business

and my men shall repair to the Bull's Head. Mister Stirling shall guide us, I think. Ladies,' he turns to Elizabeth and the other women, as though noticing them for the first time, 'you will forgive an old soldier's vulgarity, I trust.' He offers them a bow and leaves.

Rosina, meanwhile, has joined her husband and they are now deep in conversation while Long Preston Peggy has produced a pack of Italian boards, using the playing cards to tell fortunes for those that seek them.

Elizabeth helps herself to a dish of chocolate and goes to watch, for she has always had a fascination towards the skills of divination, though they border on witchcraft, she thinks.

'Ah, my dear,' says Peg, looking up at her, long hag's hair the colour and texture of dried straw. 'I need no tarots to see your future, lady. For I perceive you all dressed in bridal attire. And no more than two months hence! Give you joy of your fortune, Mistress.'

Bridal attire! She thinks of the Bride's Pie glass ring, too. A further confirmation that she may be wed. But not in the conventional sense, surely. Yet there has been this other new development in her life. *Could it be...?*

Here come the families of the prisoners at last, bringing with them their respective bankers, Childer the Goldsmith and John Dickenson, Samuel's father and far from pleased with his son, it is clear. But the business is soon dispatched. Promissory notes issued to the Sergeant for their respective fines, he being reluctant at first to accept the documents but persuaded by all around him that, in Manchester, the papers and signatures of these two gentlemen are more valuable than gold. Dickenson and Childers give assurance that the notes will be exchanged for coin as soon as the Prince arrives.

The prisoners themselves each required to reaffirm their parole, while Sydall returns with Thomas Walley so that they might now convey James Bradley to the House of Correction in his turn. Walley, poor fellow, finds it impossible to do the deed.

'Come, dear fellow,' Bradley says to him. 'You can do me the honour of walking with me in that direction. And perhaps my dear wife will join us.' Rosina does so, never a word passing between her and Elizabeth.

Yet, at the end of this strange day, with Hoole's boggart dancing a jig of Jacobite joy, the last of the volunteers signed, Crableck making arrangements for Dickson, his drummer and his whore to bed upon the floor of her coffee house, it is Long Preston Peg's words that remain with her.

The Bridal attire. And thoughts of the new passion that fills her. Memories of Sir Edward Stanley's Militia. His Warrington Company. The handsome woman masquerading as that fine Ensign, Harry Tobin. The new love in Elizabeth Cooper's life!

Chapter Forty-Five

The view from Aran Owen's lodging is very different today. Apart from anything else, while the cold weather persists, it no longer brings clarity in its wake. For, this morning, there is rain again.

The troopers below are another novelty. They fill the Market Square with the silvered chiming of their horse harness, look up into the sombre clouds and the sharp shower, tighten chin straps of fur caps, unlace redingotes and struggle into their protection, hiding the glory of splendid tartan waistcoat beneath, and almost entirely covering their cavalry boots once mounted.

They have made no secret of their destinations. Foraging for food and supplies in Bolton, Bury, Cheadle, Altrincham, Oldham and Stockport. Or spreading panic in Gatley, Saddleworth, Warrington and Macclesfield. Creating confusion about the Prince Regent's true intentions. A rumour too, from Samuel Dickenson again, who has it on the good authority of his father. That the Excise collector in Ashton-under-Lyne, Mistress Findlow, has not yet been relieved of the duty gathered at Michaelmas. Well, not *yet* at least!

And not simply Pitsligo's men but a goodly host of other mounted units that have come in all through the hours of darkness, affording Aran little sleep.

But how *could* you sleep with all this excitement? And yesterday evening. That cove Robert Jobb pleading poverty and then forced to pay his ten pounds like all the rest. Jobb could hardly claim any *droit de seigneur* last night as he had apparently attempted after Rosina's wedding. Some sympathy for Hibbert, Bower and Hawkswell, however, hauled off to that damp House of Correction to spend the night with Daniel Sourwood's restless ghost. But no such sentiment about James Bradley. That fellow's evils may have been forgotten by everybody else, but not by Aran. His attempt at blackmailing the Redmonds. His claim to have fathered poor Maeve. His seduction of Maria-Louise, for it can surely have been no less than lechery on his part that created their liaison. Even his marriage to Rosina, arranged by her family though it may have been, is still a crime for which Bradley should be punished.

In the Square, Lord Pitsligo himself now prepares to join his squadron. He seems so very frail, and a boy from the Bull's Head runs out with a stool to assist him, the old nobleman being some distance from the nearest mounting stone. But the gesture is met with an initial display of bad temper, softening as Forbes sees that the lad can be no more than six or seven.

469

'Little fellow,' he says, 'this is the worst rebuff that I have suffered throughout the entire campaign. No, I thank thee!' And he hauls himself with obvious difficulty but grim determination into the saddle, leading his men past Cross and Conduit to disperse on their various missions.

For a moment, Aran almost envies them. He is reminded of Elizabeth Cooper's taunt about his enlistment. Well, she may cast as many jibes as she likes and it was worth suffering her barbed tongue a thousand times for the pleasure of seeing her humiliated in her own coffee house. And he *does* have other duties. What? Does she suppose that he would march off with Francis Townley and his blades to leave the murals unfinished? He should be working on them now, in fact, and it has been amusing him lately to include some hidden imagery within his allegorical sketches. Sir Edward Stanley, for example, included at Bradley's insistence, now bears an uncanny resemblance to the recently deceased Old Tarquin. But there will be no work on them today since he has promised Scatterbuck that he will help with the printing being prepared for the Prince Regent. Besides, the Byroms' house, like many others in town, is all a-turmoil at the prospect of being required for billets, as the Bellman has been announcing every hour.

Yet at Scatterbuck's, with the Blaeu machine churning out copies of the Royal Proclamation, two to each page – the original to be read later at the Cross – and barber-chirurgeon Whitlock using his considerable medical skills to slice each page in half and bind batches for distribution around the town, Aran is confronted by Titus.

'You told me that you knew something of this fellow, William Owen, from Josiah!'

Aran had not altogether expected to see Titus here, for the news that the Prince shall lodge at the Redmonds has spread like tongues of flame, and he had supposed that the entire family would be taken up with the preparations.

'The fellow who had been Secretary to the Rector of Hawarden and then took service with Sir Watkin? Yes indeed but, as you say, only from your brother, sir. What of him?'

'You have not met him then?'

Well, he can be honest about this. Striker may have confessed that William Owen is his *alter ego*, a 'trusted adherent of the Welsh Jacobites', but he has never actually encountered him in that guise. Chosen Aran's name, though. Through respect, he had said. And, 'Why, it makes us almost brothers, does it not?' The very suggestion had sickened him.

'No, sir,' he says. 'As you recall, he did not accompany Sir Watkin when he came here. Why do you ask?'

Titus scrutinises him carefully.

'I have seen the cunny-sucker. In Preston. Two days since. Sent by the Prince Regent's Quartermaster-General with messages to the Welsh.'

'It is understandable, I expect,' says Aran, as calmly as he is able, 'though

470

I still fail to see the significance.'

'Do you indeed, sir? Then I shall tell you, for it was the eyes that I recognised. Unforgettable. This *William* Owen is the same lick-spittle that confronted me at Mother Blossom's.'

'Can that be possible? Though I suppose that we can find out more about him from the Squire, or possibly the lawyer, Morgan.'

'Morgan will be here later. I saw him in Preston also. Though I doubt that we shall discover much about this cove if, as I suspect, he is actually one of Newcastle's agents. And you know what I also suspect, friend Aran?' *I dread to think.* 'I fear he may be the same that was responsible for Jacob's death. And how Driscoll would have celebrated this day! But I feel myself a step closer to avenging him. And we can question Morgan tonight, for you have the honour, sir, of being invited to dine in the presence of His Royal Highness, the *Prince* of Wales. Fitting, do you not say so? Seven o'the clock. Sharp, mind, and not a minute later. Now, let us see how Scatterbuck is progressing. And not a word to the fellow about the dinner. I doubt that Charles Edward could cope with his verbosity.'

The secret is easily kept. For the proclamation copies are all printed and sent for dispatch across the town, while Whitlock has gone to purchase blue and white ribbon for the manufacture of more cockades. And there is news, too, that William Augustus, Duke of Cumberland, youngest son of George the Second, has been appointed to supreme command of the armies in England and just arrived in the Midlands, it seems, to join his forces.

'They say that he is revered by his battalions,' says Scatterbuck, 'though it is hard to understand the reason when he has so recently led them to disaster at Fontenoy.'

But Aran begs to be excused if he is no longer needed since he wishes to see the rest of the army come in and hankers to sketch them crossing the Salford Bridge. It should make a dramatic scene for the *Journal* perhaps, though Scatterbuck reminds him that he should not tarry, for he also needs an illustration of Hoole's funeral, due to take place at midday.

So he cuts through Pool Fold, Hanging Ditch and Smithy Bank with the rain coming down. Over the sandstone arches that span the Irwell, the ancient chapel turned prison tower clinging to its further parapet. A great number of others have joined him by now, a carnival atmosphere pervading the town since, last night, hardly a soul had failed to light their windows as a display of support for the Jacobites. Of the Scots themselves, however, there is no evidence and Aran finds himself swept along the same route that he had followed on the night that he came to meet Striker at the end of September.

And shall Striker ride with them? he wonders. *Surely he would not take the risk for there are so many in Manchester, it seems, who have seen his face.* Titus, of course. Rosina and O'Farrell from their encounter with Bradstreet. All those amongst Townley's crew with whom it pleased him to converse so freely.

Lewthwaite, of course, though the Assistant Curate, like himself, is more likely to be exposed than make a denunciation by the spy's presence in town.

He reaches the Ship Inn and follows the throng right into Chapel Street, then left into Greengate but, by the time he arrives at the Salford Cross there is no possibility of proceeding further, for the feverish crowd now filling the market area with its ancient Exchange has been transfixed by the unmistakeable wail of bagpipes from the street's extension into the Wigan Lane, not the best of thoroughfares, a poor and neglected road but one that now brings the might of Charles Edward's army.

Aran sees many folk from both Salford and Manchester that he knows within the gathering, but there is little scope for general discussion in the press. Hands raised in greeting. Exuberant smiles exchanged. Hats raised. White cockades everywhere. Some musicians on the steps of the Exchange with drum and flute attempting to make themselves heard above the background noise, the pipers coming nearer until, with a sudden break in the rain, a clearing of the skies, they are here in the square.

If he stands on the tips of his toes, he can see them well enough, halting but still playing at the shouted command of a blue-coated officer riding behind them, just a little beyond Aran's own position. Twenty of them, at a reckoning. Some old, grizzled and bearded. Some remarkably young. All tired, each one shrouded in a belted cloak of chequered wool, each with bonnet and feathers, many with hide-covered shields and weapons slung at their backs beside the instruments that they bear.

And such an instrument. Pipes are common enough, of course, but he is accustomed to the thin warbling of those you sometimes hear on the drovers' roads, a much smaller version of this fearsome Highland creature, its three long drones of ochre wood and horn inlay terminating in bell-ends almost the size of a large wine glass, laced together with cordage so that they rest comfortably on the player's shoulder, extending upwards from the bladder sack that he grips between forearm and waist, leaving both hands free so that his fingers dance upon the chanter. Music such that Aran has never heard before, setting the hairs upon his neck, beneath his bobbed wig, to rise and bristle.

A second command and the drones fall silent.

More blue-coated cavalry and then the Prince himself. Light-coloured tartan trews and jacket, blue silk waistcoat and silver lace, a wide sash across his chest. His own whitened wig beneath a bonnet sporting the letters 'JR' and a white cockade. Two years older than Aran himself, just twenty-five. His full cheeks are weathered and his lips, protruding a little, give him a serious, pouting expression. His horse, by contrast, is a whimsical beast, dappled grey and side-stepping across the part-paved space to the huzzahs of its rider's supporters and the merely curious alike. And there is some further commotion on the far side, with Charles Edward halted amongst his Lifeguards while his regiments continue to march past him, progressing through the streets.

472

It is hard to see now, with both spectators and tramping Scots to impede his view, but he is sure that it was the cassocked figure of Doctor Clayton that he had spotted, on the corner of Gravel Lane, and falling to his knees before the Prince. In any case, Charles Edward has now dismounted and vanished amongst a swarm of well-wishers, so that Aran joins many of the other townsfolk, falling in alongside some group of Highlanders as they proceed towards the river and the crossing from Salford into Manchester. Few words are spoken between the clansmen and those in a sibilant tongue that he cannot understand. He had expected the Gaelic to perhaps bear some resemblance to his native Welsh but there is none. Plaids and plumes though. Grime and grit on bare shanks. Tartan array. Stench of stale sweat. Muskets on shoulders. Broadsword and target. Pole-arm and dagger. Pistols in girdles. Powder horns. Pouches and satchels for ball and wadding.

The bridge, then Deansgate, into Market Street Lane where Aran notices Sergeant Dickson with a few of Pitsligo's troopers, each armed with blunderbuss and hanger. Dickson's whore is there too, dancing a jig for the blind fiddler while the regiments divide, some continuing towards the Cross and others turning into the alley that leads to Acres Field and Saint Ann's, with the town's bells all striking twelve.

There are eight burial grounds within the limits of the town itself and another twelve just beyond, but where else would Joseph Hoole have been buried except in the small patch of fenced and consecrated earth that sits below the eastern end of Saint Ann's at the far corner of the Fair's ground? They will lay him close to the tomb of the first rector, Nathaniel Bann and, in due course, there will undoubtedly be a fine headstone to mark Hoole's resting place also.

For Joseph Hoole has attracted his own modest crowd today. The Dissenting Methodist, Reverend Mottishead, from the Chapel in Pool Fold, has agreed to officiate at the service but he, like the rest of the mourners, has fallen silent as the Highlanders spill out of the alley and into Acres Field itself, gaze around at the trees, now bare of leaves, that line the square and the fine houses beyond them – where some of these men, no doubt, will be provided with quarters. The mourners all fallen silent, that is, except for Hoole's widow who, surrounded by her children, and clad entirely in sable satins, begins to keen loudly, presumably fearing retribution from the very savages that her husband had damn'd from his pulpit.

Such is her distress, the wailing so loud, that the Scots are slowed in their tracks, look to the far end of the enclosed square in which they now find themselves, fall to whispering amongst themselves, and one of their young officers approaches Aran, speaks to him in a gently accented English.

'Who is it for whom yon' lady grieves?' he says.

'Her husband, the Rector of the Church that stands before you. Though he was no friend of your Cause and the Widow Hoole fears that she shall not be allowed to lay him peacefully at his rest.'

The Highlander makes a soft noise with his tongue, shakes his head and moves quickly to confer with some of his fellows before, taking a lead, he halts the warriors at a respectful distance from the burial ground. They uncover their heads and stand in absolute silence. A few even fall to their knees in supplication. Reverend Mottishead offers quiet words of comfort to the widow for a moment before continuing with the service and, throughout the entire proceedings, the Highlanders maintain their vigil.

At its end, Aran finds Scatterbuck, exchanges a cold greeting with Elizabeth Cooper, with Lewthwaite and others, then spends an impossibly long spell trying to find somewhere he might eat. The King is to be proclaimed at four and, as he decides to buy a hot mutton kit-cat from the Pie Man near the Conduit, he sees Beppy Byrom and her sisters watching the various regiments still arriving. Each of the girls is dressed in her very finest, Beppy in a resplendent dress of purest white, blue ribbons in her hair, a woollen shawl about her shoulders against the weather and to which she has sewn a Saint Andrew's Cross.

'My dears,' he says. 'Give you joy. Such excitement!'

'La! Mister Owen, I can scarce tell you. We have seen such wonderful gentlemen. The Duke of Atholl gone to Mister Marsden's. The Duke of Perth to Gartside's. And Colonel O'Sullivan to the Saracen's Head. Yet no sign of the Prince himself. But do you know that we are to be received by His Royal Highness tonight? At Mister Redmond's where, I understand, you will dine with him. How I envy thee, friend Aran.'

'And the regiments themselves. Are they accommodated? Some in your own house perhaps.'

'Not yet, and Papa fears the prospect so. But companies are being dispatched along Market Street Lane, Deansgate and Ridgefield. We so hope that they need Hanging Ditch too, do we not girls?'

'I suspect that Mister Bradley might not share your enthusiasm,' says Aran. 'And Rosina – have you seen her since last night?'

'Early this morning. On her way to the House of Correction. She told me that she would not leave until he is released. She has so *many* reasons to now consider her Marriage Settlement breached, do you not find? I swear that I do not understand her. The effects of the laudanum, I am certain.'

What reasons? he wonders. Bradley may be a Whig, a Hanoverian, an active opponent of the Stuarts, but this hardly seems a reason that would justify a claim against the Settlement. But here, at last, comes Charles Edward Stuart to the very heart of Manchester.

No pipers now to herald his approach but a wave of approving cries and applause building away in the streets approaching the Market Square and then breaking around the Shambles as he finally appears, on foot now, the dappled grey following behind, led by an equerry at the head of his Lifeguard escort and an Ensign bearing a white Stuart standard, while other troopers form a small cordon to either side of their royal charge and maintain some clear passage through which he might walk unhindered.

'Oh,' says Beppy, 'I fear that my heart shall burst with pride. Such a handsome fellow. So tall. The Hanover pack are so very obese, do you not find? I imagine that it must be the quantities of German pudding and pickled cabbage that they consume.' He has never actually *seen* any of them but, yes, they are usually illustrated as tending towards the corpulent. As to their eating habits... 'And see,' she points to Mary and Dorothy, 'Mister Townley!'

Townley indeed, amongst a group of other gentlemen riders, including David Morgan, following close behind the blue-coated Lifeguards and pressed on each side by cheering well-wishers.

The Prince, meanwhile, has continued across the Square, past the Conduit and away towards Market Street Lane.

'He must visit the Redmonds, I imagine,' says Aran, as the bells in all the churches begin to toll three o'clock but then continue pealing as still more regiments of Scots, Highlanders and Lowlanders, begin to take station around the Cross.

Some of the townsfolk call for them to be given water and sustenance, and flagons are produced from the Bull's Head, from John Shaw's Punch House and even, reluctantly he assumes, from the Angel, all to be distributed amongst the soldiers until their officers eventually forbid it. But water? The pumps on the Conduit would normally stand locked for another two hours and there are some feeble and vain attempts to smash the heavy iron fastenings until, at last, William Fowden arrives with the keys and the waters of the Isabella Spring are summoned forth to quench the Scotsmens' thirst.

The Bellman is also summoned and Thomas Walley too, though he almost has to be dragged to the place, and his arrival coincides with that of a fellow that Aran has not seen before. He wears no military attire and, uniquely, no sign of chequered tartan either, but his bearing shows him to be a person of authority.

'Colonel O'Sullivan, I believe,' says Beppy. 'I saw him come in earlier. The Prince's Adjutant-General. So very eminent.'

O'Sullivan directs questions at Fowden and Walley in a voice so sonorous that it carries quite clearly to Aran. They will direct him, if they please, to the Lord of the Manor. But Sir Oswald has fled to Staffordshire, it seems. The Borough Reeve then? Yet Thomas Fielden appears to be away from town also. Well, how vexatious! In that case, the duty shall fall to the Constables to read the Royal Proclamation. The ceremony has so much more meaning when conducted by representatives of the township itself. And the Adjutant-General issues some hasty instructions to an officer of the Lifeguards who, in turn, fetches an equerry, relieving him of the regal document and ignoring whatever dispute has broken out between Walley and Fowden, each looking dejected, nervous, agitated.

They remain so when, ten minutes later, the Prince returns, mounted once more and walking his horse to a spot some twenty yards distant from the Cross itself. He is joined by Colonel O'Sullivan and another of the senior staff. Lord George Murray, Beppy tells him, while the former gestures to the Lifeguards' officer that he may commence.

So the Proclamation is pressed into Walley's hands, the Bellman summoned forth.

'Good people of Manchester and all others present this day! Pray silence for the Proclamation of His Majesty, King James the Third.'

Silence indeed. Walley unfolds the scroll, stares at the parchment, looks out at the expectant crowd.

'I c-c-cannot...' he begins. 'No! I fucking w-w-*will* not...'

The Lifeguard officer hastens back to his side, whispers something in his ear, Walley responding only with a rigid shaking of his head, the Prince gazing at something interesting away in the distance..

The scroll wrested from Walley's fingers and passed to Fowden.

'Yet I have no spectacles!' Fowden protests.

The officer summoned to Colonel O'Sullivan's side while Lord George Murray fumes angrily and Charles Edward appears vaguely amused. The Colonel reaches inside his coat, passing a pair of spectacles to the young subaltern and these, in turn, are conveyed to Fowden. He adjusts them upon his nose, glares at his fellow-Constable, moves the Proclamation back and forth until it comes into focus and, at last, the thing is read in a querulous voice barely audible to most of the spectators.

'Whereas it hath pleased Almighty God...'

We shall be here for the remainder of the day unless Fowden can be moved to some greater perspicacity!

But Beppy, he notices, the entire crowd in fact, seem entirely bewitched by the carefully amended version of a more traditional announcement. Yet, he supposes, it must have been adapted to fit all manner of historical peculiarity in the past.

'...Do now hereby with one full voice, and consent of tongue and heart, publish and proclaim that our only lawful, lineal, and rightful Liege Lord, James the Third, is now by the Grace of God King of England, Scotland, France and Ireland. To whom we do acknowledge all faith and constant obedience, with all hearty and humble affection, beseeching God by whom Kings do reign, to bless the Royal King James the Third with long and happy years to reign over us. God Save King James the Third.'

No mention of Hanover George then. And we seem suddenly to have acquired France too. Though it is, he knows, simply a wishful and historical ambition, harking back to those ancient days when English Crown had, indeed, held considerable French territory.

Fowden though is now just punctured by the relief of reaching the declaration's end, the wind escaping from him in a sudden rush that will cause his whole frame to collapse, his legs too vacant to sustain him any further.

'The prisoners to be brought forth!' calls the Irishman, O'Sullivan, and on the far side of the Shambles the ranks part to allow a three-strong escort of Lowland soldiers, Sergeant Dickson at their head, to lead forward both Hawkswell and Bradley, neither of them shackled but each of them unkempt, dishevelled.

Aran sees Rosina attempt to push through the cordon also, to follow her husband across the open space, and he steps forward to intercept her.

'Perhaps, Mistress Bradley,' he says to her, gently, 'it may be preferable to join your friends awhile. For see, Beppy Byrom is here with me. Dorothy and Molly too.'

She is almost asleep on her feet, he sees, needs physical support to keep her upright.

'It was my *friend*, Beppy Byrom, who condemned my husband, I am told. Was it not so, madam?'

'Rosina,' says Beppy, 'I should not distress thee for the world, of all things, but I spoke nothing except the truth about James Bradley. And, my dear one, thou art hardly obliged to show him any conjugal loyalty given... Well, you understand me, I think.'

Hawkswell, meanwhile, has been brought to the Cross where Dickson has listed charges against him, his instigation of an assault upon the Sergeant's own person whilst in the prosecution of his duties.

'Fined ten guineas and pressed to the service of His Royal Highness, assigned to the Manchester Regiment.'

Hawkswell taken away, mouthing unheeded protest.

So we are to have our own regiment after all!

'It is understandable,' says Aran, 'that Rosina should be distressed by Mister Bradley's incarceration, regardless of any strangeness in the circumstances and conduct of their marriage.'

'Strangeness?' says Rosina. 'It is not strangeness to which Beppy refers but, rather, to Mama's trysting once more with that *same* Mister Bradley.'

And, shocking though this news may be to Aran, he cannot avert his attention from Dickson's further list of charges against Bradley himself. Leader of the town's Whiggish and seditious faction, personally responsible for raising a considerable Subscription and, therefore, armed insurrection against His Royal Highness.

There is brief discussion between O'Sullivan and the Prince.

'Will Mister Bradley speak to these charges on his own behalf?' asks the Colonel.

'Me, sir?' says Bradley. 'Yes, I shall speak, for I have had the privilege of serving upon the Court Leet of this Manor for many years. Our duties are modest. To keep wandering vagrants from the town. To prevent the unwholesome spread of middens from our streets. To ensure that our citizens are not cheated by scoundrels posing as honest men. But we have failed in those duties, it seems. For Manchester now swarms with those who have no place here and sleep on straw. We are plagued with fellows who shit from our windows and upon our thoroughfares. Our citizens are promised that which cannot be delivered and for which they must pay an excessive price. It was my simple responsibility, sir, to raise additional revenue that our by-laws might be enforced against the exceptional level of this temporary civic nuisance. And the Subscription of which this fellow speaks is no more than the additional revenue needed to meet that end. There is no sedition in exercising the duties of one's public burden.'

Jeering and rage within the crowd accompany his every word, even from many who would boast themselves Whig supporters in any other circumstances.

Further debate between the Prince and his Adjutant-General.

'Our Lady be praised!' says O'Sullivan. 'Johnny Cope had need of *you* at Gladsmuir, Mister Bradley.'

Charles Edward sets a hand upon the Colonel's arm to still him.

'Mister Bradley,' he says. Aran, others too, it seems, is surprised to realise that his English, though perfect, is accented, a perceptible hint of some other European tongue. 'We observe from your expression that you believe Colonel O'Sullivan to be mocking you. Yet you are in error, sir. For we do not mock brave Englishmen, my father's subjects all, no matter whether, at this juncture, we may happen to share no common view. But we trust that a day may soon dawn when this nation shall no longer be divided and, when that day comes, His Majesty King James, or oneself as Regent in his stead, shall yet need gentlemen of bold endeavour to maintain our Realm, regardless that they may formerly have belonged to this faction or that. And there is one thing more, sir. It is this. For you have spoken fears that we have heard previously elsewhere. Some misconception that our loyal Scotsmen are, somehow, lacking in certain disciplines. Well, sir, we give you this assurance. That you shall not find a more regulated soldiery in all Christendom. Every man here knows that any who contravenes our royal expectations shall answer for it. Sergeant, you shall release this man forthwith and you shall likewise fling open the gates at the House of Correction for any others still in our custody. In this most loyal of our English towns all should be at liberty to follow us or not, as heart and conscience dictate. But, Mister Bradley, there is this also. For I doubt that you are similarly able to vouchsafe the behaviour of your entire Party. On this basis, and in the role of leadership that we would have you maintain within the Court Leet, you are charged by your Liege Lord, so recently proclaimed, to sign a bail bond of five thousand pounds, a promissory note against the good behaviour of those amongst you who might, indeed, have sedition in their hearts.'

James Bradley prepares for a further demonstration of defiance but the moment is lost to him as the Prince's party turns away to leave the Market Place while Sergeant Dickson abandons his former prisoner also, leaving him standing alone near the Cross.

The regiments are dismissed, with townsfolk and Scotsmen quickly mingled and Aran knows that, if he does not put his question now, their small group will be swept apart, for Rosina is already intent on joining her husband.

'Rosina, my dear,' he says, 'it pleases me that your husband is released. But will you not tell me? Can it be true that Mister Bradley and your mother…?'

'I am sorry, sir,' she replies, her voice slurred and slowed by the Sydenham's, 'for I know that you have some affection and loyalty towards Mama. But I tell you, Aran Owen, that she is more the harlot than any of my father's other bawds. You will ask why I should care about such a thing, of course, in the circumstances and, if I am entirely honest, I should find difficulty in providing an answer. But it wounds me more than I can say, sir. And you may find this even more strange, but I hold Mama accountable rather than Mister Bradley. Now, if you will pardon me…'

And she glides away to Bradley's side, a modest display of concern for his health.

'As I said, Mister Owen,' says Beppy, 'the effects of the opiate, I am certain. Yet do you have plans for this next hour?'

He does not, and is thus persuaded by the Byrom girls to join them, first at a five o'clock service in the Collegiate Church where King James and the Prince of Wales are both blessed by Charles Edward's chaplain, Thomas Cappock. They meet Francis Townley there and he, like Aran, is invited back to the Byroms' house for a glass of wine and a Queen Cake before all walk together to Camp Field where Townley must apparently join the Manchester Regiment. when it is embodied and reviewed.

Aran might almost pity the fellow for, whilst he is generally of high spirits, this evening he seems uncommonly low, having expected to hear by now at least that he may be offered a commission within its ranks, if not its leadership. But he goes off with good enough heart and they reach Camp Field itself, the pasture illuminated by a score of beacon fires and the ground mercifully hard underfoot except for those areas churned by the Jacobite artillery pieces, a dozen of them, lined here for inspection in the charge of their gunners, some kilted and others in formal uniform.

On the opposite side, the volunteers are mustered, perhaps three hundred of them in total, and assembled by various officers and sergeants from the existing regiments, calling instruction to them, attempting to instil some structure, some sense of the military, into these inelegant and irregular files.

Yet they are more impressive than the fellows raised by Sir Edward for his Militia, thinks Aran. *More impressive by far! Or perhaps simply seem so in the dark.*

It takes some time but finally they are sufficiently presentable for the Prince Regent and his commanders to ride along their shadowed front, though it seems more formality than anything purposeful, a cursory review only. But Colonel O'Sullivan is soon reading from a prepared speech, a subaltern holding a lanthorn above the page.

'His Royal Highness having thought fit to raise a Manchester Regiment of Foot under the command of Colonel Francis Townley...'

Cheering and hats thrown in the air by spectators and volunteers alike. *So he has his regiment after all!*

'...To consist of six companies, with two sergeants, two corporals, one drummer, and fifty effective private men in each, besides commissioned officers. His Royal Highness grants a warrant for allowing five guineas for each private man as levy-money, and for the Quartermaster-General to deliver such orders as may be necessary for issuing arms, as usual, from His Majesty's store of ordnance. Also to the Paymaster-General of the Forces to commence the provision of subsistence to the whole regiment, effective this Twenty-Ninth day of November in the Year 1745.'

Polite applause from the onlookers. Chaplain Cappock provides a blessing, and then a second document to be read. The Commissions confirmed.

Adjutant Ensign to the Colonel, Thomas Sydall.

Ensigns, six, who include the two youngsters, Charles Deacon and William Brettargh.

Lieutenants, also one for each Company. Thomas and Robert Deacon. Thomas Chaddock. John Beswicke, one of Beppy's cousins. John Holker. Thomas Furnival.

And Captains, six too, of course. Another of Beppy's cousins, James Dawson. Andrew Blood. Peter Moss. John Sanderson. George Fletcher. John Daniel of Garstang, who had brought forty volunteers himself from that village.

The new regiment dismissed and congratulations all around, Beppy promising to manufacture sashes of white satin and some tartan attire for the officers, Aran experiencing a momentary regret that he has not joined them. But it passes quickly and, by eight o'clock, he is at table for supper with His Royal Highness.

Mistress Hepple had once again been contracted and planned *un petit couvert* for ten places, the blue *motif* Chelsea porcelain and Indian China, sufficient for the Redmonds' dining room but with just a hint of informality. The table is a model of invention, the confectioner having sculpted two perfect miniatures of circular temples in meringue and sugar icing. The guests admire them greatly with, in turn, Chaplain Cappock, Anna-Marie, Captain Townley and Colonel O'Sullivan on one side whilst Titus, David Morgan, Katherine and Aran occupy the other, with the Prince and Maria-Louise taking each of the end settings.

Two main courses and a dessert course naturally, ten dishes in each course to match the number of guests. Soups, stews, vegetables and much of the fish first, each dish placed in its formal order by O'Farrell acting as butler, Mistress Hepple as his assistant. Five servants on hand, hired for the occasion, though not to serve food, of course. Etiquette dictates that dinner guests must do this for themselves. So they here simply to pass the oil, the vinegar, the bread, or to replenish drinking glasses after washing them at the sideboard fountain imported for the purpose.

Mistress Hepple, good lady, has tried to ensure that Mudge is kept at a safe distance from the proceedings but it is almost impossible when, at the end of the first course, the remove centre-piece dishes must be fetched for the second, on this occasion the salmon, the suckling pig, the wildfowl and pigeon pie.

The Prince, initially uncomfortable but now visibly relaxed by the easy charms of Maria-Louise, has delivered apologies on the part of the French Ambassador, sadly indisposed. *And thank Our Lord for it,* thinks Aran, *else he might have remained permanently thus had Mistress Redmond drawn his blood.* Charles Edward had then variously recounted details of his journey to Scotland, expressed his pleasure that Captain Townley's brother had been made Colonel largely in recognition of his former commission with the French Limousin Regiment, and expressed similar pleasure that he would have at least *one* bold Townley at his side since the Captain was due to embark tomorrow on his circuitous journey back to France with the Marquis d'Eguilles. *Yet Titus, at least, clearly does not share the Prince Regent's enthusiasm for the younger Townley's abilities! He so despises the fellow. See how sourly he received the news that Francis was made Colonel.* There are polite questions and acknowledgements from the Manchester guests but these fall unanimously, utterly and simultaneously silent, breath inhaled and held, at the entrance of the former whore, balancing a charger of fresh salmon that still swims, it seems, in wave-like motion to match the bobbing of Mudge's head as she drags her crippled leg towards the head of the table.

The Prince, the Chaplain, the Captain, the Colonel, the Lawyer take collective pause at the shocked expressions, the slightly parted lips, the fearful stares shared so completely by their hosts. And not the Redmonds' party alone, it seems, but their servants too as O'Farrell bursts through the door behind her, just too late.

'Bitch!' mutters Mudge, directing her comment towards the demure Mistress Hepple who stands near the flower arrangement.

And, as each head amongst the regal party turns to the object of the housekeeper's ire, Mudge trips, the charger leaving her hands with just sufficient forward momentum to propel the plate and its content towards the sash and bright tartan of His Royal Highness, the Prince of Wales.

It is fortunate for the young man, perhaps, that he had attended so well during the fencing lessons of the aged Maître André de Liancourt, and particularly his mastery of Signore Marchelli's *Passata Soto*, that enables his instinct now to bring him upright, turning, dropping instantly below the charger's trajectory, extending the lunge position of his right hand and placing the non-sword fingers upon the table edge as a brace. It is a perfect catch and retrieval, though there is some spillage of the liquid, while Mudge has sprawled to all fours, David Morgan rising from his place to help the poor woman back to her feet and receiving a drool of spittle down his admittedly already shabby coat sleeve by way of thanks and reward.

'So Monsieur le Marquis,' says Titus, as though the episode had never occurred, 'is returning to France. Not his illness, I trust? He seemed well in Preston and I enjoyed his kindness so, Your Highness.'

The Prince sets the platter in its proper place, resumes his seat with the assistance of a servant.

'We are pleased to hear it, Mister Redmond. Yet we fear that the local *cuisine* has affected him badly and this morning he was entirely incapable of leaving his bed, was he not Captain?' Townley affirms. 'But he must be fit enough to travel by the time that Captain Townley returns to Preston and thence to Peterhead so that they may sail at the earliest possibility. The Ambassador is convinced, and we share his enthusiasm, that our royal cousin, King Louis, shall now proceed with his promised embarkation of French regiments to secure the south coast on one's behalf.'

O'Farrell has now taken charge of Mag Mudge from Attorney Morgan and leads her, far from gently, back to the door. A final 'Fucking bitch!' echoes in the hallway beyond and occasions a movement in the royal eye-brow but little else.

'Then the invasion shall still happen, sir?' says Morgan, sitting once more and dabbing at his sleeve with a napkin. 'Sir Watkin shall be pleased to hear it.'

'An invasion,' replies the Prince, 'implies some enemy action, does it not Mister Morgan? Why, *Monsieur*, we shall require more precision from your new position. Do you know, my friends, that Mister Morgan had also been nominated as a potential Colonel for your Manchester Regiment?' *Now I wonder who might have recommended such a thing?* Aran thinks, looking towards a stone-faced Titus Redmond. 'But he modestly declined the opportunity and we have decided to utilise his talents differently, in any case. In the position of Royal Councillor.' Congratulations. A glass with you, Mister Morgan. 'Besides, Francis Townley was the obvious choice, we believed. He has accomplished so much in raising the volunteers. Meanwhile, Councillor Morgan must return to Wales and join his companions in those parts to whom one has already sent word of our plans and aspirations for them. A Welsh Regiment will be most welcome. The intervention of King Louis also. But not invasion. Mister Morgan. Never in life, sir. As valued and invited allies, naturally.' He pauses a moment, uncertain whether to continue, perhaps. 'Do you know, I wonder,' he says, at last, 'that such an intention existed earlier in the campaign, but suffered something of a reversal?' He looks around the other guests. 'Yes, one imagines that this company would be quite familiar with the detail.' Aran feels Maria-Louise tense beside him, her knee suddenly pressing against his own, almost the only time that she has acknowledged him since his arrival, she still being vexed with him about Sir Edward's ballad sheets. *The hypocrisy of the dear woman, in all the circumstances.*

'I believe that we may know something of that matter, Your Highness,' says Morgan, 'yet all is far from lost if King Louis is still prepared to intervene, as you say. And considerable numbers of the Irish Brigade now landed in Scotland too, Captain Townley, we understand?'

'Indeed, sir. Yet I always feared that there might be some devilry at work in the misfortune that prevented earlier and more substantial French reinforcements.'

'What,' says Colonel O'Sullivan, 'from Newcastle's agents, you mean? If so, I would see the wretch responsible hung, drawn and quartered. Begging your pardon, madam.'

And Maria-Louise seizes the opportunity to drive the conversation at their end of the table to more tolerable matters. The Colonel's upbringing in County Kerry. Shared acquaintance. O'Sullivan's own sojourn in Paris, five years before her own. The plans, soon abandoned, for him to join the priesthood.

Meanwhile, at the opposite end of the table, Prince Charles Edward Stuart cannot quite so quickly discard his own remorse at the loss of so much revenue. But where should they have been without the subscriptions and finances raised by this loyal family? And the tea trade, how does it stand these days? The news shocks him. So many twists of ill-fortune.

The dessert course, the confectioner's masterpiece. Elaborate cake plates, tier upon tier of gumballs and cheese wigs, the only concession to a savoury element, amongst the sugared fruits, *patisserie*, sweetmeats, jams, jellies and creams.

O'Farrell returning to announce Lord George Murray, that gentlemen in turn advising His Royal Highness that those invited to be received this evening are presently waiting in the hall. The Prince thanks Maria-Louise for the excellence of the supper in close enough proximity to Mistress Hepple for that lady to also bathe in its glow, and the whole party ascends by the back stairs to the first floor, the *piano nobile*, and the larger Entertaining Room. A long carpet runner has been set down the centre and a raised dais fashioned at the farther end upon which the town's most elegant chair has been placed, brought in haste from the Court Leet chamber at the Exchange.

I wonder if James Bradley would take comfort from, henceforth, his own arse now forever sharing the cushion that the royal posterior is about to honour?

The servants stand ready at the long boards where wines and cordials are once more available, and Phelim O'Farrell has been trusted with a list of those who are to be ushered into the Prince's presence. Sir Oswald and Lady Ann Mosley have been unceremoniously scrubbed from the top of the list, naturally, now that their extended absence from Manchester is understood.

So first comes the Duke of Perth, accompanied by his own hosts, Robert Gartside the fustian manufacturer and wife, Alice Gartside.

Adam Scatterbuck, printer, and Thomas Tipping, yarn merchant.

The linen drapers Peter Moss and George Fletcher, now both Captains in the Manchester Regiment, and their wives, Mary and Susanna.

The Byrom family. Mistress Elizabeth Byrom. *Miss* Elizabeth Byrom also, and her sisters Dorothy and Mary, with brother Edward.

Yet no John Byrom?

Colonel Francis Townley next, joining Beppy as soon as he has been received.

And Aran hastens to their side also, finding himself temporarily and gratefully abandoned by Katherine who has clung to him like a limpet throughout the earlier part of the evening.

'Well,' he says, 'give you joy Colonel Townley! I am delighted for you, sir. Yet your Papa, Beppy, he is unwell, perhaps?'

'Unwell? It depends on thy definition of the word. He has embarrassed Mama so terribly. First, he had made such a scene with the Adjutant-General about Mister Bradley's incarceration. He described it as a barbarity. And then refused to allow any of His Majesty's soldiers to be quartered in our house. Yet it is so *very* large. It was only the intercession of Colonel Townley that saved him from the House of Correction too, I fear, though he is now restrained and under discreet guard at home. But Mama perfectly refused to remain with him and insisted on being received despite my father's protestations that he himself has not yet entirely declared for the Prince's Cause in light of all these *developments*, as he describes them.' She turns to an excited whisper. 'You know, Aran, that somebody had informed His Royal Highness about my actions at the bridge, modest though they might have been. He called me the Saviour of Manchester. La! Can you imagine? And such news. Complete panic in Liverpool, we hear, the entire population fled to the Mersey's western bank following the movement of their militia to Chester and believing themselves abandoned to the mercy of our own dear Prince.'

'Not militia, my dear,' says Townley, 'for the Liverpool Blues were raised as a regular regiment, like my own. But such an excellent thing, this concentration of Hanoverians at Chester. For it surely betokens their real fear of Sir Watkin's forces in Wales. Ah, it shall be good to see the Welsh arise and cast them aside.' His own passion betokens something else, that fine saliva spray which accompanies so many of his words but seems not to trouble Beppy in the slightest. 'And you, Mister Owen, will you not now join our ranks?'

'I should make a poor soldier, I fear, though I had hoped that some of my other skills might be useful to you. Cartography, perhaps, though I note that all the commissions are now awarded.'

But Townley is sure that one more might be possible. When all is said and done, despite the announcement that the Regiment would be receive regular pay, it was their own Subscription that would fund the thing. So an engineer's position, perhaps. They arrange to meet again later, at the bonfire, or perhaps at the Byroms' house since Beppy expects to be occupied until the early hours, along with Dolly and Molly, in making sashes for Colonel Townley's officers and Saint Andrew's Crosses for the morrow.

Yes, perhaps. Though, in truth, Aran has no intentions of further conversation with Townley on the matter. All the same, he had forgotten that the next day would mark the Feast of Saint Andrew. There will be great celebrations, Beppy assures him. Services held in all the churches, except for Saint Ann's. A further review of the Manchester Regiment once issued with its muskets. And more patrols. More forays across the upper reaches of the Mersey.

Doctor Thomas Deacon and the Reverend Doctor John Clayton ushered now into the presence of His Royal Highness.

And Mistress Rosina Bradley.

Aran turns sharply at the announcement, sees Rosina advance alone along the carpet, her best green silk shimmering in the candle-light and those proud ringlets, catching the flames to shimmer like burnished copper. The interview is prolonged, though finally she takes two steps backwards from the Court Leet's throne, dips in obeisance to the Prince Regent, and retreats the requisite number of paces before turning away. She hesitates for a few seconds as others are called forward, more Jacobite merchants, while she plans a route to escape the room. On one side, her mother has broken off her own dialogue with Alice Gartside and the Duke of Perth, clearly expecting that her daughter will speak with her while, on the other side, Beppy also shows a positive intention of resolving any recent misunderstanding with her friend.

Yet Rosina determines to steer a path clear of them both, a partial smile for her Papa, a rapid yet dignified manoeuvre towards the doors. Aran had, to some extent, anticipated this and, keeping to the edge of the Entertaining Room, he reaches the landing just a yard or more behind her at the head of the splendid winding stair that descends to the ground floor.

'I do not crave any company, Aran, I thank you,' she says.

'Your cravings are no concern of mine in *any* of their various guises, Mistress Bradley. Yet I am reminded of my own past errors in spurning those who only wished me well. You will not make the same mistake, I trust?'

'We speak of Beppy Byrom, I collect. Well, sir, she should learn to curb her tongue!'

'A tongue that could be the duplicate of your own. For what words has *she* said that you would not have spoken in her place a mere six months past. It may be true that she was less than compassionate in her comments about your husband, yet she had no thought to wound *you*, my dear. And it is difficult for each of us to think of Bradley by that term in any meaningful way.'

'And myself neither. Yet I had not appreciated the closeness that can develop by sharing a marriage even without sharing its bed. He has not treated me ill, Aran. Nor sought to control my affection for Elizabeth though, Our Lady knows, Elizabeth affords me little affection in return these days. And his family. His Ma and Pa. They show me... Well, I do not know how to name it. But I had so longed for this day, when our noble Prince should come to free us, when Manchester should rise to his standard. And yet it was all so marred by the way my husband was practised upon. But you are correct and the fault does not lie with Beppy Byrom. Please offer her my apologies, Aran my good friend, for I cannot return to that room. And Mister Bradley, I fear, has contracted something of an ague during his imprisonment.'

'Do you have a message for your Mama too, daughter?'

It is Maria-Louise, stood upon the landing above them, and Aran sees the brief glimmer of affection in Rosina's eye extinguish entirely. There is no hint of opiate influence in her now, just a cold anger. He thinks of Congreve. 'Heaven has no rage like love to hatred turned.'

'It must have amused you so *very* much, Mama. Such a clever plan. To marry me against my will to Mister Bradley. Not even a man that I simply did not love but one who I felt to be distinctly odious. I could not even trust Elizabeth Cooper's part in the thing. *Oh, marry him, my sweet, and he shall leave us to our own affairs.* Well, naturally he should do so when, all the time, you were provided with the opportunity to fuck him afresh! So, a message, Mama? Let me think.'

But Titus has also now appeared upon the landing.

'Please, my dear,' he says to Rosina. 'Perhaps you might lower your voice? I am trying to persuade Mister Morgan that he should not trust this fellow who has inveigled his way into the confidence, it seems, both of Sir Watkin and the entire Jacobite command. For I believe him to be the very same fellow who killed Jacob Driscoll.' Maria-Louise exchanges eye contact with Aran, and Rosina sees it too. But Titus has turned to his wife. 'And I had not realised that you are still trysting with Bradley, madam. There is no longer any need, I assure you. For I can glean whatever intelligence I need from the cunny-sucker. Oh, my regrets, Rosina, I had not intended... Well, I can simply *ask* the fellow. And it would not seem entirely the thing, he being now related to you in a way.'

Rosina looks at them both for a moment. Each in turn. Disbelief. Then at Aran. And she walks slowly down the remainder of the stairs, her head shaking slightly as she opens the front door and leaves without even the cloak that she came in.

Chapter Forty-Six

On the shelves of the library that he helped to catalogue for Richard Williams, Striker had discovered a copy of Walter Map's *De Nugis Corialum*. It may have been written six centuries earlier, yet its description of the Welsh, Map himself being a native of these same Marches, seems entirely apposite today. 'They are treacherous to each other as well as to foreigners, covet freedom, neglect peace, are warlike and skilful in arms, and are eager for revenge.' Well, that had been Striker's translation of Map's Latin anyway.

But his impending reunion with Sir Watkin has brought to mind a more modern view. 'The older the Welshman, the greater the madness.'

He had received his instructions from Colonel O'Sullivan two days earlier, on the evening of the twenty-seventh, at the house on Friargate in Preston, along with the sealed orders for Sir Watkin himself and, turning along the line of supplicants waiting to crave the Irishman's grace and favour, Striker had found himself momentarily face to face with none other than Titus Redmond. And there was no doubting the recognition in the fellow's eyes neither, the involuntary gesture towards the moustache that Redmond insists on sporting. Yet he supposes that such appendages shall now become *de rigueur* with this new obsession for all things military.

Still, he had certainly recognised Striker yet not denounced him. What did this mean? Possible, of course, that it had taken Mister Redmond just a moment too long to associate the face with a location. It was common enough. But it would not have taken him a great while. The memories would have flooded back quickly, he supposed, and he recalls the unexpected tears that had filled the merchant's eyes on seeing the red ruin of that old bawd's face. Striker had played such a pretty pattern upon Mother Blossom's nostrils! But tears. And then Wolfe's man had damn'd near taken off the back of Redmond's head with his hanger. What had been his name? Yes, Dubbins. A heavy-handed clod. But no hue and cry before Striker had left Preston itself. Not that O'Sullivan or anybody else would have been likely to accept any denunciation as fact. Far from it. A momentary encounter? Mistaken identity surely. And Lieutenant William Owen is a respected officer within Sir John MacDonald's Company of Rangers.

Somebody like Titus Redmond would not have left the dog to sleep there, however. He would have stirred it with his foot, worrying at the beast until it was fully awake. And what? Perceived Jacob Driscoll's long-dried blood upon its fangs too perhaps. Aran has already told him that Redmond is intent upon revenge for Driscoll's death. Yet it had been Driscoll that set the trap. He had, thinks Striker, rather been hoisted upon his own petard. Still, once a man has vengeance in his heart it blinds him to any form of reason. Just as well, therefore, that Striker has not joined the Jacobite march on Manchester. And the main force must surely reach that town today. It would have been good to renew his acquaintance with young Aran though. *Why, we are almost brothers, are we not?* But since he is *not* in Manchester, and since Redmond will have overheard his destination at the very least, knows Sir Watkin so intimately too, he must exercise caution.

He had been cautious since leaving Preston, as it happens, taking advantage of the excellent turnpiked road south to Warrington by travelling overnight. A few hours rest in that pretty place, now riven with panic at the approach of the *Chevalier*, before pressing on to arrive in Chester just a little after four on the previous afternoon. Yet hardly the Chester that he had left, the town now being a fully armed camp, with several thousand soldiers within the walls, though many of them newly raised and no match for the Scots army that Striker has so recently left. There are several thousand more, apparently, within easy reach of the town too if, as seems to be the general impression, either the Jacobite army marches this way or, more likely, there is a rising in Wales with Chester as its immediate objective.

So Striker had been able to secure no more by way of accommodation than some straw bales and a few blankets in the same Livery where his bay mare is stabled in shameless luxury. But he had too much to occupy him in any case, finding a quiet table and a decent light by which he could study the sealed orders from O'Sullivan to Sir Watkin. The Welsh forces were to be assembled immediately and, contrary to earlier instructions, should now avoid Chester and its greatly strengthened garrison at all cost but march by way of Nantwich and Chelford. The Colonel stresses that no other route should be attempted, so that they may reach Macclesfield where all forces will rendezvous on the evening of Monday, the second day of December. It is a difficult itinerary but O'Sullivan must have relied on Lieutenant Owen delivering it expeditiously.

Then to his more usual lodging, where two messages from Newcastle had awaited him. First, coded, an instruction that he should do all in his power to disrupt the Jacobite communications. And the second...

He reads it again.

His Grace, the Duke of Newcastle, is pleased to inform whomsoever it may concern that a Warrant has been issued to the bearer, Dudley Striker by name, for a Commission to the rank of Captain within the armies of His Majesty, King George the Second, by the Grace of God, King of Great Britain and Ireland. The bearer to be treated with the respect and deference due to this rank since he acts with the Secretary of State's full authority in all matters pertaining to his immediate duties.

Captain! By God, sir. Lieutenant in one army, Captain in t'other, thinks Striker.

But the letter is vague on the matter of what those immediate duties might be! And the Duke not so free with King George's purse as *le Prince Edouard* with his own. For no reference to pay here. Well, a detail to be resolved at the next encounter with His Grace, perhaps, for he needs to know that he will have adequate investment for his future welfare once this whole thing is settled.

Yet, meanwhile, there had been some modest forgery to be performed. A visit to the admirable Mistress Adams, a suitably impressive parchment purchased, and then the simple skill of reproducing a passable facsimile of O'Sullivan's hand, good enough to convince any but those closest to him. The seal carefully lifted and transferred, affixed, to the new document.

A coded response to Newcastle. Thanks, of course. News of the planned *rendezvous* at Macclesfield, hopefully dispelling any further doubts about the Jacobite intentions, for Newcastle's advisors had been convinced that these moves across the border are simply a feint, the real intention being a return to the Highlands. Advisors? *Fools, more like!* And his predictions for the Welsh over the next few days, of course.

Finally, an excessively long wait at the Headquarters of General Cholmondeley in Chester's Castle, his letter from Newcastle produced and his plan sketched in the merest outline, for Striker has never been one for committing himself too closely to specifics. The world is excessively fluid for anything approaching certainty. In any case, Cholmondeley had not taken to him. Few do! Besides, the General has his own ranging picquets, KIngston's splendid Light Horse. Well, thankfully Striker's plans do not rely too heavily on military assistance.

But he had finally been able to settle amongst his blankets and straw bales, remarkably enjoying his best sleep for several weeks. Then, this morning, an early start on the bay mare for Wrecsam and, beyond to Wynnstay Hall.

He pauses at the Ruabon crossroads, Saint Mary's Church before him, then turns left, riding the lane alongside a high brick wall surrounding the estate's extensive park, turning in at the gates and following the broad tree-lined avenue that leads to the Hall itself, scattering hundreds of fallow deer from his path. Rather, Wynnstay is a collection of dwellings, large stable blocks and coach houses, then a half-timbered Jacobean pile and, finally, the main building, most of it constructed by Sir Watkin himself during the 'Thirties.

A groom takes his horse and Striker is escorted to a closet where he might wash and entrust his valise to a servant before being ushered to the reception room where Sir Watkin is taking tea with his wife, Ann, and with

Sir John Glynne. George Shakerley of Gwersyllt is also present, along with Richard Williams while, near the hearth, a harper runs gentle fingers along the rippling strings of his instrument. Acquaintances renewed and a formal introduction to Lady Ann.

'Such a splendid house, Mistress,' he says. 'I have rarely seen such exquisite architecture.'

'Do you say so, sir? My husband spent a great deal of time and money on its design. He employed two fine architects to assist him. Lavished wealth to ensure that all should be completed to its correct standard and specification. Thus, you might assume that he would have been capable of achieving just a little more in the service of King James, might you not? And certainly after so many years of the White Cycle Club and other great schemes.'

'Yet here is our noble friend William Owen returned safe to us after so many adventures,' says the Rector of Hawarden, delight and adoration each glowing in his eyes.

'Now *Lieutenant* Owen, friend Richard!' replies Striker, but thinking of the other, more senior Commission hidden within his valise.

'Well, give you joy, sir,' says Glynne. 'But, dear lady, I fear that you do Watkin little justice here. The muster is going well and more are bound to arrive during the night.'

So what has happened? O'Sullivan was expecting that there would be no less than one thousand under arms here.

'Please forgive this want of hospitality, Lieutenant Owen,' says Lady Ann, 'yet refreshments are on their way. More than can be said for any reinforcements to my husband's muster. Less than three hundred, it seems. And if you believe that significantly more shall join at this late stage, I fear that you are more the fool than my husband.'

'Three hundred is a considerable figure!' the normally ebullient Sir Watkin says at last. 'And more than half of them mounted. Gentlemen, no less, bringing fine weapons with them. His Royal Highness will no doubt be delighted. It is less than we might need for an outright assault on Chester but we shall raise more yet and all depends on whether the Lieutenant has brought further instruction.'

'I do, sir,' says Striker, 'and I have recently passed through Chester itself. At considerable risk, you understand. An attack upon the town with such numbers, unless by some stealthy ruse, would now be out of the question. Yet I think that Colonel O'Sullivan's orders may suggest a different strategy.'

'I do not hold with all this spying and skulking about the country,' says Shakerley. 'It is time that we struck a proper blow against the Hanoverian rabble. They tell me that Cholmondeley's regiments at Chester are all witless youths who still cannot load a musket, let alone point the thing. New orders, you say? Why, I have promised my men that Chester shall be theirs!'

'Your *thirty* men, George?' Lady Ann rebukes him. 'Is Chester so important to these Gwersyllt fellows?'

'Not just Gwersyllt, Lady Ann,' he replies. 'We have gentlemen here from Hope. From Caergwrle too.'

'Live in Hope, die in Caergwrle. Is that not what they say?' Striker interrupts. 'Though in this case, Mister Shakerley, I fear that it would be the Dee Bridge on which they should perish. Now, if you will allow me, here are the orders from His Royal Highness.'

He reaches into the satchel, removing the parchment and passing the document to Sir Watkin, who examines the seal and, once satisfied that all is well, breaks the wax to unfold the contents. He reads it carefully, then aloud.

'To Sir Watkin Williams Wynn, etcetera, etcetera. Preston, this twenty-seventh day of November. Please be advised that our loyal Welsh forces should proceed to Farndon, crossing the Dee at that place, and thence to the district of Tarporley, where they should occupy the town and, it being possible, also the fortification of Beeston, thus interposing themselves between His Majesty's army and the Hanoverian battalions of West Cheshire. This position to be held until further instruction. In the name of His Royal Highness, etcetera. Well, it is clear enough!'

Such an elaborate plan! If I had but known that they were less than three hundred, it would have been easier to send them to their doom at Chester as that fool Shakerley desires.

'So the Prince intends us to protect his flank,' says Sir John.

'A noble role, I am sure,' says Lady Ann, 'yet hardly the glory that you sought, gentlemen. And do we have enough even for *this* modest task, husband?'

'Remember Herodotus, my dear,' replies Sir Watkin, 'and recall those three hundred Lacedemonians who defended Thermopylae against the might of barbarous Persia.' *Though were butchered for their pains!* 'And I doubt that Manchester will have raised so many. What say you, Lieutenant Owen? What of Manchester?'

'I cannot say, Sir Watkin. For, as you will collect, I left the Prince in Preston. Though some Manchester folk had come in by then, and others from Lancashire too. There was talk of a Regiment, and the possibility that a gentleman named Francis Townley might become its Colonel. I met his brother, Captain Townley, who was then in service with the French Ambassador.'

'Captain Townley. Yes, I met him last year. His brother Francis too, who was also with me in Manchester some months ago. A fine young blade. And the French Ambassador, you say? Why, His Royal Highness has made remarkable progress but how much more could have been achieved, if only we had the armies of France at our side. An unfortunate episode. Unfortunate, indeed! And how foolish now must seem the concerns of those Manchester merchants who spoke against French involvement.'

'And what value in the fellows now, eh?' says Sir John Glynne. 'With the tea trade collapsed? No revenue to be raised from it?

They proceed through a series of ailments. The Earl of Barrymore a disappointment to them. The Duke of Beaufort's death such a loss. David Morgan's failed mission to Connaught. Cumberland now Commander-in-Chief of the forces pitted against them.

And Sir Watkin weakens with every word, thinks Striker.

They are called to supper at last, Lady Ann escorting the harper who, Striker notices for the first time, has sightless eyes. She introduces him as John Parry and, after he has taken a little food, the strings sing to the company once again in the baronial dining chamber, with its high ceilings, its armour, its mounted heads of boar and stag.

Why, they live in some lost world of Owain Glyndwr and Llywelyn ap Grufydd!

Yet such fabulous riches. The caffoy upholstery, the matching drapes and hangings. The exquisite walnut furniture. The gold leaf worked into the wall covering. But Striker particularly admires the four large table candlesticks, made for them ten years ago, says Lady Ann, by the French silversmith, Pantin, bearing Sir Watkin's crest, each *repoussé* and chased with delicate scrolls, flowers and shells. But he must sing for his supper, it seems, requested to recount his various adventures since last he was in Wales.

There are questions and a renewed quickening of pulse as Sir Watkin's wine takes effect but, late into the evening, Sir John Glynne and George Shakerley decide that it is time for them to return to the Wrecsam encampment where Sir Watkin, Richard Williams and Lieutenant Owen will join them before dawn, it being generally agreed that Colonel O'Sullivan's orders should be followed as soon as possible, with any other Welshman able to follow them easily enough to Beeston Castle.

Yet it had not occurred to him that the good Rector would himself enlist in this Welsh Regiment.

All those weeks, he thinks, *during last Christmas-tide when I was broken from that encounter with Driscoll. Do I have a debt to Richard Williams for the ministrations that he showed me? And his silver too, which I claimed to have been stolen, what of that?* Striker has never considered himself in debt to any man. It is a dangerous weakness. And he knows that the Rector sees him as more than a simple friend. *My work seems much influenced by sodomites on one hand and tribades on the other.* But there had been moments before the hearth at the Hawarden manse, the readings from Richard's Bible, when Striker had experienced a sensation entirely unfamiliar to him. He could not name it, though he suspected that it might be that illusory thing called *peace*.

So, once they are lit to their respective apartments, the warming pans removed from the beds and finally left alone on the landing outside their rooms, Striker bids Richard Williams a good night.

'Yet, do you know, Richard, that you might be wise to abandon this expedition and return to Hawarden?' he says, quietly.

'My good fellow,' says the Rector, 'you surely cannot intend such a thing. What does it signify? When we are so close to victory, friend William.'

'Less close than I should care to allow, sir. But, if you will attend me, you would do better to repair forthwith to your manse and remain there these next few weeks.' The Rector peers through the tallow light with curiosity. 'And you should press me no further on the matter, sir. Heed my words and get thee gone in the morning.'

He closes the door and undresses. At least, partially so. For he has erred in his warning, stepped beyond a line that he has never before crossed. And if the Rector now denounces him...

Still, what is there to lose? If he alerts his Jacobite associates, what shall they gain? *They know nothing of O'Sullivan's actual order to meet at Macclesfield and there lies their only hope of salvation. For three hundred of them, left to their own devices here in the Marches, or wandering through Cheshire? No threat, I think. Though perhaps I should have been entirely honest with the Rector and confessed that, should he return to Hawarden as I have suggested, he is likely to find Cholmondeley's men there waiting for him.*

He sleeps with turn-off pistol beneath his pillow and paring knife within easy reach in his boot but is awakened by a manservant without having needed the assistance of either. Yet when he is shown to the kitchen, he finds Richard Williams there ahead of him, sat at a bench, unable to meet his eye, while Sir Watkin assumes a restored air of pomposity, three retainers at his back and one armed with a wicked fowling piece, and Lady Ann busy beneath the enormous kettle tripod, feeding papers into the fire.

'Reverend Williams,' says Sir Watkin, 'tells me that you have tried to persuade him against listing with the Regiment, sir. What do you mean by it? And told him that we are a great distance from victory. It is seditious, Lieutenant Owen. Seditious, I say.'

The fowling piece is no threat, Striker calculates, *though I might need to be closer if I would wish to ensure a clean kill. I could slice this Welsh peacock's windpipe at the same time. Though it would surely rouse the whole house. I do so wish that I had not allowed myself last night's indulgence.*

'Sedition, Sir Watkin?' says Striker. 'I protest that you cannot accuse *myself* of such a thing when you have conspired all these years to overthrow the anointed King of the same realm that you have sworn to protect as part of your Parliamentary Oath. How dare you, sir!'

'What, Mister Owen, you have turned your coat? You see, my dear, I told you, did I not, that the fellow could not be trusted when he first came upon the scene. And from Squire Redmond. Another of those Manchester coves!' But Lady Ann is too occupied with burning her husband's documents to show much interest. 'And secured a Commission in the forces of His Royal Highness. You should be ashamed, sir, and it will not answer!'

'I earned my Commission honestly enough, Sir Watkin, under arms for your *Chevalier* at Edinburgh. More service to the poor misguided fellow than you have given with your Jacobite dinners, I collect. Yet you should know, sir, that I hold a superior Commission in the service of King George which required me to make certain arrangements with General Cholmondeley and, in short, will mean that your park and houses shall be invested by his troops very shortly. You should not add harming myself to the crimes with which you shall undoubtedly be charged.'

'Charged, sir? I am the Member of Parliament for Denbighshire. A Baronet. You believe that anybody will pay any mind to these *charges* of which you speak? And then only in the unthinkable event that His Royal Highness should fail to restore the Stuart line. In such a circumstance, is there one single shred of evidence against me? Unthinkable, sir. You are quite ditched, I say.'

'You are sadly lacking in the relevant facts, Sir Watkin, I fear. For though he does not yet know it, the Pretender is surrounded on three sides by armies that are each larger than his single force. There is no choice left to him, now, except retreat on Scotland and there, you may be sure, he shall be destroyed.'

'And let us suppose that you are correct on that point, Lieutenant. You are also ill-informed, it seems. For I have already been questioned by my good friends, the Dukes of Bedford and Richmond. They found no fault and will vouch for me. You believe that the word of Newcastle's spy will count against such men of noble birth, and one of them the First Lord of the Admiralty?'

'My word, sir? No, I suppose not. But there *is* the evidence!'

Evidence, Lieutenant? *There* is your evidence.' And he gestures towards Lady Ann, now having almost completed the task of burning every scrap of paper that might condemn him. 'And are you, indeed, a Lieutenant, sir? Is your name even William Owen? That whole episode of the assault in Chester, a charade I assume?'

'Why, bless you, Sir Watkin. What sort of spy should I be that travelled under his own name.' Striker sees that Richard Williams has looked up at him for the first time. 'What, Richard. You feel betrayed? Then imagine my own disappointment that I tried last night merely to save you from the gallows. Yet this morning you could not wait to expose me. You are an ingrate, sir. And the gallows now await you both. Treacherous dogs that you are! The Dukes of Bedford and Richmond may have found no earlier fault with you, Sir Watkin, but they cannot ignore written corroboration of your misdeeds.' He reaches within his coat, prompting Sir Watkin's man to raise the fowling piece. 'You will allow me, sir?' Striker says to Sir Watkin, who waves the fellow to stand down. 'I think you may find, Lady Ann, that there is at least one document that you may not be able to destroy.' And he brings forth Sir Watkin's stolen ledger. 'The one that details every financial transaction conducted by him on behalf of the Stuarts, and your husband's signature on every page.'

The colour has drained from Sir Watkin's face, and Lady Ann has stood, her hand to her mouth. Striker holds the ledger just in front of him, raised slightly, an invitation that Sir Watkin cannot resist. He steps forward, his hand outstretched.

'A common criminal too, I see,' he says, though his voice is shaking. 'And those Manchester scoundrels some part of this too, I assume.'

He approaches, his hand outstretched towards the accompting book, which Striker snatches back, pulling the small pistol from his other pocket, levelling it to Sir Watkin's forehead.

'Now, sir,' says Striker, 'let me tell you how matters shall proceed from this point. First, there shall be nobody from this house riding to meet Sir John Glynne except myself. I suggest, Sir Watkin, that you return forthwith to London, to your house in Downing Street. It is possible, I suppose, that by doing so you may escape the executioner that you so greatly deserve. The Rector, here, is free to go wheresoever he may please, so long as he also gives wide berth to Sir John.'

'You are bold, sir,' says Lady Ann, 'whilst you may have a pistol to my husband's head. Yet how shall you impose your will once we are all parted?'

'Madam, it is no matter to me. Sir John Glynne's force is lost regardless. But I swear this to you, that if I find any from this house, or any dispatched on your behalf, within hailing distance of your Welsh Regiment I will come for you, Lady Ann, and I shall open your innards, feeding them to your own dogs while you yet live.'

She recoils from him, Striker knowing that she can picture her fate in the pale barrier of his eyes, and she collides with the tripod. Sir Watkin moves back to her side, holds her, while Richard Williams is on his feet at last, some inane protest on his lips.

'Enough, sir!' says Sir Watkin. 'It is intolerable to speak so. Yet I think we understand you. And you imply that there is a second matter?'

'Indeed, Sir Watkin. Those that know me better are familiar with my *penchant* towards tokens. To ensure a measure of good faith between us, do you understand? And I can think of several attractive possibilities. Yet time does not allow me any further pleasures, I fear. Though there *is* something. Those fine silver candlesticks that graced your dining table yesterday evening would make a suitable dowry, do you not think?'

'No more than a thief, sirrah. And those sticks are...'

'Priceless, Sir Watkin? Unique, of course. Sadly too florid for my taste, however. So I shall simply relieve you of one brace and you shall retain the other. Thus, whenever we regard them, we shall think of each other across the miles. And a thief, sir? As Francis Bacon might say, it is opportunity that makes me so.'

Striker takes the silver, wishing that his valise had been large enough for the remaining pair, and makes his cautious retreat from the Wynnstay Estate, checking regularly to ensure that he is not followed, then following the winding lane back to Wrecsam where, upon the open ground of Eagles Meadow, he finds Sir John Glynne's regiment already on the move.

'Good morning, Lieutenant,' cries Sir John, huddled in his redingote. 'A damn'd miserable day for it. This wind from the north shall bring rain shortly, I swear. But where is Sir Watkin?'

'He is somewhat delayed. A concern that he should not leave behind any papers that might cause difficulty to Lady Ann in his absence. A trifle late to be considering such things perhaps, but he promises to join us swiftly. It is a simple enough route when all is said and done. And we have many a-foot, I see. He should catch us easily.'

But he has not done so by the time they reach the hamlet of Holt to cross the fine sandstone bridge over the Dee into Farndon, with a cold sleet driving against them as they climb the hill through that town and on to the exposed ground beyond. Nor has Sir Watkin arrived when they make a stop at Broxton, five miles further on.

'Perhaps we should send a rider to check that the old fellow has not fallen into some difficulty,' says Sir John.

'It is possible that he might have crossed paths with one of Cholmondeley's patrols, I suppose,' says Striker, 'though we have seen no evidence of them and he would be unlikely to raise any suspicion. No, Sir John, I am sure that he will reach us in due course. He knows our destination and we should press on with all haste, I believe.'

So they do. Through undulating woodland, across Fuller's Moor, and then up through the lane that skirts the Peckforton Ridge, a difficult route for the several carts that accompany the regiment, though the volunteers who have filled them since leaving Wrecsam are now forced to climb down and help push the things through the steepest and muddiest sections of track. Finally down to Beeston village, with the castle and its rock before them.

The ground that rises westward from the settlement to the eminence is steep, though not sheer like the other three sides, and its lower slopes are coppiced before giving way to the enclosures and pasture lands surrounding the hill itself. Suitable ground is selected for the horses and Striker, like the other riders, dismounts at the crest to remove saddle, harness, blanket, feed bag, valise and portmanteau before leading the bay mare by her halter back to the lower levels. The castle that fills the summit must once have been imposing, though Cromwell's Parliamentarians had seemingly ordered much of its forward fortifications to be demolished after the place had been held against them for a year by a mere handful of their Royalist opponents.

Sir John Glynne, George Shakerley and the other gentlemen therefore agree that it is entirely appropriate for them to hold it now for King James, he being Charles the First's grandson, and preparations are begun for its defence, though the men under their command seem far from enthusiastic, grumbling about lack of food and evidently nervous at being across their own borders into England.

The Welsh seem also never to have learned the lesson, thinks Striker, *that an apparently impregnable and isolated hilltop must inevitably fall to a siege through want of supplies alone.*

There are fine views from the castle itself, however, out across Tarporley and the Cheshire plains, and Striker finds shelter within the walls, takes some cheese and bread as the cooking fires are lit, and ponders his next move. He feels satisfied that Sir Watkin will not put in an appearance and that this unexplained absence of the Welsh insurrection's principal figure will take its toll on the morale of others. Indeed, he has noticed Sir John, in particular, look ever more anxiously to the lane below for sign of his approach. But, no, Sir Watkin will not come. And Striker, at this point, could simply slip away in the night, for he should attempt to rejoin the Pretender's army either tomorrow or the day after, the second at the latest, assuming that the Jacobites can meet their own schedule to march south from Macclesfield on the third. And these Welshmen? *Why, if Cholmondeley takes my advice he will simply find them tomorrow, neatly packaged, as I promised. Or, if he does not, they will merely drift away in twos and threes as doubt and boredom overtake them. Though perhaps I could assist matters in either eventuality!*

Here, the fires are now blazing, most of them sheltered from the winds and outside observation, camp kettles or pots brought to the boil. Makeshift shelters are being erected, some of the tents that Sir John had seemingly managed to secure before their departure from Flint. The curious assortment of weaponry is stacked in three different locations and, again, protected from the elements. Beyond the walls, men scavenge for dried wood, chop timber, or struggle with feed for the horses, while the mounts themselves are taken in groups of three or four to drink at the brook before being tethered in the shelter of the trees, some to stakes and some to lines strung between the birches.

Belatedly, somebody recalls that this is the Feast of Saint Andrew, and spirits rise again as the Welsh Regiment recalls its greater purpose, agree that they should pay some tribute to their Scots allies. Amongst the stores there are some kegs of ale and a scouting party is dispatched to the thinly populated village which, at least, seems to boast a small tavern, though the Welshmen are unlikely to be greeted with any warmth.

But, as the celebratory atmosphere develops, Striker slips through the darkness, carefully carrying his own accoutrements, having to make three separate journeys down the hill and up again before he has everything assembled near the bay mare. Thankfully, there is little moonlight and he is challenged only once, though the fellow readily accepts that he is sent on a mission by Sir John Glynne. Yet Striker curses himself for a fool that he had not thought about the thing more carefully and saved all this effort, the weight of Sir Watkin's candlesticks playing on his back more than on his conscience.

He saddles and cinches again, adjusting the harness that he had only so

497

recently removed, and secures everything in its place except his blanket, that he drapes over the horse's back. Then he waits amongst the trees until the Welshmen are largely returned to the castle before starting along the tethering lines, freeing each mount in turn or, where he is able, using his paring knife to cut through the longer ropes slung between the birch trunks and to which larger groups are secured. A few begin to wander off but most remain in their places until, with ninety or more released, Striker throws the blanket across his shoulder and mounts.

Using the coarse homespun to flick here and there, he starts the herd moving slowly through the trees and out towards Beeston village until, minutes later than he had dared hope, he is finally observed by one of the few sentries. An alarm is shouted, a shot fired, then another. But even these serve Striker's purpose, agitating the now nervous beasts while he yells at them, urging them to a trot and then, the blanket flailing above his head, to a canter before, finally, they break to a stampeding gallop. Along the lane, past the houses, doors thrown open as they thunder past, the leading horses following the track as it swings east and then south. Striker stretched along the bay mare's neck and she belly-down. He pushes them for a mile through the night. Then another until, after five minutes, they begin to slow, spreading out onto open land, a common of some sort. And, though slowed, they do not stop. They would have run further during daylight, he thinks, but this will suffice. It will take the Welshmen several hours to catch them and all the while scattered to the winds.

Striker returns to the lane, another recently improved it seems, and must therefore be the turnpike from Chester to Stone, so he follows it away from Beeston and, he hopes, in the direction of Nantwich. After an hour, he finds himself, as he had hoped at one of the local Turnpike Trust's tollgates, the gatekeeper's cottage alongside. Burford, he is told when he rouses the old fellow from his bed and, yes, he can stay the night in exchange for a silver shilling.

The following day sees his journey continue to Nantwich, then north again towards Middlewich, where he turns east to Holmes Chapel. He has decided to avoid a significant encampment of Cholmondeley's redcoats there. And then the lanes up to Chelford, where he arrives as, once again, darkness is falling. There is light enough to see, however, that Chelford requires little description. A cluster of dwellings, an ancient chapel of crumbling wattle-and-daub, and an undistinguished manor house but, at the least, a splendid inn, belonging to the Egerton family apparently, though the place all aroused by news that the Jacobite army may be near.

Despite some initial suspicion, his horse is stabled, a room found for the night but, as he descends to take supper in the parlour, he is surprised to find David Morgan there, also seeking shelter for the night. And not alone, either. For he is travelling with William Vaughan and none other than

Lieutenant Owen's former messmate, Charlie Radcliffe, the Northumbrian.

Vaughan, Striker recalls, is cousin to Sir Watkin's wife, Lady Ann, and he had met the fellow during that dinner at Wrecsam in March. Radcliffe he had last seen in Preston.

'Lieutenant,' says Radcliffe, 'what fortune, sir! We were set upon findin' yersel' with the Welsh volunteers. And by God, here ye' be!'

'And Sir Watkin, Lieutenant Owen,' says Morgan, 'where might he be, sir?'

'He had some notion that they might seize Beeston Castle,' replies Striker. 'I remonstrated with him, naturally, for it was entirely contrary to his orders from Colonel O'Sullivan. But he would pay me no heed.'

'Do you say so, Lieutenant?'

This cove doubts my words, thinks Striker. *Now why should that be so?*

'I do indeed, Mister Morgan. And Mister Vaughan, I bid you good evening, sir. It is a pleasure to meet you again. Yet I considered it my duty to return to the army rather than tarry with your countrymen. However, should you wish me to direct you to Sir Watkin's position, it would be an easy matter to do so.'

'And can you tell me, Lieutenant, how Sir Watkin – Sir John too, I assume – came to choose Beeston as his destination? It must be at the very heart of the Jacobite deployments.'

'As Sir Watkin was keen to advise me so recently, Mister Morgan, he is the Member of Parliament for Denbighshire, a Baronet, a gentleman with friends of the highest stratum in our society. I cannot presume to know his intentions entirely though I believe that he had some fear of leaving General Cholmondeley's considerable force on the Prince's flank. Yet I feel, sir, as though I am subject to your attorney's skills. Almost as though I stand accused of some offence.'

'I am sure that Councillor Morgan had no such intention, Lieutenant,' says William Vaughan. 'For did you know that he is made *Royal* Councillor to His Highness the prince Regent?'

'Then give you joy, Councillor,' Striker replies, 'but my offer stands, sir. If you wish me to guide you to Sir Watkin, I shall be pleased to do so. But, for the nonce, I would take supper. And if you should care to join me, perhaps Mister Radcliffe can give me news of our company.'

But Morgan declines, and with such little grace that William Vaughan seems almost shamed, though he agrees to eat later with his companion. Charlie Radcliffe has no such difficulty, however, and is soon relating the day's events between mouthful's of the inn's best beef and attempting to keep their conversation private.

The Jacobite army had assembled in Market Street Lane at five o'clock in the morning and marched with the Prince at its head just after six, while some of the Horse had ridden west towards Stretford for a diversionary thrust to Altrincham. Sir John MacDonald's Company of Rangers had been posted near the forward position of the main body, crossed the Medlock and on through the prettiest place, Ardwick Green, to reach Slade Hall. There, the army had divided, the Prince and Highland Division making for Stockport, taking the most direct road for Macclesfield while Lord George Murray, with the Lowland Division and the Manchester Regiment had headed for the Mersey fords near Cheadle. Since Mister Morgan was intent on meeting Sir Watkin's force as soon as possible, it had been agreed that he, along with William Vaughan, should attach himself to this latter company, and Radcliffe ordered to accompany them for their security once the time had come for the Welshmen to leave Lord George and travel independently.

The Mersey's strong current, its chest-high waters, had given them difficulties yet nobody was lost. South to Wilmslow, then under the shadow of wild Alderley Edge to the crossroads at Monks Heath, the Lowland Division swinging left to Macclesfield, barely an hour previously, while Morgan, Vaughan and Radcliffe had proceeded west to this place.

'And Mister Morgan, Radcliffe,' says Striker, 'seems not altogether himself. Has he spoken to you of the matter that ails him?'

'I should not speak of it, Lieutenant,' Radcliffe replies, shifting nervously on the bench.

'Damn your eyes, Radcliffe! If you know something, spit it out, sir!'

'Yes, sir. Simply a conversation I overheard between the Welshmen, Lieutenant. Seems that Mister Morgan was approached by that Manchester fellow, Redmond. Some nonsense that he had seen you before, involved in some mischief, though I did not hear the detail. Aye, but insistent that ye'r not to be trusted.'

'Confound the man! Such foolishness. I should broach the matter with him, Radcliffe. Now finish your beef and I shall enquire whether Mister Morgan requires me to guide him further on his journey.'

And he returns to his room, considers his dilemma for a few moments before taking paper, quill and ink from his valise. The dispatch is quickly written and Striker returns to the ground floor, craving a word with the innkeeper.

'You are in the employ of the Egertons, are you not?' says Striker. And yes, sir, indeed he is. 'A family loyal to His Majesty, King George, I believe?' Of course, sir. 'Then as God is my witness, good fellow, you must send a boy without delay to the company of regulars now encamped at Holmes Chapel. Forthwith, do you hear? To carry this note. And not a word to any other living soul. Do you understand me?'

The innkeeper repeats the instructions, fetches a boy from the stables and whispers Striker's requirements to him. The boy is entrusted with the note and gifted with a sovereign for his trouble.

Once he is seen safely on his way, Striker invites David Morgan to join him, Vaughan and Radcliffe also, for a cup of the inn's finest wine. He is all charm now, William Owen at his companionable best, but he does not mention Titus Redmond and plans are soon set for them to ride together on the morrow, to meet Sir Watkin and persuade him that he should rejoin the prince's army immediately.

But, in the morning, as they ride from the inn's stables, they find themselves suddenly overpowered by an entire company of Hanoverian soldiers. It is quickly over, the Captain in charge of them astonished at his fortune in taking such eminent prize as the Pretender's *Royal Councillor* without a single drop of blood spilled.

Striker is equally astonished, delighted in fact, to find that the Captain in question is none other than his former acquaintance, James Wolfe, the very same that had allowed him use of his men for the raid on Redmond's bawdy-house.

And there, thinks Striker, having displayed his own Commission to this fellow-officer, *ends rebellion against the Crown, at least so far as the Welsh are concerned. Let us hope that it shall be their last!*

Chapter Forty-Seven

Show me his friends, James Bradley has always believed, *and I shall give you the character of the man.*

And, as he surveys those of his associates surrounding him in the sparse congregation at Saint Ann's on this cold and murky Sunday morning, he realises that he should have to give a scathing opinion of the fellow who had *these* for intimates.

Robert Jobb, stay maker and Groom's Man at his wedding, a man with a wonderful family, loyal to Bradley, but a lecher as Rosina has correctly described. John Clowes, breeches maker, morally no better than Jobb and lacking even his intellect. The Attorney, Matthew Liptrott, a lawyer who often cannot see the wood for its trees, obsessed with detail to the frequent exclusion of common sense. Thomas Fielden, the Borough Reeve for this year, though he is a ponderous, slow-witted fellow who had disappeared at the first approach of the Jacobites. Thomas Walley, clock maker, a stammerer but at least one who has showed mettle in his defiance of the *banditti*. And Elizabeth Cooper, of course, a woman who has faced adversity to establish her business yet that strangest of creatures, a tribade. *But I count them all as friends. So what does this say about me?*

Yet perhaps if he looks beyond this clutch of worshippers, at the two women who seem, oddly, to care for him, Maria-Louise and Rosina, he sees characters of strength, whose reflected light will bathe him in their qualities.

> *When I survey the wondrous cross*
> *On which the Prince of Glory died,*
> *My richest gain I count but loss,*
> *And pour contempt on all my pride.*
> *Ah yes, my pride!*

Though this is a peculiar hymn that Lewthwaite and Nichols have chosen for the service. *The Prince of Glory? The thing could be so easily misinterpreted.* Perhaps the new Rector shall be more careful in his selections. They say that he is a young fellow, recently graduated from Queen's College, Cambridge.

'That was a damn'd unfortunate song,' says Bradley to Elizabeth as they file from the church.

'It is Lewthwaite! He is seemingly a convert to the Jacobites, though I perceive that this arises from his new-found passion for the Pretender himself. He is quite enamoured of him. Described him as *beautiful*, it seems. And will dine with the Byrom girl tonight, he says, so that they can exchange infatuations.'

'Well, I suppose that we should at least be grateful for the service, since there are no others being celebrated today in this town that God, it seems, has so recently forsaken.'

At the coffee house, Crableck has lit the fires and prepared the day's first pots of coffee and chocolate.

'But perhaps you should prefer a dish of *Assam*,' says Elizabeth, 'now that the leaf is no longer procured illicitly? I recall that once you declared the source to have an impact on the brew's flavour.'

'The flavour of all things, Mistress Cooper, is improved today simply through our deliverance from those brigands. But yes, a dish of tea would be most welcome. And Lewthwaite? Does his adoration of the *Chevalier* explain his readiness to abandon you to their less than tender mercies?'

'I so hated their presence here. And not just those Scottish heathens but all the Tory and High Church demons from the town who would not otherwise set foot in my establishment. I felt defiled by them, James. Can you understand that? Yet, even in the midst of that defilement, there were words of cheer. From that bawd of Sergeant Dickson's admittedly, but I believe that she truly has the gift of sight, of premonition. And do you know the words she spoke to me, sir? She told me in all certainty that I shall soon wear bridal attire. Such news!'

'Then give you joy of this fortune, Mistress. Yet it seems to me – and I trust that you will not take my comment amiss, my dear – that there is some small flaw in your expectation, a flaw that arises from, well...'

'Yes, Mister Bradley, your point is well taken, yet there are passions within me that you cannot know.'

'I fear that I do not understand. But might I enquire whether this development may have some impact upon my wife? I intend, you understand, to know simply whether her recent display of concern for my welfare is a portent that the nature of our marital state may ameliorate?'

'And is that important to you, James, when you seem so obsessed once more with her Mama? No, prithee, do not trouble yourself to answer for it was purely a rhetorical matter. So far as your marriage is concerned, amelioration is not something that I could guarantee but it shall certainly change. Now, I shall fetch the *Assam* and perhaps even join you in a dish.'

'Tea, James?' says Robert Jobb as Elizabeth goes to prepare the pot. 'Do you not fear that the leaf itself is responsible for our troubles? It should be banned from English society, sir, or mark my words, it shall lay us low!'

'Tea is a beverage, my friend, no better or worse than any other. Coffee or chocolate, or anything. Tea leaves are as good or bad as the man who buys or taxes them. Remember that! Yet you are closer to the truth than you may know. For without the funds secured by Titus Redmond and others like him through their enterprise it is unlikely that this rebellion would even have begun. And there are others to thank, you must believe, for it not being better financed and, therefore, better supported.'

'Is it not bad enough that they took Manchester with such ease? And where was *our* support, sir? We raised our own Subscription, did we not? Yet neither the Earl of Derby nor any of His Majesty's forces were in evidence at our hour of need. Why, even the Invalids, useless though the poor fellows might have been, remained bottled at Shude Hill.'

The Constable, Thomas Walley, joins them, blowing gently upon a bowl of steaming chocolate.

'The Invalids, Mister Jobb?' he says. 'Why, I t-t-told those gentlemen myself that they should stay in their quarters. Those with the least injuries and still possessing any form of weapons were taken by B-b-blakeney's and Gower's when they came through in October. There were only the entirely crippled and the ancient left behind.'

Bradley knows this, naturally, for the cost of maintaining those veterans from the area lamed, maimed, or infirmed from His Majesty's wars falls to the Court Leet. In Manchester, they have chosen not to provide a formal uniform as other towns have done, but the price of food, stockings, shirts, neckcloths, nightcaps remains a burden on the public purse, and the most able amongst them formerly at least been put to work on occasions for the benefit of the citizens by way of repayment.

'That was the correct thing, too, Thomas,' says Bradley. 'And, incidentally, when the Jurors are next in session I intend to bring your creditable action to their attention, sir. Your defiance of those *banditti*. Your refusal to read their damn'd proclamation. You have bottom, Constable. True bottom!'

Walley waves aside the honour, takes his chocolate to join some of the other customers, as Elizabeth returns with the tea.

'Mister Walley is enjoying his moment, I see. And shall you take a dish of *Assam* also, sir?' she says to Robert Jobb. But he declines, always uncomfortable in Mistress Cooper's company, making some excuse to join Walley and the others. 'And what now, James? Have we seen the last of the Pretender, do you think? They were so numerous. So confident.'

'And confidence is sometimes sufficient, of course, my dear. Audacity is an undervalued asset, and that young fellow has the animal in trumps. He could easily ride it all the way to London, I fear. But if we have not seen the last of him, *those* folk are set for a surprise, I collect!'

For, through the window, there is considerable traffic on Market Street Lane, with many of those who had fled the town already returning even though the dung from the Jacobite Horse still steams upon the street.

'They fear to leave their property vacant for longer than necessary. Fear what they might find when they return too. Yet Rosina rode out at the Pretender's side, I hear?'

'She took the carriage at first light to follow in their wake so far as Stockport, I think. And many others too. Why, it looked more like a *carnevale* parade than an army on the march. But we have sent word of their movements at least. There were sufficient riders willing to carry our express to Chester and elsewhere. It is all that we could do in the circumstance. But I hope never to live through another few days like the last, my dear. That dungeon! It is quite ghastly. And on the few occasions that I could sleep for the cold and damp, it was only to be woken by the nightmare of poor Sourwood's spectre driving a stake through my own heart.'

He returns to the house on Hanging Ditch to find Titus Redmond there before him.

'Why, Father-in-Law!' he says. 'A truly unexpected pleasure.'

'And how are you, Mister Bradley? Recovered from your ordeal, I trust. I should not have seen you treated thus, sir, and wish with all my heart that it might have been prevented. I came across that scoundrel Dickson in Preston. A raucous cunny-sucker, full of his own importance. And then the audacity to claim reward for those who volunteered in Manchester when others had already undertaken the work.'

'It sounds, Titus, as though you are giving credit to Francis Townley for the deed. I had never, in life, expected to hear you praise the fellow for anything. You have accepted his command of this Manchester Regiment with good grace, I see. But, yes, I am recovered. I thank you for the concern.'

'Accepted? No, not that, sir. I have never truly believed in simply accepting *anything* that I found before me. It is not necessary to accept the world as we find it. We must merely understand the world that we may seek to change it. I have my own affairs to reconcile with Colonel Townley at the proper time. And I am pleased that the House of Correction has not left its mark upon you. Yet the Court Leet has confined souls a-plenty there in the past, and many with no greater crime upon their shoulders than your own, I protest.'

It is unfortunate that the fellow should have been shown to the library, thinks Bradley, as Titus surveys the shelves, *given the pleasures that I enjoy so often from his wife on that very desk and sofa.* Some whimsy on the part of his manservant, perhaps? He shall have words with him later. But he starts as Titus, almost perceiving his thought, turns to the desk-top, runs his fingers along its olive green leather, lifts them to his nose. *Oh God. Does he sense her presence?*

'I can assure you that we shall be more discerning in the future, sir,' he says. 'Yet I was recently asked whether we have seen the last of your Prince

Regent, Titus. What think you?'

'Unless those lick-spittle cravens now returning to the town in such numbers know something that we do not, I must assume that we shall see considerably more of the royal gentleman, Mister Bradley. I have every confidence that he shall be crowned King in due course and we shall all see the head of Charles the Third on every coin of the realm. And Our Lady bless him, sir!'

Titus touches the desk's mahogany for luck as he speaks.

'And then the new order?' says Bradley. 'You must be well placed within its ranks, I think, having so recently provided dwelling and sustenance to the Prince. Why, I shall deem it an honour to have you listed as the first Catholic Juror of this town, sir.' Redmond's thumb strays to the moustache.

'I shall be pleased to concentrate on the fustian trade once more. Though perhaps I might dispose of the business entirely. Perhaps Mister Rivers or Mistress Cooper may care to diversify still further. Or you, James. What say you? I envisage for myself a more peaceful life when these greater schemes are all resolved. I intend to ask my wife whether we might travel abroad. Once these interminable continental wars are ended, naturally. Though it is inconceivable that they should continue with the Stuarts restored.'

And Bradley feels something cold close upon his heart.

'Truly, sir?' he says. 'I still maintain designs upon becoming recognised as a more prominent builder, since there remains room for some little expansion here in Manchester I believe. Though I should not be averse to considering your own trade in addition. A family business, when all is considered. I believe that your daughter might be taken with the idea. I think that she rather envies Mistress Cooper in that regard. The Age of Women is almost upon us, I fear. We shall not be masters of our own destiny much longer, do you not say so? Yet if you travel abroad, what shall become of those *other* interests from which you profit?'

What indeed? He would give up his bawds and a thriving trade in geneva to take Maria-Louise touring Vienna? Paris? Rome? She would not abandon me, surely?

'Well, there are details to be considered, that it so. But it was about my wife that I wished to speak, sir.' *Dear God, does he care after all about our trysting?* 'It is a sensitive matter, yet I am not one of those cunny-suckers who will use a score of words when six will suffice. If I may be blunt, therefore, it seems to me that yourself and Maria-Louise have, at times, shared intimacies.'

'Well...'

'And I must confess that, in times past, I had rather encouraged the thing. We are men of the world are we not?'

'Mister Redmond, sir, I...'

'And I know that there is no more substance to the thing than my own predilection for the whores at Mother Blossom's. My dear wife can be a bitch on heat too, when she chooses. I have told her so. Frequently.'

'Sir...'

'But there is this, Bradley. When you have been in my wife's company, has she ever mentioned a fellow called William Owen?'

'William Owen? Why...'

What, by God's Hooks, is the fellow talking about? William Owen? No, not that name. But the other...

'I see by your expression that it means nothing to you. I had thought... Well, never mind. Yet perhaps I might also speak with my daughter. For there was this other cove that *she* mentioned. Bradstreet, I think. It is a long shot but Rosina might recall his features.'

'I fear that I am somewhat lost, sir. But Rosina is not at home anyway. She has joined those well-wishers who intend to escort your *Chevalier* to the Cheshire border. But she will return shortly I think...'

A knock on the library door, and Bradley's manservant enters.

'Begging your pardon, sir,' he says, 'but there is a gentleman at the front. He says that he is your father.'

'My father? Well bid him enter, man.'

'Perhaps I should leave you,' says Titus. 'A private matter, no doubt, and I may return later once Rosina is at home.'

Rosina? Yes, of course. But why would Pa be here. Come too late to join the other Jacobites, perhaps. What joy!

'No, sir. I should be obliged if you would stay. My father has spoken of your family many times but never had the pleasure of meeting you. I am sure that he would wish to shake your hand, Titus.'

The old fellow enters, so frail now that Bradley is surprised he could even have survived the journey from Droylsden.

'Pa! What in the name of Heaven are you doing here. Is it Ma?' He can think of no other reason that would have occasioned such a trial for his father. 'But allow me to name Mister Titus Redmond. Rosina's father.'

'Redmond?' says the old man, his voice cracked and shattered. 'I knew your father, sir. Good man. Broken by the trial. Same age. And your daughter, Mister Redmond. A beauty. She has fire too. Though why you should have allowed her to marry Jim I shall never understand. Did you know that he is a Whig? Yet it is Rosina I have come to see. For she loved his Ma, I think.'

'What has happened, Pa?'

'Much you would care! But your Ma is passed. I came on a cart to tell Rosie myself, poor girl. And in hopes that I might catch a glimpse of the Prince. But I am come too late for both. And my bones all ache like they have been thrashed with cudgels. I threatened often enough to sell the old girl at market. And they say that we do not truly cherish anything but that which is gone. It is well said, Mister Redmond. Well said indeed.'

'My condolences, sir. And to you, Mister Bradley. You must feel your mother's loss keenly, I collect.' *No, barely at all.* 'If there is anything that I can do to assist. Any succour that we might provide?'

'A warm bed for the night, Mister Redmond,' says Pa Bradley, 'for I would not impose on this Absalom.' Titus looks to James Bradley for an indication. *It would do me a favour, for I could not tolerate too much of the old man's complaints.*

'Of course, sir,' says Redmond. 'And you shall at least have the pleasure of sleeping in the same bed so recently vacated by His Royal Highness. What say you?'

'You are kind, sir. Tomorrow I return to Droylsden to bury my wife. I do not imagine that James will attend. But I know that Rosie would wish to be there. And I bring a message too,' he turns towards his son. 'Your mother's last words. For she says that she will see you sooner than you might think.'

'Ma was a great one for premonition too. Though I have never known one come to fruition. And we shall *all* leave this life earlier than we might expect, Pa.'

Bradley feels a moment of guilt once his father is finally gone with Titus and he will, of course, attend tomorrow's burial, though he has not told the old fellow as much. But he shares the news with Rosina when she arrives home, two hours later.

'And you did not persuade him to stay under your own roof?' she says, incredulous, and badly shaken by word of Ma Bradley's death. 'Did you ask the cause?'

'Cause, my dear? Why, she was aged beyond days. What, do you fear that Pa may have murdered her? It is possible, I suppose. I never thought to question him.'

He is simply pleased that one more link to that insipid upbringing in Droylsden is now severed. *And Pa cannot survive her for long, to be sure!*

'I did not intend to amuse you, sir. Why, I wish now that I had left you in the House of Correction. You deserve no less! And the funeral. Did you ask your father whether he might need any assistance?'

'You must dry those tears, Rosina. And the burial, I am sure, must already be organised, else Pa would have said so! Why, my dear, you barely knew my mother. Oh, I apologise. That was harshly spoken in a manner that I did not intend.'

'I am inordinately fond of your Ma and she did not deserve your neglect. An annual visit, sirrah! Your pension to them may have been fine enough in its way but no substitute for filial obedience and affection. Well, she has gone to a better place I suppose.'

'Upon my word, wife, such hypocrisy! You have exchanged barely a word with your Mama for almost a twelve-month. And a better place? It has always surprised me that, giving praise as we do for the wonders of the Lord's Creation, we cannot wait to forsake them for something finer. Yet shall you not tell me your own news? The Pretender is safely gone from our County, I trust?'

'I think you are hardly well-placed to accuse *me* of hypocrisy where my mother is concerned. And where was *she* today when our brave fellows were marching to glory? Myself and Beppy followed them all the way to Cheadle Ford. And such a sight! The Prince himself waist-deep in the Mersey's freezing water and, on the further bank, many gentlemen of Cheshire there to welcome him.'

'And did they join his ranks, or merely cheer him on his way?'

'I think that it is barely pertinent, sir. For he has a force strong enough to drive all before him. And there was an astonishing moment. An old lady, ancient beyond imagining, Mistress Skyring, they said, whose own father had fought for our Royalist Cause during the Great Rebellion itself. Her eyes were grown so dim that she could barely see the sweet Prince yet fell on her knees and laid before his feet a purse containing all the savings of her long life and each of her precious jewels, saying that she could now depart in peace and would be in Heaven within the week.'

'My goodness. Such attachment to a conviction that was spent even a century ago. Such wickedness in those who would sow bitterness for its passing, generation after generation. And such a week for portent too! For presage. For presentiment. Why, first, Mistress Cooper tells me that the Recruiting Sergeant's bawd has predicted her imminent acquisition of bridal attire. Then my father brings news that Ma expects me to join her very soon. And now this of Mistress Skyring. Fie! The Pretender has not even succeeded to the throne and we are already beset by the superstitious idolatry of Papism.'

'How dare you insult and demean my Faith, Mister Bradley. I had considered you to have assumed a better degree of tolerance but your renewed association with my mother, I must assume, has dulled this quality once more.'

'It is more likely that it was my treatment at the hands of your Jacobite *banditti* that has caused any sharpness in my demeanour. It has nothing to do with your Mama.'

'Does it not, sir? And where is my lincture? I left the bottle upon the dresser. There! Now it is gone. And *banditti*, you say? Yet it seems that your Hanoverian heroes refused to engage them on Sale Moor this morning. They fled like fools at our troopers' approach. Fled, sir, as your Hanoverian rabble will continue to run until our forces reach London and drive all before them.'

'I expect that your damn'd Sydenhams has been cleared away by the servants. And good riddance to the evil brew. It so badly affects your humour, my dear. Feeds your delusions too, I collect. For the Pretender shall never secure the throne of this nation, madam. Do you seriously suggest that he can hold a kingdom with a few thousand men? It is *he*, Rosina, that acts the fool.'

'My Sydenham's gone, sir? And if it affects my humour, you must blame my mother for this also, since it was *she* that first introduced me to its delights.

509

Did you not know? You seem woefully lacking in all manner of knowledge, I perceive. For there will be more than a few thousand at the Prince Regent's side when he enters London. More honest Englishmen I am sure, but an army of brave French soldiers beneath his standards too.'

'You told me previously that it was Mistress Cooper who first tempted you to the opiate, I collect. But the French, my dear? Oh, how amusing. How utterly jocose. I fear that I shall suffer an apoplexy if I laugh any more. I shall burst my sides, sweet wife. How deliciously droll. For the French shall not cross the Channel unless there is silver and gold to pay them. And your Stuart coffers are too empty to accommodate any such iniquity.'

'The fool is *you*, James Bradley! The Stuarts have a great Exchequer, protected for them all these years in Rome by His Holiness. Enough gold and silver to purchase a dozen French armies.'

'Oh, hoity! Toity! You truly do not know, dearest? Even your father has kept the thing from you? Extraordinary! And your mother, Rosina, may have applied herself to the laudanum at times but, if so, I am certain it has been for good intent. For dispelling the megrims, perhaps. For dealing with a woman's monthly curse. But generally for good purpose. In the same way that she has put the greater good of this country before her own narrow beliefs. For the Jacobite Exchequer is lost, wife. Gone beyond the reach of the Pretender and his son. And it was your Mama who inflicted the loss upon them! Your *Mama!*'

Chapter Forty-Eight

'Please, eat some more of the stew. It shall fortify thee on thy journey,' says Mister Toft, his sleeves rolled and an enormous apron covering his waistcoat.

The Quaker's boiled beef and potato has, in fact, fortified Striker, indeed, the entire Jacobite army, since their arrival in Leek eight or nine hours ago. And now, in these first minutes after midnight on the fourth day of December, it must strengthen them once more for the road ahead. The Meeting House on Hareygate is packed to overflowing, mainly with Highlanders at this time, for the regiments have been fed in rotation by Toft's assistants and glad to escape the bitter cold outside for a while.

'We have consumed prodigious quantities of your provender already, sir,' says Striker. 'I wonder that you can spare such amounts. Do you not fear starvation as the winter deepens?'

'The Lord shall provide, Lieutenant. And He has bestowed his bounty upon us for the reason that we may share it amongst our fellows. Though I might wish that the fellows in question should leave the sharpening of their swords until they are finished eating.'

'It must be a sore trial of your Faith, Mister Toft, that you should be required to feed such warriors at all. An offence to your pacific testimonies, sir. Yet to have them prepare their weapons in your temple!'

'Why, Lieutenant, it is their digestive juices that concern me. For they will not flow so readily, I understand, if they pay such little heed to the proper consumption of their food. Our Society is without temples, and this House is simply the place where we gather, sharing a commitment to peace along with our other beliefs. We attempt, here, to understand the nature of how we should live together in this confused world. We try to find ways of resolving conflict, rather than promoting it. Yet, sometimes, we can do no more than bear simple witness to a better road. And there is no process more simple than the giving of food and warmth to those who need it, no matter their purpose. Nor should thee believe that all those within the Society have always been entirely pursuant of peace. It is certainly true that any rare breach of this tenet would be a disciplinary matter. Still, in the end, such issues are for the conscience of individuals.'

'And it does not trouble your own conscience in providing succour to those who many would see as traitors?'

'The Society sees only the cold and the hungry, Lieutenant. For my part, I see those who follow the heirs of King James, the same that assisted Friend William Penn to escape persecution here and to establish our Quaker Colony in the New World.'

'Yes,' says Striker, 'I recall the thing.'

'And the recollection causes thee distress, I see.'

Distress? No, but I recall those Quakers who had spilled down from Penn's personal utopia, his 'Sylvania', across the poorly defined boundary with Virginia. I recall the affection that they showed in the Valley towards the Lenape. I recall the horrors inflicted on some of them by the Catawba for their pains.

'Indeed not, Mister Toft. Whatever may have caused you to think such a thing? Never in life, sir. A mere lack of sleep, you will understand.'

'Thou art always welcome here, Friend, if they fail to hang thee. It is not easy to live our lives by truth and integrity, by justice and community, by simplicity and equanimity. Yet it is our task to keep trying.'

'Then I give you joy of your attempt, sir, and wish you success. For I fear that we shall find few of those qualities on the road that *we* must now tread, though I shall endeavour to avoid the executioner if I am able.'

He touches the old fellow's arm in farewell.

Such radical ideals, Striker thinks. *The Diggers and Ranters before them too.* Yet these Quakers, he knows, differ from their forebears by the devotion with which they listen for God's voice in the world around them rather than their own. *And another reason for me to take Newcastle's mission in the Americas. Perhaps I could help them finally resolve that dispute between the borders of Virginia, Maryland and Pennsylvania. What a good thing that should be!*

But here is a messenger, sent to summon him, bring him to that Greystones House in Stockwell Street where the Prince has his lodgings and where, in a downstairs room, some of the Council are meeting.

'Lieutenant!' cries O'Sullivan. 'Pray tell the gentlemen, in your own words, that which you reported to me about the Welshmen.' So, for the sake of these Clan Chieftains and Lowland Lords, he repeats the tale that he had spun for the Irishman when he had arrived in Macclesfield, following his departure from Captain Wolfe, on the second. The delays occasioned by Sir Watkin Williams Wynn's insistence on taking Beeston Castle. His own remorse at not being able to shift him from this purpose. His decision to return alone to seek some instruction which, perhaps, he might convey back to Sir Watkin and to Sir John Glynne also. The disappointing numbers of the Welshmen in any case. Chance encounter with the Prince's Councillor, David Morgan, and his two companions. Their unfortunate interception by a Hanoverian patrol, an incident similar to the earlier scuffle in Coldstream, the Colonel may recall. And, yes, William Owen again the only one to escape. The Lord has protected him once more. 'So

512

you see, gentlemen,' O'Sullivan continues, 'there is little chance that the Welsh shall join us and, therefore, no point in delaying further. It is possible, I suppose, that Lord George's diversionary manoeuvre towards Congleton and the west may have come up with them but, if so, he will bring them in when he returns. And you, Lieutenant, have you heard the news of Cumberland?'

'Indeed I have, sir. I received the briefing earlier when our scouts returned.'

For the Duke of Cumberland, deceived in part by Lord George Murray's feint towards the Welsh border, has marched his army north from Stafford, taken up a position on the bleak ground of Stonefield, and is now fixed there, fifteen miles to the west.

'So there we have it, gentlemen,' says O'Sullivan. 'The road to Derby stands open before us and, God willing, the road to London also. We can step straight past Cumberland and be at Westminster within a week.' There are the usual protestations that they would be better to destroy Cumberland now, a march overnight, catch him in the early light as they had done with Johnny Cope. But they still lack Lord George Murray's considerable force, and there is no real enthusiasm for the plan. So the Colonel gives final instructions for the commanders to get their regiments upon the frozen road to Ashbourne, and to Derby beyond, while an equerry is sent to waken the Prince from his few hours of sleep.

'Is there anything further, sir?' asks Striker.

'Perhaps you should report to your senior officer, Lieutenant. I am sure that he will have work for you. But before you go I should have a word with you. I am not sure whether there is any relevance but, in Preston, I had that Manchester fellow, Redmond, making enquiries about you. He implied that you could not be trusted but he seemed unable to explain his allegation. I know that he spoke with Mister Morgan also, and now that gentleman has been taken. Is there something that I should know, Lieutenant Owen?'

'I do not believe that I have ever had the pleasure of Mister Redmond's acquaintance, Colonel. Though I was briefly familiar with his brother, I believe. Thus I cannot imagine why he should find cause to speak of me in that way. You say *implied*, sir, but can you not tell me his exact words? And I would have saved the Prince's Councillor from capture if the deed had been possible. Yet they were taken and trussed before I happened upon the scene. Any intervention...'

'Please, Lieutenant. I know your mettle perfectly well, sir. I share none of Mister Redmond's doubts. Perhaps we may clarify the matter at some later date though, for the present, it seemed improper that I should mention the thing. For now, our destiny awaits, sir!'

So they march to meet it, leaving Leek at a little after two in the morning.

Bitterly cold, a clear halo sharp about the moon, as they progress through Swinscoe, then down the valley of the Dove to the monumental Parish Church

513

of Saint Oswald in Ashbourne, as day breaks, with Lord George Murray's diversionary force waiting for them. But there is no time to mark the reunion for they are hurried through the town.

The long main street of Brailsford, white sheets hung from windows to welcome the Jacobites. Then on to Mackworth and Kirk Langley, breads, cheeses and meats pressed into their hands and some men come to meet them, to guide them on their way, the regiments strung out along the route so that, by two of the afternoon clock, Striker and the Company of Rangers are able to enter Derby's Market Place ahead of the reformed Highland Division, their pipers, their banners.

At the George Inn, on Irongate, lists of billets are posted. Camp kettles steam. Every available shelter, it seems, is occupied by sleeping men, swaddled in blankets or plaids. But it takes little time, Striker has realised, for the spirits of these fellows to revive and, as darkness falls, bonfires are lit about the town, the bells of every church peeling and tolling. They celebrate the arrival of Charles Edward, on foot as usual, coming from the western suburbs and Markeaton Brook, along Sadler Gate to reach his lodgings in Exeter House on Full Street, at the back of All Saints and near the great water wheel of the Silk Mill.

And the evening, this historic evening when the Scots realise how close they have come to the English capital, turns into a triumphant revelry. There are musicians everywhere, it seems. Fiddlers naturally. Harpers, players of the *cláirseach*. Pipers. Drummers of the *bodhrán*. And a singer, a copper-haired woman with a voice that haunts, a voice that calls forth everything that any of her audience has ever lost, will ever lose in the future.

Alasdair à Gleanna Garadh,
Thug thu 'n-diugh gal air mo shùilibh...

A lament, it seems, for Black Alasdair, Alasdair *Dubh*, the MacDonald of Glengarry, hero of Sheriffmuir.

And how these Scots love to rejoice with the saddest of requiems!

But, regardless, this woman leaves barely a dry eye amongst the Jacobites, whether or not they can understand the Gaelic. Even the Manchester Regiment, many of them grouped here around their Colonel.

'Quite a performance, sir,' Striker says to Townley.

'Indeed! Yet you have the advantage of me.'

'Lieutenant Owen, Colonel. Sir John MacDonald's Company of Rangers.'

'And a Welshman, Lieutenant? Am I correct, sir?'

'Indeed, Colonel. Formerly Secretary to the Rector of Hawarden and then assistant to Sir Watkin Williams Wynn before gaining my present Commission.'

'And where *is* Sir Watkin then? Do we know? He was supposed to join us at Macclesfield, I think.'

'I was with him some days ago, sir, though he insisted on a detour from his route so that they might place a garrison within the castle at Beeston. He acted upon sound military principles, I believe, but I am surprised that his column has not yet reached us.'

'And that lawyer of his, David Morgan, taken too, I gather. You were there, Lieutenant?' Striker describes the fictitious incident. 'Then it seems that you succeeded, Lieutenant, in losing the Prince's Councillor, the Members of Parliament for Flintshire and Denbighshire respectively, and the entire Welsh Regiment all in one day. How astonishingly reckless, sir!'

Oh, it was nothing except my duty, Colonel Townley. But Striker offers some grovelling protest. Lieutenant Owen, it seems, had done his best to persuade the gentlemen and, at Chelford, he had been fortunate to escape with his life.

'Yet give you joy of your command, sir. I never had the privilege of accompanying Sir Watkin to Manchester. My heart aches that we have not secured such volunteers from others of the English towns. What think you, Colonel? Now that we have Derby perhaps?'

Striker looks around at the fellows in Townley's immediate company, his officers mainly, and all taken to wearing some tartan in their dress. A waistcoat here. Trews there. Some of them familiar for, God knows, he had spent enough time learning the identities of these traitors. Thomas Sydall, of course, one of Manchester's barbers and his father hung, along with Jacob Driscoll's Pa, at the end of the rebellion in '15. Thomas Chaddock who, that evening in the Bull's Head, had bored him incessantly with tales of Francis Townley's military career in French service, his expertise at *canne de combat*. Others whose faces he knows. John Holker. Thomas and Robert Deacon now accompanied by two fellows who seem barely older than children, and each of these boys responsible for a white standard bearing the red cross of Saint George. How different they all seem. Townley too. He still has the swagger of the singlestick fighter, the elegant dash of his attire, the less than elegant spittle from his ill-fitting teeth. But here, so very far from their ranting bravado in Manchester, it is hard to imagine this Francis Townley leading his *Mohocks* off to attack the Dissenters' Meeting House.

'Now that we have Derby?' Townley repeats. 'Why, Lieutenant, you should have been with the diversionary column! No matter where we went the redcoats were driven before us. Lord George was reluctant to engage but we just ploughed into them, eh lads? Then, when we reached Ashbourne, we found the local militia waiting for us but we chased them off towards Nottingham. No doubt at all about which of us was the stronger, but everywhere it was the same story. Not a volunteer to be found. Pigs and cattle all hidden from us too. We took a spy though and, God willing, His Royal Highness will

515

order him gutted on the morrow.' *Well, perhaps not so changed after all!* 'No, Lieutenant. We will either take London alone or wait until the French arrive. Though they would be better placed on the south coast than arriving always in Scotland.'

'There is news of the French, sir?'

The French and their gold too, it seems. Large quantities landed at Peterhead. *Yet the fellow knows very well that the Stuarts' Exchequer is lost! Whatever French gold is arriving must be a pittance.* Troops at Montrose. Detachments from the Royal Écossais Regiment, that formation raised in Scotland but trained in France under the direct approval of King Louis to support a Jacobite rising. Companies of the French Irish Regiments too. Bulkeley, Berwick, Clare, Dillon, Lally and Ross, all formed into a new unit, the Irish Picquets. Lieutenant Owen's Company of Rangers to be merged with this formation too, apparently, in due course. Such an honour. To stand beside those same men who had driven the Hanoverians from the field of Fontenoy!

'A thousand men, Lieutenant. And more arriving all the time. By Our Lady, these English generals do not know their peril. But tell me, sir. Your name is Owen, and you are Welsh. There is a fellow in Manchester. *Aran* Owen, by name. Could you be related perhaps?'

'Do you know, Colonel, that you are not the first to suppose so? Amongst others, the coincidence was first brought to my attention by the Squire of Llanffynon. He is Josiah Redmond and, being yourself from Manchester, you must know his brother. A fustian merchant, I believe, who has in his employment a cove who shares my name, it seems. And I apologise should I offend you, sir, but I hear little of value about the man.'

'You say so, Lieutenant? Then you share my opinion. Why, sirrah, this Redmond of whom you speak, the merchant, involved him in some foolish attempt to steal the town's Excise duties last year, and young Owen ended in Lancaster prison. He came back missing a finger. Almost as careless as yourself, Lieutenant. You are *sure* that he is not related, sir? What jests, eh! And then... By the Mass, I can hardly tell the thing. He pitched his cap at Redmond's daughter. Only to find that the girl is a tribade. And her lover, yet another sapphist, now taken control of the tea trade that Titus Redmond had used to finance this very Regiment.' *Now there is a snippet that I had not gleaned from any other source. How amusing! Mistress Cooper, I assume.* 'Yet this Aran Owen has been promoted by Redmond beyond his station, I say, and now will not even list with us. The fellow is a coward, Lieutenant. Professes himself a Jacobite, yet...'

Oh, Colonel Townley, you can barely begin to know!

He changes the subject, admitting that whilst he may not know Aran Owen, he does have the pleasure of acquaintance with the Colonel's brother, *Captain* Townley. Had met him on the journey south to Preston. A polite enquiry about his health. And an equally polite reply. The Captain, supposes his brother, should by now be aboard those same vessels recently arrived at Peterhead and waiting to make the return voyage to France with the Ambassador for company.

But Striker is not left for long to enjoy the festivities, nor Francis Townley's conversations either. For the men of the Ranger Company are required to scout the lands for sign of Hanoverians and, by midnight, he is taking the road south from Derby to Swarkestone. It is easy enough to find, for another beacon is lit here, five miles from Derby itself, where a garrison of seventy or eighty Highlanders has been posted to guard the only bridge across the wide and dark River Trent anywhere between Burton and Nottingham. He is challenged several times and forced to produce his documents but, once across, he takes the quiet lanes to his left, in the direction of Loughborough.

Another clear but icy night and Striker expects, at the summit of each rise, that he will see evidence of loyalist campfires somewhere in the distance. But there is nothing, an uneventful eight miles to the outskirts of Loughborough town. All quiet. The place sleeping peacefully except for the Watchman calling the hour of three. Westwards, then, on his triangular patrol, to Ashby-de-la-Zouch. Ten more miles and nothing to report. An abandoned barn though, just before he reaches the village, and a few hours sleep wrapped in his blanket. Or at least the attempt to sleep, the edges haunted by Daniel Sourwood's plaintive face, holding aloft the severed head of Charles Edward Stuart and demanding payment of the thirty thousand pounds reward placed upon that object by Parliament. But Striker does not have such an amount. Simply two silver candlesticks that Sourwood seems reluctant to accept. So enquiries at the Bull's Head in Manchester. Will anybody buy some of his fine pastries for he needs to raise funds? Yes, says a man named Collow, though quickly pushed aside by the barber-cum-chirurgeon, Joshua Whitlock, who will wrestle him for a prize of five guineas. Yet it is not Whitlock with whom he wrestles but Rosina Redmond, naked as the day she was born. And, while he does so, the Duke of Newcastle is ripping up his precious Commission. *That fellow?* says the Duke. *No, I have never seen him in my life.*

He must have slept, of course, but as light begins to fill the barn, he searches in his valise for the *Britannia Depicta*, checks the county map and finds the prominent tower of Ashby's ruined castle marked, as he had recalled. He finds it easily enough and climbs the ninety feet of frosted masonry to its top, looking out across the rolling countryside of Leicestershire expecting that, somewhere, anywhere, there should be evidence of the Hanoverian army. But there is nothing. Merely the sediment of his dreams, that image of reward for the Young Pretender's capture.

So, his fast broken in Ashby, then seven miles back to Swarkestone, a further five to Derby and straight to Exeter House.

A message for Colonel O'Sullivan sent into the Council meeting already begun some hours ago and, according to those who have already been summoned to speak, in a considerable state of deadlock.

'So, Lieutenant Owen,' beams the Irishman when he finally emerges, 'you bring the same news as your chamber mates, your comrades, I assume. What joy! Not a sign of the Germans, eh?'

'On the contrary, Colonel,' says Striker. 'I was at Ashby three hours ago, atop a prodigious high tower. But to the south, why, you could see the smoke from cook fires quite plain, the spread of tent canvas too. At some distance, but quite unmistakeable. A large force, it seemed. And at Loughborough too. Evidence of an artillery train recently passed along the lanes. Some pieces of linstock. Horse too, in considerable numbers.'

O'Sullivan is struck dumb.

'This cannot be correct, Lieutenant. No other from the Rangers or Hussars has made such a report. You are certain, sir?'

'I wish that it were otherwise, Colonel. But I know that which I saw. Yet if others of my Company have covered the same ground and seen nothing…'

'No, not at all. We sent most of the patrols west, to seek Cumberland. And east, towards Nottingham. It will not do, sir. Lord George Murray has been arguing all morning for a return to Scotland. He says that we will have to fight Cumberland sooner or later and, when we do so, though we would likely win, we would lose so many that we should fall prey to Wade or Cholmondeley.'

'And His Royal Highness? He would wish to press on for London, I assume. To guarantee the Stuart restoration?'

'Lord George says that all here favour a Stuart restoration, and will give our lives to achieve it, yet to press on against such odds is a guarantee that we shall all die without winning that objective. Ogilvy and Elcho support him. It is a folly, Lieutenant.'

'To be sure, sir. Why, an advance on London would be certain to finally dispel any doubts amongst other Englishmen of our persuasion. And Colonel Townley was telling me yesterday evening that the French look finally set to assist us.'

'The very sentiment held by the Prince Regent and myself. His Royal Highness has letters to confirm the thing, though Murray argues that any French support will continue to arrive in Scotland, not here in the south where we need it. He is a misanthrope of the worst order, Lieutenant. They argue that, with no prominent support evident from the English, and the Welsh simply disappeared, the only sensible course is a consolidation between ourselves, those of our forces left in Scotland and the reinforcements arriving there from France.'

'There is merit in the plan, I expect. But to hold London, Colonel. Surely they see the merits? The pressure that it would bring to bear upon the Whiggish Government. Yet there are the citizens of London itself to consider, I suppose. They may be hostile, after all. And then the regiments that I saw to the south.'

'My God, man, they did not believe that we could fight *two* armies in succession. Yet the thought of a third, to the south! They will imagine the Prince killed or captured. No, Lieutenant. We must be circumspect about this news. You will say nothing of it, sir. For the moment, the arguments spin and twist, going nowhere and I think that the Council may retire soon. Return here at six, Lieutenant Owen. Speak to nobody else meanwhile.'

The town still smiles with boundless festivity, music filling the streets while a line of Whig supporters stretches to the inappropriately named Virgin's Inn where they are forced to pay Excise duties for the Stuart coffers or make donations to the Cause that match the subscriptions they had previously made to the Loyalist Fund, the details having been discovered earlier in the day.

A service in All Saints at five o'the clock, the organ played by the Manchester Regiment's Lieutenant Chaddock with the Prince in attendance and then, on the steps outside, His Royal Highness hears petitions, makes judgements, including a decision that the spy discovered by Townley's men, a certain John Vere should be spared the rope after all but kept a prisoner, much to the disappointment, it seems, of many here assembled.

Exeter House again, bustling with the Council's return, the Lords, the Chieftains, the Colonels, each with his personal entourage. So Striker waits. One hour. Two. Until he is finally summoned to the majestic dining room now serving as Council Chamber.

The table is spread with maps, refreshments as well. At its head, the Prince, pouting, angered. To his left, Lord George Murray. To his right, Colonel O'Sullivan. While, down each side, the various members of the Council that Striker can now recognise easily. Glenbucket. Lord Ogilvy. The Duke of Perth. John Roy Stuart. Colonel Townley recently included. An acknowledgement, a recognition. Lord Elcho. Ranald Clanranald. Ewan MacPherson of Cluny. MacDonald of Keppoch. Sir John MacDonald. Murray of Broughton. And Lochiel.

'Ah,' says the latter, 'this is the fellow who brought us news about the Welshmen when we were at Leek, I collect. I trust that today's intelligence may be more heartening? Colonel O'Sullivan assures us that it is so!'

'Your Highness,' protests David, Lord Elcho, a younger man even than the Prince, 'I really cannot believe that still further reports from Sir John's Rangers can affect the issue. We have heard from so many already! And one more, sir, how can it possibly assist? I repeat that I would be happy to support a march on London if only we had proof that the English want us to do so. Forgive me, but there is no such evidence, Highness.'

'And if we reach London without giving battle to Cumberland,' says Lord George, slapping the table with his hand, his nerves frayed. 'What then? Shall we in turn be besieged in that damn'd place? A fine spectacle *that* should present. Our strength lies in our ability to manoeuvre. To march faster than the English. We lose all that advantage once we are trapped inside London. For what? The principal claims that support awaits us in that city, our only contacts for those supporters, came from Sir Watkin Williams Wynn and his Attorney, Mister Morgan. And where are they, Your Highness? By the word of Lieutenant...'

Murray looks to Striker for assistance.

'Lieutenant Owen, sir.'

'Quite so! By the word of Lieutenant Owen here, they are respectively lost and taken.'

'Yet if we fall back on Scotland, Lord George,' says O'Sullivan, equally frayed it seems, 'there is worse danger that Cumberland and Wade will have closed the road behind us, while the road to London is most definitely open. Is that not so, Lieutenant?'

Striker pauses for a moment and looks to Charles Edward Stuart.

He seems petulant, yet confident too. He knows that he can carry the day, finally, by appealing to their loyalty and tempting them with the open road before them. Even a fool would know that he can reach London before Cumberland. And he will wipe aside anything that Newcastle may have placed in his way. The thing is finely balanced but, as things stand, with the open road...

Charles Edward lifts his eyes to meet Striker's, the spectre of a smile upon those Polish lips.

'Your Royal Highness,' says Striker, 'I respect you more than words can say. It would be a dereliction of my duties to inform you falsely.'

The smile disappears, the royal head turned sharply to O'Sullivan, the whispered words carrying clear to the whole table.

'This fellow will do me more harm than all the Elector of Hanover's army, sir!'

Consternation from the Irishman, a hand raised in an attempt to silence the Ranger's next words.

'Speak, Lieutenant Owen,' says Lochiel. 'Do you have different news for us?'

'I do, sir. For this morning I stood upon a tower at Ashby-de-la-Zouch and saw the encampment of a large force to the south of us. I could not guess the exact number, gentlemen, Your Highness, but I calculate many thousands. The Divisions of Hawley and Ligonier, I imagine.'

'By the Mass, I knew it!' cries Lochiel. '*Three* armies, Highness, and the road to London no longer open to us.'

Dismay on the face of John William O'Sullivan Triumph on the features of Lord George Murray and most of those sat here. Charles Edward gazes around the table, biting back a bitter tear, but it is upon Dudley Striker's face that his dark eyes settle. A long silence.

'You ruin, abandon and betray me,' says the Prince finally, almost choked by his emotions. 'Yet, though it shall be a Black Friday, on the morrow we begin our retreat!'

Chapter Forty-Nine

To be under siege in her own home is the ultimate desecration of Maria-Louise Redmond's Faith. It clutches her throat with the taunts of that loyalist rabble gathered beyond her front steps. It screams with an ice-layered wind through the broken window of her front parlour. It shakes her nerves like the shattering of glass. It overpowers her with the taste seeping from the silver censer now lying upon her carpet. It stinks of Father Peter Scobie's fear and excrement, the poor fellow's illness no longer in remission and he having found sanctuary here just ahead of these rascals who have ransacked the Catholic chapel in Roman Entry, chasing him with his own altar vessels, one of which had been the very object hurled in defiance through her casement. But, of all things, it threatens her brood, her girls, when just a week ago these worms would have fled the town rather than confront Charles Edward Stuart's army or its supporters.

Only a se'nnight past, too, that her home had been chosen for the Prince Regent's residence. She had dined with him, by Our Lady, here in this very house. Yet now she has a self-soiled priest cowering, gibbering Latin, in the corner of her favourite room. And, they say, the Prince is returning to Manchester, swung about at Derby. The north post has come in too, the post master being at last returned from London, with the post boy claiming General Wade already at Rochdale.

'Mistress Mudge,' she calls, until the housekeeper finally drags herself through the door. 'You will show Father Scobie to the backhouse, if you please, and provide him with a bowl that he may refresh himself. Then fetch him a pair of my husband's breeches.'

'Smells like shit!' Mudge drools, pushing him ahead with her heather besom, lance-like in the crook of her ruined arm, while the other hand clasps across her face and nose.

Even Phelim O'Farrell recoils from Father Scobie as he encounters Mudge and her charge in the reception hall, on his way to the parlour also and reporting that the three girls are safely installed at the farther end of the upstairs entertaining chamber. So she bids him stay here, keeping careful watch on those in the Lane but insisting that under no circumstances should he confront them. Then up the staircase to speak with her daughters, now engaged – albeit peripherally – in a game of *Gleek*.

521

'His Royal Highness will see those rebels dead when he returns, Mama, will he not?' says Maeve. 'It should be the very thing to watch them dance!'

'Come, sister,' says Anna-Marie, 'Our Lord would frown on such a display of malevolence. He Himself would surely have sought a way to guide the creatures back onto the paths of righteousness.'

'Oh,' says Katherine, 'I doubt that even Our Lady could display goodwill and understanding towards Whigs. And what say you, Mama? Do you think that Mister Owen is safe from this pack of curs?'

'I am sure that Aran will be perfectly safe, Katherine, and would find your own concern more than kind. I am sure that he will be more preoccupied with *your* safety than his own.'

Such delight on her face at the possibility. No such joy evident in my husband, however, I see!

'Can somebody explain to me, prithee,' shouts Titus from the doors, 'why Father Peter is sporting my most commodious pair of breeches?' And she intends to explain, but cannot for the new storm that has erupted below. 'What *now*?' Titus says, and he exits, closely followed by Maria-Louise.

For a moment, she thinks that O'Farrell has entirely ignored her prohibition, for the front door stands open and he is gesturing wildly towards the thoroughfare. But not for long since he is almost pushed to the floor as four individuals crash past him into the house.

'Lick-spittle...' Titus begins until he realises that these are friends, Phelim slamming the door behind them and the *thud, thud* of missiles hurled against the now closed portal.

Maria-Louise recognises each of the newcomers. Tom Sydall, Townley's Ensign Adjutant. Daniel Holker, now a lieutenant in the Manchester Regiment. Finally, those two almost-children, Thomas Deacon's youngest boy and his friend, Billy Brettargh. And today their infancy betrays them, each fighting back tears.

'O'Farrell,' she says, 'take those two boys to the kitchen at once and provide them with refreshment.'

'Give you joy, gentlemen,' Titus says to Sydall. 'His Royal Highness has returned so soon?'

'We should not have been handled so by those dogs if there had been a few more of us, sir. We may be home sooner than expected but this is no retreat. And Colonel Townley believed that we might still find new recruits if we arrived ahead of the main column. We have ridden like the devil to get here and now find the whole town, it seems, turned against us.'

'Not the town entire, Mister Sydall,' says Maria-Louise. 'But enough of them to make mayhem. They have been parading about since late afternoon but seem to have made this house their peculiar target. It is reasonable, I suppose, in the circumstances. Though there seems to have been no attempt to restore order by the Constables. Now, I must go and tend those children.'

'Some coves set upon us as soon as we came close to Acres Field,' says Holker, 'and I weep to find your daughters under threat, madam.'

'It was not my daughters to whom I referred, Mister Holker, but those two boys barely free of their mothers' teats. They are both frightened beyond their wits, I think, and I pray to Our Lady that they never have to face true battle. You will excuse me, gentlemen.'

She leaves them to their affairs, arranging a defence of the ground floor in case matters should take a tumble for the worse while, above, she happily finds the girls in their more natural humours, the two youngest playfully pushing the boundaries of their nicknames for the recent arrivals – Simple and Honker apparently – and making cruel sport of the boys' anxieties. Anna-Marie, ever the matron, admonishes but to no effect.

More commotion in the street. Raised voices. So Maria-Louise goes to the window, snuffs the candles in the closest sconces and peers around the corner of the drapes, waiting for her eyes to adjust. Some of the mob are still there, though others have now moved away but there is somebody new, a mounted fellow, his dark horse distinguished by the narrowest of white flashes down its face, the rider himself swaddled in a pale-coloured redingote. He leans over the horse's neck, addressing the spokesmen, apparently, for her besiegers, a confrontation in which they seem increasingly agitated, the horseman increasingly calm until, finally, he sits taller, looks up to her window. *Surely he cannot see me?* And he reaches down to the holsters hanging from his saddle to draw the long dragoon pistols that they conceal, levelling them at his interlocutors until, finally, and with malevolence, they depart. The rider follows them as far as the Commodities Exchange and there, with a final glance back to the house, he turns along past Mistress Cooper's coffee house and is gone.

She almost expects to see him there on the following morning when she and Titus venture forth to visit the warehouse. Her husband has insisted on checking whether damage has been done there, though she knows that, in truth, he is more concerned with the bawdy-house.

It is the ninth of December today, and still exceedingly cold though yet, thankfully, without any snow. Thomas Sydall and his companions have left the house early, with Charlie Deacon and Billy Brettargh restored to their military manhood, while the girls are once more in O'Farrell's trusty charge. But it seems that their inspection of the business premises must wait for, at the corner of Market Street Lane and Deansgate, another crowd has assembled. It is not entirely hostile, thank goodness, though neither is it altogether friendly, being rather the normal Monday morning bustlers, drawn here by the Bellman's cry yet confused by his message.

'This is to give notice to all the inhabitants of this town that they are desired to rise and arm themselves with guns, swords, pickaxes, shovels or any other weapons they can get, and go stop all the ends of the town to prevent the rebels from coming in for two hours, at which time the King's forces will be up with them.'

Some cheer and throw hats in the air. Others shout angry refusals. Most gape at each other in surprise.

'What folly is this?' calls Titus over the heads of those in front of him. 'Who has told you to announce this, fellow?'

'A summons to arms, Mister Redmond,' replies Doctor Hall. Maria-Louise had not noticed the gentleman earlier in the gathering but she now sees him plain enough, red-faced, his head bobbing up and down amongst his neighbours. 'That we should not have to tolerate a further invasion by those heathens, sirrah. And it is the Court Leet, Mister Bradley himself, who issues the demand. He and Justice Bradshaw both!'

Oh, I wish that James would desist from such follies! Though she is not surprised at Bradshaw's involvement. His appearances in Manchester are rare, since he has responsibility for the Quarter Sessions of the entire Salford Hundred, a considerable workload. Yet he commands considerable fear, a man whose sentences are harsh though they seldom betoken sound judgement.

'Then those two men represent a conspiracy of fools,' says Titus. 'For the Prince Regent's regiments will be here this afternoon while the forces of your King Usurper will certainly not be two hours behind them. You should know better, Doctor Hall! Get you back, sir, to your ailments and fractures.'

'You says so, sir' the Doctor replies. 'Well, we shall see. And who shall join me, good people? Let us arm ourselves in the name of the Law and in defence of this town!'

A few feeble huzzahs and some follow him as he stalks away towards Saint Ann's Church while the Redmonds remain several minutes at the corner, Titus attempting to reassure those with Tory and Jacobite tendencies. Yes, he tells them, the Prince will indeed be here today, some of his forward scouts having spent the previous night in his house.

'And you, my dear,' says her husband. 'Do you not think it safer to remain with the girls?'

'What, husband? That you may whet your appetites among Susannah Cole's doe-eyed bunters? I think not. No, first to the glazier for the window repair. It will not answer if His Royal Highness returns and the house is all askew. Not at all. Though we might have suffered far worse but for the fellow who dispersed those cankers last evening.'

'Most likely one of Pitsligo's picquets. I could not tell, he was so wrapped against the cold. But I doubt that the Prince will lodge with us again. We must wait and see his bidding, I fancy. At least we shall discover the reason for his return. I am sure that he must have some strategy in mind. To draw Cumberland into a trap is the most likely. Reinforcements coming from the north. But this talk of retreat must be foolishness. I shall hear no more of it!'

I so hope that he is correct. For how can an enterprise that began so well now turn in such a way?

'And the Welsh, perhaps,' she says. 'We have heard nothing from Sir Watkin and his forces. If the Prince does indeed draw Cumberland north, the Welsh might close the trap behind them perchance.'

Warehouse and bawdy-den are both secure, though Titus Redmond's gaze lingers over-long, she thinks, on the condums at the brothel's upper mullions.

'I have been wondering, d'you know, whether we might travel,' he says.

'Another trip to Preston?'

'A trifle further than Preston.'

'You have some scheme to visit London for the victory celebrations?'

'They are certain to occur and it is possible that we shall be invited to them. A grateful new monarch is sure to favour us with his blessing, I collect. And that might, indeed, provide a beginning. Yet I still envisaged something more occasional. That we might repair, perhaps, to the Continent. After the war is ended, naturally.'

'The Continent? What stuff! We should never afford the thing. And the girls. What should become of *them*?'

'I had rather thought that we should take them with us. Though I doubt that Anna-Marie should wish to repair so far. Maeve and Katherine, however, would benefit greatly from the experience. And O'Farrell could assist.'

'The poor fellow can barely move around the house, let alone the entire Continent. And Katherine is so very taken with Aran Owen that she would simply pine like a lovelorn lamb. Then there is Mudge. Or had you planned on delighting the rest of Europe with her charms?'

'Mag Mudge, yes. I have been considering her future, poor creature. I need to be rid of Mistress Cole, my dear. She takes me for a cull and I must be shot of the woman. And Mother Blossom will not answer, neither.'

'You cannot signify...'

'Indeed I do! The bawdy-house provided Mudge with her livelihood for long enough and she might act the crippled clown but she has a jester's wit inside that shapeless head. She would serve perfectly well.'

'And the fustian?'

'If we could ever persuade your *enamorato* to abandon his misguided creed, I could sell him the business. I have already broached the matter with him. It would provide all the funds that we would need for the journey.'

'Indeed, sir? You have broached the matter with Mister Bradley, you say? Yet I prefer to consider that we are leaving the trade in the hands of our family.'

Yet could I leave James behind me? Any more than Titus might leave his whores? Yet harlots he may find wherever he travels, whilst I...

'I have never known you so sensitive, but as you will! With our son-in-law then, rather than with your plaything, your suitor, your swain. We need to plan a route, of course. But I thought that your cousin in Geneva, perhaps…?'

'Cousin Katherine, yes. But Bradley is hardly a suitor, husband. He cannot be suitor nor swain when I am already spoken for. I am no Penelope. And James is my peculiar physick, no different than that which you spoon from those good-natured doxies. But you mention geneva…'

'Physick, you say? Perhaps. Yet the gin concession is all resolved. That decent fellow, John Shaw, will take the trade. Then we are settled, it seems. I will make some tentative arrangements, to be finalised once this thing is finished. I shall write to Josiah also. Or maybe a visit to Llanffynon.'

But this is all so sudden. How long shall the journey be? And neither of us given mention of Rosina. The obvious issue that we choose to overlook. The suckling pig past which we charge to chase the chicken. She will stay with Bradley, naturally. yet shall we part without a word of farewell or reconciliation? And there is James himself. So much more than a mere dalliance now. I never sought attachment to the fellow. Merely a means to pleasure myself from time to time. Yet we sometimes find attachment at the very moment, in the very place, when we are least expecting it.

'And the duration of this journey, husband? You cannot imagine that we shall be gone forever.'

'A year perhaps. But look!'

They have walked back from the warehouse and taken the alley from Deansgate to Acres Field, each of them aware that the town is unusually quiet but not remarking the fact due to their focus on future plans. It is far from quiet here, however. There must be two hundred at least surrounding the church door, and Titus reaches out his arm to prevent Maria-Louise approaching further towards them. Doctor Hall again. And the cadaverous old stick that the town knows as Captain Hilton, though there is general doubt that he has ever held such a commission. But he is one of the Shude Hill Invalids, that much is certain, and he has a score of his fellows for company today, each with an orange sash or ribbon tied at his shoulder, each carrying his weapon of choice or capability, farming implements mostly and a single venerable musket. Damaged fellows, spoiled by war. Dribbling simpletons, some of them. Others lacking limb, or part thereof. Or hand. Or eye.

'The dubious doctor and the curious captain,' she says. 'Yet look how they bestir the crowd!'

'They are dangerous,' says Titus. 'Fowden will need to be careful.'

Constable Fowden and two deputies have now also arrived at the entrance to Saint Ann's, remonstrating with the ringleaders and seeking their dispersal.

'I see that William has brought his whip,' Maria-Louise observes. 'At least he is better prepared for his duties than last week, I collect.'

'He may need to use it too, if Miller Tomlinson continues to prod him thus. Ah, Fowden has had enough at last. Look. Tomlinson is bound for the

House of Correction now, to be sure.'

The deputies are, indeed, dragging the ancient miller away, Fowden acting as whip-wielding rearguard and Doctor Hall's assembly in bitter pursuit.

'At least we may now proceed,' she says.

Yet in Market Street Lane they see more evidence of rowdy gatherings, and then none other than Bradley himself entering the Old Coffee House.

'Mister Bradley,' says Titus, 'a word with you, sir.'

James looks uncertainly from Maria-Louise to her husband.

'I was about to take tea,' he says.

'Then we shall join you, sirrah. Though I cannot say that I approve of this rabble you have aroused.'

'They are loyalists, Titus. A rare but honest breed of citizen in this town. And you are welcome to join me though Mistress Cooper's other customers may not be so obliging. There are many who have not forgiven the affront to their sensibilities from Sergeant Dickson and his crew. There are many who will oppose any return of such poltroons, myself included.'

'We shall join you regardless, Mister Bradley,' says Maria-Louise. 'Yet the Prince Regent's army will indeed return, and this very afternoon, sir. You should not put yourself in harm's way so.'

'Such sweet concern!' says Titus. 'How touching. But come...' And he pushes open the door to the coffee house. They shrug themselves free of their outer coats as soon as they feel the warmth within. Faces turn to them. Crableck's. Lewthwaite's. Elizabeth Cooper's. Those of a dozen more. 'Though you may wish, my dear,' Titus continues, 'to share our news with Mister Bradley yourself. I did mention our possible travel plans to him a week since. Perhaps he failed to tell you.'

'As *you* seem to have done also, Titus, and I have not *seen* Mister Bradley this past week.'

'Mister Redmond. Madam,' says Elizabeth, her composure recovered as she comes to greet them. 'What a surprise! Why, this must be twice in a little over seven days. Come, warm yourselves by the hearth.'

She leads Titus towards the fire, while Maria-Louise turns to Bradley.

'So, you knew about this?'

'I did, my dear, but it has been impossible to speak with you alone the whole week through. And, in any case, my own news is far worse, I fear. For in a momentary lack of caution, and being much goaded by your daughter about the Jacobite scum with whom you associate so freely, I inadvertently told her that it was *you* who was responsible for the loss of their damn'd Exchequer.'

'You told...'

'Rosina, yes. My dearest, I am so dreadfully low about the whole thing. She barely spoke with me throughout Ma's funeral and she stayed behind at Droylsden to help settle their affairs. But she will be back later, I fear. To tell you true, I do not know what to expect from her.'

'As always with my daughter it is probably safe to expect the worst.'

'And I have had a full year of experiences,' says Bradley, 'to confirm how bad Rosina's *worst* can be. Though these past few months, I had come to imagine something else within her. But whether it is her worst or her best, the precise form of Rosina's response is usually unpredictable. When I made my foolish declaration, she was at first simply incredulous. Even her mother, she said, could not do such a thing. Then asked me how, exactly, you had performed this deed. And I had to confess that I did not know.'

No, at least I had the presence of mind to say nothing to him about Aran's part in this.

'Mister Bradley,' calls Elizabeth Cooper, 'a dish of *Assam* with you, perhaps?'

So they take tea while, outside, mobs of different sizes march about the streets, shouting, hurling filth and stones at the houses of those known to be Jacobites. She has not seen Aran for several days either, since he has immersed himself once again in those murals for the Court Leet. But at least he will be safe there, for the Byroms' house seems immune from these attacks.

'Have you decided then, Mister Bradley,' says Titus, 'how long you will allow your rabble to continue before they are penned?'

'I feel, sir, as though you have misunderstood. It was not those townsfolk who inflicted bloody war upon this nation, I think. And it haunts the lives of your own supporters too, does it not, this conflict? You think that fathers like Thomas Deacon wish to see their children taken from them? The Law may not be perfect but we possess nothing else to separate right from wrong. It should not matter whether the arm that brandishes the Law is weak or strong. So those citizens may themselves be breaching the peace yet they are doing so to protect this nation's Rule of Law. But you are correct. They cannot be permitted to *break* the Law simply so that it may be preserved. Mistress Cooper, might I enjoy the services of Crableck a while?'

And so, less than an hour later, the Bellman is back, accompanied by both Constables and several deputed assistants.

'Whereas a tumultuous mob has been raised, this is to desire that everybody will lay down their arms and be quiet.'

A while later, Justice Bradshaw himself is escorted to the Cross, at Bradley's request, so that he can formally read the Riot Act in full.

'Our Sovereign Lord the King chargeth and commandeth all persons being assembled, immediately to disperse themselves and peaceably depart to their habitations, or to their lawful business, upon the pains contained in the Act made in the first year of King George for preventing tumults and riotous assemblies. God Save the King.'

How it must hurt the fellow, she thinks, *to call out the mob at one moment and have to disperse them again at the next.*

Yet many have no desire to comply and are still on the streets when the drone of distant pipes announces the return of the first Highland regiments.

Justice Bradshaw has lifted the lid on Pandora's Box and may not now restore its contents, she thinks, as an advance party of Scots march up the Lane and halt at the Exchange. *Well, they certainly do not resemble an army in retreat. Titus is correct.* Their plaids are wrapped about them and, while they may bear the signs of a strenuous journey, all seem in high spirits. They are followed by a line of pack animals, a knot of horsemen, probably their quartermasters for men are soon dispatched to mark billets, literate men who can daub *Atholl* or *Perth* or *Cameron* or *Mac a'Phearsain* in stark white chalk across door or wall, but their work interrupted by the mob's return.

'These are cocks that have never crowed except amongst their own hens and on their own dunghills,' says Titus. 'What stirs them now to strut so bold?'

'They are patriots, sir,' Bradley replies, sucking at his teeth and pointing towards the line of older fellows and younger boys now lined ahead of the Jacobites and, it seems, denying them access to the Market Place. Taunts and chanting, the Highland officers initially unsure how to respond as the anger builds amongst their own ranks.

For these are men too, she thinks. *Far from their homes and, set down here in Manchester, distanced from their own place in time too. She has seen illustrations of those native tribes in the Colonies, swathed in blankets also, somehow unreal, as though the progress of Mankind, under the guidance of Our Lord, has left these people abandoned on their remote shores. And these tribal Highlanders are no different. They are alien to us and we fear them, all of us, for their unfamiliarity. Yet those rascals out there fear them to extremity.*

The noise is now fearsome too, rattling like hail as stone and insult alike fall upon the Scotsmen's bonnets. They fall back, the billet markers running to a place of greater safety amongst their clansmen, their kinsmen, their comrades. And, though they may retire, they also reform, executing a change from marching column to a line that spreads from one side of Market Street Lane to the other, their officers adjusting them as they walk slowly backwards, sword arm outstretched to indicate the new formation.

Townsfolk follow, men running forward to throw small rocks, pebbles, anything that comes to hand, then skittering backwards to find some new munition.

Inside the coffee house, Maria-Louise and the others cower behind tables. A window shatters. A wounded Highlander falls against the now empty frame, blood pouring from a scalp wound.

A command in Gaelic and, in one fluid motion, the front ranks of the Company cock their muskets. Command! They present, right foot moved backwards by six inches to brace them, musket butts brought up into the shoulder. Command! Muzzles lifted. Command! And the volley roars, shaking the coffee house to its foundations, acrid white smoke stabbed through and through with yellow flash, the sulphurous, rotten cloud drifting through the smashed window.

Then silence. Profound silence.

'By God's Hooks,' says Bradley, his words falling into the void, 'what have they *done?*'

They stand, peering through the dissipating haze while the Jacobite soldiers charge their pieces afresh. But when the smoke has finally cleared, they see... Well, nothing. They expect carnage. Yet there is none. Simply Market Street Lane as it has always been. Almost. For now it is entirely empty. The Highlanders' volley, discharged into the air, has served its purpose.

The cockerels dispersed, returned to their middens, while the army's work resumes in earnest. Regiments come in, one after the other. Billets are commandeered. The Prince will, indeed, lodge once more with the Redmonds. And the Bellman, no longer under the control of Bradley's Court Leet, is back at the Cross by three o'the clock.

'By order of his Royal Highness, Charles, Prince of Wales, I give notice to all persons that no two people shall be seen walking together in the streets after nine o'the clock tonight, except that they be guarded by troops of His Royal Highness, on pain of being deemed mobbers and rioters, and by them be punished as such.'

There is no formal dinner on this occasion, however. No grandeur to match Charles Edward's previous sojourn at her house, for their royal guest spends much of the evening in his own rooms, working privately with his secretary and a seemingly endless succession of messengers, advisers, commanders and petitioners.

Yet these *buffets*, laid with an array of food by which this plumb-line of people might refresh themselves, have proved even more taxing than the previous repast. Mistress Hepple and her good folk have been enlisted once more, naturally, upon the advice of Mister Gibb, while Mister Strickland has again received details of the necessary disbursements to be made.

Though I must remember to provide that gentleman with a receipt for firewood. It does not grow on trees, when all is said and done. La! What a foolish thought. But it is the very devil to keep the house warm when the doors are opened so frequently. All this coming and going. I am quite giddy.

But at least there has been no sign of Rosina. Not so far.

Colonel Townley is here, however.

'Good evening, Colonel,' she says. 'You are pleased to be home?'

'I am not, madam. We were close enough to London that we might have spat upon Westminster's Palace. And now turned about, running before Cumberland on the word of one Welshman, they say?'

'One of Sir Watkin's men?'

530

'Do not speak that name to me either, lady. A pox on the fellow and all his kind. They promised to come out. Your husband heard them swear it. Yet not a sign of them.'

'But Mister Morgan. He dined here last week. So full of fire, like yourself, sir.'

'Taken. At Chelford they say.'

'Who is taken?' asks Titus, coming up with them.

'The Attorney, Morgan, my dear. And Colonel Townley tells me that the Welsh have not come out. After all that bluster.'

My husband still blanches, I see, at the use of Townley's title.

'I am hardly surprised,' says Titus. 'I could never quite fathom Sir Watkin. Such wealth to cushion him from the Cause.'

'Traitors at every turn, it seems,' Townley whispers, with venom. 'The Welsh. Those Lowland Lords who sowed the seeds for this retreat. And that fellow who brought news of the Hanoverians blocking our further advance. I should see them all hanged, sir. But I blame the Prince, above all. For accepting the word of a single Ranger without verifying his intelligence.'

This talk of traitors disturbs me so!

'And the journey back from Derby, Colonel,' she says. 'Was it fearful?'

'For the first day, I think, nobody knew our direction. We saw no sun and the whole army believed that we were marching to find Cumberland. It was only when we reached Ashbourne again that we began to wonder. The mood was bitter for a while. And there were rumours at every turn. This commander removed from his post. That chieftain deserted back to the Highlands. A new one with every hour. Foul weather too. Snow and ice on the uplands all the way. Leek and Macclesfield again. Then the Mersey at Stockport.'

'But our fellows in good spirits again, I collect?' says Titus. 'This is a temporary reversal, to be sure. I shall have no mention of *retreat* in this house, sir. I have told my wife so already.'

'You may use whatever word you choose, Mister Redmond. The effect is all the same. Though spirits *are* restored, that much is true. Albeit the men are more snappish than before. And, I am ashamed to say, there has been some looting at times.'

'And you mention cunny-sucking traitors? The Ranger who persuaded the Prince to abandon the London road, for example?'

'Another Welshman, I fear. A former assistant to Sir Watkin, it seems. Ah, but see! You have simply to mention the breed and one of them appears before your very eyes. So, Mister Owen, shall you now enlist, sir? You will notice that we have returned all these miles to fetch you.'

They have been joined by Aran and Adam Scatterbuck too, the former blithely swatting aside Townley's taunt.

'A timely entrance, Aran,' says Titus. 'You will recall that I mentioned the fellow in Preston. The same, I thought, that I had encountered in Mother

Blossom's?' Aran seems unsure whether he remembers or *not*. 'You *must* recall our conversation, sir! Of course you do. In any case, I fancy Townley was about to tell me that, by pure coincidence, the cove who persuaded the Prince to head north again was a *Lieutenant* Owen. Am I not correct, sir?'

'By Our Lady, Mister Redmond, correct indeed!'

'I thought as much! My dear, I warned Colonel O'Sullivan himself to beware this lick-spittle.'

Aran's turn to blanch, she sees.

'Come, husband! I think we can hardly hold Aran accountable for the actions of all those who bear his name. And I must take him to see Katherine in any case. The poor girl has been worried for his health ever since those mobbers began to gather.'

She draws Aran away, leaving Scatterbuck to regale Colonel Townley with the news that members of his Manchester Regiment have attacked Doctor Hall, left him badly but deservedly wounded.

'I thought that this talk of Lieutenant Owen might distress you,' says Maria-Louise.

'Never so difficult, in life,' Aran replies, 'as seeing the fellow in person. And at your daughter's house, my dear!'

'Striker?'

'Yes, the same. And greeted Rosina as though they were old friends. Reminded her that they had met before. Apologised for deceiving her and masquerading as a purveyor of fine pastries. She would understand, of course, for he was acting on behalf of King James. Travelling *incognito*, naturally. To visit his secret contacts. A certain Aran Owen. Told her his *real* name, of course. Claimed that we are distant cousins.'

'And she believed him?'

'He is a plausible fellow at the best of times, and in company with so many of the Prince Regent's senior officers…'

'In Rosina's house?'

'Indeed. She had issued invitations to all the houses on Hanging Ditch.'

'And *Mister* Bradley?'

'You might ask him yourself, perhaps.'

For James Bradley has himself been ushered into the room. He looks angered. Flustered. Confused.

'Do you mind, Aran my love?' she says. 'He looks so forlorn.'

'Well, that would *never* do! Please give him my regards.'

Maria-Louise crosses the room to Bradley's side.

'I would bid you welcome to my house, James, but you do not seem especially happy to be here.'

'Well, I cannot decide which I resent most, whether it is suffering the indignity of having my own home invaded by those *banditti* friends of yours, or whether it is the injustice of being summoned *here*, of all places.'

But Mister Strickland has arrived to escort Bradley into audience with the Prince Regent and Maria-Louise returns to her husband.

'My dear,' says Titus, 'I see that Bradley has gone to answer for his misdeeds. But no matter his Whiggish tendencies, he has less to answer than this Lieutenant Owen that I mentioned to you. It is astonishing. He attacks me at the bawdy-house. He persuades the Prince to turn back from Derby. And when I saw him in Preston, he was on his way to take instructions for Sir Watkin – who subsequently disappears with his entire force. The cunny-sucker then spins a tale that, at Chelford, he was ambushed along with David Morgan – and, miraculously, Lieutenant Owen was the only one to escape. I am convinced that the fellow is a traitor, madam. And worse, I am certain, beyond life, that he is the man responsible for Jacob Driscoll's death.'

Yet how much more astonished you would be, husband, if you knew that he is presently being nourished by your daughter!

'And you think he may be here in Manchester, my dear?' she says, as demurely as possible.'

'The Company of Rangers has been away from the column almost continuously since Ashbourne,' says Townley. 'We have seen little sign of Cumberland but he is there, to be sure. Beppy's father has received an express, she tells me, confirming that the Hanover pack will be here by tomorrow. so it is unlikely that this Lieutenant Owen should be in town. But I shall make enquiries. Your theorem is interesting, sir, but there is not a shred of evidence to support it.'

'The evidence of his own eyes at Mother Blossom's,' says Scatterbuck, 'is incontrovertible, I protest.'

She sees Bradley again, crossing the doorway out on the landing.

'Excuse me, gentlemen,' she says, and hurries out to catch him below, as he reaches the reception hall. 'James!' she calls, while O'Farrell fetches his coat. 'Your audience is finished then?'

'As you see, my dear. I have been called to account for the town's *humours*, as your Pretender described them. The fellow seems to have aged five years this past week, do you not think? And so replete with ire now. I feared for my life. Recalled Ma's premonition that I should not be long in following her.'

'Yet you have survived to tell the tale, sirrah. Give you joy. And a free man still.'

'Free? Hardly so. The *Chevalier* reminded me that a bail bond of five thousand pounds had been posted upon the town against its good behaviour. He now insists that this amount should be forfeit to the Crown – his father's, I assumed – for the insolence of the mob. And this mulct to be paid in full by nine o'clock tomorrow morning.'

'Five thousand! And if you cannot raise this sum...'

'Then my own freedom is forfeit in its place, it seems. And he would not answer for the safety of our people. The threat, I think, is real enough. But I have told him that the thing is impossible, of course. Better to hang me now, I said. At which point he graciously agreed to cut the amount by half.'

'But still…'

'Do not trouble yourself, my dear. I shall do my best to meet the demand. And, to be frank, the task troubles me not half so much as the memory of Rosina reeling from her opiates and demanding that the Jacobite *gentlemen* who now fill my home should ensure that she might kiss the Prince's hand before he leaves Manchester.'

Maria-Louise does not sleep easily this night. In part it is due, incredibly, to the mob being on the rampage once again despite the troops in the streets and the strictures against such things, the threatened reprisals. But it is also partly from concern for Bradley and his Herculean task, partly from fear that Aran might somehow be exposed by this Striker.

So the next morning requires more effort about her toiletry than usual. But less turmoil in her own preparations than those engulfing the rest of the house. For whilst an army's arrival at its destination might seem irregular, confusing, its departure seems nothing short of chaotic. There have been units set upon the road since seven, squadrons of horse for the most part. But for two hours before that even, her home has been a hive. Another swarm of messengers, runners, creditors, colonels and captains. They hover from room to room, gather in clusters upon her stairs. A blur of insect blues, greens, reds, silvers and steel greys. Visitors too, it seems. For she has seen Mrs Starkey in company with a Highland officer. The entire Byrom family too.

And at nine o'the clock sharp, James Bradley is back.

They exchange formal greetings and she follows him to the *piano nobile* where, by this time, the Prince Regent is holding court in the Entertaining Room, more *buffets* set with food so that visitors can break their fast while they wait, maps, books and documents spread across a table, and his senior officers clustered about his shoulders.

'Mister Bradley!' says Lord George Murray. 'Come forth, sir. You can furnish the mulct, I trust?'

'I have the list here. Two hundred pounds from James Chetham. The same from Robert Jobb. One hundred pounds from John Clowes…'

'Your pardon, sir,' Murray interrupts. 'But we have much work to do this day. No need for the detail, I am sure.'

'If you please,' says the Prince. 'We are sure that Mister Bradley has purpose in his list, Lord George. We shall hear him.'

A thin smile of acknowledgement from Bradley and the names continue. Lloyd. Birch. Ayrton. Bancroft. Allen. Woolmer. Tomlinson. Walley. Dickenson. Childer. Two dozen more. And, finally, his own promissory note.

'A total of two thousand, five hundred and four pounds, and thirteen shillings, sir,' says Bradley. 'The additional four pounds and thirteen shillings,

534

I suggest, you retain to garnish the executioner's hand, for I hear that those paid to do so may dispatch traitors humanely with a mallet before drawing their innards.'

His words produce aggressive, protective instincts amongst those close enough within the hive to hear, but Charles Edward waves a hand at them dismissively.

'Gentlemen,' he says. 'Mister Bradley is passionate in his beliefs in equal measure to our own. We have already said, during our previous and more pleasant visit to this town, that we shall need fellows of his mettle soon enough. We thank you, sir, and the town may consider its duty fulfilled. Yet we were minded, in the commotion of the wee hours, to increase the fine. Manchester, it seems, is an unruly place. But we urge you, Mister Bradley, to maintain good order throughout the rest of the day, for any further infringements shall be treated expeditiously. Mister Strickland, you will relieve Mister Bradley of his burden!'

Strickland takes a brace of purses and a sheaf of notes from Bradley's hands and leads him back towards the doors but they are no more than half way to the landing when yet another party enters. The Duke of Perth is amongst them. Townley too. A glittering contingent of officers, Beppy Byrom upon an arm. And Rosina too, at the very peak of her beauty, catching her mother's eye but with a pretence that she has not seen her, ignoring her completely and Bradley as well.

Maria-Louise steps forward to intercept her daughter but the moment is passed, and the Duke, James Drummond, with the long nose and wide, thin lips of his family, elegantly presents Rosina to the Prince.

'Your Highness,' he says. 'You may recall Mistress Bradley? She entertained us most nobly last evening and craved only the indulgence of kissing your hand, sir, by way of reward.'

'Bid you good morning, Mistress,' says Charles Edward. 'And how might it be possible to forget such a picture? Why, madam, we had the pleasure of receiving your husband again just these few minutes past. You are fortunate to have such a fellow. A veritable lion, sirrah! But please...' Rosina has sunk to the carpet before him, her hoops spread and the dark silk of her skirts billowing about her. He offers his hand, and she takes it reverently, placing a respectful kiss upon the royal fingers. 'And do you truly wish no more for the care that you have lavished on my friends than this most modest of tokens.'

'If it is not too much to ask, Your Highness,' she says, 'I should perhaps crave one more boon.'

'Then name it, lady!'

'I seek simple justice, sir,' says Rosina. 'For I know a little of the plight faced by Your Highness and our most loyal army. From my father, Mister Redmond, you will understand. I think, sir, that our Cause would have been aided greatly by a certain shipment that was lost.'

535

If she continues in this vein she shall embarrass herself. Is she still in the laudanum's embrace, I wonder?

The Prince looks about the room, locates Titus with several members of Townley's Regiment, graces him with a flash of annoyance.

'These things are not for public debate, Mistress. But you mentioned a boon?'

'Yes, Your Highness. The justice that I mentioned. I would not dare to debate matters of state, sir, but if there was a single person, a traitor, responsible for the loss in question...'

She would not! I may have lost my daughter's respect but surely...

The Irishman, Colonel O'Sullivan, moves forward, as though to shield Charles Edward from some nameless harm.

'If you knew of such a traitor, my dear,' he says, quietly, 'it would be your duty to tell us, would it not?'

I shall simply deny the thing! By Our Lady, they must see that the Sydenham's has made her insensible. No proof...

Titus is beside her, gripping her arm, gently patting his wife's hand in sympathy for their daughter's foolishness.

'My poor girl,' he says in a whisper. Then louder. 'Your Highness, I would ask permission to escort my daughter below. I fear that she is overcome by the emotion of the moment.'

Our Lady bless you, husband! Yes, stop her before this terrible thing comes to pass.

Titus looks to the Prince, seeking his approval, and Charles Edward lifts a hand, palm up towards the ceiling. Please, it says, take your poor daughter from our presence. And the Prince glances from one to another of his two commanders, Lord George on one side, O'Sullivan on the other.

'Your family,' says the Irishman, 'has a propensity for identifying traitors it seems, Mister Redmond. First my finest Lieutenant of Rangers. Now your daughter on this other matter. Are you *all* overcome then, sirrah?'

Please, Titus. Do not react to the Colonel. Just take the stupid girl and leave. I shall explain everything as soon as we are alone!

But Titus, she sees, is stung by O'Sullivan's comment. The creases deepen on his face. He touches a thumb to the moustache. And a chance is lost forever, falling somewhere down into a pit within her.

I had forgotten. This is the shortest day. La! And Maria-Louise Redmond's mind drifts to another place entirely. *My father*, she thinks. *That damn'd curse upon Titus!*

'I am overcome,' Rosina says, rising to her feet with the Prince's hand to steady her, 'only by my grief for *you*, Papa. Since the person who has betrayed our Cause, who has destroyed all your work, who has stolen from us the prospect of meaningful French support. *That* person, *that* traitor, is standing by your side!'

536

Chapter Fifty

'It is something of an irony,' says Rosina, 'that I am now revered by the Whigs in general as a heroine yet so reviled by the leader of the faction that I am ejected from his house.'

Beppy examines her father's shirt for further creases, spreading it across the smoothing board in the laundry room, and setting the heavy slickstone down for a moment as she does so. Dark glass, shaped like a large inverted mushroom.

'So it has reverted to being Mister Bradley's house?' says Rosina's friend. Apparently the only one left to her. 'And I shall need the marble for this, my dear, it seems. The sleeves will never answer.'

Rosina wraps a cloth carefully around the upright handle of the slicker's stone twin and lifts it from the copper boiler, setting it down so that Beppy can restore the offending sleeves to their natural good order.

'I suppose that it was never truly mine,' Rosina replies, her voice still dull from the effects of so much opiate. 'And I cannot go home, not now!'

'Papa says that you may stay here as long as you like. There! Let me fold this and we can stack the whole pile within the airing closet.'

'Mister Byrom is so kind. Yet harsh, too, that he forces such penance on you.'

'The smoothing? La! I enjoy it, but you may not tell him so. Since the servants normally make such a huff of the task, he assumes that it must be onerous, and therefore a fitting punishment for my misdeeds. To be fair, on this occasion I rather agree that some sanction is my due. After all, if I had not encouraged you in this foolishness of kissing the Prince's hand...'

Yes, much may perhaps have been different.

But this business of the Prince had always been something of a pretence, she knows. She had brooded and worried on Bradley's disclosure about Mama's betrayal of the Cause for nine long days, all through the time she had spent in Droylsden at the old lady's funeral and afterwards when, for some reason, the deed had assumed the aspect, almost, of a personal attack. Rosina knew, of course, that her sadness at Ma Bradley's demise, potently combined with the Sydenham's had been responsible for the transmutation, yet she had become blinded to this logic on her return to Manchester only to discover Charles Edward in retreat and lacking the support that he so richly deserved.

Support of which he had been deprived in no small part, she now knew, by her own mother. All this, however, she could have handled too except for one factor – the gargantuan and entirely inexplicable jealousy that had arisen from Mama's renewed liaison with her husband.

So, in the presence of the Prince, and dosed with laudanum once again, it had seemed the most obvious thing to denounce the woman. There had been stunned silence, filled by Rosina's hasty explanation about her mother's burning hatred for the French, that Mama had confided in Mister Bradley who, in turn, had seen fit to share the knowledge with his wife, herself. *Why not put the charge to her, Your Highness? Let her deny the thing. There, sir, your Bible. Let her testify on your Bible that I speak false.* And how she had hoped, in that moment, that Mama *would* deny it. But she had not. And her poor father, rooted to the spot. *Tell them, my dear. This is a mistake.* No mistake, simply a weak smile from Maria-Louise to Titus. No mistake. So the Prince had been left no alternative except to command her arrest. A charge of sedition, naturally. Mama would be held, taken as a prisoner when the army departed, to answer the charge later. *We are sorry, Mister Redmond. Yet we shall ensure that your wife is treated with every possible courtesy.* Titus had looked at his wife for a long moment, puzzled, touching his moustache. *You may take her, Your Highness*, he had said, *and treat her as you please!*

'You are very gracious, Beppy,' she says, 'but I can hardly attribute any blame to yourself for my actions, the memory of which haunts me like an evil chimera.'

'Your father will resolve the matter, I am certain. He is a man of great purpose. Now, my dear one, we need to tackle the bed linen. Shall you help me with the battledore?'

So for the next thirty minutes they work together, winding sheets onto a long wooden roller and pressing them with the flat paddle. The exertion prevents chatter but it cannot block the memory of Maria-Louise, huddled in the back of a cart as the Jacobite army trundled northwards in the late afternoon. Assassin shots fired from a garret window, a Highlander wounded. The Scots threatening revenge and brands lit, that the town could be torched. That charming cousin of Aran Owen's, the Lieutenant of Rangers – charming for a self-confessed spy, that is to say. Intervening to diffuse the situation. A last vision of Mama crossing the Irwell Bridge. Then repercussions of her own to face. Papa unable to even look at her. The bitter, bitter recriminations from Bradley. *Should you be glad to see me gone then?* she had asked. *Well, since you have broached the subject, Rosina…*

It had not taken her father long to repent his initial rebuttal of Mama's crime, however, and by the time Rosina had reached the Byroms' house, hoping to find shelter there, Beppy had been able to furnish the news that Mister Redmond was already on the road to Wigan in pursuit of the Jacobite column.

Then two days in which the Whigs had come out of their verminous nests once more. And with a vengeance. Mobs again, a bruised, bandaged, yet buoyant Doctor Hall at their head. More attacks on Jacobite homes. The Bellman crying for the imminent arrival of Cumberland, a requirement that all townsfolk must prepare provisions for the loyalist army. A further announcement that all houses faithful to King George should illuminate their windows to celebrate Cumberland's visit to Manchester. This announcement cancelled once it was clear that the Duke would not reach them for two days more. Not the Duke himself, perhaps, but his forces had certainly appeared. Two hundred dragoons first. Then Handasyde's Thirty-First Regiment of Foot, several of its officers being quartered here with the Byroms.

'And how do you feel now?' asks Beppy, as they store the last of the pressed and folded linen within the warming cupboard that backs the kitchen chimney.

How do I feel? Like a jelly that has not properly congealed. Like the worst megrim of my life. Like all the music of my years lies torn and burned. Like some ugly animal invention of Dean Swift. She had spent the night of her arrival at the Byroms' house, all the following day – yesterday – too, lying in bed with a raging fever and shaking fit. She is only little better today, craving the laudanum that Beppy has refused to allow in the house. It is the price that her friend has set upon the accommodation they provide. A heavy price.

'I feel like I need a dose of Sydenham's,' she says. 'But might we not discover whether Aran is at work in the Academy rooms? I do not expect that he will entertain my presence but perhaps…'

'Of course, my dear. If you feel strong enough. He did enquire after you yesterday though I could not tell his mood. Let me remove my apron and we shall see.'

Aran is, indeed, at work on the murals. Or at work, so far as he is able, with so many interruptions. His initial reaction to their entrance is one of annoyance, though his face softens perceptibly, she thinks, when he turns towards her, meets her eyes, greets her with a well-mannered bow and a look of deep sorrow.

'Rosina,' he says, 'have these gentlemen yet been named?' The two redcoat officers desist from some foppery with Aran's brushes and paints, the elder of them peeking from behind a canvas with a fool's grin.

'How exquisite!' he says. 'Eh, Harris?'

'I have the honour it seems,' says Aran, 'to present Lord Lempster. Lieutenant Harris too. Both of Handasyde's Regiment, I collect. And this, my good sirs, is Mistress Bradley. Miss Byrom, I assume, you have already met.'

There follows an excessive fondling of Rosina's hand. Beppy has already mentioned Lempster, naturally. The pampered eldest son of the Earl of Pomfret. They are delighted, of course. But Mistress Bradley? Let them see. The wife of the Court Leet fellow? Oh, admirable.

Are they mocking me? she thinks. *Those supercilious smiles. The barely concealed amusement.*

'And should you not be away catching those villainous rebels, gentlemen?' Rosina asks, with as much sarcasm as she can muster.

'We can safely leave those grubbing *devoirs* to the Duke's Flying Column for the moment, I think,' Lempster replies. 'Though we enjoyed good sport yesterday. Some of the dragoons brought in a turnpike man who had practised upon us. The devil attempted to set us on the wrong road, madam. Can you credit such a thing? We hanged him for a Jacobite dog, you will be pleased to know.'

'A heroic deed, Captain, to be sure,' says Aran. 'And where is this Flying Column now, exactly?'

'At Wigan, Mister Owen. There has been some damnable rumour that the French have landed on the south coast. Nonsense, of course. For there is no Jacobite army near to meet them, now that the rabble has run north again. And the French will not fight without gold to grease their palms.'

Rosina sees her mother again, clinging to those food sacks as her cart kicked upon the sandstone slabs of the bridge to Salford, the same that Beppy had so heroically saved from destruction. *When was that? It seems so long ago.*

'A rumour, sir,' says Beppy. 'Then why are you not about your business?'

Beppy, poor dear, still believes that this whole thing is a ruse on the Prince's part. That he shall draw Cumberland north to Lancaster, defeat him there, and then return to free us once again.

'The Duke merely needs to confirm that the rumour is no more than that, my dear. Though it cannot be otherwise, for we have left Admiral Vernon to guard the Channel. No Frenchman shall slip through, you may depend upon it. But come, Harris, these ladies are correct and there is still work to be done. Bid you good morning, ladies. And you, Mister Owen. Admirable work, sir. Admirable.'

Rosina somehow regrets their departure, for she must now confront Aran with her guilt. But she is confused by the anguish that he so evidently displays. She had expected anger. Perhaps coldness and a refusal to speak with her at all. Yet he seems more distressed than anything else.

'Dear Rosina,' he says, 'I see that you expect me to reproach you. And, indeed, I might have done so most vehemently. For I still cannot believe that you would cause this tragedy to befall your Mama. But I find that I owe you a certain loyalty too. More than you may deserve, I think. Yet there is misery upon misery here, I fear.' He produces a folded note from his pocket. 'It is your Uncle Josiah. An accident, it seems. A fatal accident.'

The truth is that she has never been especially close to her father's older brother, has never really known him as Aran has done. But it is another of God's punishments for her wickedness and she feels her face crumple uncontrollably, Beppy's arm about her shoulders.

'Does my father...?'

'I fear not, my dear,' says Aran. 'The message arrived at your father's house after he had left for the north. And your mother, of course... Well, I shall arrange for an express to follow him without delay, though I suspect that none of us shall reach Llanffynon for the funeral.'

'And your cousin, the dashing spy, he was acquainted with Uncle Josiah also, I collect?'

'Yes, my dear. To be frank, I had wondered whether there might be some connection. But if, as I suspect, your father comes up with him, I am certain that he will convey an appropriate message to the fellow. And you should know, Rosina, that he is not *truly* my cousin. The link between us is considerably more remote than he will have given you to understand.'

'Indeed? He intimated a degree of intimacy between you. And so far as my uncle is concerned, I had almost imagined that you would have mounted a charger and delivered the message to my father in person, taking the excuse to attempt Mama's rescue yourself, Aran. Indeed, I had almost hoped that you would do so.'

'Your father quite properly sees it as his peculiar responsibility. I have rarely seen a man driven by so many disparate causes towards one singular purpose. You may not know, for instance, that Susannah Cole has emptied the bawdy-house coffers and absconded with the proceeds to become a camp follower of the Prince Regent's army. But his main goal, of course, is to save Maria-Louise from whatever cruel fate awaits her. No, I offered to accompany him but he would not permit the thing.'

'Aran, my friend!' cries Beppy. 'Thou cannot believe that Rosina's Mama faces any true threat?'

My mother has always believed that she is fated to die young. Though I never imagined that I might be the instrument of her premature downfall. I have prayed to Our Lady that she should allow me this week over again, but the scale of my evil apparently surpasses all hope of redemption.

'You may discern from Rosina's reaction that she fully understands the danger of her Mama's predicament. I have never known above one reward for those convicted of treason though, God knows, as I do also, and only too well, that she should not be standing alone to face that charge!'

What then? Is Aran aware that others were involved with my mother in this thing? Yet he will not be drawn further and Rosina has more pressing matters to pursue. For she has not seen Elizabeth Cooper, either, since her return from Droylsden and the one attempt to visit her *inamorata* has been met simply by Crableck's insistence that his mistress was indisposed.

So she persuades Beppy to one further favour, to accompany Rosina on a visit to the coffee house at a time when she is certain to find Elizabeth there. Just a little after noon, as it happens, on a day so cold, the worst of the year so far, that it claws at her face, freezes her brain to such a robin's egg blue that she can barely think. Their arrival at Crableck's high desk, the payment of their pennies, exposes them to a heat that shocks their numbed systems to quaking resurrection and the momentary illusion that the sudden warmth emanates from Elizabeth's flushed welcome.

'Ladies,' she says, from a table of uniformed customers, 'you have arrived in time to share this revelation with us. See, the latest copy of Mister Scatterbuck's *Journal*. But Crableck, do I not reward you enough to ensure that my customers receive the beverage for which they have paid so handsomely?'

The crook-back mutters some comment and climbs down from his perch to take their orders. A dish of chocolate for each of them, please. And they are drawn to study Scatterbuck's new editorial.

The EDITOR was witness, on the tenth instant, Tuesday last, to the remarkable good order in which His Royal Highness departed this town for the more northerly parts of Lancashire County where, we hear, he shall give battle to the regiments of the Usurper's son, William Augustus, Duke of Cumberland. This demonstration of fine conduct must contrast strongly with the wicked behaviour exhibited by a small number of Manchester's residents who discharged firearms in the most cowardly fashion against the innocent and marching Scotsmen and who murder'd butcher Cringle, mistaking him for a Highlander. The Prince Regent's forces number'd full ten thousand and would be united at Lancaster with a second army of those loyal patriots formerly exiled in France, at which time the entire course of this present conflict shall be resolv'd. His Royal Highness was pleas'd to acknowledge all those additional volunteers who have swelled the ranks of our own Manchester Regiment, as well as the presence of Mistress Redmond, wife of the illustrious Titus Redmond, Esquire, who shall remain a guest in the household of the Prince of Wales at least so far as Lancaster. The EDITOR takes no responsibility for the veracity of any detail included in this column.

'There!' whispers Beppy. 'Did I not tell you? We shall settle with Cumberland once and for all.'

'La! Miss Byrom,' says Elizabeth, 'what a fancy you have. Inherited your father's flair for imagination and gullibility both, I see. I rather recall that Mister Scatterbuck utilised this same disclaimer when he announced the impending performance of the Bottle-Conjuror. I expect a similar level of accuracy in this present prediction. Do you not see that the town is now brimming with the armies of King George? And here, see, the officers of Sir Edward Stanley's Lancashire Regiment of Militia, come to our protection at last.'

'And do I merit no greeting from you, Elizabeth?' Rosina says.

'My dearest! Of course. A fie upon me for my excitement. Yet how *should* I greet you, my sweet? With reverence, as the honoured daughter of the woman who, it seems, has thwarted this evil rebellion single-handed? Or with disdain, as the person who has caused our recently beatified Saint Maria-Louise to be martyred upon the heathen Jacobite altar. *Guest in the household of the Prince of Wales* indeed!'

'In either case,' says Rosina, 'I do not see how this affects our own relationship. I bear such a weight of guilt for my deeds. Yet I should have thought your own affiliation to cause you satisfaction at this state of affairs, you having so little regard for my mother besides.'

'I am only pleased, dear heart, that you did not find cause to damn *me*! If you could sell your own mother in such a way...'

Crableck fetches the chocolate, although Rosina finds that she is barely able to hold the *saucière* for the trembling of her fingers. *This behaviour of Elizabeth's must pass, surely. She loves me. I know it!* But they are joined by an exceedingly handsome young Ensign.

'Ladies!' he says. 'How perfectly charming. Might I have the pleasure, Mistress Cooper?'

'Indeed you may,' says Elizabeth and, to Rosina's surprise, in her most flirtatious tone. 'Please allow me to name Miss Elizabeth Byrom, daughter of the town's most eminent author. And Mistress Rosina Bradley, wife to the Leader of our Court Leet, daughter to Mister Titus Redmond, our most illustrious merchant. Daughter too, I should say, to the dear woman who has so recently been taken hostage by the Pretender's *banditti*.'

'Then have no fear, madam. We shall lay them by the heels shortly and restore your mother without procrastination.'

'You do not fear the Highlanders then, sir?' says Beppy. 'Might you not face the same fate as General Cope?'

'Bless you, miss. The Duke has more Highlanders in arms against the Prince than those who march at his side. The Black Watch. The Royal Scots. The Sixty-Fourth Foot.'

'And most of these so loyal,' says Rosina, 'that the Duke of Cumberland must keep them in reserve, we hear, fearing to have them face their countrymen in open battle.'

'Ah,' says the officer, his melodious voice assuming a note of gravity and regret, 'I perceive that your sympathies lie elsewhere. Yet those same regiments were crucial to the defence of London when it seemed as though the *Chevalier* might dare an advance on the capital. Now that the threat is past, I am sure that His Grace will bring them up. Alas, that may signal the end of this pleasant vacation in your town. Very pleasant indeed.'

Rosina is surprised to see that he turns to catch Elizabeth's eye, that some intimacy passes between them.

'But you are from the County too, sir, I collect,' says Rosina.

'Almost a neighbour, Mistress Bradley. I am your servant, madam.

Ensign Harry Tobin of the Lancashire Militia's Warrington Company.'

The fellow bends his knee, an elegant gesture that almost distracts Rosina from the look of amusement that lights Elizabeth's face as she gazes towards the door.

'By God's Hooks,' she hears her husband's unmistakeable tone behind her, 'it is cold enough to freeze the balls from a brass monkey! Give you joy... Aaah!' Bradley is still removing his redingote and a long woollen muffler when he sees her. 'You are well, my dear? Your colour is somewhat improved from our last encounter. Life with the Byroms must agree with you, I think.'

'And should you care, sir, if it did not?'

'Not excessively.'

'I am surprised to find you still in town, sirrah. From your outrage at my deeds I should have supposed that you would take horse and bring Mama safe back to your trysting place. Or do you, like Mister Owen, have some plausible reason to leave her rescue for others to perform?'

'Aran Owen, you say? Why, I was thinking about him only earlier. I recalled the dinner during your Naming Day, when the fellow almost choked on the pickled walnut at Sir Edward's mention of friends here in Manchester who had helped to ditch your Jacobite Cause. It was your Mama it seems, and your dear friend, loyal Aran Owen, knew it all along!'

But Rosina is no longer listening. She has dashed the dish of chocolate to the floor and, with a final glance backwards at Elizabeth's sardonic smile, she sweeps out to the more welcome bitterness of Market Street Lane.

If she was ever going to resume her infatuation with the opiate, it would have been tonight. The incontrollable trembling, the vicious stabbing pains in her stomach, the feverish sweats, begin again and Beppy, dearest Beppy, spends most of the darkest hours at her side, bathing her forehead and soothing her fears.

Late in the following morning, it is the fourteenth day of December today, a Saturday, she takes some gruel. She knows that she must appear frightful but there is no time to undertake her *toilette* before the Byroms' front door is almost beaten to the ground by somebody hammering for entrance.

'Open, in the name of the King!' echoes through the house.

'What can it mean?' says Beppy and they huddle in trepidation near the kitchen fire while the servants run hither and thither and the sound of military boots fills each passage and staircase.

Voices in the reception hall. Beppy's mother and father demanding to know the meaning of this intrusion. Lord Lempster's primped response. An apology of sorts. No time to advise them beforehand. No cause for alarm. But they are to receive a visitor.

Curiosity entices the young women from the confines of the kitchen, though each is still dressed in bedshirt and winter nightgown. Yet only Mister Byrom himself seems concerned at their attire. Neither Lord Lempster nor

Lieutenant Harris spares them even a second glance, being much preoccupied with arranging their redcoats in proper order.

'My dears,' Byrom says, 'you are undressed, *négligées*, unfit for polite society!'

'In my wildest dreams, Papa, I could never have described such an invasion of our privacy as *polite*. La! There is a sentry at every door and turning. Pray, what is happening? I had thought us all arrested for sedition.'

'Do not say such things, Beppy!' cries her mother. 'I am sure that there is a reasonable explanation.'

'Explanation?' says Aran Owen, who has appeared at the end of the corridor, also now posted with a redcoat, leading to the Academy rooms, paint brush still in hand and his shirt sleeve daubed with a stain of yellow ochre. 'My goodness, I see! I would give you joy of the morning, ladies, Mister Byrom, but my instincts tell me that I should wait to see what transpires next from this tableau.'

His sentence is not complete before further disturbance out on Hanging Ditch announces the arrival of their intruder.

Prince William, Duke of Cumberland, Marquess of Berkhamstead, Earl of Kennington, Viscount of Trematon, and Baron of Alderney Isle. Younger brother to the unpopular Frederick, Prince of Wales. The *other* Prince of Wales. William is an educated man, they say, tutored by Halley and Fountaine, amongst others.

A *coterie* of senior officers follow him across the Byroms' threshold.

'Your grace!' says Byrom, bowing low, his wife offering a curtsy.

'Mister Byrom. So good to see you again, sir.'

Rosina had forgotten how frequently her friend's father had been a guest at the Usurper's Court and this young Prince seems genuinely pleased to renew their acquaintance. *How old is he?* she wonders. *Only a few years my senior, I collect. Twenty-four, perhaps? Twenty-five?* Comparisons with Charles Edward are impossible to avoid. Similar height, she supposes, but this Cumberland carries more weight, a pugnacity in place of the Prince Regent's dash and elegance. Eyes piercing blue rather than Charles Edward's bovine brown. But they share that sense of breeding from Continental stock, an alien quality, natural perhaps for a second son from the coupling of Hanoverian George with Brandenburger Caroline of Ansbach. *And, to speak of coupling, there had been that strange rumour that she and Mister Byrom had once...*

'Yet I may hardly dare to think that we owe your most welcome attentions simply to the revival of past familiarities. Though I am remiss, Your Grace. My wife you already know, of course. And this, my daughter, *also* Elizabeth. You must forgive the negligence of her attire, I fear. This other lady, too. Mistress Bradley.'

Rosina is awed by Cumberland's presence, despite herself. She had expected a weaker man, this general defeated at Fontenoy, had assumed him merely a pale imitation of his father, George the Second, who had at least succeeded in leading *his* armies to English victory at Dettingen.

'Bradley? A common name in Manchester, it seems,' says the Duke. 'But no, Mister Byrom. Pleasant as this interlude may be, I have come to seek a more exotic commodity. *That* fellow, I think!' He raises the royal arm and points a thick finger towards Aran Owen. 'The painter, I assume?'

'Indeed, Your Grace,' says Lempster.

Cumberland places his hand upon the top of his powdered wig, rubs vigorously at whatever creatures may live beneath it.

'Extraordinary!' he says. 'Ligonier, are you *sure* about this?'

Lieutenant-General Sir John Ligonier, born in France to a Huguenot family, émigrés to England at the close of the previous century. He is well into his sixties, horse-faced, hog-jowelled and apparently ailing.

'His Majesty's dispatch was quite specific, Your Grace,' he says.

'Very well,' says Cumberland, 'if we *must!* Mister Byrom, I would inspect the work being undertaken by this artist of yours, if you please. His name?'

'Mister Owen, Your Grace, though...'

'Lead on then, sir,' Cumberland says to Aran. 'As pretty as you please, Mister Owen. We have traitors to pursue.'

Rosina feels the familiar anger rise within her.

'And shall you hang them all when they are apprehended, Your Grace, like the poor turnpike-keeper at Warrington?'

'This town has a fine packet of Jacobites, eh Byrom? They call us usurpers yet react in outrage when we defend the lawful governance bestowed on us and which, they themselves contest, we hold so tenuously. It never occurs to them that the more they deem us usurpers, the less quarter they shall receive for their treasonous rebellion.' Cumberland sweeps past Rosina contemptuously, following a confused Aran Owen along the passage to the Academy rooms. 'I am told that the old printer, Scatterbuck, squealed like a gutted pig when we smashed his presses this morning.'

Aran stops.

'Adam Scatterbuck?' he says. 'You smashed his press, sir?'

'Indeed, Mister Owen,' says Ligonier, 'and turned out the families of every officer in this so-called Manchester Regiment onto the streets in the bargain. Do you object, sir? Are you another of these damned Jacobites?'

'I was apprenticed to Mister Scatterbuck, Your Grace. He is a kind man, though sometimes prone to foolish enthusiasms. And, yes, for my own part I share many of his beliefs.'

'Then you have been the Jacobites' apprentice too long, sir. Time now to serve as journeyman to the Crown, perhaps. Let me see your work, Mister Owen.'

So the entire party enters the salon where Aran's six canvasses stand upon their easels.

The first is well advanced, the panorama of all Manchester, imagined from a point above and to the south of the Commodities Exchange, its proportions exaggerated slightly to flatter the Court Leet, and the town's various churches arranged at the cardinal points to add symmetry. Acres Field provides a perspective that leads the eye towards the picture's central feature, and the foreground corners are decorated with assorted livestock, tidied from the streets to the outlying pastures for the sake of this invention, and that porker in their midst with the strangely human features. Cumberland glances involuntarily at Ligonier when he sees the beast, but then touches his finger to the Prussian pigment with which Aran has so recently begun to add background depth within his sky. The royal digit comes away blue.

'Still wet, Your Grace,' says Aran, taking a cloth from the table, next to the turpentine pot that hold his brushes, the liquid stained to the same shade and filling the room with its heady aroma.

Cumberland cleans his hand.

'And these others,' he says. 'This one must be the Court Leet Jurors themselves, I collect. You are a fine portraitist, I see.' He peers closely at the detail, passes to each of the remaining four with their charcoal outlines sketched onto the dried *gesso* and the first flashes of colour beginning to bring the allegories to life. 'Are you a student of Mister Hogarth, I wonder?'

'Hardly a student, Your Grace. As you must have gathered, I am largely self-taught and my trade did not prepare me for this work. But I had the fortune to once examine a likeness of his *Rake's Progress* at our school library, at Chetham's, sir.'

'And you admire him, Mister Owen?'

'Indeed, sir. He is exceptionally gifted, I believe.'

'No, sir. He is a rogue, sir. His Majesty commissioned the fellow to depict the glory of our forces, Mister Owen. Glory, sir! It is common enough upon the Continent to celebrate martial prowess in such a way. But here? In these damp islands it is all trumpery and trivialities. Hounds and horses, sir. Yet Mister Hogarth seemed of a different stamp. At least, until His Majesty saw the cartoons. They will not answer, sir. He attended at Tottenham Court Road when the Guards were assembled for Finchley and took some sketches. Submitted them as though the Court should approve. Damn the fellow. They are burlesques, sir. Burlesques!'

'You could have him hanged in place of his pictures perhaps, Your Grace,' says Rosina. 'Though I hear that, more inventively, your men have become fond of tying prisoners to their horses' tails and dragging them to their death. What better punishment for a recalcitrant artist than execution by horse-hair!'

'You speak nonsense, girl,' says Cumberland. 'But, in any case, we cannot use Hogarth now for this noble purpose. And we have no decent artist at our immediate disposal, Mister Owen. I should have rather chosen Monamy but the fellow will only paint ships. You will have to suffice, sir.'

'Suffice, Your Grace. As what?'

'Have I not explained myself already, sir? Must I spell the thing for you? As my propagandist, of course. It shall be *your* paintings, Mister Owen, that will have the honour of recording our achievements in the forthcoming campaign.'

For a moment, Rosina assumes that Aran must surely refuse. Yet she knows he may not, in truth, do so. And, in a moment of impulsive weakness, she decides to take matters into her own hands. It may not be a decisive act such as Beppy's raising of the alarm to save the Irwell Bridge, but there is satisfaction of sorts derived from her clumsy stumble against Cumberland's side, the collision of her fist with the turpentine pot, and the thinned Prussian blue stain that so permanently ruins the Duke's immaculate white breeches.

Later, with Aran allowed only enough time to gather his equipment and some possessions from his lodging, and then marched to Ligonier's headquarters at the Angel, Rosina confesses to Beppy that she may have been foolish to visit Elizabeth yesterday when there were so many customers in the coffee house. Surely better, she argues, to catch her when the premises are closed.

So she spends the afternoon, that cold Saturday afternoon, washing every trace of stale sweat from her person, applying her powders, dressing her hair and smoothing the few clothes that she has so far been able to bring from Bradley's house. She borrows a heavy outdoor coat from Beppy and, at the proper time, she cuts along Pool Fold, across the Market Place, and knocks gently on the coffee house door. There is only a single candle lit within but, by its weak light, she sees Crableck coming to open for her.

Elizabeth shall at least be pleased that I have now passed two full days without a drop of Sydenham's, she thinks, as Crableck slides the bolts.

He says nothing, smiles enigmatically, gestures towards the stairs that lead to Mistress Cooper's private rooms, those same that Rosina has come to know so well.

She gathers her skirts, climbs to the top of the flight, and quietly opens the door to Elizabeth's parlour.

I have made my confession to Father Scobie, she thinks, recalling her visit to the partly restored room in Roman Entry. *I have disclosed my sin. I have shown contrition. Yet it is never sufficient. We sin and, as Catholics, we pay the price for our guilt. We pay the penance. My mother is taken, though I cannot blame Our Lord for that particular. My father cannot bear to speak to me. My husband turns me out of the house that I have shared with him. I am abused by my former friends. Elizabeth humiliates me in public. My friend Beppy must be punished for supporting me. My Uncle Josiah is dead. Aran Owen is taken for Cumberland's personal artist. And now this! No, confession is never enough.*

Elizabeth Cooper lies spread upon the couch. Her left hand rests, palm upwards across the lower part of her face, the fourth finger, sporting the bride's pie glass ring, gripped in ecstasy between her perfect white teeth. She is wearing the blue silk dress that Rosina had worn for the wedding and which she had last seen, of course, in her closet at Bradley's house. Her bridal attire. *It will crease so badly*, thinks Rosina, seeing the way that the material is pulled up across Elizabeth's naked belly and nether regions, her pale stockings pulled down to her shins. Her legs are spread so wickedly of course and there, between them, with his hand – no, *her* hand – thrust deep within Elizabeth's quim, kneels the person previously introduced to her as Ensign Harry Tobin.

Chapter Fifty-One

'You shall never succeed in shifting the thing,' shouts his wife, against the driving rain and the torrent's roar, 'with my additional weight to hinder you!'

Titus struggles to keep his footing, clutching the wagon's side to prevent himself being swept away by the deep and dark waters of Bannisdale Beck. Its brown and foaming current rises above his weight, snatching at his coat as he tries to get a grip upon the spokes while two drivers whip the four horses, urging them towards the steep bank on the farther side. Still more fellows drag at the bridles, splashing and stumbling backwards with every tentative movement of the wheels.

'I should prefer that you stay there, my dear,' he calls. 'We shall have you out of this in a trice!'

It is a foul day and the army has left Kendal early. The lick-spittle locals have torn up the Orton Road, so the main column has taken the narrow and possibly treacherous road to Shap. But the challenge seems, at least, to have animated the Prince and he has led them off, on foot, crying encouragements and two pipers at his heel.

The baggage and the artillery, however, present a different problem, for the picquets have confirmed that the Shap road simply cannot accommodate them. So they have waited at the rear, under the command of Lord George Murray with the Manchester Regiment and the Glengarry MacDonalds for escort, then followed northwards so far as Garnett Bridge, where they cross the Sprint but soon take their own route over the older drove road that skirts Whiteside Pike.

All has gone well until they reached this raging stream, made more difficult by the sharply twisting approach. Lord George has instructed that the horses for each cart or wagon should be twinned with another pair, doubling their pulling power but, even so, various Manchester volunteers have now spent two hours already immersed in the icy depths, while the Highlanders either call encouragement or impatient insult. It is difficult to distinguish in the Gaelic. Tempers rise as those willingly engaged with the struggle become increasingly frustrated by those who refuse the task, and a sullen silence has fallen between the two groups as, well into the afternoon, with the final gun hauled up to safety, they take whatever shelter from the elements that may be available to them so that they can eat some bread.

'You should not risk your life in that way,' says Maria-Louise. They are eating alone for few of the Manchester men will even waste spit on her any more. 'It is perfectly foolish and you shall freeze, sir. I have caused you such a burden, dear Titus!'

If I was honest, I should have to admit that you were not my primary concern. Not at first, that is.

He had been astonished, incredulous, when Rosina had made her allegations, certain that Maria-Louise would deny this infamy. But she had not done so. And his emotions had been confused. Betrayal by virtue of his wife's failure to share her guilty secret with him. Shame occasioned by his public humiliation, all the work undertaken on behalf of the Jacobite Cause shattered in that one revelation. Paternal incompetence that his daughter should have been so easily infected both by tribady and betrayal. Self-righteous indignation that taunts his manhood with the thought that Maria-Louise had shared her sedition with Bradley, perhaps even shared complicity with him. And impotence, fuelled by his inability to influence the outcome despite being in his own home, the small palace built through such tireless dedication to his enterprise.

The impotence had driven him to dialogue with his old companion, the geneva jug, and the jug had suggested a visit to the whore-house that his humours might be restored. But the place had been almost deserted, Susannah Cole having vanished along with most of his doxies and the proceeds of their labours. So he had sat there brooding until late in the evening before it occurred to him, first, that the bawd could only have gone with the army and, second, that somewhere within the column he would find the Ranger, Lieutenant Owen, now become the epitome of every evil that has ever befallen him.

Titus had staggered back to Market Street Lane, given instructions to O'Farrell for the girls' care, scribbled a note for Aran Owen concerning the business, packed a valise and taken himself to the Livery to hire another beast. The town had still been fraught with its own anxieties, opposing gangs wandering the streets, torches a-blaze, and the name of the murdered Salford butcher, Mister Cringle, on every Jacobite lip, the foolish fellow having decided to march alongside Lochiel's Camerons a while and been shot by a zealous Whig marksman for his troubles. But Titus weaves a path between them all, slumbering in his saddle despite the ice and snow, astonished to find himself, in the morning, fifteen miles away in Wigan.

'More foolish than you can imagine, wife,' he says. 'Would you believe me, madam, if I told you that I feel free from burden for the first time in more years than I care to remember?'

He had stopped in Wigan for most of the day. For one thing, his hopes of finding Susannah Cole or Lieutenant Owen seemed shattered. He had thought to find one cohesive body encamped as they had been in Preston or billeted in the fashion of their quarters at Manchester. But the army's cantonments here had been scattered from Leigh in the west, through Wigan itself, and so far as Standish in the east. His two quarries could have been almost anywhere, though he suspected that the bawd, at least, would not venture far from Townley's Regiment.

His enquiries had eventually persuaded him that Townley was long gone, however, on the road to Preston, so Titus had followed and, in the process, begun to consider his wife's crime afresh.

'Do you know, sir,' she says to him, 'that I feel the same? I cannot remember ever being cold for so long, and the damp is eating at my flesh faster than the fleas in this blanket.' She adjusts the plaid around her shoulders. One of the Highlanders has gifted her the garment. It is so alive with vermin that Titus almost imagines the chequered wool to have shifted of its own accord. 'Yet I am not troubled here by anything except my bodily discomforts. I feel no guilt at my actions, my dear. And, while the blame is all my own, you must believe that some part of me imagined that my deed would be a blessing for our Cause, not its curse.'

He had come to the same conclusion on that road from Wigan to Preston.

How many times, he had thought, *have we both damn'd the principle of French intervention? I have encouraged this thing. I willingly shared the information with my wife about the Prince's plans for the Exchequer's transport. It was Titus Redmond who placed this weight upon his wife.*

The army had camped in its old ground to the south of the Ribble and remained there all through the following day.

A Thursday. That must have been the twelfth, I think.

There had been talk of the Prince standing here to fight. Then news of the Duke of Perth taken ill and sent north in a carriage with some of Bagot's Hussars and the Company of Rangers so that he might make contact with the considerable Jacobite forces now in Scotland and, perhaps, effect their conjunction.

That cunny-sucker has escaped me again, it seems! Titus had thought.

But he had at least succeeded in renewing his acquaintance with O'Sullivan, pleaded his wife's case and sought leave to visit with her. Been refused. Any vestige of former amiability between the two men now quite lost. Might he petition the Prince perhaps? He could petition God Almighty but it would change nothing. The traitor was safely ensconced in Preston's House of Correction and there she would stay until His Royal Highness chose whether to remain or to proceed.

He had passed the House of Correction on his previous visit to Preston and had journeyed there again now, to the town's eastern edge where, although unable to see Maria-Louise herself, the gaol being more formidable than he remembered, he had at least provided some garnish to the cell-keepers so that she would receive additional food, a little warmth.

'I know it,' he says, as the artillery and baggage column prepares to resume its journey. 'It is a pity though that Rosina did not also trouble to consider your motives before condemning you to this fate, my love!'

Fate? It had been fate, certainly, that led him to find the Manchester Regiment's canvas, the spare tents that they had allocated for their pleasures and the thin line of fellows waiting to take their turn at the bulk-mongers within. The weather being so cold, he could have passed for anybody, his redingote tight about him and a muffler around his face until, finally, he had come to the front of the queue. He had ducked through the flap, found Susannah Cole within, adjusting herself from the previous customer, greeting him with her usual prattle and prices until, inevitably, she had recognised his eyes. But by then his hands were about her throat. *Thieving bitch*, he had said. *No Billy Bender to protect you here, Suzie. By choice I would feed you to the pigs as well!*

He had his money back at least, and a little more besides. Enough to pay for decent lodgings in the town. Enough perhaps to provide a decent bribe for his wife's freedom. If only the right person could be found. Strickland perhaps? Mister Gibb? He would work on it.

'And what, precisely,' says Maria-Louise, 'do you consider shall be my fate? Shall they hang me, do you think? It is a long and cruel road that they make me take simply to release me at its furthest end.'

'It is a curious obsession that you have, wife, with the possibility of dying young. Why, do you not know that you shall be forty next year? There must come a point, surely, when you can no longer flatter yourself with this illusion! We should ask Colonel Grant his opinion on the matter. He understands your Irish ways better than me.'

Grant has come to check that all is ready. It is thanks to him that Titus is allowed to accompany Maria-Louise in this way. For they had taken a liking to each other from the moment of their first meeting at the Mitre back in November and, at Lancaster, when it had been clear that she would be attached to the baggage and artillery train, he had gone to seek out Colonel James Grant, now Baron of Iverk, and begged this favour from him. Grant had been only too obliging. He had already ensured that she should be treated with all possible dignity and spent time with Mistress Redmond, recalling the friendship between his own people and the neighbouring FitzWilliam family, reminiscences of her father. Grant had subsequently spoken with Lord George, told him how O'Sullivan had dismissed Redmond's request already, and such was the animosity between these two commanders that Murray had readily agreed to Titus remaining near to his wife.

'Quite ready, Colonel Grant, I thank you,' says Maria-Louise. 'Such comfort and quality of fare that I could quite imagine myself at home here.'

Grant offers his usual apology and, over the next hour, as they slide and ooze their way north, the Colonel's artillery officers come to check that she is well. The Aberdeen Captain, Burnet. And the Frenchmen. Du Saussey. Bodin. D'Andrion.

Yes, the Frenchmen. Another cunny-sucking irony!

The afternoon is interminable. Impossible to get dry after his soaking this morning, the shivering damp dragging at his back, his shoulders, his arms, his numb fingers.

The dark rain of Lancaster seems almost a pleasant memory. The army had been scattered there again, called chaotically together with rumours that Major General James Oglethorpe's considerable cavalry had arrived in Preston, just behind them, having completed a prodigious cross-Pennine one hundred mile march from Barnsley in less than three days. But when some of Oglethorpe's green-clad troopers had been captured and brought to camp, they were poor specimens on spent horses. So the regiments had been stood down, dispersed again until, almost immediately, they were called together once more, on the high ground south of Lancaster where they will fight Cumberland at last.

'Good ground,' Grant had said to him. 'Good timing too. Cumberland still has fewer men than us and half of them cavalry. This is our chance to defeat the devil, Redmond!'

But they had not fought. No further sign of Cumberland's army. Simply a solitary rider. A messenger, bringing the express from Aran and news of Josiah's death.

'Do you think my brother will forgive me?' Titus says, gripping the cart shaft and plodding resolutely through the gathering snow, his mount abandoned back in Lancaster.

'For failing to attend his funeral?' she replies, shouting above the gathering breeze. 'I think that Josiah should expect you to be precisely here, with your wife. He would approve, I protest.'

'I was thinking rather that the poor fellow might not have died if I had caught up with this Lieutenant Owen earlier.'

She looks unduly shocked each time I mention the cove. Why is that?

'You are developing an ague, I fear,' says Maria-Louise. 'How can you place blame on the fellow when, so far as you tell me, he has been with the Prince's army these many weeks past.'

'That which we sometimes describe as feverish rambling will always contain a germ of reality. It takes the merest assumption that this fellow may be a *double* agent, does it not?' The wind carries away his words. 'I think that he is a *double agent*,' Titus repeats, louder now. 'Newcastle's agent. Sent to Manchester and thwarted our attempt upon the Excise duty. Come face to face with Jacob Driscoll on Chat Moss. Then myself at Mother Blossom's. Jacob again at Liskard Moor, somehow. Kills him there. Discovers my family's history. Needs to insinuate himself with the right people. But cannot do so through Manchester. But he knows of Josiah. Makes a link through him to

Sir Watkin. He is trusted. Works his way into O'Sullivan's confidence. Joins this Company of Rangers. And I pass him, by chance, in Preston. On his way to take dispatches for Sir Watkin. Of whom we hear no more. His Welshmen disappear without trace too. Then Attorney Morgan is taken. Yet this damn'd Lieutenant arrives safe enough in Derby. Just in time to persuade His Royal Highness that he should abandon his attempt on London. And, within days, my brother is dead. Another link to this fellow closed forever.'

He had tried to explain all of this to O'Sullivan when they arrived in Kendal the previous night, for the Irishman was in session with the Prince and, to Titus Redmond's surprise, his request for an audience had been granted. He had been ushered into the Prince Regent's presence to find him sharing a bottle of his favourite muscatel with the Quartermaster-General. O'Sullivan had been dismissive, however, aggressive in fact, although Charles Edward had listened carefully enough, patiently attending each line of argument that Mistress Redmond's actions had been undertaken with the best of intent while this Lieutenant of Rangers...

A waste of breath. The Company of Rangers is under the command of Sir John MacDonald, a most capable fellow whose troopers are all Chosen Men. Beyond reproach or suspicion. And as for Mistress Redmond, she will face a military court when they finally reach Carlisle.

'Do you understand, Mister Redmond?' the Prince had said to him. 'Can you possibly comprehend the damage that your wife has done to our Cause? King Louis has promised us support a-plenty. Yet our father had insisted that any such assistance must be the subject of a commercial arrangement. That King Louis must not act unless payment was made. And do you know why, sir? It is because His Majesty King James the Third, shares precisely the same fear as your wife. He does not altogether trust French motives either. But with a hired army, a mercenary force, he should feel more secure. And now, with the Vatican silver lost? Oh, cousin Louis will still send help, we are certain. And we must ensure that it is used wisely. But it will be modest help, Mister Bradley. And we fear that it may not be sufficient for our purpose. It is your wife, sir, who has created this jeopardy and she must answer for it. In the meanwhile, of course, we will continue to ensure that she is treated as decently as may be possible in these difficult circumstances. But if you will forgive us, we have the pressing question of horse shoes to be resolved.'

Titus, naturally, has only relayed the first part of this response to his wife.

'I could hardly blame His Royal Highness,' says Maria-Louise, 'for dismissing your opinion, my dear. The idea that one man could have been responsible for so many misfortunes, for the disappearance of the whole Welsh regiment, for causing the army's entire retreat seems fanciful even to your *wife*, sir!'

Darkness has fallen as they arrive at a cluster of buildings, an abandoned farm or settlement, alongside the drove road on this higher section of fells before it drops down towards Borrowdale. The ruins do not provide great shelter but they are better than the alternative.

Some of the Glengarry men beckon for them to share their meagre accommodation, and there must be fifty of them packed into one tiny space. They chat in the sibilant melody of their native tongue. Fires are lit. Meagre rations are shared. Some blankets too. And Titus is able to peel off his breeches to dry them, dozing with Maria-Louise huddled against him while a fine billow of steam builds and, outside, the snow thickens and whips around the door-posts.

Lanthorns. The officers' inspections. Townley taking his turn at the rounds.

'Ah, so this is where you hide,' he says. 'These Scots likely do not understand the hazard that they harbour in their midst. Yet I am surprised to see you here too, Titus. When this creature was revealed as the Whore of Babylon, I thought that you had forsaken her. Finally, I thought. My old friend has seen the truth of this woman.'

Townley's cheeks are sunken, his face drawn, his eyes somewhat crazed. *And with those crook-raked teeth, he looks like a hunted hare.*

'You should do better, Francis, to spend time seeking your missing men. It shames us both, I think, that you have already lost a full third of those who volunteered to list in Manchester.'

'Shame? You speak of shame when this harlot has brought such damage upon us. If she had not betrayed us, the Prince would have had enough gold at his disposal to finance a French invasion five times over. Our allies would have landed and the road to London been unblocked. Instead of this... This disgrace!'

'The French would have been perfidious friends, sir. And the only disgrace is that I have allowed you to call my wife harlot and whore so many times and allowed you to live, Francis Townley. Do not repeat your mistake, sir!'

'Old fool! I said that you were a spent force once before but *now* look at you. Breeks warming at the fire. Your rooster's legs wrinkled and wrapped in a blanket. What price your moustache now, Titus Redmond? You still hope to be accepted as a burgess? To shave the foolish thing in celebration? You should think again, sir. There shall never be a Catholic burgess while Hanover holds the throne. And if we fail to wrest it from him, the fault shall fall to your wife. And you will always be a pariah so long as you adhere to this woman. Think yourself fortunate, Titus, that you shall be rid of her soon. For in Carlisle we shall see her hung. The whole Manchester Regiment has petitioned to have it so!'

'Then the whole Manchester Regiment shall be damn'd to Hell, Townley. And you shall lead them there unless I am much mistaken.'

They sleep little when Townley is gone, Maria-Louise weeping softly against her husband's arm, while Titus imagines the retribution that he might pour on the cunny-sucker's head. If only he had the strength. For the meanwhile, he satisfies himself by pulling a large thorn from his buttocks.

But I need whatever strength remains to me, he thinks, *for what I must attempt tomorrow. If Townley believes that I would leave her to hang...*

In the morning of the seventeenth, they are roused before daybreak. Lord George has sent out scouts all along Borrowdale to purchase as many smaller carts as they are able while the existing wagons and the field pieces are trundled over the thickening ice down towards the Borrow Beck. It is not such a fearsome obstacle but a halt is called all the same while the larger vehicles are unloaded and their cargoes transferred to the lighter two-wheelers that have been acquired. At least, Murray orders the transfer of all that may be useful for, buried under their protective sacks, they discover boxes of bayonets that will never be used. Three cases of ceremonial cockades. And four barrels of biscuit.

'Dear God!' says Colonel Grant. 'We have been dragging this stuff with us ever since we left Edinburgh. All the way to Derby. And all this road back north again.'

'Well,' says Titus, 'it seems that we shall have breakfast today.'

For Lord George has deemed that everything except essentials should be jettisoned and the biscuits broken open for immediate consumption.

Fed and somewhat refreshed, they cross Borrow Beck without incident, still following this drovers' track as it runs north into the lower reaches of Crookdale, where the Crookdale Crags rise to their right and the Highhouse Bank to their left. Here they must cross another torrent, but there is no problem since Crookdale Beck has its own wooden bridge, narrow but just wide enough for the pair of four-wheelers still with them and especially easy for the smaller carts.

While Lord George arranges the order of passage, Titus surveys the surrounding countryside, the wooded ravine to their left, partly shrouded in a cold fog, and the sheer cliffs to their right. A dramatic landscape, right enough, and one in which the Highlanders seem perfectly at ease.

Perhaps, one day, I shall see the land of forest, lake and mountain that has spawned these fellows.

But, for now, he must leave Maria-Louise, walking today just a little further along the line, and go to help guide the first of the larger wagons over the bridge.

'Careful!' shouts the driver as he eases the draught ponies onto the slippery wooden planks, Titus on one side and a Manchester fellow – Collow, Titus thinks – on the other. The cart is particularly heavy, loaded mainly with cannon balls, so each of them keeps a hand on the hames of the collar, walking backwards and gesturing for the fellow to ease the reins, first this way, then that, to maintain the wheels just within the limited margins that the bridge's width allows.

Titus waits patiently for a moment, then motions quickly for the driver to steer to the right.

'More!' he cries. 'This way! More!'

The wheels move perilously close to the edge. The driver stands, peering over the side.

'What, in Christ's Name, are you about?' he shouts

And Titus takes the thorn from his pocket, grips it tight in his fingers, to drive the thing deep within the pony's flank.

The beast bucks and tries to rear, but is restrained by the wagon shafts and belly-band, so it side-steps across the bridge, forcing its partner sideways too and spilling Collow into the stream. The pony reacts again, shying backwards against the breeching strap around its haunches which would normally allow it to set back, to slow the vehicle. But now the movement serves only to push a rear wheel over the edge.

Titus dances backwards, clear of the ponies as they struggle for footing on the frosted timbers, watching as momentum and gravity do their evil work.

With one wheel over the edge, the shifting load of iron shot, and the animals frantic scramble, the second wheel soon follows, the whole wagon heaving into the torrent, the driver washed downstream and the ponies crashing down too in a tangle of harness, flailing in their traces, terrified and screaming as the water floods over them.

Titus sees Lord George leap into the Beck, knife in hand, to release the animals. A score of others join him, while others attempt to calm the rest of the horses further down the column, all of them infected by the desperate scene of panic being played out here beneath the bridge. Those not engaged with steadying the carts are now flocking to the banks, every eye focused on the drama, not a single eye on Titus or his dear wife. He eases his way back through the crowd to the far side of the bridge, checks once more that they are not observed, and takes Maria-Louise by the arm, pulling her towards the rocky cascade to their left, a short climb into the fog-rimed trees and freedom.

Chapter Fifty-Two

It is Sir Edward Stanley's moment of glory. The prospect of a cavalry charge to rout the enemy, those damn'd Jacobite rebels. He rests a hand against the troubled side of his stomach, now constrained by the taut fabric of his scarlet coat. He belches. He farts. His mount moves uneasily beneath him.

Beyond Shap, the countryside is considerably more benign and the road to Penrith climbs steadily with still higher ground to each side. The highest of this terrain, on the western side, is Thrimby Hill and, from its summit, the Earl of Derby can look down to see the Pretender's artillery and baggage train moving slowly northwards. It is escorted by several companies of Highlanders, the whole column halted now in the shallow and snow-smeared valley, since they have spotted the Hanoverian presence.

For Sir Edward is not alone. Stretched out on either side of him are sixty men from the Lancaster and Lonsdale Company of his Lancashire Militia Regiment, mounted infantry now and incorporated into the Duke of Cumberland's Flying Column.

'What say you, Bradshaw?' says the Earl to the Company's Captain. 'Action at last, eh?'

'I hope so, My Lord,' replies William Bradshaw, standing in his stirrups so that he might better see the troopers further along their front. Two hundred of Bland's Dragoons and another fifty men from the Yorkshire Chasseurs, part of Oglethorpe's famous Light Horse.

Another line of Oglethorpe's men sit on the heights opposite, fewer in number and on lower ground but still it signifies that the Jacobites are caught in a trap.

Sir Edward reaches down to touch the sword hanging at his side. A gift from his wife. The scabbard is red leather. The weapon itself forged in Toledo, signed with the name *Sebastián Hernández*. Shell-hilted in that style the Spaniards call *boca de caballo*. The quillions and knuckle beautifully rendered, the pommel faceted. The grip leather matching red, wired with silver. His Elizabeth had arranged too for a London swordsmith to engrave the fine blade with the Royal coat-of-arms and *GR* cypher on one side, the Stanley emblem on the other, along with the motif *Sans Changer*. It is an elegant piece, too fine to use in anger, he supposes, but presented to him with all his wife's usual exhortations to be careful with his food, careful with his health, careful to avoid the demon snuff.

Careful? If only you knew, my dear!

First there had been the disgrace of that useless Manchester Company, disbanded almost as soon as it was embodied.

Then most of the remaining Companies marched across the Pennines to Yorkshire. Yorkshire, of *all* places! To Huddersfield, in fact. Rumours everywhere of Jacobites. From Huddersfield to the village of Mirfield, only to find the place deserted, the foolish folk of those parts mistaking the Lancashire accents of his men for some Highland brogue. Back and forth. Back and forth. And the Pretender's army nowhere near, had marched unhindered through his own County in fact, while *they* slogged across the desolate moorlands of thrice-cursed Yorkshire. And back to Lancashire the Militia itself had finally been dispatched. Too late again, the Pretender having lost his nerve, foreign dog, at Derby and tramped all the way through Manchester again just days ahead of them. There had been such whimsy amongst his officers at the news, naturally. The *Chevalier* brought to a halt by Derby. La! Such whimsy. It had been the very thing.

As instructed, Sir Edward had left the Warrington Company in Manchester town as a partial garrison, the dung-hole being still so very full of traitors. Traitors and livestock, he recalls. While the remaining Companies had marched north to join Cumberland's forces on the previous day in Kendal, the seventeenth, where they now rest. They had been briefly reunited there with the Lancaster Company, however, already part of the Duke's strength, and the Earl of Derby had naturally been invited to join this unit of his command for today's expedition.

'But there is little happening, Captain, do you not think? I shall ask Honeywood whether we might attack the fellows.'

He pulls his mount back from the line and trots across the broken ground to the Dragoons, Bland's Dragoons by name but under the command of Lieutenant Colonel Sir Philip Honeywood. The fellow is in his mid-thirties. A veteran of Dettingen. Bad-tempered, though this might be attributed to the twenty-three broadsword wounds that he had received in that fight, as well as the two musket balls still lodged in his flesh.

'What now, Sir Edward?' says Honeywood. 'I do not expect my officers to be prancing about our positions, *regardless* of their station.'

Damn'd impertinence!

'I simply wondered, Colonel, whether we might advance and take those field-pieces while they are yet unprotected. It is their entire artillery train, I believe.'

'Unprotected, sir? Unprotected. They already have as many men down there as we possess and, unless my eyes deceive me, there are two more companies of the heathens coming up behind.'

Sir Edward reaches for his spyglass, brass and hardwood, one of

Matthew Loft's finest, single draw, and he snaps it open to survey the scene more carefully.

What have we then? Six light cannon. Four-pounders unless I am mistook. One wagon. Six curricles. A single piece with long brass barrel. Then all those small carts. Must be two dozen of them. And what might this be at their tail? A woman? Perhaps.

These savages must have their pleasures too, he supposes. He runs the spyglass along the Highlanders strung out on either side of the convoy.

They are walking potato sacks! I cannot imagine why we have not dealt with them sooner. Yet these fellows coming up from Shap look like they have more bottom.

The newcomers at least have uniforms, blue like Frenchmen. Green facings.

Some of those Irish traitors serving the French, I should think.

'Yes, Colonel, I see,' says Sir Edward. 'Those regulars at least might give us some difficulty. Yet a charge, sir? Downhill? We should have the advantage, surely!'

'A charge, you say? Down a slope so littered with rocks that we should arrive at the bottom with less speed than a man might walk, and under their fire for most of the way. Does it not occur to you, Sir Edward, that we would do better in chasing that column back to Shap and await the Duke's arrival with his reinforcements?'

'A capital idea, Colonel. Of course! Yet how might we persuade them to retire, sir?'

Honeywood turns towards their rear, to the reverse of the slope where so many of his non-combatants remain.

'By choice I should not have brought them,' he says. 'They are an encumbrance but...' He looks for a moment at the Regiment's assorted kettle-drummers, trumpeters and musicians gathered in the sparsely wooded hollow below them. 'Ensign Midgeley, if you please! Have those fellows beat up the band, sir. As much noise as they like.'

'Which tune, Colonel?' says the boy.

'You bloody fool, sir! Anything that they choose, so long as it is loud.' The Ensign rides down to issue the order. 'Well, we shall see. Pray God they think it is Cumberland's entire army come to get them. Now, Sir Edward, you will return to your post, sir. And do not let me catch you away from it in future. Discipline, sir. Discipline.'

A contrite Earl of Derby rejoins his Company while the trumpets and drums begin to play merry hell behind them.

'Now you shall see a spectacle, Captain Bradshaw. The very epitome of military stratagems, sir. Watch this!'

And indeed they do. They watch as the commander of the uniformed fellows moves up to consult with the apparent Chieftains of the Highlanders at the baggage train. They watch as the Jacobites form up below. They watch as the savages draw swords, check the charges in their muskets. They watch as the Scots cast aside their cumbersome plaids, throw them on the hillside. They watch in disbelief as one tartan-trewed officer steps to the front, raises his spiked and studded targe and screams a Gaelic command. They watch as the entire force takes up the cry, springs forward, a monstrous deer hound, bare-arsed amongst the rocks and bracken, bounding towards the summit. And they watch as their line of Hanoverian horsemen begins to buckle, not a shot yet fired. To buckle, to bend and to break. Scattering to their rear, colliding with the musicians in the dell, kettledrums and trumpets discarded now in the panic until they have put distance between themselves and their former position.

Sir Edward halts as he reaches the flatter ground on Knipe Moor, turns to see the Highlanders two hundred yards behind, the summit of Thrimby Hill now taken and one hapless drummer, knocked from his horse at the mercy of his captors.

The final scene. This drummer, upon the ground, arm upraised in a plea for clemency. But the broadswords rise and fall. Rise and fall. Chop and slice. Until the fellow is hacked to small shreds.

It is just after noon and the sun has finally begun to shine for the first time in two weeks.

An hour passes while the scattered troopers are rallied and returned to some semblance of order while Honeywood rides about the moor in an ugly mood.

'Which pox-faced son of a whore broke first?' he cries. 'I shall have him horse-whipped, by God I shall!'

He is only placated by the arrival of Major General Humphrey Bland, come up with a company of Kingston's Light Horse and himself cursing because he cannot find Oglethorpe, somewhere off in the hills to the south-east and the Duke himself three miles behind, still in Shap.

Bland is almost sixty, a contemporary of Sir Edward's, but renowned across Europe and beyond as a military tactician.

I remember the presentation of his treatise on the philosophy of warfare at the Royal Society. Remarkable. It is now the bible of the British Army, they say!

'All is not lost, gentlemen,' he calls to the officers now gathered about him. 'This lane from the moor northwards runs parallel with that taken by their artillery train and rearguard. If we follow it so far as the Lowther enclosures we can turn east and cut them off before they may reach Clifton village.'

It is a decent plan but, when they reach the track where they must turn right, the walls and hedges on either side slow them almost to a halt so that, when they finally break into the fells again, they find themselves still behind the rebels. But only just.

In the distance, they can see the enemy's field pieces and carts but before them are the same companies of Highlanders and blue-coated Irish that had chased them from Thrimby Hill, spread in a line perhaps a quarter-mile across. But they are less numerous, at least matched by Bland's force, and the Major General deploys his own units, employing traditional dragoon tactics.

Thank the Lord that Bradshaw has at least some experience of this, thinks Sir Edward, though the manoeuvre is rarely used in these modern times, as the Lancaster Company canters forward within range of their muskets, dismounts, one man from every eight remaining on his horse to hold the reins of his comrades. Present and fire. The smoke rolls away across Clifton Moor. They watch for sign that the Scots may advance and, if so, they retire to the horses, mount again and fall back. If not, they charge their muskets afresh and fire another volley.

They call this a running fight, I think. But there is no running at all. A plodding fight, rather. Step by step.

It lasts for nearly an hour and they have advanced less than a mile, over the slight rise of Brackenber Hill with the village of Clifton in sight. Casualties are few, a dozen or so on each side perhaps. And there are now three things to dismay them. First, from the higher ground they can see that their main quarry, the artillery and baggage carts, are well on the far side of the village itself and approaching the Lowther Bridge, where there is considerable evidence of additional Jacobite infantry. Second, the Highlanders and uniformed troops ahead of them have succeeded in reaching the safety of the enclosures around Clifton whereas any further advance of Major General Bland's part must be over open ground. But third, away to their right, coming hard across Clifton Moor, is the Jacobite cavalry.

'We shall be caught like rats in a trap, gentlemen,' calls Bland. 'If Oglethorpe had been up we could counter them and still take those damn'd pieces, but not now! We must await the Duke, I fear. And the only safe place to do so is Lowther Hall. Due west, gentlemen, I think. Due west. At least we have the sun.'

Our second retreat in one day! God's Hooks, this is becoming tedious.

But at Lowther Hall there is good news, for a party of Cumberland's Georgia Rangers awaits them, green uniforms and small black caps, with two dispatch riders from the Duke himself, now come up with his main strength to Hackthorpe, only a mile distant.

'You should not tarry here too long, Captain' Sir Edward calls to the Rangers' officer, 'for the devils are at our heels.'

And he spurs away to the south-east and Hackthorpe.

Be careful with my food, Elizabeth told me, he thinks, dismounting in the hamlet and passing his reins to Ensign Sandys. *I should count myself lucky was there any to warrant such attention. I shall starve to death before long!*

'Is there no food, William?' he says to the Lonsdale lad.

'Biscuit, sir,' replies Sandys, a boy with ineffable good humour, Sir Edward has discovered. Irrepressible to an infuriating degree.

'Sir Edward,' calls Captain Bradshaw. 'His Grace requests your company, sir. The second house along the street.'

The Earl of Derby digs his fingers into the pain-wracked muscles of his backside, groaning as a spasm ricochets around the flesh of his oversized thighs. He lowers his head to enter the hovel currently serving as Cumberland's headquarters. The others are already here. Bland. Ligonier. Kerr. Cobham. Honeywood. And...

'Mister Owen! Can that be you, sir?' he says.

The Duke turns towards the young painter, back to Sir Edward.

'You have met already, gentlemen!' says Cumberland. 'In Manchester, I suppose. Then give you joy of Mister Owen's elevation, Sir Edward. He is become an artist to the Crown as you see, it seems.' Aran smiles weakly at the Earl of Derby. 'Now, to business. We need to test their strength. They cannot be more than a few hundred else they should not have sent their artillery so rapidly to the rear. We will probe them, gentlemen, though gently, I think.'

'I should be pleased to volunteer my Company for the task, Your Grace,' Sir Edward hears himself saying, almost as if somebody else had spoken.

'Regulars only for this one, I fear, Sir Edward.'

Conceited young pup!

'Of course, Your Grace. Perfectly understandable.'

'In that case,' says Cumberland, 'it shall be Kingston's, Bland's and the Georgias, I believe. We shall form up beyond the hill and Honeywood shall take in the advance guard. Open order, if you please, Colonel.'

'And my own role, Your Grace?' says Aran Owen.

'To observe and to replicate, sir, naturally. Yet you shall only replicate so much as the times permit. The stature and heroism of our dragoons, I collect. The dismal and starved appearance of the enemy. And bloody them, Mister Owen. As *we* may do!'

Within twenty minutes, the British regiments extend in a line that spans the Shap to Penrith road, with Cumberland just behind its centre on the rise of Brackenber Hill. He is surrounded by his personal guard, the Austrian Hussars who attached themselves to him in Flanders. Dashing fellows, all crimson and green. Ligonier's Eighth Horse are out on the left flank, the dragoons of Cobham and Kerr in the centre, with most of the mounted infantry on the right. Montagu's Horse are in reserve and the advance guard is, of course, precisely where such a force should be. To the fore.

From his position, Sir Edward can see the village clearly. All seems peaceful enough and, facing them, is a seemingly unbroken line of enclosures, on each side of the road, and extending to about the same width as Cumberland's own line. The road splits these fields, with their surrounding hedges and walls, into two equal halves. Behind the fields, on the extreme left, is a substantial huddle of farm buildings and, after another couple of enclosures, the single street of cottages and mean dwellings along each side of the town's only street, running back to a church on the rising ground at the settlement's far side.

Honeywood glances back to Cumberland for confirmation. It is given, and the Colonel barks an order that sets the dismounted dragoons marching resolutely towards the fields and farm. Tricorne hats, scarlet coats with long, loose skirts, square-toed, thigh-length boots. Carabines at the ready. The lighter troops of Kingston's Horse and the Georgia Rangers behind them.

Now what? A boy. From the farm.

The lad runs out onto the road, making directly for Honeywood, who signals for his men to halt.

'Who *is* that boy?' says Cumberland but, as he does so, the young fellow is gesturing towards the nearest of the enclosure walls, perhaps twenty-five yards distant from the leading troops. The Colonel shouts an order to his men, drops to one knee as he does so, throws the boy to the ground as a line of Highland bonnets appear above the hedge and parapet. There is a volley, a line of smoke followed just afterwards by the crash of muskets. The dragoons reply. Another volley from each side and then a further group of Jacobites emerging from the farm itself, spread across the lane.

A signal from the Duke and Montagu's Horse advance at a walk, sabres drawn, down the road towards the village. A party of Jacobite hussars also appear, away towards the church but do not engage, and the ambushers from the farm and surrounding fields are soon falling back, hotly pursued by Honeywood's men and their supporting cavalry.

Cumberland releases his Austrians, their long side-plaits blowing in the breeze as they rush the barns and outbuildings. There are shots, prisoners taken, and Cumberland's trumpeter sounding the recall.

Honeywood falls back to the Duke's position, bringing the boy with him and soon followed by the lad's father, it seems.

Sir Edward is called to conference with his Commander-in-Chief, along with the other senior officers, and Aran Owen sketching in the background.

'It seems that we owe this young spy a huge debt of gratitude,' says the Duke, and Sir Edward sees Aran's head jerk up in surprise, then lower again to focus on his work. 'What do you say, Honeywood? You might have been ditched without the lad's warning. And you, sir? His father?'

'I am, Your Grace. Thy servant, sir. Thomas Savage. And thou art welcome to succour in my home once this rabble is cleared from the field.'

'You are a Quaker, I collect. Am I correct, Mister Savage?'

'I have the honour of belonging to the Society, indeed, sir. And whilst many of the Friends are supporters of the Pretender, I find myself unable to condone the pestilence that he has spread upon the land.'

'Well said, Mister Savage. There is no pestilence to match civil war, I find. And what have we here, Colonel? A brace of prisoners, though this one

565

cannot be long for the world, I fear.'

'He says that his name is Ogden, Your Grace. A Manchester fellow, separated from his Regiment. The rest are already in Penrith it seems. One of your Hussars took him apparently but he begged for his life. Then, when he was spared, drew a pistol and shot at the man who had pitied him. The Austrian was not about to make the same mistake twice, however.'

The fellow's head is almost clove in two, the right side of his face split like a ripe watermelon, flesh and bone spilling out of the wound.

'He will not survive,' says Cumberland, 'but we shall hang him in any case. And this one?'

'From Edinburgh, Your Grace,' says Honeywood. 'Calls himself Captain Stevenson.'

'So, Captain, what have you to say for yourself?'

'I was a lawyer in Edinburgh, Your Grace, and volunteered to join the Prince as many other ha'e done before me. But in my youth I also served King George, sir.'

'You say so, by God?' says the Duke. 'Well then, you are twice the traitor, Stevenson. And an ambushing assassin in the bargain. Hang them both!'

'Your Grace,' cries Thomas Savage. 'For pity's sake, sir. My Society abhors violence. My son, Jonathan risked his life to warn thee of the ambuscade. My good wife remains hidden in her cupboard, not knowing whether her boy yet lives or is dead. For *our* sake, Your Grace, will you not spare the lives of these two foolish fellows? There may be precious few opportunities for you to show mercy if this campaign runs further.'

The Duke considers the Quaker for a moment.

'I cannot spare traitors, Friend Thomas, for we are too near the edge. As you have seen, each one to whom we show clemency will return to bloody us again in the future. But the price of a bed for the night, sir, that is incalculable. You shall have their lives in exchange for your family's hospitality. If ever we triumph this day.' He turns to his officers. 'For I tell you, gentlemen, that I did not expect such a battle on this ground. It seems that neither myself nor my cousin, *le Prince Edouard*, has chosen the field, but here we shall fight all the same.'

The prisoners are led to the rear although it is doubtful whether Ogden will live much longer.

And the rest of those Manchester scum already in Penrith? thinks Sir Edward. *How I should have enjoyed a reckoning with them, the blight of my County!*

His own thoughts turn suddenly to hospitality as well. To the night at Bradley's house. Aran Owen's unexpected presence here, perhaps, that has sparked the recollection. The dinner to mark the Naming Day of that wayward wife, the tribade. *Such an arrangement. Elizabeth would scarce believe me, though God knows I could not fully explain the thing. She has led a sheltered life, I fear, and they do not call it the Silent Sin for nought. Such a singer though! Fine voice. I wonder what has become of them both?*

By some miracle there seem to have been no casualties amongst the Duke's ranks but now, at four in the *post meridiem*, and darkness falling, it is just possible to discern large bodies of Jacobite reinforcements – two full regiments, report a couple of bold Rangers who have ventured forth to reconnoitre – arriving near the distant church.

'We shall have no such easy time of it now, I fear,' says Cumberland. 'We must not retire and yet they will have the advantage of night. It is the Highlanders' friend, while our pipe-clay shall shine like a beacon for their shooters. And this rearguard – we are agreed that it is only the rearguard, I think – is commanded by Lord George Murray. I know the fellow. He is competent, gentlemen. Now, let us consider our dispositions.'

By five, with no real intelligence about what they face, the Duke has made the best calculations available to him.

Ligonier's Horse remain on the left but sent forward to watch for one of the flanking attacks that so destroyed Cope at Gladsmuir. The dismounted dragoons of Cobham and Kerr remain in the centre, with Montagu and Kingston's Horse in reserve. And on the right wing, Bland's Dragoons and Sir Edward's Militia Company, once again led by Honeywood.

'Do you have protection, Sir Edward?' whispers the Colonel as they await the signal to advance. 'Well, sir, do you?'

'Your pardon, Colonel?' the Earl of Derby replies, 'I fear...'

'Your head, fellow. Your head! No, I suppose you would not.' He removes his tricorne and reveals the iron skull-cap that dragoons alone so habitually utilise to protect themselves from sabre cuts, though it seems to have done Colonel Honeywood little service in previous encounters. *Twenty-three broadsword wounds at Dettingen alone?* 'Here,' he says, 'take mine, if you will.'

Sir Edward finds himself somewhat overwhelmed.

'Too generous, Colonel,' he says. 'How gracious!'

And, to their rear, a trumpet blows.

There is little light. Night has come and turbulent storm clouds cartwheel across the sky. The moon is no harsh mistress this evening, simply a weak and timid creature sheltering in sombre corners. But away to the west, two distant eyes, far apart, glow from some hilltop beacon or alarm fire.

They advance into the unknown, step by tentative step.

Five minutes pass and they come to the first of the drystone walls, surprised to find the enclosure undefended. They scramble across.

'Steady, my boys!' shouts Sir Edward. 'Keep the line. Keep the line!'

And, to their left, a volley from the village houses is a ragged burst of lightning.

Kerr's fellows come under fire, I think, upon the road.

Then another volley, more distant.

Cobham shooting into the village from its rear, its western side. Then the ragged crackle of continuous musketry to their left, shots in every direction, illuminating that part of the battlefield around Clifton.

But here it is hard to know even in which direction we should move.

A hedge. Sacrilege but he must draw the Toledo blade and use it to cut through. Snow has drifted against the thing.

It is impossible. We shall never breach it.

But they crawl, and tunnel, and hack. They reach the farther side, their formation more or less intact. Then find that the ground slopes sharply downwards, though they had not expected this. Down. Down. And they are in water up to their thighs, splashing and cursing in an icy ditch that sucks at their boots, another hedge to their front, though threadbare.

By God's Hooks, if we do not draw their fire now...

A volley from up beyond the hedge. It lights up the Highland regiment waiting there for them. Yet the shots go high.

'Present!' calls a voice to Sir Edward's right. Honeywood, he thinks.

'Fire!'

The turn of the ditch and its occupants now to be revealed, the Militia's muskets and Bland's carbines barking out, roaring death and defiance at the Jacobites.

Cries in the dark, the shrieks and groans of wounded men.

Then a second's silence and an order, clear and loud from the Highlanders' ranks.

'Claymore!'

The yell is taken up by others. Gaelic oaths.

Sir Edward will never properly be able to describe the next few minutes. He feels the ground shake as the Scots come pouring down the slope towards them. More properly, he feels the vibration of it through the water that now fills his boots. Then jarring shock as the two bodies of men collide, the impetus of course being with the Jacobites so that the Earl of Derby, like many others in his Company, is pushed backwards. His blade comes up by accident more than instinct and is wrenched from his hand as his assailant falls sideways, the steel deep within his chest.

Clawing and gouging. Some dragoons being butchered to his left. No, to his right now, for he has turned himself over, shaken off his boots and wriggles back up the bank.

I must retrieve Elizabeth's sword, he thinks.

'Come, Sir Edward,' calls Honeywood, hauling him to his feet. 'No time to be prancing about here, neither. What a fellow you are, to be sure!'

He is taller than the Earl of Derby, heaves him upright, still carrying his own sabre.

'My sword...'

'No time...' But Honeywood cannot complete the sentence, for his feet have slipped on an exceptionally large cowpat and the turd has laid him low. Worse, two Highlanders have appeared out of the gloom immediately behind the Colonel.

One bends to grab Honeywood's shoulder, the other lifts his claymore for a fatal blow. But Sir Edward, seizing the Colonel's own blade from the snowy ground, slashes two-handed at the Scotsman's arm, all but severing the thing while, on the other side, a militiaman drives his bayonet cleanly through the second Highlander's neck.

Between them they pull a protesting Colonel Honeywood to safety although, by now, most of the conflict seems to be over.

With much of the village cleared, Cumberland has moved his position to Quaker Savage's farm where Mistress Savage has finally been persuaded to emerge from her cupboards. Lanthorns are lit and it is now evident that Honeywood has gathered a further three sword wounds to his head tonight.

Twenty-six in total. By God, there shall not be an inch of him left without a scar!

Sir Edward, on the other hand, has come away unscathed, but barefoot, returning the iron skullcap to Honeywood with grateful thanks.

At least, he is *almost* unscathed.

An unspoken truce has been declared, the clear sounds of withdrawal coming from along the lane to the north, pipers leading their regiments away.

And there, not fifty yards distant from them, on the opposite side of an enclosure, the Scots have their own torches lit. They are few in number but the cove at their centre is, from his bearing and dress, a warrior of some renown.

'A victory, Your Grace?' asks Sir Edward.

'Victory? It depends on the butcher's bill, I suppose. But we seem to have lost no more than a score dead and perhaps twice that number wounded. Yet somebody once told me, Sir Edward, that any time your enemy surrenders the field, you may claim it as a victory. So, yes, a victory. Perhaps the last battle ever to be fought on English soil. What think you? All this might just be worthwhile if we could make it so.'

'I agree, Your Grace. But tell me, sir. That fellow over there. The Highlander.'

'Your glass, Sir Edward, if you please!' He examines the fellow. 'Ah, it is Ewan MacPherson. Cluny. Chieftain of Clan MacPherson. I met him once, in better days. And you, Sir Edward?'

'Me, Your Grace? No, I have not had the pleasure. But the bugger seems to have my sword!'

Chapter Fifty-Three

The letter had arrived this morning. Christmas morning. Rare for express boys to be working today but not exceptional. Bradley had stood upon his threshold, night turban still upon his head, banyan pulled about him, watching the snowflakes blow along Hanging Ditch a moment. He had lifted his eyes to Heaven.

'Thankyou, Lord,' he had said. 'You sent your Son to us this day. I pray that you shall forgive the profanity but, for my part, I could not have received a gift more precious than this sacred epistle.'

He had prayed for this too. Last night. The service at Saint Ann's where he had thought about her so much, though Maria-Louise herself would have attended the Eucharist Midnight Mass at the Collegiate Church, of course. Why, for the sake of seeing her, he would gladly have entered that nest of Papists himself.

But the letter itself had been an answer to his supplications. All these weeks without a word! And now this, in her own hand.

Dearest James, she had written. *The challenge I set myself is a simple one. That I should write you this letter. Yet how might I undertake such a task and, at the same time, deal with all the guilt that this one act shall heap upon my head?*

He had not immediately read any more.

'She is alive! Oh, Most Heavenly Father…'

He had almost skipped to the library, set the pages down upon his desk, called for his manservant.

'I shall take a little oatmeal with sweet cream, a brace of smoked herrings and some grilled kidneys, if you please. Oh, and some bread. Raspberry conserve. A glass of Spanish brandy too. It is Christmas, after all!' The fellow had looked at him in astonishment. Reasonably, Bradley concluded. For he had barely eaten at all in the previous few weeks. 'And prepare my shaving bowl. I shall look like a vagrant no longer.'

Restored to himself once more, he picks up the letter again.

Now, he thinks, *the dear lady spoke of guilt, I believe. Well, Maria-Louise is a Catholic, after all. Guilt is her natural environment. Yet the level of her own guilt must be but a miserable reflection of my own!*

The letter is dated this twenty-first day of December, 1745. Four days ago.

First, there is Rosina to consider. Visions of my daughter are always with me now. Not the image of anger and resentment that I witnessed on the morning that we were last together, my dear, but that of Rosina in gentler days. As a child. Before foolish fancy came between us. And, strangely, as I saw her last. I was on the cart, I recall, being taken by the Highlanders towards the Irwell Bridge and I caught a glimpse of those distinctive curls within the crowd. There was shooting, I fear. A Scotsman, a kind fellow who had offered me water, so badly wounded, and his fellows intent on revenge. They would have burned the entire town, I am sure, and Rosina seemed in such peril. Yet a rider appeared. I swear it was the same fellow who had dispersed the mobbers from my house. The same horse. Quite distinctive. The same pale redingote too. And I noticed that, wherever the Scots attempted to move – they not being at once persuaded to abandon their retribution – this fellow kept his mount always betwixt them and my daughter. How strange! A mere coincidence perhaps, yet it moved me to ask that you should speak with her. Tell her that, whatever may have come to pass, I love her very dearly. And I always shall.

But Rosina is no longer in Manchester either and he has not seen her since their last brief encounter at the coffee house. A few days afterwards, he had learned from the Byroms that she had repaired to Wales, bound for the village of Llanffynon and her uncle's interment. There are affairs to be settled, it seems, and no other family members available for their execution. Family. He had barely troubled with his own mother's funeral and has certainly spared no further thought for Pa Bradley. *Guilt.*

He misses Rosina. Not in the same way that he has missed Maria-Louise. But still a painful separation. The music. Even her addictions. Yet he had not felt entirely distant from her either for, amongst her belongings, those belongings that so embody her very essence, he has discovered her personal journal. *So here is guilt, my dear Maria-Louise. That I delved into the depths of another's private thoughts.* The trivialities had amused him but he had soon tired of them. So he had begun to skim the pages, seeking those paragraphs in which *Mister Bradley* might be mentioned. There was a danger in doing so, but it was a calculated risk. Yet he could never imagine the wounds that her words would inflict on him as he turned those damn'd pages.

Bitterness had gnawed at him and, on the evening of its discovery, just a few hours after seeing Rosina herself, he had summoned Elizabeth Cooper, requested her help in removing the girl's possessions, turned now so swiftly from fond memorabilia to miserable torments. *Oh, and how Elizabeth's face had brightened when she discovered the bridal dress. You speak of guilt, cara mia?* Imagine how I felt, afterwards, that I had given away that particular item.

He had been drawn back to the book like iron to a lodestone, however, plumbed its depths and discovered all the secret *minutiae* of Rosina's life, her intimate discussions with Elizabeth, Mistress Cooper's outspoken views about all manner of things. The Earl of Derby's incompetence, hints of corrupt association with Titus Redmond. Tom Lewthwaite's sodomy. *Oh, guilt.*

Yet, in the end, the guilt that truly etches his soul as he reads the letter, here in the leather comfort of the library in which they have pleasured themselves so often, pours from his bottomless failure to pursue Maria-Louise Redmond northwards. Yes, Titus had already gone. And correctly, as a husband's duty. But the responsibility was Bradley's own. It was he who had flaunted his liaison with Mama in Rosina's face. It was he who, in childish pique, had revealed the secret of the Jacobite coffers to the one person who was bound to use the intelligence against Maria-Louise. It is almost as though he had committed the action deliberately. *Guilt.* And then there is the ghost of Sir Edward Stanley at dinner with them, his gloating glee that the Jacobite Cause had been ditched by friends of the Crown here in Manchester. The very idea that it should have been Maria-Louise Redmond. It is still impossible to believe!

Meanwhile, I should tell you that I am in Carlisle. Imprisoned, though my condition is comfortable. There are some pitiful dungeons here in the Castle, a true 'oubliette' where one may indeed become forgotten. But I have the fortune to be housed in a servant's room adjoining the Governor's apartments. He is a dear but elderly fellow, Captain Hamilton, a Scot left here as warden by the Prince Regent when they captured the town last month. And still in charge, though His Royal Highness himself marched north with most of his army yesterday. He has left a small garrison to hold the place against Cumberland.

The Duke's regiments arrived this afternoon and are now encamped on all sides of the town walls. I was allowed upon the parapet to watch them but I could see little of their cantonments. They have no artillery, however, so the garrison feels no threat, especially since Charles Edward has left many of his own pieces behind, they now being arranged in batteries at various points about the walls and on the castle battlements too. The gunners seem mostly French – a strange thing for me, in the circumstances – and they join one hundred men of our Manchester Regiment with perhaps twice that number of Lowlanders besides, all charged with Carlisle's defence.

Bradley wonders about her ability to still describe the Jacobites as 'our' forces when she is their prisoner, but his shaving bowl is now ready, it seems, and then his breakfast.

572

There, he thinks, *I feel perfectly myself again.* And he takes up the letter once more, having carried his brandy, a dark *Lepanto*, back to the library.

There are so few of the Manchester boys still here, however. Most of the officers but perhaps only eighty of the men. They have treated me with such contempt, I fear. Except for Doctor Deacon's three boys. They have been kind. Thomas in high spirit, Robert suffering from an ague, and the boy, Charlie, repining over such protracted separation from his Papa. I wonder frequently whether their fortunes might have been improved had I not interfered in this history.

But there is then the possibility, he reflects, that if Maria-Louise had not intervened, London might now be awash with Frenchmen.

Oh, and Mister Strickland is here too, though also suffering from a fever. That gentleman tells me that the Prince is hurrying north to be united with the new forces rallying to his standard in Scotland. He will consolidate there, it seems, and march back to England in due course, though I doubt I shall still be here to witness the event.

He ponders these words. Does she mean no longer in Carlisle itself?

Meanwhile, Captain Hamilton must perforce share his Governorship with Francis Townley, and I shall tell you more of the Colonel anon. Yet you must wonder at the odyssey that brought me here. A harsh journey, I fear, sometimes upon the bed of a wagon, sometimes walking. But the weather fearsome and, as I have said, treated with utter disdain by the Manchester fellows in general, and by Colonel Townley in peculiar. By Standish first, where I set eyes upon my husband's bawd, that intolerable whore, Suzannah Cole. She spat upon me. Though I have never seen her since that night. Thence to the House of Correction at Preston, where I first received news, from the turnkey, that Titus was in that town also, had left some coin that I might be better fed. Though, as Our Lady knows, I had little appetite for sustenance. La! You should hardly recognise me, I have grown so sparse. That matters little now, however.

Bradley has begun to feel the first sense of unease at the tone which is developing.

At Lancaster, Titus was allowed to join me. To walk beside my cart. Such a comfort, my dear. And he tried several times to seek my release, yet without success. In my husband's fashion, he therefore decided to take matter into his own hands and, to the north of Kendal, he attempted an escape. We spent several hours, scrambling amongst trees and boulders, believing that Lord George would be too concerned for the safety of his artillery and baggage than to seek two flown birds such as ourselves. But we were mistook. And some Highlanders discovered us quite casually. They seemed perfectly amused although Colonel Townley insisted that we should each be bound and poor Titus was practised upon quite cruelly. He blamed my father's curse again, of course. Poor love! He says that he shall have his revenge upon Townley before long and shall then take delight in scripting an obituary to damn the fellow – he used a different word to describe him, as you may imagine – and for Scatterbuck to publish in his courant. We have spoken but little since that day, to my great chagrin. Though whenever we have managed to exchange words, he has always tried to comfort me with his promise that we shall travel. I understand that the thought distresses you but you should not fear on that account. For I know now that it shall never come to pass.

Unable to read further for the moment, Bradley folds the letter, then rings once more for his manservant. He is helped to dress, to wig, to pull on sturdy boots and heavy cloak, to don his hat.

What does she mean? he thinks, but his earlier unease has now developed to something more approaching dread. And he does not leave the house immediately, choosing instead to seek some vague reassurance by visiting the rooms presently occupied by the Redmonds' three girls. Anna-Marie. Katherine. Maeve. Two further rooms in the servants' quarters cleared to accommodate that strange creature Mudge, and the decaying Irishman, O'Farrell.

He wishes the girls joy of this Christmas morn, though their mood is understandably less than festive, but they cheer slightly at the news that he has received a letter from their Mama. He must go out, however, so will share the contents with them, perhaps at dinner. He will return to eat with them. A modest repast only, do they not agree? The smallest of ducks. Then he leaves them to their game of cards, braving the snow to set himself for town.

The church bells rhyme their Christian clarion to the world, sharp with woodsmoke and blanched alabaster, icicles at every edge. The town looks beautiful today, its tiles and thatches thick with yesterday's fall. But Pool Fold is a stark reminder that this is a world still at war, for the second cottage stands empty, its Jacobite family turned out and fled Manchester almost three weeks ago. There are many similar echoes of Cumberland's visit, an entire fullers' row in Long Millgate now deserted for the same reason, two houses in Withy Grove, Townley's place in Toad Lane, Sydall's near the Apple Market at the Grammar School. But there is no symbol of defeat to quite match that which stands obliquely opposite the Commodities Exchange. A reminder to Bradley of his meeting with the Duke every time he attends the place to meet with his Court Leet fellows.

'And this?' Cumberland had said, twelve days ago, following his inspection of Aran Owen's work in Byrom's Academy. 'I collect that the *Chevalier* was given lodging here. Entertained like royalty, they tell me.' He had pointed his tricorne towards the proud façade of the Redmond house, its front steps, the balustrades below the roof.

'The house belongs to Titus Redmond, Your Grace. Himself the fellow who did so much to raise funds for the Jacobite Cause, his wife a dear lady who, we are told, has served your father well by exposing plans for the secret transport of the Stuart Exchequer. Now safely within our Government's hands, I am pleased to say. Yet Mistress Redmond a prisoner of the enemy.'

'Redmond? Yes, tea. I had the explanation from Newcastle who now seems intent on using the same revenue source to make our country rich again, sirrah. And the wife? They say that she is only a whore. In any case, this merchant's palace is become something of a shrine, it seems. Burn it!'

'Your Grace?'

'You are a builder, are you not, Mister Bradley? You construct things. Yet must you not also sometimes demolish them? Of course you do! So I leave the technical detail to yourself, sir. Either burn it or pull it down stone by stone. I do not care. Yet the deed shall stand as a reminder for all Lancashire, which has done nothing to oppose the fleeing rascals. Nothing, Mister Bradley. Tear it down, if you please!'

And he had left Sir Edward's Militia behind to see the task completed.

Bradley could not comply, naturally. So he had visited the house, spoken with O'Farrell and agreed an acceptable course of action. His labouring men had shifted the furnishings to rooms at the rear, storing them carefully, and his best craftsmen had removed every front-facing window, set dark sheets behind, to give the impression that the interior was gutted, then boarded the front door.

It stands now as a sad reminder of other days, casting a gloom upon the whole of Market Street Lane, so that Bradley turns quickly, hoping to find more cheer at the coffee house.

Crableck takes his penny, offers a pipe and tobacco bowl.

'Do you know, sir,' says Bradley, 'I think I might partake of the weed, this being Christmas.'

'Mister Bradley!' cries Elizabeth. 'Give you joy, sir. Shall you join us?'

She is with that young Ensign again. By God's Hooks, they are become inseparable. Has she forsaken her sapphic ways, I wonder?

'I thank you, madam. A dish of *Assam* with you and the season's blessings upon you, too. Though I suspect that the collection will be thin today. All this coming and going. Too many excuses, I collect. Too many transactions undertaken with one army or the other, eh, Mister Tobin?'

'I do not have a head for business, Mister Bradley,' says the officer, his voice like heather honey. 'Yet I have never understood the logic of collecting rents and duty on this most auspicious of days. I am not convinced that Our Lord Jesu would have quite approved.'

'Why, it is a Quarter Day, sir,' says Bradley. 'Mistress Cooper would be failing in her duty as a representative of the Crown if she did not do so. And you, Ensign Tobin. If the Jacobites appeared again in town to day, should you throw up your arms and wail *Ah, it is Christmas Day and we may not fight?* I think not, sir.'

'Yet there are enough of them arrived already, James,' Elizabeth says. 'Another clutch of Jacobite deserters returned and too many of them, I fear, with homes still waiting for them. We should have burned out every rat's nest while we had the chance. But your Court Leet Constables have been too weakened by your own show of pity, I think.'

'There seems little profit, my dear, from turning families upon the street simply to have the Parish then required, by law, to provide for their welfare. The possessions of their leadership are all taken. Scatterbuck's infamies silenced, his presses being broke and shattered, his print shop destroyed. Is that not enough? I dare say that those running back for their holes will be arrested and brought to account.' Crableck arrives with his tea. 'Yet have there been any more rumours? Even true intelligence, though I doubt we should be able to distinguish those two things anymore.'

The past week has been full of tales. Claims that Cumberland had abandoned the army and returned to London. The Duke's army in disarray. A battle fought at Lancaster. Yet another French invasion. Cattle moved twenty miles from the south coast. King George died of an apoplexy. King George fled to Hanover. The Pretender on his way back to Manchester again. All false.

'Nothing of general interest, I think. Though I might have some news of my own to share?'

'Indeed, Mistress. Then later perhaps. Shall you be at Saint Ann's for the midday service? Good, then perhaps I shall join you there. For the nonce, I see that the corner table is empty and I shall smoke a while. I have a letter to read.'

So he settles himself for the next page.

Thus, dear Titus has been held under arrest since our failed bid for freedom. He was taken ahead with the Manchester Regiment and is now held in Carlisle's House of Correction. Captain Hamilton brings word of him whenever he is able, though this vexes Townley so considerably. My husband would be obliged, I think, if you could speak with Aran Owen and ensure that all is well with the fustian business. He will fret about it so, yet I persuaded him before we parted that he should make no further attempts at escape. Townley made it clear – and he would relish the prospect, I think – that my husband would be shot if any such attempt was made.

How strange it seems that their two worlds should have drifted apart so entirely, for Aran Owen must, by now, be almost within sight of her and, oddly, in the service of the Crown. Meanwhile, the murals for which the Court Leet has paid so handsomely, and with Mistress Redmond's beguiling, persuasive and skilful hand in the deal, stand unfinished in the Byroms' house. And barely an hour goes past without young Katherine enquiring whether he might have heard anything from the fellow.

Yet I have not recounted the battle to you, though surely you will have heard this tale already.

He has not.

In any case, we had arrived at a strange place called Shap. I suppose that it might be a village though it was merely a string of humble dwellings stretched out along the wildest and most desolate length of road in the world. The Edinburgh Regiment joined us there before the Prince marched on, being keen to reach Penrith without delay. The artillery, the baggage, myself tied to a cart-tail, were all left behind with a small escort, just a regiment or so. And when we finally moved off, we had not gone far before Hanoverian horsemen appeared on the ground above us. I thought that we should be attacked or killed but the Highlanders charged up the hill and scattered the fellows.

You will recall Sergeant Dickson, I think? He that took the whole town of Manchester almost alone? Well, he was with me about an hour later when the cart to which I was attached shed its wheel. Such panic, for the dogs could not be far behind. And then the good Sergeant saw the same horsemen, though away westward, across country. The wheel was fixed very quickly, as you might imagine, and we gained the hamlet of Clifton just in time. Dickson and our soldiers stayed behind to fight the English. We passed still more of our regiments heading out from Penrith again to support Lord George and a full-blooded fight began.

Our regiments retired in good order at about six, they say, but Sergeant Dickson was not amongst them. He died with a gentleman's sword through his chest, I believe. And the sword itself quite the thing. MacPherson of Cluny has it now as a prize, and it has gone north to the Highlands.

We left through Penrith on the following day, though coming under fire as we did so, causing His Royal Highness to order the town destroyed. And so we came to Carlisle.

'I have received an express,' cries Bradley. 'From Carlisle. It recounts a battle in Clifton Village. Have we no other word of this?'

Yet no such word has arrived. Not in the coffee house, at least. Though, by the time Bradley arrives at Saint Ann's Church, a little before noon, the congregation is all a-buzz with variations on the theme. A victory for Hanover. A victory for the Jacobites. Casualties fluctuate. Maria-Louise has not mentioned the figures and here, some claim, the Duke has lost hundreds dead, the Prince none at all. Others set the numbers even but some at fifty for each side, some at six or seven score. All accept the authority of Brigadier General Lord Sempill, however. Arrived yesterday with two regiments of foot for the north, staying two days only in Manchester for no better reason, it seems, than he had married here his wife, Sarah, thirty years before. So, Cumberland's casualties negligible. The heathens driven from the field and carried their many dead with them.

It would have been hard for these loyal Whigs to concentrate normally on this Christmas service after such news, but they are soon shocked to reality when, to the horror of most, the pulpit steps are mounted by the Reverend Thomas Deacon.

How strange, thinks Bradley. *It is barely an hour since I received word of his sons from Maria-Louise. I wonder whether he has heard from them too? Yet the fellow is a Jacobite dog. A Non-Juror in the bargain. What can the Curates be thinking of?*

It is certainly true that Deacon's position has moderated considerably since losing his wife, also named Sarah, as it happens, earlier in the year. But many in the congregation are not willing to await his message. They bang and clatter and complain their way to the doors, a substantial protest, while Deacon explains that he has been invited simply to welcome their new Rector, the Reverend Doctor Abel Ward.

Ward in turn offers an apology. A young man's folly, he says, though he had sought simply to heal some of the town's evident wounds in his own manner. The remaining church-goers hear him in sullen silence. The Assistant Curates, Lewthwaite and Nichols, listen with arms folded, chins on chests, furious it seems that the post has not been conferred on one or the other of *them*. Yet all is soon concluded and Bradley pushes through to reach Acres Field, arriving on the church steps at the same time as Lady Darcy Lever, just descending from her private box in Saint Ann's gallery.

'La! Mister Bradley. The very fellow. Did you see that audacity, sir? That self-styled Bishop?'

'Indeed, Lady Darcy. I fear that the new Rector has a lot to learn.'

'You cannot blame Mister Ward, sirrah. What stuff! It is Deacon. I had been minded to ignore his sedition for the sake of his dear wife. God rest her soul. She was a brighter star than her husband, I fear. Yet here he is, presenting himself as a genuine clergyman. It will not answer, Mister Bradley. Now, sir, you shall seize the fellow's goods, if you please.'

'Lady Darcy, do you think…?'

'I think *this*, young man! That in the absence of that coward Mosley, and following the demise of my dear husband, I am the closest thing that this town might possess to a Lord of the Manor. Do you think your position within the Court Leet might set you above me, sir? Now, where are your Constables. Ah, you…!'

Thomas Walley is hovering at the rear of the gathering crowd, an amused spectator merely, at this point.

'M-m-me, Your Ladyship?'

'Of course, Mister Walley. You will take some fellows forthwith and repair to the house of Thomas Deacon. He is a renowned Jacobite and father of a brood more, as you know. You shall seize all of his goods. Do you comprehend me, sir? No, Mister Walley, you shall not look to Mister Bradley, sir. You shall attend *me*! And when you have finished at Deacon's, you shall go straight to the house of that devil Clayton and do the same.'

'But Lady Darcy,' says Bradley, 'Doctor Clayton is a resident of Salford, not Manchester. Neither Mister Walley nor myself…'

'Do not use the word *jurisdiction* to me, Mister Bradley. I shall not hear it. Did the Young Pretender trouble himself about *jurisdiction* when he crossed the Irwell Bridge, sir? No, he did not. And it has clearly escaped your notice that Deacon has the misfortune of renting his property in Salford from myself. Now, Mister Walley, away to your duty and have it done, sirrah. And before you sit down to your dinner. A joyful Christmas to one and all, naturally.'

Lady Lever's carriage arrives and away she is whisked to the house at Daub Holes, on the very edge of town beyond Market Street Lane. Walley awaits a final approval from Bradley, who feels himself with no option in the matter.

The congregation disperses as the bell of Saint Ann's rings its own welcome for the new Rector, and James Bradley begins to walk slowly back to his house for dinner with three daughters of his *inamorata*. The fourth daughter, his wife, is estranged from him, their Marriage Settlement now a cruel jest. The girls' mother, his lover, is imprisoned in Carlisle. Their father too. *How strange are the ways of fate!* Yet he must decide how much of the epistle can be shared with the girls. Perhaps he should invent some additional paragraphs. But that can wait a while at least. First, he must summon his courage. A task that he has avoided all morning. For he must read the final portion of the letter. And he does so in the centre of Acres Field, the naked hornbeams on either side and the sound of family merry-making in the houses beyond. *They are fine houses*, he reflects. *One terrace built by his own hand. Fine houses.*

And, dammit, he has forgotten after all to ask Elizabeth Cooper about her own news. But that can wait also.

Thus, too, we come to the most difficult part of this letter. For I have news, dear James, and I know that it shall be hard for you to bear. His Royal

Highness told me that I should stand trial for my sins. And I did not fear such a thing for I was certain that either he, or his Councillors, would see the honesty of my motivation. Not a blow against the Stuart Crown but the attempt of one foolish woman, the most loyal of Jacobites, to prevent our Holy Cause from being held to ransom, impressed in the service of the French. Perhaps, if I had known that the entire Treasury would be lost, I may have acted more judiciously. But I cannot say.

The only thing that I may declare with certainty, dear heart, is that Charles Edward has forgotten me as efficiently as though I were, indeed, cast into the 'oubliette'. But Colonel Townley has not forgot. He despised me long before he discovered my guilt, and he has declared that a trial shall, indeed, take place. To be conducted by the Garrison Council very soon. With the exception of Captain Hamilton, perhaps the gunnery officer, Burnet, they are all Townley's creatures.

There can therefore be no question and you must be strong, my love. Neither Titus nor anybody else can save me now. They shall hang me before the month is out. So you must go to the house – how I love that house, and can see it now, clear in my mind's eye – and kiss the girls for me. Kiss them, dear James. Kiss them, for the Love of God!

Chapter Fifty-Four

Striker adjusts his eyes to the almost impenetrable gloom of the cell. *I have spent too much of my time in such places*, he thinks. It is dank and cold, this House of Correction.

Entry to the wholly walled town of Carlisle from the south or east is only possible through the bastion known as the English Gate that leads, predictably, onto English Street. They have little imagination, these Carlisle folk, it seems. There are some dwellings to the right and then an open space for the Bowling Green. Elegant. Yet, to the left, there is a narrow wynde of filthy hovels and, in their midst, this two-storey gaol.

He has not arrived here today from this direction, of course, for the English Gate is now blockaded by Cumberland's army, although a considerable amount of traffic still passes through. Striker himself travels back and forth with impunity and has done so since his arrival with the Jacobite column nine days ago. His wound is not healing well, however. Such a modest scratch and so ignobly gained. In truth, he still has no idea whether it was inflicted by friend or foe since he had chosen entirely the wrong cottage in which to shelter when he found himself, almost by accident, in Clifton Village. Highlanders climbing through the window on one side and English dragoons on the other. A sword slicing his ribs as he stepped back to let them settle the thing. The bruising has now largely subsided but this damned crease in his flesh, though shallow, weeps like a stone saint.

The wound provided him, however, at least with reason to be left behind, albeit with instruction from Sir John MacDonald that Lieutenant Owen should put himself at the service of Captain Hamilton, the town's Jacobite Governor. The Pretender had stayed here only two days, leaving this garrison against his future return to England, and marched off northwards on his birthday, the twentieth of December. Then, on the following day, the Duke of Cumberland had arrived to find his bird flown and the town to be invested.

'I see that you sleep in a truckle bed, sir,' whispers Striker into the darkness. With his face pressed against the damp bars, he can just perceive the prisoner hunched upon his cot.

'Cunny-sucker,' says the other. 'If you think me some tame servant then unlock the door and see for yourself whether or not I am truckled.'

'Stand easy, Mister Redmond. I intended only to comment on the nature of your furniture. It has wheels, after all, I perceive. Nothing more.'

'Fucking lick-spittle. What do you want of me, sir? And in God's name, what is that infernal noise?'

'Ah, the noise!' says Striker. 'That I can explain. It seems that the good folk of Whitehaven have loaned a considerable quantity of eighteen-pounders to His Grace, the Duke of Cumberland, along with all the powder and shot which that admirable general may need to reduce this entire city. According to my time-piece, they opened the game at eight this morning and are already inflicting prodigious harm.'

So far as the first part of your question is concerned, however, I should not know how to respond. What do I want of you, Titus Redmond? To satisfy my curiosity, perhaps.

And then there are his various commitments to Aran Owen. That his invaluable information should not be used to betray or harm the Redmond family. That his intelligence should serve only to lay the conspiracy's leadership by the heels. Striker could never have imagined how far his tokens would bring him, that this one informant would allow him both to thwart all Welsh involvement in the rebellion while, at the same time, depriving the whole enterprise of its principal coffers.

The plan had failed in one significant regard, however.

I imagined that this clever ruse, this player, this trusted Lieutenant of Rangers, would bring me close enough to the Young Pretender that I might find opportunity to take the outlaw and claim Newcastle's reward. Thirty thousand pounds, sirrah. Thirty thousand.

But the opportunity had never presented itself and, when Charles Edward crossed the Scottish border again last week, Striker had given up the idea. At least for the time being.

Then if no reward, how is a man to turn an honest guinea from this enterprise?

'I had not thought to find an admirer of Cumberland here,' says Titus. 'What are you then. Some local spy for the Elector? If so, how did you pass the turnkey?'

What should I say to you, sir? That I feel an obligation to Aran? That I may have practised upon your family but, for his sake, would not willingly see them harmed by another's hand? That one of your daughters haunts my dreams? That your wife shall die on the morrow unless we are capable of some sorcery between us? That this same wife has saved this realm from the heel of King Louis? Or that you might, perhaps, be willing to pay handsomely for her deliverance?

'Oh, the turnkey and myself are old friends,' Striker says. And it is true. He had shared ale with the fellow on his journey north to Edinburgh. 'Yet you only need to consider that I am your ally, Mister Redmond.'

'Do I know you?'

'Alas, we have never had the pleasure of an introduction.'

The shadows shift. Titus has stood from the bed but does not come forward. Not at first. But he slowly shuffles across the slabs, setting his hands upon the iron rods of his cage. Striker moves back two paces.

'Do you fear me then?' says Titus. 'Come forward, fellow.'

Striker does so and, for a long moment, their eyes are merely inches apart, reflecting each other's orbs in the dungeon's only light.

Redmond's hands shoot forward, clawing for Striker's throat. Fast, snarling, face contorted in hatred.

'Lick-spittle bastard!' he cries, as Striker dances backwards away from the questing fingers.

'You are quick, Mister Redmond, but never quite quick enough, it seems. Or you should not have been recaptured so easily, I think.'

'You scum! You killed my brother.'

'I? The Squire? I did not even know that the old fellow is dead. And you need not trouble yourself to believe me, sir, but I am sorry for it. He was a good man who had distanced himself from your Jacobite foolery.' *Yet I wonder. I taunted Sir Watkin with the ledger. He lost the thing in Manchester. Knew that I had been put into his confidence through Josiah initially. I would not set it past him.* 'It would take too long to explain, Mister Redmond. But if your brother's death was unnatural, as you seem to suspect, you might look rather to those Welsh friends of yours, and to Sir Watkin Williams Wynn in particular.'

'You talk nonsense, sir! And will you deny Jacob Driscoll's murder too?'

'Murder, you say? La! The fellow tried to lure me into a trap, sir. The world and its dog knew that he had sworn revenge upon me for thwarting the fucking whoreson on Chat Moss. I owed him a reckoning, Mister Redmond, but Driscoll provided the means to his own end, I fear.'

'And Mother Blossom. You mutilated that poor woman's face to red ruin. Or had you forgot?'

'Ah! Now *there* you have me, sir. *Touché*, I believe. An especially evil mood was on me that day. An inventive spirit moved me... Oh, and speaking of spirit!' He reaches into his pocket and removes a stone bottle, sets it upon the floor and slides it carefully between the bars. 'Your favourite, I think. And I must thank you too for the inspiration that your geneva distribution system has afforded me. When I return to the Colonies I shall modify the thing for local conditions, but the essence shall be the same. Where was I? Yes, the inventive spirit. To set yourself and Mister Bradley at each other's throats. Pointless as it transpired. And perhaps insensitive that I should mention the fellow, eh?'

Now that I think of the thing, much that has transpired within Redmond's family arose from the bout that I sponsored between those two. The fire. The raid on the bawdy-house. Oh, happy days!

Titus removes his hands at last from the iron bars, retreats again to the rear of his cell, sits once more upon the truckle bed.

'You have come to torture me, I see, Lieutenant Owen. Is that even your name, sir?'

'It will suffice for the nonce. But torture was not on my mind today, Mister Redmond. I came with news, sir. Do you know that Colonel Townley intends your wife to stand trial tomorrow?'

'Maria-Louise? You have seen her?'

'Not recently, I fear.'

But he does have an image of Maria-Louise Redmond. She is casting about the ground of Acres Field back in Manchester. It is their Annual Fair. And, though she does not know it, her lost daughter Maeve is being held high on the church tower by that sodomite, Lewthwaite.

I still wonder whether...

'Townley will see her dead, I think. But why should you care for my wife's fate, I wonder?'

'Colonel Townley has certainly become somewhat deranged, Mister Redmond. That much is true. And my motivation, sir? Might you accept that any support which I may offer shall come your way due to that loyal servant, Aran Owen?'

'Aran...?'

'Indeed, though it is another excessively long tale. We could spend many happy days in reminiscence, I think. Alternatively, we could remonstrate with each other about our respective weaknesses and past misdeeds. But none of that would help to save your dear wife, I fear. Do you not agree? And if you seek a more banal reason for my concern, we could perhaps discuss a monetary disbursement perhaps?'

'I do agree, sir. If you have a plan then perhaps you might share its details with me, either before those scoundrels murder Maria-Louise or Cumberland succeeds in reducing us both to rubble! And I should expect nothing less than to pay your fee. But when this is done, Lieutenant Owen...'

The threat hangs between them as Striker explains his intentions. He slips the gaoler an additional shilling as he leaves, turning north-west along Back Street, Saint Cuthbert's Lane, the Customs House, Market Cross Place, the Cathedral Precincts and Castle Street, before crossing the lifting bridge over the flooded moat. Townley has had a *chevaux de frises* constructed here but there is still enough room for a small wagon to pass between the sharpened stakes and enter the main bailey of the fortress proper, below the portcullis and through the double gates of Ireby's Tower.

From here Striker can mount the steps to the battlements where he walks the walls, exchanging pleasantries with the nervous sentries as shot follows shot against the furthest corner of the fortifications. The Artillery Captain, John Burnet, had mounted a four-gun battery at that place but there is little evidence remaining of it now.

Striker peers cautiously through an embrasure to one of Cumberland's

584

positions across the Caldew on Primrose Bank, though it is almost permanently cloaked in smoke as the Duke's own batteries play with this western wall.

My God, he must have four thousand men with him by now, if I am any judge.

He has seen enough here, so retraces his steps past the gatehouse. Another lower wall takes him to the top of the Half-Moon Bastion, stinking with the soiled waters and shit of its inner moat, and past the gates of the Captain's Tower to the inner bailey. And all the while Striker is surveying and calculating, measuring distance pace by pace, until he reaches the highest point on the walls, where he finds Burnet himself. Yet, even here, one of the pieces has been dismounted, blown from its carriage, and two of the gunners dead.

'And where, pray, are the rest of your fellows, Captain?' says Striker. 'Fishing perhaps? A stroll around the town? God's Hooks, sir, you may not manage with so few.'

Burnet looks ill, his face grimed with smoke and sweat pouring from him despite the snow flurries that beset them. And while his larger group of eight guns, away to their right, still seems reasonably crewed, the Captain is here left to his one remaining four-pounder entirely alone. He is from Campfield, in Aberdeenshire, and Striker likes him though, Heaven knows, he must be the most unfortunate fellow that ever sported a uniform. For he has been upon the walls, with little respite, for a full week, eighteen cannon in total under his command. They are not heavy pieces, admittedly, but to Striker's certain knowledge they have yet to inflict even a single casualty upon the besiegers. Several cattle, it seems, *have* met a premature end in the process but not one Hanoverian soldier.

'Deserters, Lieutenant, I fear,' says Burnet. 'We lost another six last night. Two gunners and four matrosses. It will not answer, indeed not!'

'And have you hit any of the scoundrels yet, sir?'

'You practise upon my good nature too much, Lieutenant Owen. Why, wi' these pieces I should fare me better by taking a wee pile o' stones and throwing them at Cumberland's head! Yet give me a battery of siege guns the like o' which we had in Flanders and I should play thae Germans a merry tune.' Once again, Striker has used this interlude well but, as he takes his farewell of Burnet, one of the Duke's longer-range shots crashes against the masonry below. The shock knocks both of them backwards. 'These old walls cannae take much more o' this!'

'Then you will be at this afternoon's Council to provide Townley with your opinion?'

'Indeed I shall, Lieutenant, and I curse the day that Colonel Grant abandoned me to this duty.'

The Garrison Council meets every day at noon in the long gallery near the Governor's own apartments.

'Well, gentlemen, let us begin,' says Captain Hamilton as soon as they

585

have all taken a place at the table. All except Strickland, of course, who has been carried here on his sick bed. Fourteen of them in total. Three of Townley's Captains. Townley himself. Four Captains from the Edinburgh Regiment. Arbuthnot from the Royal Écossais. Burnet. Strickland. Thomas Cappock, also too ill to travel. Lieutenant Owen, of course, as acting secretary to Hamilton. Hamilton himself. The old fellow had distinguished himself forty years ago, battling alongside Dutchman, Russian and Swede. He presides now over these meetings, today to the tuneful and regular background beat of crashing sandstone.

'Captain Hamilton,' Townley replies. 'I intend to repeat my request that some of the Edinburgh men be detached to help me with the defences. Another forty will suffice, sir.'

'They cannot be spared, Colonel, I fear,' replies Hamilton, leaning forward in the chair, one hand upon his cane. 'The townsfolk complain that they cannot move already without a stake sticking in their arse.'

'It is not the *chevaux de frises*, sir. It is the walls. They must be reinforced.'

Burnet raises a hand, still grimed from his labours.

'Colonel Townley,' he says, 'I fear that no amount of reinforcement will save those stones. Have you no ears, sir? They have not been strengthened since Old Henry's day and they were never designed to withstand the constant attentions of so many eighteen-pounders.'

'Nonsense,' cries Townley, a fine spray of spittle settling upon Peter Moss at his side. 'With sufficient men, we could dismantle some of the older buildings, construct gabions and support those positions most at risk.'

'It is the lack of men that sinks your plan, Colonel, is it not?' says Hamilton.

'Why, sir, there are men a-plenty,' Townley replies, 'if only you should release them. It was my understanding that you and I were to share this command, Captain. Yet here I find myself, once again, bonnet in hand to request additional labour. Better working on our defence than endlessly patrolling the streets, I protest!'

'It is my recollection, Colonel, that His Royal Highness agreed that we should divide responsibility only so far as the Manchester Regiment is concerned. You *are* a Colonel, when all is said and done. I, merely a Captain. Yet the Prince Regent saw fit to make me Governor of this town and its castle, sir. I have kept order here since we took the place from Durand, despite the protests of the townsfolk, and in so doing we have turned them to our Cause in the main. I will not jeopardise that peace by allocating much-needed sentries to useless endeavours!'

'Useless?' Townley hammers the flat of his hand upon the table. 'Useless? You think it useless, sir, to prepare defences against Cumberland's scum? To deny him a breach through which to assail us?'

Francis Strickland raises himself on one arm from the cot that has been set down closer to the fire.

'It seems to me, Colonel,' he says, 'that it may be foolish to assume Cumberland such a bad general that he would risk his men on some futile attempt upon a breach when he can so readily starve or pummel us to submission.'

Townley whispers something under his breath. There is no love lost here. Strickland has grown up around the Stuarts. They say that he has been Charles Edward's closest friend, though despised by James the Third for leading the boy into unruly ways. An opinion apparently shared by Townley. Strickland has been suffering some serious malady this past two weeks and is now almost too weakened to speak further. He slumps down again on the bed.

'Submission again!' cries Townley. 'Why do these damn'd meetings always turn to the subject of submission?'

'Because, Colonel,' says Arbuthnot, 'in the end we must try to discuss terms. The Prince Regent did not imagine that Cumberland would lay siege to Carlisle. He believed that the Duke would follow him quickly to Scotland and would be brought to battle there. This was an unforeseen development. But we do the Cause no service if we are simply butchered here. Even less if the townsfolk are butchered too.'

'Then let me lead a sally,' Townley says. 'With three hundred men we could spike their guns. Or most of them, I say!'

'No, Colonel,' says Hamilton. 'It would be a useless sacrifice. Cumberland made it clear that we should receive no quarter from him once Carlisle was taken. But if we seek terms now, it is just possible that we might leave here with our honour intact. For Cumberland now has wiser voices, older heads about him. I shall draft a letter, gentlemen, with your agreement. And perhaps Lieutenant Owen shall be good enough to deliver the thing?'

All are agreed with the exception of Townley and his three Manchester Captains, Moss, Fletcher and Tom Deacon, but there is one more matter to discuss.

'Before we leave, Captain,' says Townley, 'there is the question of the traitor's trial. We can delay no longer and, just as you insist on the civil laws being enforced, so too must we conform to the Prince Regent's prerogative that the Redmond woman should face the charge of sedition and, if proven guilty, pay the appropriate penalty.'

Hamilton bangs the tip of his cane upon the stone floor in frustration.

'Do we not have more important matters with which to deal, sir?' he says. 'I have argued before that His Royal Highness, having abandoned the prisoner to our charge, must surely have intended that we use our own discretion here. And discretion, I think, argues for the lady's release, does it not?' But this time it is Hamilton's turn to be shouted down. 'Very well, gentlemen. Very well. In that case, I should rule as follows. That Lieutenant Owen will deliver our proposals for terms to the Duke of Cumberland this evening. That this meeting shall reconvene at nine in the morning. And that Mistress Redmond's trial shall begin as soon afterwards as our business is complete. Are we agreed?'

'Just one minor point, sir,' says Striker, 'if you please. I wonder whether it might not be prudent to also summon the prisoner's husband? Mister Redmond is, as you know, currently at the House of Correction. He faces lesser charges but, given his prominence amongst our supporters, it might be wise that he should witness the proceedings?'

They are all in accord and, just two hours later, Striker is making his way, with Hamilton's detailed truce proposals, for the lines. He stops first, however, at the stable blocks and hay lofts on the far side of the outer bailey. The bay mare is here, tethered with the other officers' mounts. The cannon fire makes her nervous, so he sets down his valise, puts one hand under her chin, fondles her ear with the other, smoothes her forelock and strokes the firm muzzle with its thin blaze, over and over again until she settles.

Dear Ginnie, he thinks. *You have carried me far, my girl. But I cannot see beyond the morrow, I fear. I wonder whether we shall ever ride together again. Still, I have a gift for you.*

He reaches down, takes an apple, stolen from the kitchen barrels, and the mare takes it greedily from him but making sure, as she always does, to bite his fingers in the process.

'Ungrateful bitch!' says Striker, as he heads again for the English Gate.

Once more, he is surprised at the number of regiments still arriving and all, it seems, in a state of readiness. Even the militia units now seem to have found their form and, near the Priestbeck Bridge, he smiles at the sight of Sir Edward Stanley, Earl of Derby, Lord Lieutenant of Lancashire, watching his various companies at their drill.

How long is it, he wonders, *since I met the fat Earl in Newcastle's office? It must have been July last year. August perhaps.*

He has seen Sir Edward several times already as he has passed between the opposing camps but the old fellow has not recognised him and Striker has not troubled to renew their acquaintance.

But nothing can prepare Striker for the reunion that he *is* about to enjoy since, as he is ushered into Cumberland's command tent on the Stanwix Bank, he finds himself face to face with none other than Aran Owen.

'What a curious fellow you are, to be sure, Mister Owen,' says the Duke. 'A familiar to the Earl of Derby at Clifton. And now it seems you are associate of Dudley Striker. By Heaven, sir. Your reputation as an artist must be better established than I knew!'

'My dealings with Mister Striker have been quite distinct in nature, Your Grace.'

'You say so? Well, he is *Captain* Striker, of course. But you may renew your friendship later, eh? For now, Captain, what news?'

What fortune, thinks Striker, as he explains details of the Garrison Council meeting and hands Hamilton's document to the Duke. *I had imagined this thing with the Redmonds almost impossible, but if I can persuade Aran Owen to assist...*

'So they propose a truce? Tell me, Striker, how matters proceed in the town.'

Townley's meagre defences are described in detail. The weakening morale of the defenders. The deserters, another group of the Manchester men having disappeared this morning. And, as if to underline the message, Burnet's battery on the wall to the south of them fires a salvo in their direction, to be followed by the desultory *plop, plop, plop* as the shots fall one after the other into the deep waters of the River Eden.

'Have they still not reached you, Your Grace?' says Striker.

'Not a single casualty. Not one. We could stay here all winter through and never suffer a scratch. But there are grumblings. Complaints about the paucity of comforts. Is that not correct, Ligonier?' His commanders confirm that, sadly, it is so. 'Thus, we shall have to end the thing sooner rather than later. Tomorrow at noon, I think. Meanwhile, I have read this insult that Hamilton sends by way of a treaty for truce. For my own part, I should put every one of the dogs to the sword, or worse. Shall do so, too, if they resist. But Ligonier and Richmond persuade me to another path, Captain. So you may tell them this. That should they surrender then they shall be treated accordingly. Not put to the sword but, rather, reserved for the King's pleasure. Should they wish to be so treated then they must show the white flag. If that is clear, sir, then I shall leave you with our Royal Artist. If you are fortunate, he may show you some of the remarkable sketches he has made of the town and its walls. And some stirring stuff from Clifton.'

'You was at Clifton yourself, Captain Striker?' says Sir John Ligonier.

'A fie upon you, General,' Cumberland says. 'Of *course,* Striker was there! But the question you must always put to *this* gentleman, sir, is which *side* was he on. Hah, Striker. Is that not so?'

Striker's hand moves to his ribs but he smiles appreciatively at the Duke's fine sense of the comedic.

'I should never have thought to find you here, Aran Owen,' he says when they are later alone, walking the Eden's margent. 'It pleases me of all things.'

'You have come from the garrison, Striker. Do you have news of Maria-Louise? Of Mister Redmond too, perhaps?'

'Well, I am gratified that you share my joy at our reunion, my friend. Yet I suppose that I deserve no better. But I see that you already know they are imprisoned.'

'Of course. I told the entire story to Sir Edward, though he was little help. He says that they shall be freed when the town is liberated. He could barely believe that it was Maria-Louise who had ditched the entire Stuart

Exchequer. And I could barely believe that I have assisted her in the iniquity, Striker, then left her with all the blame. But Titus imprisoned too? On what grounds, sir? I knew that he was intent on seeking his wife's release but…'

'He chose, apparently, to free her without her captors' permission. Cried havoc and caused the death of two men, two horses in the process. Though he is not personally at risk, I believe. His stature amongst your Jacobite friends is too high. Do you still *count* them as friends, by the by, now that you are employed so profitably, it seems, by His Grace?'

'I had little choice in the matter. But Maria-Louise? You seem less positive about her own future, I think.'

'She stands trial tomorrow morning. Townley insists upon the thing. And the outcome can be in no doubt. They will hang the woman, Aran. Believe me, they shall! Yet I have discussed a plan with Redmond this morning.'

'You? Have spoken with Titus Redmond? And lived to tell the tale? I cannot believe you, sir.'

'It was devilish tricky. The fellow believed that I had a hand in his brother's death. The one thing in which I stand entirely innocent. So let us just say only that we have found common cause in releasing his wife. There are but two small problems.'

'And they are?'

'The first, that it cannot possibly succeed. Not in my wildest dreams. The plan requires a third person, I fear.'

'You cannot intend…'

'The Lord will always provide, or so said my dear mother. And it seems that she was correct after all. For look, here you stand. And you have, as I recall, a certain fondness for this Redmond woman, do you not? Fine wench. You will have dipped your wick in that sweet lamp, I imagine. Young rascal that you are! And such secrets between you. I am quite envious!'

'I count Mistress Redmond as a valued friend.'

'Yet you colour so to speak her name. La! We are both men of the world, sir. And at least you now have a chance to show your worth to this *valued friend*.'

'And for what purpose do you need a third, Striker, though I almost dread to ask the question.'

'Ah! A simple matter. At some point tomorrow, either during the trial or afterwards, myself and Redmond will free his wife. We shall wait for the most propitious moment and must then get her from the outer bailey into the town. It will be impossible unless there is some diversion.'

'And what form of diversion do you have in mind?'

'I have something. No real peril involved, I believe. But might I first crave a boon from you, dear fellow?'

'It involves no exchange of tokens, I trust?' says Aran, holding up his left hand with its missing digit.

'A cruel reminder of harsh times, sir. It ill befits you to confront me with such things. Much water under many bridges since then, eh? But no. No tokens. Just this.' He unslings the valise from his back. 'My possessions. I should be grateful if you can ensure their safekeeping until this thing is done. The outcome is, after all, far from certain. I should not, however, be able to carry it tomorrow.'

Aran agrees and takes the valise, hefting its weight in his hand.

'What, in the name of God, do you carry in the thing?' he says. 'But, yes, I shall ensure its safekeeping. Now, sir, the diversion?'

'In truth, I did not know. It was the Duke that inspired me. The most simple of inventions! The castle's surrender!'

'Your pardon, sir?'

'Nothing less will suffice. And I mentioned a second small matter, I think?'

'Tell me!'

'Ah, this is a significantly easier problem. You see, Titus Redmond, generous soul that he is, has offered to recompense me for my part in the rescue. You, Aran, shall reap rewards in your own way, I am sure. It is simply this. That should your employer fail to honour his agreement, for whatever reason, I would seek your word that you might intercede with an alternative source of payment. Mister Bradley, perhaps? Or his charming young wife…?'

Striker stays the night in the encampment but, at first light, he escorts a troubled Aran into Carlisle, that has suffered Cumberland's bombardment the whole night through. The guards sheltering within the protection of the English Gate know him well enough and he vouches for his companion as a messenger come from Manchester with a message for Colonel Townley. It is too early to visit Titus just yet and, anyway, Aran has a yearning to discover Scarrow's Coffee House with which he and his Fly Wagon have had so many dealings. He is treated there like an old and familiar friend. Scarrow is proud of his Fisher Street establishment, proud too that it served as a gathering place for so many Carlisle Jacobites even when they were badly persecuted here. Aran accepts a pipe of tobacco. Inevitably, they discuss tea. The *Twankay* and *Singo* that the locals favour. Criminal that Mister Redmond has been forced to sell the business. And to a Whig as well, they are told. A scandal. Yet not such a scandal as the poor fellow now being held at the House of Correction. What is the world coming to? Yet they will withstand this siege, never fear, though his other customers seem not so certain and several houses near the eastern wall have been fired by those damn'd coehorn shells.

'Listen, my dear,' Striker says, as he walks with Aran back towards the gaol, 'I have been thinking. It may be best that we keep the precise nature of your own part in this endeavour from Mister Redmond. You may find him somewhat disorientated from his time in that dark place and too much detail is apt to confuse him. Simply remember, friend Aran, that you must be promptly at the linen store. You have the diagram I made for you? Excellent. The linen store and then, at twelve sharp by the Cathedral bell, upon the battlements of Ireby's Tower. You shall pass through its gates on the way to the keep. Mark it well, sir.'

He leaves Aran at the entrance to the House of Correction, garnishes the turnkey with a full sovereign and makes clear his instructions. When the escort comes to collect the prisoner, this young man must go with them. Under instruction of Lieutenant Owen, and the authority of Captain Hamilton. It takes a moment before Striker is satisfied that all is understood and he leaves Aran with the difficult task of providing a limited explanation to Redmond for his presence and purpose here.

Though the fellow is a fine liar, I have found, to his credit. A pity that his talents are wasted so!

The Garrison Council is reduced to an inauspicious thirteen members this morning. For Francis Strickland has died during the night, of his dropsy, choked on his own vomit, they say. And it has cast a strange doom about the place. Strickland had never been a popular fellow despite being so close to Charles Edward. Yet he was, in the end, one of the Seven Men, that small band of intimates who had sailed with the Prince on his adventure and landed with him at Moidart. They have assumed an almost religious reverence in these past months. O'Sullivan possesses the same, Striker has noticed, being another of this mystic group.

And they shall bury Strickland at noon, it seems. A stroke of luck, at last!

Captain Hamilton invites Cappock to read a short prayer from his missal. It takes longer than they should have liked, for this former-Chaplain to the Prince coughs and chokes over every line. Impatience grows, and the collective *Amen* still hangs in the air when Townley demands to know Cumberland's response.

Striker cannot resist the dramatic, naturally, but he sets out the Duke's answer plain enough. If they surrender, they shall not be put to the sword, nor the town suffer pillage, but shall be reserved for the King's pleasure.

'Well,' says Hamilton, 'that is some progress, at least.'

'Progress?' Townley cries, leaping to his feet. His eyes are wild, red-rimmed. 'Progress? They will simply butcher us on the scaffold, sir, rather than upon the streets.'

Yes, and slowly, I trust.

'I do not see that we have a choice, Colonel. What would you have us do, sir?' Hamilton says, his own temper rising.

'Strengthen our defences, Captain. And you, Lieutenant, did you glean any details of when Cumberland intends to attack if we reject his kind offer?'

'I did not, Colonel,' Striker lies. 'Though he seemed in no great haste.'

'Nor should he need any,' says Burnet. 'For soon there shall be no defences left to us. They have been firing continuously now for twenty-five hours, gentlemen. We count that, in this time, they have fired a thousand shot. Eight score hundredweight of iron! It will not hold, Captain. The parapets are crumbling and the walls are split wide in four different places.'

'Whether the walls hold or fall, I shall not be taken alive,' says Townley. 'We have seen some of Cumberland's justice already. No, gentlemen, I tell you this. That when the attack begins, I shall make my stand here, sword in hand, with any who will join me!'

There is no vote on the matter, simply a general clamouring of support for Townley's principle. A final stand it shall be.

'And I collect then,' says Hamilton, 'that we should want Mistress Redmond's trial to proceed. Though I should tell you that I would not wish any part of the thing personally.'

'Then allow me to remove the burden from you,' says Townley. 'Our joint command can stretch thus far, surely. That I might preside in your stead.'

Hamilton hesitates but finally agrees, and the prisoner is sent for. Her husband too.

'Colonel Townley,' Striker whispers. 'A word with you, sir? You recall that we once discussed the fellow employed by Redmond. Aran Owen, by name?'

'Indeed, Lieutenant. We were still at Derby, I collect. With victory imminent. Until you brought word of the Elector's armies on the road ahead. Am I correct?'

'That *was* the time, I believe. Yes. But I have met that same fellow at the House of Correction. On my return to town I passed the gaol and the turnkey drew my attention to the man. He had been making enquiries about Mister Redmond. I instructed that he should be detained there and, perhaps, brought to your presence when Redmond himself is fetched.'

'Aran Owen, here? I cannot believe it. He has left it late if he wants to enlist, do you not think?'

'I sense that he came from loyalty to the Redmonds, Colonel. Messages from the family, perhaps.'

'Family, sir? You call *that* a family? Their eldest is a tribade, Lieutenant. Can you imagine, sir? And worse, the girl that I should have chosen for my wife, Miss Byrom, so taken with this Rosina that I fear she may share her affliction. It is infectious, they say, this Silent Sin. Is that not correct? The youngest is a feather-brain child. Another permanently in a trance. Yet the fourth, Katherine, is fair enough. Well, no harm done. It will pleasure me to have them both witness the whore's fate.'

Anxious minutes pass with no sign of Maria-Louise, though she is only a few rooms distant. Townley, pacing the floor now, calls for Peter Moss to find out what has happened and, meanwhile, a small escort of Manchester men arrive, bringing a shackled Titus Redmond, with Aran following just behind.

Titus has spent ten days in the House of Correction. His wig is gone, the stubble of his head almost entirely white, and the creased skin of his face barely better. His shirt is filthy and he brings the stench of ordure into the chamber with him. A heavy blanket is wrapped about his shoulders.

'Are the fetters really necessary, Colonel?' says Hamilton.

'Indeed, sir. Mister Redmond has committed a serious felony. We shall see how he comports himself during the trial perhaps. And Mister Owen! Give you joy of your decision to join us at last. A welcome addition to our ranks. As soon as these proceedings are done, we shall list you for the Regiment, my friend. And what news of Manchester?'

How admirable, Striker thinks, as he listens to Aran's account, *to modulate himself so. He is quite a fellow. He must feel such glee that Townley and the others are dispossessed, yet he tells the tale with so much sorrow. And he leaves out a great deal, I sense. Those parts that might wound Redmond, I imagine.*

'You see, Titus?' Townley bellows when Aran's news is all told. 'Yet more crimes for which your wife shall answer!'

Titus looks at the Colonel coldly, any retort that he might have made now silenced by the arrival of Maria-Louise.

She is, indeed, a beauty. Like a veritable image of the faerie queen herself. And the sprite has prepared herself for this ordeal. Powdered and primped as though for a rout. Yet God alone knows how she has done so! No more than the flicker of an eye to acknowledge her husband. The same for poor Aran. He looks fit for tears, does he not? But I know that look in her eye. She has composed herself for a fight that only she can undertake. Redmond knows it too. See how his chin comes up. And what is that sign he makes with his fingers? Defiant fuckers, both of them.

They have set a chair for Maria-Louise a little apart from the table.

Townley has prepared some papers, more for effect than anything else, and he studies them now, sitting at the table's head.

'Do I face my accusers alone then?' says Maria-Louise, without waiting for Townley to finish his mummery. 'Shall there be none to defend me? To act as my counsel?'

'You are suspected and accused of treason, madam,' Townley replies, setting down the papers. 'Those so accused are never allowed Counsel. It is the law of this land.'

'I hope that you may live to regret those words, Colonel. Yet I do not know the laws by which this trial is held. Can somebody describe them for me?'

'Why, madam, we proceed by equity and right.'

'Then by equity and right might I not refuse to attend? For I do not recognise the authority of those around your table.'

'As you please, Mistress Redmond,' says Townley. 'We may deal with the charges in your absence, however, I collect. It is a normal process when dealing with cases of sedition.'

'Charges, you say? And will one of these gentlemen advise me of their substance? What are these charges, Colonel Townley?'

Townley turns to George Fletcher, one of his Manchester Captains, who lifts a parchment, reads it with painful deliberation.

'Mistress Maria-Louise Redmond, of Market Street Lane in Manchester...'

Oh, they have rehearsed their lines. Clever dogs!

'...Is hereby charged with receiving intelligence from her husband, Mister Titus Redmond, at a date yet unspecified, and Mister Redmond being a conf...'

'*Confidant!*' says Townley.

'...Being a confidant of the Prince Regent's agents and advisers, this intelligence being sensitive in the extreme and concerning passage of the Royal Exchequer from Rome to Scotland, a matter vital to the future welfare and security of this realm, and with then sharing said intelligence to representatives, as yet nameless, and on a further date yet unspecified, resulting in considerable loss to the Crown and harm to the common wealth of this nation. These charges constituting an act of high treason...'

'Enough, I think!' Townley says. 'Mistress Redmond asked only for the charges. She has them now.'

'Indeed!' she says. 'Dates unspecified. Nameless representatives. Your charges, the evidence with which you hope to support them, circumstantial I think, Colonel. At the least.'

'You were accused by your own daughter, madam. Many of us were present to witness the thing. You were offered the chance to deny the charge by swearing upon the Holy Bible, were you not? Should you like to foreswear now, Mistress? Reverend Cappock could accommodate you, I am sure. You could be free within the hour. What say you, madam?'

'I could not so profane myself.'

'Then you do not deny it?'

'I cannot. Yet I may perhaps explain. For my action was not malicious in intent, as you imply.'

'Then please, madam. Explain to these gentlemen how sedition might be something other than malicious.'

'It may be so when the act is intended to benefit the nation, rather than harm it. I had believed that only part of the Exchequer would be transported to Scotland, and that part destined to finance French invasion. I am hardly alone in staunchly supporting the Stuart Crown while, at the same time, mistrusting that of French Louis.'

'You thought, then, to set yourself above the judgement of His Royal Highness? Is that not also seditious?'

'I believed that Our Lady had given me guidance on the issue. A higher authority, Colonel Townley.'

'I think, madam, that you add blasphemy to your crimes. But let us leave that aside. You considered the act, therefore, a virtuous one?'

'I intended it so.'

'And you are a virtuous woman, Mistress Redmond?'

'I do not understand your meaning, sir.'

'Your daughter, I collect, said that you had informed her husband, Mister Bradley of your deed. Is that not so?'

'Yes.'

'And Bradley is the leader of the Whiggish faction in Manchester. Is that so?'

'He is.'

'A *confidant* of the Lord Lieutenant of Lancashire, too?'

'I believe so.'

'The Earl of Derby had dinner with your daughter and her husband, recently. Is that correct?'

Maria-Louise darts a glance at Aran.

'I believe so.'

'And you have a lustful liaison with this fellow Bradley. Is *that* not so?'

'Your pardon, Colonel Townley?'

'Should you care for Reverend Cappock's bible at this point?'

'No, there is no need.'

'Then you do not deny the thing?'

'No.'

'This woman is a whore!' cries Townley. 'She has no virtue in her body. She does not understand the meaning of the word. She sold the secret because she is a traitor, seduced to a traitor's ways by her lover? Is that not so, madam?'

'No.'

'Then explain it, Mistress Redmond. How else might this intelligence have passed from yourself to the Duke of Newcastle?'

'I cannot say.'

'Then you shall hang for it, madam. You have heard, gentlemen. Mistress Redmond neither denies the charges nor her association with the Whig leadership. As President of this hearing, I do not need to hear further testimony. Does any wish to speak? No? Then what say you? Those who find the defendant not guilty of the charges...?' Hamilton's hand is raised. Burnet's. Tom Deacon's. 'And those who find this woman guilty of sedition?' The rest, with the exception of Lieutenant William Owen, whose abstention is not even noticed. 'Very well. The sentence of this military court, Mistress Redmond, is that you shall be hanged at one o'clock this afternoon. And may Our Lord have mercy on your treacherous soul!'

He slaps his hand on the table, and the escort lift a now silent

Maria-Louise from her chair, taking her back to her room past the lowered heads of the spectators.

Yet Redmond does not seem cowed. Look at him. Vain fellow! Not a flicker of fear.

'Colonel,' says Striker, 'what of *Mister* Redmond?'

Townley looks at Titus, a barely concealed smile on his lips and Striker imagines that he hears the word *spent* whispered on the Colonel's breath.

'Mister Redmond may pass the time between now and noon with his wife, though they shall remain under guard at all times, Lieutenant. His shackles may be removed. At twelve, he will leave her so that she can prepare herself with Reverend Cappock.'

Titus is also escorted away, to the room occupied by Maria-Louise.

Hamilton comes forward.

'And where, precisely, shall the execution be conducted, Colonel. We can scarcely ask Cumberland's permission to use Gallows Hill, I suppose.'

'There are two possibilities. The hoist for the hay loft. Or the lifting bridge over the moat. Either will suffice, though the bridge may be more appropriate. More public. I will ask Captain Fletcher to make the arrangements.' Striker turns towards Aran Owen, a quick gesture of the head. *Go, you fool, while you remain unobserved.* And Aran is gone. Hopefully to the linen store, as Striker has instructed. 'Now, gentlemen, let us get Mister Strickland in the ground.'

It is morbid fascination that, shortly afterwards, leads Striker to follow Strickland's funeral procession as it passes through the gateway of Ireby's Tower and over the very bridge towards the Cathedral and its burial ground. But he goes no further, waiting with Fletcher's smaller party, head bowed in solemnity, until the short *corteggio* has gone past.

'Right lads,' says Fletcher to his Manchester men, 'let's get this done!'

And prettily too! Efficient. For the design of the bridge follows the normal counterweight pattern, its upright frame on the moat's edge nearest the castle, its arms pivoted and joined to the further end of the lifting section by chains. Counterweights at the other end so that, with little effort, the bridge can be pulled to its upright position. With a noose slung forward, near the chains, Maria-Louise will simply need the lightest push over the side, the bridge lifted and…

Striker's preparations follow their normal pattern. He checks that the small room he shares with a dozen men of the Edinburgh Regiment is empty and he pulls the square portmanteau box from beneath his cot. Here is the case with its brace of martial pistols and tools. Flint checked. Touch-hole cleared. Lock oiled, then dried thoroughly along with the bore. Half-cock. Frizzen open. Powder in the outer pan. Frizzen closed. Barrel charged, Ball and wadding rammed home. Left half-cocked in the safety position. Second pistol the same.

Then the Queen Anne's turn-off piece, cleaned and readied. He would never again make the mistake of forgetting the tiny gun's potential. The paring knife too. And a further weapon. A beautifully sharpened carpenter's axe, a shingling hatchet, he thinks, for it has a long blade and, at the rear, a pair of wickedly sharp claws for drawing nails.

The military pistols are tucked into their leather holsters, beneath his redingote, the paring knife in one of the coat pockets, the turn-off gun down his boot-top. The hatchet in a belt worn over his waistcoat and also carrying his powder horn. A few extra bullets. Some of the *cartouches*.

He looks for a moment at the pistol case. It is very fine but he cannot take it. The tools, however, he also stuffs into a pocket.

I should not want to lose them and, after all, this is unlikely to be a stealthy adventure.

He checks the Graham timepiece with Sir Peter Leighton's monogram. Thirty minutes past eleven. *Time to go!*

Striker walks across the outer bailey, counting sentries though most are sheltering from the whistling iron of the bombardment. Then Ireby's Tower. Six flights of steps to the top. No sign of Aran Owen but there is still time. The walkway to Stephen von Haschenberg's Half-Moon bastion, the Captain's Tower once more and then the keep itself. He checks the chapel on the ground floor.

More flights of steps and, so far, he has attracted little attention.

Yet why should I? They have seen me here and there for a week.

Ten minutes to noon and Striker has reached the room where Maria-Louise is held, now doubly so with her husband's arms about her. He is whispering into her hair. Comforting and caressing. But with little intimacy permitted for there are three of the Manchester men in the room also. Three more outside and the young Ensign, Charlie Deacon, in charge.

'Ah, Mister Deacon,' says Striker. 'My compliments, sir. I am sent to fetch the prisoner. Reverend Cappock will attend her confession in the chapel rather than here, it seems.'

'I was told, Lieutenant, that under no circumstances…'

'I think you forget yourself, Mister Deacon. I act on behalf of Captain Hamilton.'

'And I for Colonel Townley, sir. He has authority in this matter of Mistress Redmond, I collect.'

'Well, damn your eyes, Ensign. We shall see about this later. Yet you can escort the lady yourself to the chapel, surely? You have six men and myself to ensure that all is well, after all.'

The boy looks about him. Maria-Louise gives him the smile of an angel. No, better, that of a mother.

'Very well, Lieutenant. If you please, madam. Reverend Cappock awaits you in the chapel, it seems. And, if I may say so, Mistress Redmond, how very much I regret the turn that events have taken.'

'All is well, Charles. And do not fear, young man. Perhaps I shall see your Mama soon. I shall give her your love, my dear. I promise.'

Charlie Deacon's fifteen-year old face flushes and he rubs a fist hard at his cheek and eyes. But he does his duty. Four guards in front. Two at the rear with himself and Lieutenant Owen. Down the stairwell, boots ringing on the stone treads. Along the ground floor passage and the chapel doors, both flung open. The forward guards take a few paces towards the central aisle while Titus and Maria-Louise pause for a last embrace before... Before Striker sends the two following guards catapulting into Deacon's back. A tall candlestick crashes to the ground also, entangling the struggling group while the other four fellows lift and cock their muskets.

But by this time, Striker has taken one of Mistress Redmond's arms, Titus the other, and they have wrenched her back through the doors, slamming them closed as the first bullets hit the oak panels. They each turn the keys that Striker has left in the locks and, while the Ensign and his men begin hammering for release, they make their way out once more to the inner bailey, colliding with Reverend Cappock as they do so.

The priest smiles at first, thinking himself pleased to see them, then hears the shouting from the chapel beyond.

'Lieutenant...' he says. But no more than that, for Titus has laid the fellow cold.

'Father, forgive me!' he says, genuflecting as he does so.

Striker jumps over Cappock's sprawled body.

'Come on!' he shouts. 'No time to waste.' For Maria-Louise has chosen a most inappropriate moment to start seeking explanations.

And now what? Is this damn'd timepiece slow?

He had not noticed before but it is suddenly very still. The bombardment has ceased. Then the alarm bells shatter the peace, begin to clamour all along the walls. And, from the far side of the town, an explosion. A petard perhaps. And the hailstone clatter of distant musketry.

Cumberland has started early!

The battlement should still have been clear along the castle's southern wall but it is now filling with men. Worse, the portcullis of Ireby's tower gatehouse is falling and the great gates are being closed behind it. They are trapped within the outer bailey.

Trapped and pursued. For somebody has released Deacon and his men.

'Stop those traitors!' he cries, though he is still some way distant, only just on the walkway from the Half-Moon Battery.

One defender alone is near enough to hear, turns just in time for his face to be split by Striker's hatchet.

'No!' shouts Maria-Louise. 'You must not.'

'Come, my dear,' says Titus, stroking her hand. 'You must avert your eyes, I fear.' And he pulls her after Striker towards the gatehouse tunnel. 'Look,' Titus continues, 'here comes Aran Owen too. He will look after you, I think!'

Though Titus looks strangely at Aran, struggling towards them from the buildings on the far side of the yard, his stomach monstrously distended beneath his coat.

'The steps!' shouts Striker. 'We must get to the top. Nothing else for it!'

They push through the confusion of milling Jacobites in the tunnel, enter the gatehouse proper and start up the stairs, running as hard as they may until they come through the door on the roof, five floors above the ground. The door opens inwards, however. There is no key to lock it behind them, and there are already sounds of pursuit from below. At the parapet embrasures are three sentries, but entirely occupied with the attack developing below them, in the town.

'Now what?' says Titus.

'Just hold the door against them. Use this!' And he hands the hatchet to Redmond.

Striker draws and cocks his pistols, moves close to the nearest. But not *too* close.

He levels both pistols, the left at the farthest fellow, the right at the Scotsmen in the middle embrasure. He pulls the triggers and, before the smoke has cleared, he steps quickly to the third guard, now turned towards him but felled by the butt of Striker's gun, his mouth a bloodied mess.

Paring knife, he thinks, rushing through the still hanging smoke to cut the throats of first one, then the second and, finally, the third.

Maria-Louise has her head buried in Aran's shoulder, while Titus has pulled the door closed to the best of his ability. The fools inside are too packed for the use of their muskets but they keep pulling the door open again and Titus is hacking at them with the axe.

Striker pulls the turn-off piece from his boot, runs to Redmond's side and points it blind through the opening gap. *Crack.* A scream within and the door goes slack, quickly closed again by Titus.

Sliding his back down the wall, Striker loads the brace of pistols again but does not bother with the turn-off piece.

'Here!' he says to Titus. 'Take these. Just shoot anything that tries to come through.'

He runs to the embrasure nearest to the tower's flagpole, gazing up at it a moment, then surveying the chaos below, looking south-east along Castle Street where a party of Jacobites is fighting a rearguard action against large numbers of advancing redcoats. Smoke and musket fire everywhere.

The Jacobites – Townley and the officers from Strickland's funeral – have now reached the open ground, snow-covered, just ahead of the moat, with its lifting bridge. Striker realises, too, that the tower's gate has been opened again to allow as many of their fleeing Jacobites as possible to seek refuge within the castle once more.

For their last stand, they imagine!

There is a shot behind him. Another scream. Titus taking control of the door once again.

If the gate is open...

But the wild thought blows away on the gathering breeze.

We would never get through. Not all of us.

'Aran,' he calls, 'do you have it?' And he starts untying the flagpole lanyard from its cleat.

'It has not struck twelve,' Aran replies.

'You bloody fool, just bring it!'

Aran releases Marie-Louise, fumbles with his coat, pulls an enormous while linen sheet and crosses to the flagpole.

Another glance below. Townley now across the bridge but a press of men at his heels so that it cannot be closed and the redcoats bringing down one after another amongst the packed fugitives.

Aran behind him with the sheet. Titus peering through a crack, the door just ajar.

'They have gone down,' he calls.

More for them to worry about below, I imagine!

He begins to tie the lanyard around one corner of the sheet.

'For God's sake,' says Titus. 'What are you doing?'

'To surrender the castle, my friend. We shall prevent a shambles if we hoist now.'

'You cannot, sir,' Titus replies.

'Are you mad, Redmond? You want to die? Your wife too?'

Titus looks a moment at Maria-Louise. She smiles at him. Redmond raises the remaining loaded pistol.

'The only thing certain upon this rooftop, Lieutenant Owen... Will somebody tell me this cunny-sucker's *true* name?'

'Allow me to introduce Captain Dudley Striker, sir,' says Aran.

'Then it is *this*, Captain Striker. That *you* certainly do not wish to die here and, this being so, you will release that infernal sheet, sir. Aran, if you please.'

Aran takes the sheet from Striker's hand, starts to untie the lanyard while Titus gestures for Striker himself to move back. He does so.

Titus Redmond runs to the flagpole to help his young associate and Dudley Striker smiles to see them at work together.

'That useless left hand, boy!' says Titus. 'It is fit for nothing. Now, Captain Striker. You should know this also. We are Jacobites, sir. Each of us that you see here. We have worked these God knows how many years to clear this land of the Hanover Usurpers. Ah, there!' The sheet has finally come free and Titus steps back to the wall. 'It has been a long story,' he continues, 'and, for we three, at least, this is likely to be the final chapter. I had promised my wife that we would travel together. Venice perhaps. Paris, though she despises the French so much that we may have tried to pass through that country with

601

indecent haste. But not now. It is more likely that we are soon to see glories beyond our imagination, Captain.'

Maria-Louise has moved forward to the flagpole too, while Striker is now sheltering just past the next embrasure. He risks a glance below. Redcoats everywhere, the bridge taken but the gates closed against them, a ragged fire upon them from the walls to either side but not from Ireby's Tower itself. And there, just this side of the bridge, is a large gentleman, Sir Edward Stanley. He has a dragoon pistol in his hand. He aims it up at the walls.

Too far, surely!

'And I may despise Townley for a lick-spittle, Striker, yet we would prefer to die here with him, as free Jacobites, than go to Cumberland's gallows or, worse still, to continue living under Hanover's heel.'

Sir Edward's pistol discharges, its report only just discernible amongst all the other gunfire.

Six feet below the embrasure, a pistol bullet hits sandstone, whines away into the distance. Titus Redmond turns at the noise, lifts a finger to his moustache and, as he does so, Colonel Francis Townley bursts through the door onto the roof, his own pistols cocked and ready.

Titus takes a step forward.

'You fool, Townley,' says Titus. 'Impatience was always bound to be your downfall!' Then he looks past Maria-Louise at something only he can perceive. 'Your father, my dear...' he says to Maria-Louise. And the pistols bark. Once. Twice.

One ball takes him in the chest and his hand moves there, still clutching the linen sheet. He staggers back. The second catches him square in the brow, just above those piercing blue eyes. His head jerks back. He drops Striker's pistol. It discharges too, but harmlessly. And he lifts his fingers to the stubble where his wig should be.

'Cunny-sucker!' he says, and collapses back through the embrasure.

Striker leaps forward to catch him, succeeds only in grasping an ankle.

'Help me!' Striker shouts, and Aran is at his side, holding the other leg so that Striker can catch the lanyard, lashing a quick but expert turn about Redmond's feet. 'I trust that you will remember our bargain, Mister Owen?' Striker gasps. 'A modest purse will suffice now, I think.'

'Pull him up, for pity's sake!' cries Maria-Louise.

Pull him up, madam? The fellow is far more use dead than ever he was alive!

And he heaves Titus Redmond's legs over the edge so that the body swings, suspended from the tower's parapet, the white linen sheet still gripped in his hand, billowing out its signal of the garrison's surrender and the sealing of so many fates.

Chapter Fifty-Five

Sir Edward considers the job well done. All England is now free of the Jacobite *banditti* once more, and the Duke has been as good as his word. Not one of the prisoners put to the sword. They are safely out of the way, all the same. The officers consigned to the castle's *oubliette*, left to lick whatever sustenance they may find from the damp walls. The rest virtually entombed, three hundred of them, within the Cathedral, now become a cess pit. Nobody will feed them, naturally. Five of them already dead. Dozens more will not survive the next few weeks. And the rest are already destined for the dungeons where they will await their trials – though he cannot understand why the Government would want to waste money on such a foregone conclusion.

The clergy have complained endlessly about the Cathedral but they are as guilty as the rest of collaborating with the enemy. So their fine temple turned to pitiless prison is a fitting punishment for them. It will be a long time before they clean this Augean Stable. The mayor arrested too, the town clerk, the postmaster. Collaborators, each of them. And the coffee house burned to the ground, Scarrow's nest of rats finally destroyed.

Yes, it were a damn'd fine show! he thinks as their small convoy leaves Wigan on the Manchester Road.

The Earl of Derby has been permitted a modest escort as befits his heroic status. Veteran of Clifton Moor and also the first of King George's officers upon the scene to accept the surrender of Carlisle's castle.

Though was anybody to ask me for a full account, I am buggered if I could provide same. It were all so damn'd confusing, the gate opening and closing like a trout's mouth. The portcullis run up, then down, then up again. But so many cries that they had struck, I protest that any decision was took for them. And poor Redmond's body there like a pendulum, the white flag blowing in the wind for all to observe plain enough. Strangest thing I ever saw though, methinks.

He looks back down the column to the line of carts that they seem to have accumulated on the way, including some of the loyalist families from Manchester now returning there having fled to other parts of the County. *His* County again. Though he must say farewell to some of his glory soon enough. His Companies are ordered to gather in Lancaster, six days hence, when the Lancashire Regiment of Militia will be disbanded. And the Lord Lieutenant's position will undoubtedly be abolished once more, until the next crisis at least, as soon as Parliament determines the rebellion to be entirely crushed.

But not yet. For Cumberland, presently on his way back to London, must eventually pursue the Pretender across the wilds of Scotland and, unless he misses his guess, the Jacobite army still has teeth a-plenty with which to tear its foes. And there is always the chance, the very real chance, that the *Chevalier* might find his way back to England yet again.

Sir Edward rides back down the column until he reaches the party strung out around the Redmonds' Fly Wagon.

'I were just thinking, Mister Bradley, that we should be on our guard against that damn'd Pretender sneaking back across the border again. Do you think that Manchester is still a threat for us, sir?'

'With so many of its young men taken, Sir Edward? I think not. We should have no sympathy for them, I suppose, but to leave them in such condition. It is monstrous.'

Bradley had arrived in Carlisle just a few hours after the surrender, along with that gangrel Irishman, O'Farrell. It was the Redmond woman, of course, that drew him there. The Earl had expected him to be pleased with the outcome. The Jacobites taken, including many of those who had humiliated the fellow so much during Charles Edward's occupations of the town. His rival, Redmond, dead too. Sir Edward had come to quite like the rebel merchant but he would have thought Bradley satisfied to see him dangling from the flagpole. But Bradley had wept. At the bodies in the streets. At the prisoners being herded to their imprisonment. At the sight of Redmond's body.

So Cumberland had agreed that the corpse could be taken down. The white flag had, in any case, finally come free from Redmond's hand, fluttering away to settle on the Eden's current, carrying its ebb towards the Solway Firth.

'No less than they deserve, I think,' says Sir Edward. 'Yet it were well that you arrived. If you had not insisted on the search for Mistress Redmond, she might be with the devils still. Though I suppose His Grace would have realised his artist was missing at *some* point. I have rarely seen him so livid. That the fellow should have absented himself without permission in that way!'

No sign of the other cove though. Strange tale, to be sure. Feel guilty now that I took no more note of Mister Owen when he told me the woman was taken for a prisoner. Nothing we could do though, I suppose. And she lived to tell the tale. Though quite how I do not know. Claim they escaped to the roof together with Redmond and some spy of O'Sullivan's. Frightful great scuffle with Townley. Now there is a man whose trial I shall relish! But this spy...

'I have never had any great opinion of Aran Owen, Sir Edward,' says Bradley, 'but I fear I must now moderate my views. Had he not ventured into that den of vipers, I dread to think what might have happened to Mistress Redmond. For she had no help from the rest of you! And unfair that

Cumberland should have dismissed him from his service, though Aran seems little troubled by the punishment.'

Mister Bradley remains as curt with me as the day I first met him. He does not like me, sirrah. Discourteous hound! He is merely a Court Leet Juror after all. A builder of houses.

'Well, I must confess, Mister Bradley, that I initially found their story less than convincing. And did you know, sir, that one of Newcastle's *own* agents is missing? A Captain, Striker by name, and sent to deliver an ultimatum to the rebels. Never seen again. I met him once, I think, though I do not recall him properly. Cumberland believes that the devils killed him for his troubles.'

'It would not surprise me. It has sometimes seemed to me that this whole drama has been beset by spies of one cut or another. A dirty and perfidious profession, I think. And beset with dangers. Though even Mistress Redmond, I suppose, could claim herself a member of its fellowship.'

'And how does the lady fare, Mister Bradley?'

'As you see, Sir Edward. She rides the Fly Wagon that now serves as a bier for her husband, O'Farrell beside her. I have grown fond of that creaking pirate, I find. The journey north must have been hard on him but I could not stop him from joining me when I told him my intention and he rode like the very devil, despite his joints. Will you not speak with the lady yourself, sir?'

'I think not. She still sees me as the enemy, you know. She is polite, but no more. A strange creature, Mister Bradley. I warned you once not to be naive in that direction, did I not? Yet you did not attend me. When Newcastle told me that informants in Manchester had helped deliver the Old Pretender's coffers, I assumed it to be *you*, sir. And there I were, sitting at your dinner table thinking the same thought. Yet it were *she*, it seems. But I am not deceived by the woman. She must have had her own reasons for the deed and we should be glad of it. But she is still one of *them*, Bradley, at heart. Why, we had to almost drag her from the Cathedral, for she could not bear to be parted, as you will recall, from her Jacobite friends. She will always be so, sir. And worse, she is a Papist!'

Several hours later and they are crossing the Irwell's bridge from Salford into Manchester. It is thronged with people, a very mixed crowd, most of them the town's remaining Tories and Jacobites, come to solemnly pay their respects to a fallen leader, for they seem to know only that Titus Redmond died in the defence of Carlisle against the Hanoverian foe. But there are others, a raucous and unpleasant bunch, come to celebrate Redmond's death as a symbol of the rebels' downfall.

And so it is, I suppose, but this display of ranters does our own cause no good, I fear.

He sees Bradley in discussion with Aran Owen, riding side by side, and Sir Edward joins them.

'You will forgive me, gentlemen...'

Bradley passes an object to the artist.

'Here,' he says. 'Return it to her, will you? You will find her at the Byroms' house. My apologies, Sir Edward. My wife's journal. I found the thing. We are estranged, you know. So I have asked Mister Owen to restore her property.'

'I should not have troubled Bishop Peploe with conducting the service if I had known the thing would be so temporary, sir.'

'You had reason to make the arrangement as a service to Mister Redmond, as I collect. Lordship.'

Things was different then, though. Damn'd Jacobites might have pulled it off, after all. May have needed the odd favour or two from Redmond and his ilk.

'Indeed, you may be correct, Mister Bradley. But I simply came to say that I shall ride ahead. Summon my Warrington Company. In the meanwhile, my escort will attempt to silence these ruffians. Mistress Redmond is entitled to her mourning at least, I think.'

But his Militia Company is not so easily found. He rides about the town, from one designated sentry post to another. At the Cross. At the Collegiate Church. At Deansgate's southern extremity. At Camp Field. And at the Lever's House. It is Lady Lever's pox-marked son who tells him the news. That his militiamen have mostly already disbanded themselves, returned to their Warrington homes, the officers normally to be found at Mistress Cooper's coffee house.

And there, right enough, he finds Captain Thomas Patten, Surgeon Lieutenant William Leigh and Ensign Harry Tobin.

'A word with you Captain,' says Sir Edward, ignoring the crippled cove who tries to take a penny from him.

'Lordship!' cries the fifty-five year old company commander, springing to his feet. 'We had not expected you, sir.'

'That much is evidently correct, for I find my entire Company dispersed. Not a sign of them anywhere!'

'The fault does not lie with your officers, Sir Edward,' says Elizabeth Cooper, coming to join them. 'It was Sir Oswald, I fear. He returned to town at last week's end.'

'Ah! When he thought it safe to do so, I collect. Yet what, prithee, is Sir Oswald's part in this?'

'He instructed us, Lordship,' says Patten, 'that the rebellion now being over, there was no longer any need for a military presence within his Manor.'

'His Manor? Damn the fellow, he abandoned it quick enough when he saw trouble brewing. Ah, yes. Tea. I thank you, Mistress Cooper. Most kind. And the rebellion over? Does he say so? There must be five thousand Jacobites still under arms in Scotland. Does he not realise. But you, sir! The Company was under *your* command, not Sir Oswald Mosley's. Did you not trouble to gainsay him?'

'We tried, Lordship. But they began to drift away in small groups and then, when they started the bells for the capture of Carlisle...'

'And give you joy of that victory, Sir Edward,' says Mistress Cooper. 'The town is still telling tales of your valour in the action, I understand.'

'Are they, by God. Well, there is a thing! But the bells, Captain, you say?'

'Yes, sir. The bells were rung, night and day. Great bonfires and the Bellman crying for all to light their windows. Barrels of ale upon the streets. And effigies of the Pretender carried about the town. A great mob. Smashed every window that was not illuminated. And all the town's fine gentlemen taking turns at twisting the Prince's nose...'

'What brave fellows they have become then,' says Sir Edward, his irony entirely lost on those around him.

'Indeed, Lordship. And then the effigy hung from the Angel's signpost, before they took him down to quarter and burn the thing. I believe that was the final spur to send the rest of the men home, sir. We tried to stop them but...'

'But the Captain had little assistance, I understand,' says a voice from behind Sir Edward.

He turns. It is Aran Owen.

'Mister Owen! You have something to say on this matter? And Mistress Redmond, all is well with the lady?'

'Indeed, Sir Edward. Reunited with her daughter, I am pleased to say.'

'La!' cries Elizabeth. 'I could not be more delighted. Dear Rosina!'

'You are a hypocrite, madam,' says Aran. 'And yes, Sir Edward, I have a great deal to say. For Rosina and Miss Byrom were most informative. The town has been left with a ruinous lack of control. Not altogether the Captain's fault. Nor that of the Constables neither.' Mister Owen exchanges a greeting with one of those gentlemen, Thomas Fowden, enjoying a *saucière* of chocolate in the corner. 'But this self-styled surgeon,' Aran points towards Leigh, 'was all the while dead drunk in the Punch House, while your Ensign,' he indicates Tobin, 'was being bedded by Mistress Cooper here!'

What nonsense! It were Bradley that told me about this Cooper woman. That night at the Pantomime. The whole town was aware, it seemed. Yet do sapphists turn their coats, I wonder? It is possible, I suppose. But there is some other recollection of that performance. *Harlequin's Vagaries, was it not? And a discussion about the Iniskillings' dragoon. Turned out to be a lesbian too. What is it the Spanish say again? Donna con donna? The Game of Flats? Vulgar. And still do not understand...*

'What a monstrous lie!' cries Elizabeth.

'Every word of it the truth,' says Crableck, to the universal shock of those within ear-shot. 'Tight-fisted bitch. Hoity! Toity! Fucking tribade. Him too.' The crook-back nods towards Tobin. '*Her*, I mean!'

'Ensign Tobin,' says Sir Edward. 'What *is* this fellow speaking of?'

But Tobin – *Harriet* Tobin as Sir Edward will later discover – has moved protectively towards Mistress Cooper. A significantly disconcerted Mistress Cooper.

'And there is this, Sir Edward.'

Aran is holding the journal that the Early of Derby had seen passed to him by Bradley earlier. There is a slight gasp from Elizabeth.

'You must explain yourself, Mister Owen.'

'I will, sir. As you know, I think, this journal belongs to Mister Bradley's wife, Rosina. You also know, I believe, that the young lady in question is an intimate of Mistress Cooper's.' *Intimate barely covers the thing!* 'Thus, they have shared some close confidences and some of them, Sir Edward, should interest you greatly.'

'You cannot believe, Sir Edward,' says Elizabeth, 'that I should have been foolish enough to say anything indiscreet to Mistress Bradley. For Heaven's sake, the girl is addled on opiates for most of the time.'

'Yet it was not always thus, madam,' says Aran. 'And there are plenty who will vouch for the fact that Rosina's mind was clear enough when she wrote the most significant passages.'

'And they are?' Sir Edward says.

'A considerable number of libels against dignitaries of the town. Mister Lewthwaite there, for one.' The Assistant Curate almost leaps from his table. 'A most offensive suggestion that the gentleman might be a sodomite, Sir Edward. What is the word? Ah, here. A *molly*, she calls him, according to Mistress Bradley. Yet Mister Lewthwaite is quite beyond reproach.'

'Of *course* he is beyond reproach,' says Elizabeth. 'Because I never spoke such words to the girl. They can only be libels, surely, if I wrote them myself. The fact that this foolish child attributed such words to me is no crime on my part, Mister Owen. You are not only a scrub, sir, but an imbecile too! Why, Sir Edward, would you take such accusations from a known Jacobite? A fellow who knows more about libels from the pages of their own *Journal*, now destroyed, the Lord be praised, than anybody I have ever known.'

'You should exercise caution, Mistress Cooper,' Sir Edward says, 'for Mister Owen enjoys the private ear of Cumberland himself, though he may have fallen temporarily from that state of grace. And do you say, madam, that this girl, with no apparent cause, has made such attributions with no reason?'

'There is worse, Sir Edward,' says Aran. 'Perhaps you should care to read these passages that I have marked in regard to your good self?'

Where did I put my spectacles? Ah, yes. Why, damn the woman…

'I do not know what you are reading, Sir Edward,' Elizabeth Cooper says, 'but I fear that the girl has once again written fictions…'

'I have learned a great deal lately,' says Aran, 'about the process of trials…'

'Yet I am not on trial here!'

608

'No, madam, you are not. Yet you are a devout person, are you not? A staunch and god-fearing Presbyterian?'

'I am!'

'Then the matter is simple, Sir Edward. We might ask Mister Lewthwaite for the loan of his Bible and allow Mistress Cooper to swear upon it that the words written by Rosina Bradley are lies.'

'I repeat, Sir Edward, that I am not on trial here. This is my own establishment. And I am a servant of the Crown. The Collector of His Majesty's Excise Duty.'

'All the more reason, I fear,' says Sir Edward, 'to consider Mister Owen's words carefully. I cannot believe that such things have been written about me, madam. Not just myself either but many other notables, I see. And the guilty party is either yourself or this Bradley woman. Come, Mistress, the truth!'

The coffee house door opens behind them. Rosina herself, with Beppy Byrom.

'I see you have my journal, Sir Edward,' says Rosina. 'I had given permission for Mister Owen to share its contents, but then regretted the thing. For a friendship once fostered should remain so even when it may be fractured.' She looks at Elizabeth. 'But I see that I am come too late. And I collect that Mistress Cooper may already have denied the things we spoke together.'

'She said that you were addled with opiate, my dear,' says Aran. 'But the test is now simple. These are each devout women though their Faiths may be distinct. Your Bible, Mister Lewthwaite, if you please.'

'No,' says Elizabeth, 'I shall not!'

'Then I shall have to consider you guilty, madam,' says Sir Edward. 'You may not have been libellous but, according to Mistress Bradley, you have shared your views quite openly.'

'And I will vouch for that too, Sir Edward,' says Beppy. 'You may also wish to recall that Mistress Cooper allowed these premises to be utilised by the Prince Regent's Recruiting Sergeants when they came to town.'

'Condemned by a Jacobite for being inveigled by those that she, herself, supports? What absurdity is this? In any case, I shall not be staying much longer in this town. We are leaving.'

She puts her arm through Tobin's.

'It is no matter, Mistress,' says Sir Edward. 'It is these statements that concern me. Infamous statements against myself and other. Not libellous. No, but slander certainly. And slanders that pour disrepute upon the post which you hold, madam. There is only one fitting punishment for such a crime, so far as I recall. And you shall be going nowhere meanwhile. Constable! To the House of Correction with the woman, while I send for the Lord of this Manor to confirm sentence.'

The Scold's Bridle is a peculiar punishment, a humiliation reserved for women alone. To tame society's shrews. Its gossip-mongers. Its rebellious wives. And no self-respecting town or village would be without one, nor the Constables whose task it is to manipulate the thing.

It draws such fine crowds too, for its use is now becoming rare.

I doubt that my wife would approve, however, thinks Sir Edward as he waits at the Cross, still surrounded by his escort. Captain Patten and Surgeon Lieutenant Leigh have been dismissed from his service, and Ensign Tobin has not been seen since the Cooper woman was taken away. *Yet another tribade. Amongst my officers. God's Teeth!*

Aran Owen is here too and, to Sir Edward's surprise, Maria-Louise Redmond.

Come to see the woman that infected her daughter, I suppose.

And here comes that woman now, to the great exultation of the mob.

She is tied to the back of a cart, pulled by the Constables while, around her head, the iron frame of the branks itself. Heavy, cutting into her shoulders as she is wrenched forward, filth flung constantly at her by the onlookers. But the thing is not especially tight about her features, relying rather on a different part of its apparatus for effect. The front is hinged, so that it will enclose the victims face but, when it does so, it forces a thick plate into her mouth, a plate with sharp spikes on its lower surface that bite and grind into the surface of Elizabeth's tongue with every jolt, jerk and jounce of the cart.

'Hah!' cries Sir Edward. 'It is all the woman deserves. To be attired in the Bridle!'

'Is that the Cooper woman?' asks a fellow beside him.

'Indeed, sir. Condemned for her slanders.'

'Quite so, Sir Edward! A fitting punishment indeed.'

'Do I know you, sir?'

'Why, of course. I am Striker, Lordship. We met once at the Duke of Newcastle's office?' *Did we, by God? I recall meeting one of Newcastle's agents there. Of course I do! But I was suffering so badly with the bile that day. Though it seems to have eased of late. And then Cumberland had mentioned some Striker as also missing. Could this be he?* 'But it is that other gentleman I have come to find. Mister Owen. You are acquainted, I recall.'

But Aran has already seen the fellow. And such a look from him. He takes Maria-Louise Redmond by the arm, drawing her from the crowd towards the Earl of Derby.

'Has this scoundrel accosted you, Lordship?' cries Aran Owen. 'Seize that fellow, will you!'

Sir Edward's escort look confused, turn to their commander for guidance.

'A moment, sir, if you please,' says the Earl. 'This gentleman claims acquaintance with the Duke of Newcastle.'

'Does he say so? Yet myself and this lady can identify him as the Welsh Jacobite Lieutenant who was upon the roof of Ireby's Tower with the rebel Colonel Townley.'

Why, the dog! Better safe than sorry, then.

'Hold this fellow!' cries Sir Edward, reaching for the sword that no longer hangs at his side. *Ah, I must still face my dear wife with its loss!* But his escorts are efficient enough. They have changed, these Lancaster and Lonsdale men who have so recently formed part of Cumberland's Flying Column. Muskets cocked in a trice and their prisoner edged backwards to some clearer space.

'Sir Edward,' says Striker. 'There is some confusion here, I regret. I have indeed been acting the part of a Lieutenant in the Jacobite army but Mister Owen knows only too well that I am truly an agent of His Grace, the Duke of Newcastle. And we have met, sir, in the Secretary of State's own office.' *I certainly met somebody there. But what did we discuss? And even if it was this man, is he not a self-confessed double spy?* 'I have only come, sir, to collect the valise that I left in Mister Owen's care. And a small debt that I am owed. He chooses to practise upon me, I think, in payment of certain injustices that I may have done him in the past.'

'And this lady? Mistress Redmond?' says The Earl. 'Does she have reason to practise upon you also?'

'Indeed she does not! Why, at the moment that her husband was shot upon the ramparts, it was I who threw myself at his assassin, Townley, and pushed them back down the stairs. We were separated in the subsequent confusion, Sir Edward, after I had laid Colonel Townley flat. But I was taken with the prisoners, all the same. It was several days before I was brought to Cumberland's attention and released. But by then you had all departed. Yet His Grace knows me well, sir. You need simply ask him.'

'The Duke of Cumberland is in London by now.'

'Then ask Mister Owen to end this jest forthwith, I beg you.'

'The only truths that this traitor speaks is that I hold his valise, Sir Edward,' says Aran. 'For he dropped it at the castle and I thought to bring it with me. And it is also true that he demanded payment in exchange for Mistress Redmond's life.'

Good Heavens. What a day this has been. I have never known a place like Manchester for dissemblers and confusions.

'What shall I do, gentlemen, to resolve this impasse? And you, madam. Can you assist?'

'Only in this regard, Sir Edward,' and Maria-Louise stares deeply into Striker's eyes, 'that I have seen the content of this valise. It already contains a purse of gold coins. Traitor's gold, I think. Also a brace of candlesticks, stamped with the arms and name of another traitor, Sir Watkin Williams Wynn. And, finally, a Jacobite Commission, a Lieutenant's Commission, signed by the Young Prince himself.'

'And a Captain's Commission also, Lordship,' says Striker. 'The Warrant signed by Newcastle beneath the King's own, and in my proper name, sir. Dudley Striker.'

611

'You have seen this Commission, madam?'

'I have not, Sir Edward.'

'Yet if this fellow is a Jacobite, as you say, surely you would seek to protect him?'

'Indeed,' says Striker. 'Exactly as I have tried to protect your daughter, Rosina. Exactly as I sought to save you from execution. For Aran's sake, madam. Tell Sir Edward, if you please.'

'You ask why, Sir Edward?' says Maria-Louise. 'For the cruel way he practised upon my husband, sir. For the way he tortured the best friend I have ever known. For the reckoning that my husband promised him. And if you find this fellow to be a Welsh Jacobite, as we attest, what shall happen to him?'

'If he is one of the Welshmen, he will be sent to Chester. For the Assizes there. Or perhaps those of Caernarfon. It is not altogether determined yet. But how should I decide?'

'Why, Sir Edward, it is easy!' says Aran. 'For you should know, Lordship, that in Manchester there are two sorts of people. I like to call them the Rogues and the Righteous. The Rogues always lie, of course, and the Righteous – though they are few in number. Only ever tell the truth. Yet I think that you already know this, sir.'

'Indeed I do, Mister Owen. A belief that I have long held. Yet how can the Rogues be told apart from the Righteous in this town of yours?' the Earl of Derby asks.

'I have always found that, by questioning the townsfolk, their natural honesty or otherwise will normally shine through.'

'But question *who*, Mister Owen, and on what subject? You speak in riddles, sir. You would suggest that I start with yourselves, I collect. And what? Simply ask who is a liar and who is not?'

'It is a beginning, there being three of us.'

'Then I suppose that I should ask how many of you are honest and righteous.'

'Indeed, Sir Edward. Though, personally I feel less than qualified to answer.'

'What foolishness is this!' says Striker. 'You must know, Lordship, that both Mister Owen and the Widow Redmond are each self-sworn Jacobites. Traitors, sir. I am the only one amongst us, apart from yourself, who has served King George.'

'He is a liar, Sir Edward,' says Maria-Louise. 'You may remember that I was imprisoned by the Jacobites because I could not, in Faith, place my hand on the Holy Bible and speak an untruth. Test me now by the same method, I beg you. But I swear to you that this fellow was a trusted confidant of Colonel John William O'Sullivan. He has been at the Prince Regent's side throughout his entire campaign.'

'On behalf of the Duke of Newcastle, I protest!'

Sir Edward fingers his snuff box, takes a pinch, thinking carefully.

'Apart from anything else,' he begins, hesitantly, 'this fellow and Widow Redmond cannot both be Rogues nor both be Righteous, since each has contradicted the other. So one of these two is a Rogue, and one of them is Righteous.'

'The product of an enquiring mind, Sir Edward,' says Striker, 'as befits a student of natural philosophy. But I do not see how this may benefit you, sir.'

'In this way, Mister Whoever-you-are. That if this young fellow is indeed an honest cove, there would be two of the Righteous present – and, in that case, you would not have lied and said that there was only one truthful person amongst you.'

'A reasonable assumption,' says Striker. 'But if he was a Rogue, as well as the Widow Redmond, would it not be true that there was only one of the Righteous present? Myself, of course.'

'Certainly not, for if he was a Rogue he would simply have lied to me, being unable to make a true statement.'

'And your meaning, Sir Edward?' says Maria-Louise. 'For I find myself somewhat confused.'

'It is simple, madam. Young Aran could not bring himself to tell me that there is only one of the Righteous amongst you. This other fellow must therefore have lied, being a Rogue, and your good self told the truth, being Righteous. The Jacobite dog will find himself in Chester Prison, forthwith!'

Chapter Fifty-Six

Aran quickly hides the canvas on which he has been working. But too late.

'What is it that you hide, Welsh boy?' says Rosina from the Academy Room's doorway. She looks beautiful, her colour much restored and her ringlets afire with a copper glow.

'Spy!' he says. 'I have not yet decided whether it is fit for public viewing.'

'Well, the secret is out. You might as easily show it now.' He pulls the painting free of the spare frames and lifts it to an easel. 'My dear fellow,' she says. 'It is the best, of all things. The very best.'

On the day that Aran and Maria-Louise had been released from the stinking confines of Carlisle Cathedral, they had walked slowly towards the English gate, close to the town's Bowling Green. Many of the women and children who had accompanied the Edinburgh Regiment throughout their brief campaign were still here, and thank Heaven, being treated with some common decency, unlike the barbarity meted to their men. At the edge of the Green were three small peasant girls, wrapped in plaids while, on a low wall before them, was a young boy of their same age, a lace-coated drummer from Cumberland's regiments. He was playing them a gentle lament upon a fife. No barrier between them. No bitterness of generations gone. No gulf by creed or faction. Just four small children. He had begun work on it as soon as he returned, and now it was almost complete.

'I believe that it is the first piece I have ever done which entirely satisfies me,' he says.

'And will you complete any of the paintings for Cumberland?'

'I have done so already. But how are you, my dear? You seem in good spirits.'

'And why should I not be so, sir? Mister Byrom has said that I may stay a while longer. Beppy has been so very patient with me. And Mrs Starkey has suggested that she may be able to furnish me with some work, for she now has more students than she can accommodate.'

'Then give you joy. But the Sydenham's?'

'I still crave it so desperately though I have not touched a drop for two weeks and more. I think that I am over the worst at last.'

'It has been a difficult time for you, I collect. Losing your home. Mistress Cooper's betrayal. Your uncle's funeral. Papa. The laudanum must have been

614

a constant temptation.'

'Indeed, and it remains so. Yet I came with news!'

'Not another rumour, I beg you.' They had been arriving thick and fast all through the month.

'Gracious, no. But the word is all over town. There has been another battle. Four days ago. Friday last, the seventeenth. The Prince had been at Bannockburn and General Hawley with the English army on Falkirk Muir. The Prince marched there and thrashed the fellow. The English lost nearly four hundred killed or wounded, it seems, and the same amount made prisoner.'

'And will be treated considerably better than our poor fellows in Carlisle, I suspect.'

'Indeed, but there is more, Aran. So much more.'

'And would you make me beg for it then?'

'La! Of course not, though it is difficult for me to speak of it. You will understand, I am certain. But you know that the person with whom Elizabeth has been, that Tobin creature…?'

'She listed with one of the new regiments, did she not?'

'Indeed, and has been wounded in the fight, it seems,' says Rosina.

'It is good riddance to her, I imagine.'

'But the *real* news is that Mistress Cooper holds discussions, as we speak, with Mister Rivers of Liverpool, and the intention of selling the coffee house to follow Harriet Tobin north.'

'And how do you feel about that, my dear?'

'I should count myself blessed that the woman shall be out of my life but, if I am honest, I still miss her terribly.'

'It is understandable,' says Aran. 'Yet you do not seem too greatly troubled. And your negotiations with Mister Bradley. How do *they* progress?'

'I could not face him. I have an Attorney now. That Salford fellow, Turnbull. Mister Byrom recommended him. Though it is excessively complicated. We may be estranged but the separation can only be made legal if an application is made to the Ecclesiastical Court. The law does not permit me to seek such a divorce on grounds of adultery because I am a woman, and my husband is protected from such a charge. Mister Bradley could cite such grounds, of course, but there are considerable complications arising from the peculiarities. You know the thing to which I refer, I am sure, without needing all the detail. As usual in these matters, the only people likely to gain are the Attorneys themselves, yet we must leave them to find a solution.'

'And the Marriage Settlement?'

'We are each agreed that the document is no longer valid nor enforceable. The Marriage Portion, two hundred pounds, you will recall, shall be returned to me, though I lose any right to the clauses negotiated by Papa in relation to the possible sale of Mister Bradley's property.'

And such a sale is now very likely for, as Aran knows to his considerable distress, Bradley has suggested to Maria-Louise that they should move to London, taking the three younger girls with them. O'Farrell too. Titus had been hardly a week in the ground before she had broken the news to him.

'Well,' says Aran, 'I suppose he *could* have chosen to sell you at the Market Cross. But you must be cautious in this matter of the two hundred pounds, my dear. Take some proper counsel. Mister Byrom perhaps, since it seems that you will remain under his protection a while.'

'Indeed. If he can tolerate me then I shall stay at least until the Prince returns. For he is certain to do so, do you not think, now that the Elector's army is beaten once more?'

'I certainly hope so. Yet Hawley commands only one part of the Hanoverian forces. We must wait to see what happens next. For now, my dear, I should be very obliged if we could walk together so far as Attorney Liptrott's. It is very possible, I think, that your Uncle Josiah may have left you some consideration in his Will.'

Rosina had indeed attended the Squire's funeral at Llanffynon, but subsequently the old fellow's own solicitor, Mister Price of Chester, had informed her that he would need to visit Manchester for the document's reading and Liptrott has kindly offered the use of his own office for the purpose. So they walk from Hanging Ditch to Deansgate, avoiding the coffee house at Rosina's request, but coming face to face with Bradley's good friend, Robert Jobb, as he stumbles out of the Angel.

'Now *there* is a sight!' he says. 'They say that you may now be cured of your affliction, Rosina. Is that correct, my sweet girl?'

'I think it may be *you* who is afflicted, sir. By a surfeit of ale, I collect.'

'Not so influenced by its vapours that I cannot see the ripeness of the fruit before me. And my good friend, poor James, now saddled himself with that old whore instead. The rotting windfall rather than the blushing bough apple. He is a fool. Have told him so. Now, were you to consider...'

Aran exchanges a quick glance with Rosina, then around the Market Square.

The blow that he delivers to Robert Jobb's face is not especially expert but sufficient to draw copious quantities of blood from the fellow's nose and to send him reeling back against the inn's signpost, where he now sits slumped upon the ground nursing his left eye.

'I have wanted to do that for so long,' Aran says, rubbing grazed knuckles.

And Rosina is still laughing at the thing when they arrive at Liptrott's premises. Chairs have been placed for those invited to attend. Aran himself. Rosina. Maria-Louise. Anna-Marie. Katherine. And Maeve.

Poor Maeve! She has always been such an enchanted child. But I do not think she has spoken a word since Titus was fetched home.

Attorney Price of Chester, a venerable fellow with an eye-glass bids good day to Rosina and she, in turn, greets her Mama.

Hardly the most affectionate of scenes but a considerable improvement. We must give them time, I suppose.

'Dearest Aran,' cries Katherine. 'Have you heard the news? That Mama intends us all to leave for London. I have told her that I may not accompany them. For I could not stand the thought...'

'Sweet child,' he says. 'But of course you must go. I shall miss you terribly but do you not think that Maeve might need you more than I, for the nonce at least.'

The warmest smile from Maria-Louise as Liptrott invites them to be seated.

'First,' he says, my deepest condolences, madam, to yourself and your family. Harsh times. Harsh indeed. Yet I hope it shall give you some small comfort to now be in the hands of Mister Price, who I now name for you. A most eminently professional gentleman, listed on the Attorneys Roll this fifty-five years past.'

A few preliminaries from Price and then the reading itself.

The Last Will and Testament of Josiah Redmond, of Llanffynon Hall, Esquire.

Dated the twenty-fourth day of August, 1744.

...Do make and ordain this my last Will and Testament as follows (to wit) I give and devise all my messuages lands tenements and hereditaments that I am any ways empowered to dispose of and the reversion and reversions remainder and remainders thereof unto my dear friend Aran Owen of Manchester his heirs and assigns forever subject nevertheless to the payment of my just debts which I hereby charge thereon...

Aran thinks that he must have misunderstood. He looks to Maria-Louise for confirmation, receives a reassuring smile and her hand upon his arm, a slight pressure of congratulations.

'Titus would be pleased, I think,' she whispers.

Rosina does not look so certain. She stares rigidly at Mister Price as he works his way through the rest of the document.

'Give you joy of your inheritance, Mister Owen,' he says. 'We have made some initial estimates of the Squire's debts and this represents our initial accompts of the situation.'

Aran studies the paper set upon Liptrott's desk.

God's Hooks, I had never imagined...

'You are certain, sir,' he says, 'that the amounts are so great?'

'They are, if anything, a conservative estimate, sir. If you should wish to engage my services further, of course...'

Indeed he shall. And here is Rosina, at last, come to offer her own felicitations.

Bless her heart. She had been so hoping for some better fortune, I think. And she shall not be disappointed. But I must decide the correct amount to settle upon her once I have had the chance to consider the thing properly.

Aran studies the accounts once more, lifts the paper and sees that, beneath them, are two silver crowns, gleaming new.

'Mister Price,' he says, 'you have left these coins, I think.'

'Ah! I was intent on sending out for food and drink and then became distracted by Mister Liptrott's fine account of *Makepiece versus Makepiece*. I had not appreciated his part in that drama. Most edifying.'

'I am sure, sir,' says Aran. 'But you must allow *me* to buy you dinner, will you not?'

He picks up the crowns to hand them back, notices the sharp outline of King George the Second's head.

It might all have been so very different!

And beneath the King's head, a single word inscribed. The other coin the same.

LIMA.

'I have never seen such coinage before, Mister Price, They are newly-minted I think.'

'Indeed, Mister Owen. I was in London recently. I received them at the Bank of England. I commented upon the design myself. A curious tale. Some of our brave privateers, it seems, intercepted a cargo of enemy silver from Jack Spaniard and Peru last year. The treasure was landed on the thirtieth of August and some enterprising fellow at the Admiralty, having a curiosity for such things, discovered that this same date was the Festival of a certain Santa Rosa del Lima. Government persuaded the Mint Master that, in order to commemorate their good fortune in having such an amount fall into British hands, and to denote their origin, the coins should be stamped accordingly. Remarkable, is it not?'

Aran weighs the coins in his hand.

'Indeed, sir,' he says, stealing a glance first towards Maria-Louise and then towards Rosina herself before passing the two pieces of silver back to the Attorney. 'Now, Mister Price, I promised you dinner, I think.'

He suggests that Maria-Louise and her daughters should join them, though it is merely a courtesy and he knows that they shall politely refuse.

'Yet I wonder,' she says to him, 'whether you might join me later. At seven, perhaps. No, not at the house. Wait for me at the Commodities Exchange and, when I see you there, I shall join you.'

They eat at the Bull's Head, where they receive more news. The officers of the Manchester Regiment are being sent to York, and thence to London for their trials, though no date set for them so far. All but one of the officers, it seems. For Robert Deacon has died in Kendal, of illness and neglect. The rest of the common men are still in Carlisle, with more of them dying every day. It is evil news, that plays upon Aran's mind for many hours, dampening any enthusiasm that he might have felt for his own sudden fortune.

'You have heard about Deacon?' he says to Maria-Louise, at the time appointed.

'Indeed, my dear. It is shocking news. And every piece that we receive adds weight to my guilt. Shall we always be haunted by it, do you think?'

It is a clear night, star-filled, and bitter cold. Snow lies crisp upon the ground and the pattens on her boots tap a regular rhythm as she stamps to warm her feet.

'I think so, yes,' he says, pulling the collars of her heavy cloak closer together. 'Though you shall have Mister Bradley and the girls to succour you when the phantoms come too close. For my own part, I am set on Llanffynon again, and hope that Josiah will watch over me there. You are not vexed at my inheritance?'

'I give you joy of the thing, with all my heart. It is *precisely* the thing. And as my husband should have chosen. He would be pleased, too, that Gartside has agreed to purchase the fustian business, though the poor fellow seems less certain about his neighbours. The brothel shall never be the same again, and I am glad of it! Though I should dearly love to see how it develops with Mudge as its bawd and George Blossom as Flash Man!'

She laughs. The first time he has seen her do so these several weeks.

'And you are certain? About London?' he says.

'I am, sir.' She turns to look at the house, just across the Lane. 'James was thoughtful to prevent the place from destruction. But it is not the same. I see Titus in every corner. He will always be here, I think. Or beating his path to the bawdy-house. I fancy that, in years to come, this town shall become more populous perhaps. That folk shall jostle each other as they bustle about. And in so doing they shall jostle my husband's ghost in the bargain. They shall not know. But, now and again, one of them shall hear the word *lick-spittle* whispered in his ear.'

Aran turns away, unable to look at her.

'And Striker?' he says. 'Do you think that we treated him unjustly in the end?'

She takes his hand. His left hand, of course.

'I think, my dear, that Dudley Striker deserves everything that he may receive. Titus swore revenge upon the fellow and may now rest a little easier for our actions. Yet do you truly believe that the fellow will suffer any lasting punishment? He will get word to Newcastle somehow, will he not? I doubt that any prison could hold Striker long in any case. And now, sir. Will you promise to visit me in London? To visit Katherine, at least. She will miss you so very much!'

'And you, Mistress. Shall you pine for me also?'

'Foul wretch! How could I *not*? To find such a friendship as this. With no jealous attachment. With no guilt. How precious a thing. To realise its worth only to be parted and lose it again. It will not answer. Now, kiss me, sir. Before I freeze to death!'

Epilogue

The Prince has sailed away long since.

It is just as well, I suppose, Aran thinks as he sets away his brushes for the day. He compares the painting with the view it reflects. The orchard at Llanffynon. His home again in Wales for almost a year now.

The whole country now knows the aftermath of Falkirk Muir. *Not quite the turn of fortunes that myself, Rosina and Beppy had sought.* Sickness and desertions causing a Jacobite retreat to the Highlands. Cumberland resuming command in Edinburgh and reinforced by thousands of Hessians. The surrender of Inverness to Charles Edward and the disastrous engagement on Drumossie Muir in the middle of last April. A battle that lasted no more than thirty minutes but which left fifteen hundred Scotsmen dead, many butchered by Cumberland's murder squads, they say, as the poor fellows lay wounded on the Culloden field.

Then the Prince's fugitive flight across the Highlands, protected by hundreds of loyal individuals throughout May and June, all of July and August until, finally, he was back at Borrodale Bay where, just after midnight on the nineteenth day of September, a French ship weighed anchor and carried him to France.

Did we cause this, Maria-Louise Redmond and I? The end of a dream? That a Stuart Monarchy under that kindly young man might have led to greater tolerance in this nation? That there might have been lasting peace with France, peace across the whole of Continental Europe? France and Britain freed of warfare and able to concentrate on the internal problems that so beset our peoples?

Yet could they truly carry the burden for all that has transpired between?

The wicked persecution of the Highlands in general. Whole clans transported into exile.

The hundreds of Jacobite prisoners who have died on hulks in the Thames and elsewhere.

The trials and the judgements.

A tiny number of the rich and powerful executed. Lords Balmerino and Kilmarnock in August.

But so many others.

Francis Townley hanged in public on Kennington Green in London, then cut down so that his head could be removed, his bowels pulled out and burned upon a fire. Most of the other Manchester Regiment officers too, Tom Deacon included, their decaying skulls sent north again so that they might be spiked upon the Exchange.

Not young Charlie though. No, they had been merciful to Charles Deacon, simply sent the boy to Jamaica, a slave upon the plantations until a fever took him.

I merely thank Heaven that nobody called me to bear witness in the trials.

Dozens more executed in different parts of the country.

And a few rewarded, in a strange way. Captain John Townley, for example. Destroyed by his brother's death but awarded small compensation by receiving the French Order of Saint Louis.

Occasional unexpected outcomes too, such as that here in Wales itself.

For the Great Sessions, the Welsh Assizes, held at Caernarfon in the spring of 1747, have considered the case of various Jacobite prisoners from the Principality, including one William Owen. And the gentleman set to preside over these proceedings none other than the Member of Parliament for Denbighshire, Sir Watkin Williams Wynn, of course.

The trial has attracted a fair crowd of spectators. Two reverend gentlemen from Manchester, Ben Nichols and Tom Lewthwaite. A Cheshire landowner, the young Sir Peter Leighton. A bullet-headed brothel minder and his wife, a terribly scarred old hag. Several folk from Ormschurch in Lancashire. And one lady travelled all the way from London, small, attractive in an elvish way.

But not the young Squire of Llanffynon, who has viewed Sir Watkin's rapid restoration to wealth and good fortune with amusement. There was, after all, he supposed, no legal proof of the fellow's involvement in rebellion. And he does have some influential friends, including the Duke of Bedford.

No, Aran prefers to remember Striker through his elegiac descriptions of the Virginia Valley.

Perhaps I shall go there one day! See it for myself.

But Dudley Striker will not be there. Whatever efforts he might have made to establish his true credentials, the sentence of the Session is clear. That William Owen, Jacobite officer, shall be hanged in chains until dead on Twllhely Marsh. And may the Lord have mercy on his soul!

Aran returns to the house, where his afternoon tea awaits him.

A very decent *Tippy Pekoe* that he can now buy in Chester.

Well, it did not last long, he thinks, *the relaxation of the Excise duty on tea. Just long enough to put us out of business.* And now it is taxed to the hilt once again. But demand just keeps growing. The British East India Company, with virtually no competition again, have begun to set up wholesale markets and public sales for the commodity in every major town. Thomas Twining's tea empire has doubled in size and is now operated by his son, Daniel, one of the richest merchants in England. And with the Excise duty in force, once more, tea smuggling has returned to being the mainstay of organised crime across Britain.

But somewhere in Government a plan is developing. Demand for tea in the American Colonies has reached epidemic proportion. It may take twenty-five years to drive out the smugglers but, once done, the Company will be granted the exclusive license to satisfy demand from New Hampshire all the way to Georgia. And the Government, in turn, will receive the princely sum of thruppence tax for every pound of tea imported there. Why, there is a King's ransom to be made from the American Colonies. At least, until the Colonists of all classes decide to resist. One more rebellion ready for the brewing!

The End

Acknowledgements

I had no intention that this should be such a *picaresque* novel. Several things had come to my mind at the same time. The prominence of the Manchester Jacobites in the Rising of '45. The capture of the fabulous Lima treasure, the origins of which remain disputed. And the significant part played by anti-Hanoverian tea smuggling operations during the middle of the 18th Century. Apart from that, whilst I had read some wonderful accounts of the '45 itself – and I want to acknowledge here, above all other sources, Christopher Duffy's extraordinary book *The '45, Bonnie Prince Charlie and the Untold Story of the Jacobite Rising* – I still had no *real* sense of the men and women whose names filled the pages.

So I fictionalised them and apologise unreservedly if I have offended the current generations of families whose ancestors actually took part. Like any fictionalised characters, they developed a life of their own, I fear. In truth, there is little to tell us about the actual natures of Francis Townley, Sir Watkin Williams Wynn, Beppy Byrom, Sir Edward Stanley and others. Nor, indeed, about the various and conflicting Manchester merchants who became composited to make the Redmonds and the Bradleys, or the Government spies, Dudley Bradstreet most prominent amongst them, who provided the basis for Striker, or that breed of women disguised as soldiers and typified by the real-life Hannah Snell, whose tale is more unbelievable by far than that of my fictitious Harriet Tobin.

The history too perhaps suffers in the same way, though the main chronological anchors in the story are (in my own humble opinion, at least) accurate enough. Sir Watkin's Welsh 'army' did, indeed, simply disappear from the records. The Jacobite forces were, in truth, turned about at Derby largely by the lies told to Charles Edward by the spy Dudley Bradstreet. The skirmish on Clifton Moor really was the last battle fought on English soil and happened almost entirely as I described it, including poor Honeywood's misadventure with the turd, but without the direct involvement of Sir Edward Stanley. Even Charles Edward's visit to Ancoats Hall may have a basis in fact. Only the surrender of Carlisle has been substantially 'tweaked'. But then, none of us really know the precise details of its fall. There was certainly, however, no attack through the town by Cumberland and I can personally vouch for the fact that Titus Redmond was not there. Honestly, he wasn't!

Apart from the 'history', much of the rest is pure invention. There *was* no attempt to steal the Excise Duty in Manchester on Lady Day 1744. There *was* no attack on the bawdy house. There *was* no killing of Minister Semple at the Dissenters' Meeting House. Yet similar incidents *did* take place in other parts of the country and it seemed reasonable to bring them together in order to 'paint a picture' of the lawlessness that pervaded so much of English society at the time. I accept, however, that it might be unfair to ascribe such misdeeds to one faction or the other, or to any individual.

But I must acknowledge those other source materials that helped so much. Roy Moxham's *Tea: Addiction, Exploitation and Empire*. Raymond Smullyan's book of riddles, entitled *What is the name of this book?* Almost too many websites to list. Rictor Norton's *Homosexuality in Eighteenth-Century England*. Douglas Harper's *Etymonline*. The Scottish History Society's *Prince Charles Edward Stuart: Itinerary*. The Open Library's *Private Journal and Literary Remains of John Byrom*. The Open Library's *Journal of Elizabeth Byrom in 1745*. Hundreds of Wikipedia entries and whoever it was that published the Julian Calendars for 1744, 1745 and 1746. Bradshaw's *Origins of Street Names in Manchester*. Elizabeth Raffald's 1772 *Directory of Manchester and Salford*. They were invaluable.

All dates given are, of course, 'old style', the Julian Calendar being eleven days ahead of the Gregorian Calendar that we currently use. Under the Julian Calendar, too, the 'new' year began at the end of March. Hence, the Battle of Falkirk, now always described as taking place in January 1746 would then have been dated as January 1745-46.

Further acknowledgements must include thanks to Ann, Joan, Tony, Jake and Marilyn for helping to resolve some of the economic threads during a session on the beach at Guardamar del Segura in October 2010.

And then there are the long-suffering staff at *Caffé Nero* in Wrexham and at *Monge* in Guardamar since most of my chapter revisions took place in those two very fine coffee houses.

My personal thanks go to the author, David Almond, who helped me to recognise that I 'can write' even if I do not yet consider myself 'an author'. Similarly, I appreciate the support offered to me by *New Writers UK*.

And finally to my editor, Jo Field. Herself the author of that excellent novel *Rogues and Rebels*, she provided me with a level of objectivity that I found invaluable. It was Jo who persuaded me, amongst many other things, to add the glossary that appears in the following pages and lists some of those eighteenth century words whose meaning may now be lost to us or significantly altered. The glossary is not intended as an academic work but, rather, to explain the way that I have used particular vocabulary throughout *The Jacobites' Apprentice*. Jo also queried whether Striker did, indeed, meet his end upon Twllhely Marsh but that, as they say, is a different story.

Glossary

ACCOMPT – An old spelling for account.

AGAINST – In addition to its modern meanings, 'against' could mean 'before'.

ALLOW – To admit.

AN' – An obsolete word for if.

ANSWER – To suit, to suffice.

APARTMENT – Not a rented dwelling, but a room.

ARTIFICIAL – Crafted.

ATTEND – Listen or Take Note.

BANDITTI – Common phrase for 'Jacobite rabble'.

BATING – Except for.

BAWD – A female procuress.

BIT – Deceived, duped.

BOHEA – A variety of tea, pronounced "bo-hay."

BRAVO – A hired assassin; sometimes used loosely for any thug.

BUBBLE – As a noun, a dupe; as a verb, to dupe or trick.

BUMPER – A (toasting) cup.

BUNTLINGS – (Slang) Petticoats.

CANKER – A cancer.

CAPUCHIN (CLOAK) – A cloak with a hood.

CHARIOT – A fast two-seat horse-drawn coach, popular among the fashionable set.

CHATTER-BROTH – Tea, or sometimes scandal-broth.

CHIRURGEON – An old spelling of surgeon.

CHIT – As now, e.g. "a chit of a girl" or "she's no more than a chit".

COCK-PIMP – The supposed husband of a bawd, procuress etc.

COLLECT – To gather, understand, as in "I collect that..."

CONCEIT – A notion or idea, sometimes a witty or paradoxical one.

CONDUM – A contraceptive sheath as spelled by English physician, Daniel Turner, in 1717, from un condus, something that preserves, but almost certainly nothing to do with the mythical 'Doctor Condon'.

CRICKET – A piece of simple three-legged furniture, stool or table, round-topped.

DAB – An expert rogue, as in "a rum dab".

DEVOIRS – Responsibilities or duties (from the French). Also civilities.

DICKER – To barter.

DIDDLE – (Slang) Geneva, gin.

DIRECTION – Address, as in the address of a house or building.

DISTEMPER – An illness or disease.

D'OFF – To tip one's hat, to take off.

DURST – Dare.

ELSE – Often used on its own to mean or else, or otherwise.

FIE – General expression of disgust/curse, as in "Fie upon it!" or "A fie upon you!"

FLASHMAN – (Slang) A bawdy house bully.

FULLING – The cleaning and processing of cloth, often using human urine.

FUSTIAN – Coarse, sturdy cloth made of cotton and flax.

GARNISH – Fees a prisoner paid a jailer to gain better treatment. Bribe.

GENEVA – Gin. The word and its shortened form come not from the Swiss city, but from genever, Dutch for juniper.

GIVE YOU – I wish you… As in: "Give you good night" or "Give you joy of it!" or "God give you joy!"

GOD BLIND ME! – Curse, became Cor Blimey.

GOD'S HOOKS! – Curse, became Gadzooks.

GOLD-FINDERS – Latrine cleaners, Nightmen.

HACKUM – (Slang) A fighting fellow.

HIGGLERS – Itinerant dealers in small goods.

HISTORY – Used for any narrative, including fictional ones.

HOITY! TOITY! – Riotous behaviour; flighty; frolicsome, e.g. "Such frolicsome behaviour!"

HOMBRE – A favourite card game. Also Ombre Renegado.

HUMOUR – Sometimes the modern meaning. Sometimes in the sense of mood. Sometimes one's medical condition.

IN LOOKS – Good-looking, e.g. "When she was in looks".

JAKES – A privy or latrine.

JOCOSE – Humorous, witty.

JOKE – (Slang) Word for female sexual organs.

KIT-CAT – A mutton pie.

LA! – An affectation of speech, usually by women.

LANDSKIP – Old spelling of landscape.

LANTHORN – A lantern. Jack a' Lanthorn, a spirit light.

LIMN – To paint.

LINE – The equator.

LINK – A torch.

LINSEY-WOOLSEY – Inferior mix of linen and wool/cotton; therefore "cheap".

LIST – As a verb, list could mean enlist.

MAHOMET – The standard eighteenth-century English spelling of Mohammed.

MARGENT – The bank of a river. Sometimes spelled margin.

MIEN – Face, countenance, appearance. Pronounced mean.

MOBILE VULGUS – Mob. Our word mob is just a shortened version of the Latin phrase.

MOLLY – A homosexual man, often a transvestite.

MUMCHANCE – Silent, mute.

MURTHER – An old spelling of murder.

MUSSULMAN – A Moslem.

MY PARDON! – Excuse me!

NABOB – A Briton who made a lot of money in India.

NAME – Introduce, as in "Allow me to name…"

NIGHTMEN – Latrine cleaners.

NIGHT WASTE – Night soil, etc.

NONCE – Particular occasion, such as "For the nonce" = for now, or on this occasion.

NUBBING CHEAT – Gallows

OCCASIONAL – Not from time to time, but on a special occasion. Celebrational.

OF ALL THINGS – Above all, as in "I should like it of all things!"

OWN – Acknowledge, admit to.

PATCH – An artificial birthmark or beauty mark applied to the face, often to cover up blemishes. They were most common among women, but at various times men too wore them.

PATTINS – Slip-on or strapped-on wooden/metal soles to protect shoes from mud or snow.

PECKSNIFF – A hypocrite.

PECULATION – Like the worst form of speculation, personal enrichment, embezzlement.

PECULIAR – Peculiar often means particular, with no hint of weird or unusual.

PETTY-FOGGER – Contemptuous term for unscrupulous lawyer.

PHAETON – A four-wheeled carriage drawn by two horses, open to the air.

POESY – An obsolete word for poetry.

POSSE COMITATUS – A posse. The "force of the country".

POUNCE POT – The shaker containing pounce, the fine powder used for drying ink.

PRETEND – To profess or claim. It didn't have the modern suggestions of make-believe.

PRIME – Excellent, as in "That would be prime!"

PRITHIE – Please, from "I pray thee…"

PROPER – In addition to its modern sense, proper could mean one's own.

PROTEST – To declare as in "I protest!" = "I declare!"

RAM YOU DAMN YOU – A purely nautical term for "not giving a damn".

RANTER – Somebody who talks foolishly, raves, from the Antinomian Sect of 1645.

REMOVE AFTER REMOVE – Course after course, since the table-cloth etc was taken away at the end of each course: so, "remove after remove" from the end of the first course.

RENCOUNTER – A meeting (or, as a verb, to meet). Tryst.

REPAIR – To go or to travel.

REPINE – To feel dejection or discontent, e.g. "He repined over the loss of his love".

RIFF-RAFF – Rabble. Note 18th Century use of "Tag, rag and longtail".

ROUT – As a noun, it means either a crowd or assembly, or a great deal of noise.

RUB – An obstacle, rough ground, as in "there's the rub".

SAPPHIC – Relating to female homosexuality and stemming from the 7th century BC poetess, Sappho of Lesbos. The word "Lesbian" was certainly in use in 1732 (William King, *The Toast*) but words like "Sapphist" and "Tribade" seem to be more commonly used.

SCRUB – A mean, insignificant fellow (from shrub, a stunted tree).

SEDAN CHAIRS – Carried by Chair men and led by Link Boys, carrying torches at night.

SE'NNIGHT – A week. Seven nights, of course.

SENSIBLE – Aware. Conscious.

SESSIONS – Legal sessions in which cases were decided. Assizes.

SETTLE – Older variant of "settee" but probably still in use through mid-1700s.

SHAMBLES – An abattoir.

SHORT SHRIFT – *Short shrift* was originally the brief time for a condemned criminal to confess before execution.

SIGNIFY – Often used for mean or amount to. If something "doesn't signify," it often means it doesn't matter.

SIZE – Short for Assizes, a session of the legal courts.

STUFF – A kind of light woollen fabric. Also often used dismissively, as in "Such stuff. Such nonsense!"

TAPER – A small candle.

TARTER – A stick to beat carpets etc.

TATTERDEMALLION – Untidy, scruffy, ragamuffin-ish.

TAWDRY – Shortened from As flawed as St Audrey's Lace.

TIP A STAVE – Literally to arrest somebody (with a tipstaff) but used figuratively to mean "do a bit" as perhaps in "I'll tip you a stave" – I'll sing you a verse.

TIP FOR TAP – Blow for blow, tit for tat.

TIPSY – Almost drunk.

TOILET – A dressing table, where a woman applied make-up, or the act of dressing at such a table. There's no hint of the modern plumbing fixture, which hadn't yet been invented.

TOKEN – Any small sign or indication.

TOUCH AN INSTRUMENT – To play.

TREPAN – To beguile, cheat, or entrap.

TRIBADE – Lesbian, as in William King's 1732 book, *The Toast*. A practitioner of 'The Silent Sin'.

VIRAGO – (Slang) A masculine woman.

WHERRY – A small rowboat.

WITHOUT – Often means outside of, the opposite of within.

WONT – accustomed, or habit, e.g. "She was wont to…" or "It was her wont to…"

Lightning Source UK Ltd.
Milton Keynes UK
UKOW042242191112

202443UK00002B/23/P